DESTROYERMEN: FIRE ON THE WATER

Books by Taylor Anderson

DESTROYERMEN: UNKNOWN SEAS
(SFBC 2-in-1 Omnibus)
Into the Storm
Crusade

DESTROYERMEN: FIRE ON THE WATER
(SFBC 2-in-1 Omnibus)
Maelstrom
Distant Thunders

DESTROYERMEN

DESTROYERMEN

FIRE ON THE WATER

MAELSTROM & DISTANT THUNDERS

TAYLOR ANDERSON

SFBC
SCIENCE
FICTION

MAELSTROM Copyright © 2009 by Taylor Anderson
    Publication History: Roc Hardcover, February 2009
                          Roc Mass Market, April 2010
DISTANT THUNDERS Copyright © 2010 by Taylor Anderson.
    Publication History: Roc Hardcover, June 2010

First Science Fiction Book Club Omnibus Edition: January 2012

Published by arrangement with
The Penguin Group (USA), Inc./New American Library
Roc
375 Hudson Street
New York, NY 10014

Visit the SFBC online at *www.sfbc.com*
Follow us on Facebook: www.facebook.com/ScienceFictionBookClub

ISBN 978-1-61793-413-1

Printed in the United States of America.

CONTENTS

MAELSTROM

ACKNOWLEDGMENTS

I must thank my parents again. They are, after all, my first and sometimes strictest critics. My wife, Christine, continues to endure ill-tempered remarks such as "I couldn't possibly care less what the cat did. When the door is shut, I'm *trying* to write." Thanks to my dear friends at Books and Crannies and all the helpful people I've met at maritime museums all over the country, who have bent over backward to help in every way they could without the least complaint or desire for recognition. My deepest appreciation (and apologies) to Darla and Ryan Goodrich, who never fail to remind me that I've left them out in the past. Nowhere is there a better resource for examples of acerbic wit. Sheila Cox continues to lead me through the labyrinth of online literacy—a most difficult chore, I assure you. Thanks again to Ginjer Buchanan, the most patient and gracious editor in the business, and of course, my friend and agent, Russell Galen, who continues to amaze me with his unwavering, steadfast support and encouragement. I think I've thanked the rest of my "crew" before, and if I've left anyone out, you have my most abject apologies. Trust me, you are appreciated.

Finally, I have, in general, acknowledged the sacrifices of the Asiatic Fleet before, but Alan Levine recently reminded me that it's high time I recognized the sad ordeal of a few ships and crews in particular. Unlike *Walker* and *Mahan*, USS *Pope* was actually there at the end when *Exeter* and *Encounter* met their fates. *Pope* was destroyed as well, but the torment her survivors suffered at the hands of her Japanese "rescuers" must never be forgotten. Nobody really knew what happened to USS *Edsall* until after the war, when grainy pictures of Japanese capital ships using her for target practice came to light. Apparently, a couple of her crew were "rescued," but they didn't survive internment. A similar fate likely befell USS *Pillsbury* and the gunboats USS *Asheville* and HMAS *Yarra*, but we will likely never know for sure. God bless and keep them.

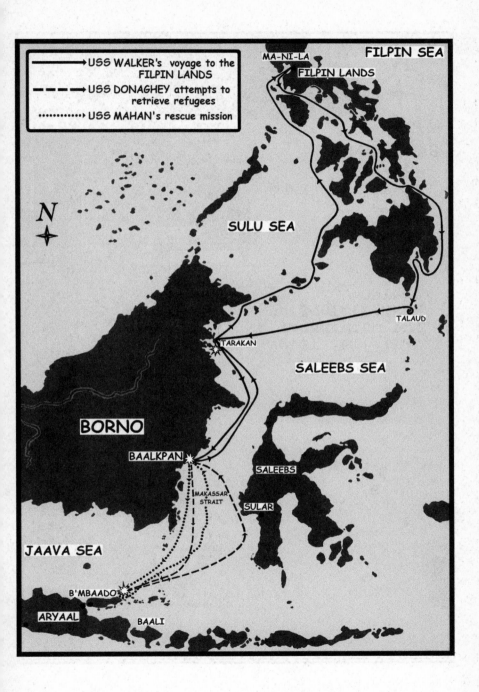

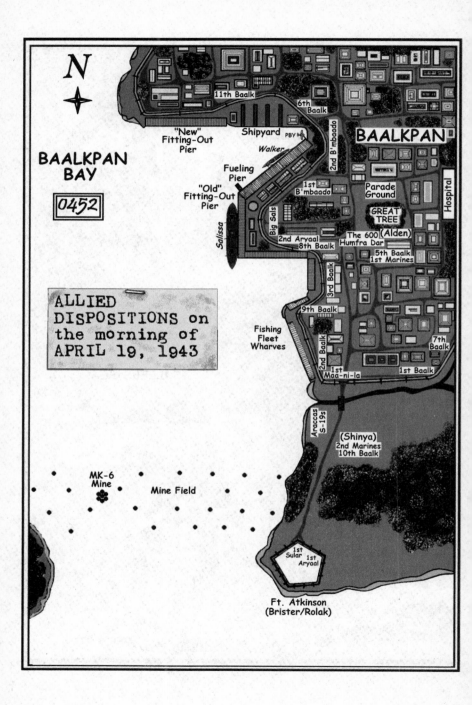

*T*here was a new rumbling sound below, but it went unnoticed by the eight-year-old girl swaying in the sailcloth hammock. Her slumber was already filled with the incessant rumbling and groaning of the working hull, and the endless, hissing blows of the pounding sea. Then came another rumble, and another, each more insistent than the last. Still, she didn't stir from her dream. In it she'd been swallowed by a leviathan, just as she'd dreaded since before the strange voyage ever began. Every night, as soon as the lids closed over her large, jade-colored eyes, the same terrible dream came again. She was in the very bowels of a leviathan, and the rumbling, hissing roar was the sound of its belly digesting the ship. The voices came—there were always voices—excited, urgent voices in a tone entirely appropriate. Of course there would be dreadful voices in a dreadful dream. She knew what would happen next. . . .

She was facedown on the thundering deck, and only her tangled bedding protected her delicate nose from the fall. Her eyes flew open, but she could barely see. The only light in the stateroom came from the meager glow of a gimbaled lantern on the far bulkhead. Slowly emerging from the dark nightmare of a moment before, she began to understand she'd entered another. The deck felt wrong, its motion contradicting what she'd come to perceive as normal. She still heard the voices, and although the words were muffled, they were louder and shrill with alarm. One word she clearly understood sent a spasm of primal terror through her heart: "Leviathan!"

The rumbling groan intensified, and the deck heeled sharply beneath her. She had the impression the ship was rising up, much of the noise coming from the mighty timbers of its very bones, stressed beyond endurance. With a screech of agony and a splintering crash, the stress fell away like a broken spring, and she tumbled against the aft bulkhead that had suddenly become the floor. With a sickening, wallowing lurch, the stateroom righted itself, but then quickly tilted toward the bow. She hugged her knees to her chest and sobbed.

The door crashed open and her heart leaped with relief to see the wispy form of her tutor, Master Kearley, stumble into the room.

"My lady!" he cried, over the rising pandemonium in the passageway.

"Master Kearley! Oh, Master Kearley!"

"There you are, child," he exclaimed in a more normal tone. He even paused to straighten the lapels of his frock coat. "Come along quickly—no, do not hesitate to dress! A simple shawl will do."

She was accustomed to following his orders, and she did so now without thought, snatching her shawl from the hook by the door and draping it around her shoulders.

"And your bonnet too, I suppose," he instructed. Obediently, she took the bonnet from its place beside the shawl and pulled it down over her long, golden locks.

"What has happened?" she asked tremulously.

"Come," he said. "I will tell you what I know as we go, but we must hurry."

The darkened passageway swirled with kaleidoscopic scenes of shadowy panic. Shrieks of terror rent the air, and bustling shapes surged aft against the increasing cant of the deck. An indignant roar rose above the turmoil, and the girl thought she recognized the voice of Director Hanes. Even his exalted status couldn't protect him from the animalistic instinct of the throng. The metallic *sheeng!* of a sword leaving its scabbard quickly silenced the dignitary.

"Hurry!" Kearley prompted as they wove, hand in hand, toward a companionway. "We have struck a leviathan—or it has struck us. It makes no difference. The ship will quickly founder. Her back is broken." The girl sobbed again, and her terror threatened to overcome her. The nightmare was true after all.

"Make way, there!" Kearley shouted at the broad back of a man blocking the ladder. "Are you unmanned? Don't you know who this is?"

The big, dark-skinned man whirled and made a fist, preparing to strike the frail scholar. His eyes were wide and white with fear, his huge, disheveled black mustache almost covering his entire mouth. Before he released the panicked blow, however, he recognized the small form below him.

"Yer pardon, young miss!" he almost squealed with contrition. "Clap onto me back, and I'll plow us a road!"

Kearley grabbed a handful of belt with one hand and took the girl's wrist with the other. Together they fought their way up the choked companionway to the tilting quarterdeck. Once there, to the girl's surprise, the big man stooped and swept her off her feet.

"We must put her in a boat this instant!" he cried. His voice had returned to what was surely a more normal growl.

"My thanks, good sir," Kearley replied. "I appreciate your assistance." The man spared him an incredulous glance. Now that he recognized the girl, there was no question he would die to save her.

The girl was oblivious to the exchange. Around her in the darkness, there was no longer any doubt: her terrible dream had come to life. Helpless canvas flailed and snapped, and the once fascinating scientific intricacy of the rigging was a hopeless mare's nest of tangled lines. A constant, deadly hail of blocks and debris fell from above. Beyond her immediate surroundings, she dimly saw the bow, twisting and bent, jackknifing ever upward until the bowsprit pointed at the sky. The fragile paddle wheels on either side, amidships, resembled twisted flowers shorn of their petals. Steam and smoke jetted from the funnel. In the center of this catastrophe, the deadly sea coursed into the ship.

Then, past the bow, coal dark against the starry horizon, she saw a monstrous form. It was clearly the great leviathan that destroyed the ship—possibly entirely by accident. It may have simply risen from the depths, unknowing and unconcerned, to inhale a cavernous lungful of air. Perhaps only then did it discover the water bug on its back. No matter, it noticed it now. Even as the girl watched with unspeakable dread, the island-size creature completed its leisurely turn and came back to inspect the wounded morsel in its wake. The big man saw it too.

"Into a boat!" he bellowed, carrying her to the larboard rail, where a dozen men frantically tore at the quarter-boat tackle. "Make way, damn ye! Can ye not see who I bear?" A wide-eyed young officer motioned them through the gathering throng that regarded the boat with frantic, greedy eyes.

"Are you a sailor?" the officer demanded of the big man. "You're not one of the crew."

"I was a sailor once," he admitted. "And a soldier. I'm a shipwright now, bound for the yard at the company factory."

The officer considered. "Right. Take her aboard under your protection. As soon as you launch, you must hold the boat close so we may put more people aboard." He cast an appraising glance. "You do look strong enough."

Before the girl could form a protest, she was hoisted over the rail by the man's powerful arms and deposited into the boat. Quick as a goat, he followed her and turned to accept the bundles hastily passed to him. A sailor jumped aboard too, encumbered by a double armful of muskets, which he quickly stowed.

The girl found her voice. "Master Kearley!" she wailed. "Master Kearley, you must come too!"

"I will, my dear," came a muted cry beyond the desperate mass. "Lower away!"

The boat dropped swiftly to the water, and struck with a resounding smack.

"Fend off, you lubbers!" came the cry from above. "Hold her steady, now! I'll send them down two at a time on the falls!" The big man looped a rope around his powerful forearm and pulled with all his might, while the seaman pushed against the hull with an oar.

"Let 'em come!"

The girl gave voice to such a sudden, piercing, gut-wrenching shriek of terror that for an instant, in spite of their own fear, everyone froze to look. A massive cavern had opened before them, wide enough to swallow half the ship. Amid a chorus of muted screams it clamped down on the settling bow with a thunderous, rending crash. The mainmast toppled forward and fell against the darkened mass. More screams came when the mizzenmast also thundered down upon the horrified humanity on the quarterdeck.

"Master Kearley!"

With a terrible grinding, crunching sound, the titanic jaws gaped open, then closed once more on the pulverized forward section of the ship. Far in the distance, a monumental, explosive splash of mighty flukes crashed down, and with a convulsive jerk the entire ship lurched bodily away from where the tiny boat bobbed in the choppy sea.

"Master Kearley!" shrieked the girl with a desolate, perfect anguish, while the rest of the ship was shattered by the impossible strength of the beast. The boiler burst with a thunderclap roar and a swirling, scalding gout of steam. Further enraged by the discomfort this might have caused, the leviathan redoubled its attack. Terrible screams and splintering timbers filled the night, but soon all that remained was the surging sound of the agitated sea.

The seaman who brought the muskets had gone over the side, so there was no hope for him. The girl collapsed into the bottom of the boat and wept with disconsolate abandon. For a while the big man could do nothing except stare into the empty, endless night. Occasionally, his gaze fell upon the ragged, pulsing stump of his left arm. The rest of it had been snatched away so suddenly, and with such force, all he remembered feeling was a tug and a pop. Now his life was coursing into the sea, and he already felt the loss. Shaking himself, he snatched his belt from his waist and wound it tightly around the stump. Shortly the cascade reduced to a trickle, but, light-headed, he sat heavily in the boat and looked down at the sobbing girl.

"Little miss," he croaked, and the girl slowly raised her sodden eyes. "Yer Ladyship . . . I truly hate to impose, but if ye could see clear to bind me a bit better, I might be of more use to ye."

Seeing his terrible wound, the girl recoiled for an instant, but then scrambled lightly across the seats to his side.

"I will do what I may," she assured him bravely through her tears, "but I'm no surgeon."

"That's a fact," he agreed with a wan smile, "but I've no doubt ye could be if ye wished." As gently as she could, the girl tightened the tourniquet, then rummaged for something to use as a bandage. She finally settled for the sleeve on his other arm.

"They will search for us, won't they?" she asked while she worked.

"Of course, lass."

"Will they find us?"

The big man's smile faded completely, and he gazed out at the dark, endless swells. They'd lost contact with their consorts some nights back, but that happened all the time. The other two ships wouldn't grow concerned until several days after they reached the factory dock and the doomed ship and her important cargo still had not arrived. They'd traveled only half the distance to their destination, so it would be weeks before they were considered overdue. Months before the news reached home and a search was mounted. The wind and current would drive them quickly westward, far beyond the lanes traveled by men.

He blinked, then looked down into the huge, trusting eyes that seemed to pierce his callous soul.

"Of course they will, Your Highness."

*T*he Great Hall was a raucous Babel when the council met shortly after dark. Nakja-Mur, U-Amaki ay Baalkpan, took his place on the platform encircling the trunk of the Sacred Tree, resuming his position as host. The Great Hall was nearly as crowded as the first time Lieutenant Commander Matthew Reddy, USNR, entered it. Then, there'd been a party atmosphere, and it was open to any who wished to come. Now, the mood was anything but festive, and only High Chiefs and the newly created "officers" were present. Matt was still surprised how many there were. He rubbed at the sticky, burning sweat film that he couldn't seem to keep out of his green eyes, and tried to banish the exhaustion. Ever since his battered, overloaded, leaking ship crept back into Baalkpan Bay three days ago, he'd been overseeing emergency repairs day and night. He'd changed into his least soiled uniform, but realized with chagrin he'd neglected to shave when he felt the stubble on his face. *Damn. It's always the details that get you*, he thought, and tired as he was, he didn't have the luxury of neglecting any.

He stifled a sneeze. Sometimes the musty, downy fur of so many "People" in one place could be hard to take. Courtney Bradford had coined the term "Lemurians" for their friends, based on their resemblance to Madagascar lemurs. They had, in fact, learned the People (they called themselves Mi-Anaaka) were almost certainly descended from the giant lemurs of that place, although they looked more feline. Most of his human destroyermen just called them 'Cats now, although a few still clung to the original monkey-cats, or cat-monkeys, depending on whether they were from the deck division (apes) or the engineering spaces (snipes). The Lemurians had become firm allies, and many were official inductees into the United States Navy. Like all Navy terms however—even slang—uniformity was important, so simply 'Cats had gradually prevailed. There were still 'Cat-apes, and 'Cat-snipes, but that had nothing to do with race. It was occupational.

He nodded a greeting when he saw Queen Protector Safir Maraan of B'mbaado, looking, as always, amazingly fresh and vigorous in her black cloak and silver breastplate. She nodded deeply and respectfully in return. She and Lord Rolak of Aryaal stood together, encircled by their respective staffs. The scarred old Aryaalan warrior didn't look as fresh as his former enemy. Not only was the "Orphan Queen" a third his age, but he'd been much harder-pressed to organize his displaced people. He'd started with no staff at all, to speak of, and because of the bitter division that had existed in his city at the end, he'd been forced to assemble one with care. Contention, under the circumstances, couldn't be permitted.

Chack-Sab-At, with his brindled fur, still wearing his red kilt, white T-shirt, and platterlike "doughboy" helmet, didn't seem to know where to stand. He was present as the commander of the Second Marines, but since *Walker* was his home, he wound up standing close to Matt, along with his lieutenants. Most of *Walker*'s and *Mahan*'s officers were there, except Nurse Lieutenant Sandra Tucker, who was at the hospital tending to the wounded and shell-shocked survivors they'd brought home. Also absent were Lieutenant "Spanky" McFarlane and Acting Lieutenant Frankie Steele, who'd been left in charge of the ships. A grim-faced Ben Mallory, head and shoulder swaddled with bandages, stood unsteadily next to Matt with Sergeant Pete Alden, and Lieutenant Tamatsu Shinya, late of the Japanese Imperial Navy. Keje-Fris-Ar, Geran-Eras, and the recently arrived Ramic-Sa-Ar, all High Chiefs of the remaining seagoing Homes—stupendous wooden sailing vessels roughly the size of an aircraft carrier—made up the rest of the naval contingent.

Fristar, and most of the other Homes collected in Baalkpan Bay, had left earlier that afternoon. Their departure came as no surprise. Their warriors would have been welcome, but only *Fristar* was armed. Everyone knew from the start where her high chief, Anai-Sa, stood. Now they were gone, on course for Manila. At least they carried the seeds of the various cultures that remained.

Nakja-Mur struck the pipelike gong suspended above the platform, calling everyone to attention with a harsh, resonant sound. Baalkpan's High Chief wore his traditional robes, and his fine, silver-shot black fur was elegantly groomed. His long tail swished behind him with dignified expectation. He was still about the fattest Lemurian Matt had seen, but he wasn't all flab. The blow he gave the pipe would have severed an enemy's head, had he held a sword instead of a striker. The sound reverberated for several moments with a bone-rattling vibration. With Adar's assistance, Nakja-Mur's aged sky priest, Naga, mounted the dais to stand beside him. It was the first time Matt had seen him since his return, and the priest appeared to have aged a dozen years. Slowly the hall grew quiet and Nakja-Mur spoke:

"The Allied Expeditionary Force has returned to us," he said in a proud, positive voice.

The mission of the Allied Expeditionary Force had been to raise the siege of Aryaal, or Surabaya, Java, as the Americans remembered it, and expel the Grik—the Lemurians' "Ancient Enemy"—beyond the Malay Barrier. The Grik were a seemingly numberless race of furry/feathery, reptilian bipeds, whose expansionist imperative seemed matched only by their merciless ferocity. Apparently centered in eastern Africa, their empire now spanned the coast of the Indian, or "Western," Ocean all the way to Ceylon and Singapore—and now Java too. Separated from the Lemurians by the vast, hostile sea for ages, they'd developed their seagoing technology to the point they could threaten their old "prey" again at last.

The campaign met success at first, before the unforeseen full might of the Grik swept down, accompanied by the mighty Japanese battle cruiser, *Amagi*. In one fell swoop, the fortunes of war had changed entirely, and contentious Aryaal had been evacuated. Also evacuated, albeit less thoroughly due to the constraints of time, were the people of Aryaal's hereditary enemy on the island of B'mbaado (Madura). The people there, led by their charismatic Orphan Queen, Safir Maraan, had been aiding Aryaal against their mutual enemy, despite their animosity, when the AEF arrived. B'mbaado had actually officially joined the alliance. But with the enemy bearing down, as many people as possible from both cities were stuffed into every available boat, as well as the four allied (cannon-armed) seagoing Homes that constituted Captain Reddy's "battle line." What ensued was an exodus unlike any since that first one had occurred countless ages ago, when all the People were driven from "paradise" by the same ravening enemy. Matt knew the Lemurian "Scrolls" gave few details about what transpired back then; the tale had been passed down by word of mouth for millennia before being written, but he imagined the trauma must have been very much the same.

"They achieved great victories against the Grik and were not defeated," Nakja-Mur continued, "but through their success, they discovered the Ancient Enemy has numbers beyond what we ever imagined. Wisely, they returned to bolster our defenses here, so together we will have the forces to destroy that terrible threat." He paused and stared out at the expectant faces. "They bring also new, veteran allies—warriors who have faced the

Grik in battle, and come to our aid as we once went to theirs. Together we will field the largest army in the history of our race! There will be no defeat like that which drove us from our ancestral home!"

There were a few scattered cheers, and Matt had to admit Nakja-Mur was becoming a skilled orator. It was also clear he'd decided to concentrate on the positive—even to the point of glossing over a few blatant facts, like the tragedy that made those forces available. He supposed there was no harm in that. Everyone knew the story already, and those who remained were committed to the fight. They had no choice. All the mighty seagoing Homes that meant to leave were already gone, either fled or acting as giant freighters for goods and raw materials from the Fil-pin lands. Once again he was struck by the similarity of their current situation to that the Americans had faced nearly a year before, when the Japanese swept the Asiatic Fleet from the Philippines and Dutch East Indies. The irony was, this time the Philippines were the distant haven, instead of the first place they got kicked out of.

Nakja-Mur continued: "Safir Maraan, Queen Protector of the island of B'mbaado, has come with her personal guard of six hundred warriors, as well as the majority of her entire defense force of almost two thousand seasoned warriors!" Nakja-Mur didn't mention that over a thousand of B'mbaado's best troops had been lost with *Neracca*. *Neracca* was the final Home to evacuate, and was intercepted by the enemy. Reddy's old Asiatic Fleet "four-stacker" destroyer, USS *Walker* (DD-163), was escorting her to safety, and even tried to *tow* the much larger Home from the enemy's clutches, all to no avail. *Amagi*, slowed by damage she received once before at the hands of the Americans, was still unimaginably powerful. She cruelly smote *Neracca* from what seemed to the Lemurians an impossible distance with her massive ten-inch guns. *Walker* saved as many as she could, becoming dangerously unstable with close to a thousand aboard, but in the end, the uncounted thousands remaining on *Neracca* were doomed.

Tassat-Ay-Arracca, her High Chief, sent his daughter, Tassana, in the final gri-kakka boat to cut the cable herself. Matt could only imagine the weight of grief bearing upon the child's heart. In a fit of rage, or perhaps genius, he used the darkness, and the glare of the burning Home, to maneuver his damaged, overloaded ship into a position to fire his last remaining, fully functional torpedoes at the mighty ship. One exploded, damaging *Amagi* even further. Not enough to sink her, unfortunately, but enough to cause the Grik to postpone their final attack and turn their armada back to Aryaal. They must have decided, uncharacteristically, that they needed *Amagi* to ensure their success against what the Tree Prey had become (and the friends they'd made) since their last, ancient meeting. It was the only thing that gave Baalkpan this precious time they now had.

"Lord Muln-Rolak, Protector of Aryaal, has joined us with a trained force almost as large. Together with the majority of the civilian populations of both great cities upon which we can draw a levy, we stand prepared to face the enemy with over sixteen thousands able to bear arms!" There was a larger cheer, even though everyone must have realized how small that force was, compared to what was coming.

Nakja-Mur motioned Matt to join him.

First the sugar, now the salt, Matt thought, stepping up onto the platform.

"Cap-i-taan Reddy was acclaimed commander of the Allied Expeditionary Force, and he is the architect of its victories. The AEF has ended now, and with it the mandate of command. I propose he now be acclaimed Supreme Commander of the Allied defense of Baalkpan!" There were hoots and cheers, and the floor of the hall thundered with stamping feet. Matt just stood and watched until the tumult died away. "Then by acclamation, it is done! Cap-i-taan Reddy will assume command of all forces gathered here. Let all swear to follow his instructions in the coming fight. Swear on the honor of your clans! Swear now or leave!" Nakja-Mur turned to him then, and over the sound of the vigorous affirmations, he spoke in Matt's ear: "It is done. I've given them reason to hope, I think. I imagine you'll temper that with a large measure of despair. Taken together, perhaps a realistic expectation will emerge."

"I'll try to keep it upbeat, but I won't lie to them, my lord," Matt answered him. "These are our officers. We'll have a chance only if they know exactly what we face." He turned to the crowd and cleared his throat. Beginning with a summation of the previous campaign, he recounted how his ship had led the newly cannon-armed Homes against the invasion fleet that invested Aryaal. He told of the great victory in the bay, and how they landed and fought a desperate battle against the besieging force—a battle they won only by the skin of their teeth, prolific use of *Walker's* modern weapons, and the timely assistance of Queen Maraan and Lord Rolak. He didn't dwell on the treachery of Rolak's king that cost them many lives, and nearly the battle. King Rasik-Alcas was surely dead by now. He told how they found *Walker's* long-lost sister, USS *Mahan* (DD-102), and the pitifully few members of her crew who'd survived their own terrible ordeal. He spoke of things they'd learned about the enemy—still far too little—but also about how they'd defeated them. The Grik were terrifying warriors, but they fought without discipline—or even much thought. They'd beaten them, and they could do it again.

Then he talked about *Revenge*. She was a Grik "Indiaman" they'd captured and armed, and Matt had sent her to harass the enemy and scout the AEF's next objective, Singapore, the most tenuous Grik outpost. Ensign

Rick Tolson had been captain of *Revenge*, and Matt had finally read his log. The narrative was inspirational. It also wrenched his soul. *Revenge* had been badly damaged in a storm, and was left to face the full brunt of a new, massive Grik fleet all alone. Mallory took up the narrative, and briefly described what he, Ed Palmer, and Jis-Tikkar saw from the airborne perspective of the PBY flying boat, and he haltingly, hauntingly recounted the sacrifice *Revenge*'s people made to destroy as many of the enemy as they could, and prevent the capture of their ship. Matt thought the example was good for all to hear. It was the story of a gallant struggle against impossible odds, something they were all likely to face before long.

Matt then described, as clearly as he could, the force that destroyed *Revenge*; the force coming there. The hall grew silent, and for the first time, probably—for the Baalkpans, at least—it began to sink in. He spoke of the courage it took for the B'mbaadans and Aryaalans to sacrifice their homes, hoping that by defending Baalkpan, they might someday see their own homes again. He described the desperate evacuation and the bravery of Tassat-ay-Arracca, who'd saved so many in the face of certain destruction, and of Tassana, his daughter, and her own personal horror.

And when he had everyone's undivided attention, he talked about *Amagi*. At 46,000 tons of iron, and over 800 feet long, she was much heavier and almost as big as the improbably huge wooden seagoing Homes of the People. Most present still hadn't seen the Japanese battle cruiser, although some survivors of *Nerracca* had. At least, they'd seen what she could do with her terrifying guns. Tassana stood beside her grandfather, Ramic-Sa-Ar, her eyes red and haunted, while Matt described the ship. Chack had seen it. He'd had a good long look from *Walker*'s crow's nest, and often, when Matt stopped for a moment, he continued quietly in his own language, speaking of what he saw. Finally, Matt described *Walker*'s vengeful torpedo attack and the damage he thought it inflicted. To those listening it was a stirring commentary, but that wasn't Matt's only intent. He massaged his brow with his fingers and glanced at Nakja-Mur. The High Chief knew what he was going to say to the hushed assembly.

"She's still out there," he said at last, and took a long, deep breath. So did everyone else. "Mr. Mallory confirmed by direct observation that she's still afloat and underway"—he managed a predatory grin—"but not very fast. We were right about the damage to her boilers. It looks like she's making only about four knots. The Grik are clustered around her, probably to prevent another torpedo attack, and she and the rest of the enemy fleet have turned back for Aryaal. Her damage is severe, and remember, she was already badly damaged after the last time she met up with us. After that fish we stuck in her the other night, I'm frankly amazed she didn't just roll over and sink. Maybe she still will," he added hopefully, "but we can't count on it. I think we can count on a little time, however, and maybe we evened the odds a little. A few enemy scouts were reported nosing around the mouth of the bay this morning, but Fort Atkinson's guns drove them off. My ship is still in pretty rough shape, but tomorrow we'll sortie and see if we can tow in some of the Grik ships we damaged in the strait. As you know, a couple have already arrived, captured by local crews. I understand the fighting against the survivors was fierce. . . ."

"So *Amagi* and the main force have retired?" Keje asked for emphasis, speaking for the first time.

"As of Mr. Mallory's last observations before the PBY got jumped by one of *Amagi*'s spotting planes. I'm sure you all appreciate how lucky we are that plane and most of her people made it back? As for *Amagi*." He shrugged. "Maybe her other boilers will choke and that'll be the end of her. We could sure use one of those Strakkas right about now," he added, referring to an intense, typhoonlike storm spawned by the slightly different climate on this very different Earth. There were murmurs of agreement, mostly from the destroyermen. "In any event, Mr. Alden and Mr. Letts have improved considerably on the defense designs I left behind. They came up with stuff I never even thought of, and then the people of this city, working themselves to death, managed to finish the job. I'm impressed. Pete explained the differences and I had a good look at them this afternoon." He looked as many of them in the eye as he could. "They're *good* defenses, and they ought to hold against a very determined assault. That's good, because that's the only kind I've seen the Grik make." He paused, measuring the mood in the hall.

"Eventually, they'll come. *Amagi* will be repaired or not, but I expect if she can be, they'll try to wait for her. That may give us months to prepare, or it may not. They strike me as pretty notional, strategically. They might just get sick of waiting. Regardless, like I said, eventually they'll come, and we have to continue to prepare as if the attack will come next week . . . or tomorrow." The mood was decidedly somber. "Without *Amagi*, I think we can hold. We've already seen that their ships are extremely vulnerable to gunfire, particularly the high-explosive shells from *Walker*'s four-inch guns and the big thirty-two-pounders—both on the Homes and emplaced here. That's good, and I've no doubt we'll thrash the lizards if they come into the bay. The landward defenses look good too, and they'll be in for a hell of a surprise if they try them. The problem is, as with any static defense, we don't have any depth. If they break through anywhere, we're done. The wall has to hold. The lizards outnumber us ten to one already. With the extra time they now have too, I expect those odds to grow even worse. They may try to force some strategic point, and keep piling in until the defenders are exhausted. That means we have to keep plenty of reserves, and we can't commit them too soon.

"We can do this, but it's going to take unflinching discipline"—he let that sink in—"and it's also going to take more troops."

"But . . ." Keje spread his hands, palm up. "Where will we find them?"

"The Fil-pin lands," Matt said simply. "Manila. It's our only hope."

The Fil-pin lands and some other Homes not yet on the front lines of the war recognized the threat posed by the Grik and gladly sent almost everything asked of them. They knew the consequences if Baalkpan should fall, but for the most part they jealously reserved the one commodity Baalkpan needed most: warriors to match the countless hordes of the enemy. Token forces had been sent; Nakja-Mur suspected that was mainly so they might learn the new ways of war taught by the Americans, but with the exception of the Sularans across the strait, their combined numbers would not make up a single regiment of Alden's "Marines."

"I know they've refused to send significant forces in the past," Matt continued, "but if we go and talk to them, tell them, *show* them what the stakes are, maybe they'll change their minds. Besides," he added with a strange expression, "we might find more friends than the Manilos. I've been thinking about those reports of an 'iron fish' in the Fil-pin Sea. If it's what I think it is, and if we can find it, *Amagi* might be in for a very big surprise if she ever comes here."

"But who will go?" asked Adar. "It is a journey of months." Matt turned to him.

"You'll go; so will I. So will *Walker*. After a few weeks in the yard she can get there, meet the Manilos, look around for the iron fish, and still be back in plenty of time. We'll establish another wellhead on Tarakan Island too. Bradford says it's a good choice, and we need a fallback fuel reserve."

"What if the Grik do not wait?" insisted Nakja-Mur.

"We'll stay in touch through the radio in the plane." Matt looked at Mallory. "If Ben somehow manages to get it airworthy again, he won't fly until and unless Lieutenant Riggs and Radioman Clancy's experiments with other types of receivers are successful. Understood?"

Mallory nodded reluctantly. "Understood, Captain."

"There," Matt said. "*Amagi can't* come before we get back, and if the Grik try to send their main force, you should be able to hold for a time, and we'll be less than a week away. This is what I propose to do. . . ."

After the council adjourned, Matt and his former executive officer, Jim Ellis—now *Mahan*'s captain—were joined by Sandra Tucker, and together they strolled slowly along the pier. Ellis, burly, once ebullient, still showed the effects of his ordeal aboard *Mahan*. His limp, caused when he was shot by Kaufman—an Air Corps captain who'd taken over his ship after they came through the Squall—was better, but he was still haunted by what he felt was his less than stellar performance as *Mahan*'s commanding officer. Most of the already shorthanded old destroyer's remaining crew had died while she was nominally in his charge. Matt knew it wasn't his fault, but Jim didn't see it that way. Nor could he and the rest of *Mahan*'s survivors dispel the sense of dishonor that seemed to have settled upon their ship, due to Kaufman's actions and their own inability to prevent them.

Sandra Tucker was as petite as Ellis was physically imposing. The top of her head, long, sandy-brown hair coiled in a bun, reached only to Matt's shoulder, but her seemingly delicate frame concealed a strength of will and character that had been tested over and over again on the grisly battlefields of her operating tables. She'd faced wounds of a type and scope few Americans ever had, since the primary weapons of this war were designed to hack, stab, and slash. The unwarlike Lemurians had never seen anything like it before either, and she and Nurse Theimer had created, from scratch, a professional, efficient Hospital Corps. The 'Cats possessed a powerful analgesic, antiseptic paste, a by-product of the fermented "polta" fruit, so wounds were less likely to fester and fewer wounded were lost to disease. But battlefield medicine—the wholesale treatment of terrible wounds— was something the 'Cats had known nothing about. Sandra was just as tired as Matt. Many in her hospital now were younglings who'd survived the loss of *Nerracca*. The ship had been shelled into a sinking inferno, and a lot of the injuries she now faced were terrible burns on tiny, whimpering bodies.

The sky was clear, and in spite of the glow from the city and the pier, the stars stood out brightly overhead. In a way it was much like that night, so long ago now, when Matt and Sandra so tentatively discovered how they felt toward each other. On that occasion they'd been serenaded by drunken men singing an off-color song as they were transported back to the ship. Tonight the background music consisted of crackly, indistinct, upbeat tunes, from the dead gunner's mate "Mack" Marvaney's phonograph, playing over the ship's open comm. The music was accompanied by loud, hoarse voices and clanging metal, as the men continued working under the glare of the searchlights.

The main difference between that night and this, however, was that back then, they still had no real idea what they faced. They'd had a few minor successes against the Grik, and their concerns about fuel had been put to rest. In some ways it was a hopeful time. Matt had chafed at their ignorance regarding the enemy, but compared to now, that ignorance had indeed been bliss. Now they knew what they faced, and the mood was more somber. Back then, things seemed to be looking up. Tonight, hope and optimism were in considerably shorter supply.

They stopped at the end of the pier, a hundred yards aft of *Walker*. In the gloom, weirdly illuminated by the ambient light, the PBY was beached near its own short pier to keep it from sinking. The plane appeared to sag with exhaustion, its wings drooping low. The only things keeping them horizontal to the fuselage seemed to be the wingtip floats on either side, supported by blocks and makeshift braces. Matt remembered something else that had changed: he'd been committed to protecting and husbanding the irreplaceable Catalina. Since then, he'd nearly used it up, as his idealistic intentions gave way to the demands of reality. It was just as well, because if they'd kept to his original plan of, basically, not letting it fly out of sight, they'd all be dead right now. They'd have never known about the approach of *Amagi* and the Grik ships that accompanied her. He still felt a deep regret.

Few of the plane's injuries were visible in the shadows, but he could see them still by memory. Bullet holes and shattered Plexiglas, shredded control surfaces, the fire-blackened cowling, the terrible, violently amputated port wingtip . . . all added to the already generally dilapidated appearance of faded blue, brine-streaked paint. He didn't seriously expect her to ever fly again, in spite of Lieutenant Mallory's assurances. Even if Ben was right, the plane couldn't have many hours left to give them, and when it was gone, there'd never be another. Of course, the same could be said for *Walker* and *Mahan*, and the destroyermen that kept them alive. He was using them up too.

Matt finally broke the silence that had descended upon them. "So, Jim," he said, "what do you think of the plan? You didn't say a lot during the meeting."

Jim didn't answer at once. Instead, he stared back at the two destroyers tied to the dock. *Mahan* lay just ahead of *Walker*, lights burning aboard her as well. Even before the war they left behind, on another Earth, both ships had been antiques, commissioned in 1918 and 1919, respectively. Since then, they'd spent much of their lives toiling in neglect with the U.S. Asiatic Fleet. When the Japanese ravaged the Pacific Fleet at Pearl Harbor and ran wild during the early months of the war, all that stood in their way were obsolete relics like the ones he was looking at. Their sleek hulls and rakish, primitive appearance little resembled their more modern counterparts, and in comparison they were sadly underarmed. A meager four 4-inch guns and a single 3-inch gun constituted their "main battery," and a few machine guns mounted on the rails were all they ever had against aircraft. Their main offensive capability had always been their speed, and twelve 21-inch torpedo tubes. Now, both ships' speed had been reduced by battle damage and mechanical failure. *Mahan* had only one propeller, for example. Her other one had gone to replace one lost by *Walker*. They also had but a single—hopefully—operational torpedo between them; an obsolete MK-10 they'd scavenged from a warehouse of condemned equipment before evacuating Surabaya. During their "old" war. They'd originally fled that place with another American "four-stacker," *Pope*, and the British cruiser *Exeter*, and destroyer *Encounter*. All three other ships were destroyed by the Japanese, leaving only *Walker* and *Mahan* to face *Amagi*— and the Squall that swept them all here.

Any realistic assessment of the two destroyers would have left them condemned to the breaker, or at least several months in a dry dock after what they'd endured, but they had no such luxury. Therefore, with monumental ingenuity, jury-rigged parts, and the tireless efforts of their human/ Lemurian crews, the ships were being prepared for yet another last-ditch defense.

"I don't like staying behind," Jim confessed, "and I don't think you should go. The stability of the alliance depends on you too much."

"Maybe once," Matt admitted grudgingly, "but I think we're largely past that now. Everyone knows what's at stake. Mr. Letts will be chief of staff in my absence—he's developed a genius for diplomacy, it seems. If anybody can keep everyone on the same page, it'll be him and Nakja-Mur. You'll control all naval forces. I still hope to get Keje to leave *Big Sal* as a floating battery and go with me, since he's been to Manila before. Pete'll have overall command of land forces. I'd like to take him with me too, but with Lieutenant Shinya's issues still unresolved . . ." He sighed. "Besides, *Walker*'s the fastest, so she's the one to go. She's my ship; therefore, I go with her. *Mahan*'s your ship, and she needs you here."

"But I'll just be sitting around," Jim protested. As far as they knew, the enemy believed they had only one destroyer left. *Mahan* would be fitted with a new dummy smokestack, to replace the one she'd lost, and painted with *Walker*'s number so any spies wouldn't suspect Baalkpan's weakened condition, or that *Walker* had gone away. Mostly, the enemy must never suspect there were, in fact, two American destroyers. Unless they got reinforcements, it was the only ace they held. Matt had given orders that *Mahan* should steam about and be seen, but never risk herself or venture far from the mouth of the bay.

"Besides, you won't be just 'sitting around,'" he argued. "The captured ships'll need refitting, and there's the new construction to consider. I expect you to use them to try to get as many of Queen Maraan's people off B'mbaado as possible. I promised her as much, and besides, we'll need them. If Haakar-Faask, her general she left behind to lead them, is as good as he seemed, we'll badly need him as well."

Jim grunted. "All right, Skipper, if you say so. I still don't like it."

"Well," said Sandra, somewhat haughtily, "now that that's settled, I guess I deserve some explanation why you're leaving *me* behind, Captain Reddy!"

Matt groaned. "We've been over this before. Karen did a good job while we were away, and now we've got our other two nurses, Pam Cross and Kathy McCoy, back. But there aren't going to be any battles where we're going. You need to continue your work here. We have Pharmacist's Mate Jamie Miller, and you know he's turned into a fine surgeon in his own right. He's certainly had enough practice! Besides, there's still that other . . . issue to consider."

He was referring to the increasingly acute "dame famine." As far as the human—and rambunctiously male—destroyermen were concerned, there were only four human females in existence. One, Karen Theimer, was clearly attached to Alan Letts, and Matt expected Letts to approach him on the subject before much longer. This was the source of considerable stress. Rumor had it that a few men had actually formed . . . romantic relationships with the local females. One such relationship, between the irrepressible (acting) chief gunner's mate Dennis Silva and Chack's sister, Risa-Sab-At, was apparently more than rumor. Silva and Risa had done everything in their power to make it *seem* more than rumor, at any rate. Chack had been livid, but recently, strangely, Matt had noticed a visible thaw between Silva and Chack. Perhaps they'd sorted out their differences without violence this time, or maybe Chack had finally decided Silva and Risa were just joking after all. Whatever. He'd rather not have the distraction of females on this trip if he didn't have to. Out of sight didn't always mean out of mind, but if there were no women aboard, there shouldn't be any fights over them. Matt remained convinced there must be other women somewhere on this Earth; there was too much evidence of previous human/Lemurian contact, and even human/Grik—witness the enemy ships built along the same lines as eighteenth-century British East Indiamen. But until they found them, they had to tread carefully. That was why he and Sandra never openly acknowledged their own mutual affection.

His thoughts were interrupted by the sound of approaching footsteps. In the dim light, Karen Theimer and Alan Letts were walking arm in arm. *Sooner than I thought*, Matt speculated resignedly.

"Good evening, Captain . . . uh, Captains," Karen said as they exchanged salutes. "Good evening, Lieutenant Tucker."

"Good evening, Karen. Mr. Letts."

For several moments everyone just looked at one another. Alan seemed uneasy. He acted as if there were something he wanted to say, but couldn't find the words. Matt had a rough idea what they'd be, and he clasped his hands behind his back and leaned forward expectantly. Letts wasn't ordinarily the tongue-tied type, so this ought to be good. Suddenly the young supply officer jerked and gasped through clenched teeth. Matt glanced down in time to see Karen's right foot reappear next to her left.

"Uh . . . Captain Reddy, I, uh, have . . . I mean, I'd like to have a . . . ah, word, sir. I mean, if it's convenient." He glanced quickly at Karen, probably afraid she'd kick him again.

"Of course, Mr. Letts. We were just discussing the plan for our expedition and Baalkpan's defense. Perhaps you'd like to add something?"

"Uh, no, sir, not just now." His eyes flicked to Sandra and Jim. "Actually, sir, what I need to talk to you about falls more in the line of . . . well, a private . . ." He stopped, unable to continue.

Jim Ellis leaned forward wearing a menacing expression. "My God, Mr. Letts!" he exclaimed, shifting his gaze to the nurse. "Ensign Theimer, if this rogue has behaved indecently toward you, I'll see he's punished severely!" He motioned with his head toward the water of the bay, full of terrifying creatures their own world had never known. "And I mean *severely!*"

The whites of Letts's eyes became visible in the dark. "Oh, no, sir, Mr. Ellis! I assure—" Karen kicked him again, surprising him completely. He hopped quickly away from her, uttering a soft moan. In spite of her earlier confrontational mood, a giggle escaped Sandra's lips.

"Just spit it out, you big dope!" Karen commanded, rolling her eyes.

"Captain!" Alan squeaked. "We want to get m-m-married!" he finally managed.

Matt waited a moment, looking at the mismatched pair. Letts with his fair, peeling skin; Karen, dark-haired, lovely, slightly taller. He nodded. "I assume you've thought this through?"

"Yes, Captain, we have," Karen replied. "Ever since the AEF set out, and we remained here, we've worked closely together." She shrugged. "Somehow I fell in love with the guy." She looked at Sandra. "I know you're the head of my division, Lieutenant, and I should have spoken to you first, but we saw you walking out here together and . . ."

Sandra nodded. "Perfectly all right, Karen. I have to agree with Captain Reddy, though. Are you sure you've thought this through? You want to do this . . . now?"

Karen nodded sadly. "We wanted to wait until things settled down, but with everything going on . . . well, there might not be a better time."

Sandra sighed. "I understand. Very well, I've no objection. Captain?"

Matt rubbed his chin. "You know, Mr. Letts, some resentment's likely to arise out of this—what with the dame famine becoming more and more, ah, acute? If you ladies'll pardon me, I'll be blunt. Our men have gone literally months without female companionship, when, before we left the Philippines, to do so more than a few days would have been . . . extraordinary. A lot of pressure's building up. If not for the unending combat against the enemy, the elements, or the deterioration of the ship to help them . . . vent that pressure, I'm not sure we could've kept them under control. It's my hope, God willing, that someday we'll explore this new world. If that occurs, it'll be my very first priority to discover whether other humans exist here." He paused thoughtfully. "It's my belief they do. But first we have to survive the coming battle, and maybe the whole damn war. That's a lot of 'ifs.'" He waved away their concerned expressions. "That being said, I don't object either, I guess. I just want you to be sure this is what you want to do. It might be . . . difficult."

Jim chuckled. "I'd say that qualifies as one of those British understatements, Skipper. I also think if I were in their shoes, I wouldn't give a damn right now." He frowned. "Whatever time we've got left, I say make the most of it. Captain?" Matt nodded.

Jim Ellis beamed at the couple. "So. You want a big, fancy church wedding? Or are you going to elope?" He laughed at their confused expressions. "Run along, children," he said. "I'm sure our illustrious supreme commander'll be happy to perform a suitable ceremony directly."

After they were gone, Jim let out a breath and turned to Matt and Sandra. "You know," he began conversationally, "everything I just told those kids about 'making the most of it' and 'living while you can' goes double for you two." Only the darkness hid Sandra's sudden, deep blush.

"What the hell are you talking about?" Matt sputtered.

Jim laughed out loud. "Oh, c'mon! You honestly think you've kept your little secret? Wow. Patty-fingers on the bridge wing, moon-eyes whenever you're around each other! Queen Maraan thinks you *are* married and asked me if you have a *child*!" Ellis laughed again at their stunned expressions. "Keje finally believes you aren't already 'mated' and thinks you're a couple of idiots. Self-sacrificing deprivation isn't the norm with 'Cats."

"Is it really that obvious?" Sandra asked in a small voice. "We've both tried so hard!"

"Who else knows?" asked Matt through clenched teeth.

"The Mice may not have figured it out," Jim drawled dryly, referring to the two enigmatic, almost belligerently insular firemen, and their female Lemurian protégé, "but I wouldn't bet money."

"Damn."

Jim held up his hands. "Hold on, Skipper. Before you think your little act was a waste of time and the men'll resent you—like you warned Letts— let me tell you something. I told you everybody knows you're nuts about each other, but they also know why you've been acting like you weren't.

They appreciate it, Skipper! They know what it's cost you, because they know how it would feel to them. I do too. Your crew admires you immensely. They'd follow you into hell. They already have!" He shook his head. "*Mahan*'s the same way. Everyone sees the weight on your shoulders, both of you, and they know you've denied yourselves the one thing that might help lighten the load. And they know you've done it for them." He grinned. "Even if they still think you're a couple of dopes."

Matt was embarrassed. Not for how he felt, but because the men had seen through his deception. He felt as though he'd let them down. He looked at Sandra and saw tears gleaming on her cheeks, the lights of the city reflected in her shining eyes. "Would you excuse us for just a minute?" he asked in a husky voice.

"Sure, Skipper, I could swear somebody called me." Turning, Jim walked down the pier toward the ships.

Tentatively, Matt put his arms around Sandra and drew her close. For the first time he didn't notice any pain in his shoulder, wounded at Aryaal, at all. She began to shake, and he knew she was crying. "I'm so sorry," he said.

"Don't be," she scolded. "It was the right thing to do." She raised her face until she was looking into his eyes. "It still is," she told him firmly.

"I know." Then he kissed her. It was a light, gentle kiss, and their lips barely touched. He didn't dare make more of it. Still, it was enough to send an electric shock clear to the soles of his shoes. Finally, wistfully, retreating from their embrace, they began walking back toward the glare and racket of the feverish repairs. "There," he said softly. "Maybe that'll tide me over a little longer."

"I guess we have a wedding to arrange." Sandra sighed, wishing it could be their own.

Nakja-Mur lounged on his favorite cushion on the broad western balcony of the Great Hall of the People, apparently taking his ease. He often did so on clear evenings, watching the Sun slowly descend from the sacred Heavens into the impassable jungle beyond the bay. Sometimes, when the light was right, and his mood and eyelids were adjusted just so, he imagined the mighty orb quenching itself in the very bay. Many of his people had often watched him thus, equally content, at the end of a day's honest labor, or the beginning of a night's. They took comfort from his comfort, as he did from theirs, because it represented stability, prosperity, and, above all, the promise that they could continue to live their comfortable lives without want, fear, or change. Those had been happy times. Times he'd thought would continue throughout his life and reign as Baalkpan's High Chief. They were the only sort of "times" he'd ever known, and he'd taken them for granted. But that was before the Amer-i-caans came, and change became the norm, a necessity. That was before the War.

The Amer-i-caans didn't *bring* the war, of course, although some had argued they did. Many of those were long gone, having fled to "safety" in the Fil-pin lands, or just generally eastward in their huge floating Homes. Most who now remained were committed to the fight: the fight that, long as the odds were, they wouldn't have had the slightest chance of winning if the Amer-i-caans hadn't come. The People of Baalkpan would probably have been slaughtered before they even suspected war was upon them.

But still, when he could, he continued to take his evenings on the balcony of the huge wooden edifice encompassing the trunk of the mighty Galla tree. The tree was so massive, it continued to soar through the ceiling and high above before branching into a dense canopy that dwarfed the bulk of the Great Hall below, as well as every other structure in the city. He'd sit there and view the city: the tall pagodalike structures housing many families, just as those aboard the seafaring homes had traditionally done. Larger structures, with many levels, sheltered Baalkpan's various industries: ropewalks, chandleries, looms, block makers, coopers ... industries supporting Baalkpan's primarily maritime economy, and her trade with the seagoing Homes. They'd once been a source of employment, prosperity, and pride. Now greatly expanded, and with the new industries the Amer-i-caans had instituted or improved, they represented the only hope of salvation for Nakja-Mur's Home.

Before, he'd gazed upon the bay and the busy commerce of the city's fleet of coastal traders and fishers with a sense of satisfaction. Sometimes as many as a dozen enormous seagoing Homes might be moored or snugged up at the piers, disgorging barrels of gri-kakka oil in exchange for services, necessities, and even luxuries they craved from the increasingly prosperous, influential, and just as increasingly resented "land folk." Occasionally, swift, tall-masted feluccas dashed across his view, hurrying to ports across the dangerous strait, or returning with cargoes from distant land Homes. He marveled at the speed they achieved with their fore and aft rigs and sleek, radical hulls. Now the seagoing Homes were mostly gone; only the transient freighters and the three ships of the Allied "battle line" remained.

With the return of the AEF, and the Aryaalan and B'mbaadan warriors it had managed to save, the city's defenses were nearly tripled, but they needed more just to survive. Nakja-Mur was skeptical that more troops would be forthcoming from Manila, beyond the hundred or so volunteers they'd already sent, and he'd come to agree with the argument Cap-i-taan Reddy once made before the AEF set out in the first place: they could prevent defeat, for a time, with static defenses, but they could only *win* if they attacked. Attack, now, was out of the question, and Nakja-Mur constantly brooded over the implications of that.

The water of the bay glowed red beneath the lowering Sun, and except for the absence of most of the Homes, the bustle of small craft seemed undiminished even as they toiled for a much greater imperative than personal profit. His heart lifted when he saw one of the Amer-i-caan destroyers—*Mahan*. His newly practiced eye could tell by her awkwardly repaired pilothouse, even if she now sported a new fourth funnel. The ship was steaming slowly toward the mouth of the bay on some errand to Fort Atkinson, he guessed, or testing some repair. She was resplendent in a new coat of light gray paint, and he still marveled at the effortless grace with which she moved in any wind, though he knew she could use only one of her "engines."

Despite the fact *Walker* had seen more action in this war, *Mahan* was the weakest, most badly damaged of the two Amer-i-caan ships that came to them through the Squall. He now understood that that damage was due to an earlier encounter with *Amagi*. As powerful and indestructible as she seemed to him—she was made of iron, after all—he had to remind himself that if *Amagi* one day came—perhaps entered this very bay—she could swat *Mahan* aside with little concern. Such a thing was so far beyond his experience as to seem unthinkable. But he hadn't been there; he hadn't seen. Those he knew and trusted who'd beheld *Amagi* assured him it was true, and somehow he managed to believe them. The thought churned his gut with dread.

A servant, a member of his expanded wartime "staff," pushed through the curtain behind him and stepped into view, waiting to be noticed. Nakja-Mur sighed. "Oh, I wish you wouldn't lurk behind me like that; I won't eat you!" His tone was gruffer than he intended, and if anything it made the young servant cringe back a step.

"He does not know you as I do, lord," came a voice from beyond the curtain. It parted, revealing the hooded form of Adar, High Sky Priest of *Salissa* Home. Adar was tall for one of the People. He wore a deep purple robe adorned with embroidered silver stars across the shoulders and chest. The hood bore stars as well. His silver eyes peered from a face covered with fine, slate-gray fur. He gestured at Nakja-Mur's stomach, which, though considerably shrunken from its prewar dimensions, was still quite respectable. Nakja-Mur chuckled.

"I only eat youngling servants for *breakfast* these days, you know." He patted his belly and it rumbled on cue. "Though perhaps . . ."

"I will bring food instantly, my lord!" cried the servant, and he vanished from view.

Adar blinked amusement. "Do you suppose he will return?"

Now that the youngling was gone, Nakja-Mur sighed again. There was no need to keep up appearances for Adar. "Of course. Please be seated," he said, gesturing at a cushion nearby. "We have much to discuss."

Adar folded himself and perched rigidly on the firmer cushion Nakja-Mur knew he preferred. For a moment he just sat there, looking at the High Chief and waiting for him to speak. Nakja-Mur was casually dressed in a light, supple robe, and sat with a mug of nectar loosely balanced on his knee, but his increasingly silver-shot fur, and the absently troubled cant to his large, catlike ears, would have belied his relaxed pose to any who knew him well.

"The Amer-i-caans are planning a 'fallback' source of gish, to power their ships," he stated abruptly. "So no matter what they say, they recognize at least the possibility Baalkpan will fall." The strange Australian, Courtney Bradford, had been an upper-level engineering consultant for Royal Dutch Shell. That occupation allowed him to pursue his true passion: the study of the birds and animals of the Dutch East Indies. Also because of that occupation, however, stuffed in his briefcase when he evacuated Surabaya aboard *Walker* were maps showing practically every major oil deposit in the entire region. There'd been some skepticism that the same oil existed on "this" Earth that they'd found on their own, but after the success of their first well—exactly where he'd told them to drill—they were all believers now, even the Mice. Tasked by Captain Reddy to locate another source, he assured them they'd find oil in a variety of places. Most, for one reason or another, were rejected, but Tarakan Island seemed perfect. It was more than halfway up the coast of Borneo, bordered by the Celebes Sea. It was beyond anything the Grik maps showed they'd ever explored, and it was in a fallback position not only toward the Fil-pin lands, but one of Baalkpan's "daughter" colonies nearby.

The "colony" was a growing settlement right across the little strait in a marshy, swampy hell called Sembaakpan. There they gathered small crustaceans called graw-fish by basketfuls at low tide. They were very tasty in their premetamorphic stage, and considered a delicacy because no one knew them to exist anywhere else. They had a short shelf-life too, and were some of the strangest creatures the destroyermen had yet encountered. They looked and acted like little horseshoe crabs till they shed their shells and swam—and ultimately flew—away. Anyway, at least there were friends nearby, but they'd never even come up with their own name for the tiny, forbidding, impenetrably blanketed island, so Tarakan it still was.

"A prudent decision," Adar said, "and one I heartily approve."

Nakja-Mur grunted, his eyes still upon the bay. "It smacks of planning for defeat."

"You are mistaken. They plan for victory; why else embark on this expedition to seek allies—and a new source of fuel? No." He blinked in positive denial. "They do not *plan* for defeat, but prudently prepare for the possibility. Even if we are defeated, I do not think Cap-i-taan Reddy can imagine such a thing might be the end of the fight. Another setback, perhaps, and a serious one, but not the end."

The High Chief gazed out upon his city, contemplating it as a ravaged shell in the hands of the Grik. "How can such a thing *not* be the end," he breathed, then changed his tone, suddenly urgent. "How soon can you leave?"

Almost two full faces of the Sun Brother had passed since the AEF returned. Repairs were taking longer than anticipated. Evidently each time they fixed one problem, some new issue was revealed.

"A ten-day. *Walker's* repairs are almost complete, but it will take much of that time to dismantle the rig at the well site and transport it to the city. By then, *Mahan* will be completely ready to masquerade as her sister, and the three damaged Grik ships towed in from the strait will be repaired, armed, and ready for sea. With the flying boat still grounded—and likely to remain so, I fear—we cannot leave you blind. If their scouts sneak past, they will see everything seeming as before. With *Mahan* pretending to be *Walker*, they will never suspect the other ship is gone, or that there are, indeed, two Amer-i-caan destroyers. That's a secret we must keep at all costs. Within another ten-day after that, the first of your own warships that you so wisely commissioned in our absence will be ready for sea." He blinked. "I understand it is a great improvement over those of our enemies."

Nakja-Mur nodded enthusiastically, his depression momentarily forgotten. "Indeed! She is far more modern." He gestured toward the shipyard, where two sleek hulls still sat on the ways. A third was down at the new fitting-out pier, undergoing completion. Even now, the ship seethed with busy shapes silhouetted against the ruddy, reflected sunlight on the bay. "I have watched them erect every frame, place every plank. Cap-i-taan Reddy and the engineer, Brister, provided the basic design, but even they say we have built them better and stronger than their people ever constructed such ships! They call them 'frigates,' but they have yet to be named. As you know, a great deal of thought must go into such things."

For the first time, with human help, Lemurians had bent their formidable engineering skills toward constructing dedicated warships. Human and Lemurian technology and techniques comingled at every hand, and at least as far as the wooden shipyards were concerned, the Lemurians gave as much as they got. Their structural designs were amazingly efficient, as well as highly redundant—in exactly the sort of way to be prized in a warship. The humans made many suggestions for lines based on speed, and the Lemurians took them to heart, but they built the ships their way. The result was, hopefully, ships much faster—and stronger—than any sail-powered vessels the world had ever seen.

Adar nodded, looking where Nakja-Mur pointed. "Of course. They are very beautiful as well. A pity . . ."

The High Chief snorted. ". . . there will be only three? True. We will never have time to build more, no matter how long the Grik delay. With but fifty such ships, the Grik would never dare attack if it weren't for *Amagi*!"

"I meant that it's a pity they will be the last of their kind. The next ones will have auxiliary steam engines, I understand. As for the Grik . . . Oh, I think they would dare," Adar murmured. "They might lose, as you say, but they would still dare. They would have no choice." He blinked discontent. "And even if we had them, we haven't the crews."

"True, and that brings us back to our original discussion. I yearn for you to be on your way. First to gain us allies, of course, but also so you might more quickly return. I cannot help but fear the Grik will come while *Walker* is away." He waved off Adar's protest. "I know Cap-i-taan Reddy believes that unlikely, and without more troops to defend my city, her presence might make little difference. But to many people, she has become more than just a ship. After all she has done, and particularly after *Nerracca* . . . her absence will be felt."

"I understand what you mean," agreed Adar.

"Do you? Do you indeed? For it is not just the ship people look to, but the people who will be with her: Cap-i-taan Reddy and his crew, Braad-furd, Chack-Sab-At, my dear cousin Keje-Fris-Ar, if he goes . . . and you, of course. As you know, my own Sky Priest, old Naga, has become increasingly . . . disassociated. He cannot accept what has come to pass."

Adar nodded sadly. Naga had been his teacher, as a youngling, and had set a high example. His ancient mind was full of the lore and history of the People, and his knowledge of heavenly paths and mysteries was without compare. He once could recite, from memory alone, every word of the Sacred Scrolls, and unerringly describe every coastline drawn upon them. Recently, however, all that priceless knowledge and wisdom was increasingly locked away, inaccessible even to himself in any coherent fashion. Even though Adar was Sky Priest to Keje-Fris-Ar and *Salissa* Home, the people of Baalkpan, and strangely—given their different dogma—Aryaal and B'mbaado, increasingly looked to him for spiritual and moral inspiration. Ever since he'd learned the true nature of the Grik, Adar's most consistent inspiration was to fully embrace what the Amer-i-caans called "Total War." Only by doing so did the People have any hope of survival.

"Perhaps," he whispered.

The promised food arrived, and both Adar and Nakja-Mur forced confident grins and stilled their twitching ears. Fortunately, their tails were confined by their postures and couldn't betray their agitation by swishing back and forth.

"Leave us," said Nakja-Mur congenially, when the servant placed the tray before them. The youngling quickly departed. "Speaking of what this war has cost our Naga, how is Cap-i-taan Reddy? I will never learn to understand their grotesque face moving and hand waving, but he does not seem the same."

"He is driven," Adar conceded. "After what happened to *Nerracca*, he hates the Grik just as passionately as I, and if anything, I believe he hates the Jaapaan-ese even more." He cocked his ears. "Tragic as *Nerracca*'s loss certainly was, it is stunning how it has strengthened the alliance."

"True, but he seems distracted as well."

"There is tension," Adar confessed. "He is reluctant to mate with their healer, although their attraction is plain to all. I believe it has to do with the scarcity of females available to the rest of his people."

"Absurd."

"Perhaps. But there is also the issue of his secondary commander of land forces, Lew-ten-aant Shin-yaa."

"Shin-yaa is a 'Jaap,' I believe they call them, is he not?"

"Indeed. An enemy, yet they trust him; rely heavily upon him, in fact. Shin-yaa is of the same race, or clan, controlling *Amagi*, and he recognizes the evil she aids—represents—but he cannot believe all the beings aboard her have become evil as well. He is . . . conflicted, to say the least. It tortures him that his own people assist the Grik and did what they did to *Nerracca*. Yet, like us, the idea of fighting his own people tortures him just as much."

"But it is not the same! Hu-maans are much more warlike than we; they are more like the Aryaalans and B'mbaadans in that respect. . . . Oh."

"Precisely. To them, belonging to the same species does not keep them from killing others of different clans, or races within that species. And among the Jaap clan, the ties that bind them together seem even closer than those that bind the Amer-i-caans. The Amer-i-caans have much freer will to decide for themselves what is right and what is not. Among the Jaap clan, that decision is taken by a leader and imposed upon all others, regardless of what they might personally think."

"I see," murmured Nakja-Mur. "Do you think Shin-yaa can be trusted? Will he aid his clan against us?"

"I think not. I believe, even if he didn't know the right or wrong of it, his perception of what he calls his 'honor' would prevent it. Remember, before they ever came here, his clan and that of the Amer-i-caans were at war, but he has given his parole to Cap-i-taan Reddy, and rather than break it, he would resolve his personal conflict by ending his own life. More likely, in a confrontation between his people and ours, he will simply abstain. 'Sit it out,' as the Amer-i-caans would say."

"A pity. He is a fine leader, and the troops he leads—our own people—have no stake in his 'conflict.' I hope, for our sakes, as well as his own, he is able to resolve it in our favor."

Adar nodded. "Regardless, that is why he will accompany the expedition rather than remain behind."

"Probably best." Nakja-Mur changed the subject. "What is involved in dismantling and transporting the 'rig'?"

"Mostly time and labor. The 'rig' itself is not complex. If we had time, I'm sure it would be simpler to just build another. We will do that anyway, so we can sink more wells here, but we know this one works, and it is not needed at its present site. It would have to be moved in any case. The labor is something else; remember, there is a gri-gaantus maax-i-mus—a Gri-maax—in the area. The one that got their Tony Scott. I believe the Amer-i-caans call them 'super lizards.'"

"An appropriate term, if I translate correctly."

"Indeed. In any event, in order to convince a sufficient number of workers to go, we have to assemble an escort of almost equal numbers. Most inefficient, but necessary."

"Amazing!" gushed Courtney Bradford, removing his ridiculous hat and wiping sweat from his balding pate. (Acting) Chief Gunner's Mate Dennis Silva had to agree. Actually, the word that sprang to his mind was "prodigious," even though it was a word he'd never used before and had, in fact, only ever heard from the Australian engineer and self-proclaimed "naturalist." It was pretty "amazing" too, though.

"Biggest damn turd I ever saw," Silva agreed respectfully, slinging his BAR (Browning automatic rifle) on his powerful shoulder and crouching to view the thing in all its glory, "and I've seen my share of whoppers. Conjured up a few myself, but nothing to compare to *that*." The coiled heap of excrement wasn't exactly steaming, but it was fresh, and about the size of a grown man curled in a fetal position—which immediately set Dennis to thinking dark thoughts. He looked at the Australian and saw his eyes glisten with anticipation. He snorted. It was late January 1943 in the world they remembered, nearly a year since USS *Walker* passed through the Squall that brought them to this twisted, alien Earth. Personality-wise, Bradford had apparently changed least of any who'd survived. Outwardly, the change was complete. He'd finally given in to the inevitable and had allowed a salty, reddish blond beard to creep across his ruddy face. In fact, it struck the fine-furred 'Cats as hilarious that he now had more hair on his face than on the top of his head. In the heat and glaring sunlight of the latitude, that might've actually been dangerous, but Bradford had replaced his lost hat with a bizarre contraption most resembling a cartoon version of a Mexican sombrero. Of course, it looked ridiculous on his fair-skinned, somewhat rotund frame—a fact not lost on their friends.

Because of their large, catlike ears, Lemurians rarely wore any kind of hat. Some wore helmets into battle, but most had been fashioned with the ears in mind. Some, like Chack, insisted on wearing the round "dough-boy" helmets of the Americans and managed to do so—uncomfortably— by wearing them at a jaunty angle that allowed one ear to stick out to the side and the other to protrude inside the crown. It worked, after a fashion, and the American helmets certainly provided more protection in battle than anything else the 'Cats had ever put on their heads. But Courtney didn't have even that excuse. He looked ridiculous and didn't care, and that was part of his charm. Or maybe he did care, and did it anyway. He and Captain Reddy had once discussed how important amusement was to morale, and sometimes, just by being himself, Courtney Bradford was very good for morale. Like now.

As entertaining as the eccentric Australian could be, he was also pro-foundly valuable—besides his knowledge of oil-bearing strata. He could be highly annoying, and the word "eccentric" wasn't really quite descriptive enough, but despite his amateur "naturalist" status, he was also the closest thing to a physical scientist they had. His specialty—if it could be said he had one—was comparative anatomy, and he'd provided many important insights into the flora and fauna they'd encountered. The Lemurians were always more than happy to tell them everything they could, but this in-formation, of course, came from some of the very creatures he was intent on studying. In addition, he was the quintessential "Jack of all trades, mas-ter of none," but in his case, that was often a real asset. True, he didn't know everything about, well, anything, but he did know at least something about quite a lot, and that was more than anyone else could say.

Silva was darkly certain that when the captain found out he'd allowed Bradford to tag along, there'd be hell to pay, and with that realization came another: he cared. For Dennis's entire life, particularly since he joined the Navy, he'd always lived for the moment and damn the consequences. He was acting chief of the Ordnance Division, now that Campeti was Walker's acting gunnery officer, but with his skill and experience he should have been one long ago. He just never cared before, and didn't want the respon-sibility. Now everyone was having new responsibilities thrust upon them whether they wanted them or not, and most had risen to the challenge.

His old boss, Lieutenant Garrett, would soon have a command of his own. Alan Letts, once an undermotivated supply officer, had risen to the position of Captain Reddy's chief of staff. Bernie Sandison was still *Walker*'s torpedo officer (not that she much needed one), but he was also in charge of developing "special weapons." Sergeant Alden, formerly of the ill-fated USS *Houston*'s Marine contingent, was now "general of the armies." Chief Gray had been elevated to something else, still ill-defined. Maybe "super chief" described it best. Even the Mice had evolved beyond the simple firemen they still longed to be. He glanced at Bradford, who'd changed his appearance, perhaps, but remained essentially the same person. In all the ways that counted, Dennis suspected he himself may have changed more than anyone.

He hated the thought of letting the captain down, but felt a moral imperative to avenge the death of Tony Scott—someone he'd barely known before the Squall. He couldn't shake a sense of protectiveness toward all those who remained. He continued to act like the same Dennis Silva everyone expected to see: careless, fearless, irreverent, happy-go-lucky, perhaps even a touch psychotic. Outwardly, except for some new scars and a luxuriant blond beard, he remained the same. But now he did care, and that was a big change indeed.

"Smells like bear shit," observed the other gunner's mate, Paul Stites, nervously as he scanned the green, nightmarishly dense jungle bordering the pipeline cut. Dark haired, and as scrawny as Silva was powerful, he was Dennis's chief minion in mischief, and the closest thing to a human "best friend" he had left. He motioned at the enormous impressions all around them in the perpetually damp soil. "Bear shit from a giant turkey."

Stites, Bradford, and Dennis were the only humans along with the guard detail sent to dismantle the drilling rig called a "Fort Worth Spudder" they intended to transport to the new site. A respectable facsimile of a pump-jack had taken its place, and continued busily pumping oil to the expanded refinery near the pier. Stites, like the other humans, had smeared grease on his exposed skin to protect him from the dragonfly-size mosquitoes, but he was experimenting with used grease to see if it might prove more effective. Even though it was now streaked with sweat, he looked like he was in blackface.

The humans, however, along with a half dozen other 'Cats, had a different, unsanctioned agenda. Silva and Stites were there for revenge, pure and simple, and Bradford, curious as ever, upon learning their plans, had extorted an invitation.

"I don't know about where you're from, Stites," quipped Silva, "but turkeys in Alabama keep to a more manageable size." The tracks did look a little like a turkey's, except the impressions were more than a yard long.

"You don't suppose . . ." Stites mumbled, gesturing at the turd. Courtney looked up at him and saw his troubled expression.

"No, no. I shouldn't think so. It's been weeks since, well . . . Of course, I can't know for sure without more information about their metabolism. . . ."

"I was just wonderin' if we should . . . you know, bury it. Just in case it's . . . Tony. In case he's . . . in there."

Silva rolled his eyes. "That turd ain't Tony. Even if it is, I ain't buryin' it. We're all gonna be somethin's turd one of these days. We ain't got much time out here, and I'd rather spend it killin' the big bastard that ate him."

Before he was killed, Tony Scott had become Dennis Silva's friend. Dennis never had many friends, but those he had, he valued. Especially now. Scott had been *Walker*'s coxswain before the Squall, and had remained in charge of the launch despite his growing, almost panicky terror of the water. He had reason to be afraid. Everywhere they'd been so far, the water seethed with deadly creatures, and he'd come to hate the sea he'd always loved. He was no coward, though. Despite his fear, during the battle to capture the Grik ship that became *Revenge* he'd jumped in the water to save Lieutenant Tucker. At the time, a storm was running and flasher fish were inactive then—but he didn't know that. Everyone knew what the act had cost him. He thought he'd been committing suicide. He'd been afraid of nothing but water, though, and once aboard the Grik ship he'd fought like a maniac.

The irony of his death was still painful. Despite evidence to the contrary, compared to the water he'd always felt as if the land were safe. In an unguarded, thoughtless moment, he'd left his ever-present Thompson in his boat when he went ashore to check the oil rig after a storm. When he never returned, there was little doubt what got him, and whether the turd was Tony or not, it was big.

They'd seen plenty of larger piles: the stupid, domesticated "brontosarries" the Lemurians used as beasts of burden created much more mass, but the droppings of the strictly herbivorous sauropods more closely resembled titanic cow-flops. The object they were studying so intently was clearly a giant, compacted turd, manufactured by an equally giant carnivore. A "super lizard," to be precise.

Bradford hated the term "super lizard," and insisted the creatures were unquestionably allosaurs, relatively unchanged from specimens in the fossil record. Also, unlike most other "dinosaurs" they'd seen throughout what should have been the Dutch East Indies, super lizards were not stunted in size. If anything, they were *bigger* than their prehistoric cousins. Fortunately, there weren't many of them, and they seemed highly territorial. When, rarely, one was killed, it was often quite a while before another took its place. They were ambush hunters that positioned themselves along game trails and the odd clearing. Bradford said they were built for speed, but they hunted lazy, Silva thought. That was probably how this one got Tony. Just snatched him up when he came ambling along the cut. Fresh anger surged within him, and he stood and brushed damp earth from his knee.

The voices of the work detail diminished as it slogged on toward the well, leaving them behind. Silva turned to a gap-toothed 'Cat with silver-streaked fur. He had no clan, and he was known simply as the Hunter. All 'Cats wore as little as they could get away with, but the Hunter wore nothing but a necklace and a quiver of large crossbow bolts. The massive cross-bow he carried, and the super lizard claws clacking on the thong around his neck, seemed to establish his bona fides. "That not you friend," the Hunter said simply, referring to the spoor. "See thick black hairs? They from . . . I think you call 'rhino-pig'?"

"Rhino-pigs" were rhinoceros-size creatures, one of the few large mammals indigenous to this Borneo, and looked remarkably like massive razorbacks. They were extremely prolific and dangerous omnivores with thick, protective cases, and savage tusks protruding a foot or more from powerful jaws. They also sported a formidable horn on top of their heads. Regardless of the challenge, they were the Hunter's principal prey due to their succulent, fat-marbled flesh. Evidently, in spite of their horn, they were also the preferred prey of super lizards.

"How long?" Silva asked.

"Not long. He hear big group, loud walking. He go."

"Afraid of large groups?" Stites asked hopefully. The Hunter's grin spread.

"He no hungry enough for all. He waste good hunting place."

"Waste—"

Silva interrupted. "Where'd he go?"

The Hunter pointed toward a cramped trail disappearing into the jungle.

"You're kidding," Stites grumped. "I thought these things were big?"

Hefting his crossbow and setting off down the trail, the Hunter called back: "Trust me, he very big."

"Well . . . how many of these things have you killed, anyway?"

The Hunter paused briefly, and fingered his necklace. "Only one," he answered quietly.

"How come you know so much about 'em, then?" Stites's tone was skeptical.

The Hunter considered before making his reply. "With you magic weapons, maybe you not fear 'super lizard,' as you call him, but to slay even one with this"—he motioned with the crossbow—"I learn as much as I can about him. Also, even while I hunt other beasts, he always hunt me. I survive him long time, so maybe I learn much." He grinned hugely at Stites's expression. "Enough? We see."

"Then what brings you along?" Bradford inquired, visibly perplexed. "We cannot pay you."

The Hunter blinked pragmatically before turning back to the trail. "If he gone, this place be safer hunting for short time. Maybe long time. The Great Nakja-Mur reward me for meat I bring. . . ."

"Oh."

For the rest of the morning they crept carefully along, the Hunter in the lead, sometimes on all fours, tail twitching tensely behind him. Occasionally he paused, studying the ground disturbance in the dense carpet of decaying leaves and brush. Sometimes he motioned them to silence and listened, perfectly still, often for a considerable time. Silva grew certain that the 'Cat was using his nose as much as his ears. Ultimately, almost reluctantly it seemed, he'd move on. During one such respite, he gathered the eight others around him and spoke in a whisper that seemed almost a shout. Strangely, for once there were no raucous cries or any of the other sounds they'd grown accustomed to. Their quarry had passed recently indeed.

"We close," he hissed. "He pass this way soon ago. He know we come; he search for place to spring trap." The others, even Dennis, looked nervously around. "No, not here. He need more space. Maybe be clearing close ahead. He be there."

The jungle slowly came back to life, and even at their careful pace, the expected clearing soon appeared. It was much bigger than they'd expected, perhaps a hundred yards wide and longer than they could tell from where they stood. Blackened stumps, and new, fresh leaves testified to a recent lightning fire. They squinted for a moment in the dazzling sunlight, accustomed to the gloom of the trail, but the sun soon passed behind a cloud. The midafternoon showers—so common this time of year—awaited only the inevitable buildup. A dull, distant grumble of thunder echoed in the clearing. Silva unslung the BAR and raised it to the ready.

"No," pronounced the Hunter. "He not be so near opening. As I say, he want get us all. That need more room, I think. We go down main trail through burn. Where trail pass near jungle on either side, that where he strike."

"Are you suggesting he'll employ a *strategy*?" questioned Bradford, amazed.

"You ask, 'he plan this?' I let you judge. Super lizard is greatest hunter on all Borneo. He not stupid." He looked meaningfully at Silva's BAR. "I not stupid. You magic weapons kill him easy? Kill him fast?" Silva nodded confidently, although deep down, he was less sure than before.

"But I must see him alive!" Bradford insisted. "I must see him move! Really, I didn't come all this way solely to view a dead allosaur!" He turned to Silva. "I know you mean to kill this magnificent beast, and I understand your motive, but I insist you allow me to have as close a look as possible!"

The Hunter strode into the clearing with a strange chuckle. "You see alive, you see move, you see close. Hope you not see *too* close."

Tentatively, in single file, the others followed him. Silva walked behind the naked 'Cat, and Stites, armed with a Springfield, brought up the rear. All the others, including Bradford, carried one of the Krag-Jorgensens they'd discovered in crates in *Walker*'s armory. They were fine rifles, probably commissioned with the ship, but weren't quite as powerful as the .30-06s carried by the two gunner's mates. Their heavier bullets and slightly lower velocity might provide better penetration against something the size of a super lizard, however. None of the massive creatures had ever faced such formidably armed prey in all of history. That was the hope, at least, for all the comfort it gave them.

Two hundred yards into the opening, the Hunter paused. "You see him, you shoot very fast?" he asked Silva. Truthfully, Dennis nodded. The BAR was a handful for most men, but he was less encumbered by it than Stites was with his '03. Certainly less than the shorter Lemurians were with their Krags. "Then stay here short time. I walk ahead. Tempt him with me."

"What you want me to do?"

"You know when time comes. Just no hesitate for Braad-furd, or I be 'turd' like your friend." Whistling a strange tune through his missing teeth, the Hunter stepped forward and continued walking, apparently unconcerned, as the trail neared the edge of the trees.

As he drew closer, even those behind thought they heard a new sound in the denseness around them. The cries of the lizard birds and grunting shrieks of the ground dwellers had largely returned. They even heard the distant bellowing squeal of a rhino-pig echo in the burn, but there was something else, indefinable—perhaps an anxious breath. The Hunter stopped about sixty yards ahead. He still whistled, but the tune had become monotonous. He appeared as casual as before, but his long tail swished rapidly, tensely, agitated. He was looking at the ground. For an instant his gaze swept across the jungle to his left; then he stooped and collected some stones. Abruptly shattering the natural quiet, he began a shrill, frightened barking sound, hopping to and fro. Whipping his arm forward like a sling, he flung his first stone into the trees. The only response was an indignant grunt, but the breathing came quicker, more defined. More barking and a second stone invited a deep, rasping inrush of air. Even before the third stone flew, the jungle erupted with a heavy, gurgling moan, and several substantial trees fell like grass blades.

Silva had been keenly staring at the jungle, BAR at his shoulder, but when the massive head rocketed from the darkness amid a cloud of leaves, branches, and fleeing lizard birds, he hesitated for an instant, despite his promise. The head appeared almost twice as high as he'd expected, and by the time he acquired the target, it was already descending, murderous jaws agape, toward the Hunter on the trail.

No one else fired either. Not even the other 'Cats had ever actually *seen* a super lizard before. Silva knew the Mice had—perhaps this very one—and they'd both emptied their rifles into it before it simply stalked off. But nothing, certainly not their surly, monosyllabic description of the thing, could have prepared them for what they saw. Bradford only gasped in astonishment. Two great, rapid strides brought the thing completely in view, and it had to be fifty feet from nose to tail. Unlike many other creatures they'd seen, including the Grik, no fur or feathers of any kind adorned its hide. The skin was coarse, wrinkled like an elephant's, but blotched and streaked with a wild variety of dull colors. Even fully exposed, it was almost perfectly camouflaged against the dense jungle beyond. Only the sun, peeking from behind the clouds at a providential moment, showed them more than a rippling blur as it stooped to seize the Hunter with six-foot jaws lined with improbably long, sickle-shaped teeth.

Fortunately, with the agility of the cat he so closely resembled, the Hunter somersaulted out of the way, but he hit the ground hard and it was clear another step would pin him beneath the creature's terrible claws.

"Great God a'mighty!" Silva chirped, squeezing the trigger. A mighty *BAM-BAM-BAM-BAM* filled the clearing. Possibly, in his haste and surprise, the first few shots went wild. But Dennis was an excellent shot, and the familiar recoil of the heavy weapon pounding his shoulder steadied him. His training and experience took over. In a businesslike fashion, he confidently emptied his first magazine into the beast. Even before he snatched another to replace it, other shots sounded.

Silva didn't know how he expected the monster to react to the fusillade; a stately collapse would have been nice. Even a dramatic tumble and a long, flailing, writhing death would have been fine with him. What he didn't expect it to do, after absorbing most of a magazine from his BAR and numerous shots from his companions, was turn in their direction. The Hunter forgotten, it produced an ear-numbing roar and charged, its long-legged pace making it shockingly swift.

"Shit!"

Magazine in place, Silva racked the bolt and hosed the creature as it came. He knew he was hitting it, but the bullets appeared to have no effect. Way too soon, he burned through all twenty rounds and the bolt locked back. He turned to run, while groping at another magazine pouch, and saw that everyone else except Courtney Bradford had already fled. Even Stites. Bradford still stood, rifle hanging slack and apparently un-fired, gaping at the charging beast.

"C'mon, you crazy son of a bitch!" Silva screamed. He tugged at the Australian's arm, and the two of them ran for their lives. They raced across the clearing, back to the trail through the jungle, gasping in the sodden air and at the unexpected, unaccustomed exertion. Silva reasoned that his shots must have had some effect or the super lizard would have caught them already, but even the confined space of the trail provided little im-pediment. The creature only lowered its head and surged after them, crash-ing through the brush and shattering trees. They gained a little, though, and Dennis managed to insert another clip and blast at the thing's head periodically as it came for them, gnashing and snapping through the un-dergrowth like some insanely huge crocodile.

"This close enough for you, Courtney?" Silva rasped.

They could see only a short distance ahead, but after only a few min-utes of running as fast as they could, the trail that earlier took them over an hour to cautiously follow widened as they neared the pipeline cut. Brad-ford was spent, gasping, coughing, staggering as Silva pushed him along. He couldn't go much farther, and Dennis couldn't leave him. If the goofy naturalist got himself killed on this trip, Silva knew he might as well hang himself. After all the fighting, there weren't many destroyermen left. He was more than average valuable, but compared to Bradford . . . He emp-tied his gun at the ravening jaws yet again.

They burst into the cut, and Silva was surprised to see a skirmish line of riflemen. Stites had somehow managed to stop the fleeing 'Cats, and he'd gathered the rest of the returning guards. Now a dozen armed 'Cats waited with the other man. Bradford collapsed when he saw them, and Silva managed to drag him aside before inserting another clip—his last— into the BAR.

"I thought you were dead!" Stites shouted.

"I thought you were yellow!" Silva growled in reply. Just then, shaking shattered brush from his back and roaring with a mindless, deafening frenzy, the super lizard appeared.

It was hurt after all. One eye had been churned to goo and dangled loosely from a shattered socket. A long, three-fingered "arm" seemed use-less, and even some teeth were splintered or gone. Blood streamed from dozens of wounds, but it was still on its feet when it saw the new prey arrayed before it. He lunged forward once again.

"Open fire!" Silva yelled breathlessly.

A ragged volley erupted, sounding dully anemic in the humid air. For the first time the great lizard screeched in pain and staggered under the simultaneous impact of more than a dozen high-velocity projectiles. Silva continued firing short, three-shot bursts, while the others worked their bolts. Focusing on Dennis as a continued source of noise and irritation, the creature roared and swerved drunkenly toward him. Silva retreated, but didn't run—even though less than three full strides would see him devoured. The other side of the cut was at his back, and he had nowhere to go. Besides, this monster was Tony's killer. He was finished running. He'd kill it or die trying. He continued firing, but with much more care, aiming at the roof of its open mouth. Its brain must be in there somewhere. A single pace away, the super lizard stopped and shook its head, apparently disoriented. Great gobbets of congealing blood rained all around.

"Just *die*, you son of a *goat!*" Silva bellowed, and emptied his rifle down its throat. The bolt locked open with an audible *clack!* Out of ammunition, he simply pitched the rifle aside and drew the long cutlass, pattern of 1918, from his belt.

"C'mon," he breathed, planting his feet a little farther apart and raising the point of the cutlass. Vaguely noticing him once more, the massive beast took a tentative step in his direction.

"Fire!" came Stites's excited cry, and another volley, more carefully aimed than the first, slammed into the massive head.

For an instant nothing happened, and the air in the cut was filled with a gray, wispy cloud from the "smokeless" powder cartridges. Then, ever so slowly, but with increasing speed, Silva got his "stately collapse." It almost fell on top of him. The earth shuddered as the monster toppled lifelessly to the ground amid the sharp crackle of its own breaking bones. The riddled head struck less than six feet from where Dennis stood, and he was festooned with a splatter of gore and snot.

Silva almost fell to his knees, but somehow managed to keep his feet. Angrily slamming the cutlass back in its scabbard—to hide his shaking hands—he whirled and faced a grinning Paul Stites, as the gunner's mate rushed to him.

"What the hell'd you do that for?" he yelled, his voice filled with indignant wrath. "Goddamn it, I was just gettin' to the good part! What's the matter with you?" Yanking his cutlass back out, he stomped over to the head until he stared down at its remaining, unblinking eye. The thing seemed dead, but its abdomen still heaved weakly, and bloody bubbles oozed from its nostrils. He touched the eye with the sharp tip of his blade, pushing until the orb popped and a viscous fluid welled forth. The creature didn't stir.

"That's for chasin' us all over kingdom come and scarin' these poor cat-monkeys half to death," he said. Then he drove the blade deeper, feeling with the point. Finally he shoved it in almost to the hilt, and the ragged breathing abruptly stopped.

"That's for Tony Scott," he muttered darkly. "That's for killin' my friend."

"Wish we had a camera," Stites said languidly, slowly exhaling a blue cloud of smoke.

"Who cares about cameras; just gimme a damn bullet, will ya?" Silva pleaded. He and Stites were lounging on top of the dead monster, sharing a carefully hoarded cigarette, while Bradford—quite recovered— scampered around the beast, pacing its length and talking excitedly with the Hunter, who'd appeared in the cut soon after the shooting died away.

"Why?"

"Because I want one, damn it!" He sighed. "Look, shithead, I shot myself dry, see? I'm *totally out of ammo*! Right now that gives me the creeps like I never had before. So just shut up and give me a bullet, before I beat you to death!"

Stites smirked and opened his bolt, then stared into his own magazine well in horror. Frantically slapping his pockets with increased panic brought no satisfaction. "Jeez, Dennis! I'm empty too!"

Silva was grimly quiet a moment, considering the long trek back to the refinery and the boat. Suddenly he brightened. "Hey, Mr. Bradford!" Courtney paused his examination and looked inquiringly at him. He had every reason to be well disposed toward the big gunner's mate. After all, he'd gotten quite close to the monstrous creature and witnessed all sorts of movement before it was killed. Silva only hoped Bradford could protect him from the worst of his captain's wrath. "You got plenty of bullets left, right?"

Bradford sheepishly hefted the Krag. "Indeed. I'm certain I fired several times, there at the end, but somehow I still have as many rounds as I set out with. Strange."

"Musta had some extras an' thumbed 'em in without thinkin'. You got plenty of stuff to think about right now, though. Why don't you let me wag that heavy rifle back for you?"

Bradford grinned uncertainly. "Oh, thank you very much indeed . . .

but I wouldn't want to be a bother. I can carry my own weight, you know! Still . . . the sling is bloody uncomfortable on my sore shoulder. . . ."

Silva tossed the empty BAR to a wide-eyed Stites and leaned down to accept the Krag. "No bother a'tall!"

U

nusually, despite the early hour, it was already raining by the time all the lines were singled up, and the special sea and anchor detail finished all topside preparations for getting underway. Matthew Reddy, captain of USS *Walker*, High Chief of the Amer-i-caan clan, and supreme commander (by acclamation) of all Allied Military Forces, stood in the pilothouse, binoculars around his neck, waiting for "Spanky" to report on the engines. Raindrops pummeled the slightly convex foredeck below him, and ran from the freshly painted steel to course down the side. Behind him the newly overhauled blower roared reassuringly, and he felt a sense of calm begin to edge out the anxiety he felt about the expedition. The routine procedures he knew so well had much to do with that: all the sounds and shouted commands, the twitter of the bosun's pipe. He was also encouraged just by the fact that they were finally getting underway. The expedition was his idea, and the mission they were on was crucial, but the time it had taken to prepare had cut deeply into the cushion he thought they had. He was glad to have his ship under him again, alive and straining for the open sea, but he was nervous about leaving all the same.

The bridge talker, Seaman Fred Reynolds, spoke: "Engineering reports ready to get underway."

"Very well. Cast off the stern lines." He nodded at Chief Quartermaster's Mate Norman Kutas at the helm. "Left full rudder. Port engine ahead one-third."

"Left full rudder, port ahead one-third, aye."

With a juddering vibration, dirty water boiled under the port propeller guard and the cramped, rounded-vee-shaped stern eased slowly away from the pier. Matt stepped into the rain on the port bridge wing and glanced aft. Immediately, water began soaking his hair beneath his battered hat. When the stern was far enough from the pier, he called back to the helmsman: "Rudder amidships. Cast off the bowlines." The orders were quickly relayed, and the human and Lemurian destroyermen on the fo'c'sle, already soaking wet, scampered to throw off the heavy ropes. "All astern, slow." He moved back into the pilothouse and quickly dried his face and the back of his head with a towel while he watched the proceedings. Quite a few people lined the dock in spite of the weather, watching the amazing ship depart. Many of their hopes rested with him and the successful completion of their task.

He noticed one person in particular standing with the furry, drenched Lemurians. Her small form already partially obscured by the deluge, he saw her sandy-brown hair hanging down in sodden strands. She raised a tentative hand. *We'll be back soon*, he silently mouthed, knowing she couldn't see, and he waved back at all the spectators, but one most of all. "We'll be back soon," he repeated aloud.

"Sir?" asked Reynolds.

"Nothing. Right standard rudder, all ahead one-third."

"Right standard rudder, all ahead one-third," Kutas replied. "Recommend course two seven five."

"Make it so. Reynolds, get the sea and anchor detail out of the rain and pass the word for the bosun and exec to join me on the bridge. Spanky too."

"Aye, aye, Captain."

To Sandra Tucker, standing on the old fitting-out pier, the new, light gray paint covering the battered old destroyer couldn't hide her many defects, but it did quickly blend with the driving rain. She felt a lump the size of her fist tighten in her chest as the ship grew ever more wraithlike and ethereal, and she wondered if she'd ever see it again. If she'd ever see Matthew Reddy again. She said a quick, fervent prayer for the ship and all those aboard her—and one in particular. With a sigh, she turned and melted into the throng and made her way through the dripping, awning-covered bazaar, back to her own duties at the hospital.

Lieutenant Larry Dowden, *Walker*'s executive officer, reached the bridge first, water running from the brim of his hat. Dowden was of average height and spare, but the young towheaded officer from Tennessee had stepped into his new job with energy and professionalism. He'd been a good choice to replace Lieutenant Ellis, Matt reflected once again, tossing him the towel. Soon afterward, Chief Bosun's Mate Fitzhugh Gray clomped up the metal ladder and joined them.

"Mornin', Skipper." He didn't salute because technically, as soon as he stepped out of the rain, he was no longer "outdoors."

Gray was a bear of a man, close to sixty, who'd gone a little to seed on the China Station before the war, but had since trimmed back down and muscled up considerably. He, at least, had thrived on all the activity and adventure they'd experienced since the Squall. He'd always demonstrated a clear—indeed, profound—understanding of the practical; that had perhaps been the very definition of his duty as *Walker*'s senior noncommissioned officer. Unlike many in the Navy who had the rank without the skill, Gray had the skill in sufficient measure to apply it beyond the insular world of *Walker*'s deck. As Spanky could, when it came to anything mechanical, Gray brought absolute moral authority to any discussion regarding what people were capable of, and his uncannily accurate assessments now included Lemurians as well.

"Mornin', Boats."

"I ran into Juan on the way up here and he said he'd be along directly," Gray said, referring to Juan Marcos, the Filipino mess attendant who had, for all intents and purposes, become Matt's personal steward. It was never discussed, and it certainly wasn't official, but that was how it wound up. Juan had seen to that. "He's bringin' coffee," Gray added ominously, but with an entirely innocent expression—quite an accomplishment for him. Matt grimaced. Juan wasn't good with coffee, never had been. Somehow he couldn't destroy the stuff that passed for coffee here as thoroughly as he had the "real" stuff, but it still wasn't exactly good.

"Maybe . . ."

Juan appeared, beaming, as wet as they. He carried a tray loaded with cups and a silver tureen. A towel was draped over his skinny brown arm.

"Good morning, Cap-tan! You slept well again, I trust? I am so pleased! Here is your coffee!"

"Uh, thanks, Juan." Matt took a cup and glanced at Gray. "Pour some for Chief Gray too."

"Oh, no, Skipper, I've had plenty already. . . ."

Matt arched an eyebrow. "Nonsense, Boats, I insist. Since you were so diligent in letting Juan know I was ready for my coffee, it's only right you should have some too." He turned to Dowden. "How 'bout you, Larry? No? Well, perhaps later."

Juan happily filled two cups, then set the tray on the edge of the chart table. "When that is gone, I will bring more."

"Thanks, Juan. You're too good to me." The Filipino smiled even more broadly, bowed, and turned away.

"Little booger should've been in the hotel business," Gray said, peering into his cup doubtfully after Juan disappeared. "There'd be few complaints as long as they kept him away from the coffee."

Matt sighed. "Yeah, but ever since my 'promotion' to supreme allied commander he's been treating me like MacArthur. It's weird and kind of . . . embarrassing." He was uncomfortable with his new title, and all the stuff that apparently went with it—in Juan's estimation, at least. But it was his job whether he liked it or not, and the people who'd given it to him deserved his very best regardless of how he felt. He briefly wondered what Admiral Tommy Hart would say if he could see him now—let alone General MacArthur.

Gray nodded. "Kinda hard to go through everything we have without makin' that comparison—all the runnin' around fightin' and such, with you right in the middle of it, and so much dependin' on every word you say." Matt started to chuckle. "Misery and strife shared by all, sword fights, for God's sake! Wounds, sudden death at any moment, *everything* wants to eat us . . ." Matt was laughing out loud. He held up a hand for the bosun to stop, but Gray continued: "Yeah, I can see how it'd be hard not to compare you to that Army idiot who let all our air cover get hammered on the ground and never even saw a Jap. The excitement and adventure. Honors and glory! It's everything *I* joined the Navy for in the first place."

"Okay, Boats, I give up," Matt said at last, still smiling at the older man. Gray never made any secret of his opinion regarding MacArthur's strategies. "I guess everyone's earned a little rest. Maybe this trip will provide one."

"Rest, is it?" Gray growled with a matching grin. "Don't say that, Skipper. I feel better than I have in years." His face became thoughtful. "You know, all that time on the China Station and in the Philippines, I was just goin' through the motions. Drinkin' San Miguel, fightin' in bars, gettin' fat. I did my job, but there wasn't any real point to it, I could see. I love the old *Walker*, sir; she's my home. But no matter how hard we tried to keep her ready to fight, nothing could've made her ready for the Japs. She was too old and worn-out. Just like me." He sighed. "Then the Japs ran us out of the Philippines. Beat us up and chased us out of the Java Sea, too. Beggin' your pardon, Skipper, but none of us were much good for anything but runnin' back then. You were right. Even if the Japs hadn't got us, *Walker* would've spent the war towin' targets . . . or bein' one, and most of her crew wouldn't have been good for much else either. After that last big fight with *Amagi*, when we got sucked up by the Squall, none of that mattered anymore."

A stormy frown creased Gray's face. "I hate the Japs for what they done to us, and I hope wherever 'home' is, our boys are kickin' hell out of 'em. But we wouldn't have been helpin' much, even if we were alive. Back there, *Walker* wouldn't have made any difference." His frown shifted into an expression of determination. "In this world, in this fight against those damn Griks, she has made a difference, and so have all her people. With God's help, maybe she will again."

"God's, and Spanky McFarlane's," Matt agreed quietly, referring to *Walker*'s engineering officer, who still hadn't arrived. The diminutive engineer had performed miracles keeping the battered ship not only afloat, but seaworthy, and three of her four boilers were probably in better shape than they'd been in years. Their arrival in Baalkpan, and the necessities of the war they found themselves in, had sparked an industrial revolution of sorts. The Lemurians had already possessed impressive foundries for casting massive anchors and other fittings for the Homes, but the Americans had taught them to make cannon, shot, and other things they'd need. The machine shops on the two destroyers turned out parts for lathes even bigger than themselves, and soon milling machines, lathes, and other heavy tools were operating in huge "factories" near the shipyard. They were running out of certain other spare parts fast, though, mostly bearings and things that Lemurian industry wasn't yet up to helping them produce. They'd have to figure that out pretty quick.

Gray nodded. "Yes, sir. Please don't ever tell him I said so, but Spanky's been a wonder. Him and everybody else."

"What?" demanded McFarlane, suddenly joining them, dripping like the rest, and striking his distinctive pose: hands on his skinny hips.

"Nothin'," Gray grumped, recovering himself. "I was just wonderin' who's gonna restow that junk your snipes scattered all over my topsides." He was referring to the disassembled drilling rig.

"Your deck apes," Spanky replied cheerfully. "That's their job."

Walker steamed past *Aracca* Home, one of the enormous seagoing cities of the Lemurians. She was moving toward the mouth of the bay to relieve *Big Sal* as a floating battery—a task all the sea folk despised, but knew was necessary. Larger than the new *Essex*-class aircraft carriers Matt had seen under construction, *Aracca*, like all her kind, was built entirely of wood. Her hull was double ended, flat bottomed, and diagonally plank laminated to a thickness of six feet in some places. Matt was impressed by the sophisticated design, and knew the ship was incredibly tough. It had to be. Despite the stresses inherent to her momentous proportions (1,009 feet long, with a beam of almost 200 feet), *Aracca* had been built to last for centuries upon a sea that was much more hostile in many ways than the sea Matt had known before the Squall. *Not in all ways, perhaps*, he reflected grimly—remembering that Homes like *Aracca* were not proof against ten-inch naval rifles.

Despite the rain, he saw her people going about their morning chores: preparing fish from the morning catch for drying, once the rain eased, and tending the polta fruit gardens on the main deck that ranged along the bulwark completely around the ship. The main deck was a hundred feet above the sea, and three huge pagodalike structures that served as apartments for many of her people towered above it like skyscrapers. Encompassing the structures were three massive tripods soaring another two hundred and fifty feet above the deck. They supported the great sails, or "wings" that provided *Aracca*'s only means of propulsion—other than the hundred giant sweep-oars her people could use for maneuvering when necessary.

Matt was always amazed whenever he looked at *Aracca*—or any Lemurian Homes. Not only because of their size, but also because of the industrious ingenuity they represented. 'Cats may have been a little backward in some respects when the Americans first arrived, but they certainly weren't ignorant. He had *Walker*'s horn sounded in greeting, and he and the other officers went back out in the rain on the bridge wing and returned the friendly waves they received. Slowly the massive ship receded in the rain behind them.

"I'm already anxious to be back," Matt said aloud, ruefully.

"We're getting a late start," conceded Dowden. He glanced apologetically at Spanky. "No offense, I know you went as fast as you could. It's just . . ."

"I know," Spanky growled. "By the original timetable, we should've been on our way home by now. But one thing led to another . . . It sure would've been easier with a dry dock, especially to get at the damage below the waterline. She won't ever be 'right' until we can do that."

"Agreed," said the captain, "but that'll have to wait. New construction has priority, and there just aren't enough hands, or hours, or days. . . ." He shook his head. "Nothing for it. You've done an amazing job, Spanky. All of you have. My question is, are the boilers in shape for more speed than we planned on, and if so, do we have the fuel? How much time can we shave off our trip?"

Spanky took off his hat and scratched his head. "We're steaming on two boilers now, numbers two and three. Our range used to be about twenty-five hundred miles at twenty knots. We can't do that well anymore. I can't guarantee we can even *make* twenty knots on two boilers. If we light off number four, it'll take half again as much fuel to gain just those few extra knots. Now, the new fuel bunker we installed where number one used to be ought to give us a safe margin, but it might not—and until we get the new site on Tarakan up and running, there won't be anyplace to top off." He shrugged. "If you're putting me on the spot, I'd say we can light number four, probably squeeze twenty-five, maybe twenty-eight knots out of her, and still get back okay, but you won't be able to do as much poking around looking for that 'iron fish' as you hoped. If we burn it now, you might wish we had it later."

Matt grimaced. "Well, let's wait till we reach open water and see what she'll give us. Maybe she'll make twenty. If she won't, though, I'm inclined to burn it now. I just can't shake the feeling we need to get back as soon as we can."

"But . . . we'd still get back before any reinforcements could arrive," said Dowden. "What real difference would it make?"

"Probably none. We'll be in radio contact, and should have plenty of warning if the Japs and the Grik get uppity. We can take it easy on the way back if we have to."

"What's really bothering you?" asked Gray. "Is it *Amagi*?"

Matt nodded. "I guess. Theoretically, we should still have months before she's seaworthy again. They don't have a dry dock either, and she's got a lot of underwater damage. But she shouldn't have been here in the first place." He paused, considering the absurdity of his remark, but they knew what he meant. "I just hate being blind. It's like the 'old' war all over again. Without the PBY, we don't really have any idea what the enemy's up to, or what they're capable of."

The rain began to slacken, and before them lay the mouth of the bay. In it loomed *Big Sal*, or *Salissa* Home.

"Signal from *Big Sal*," announced the talker, relaying a message from the Lemurian lookout in the crow's nest. All allied vessels had been fitted with some means of making a signal by flags or semaphore. "It says Keje-Fris-Ar would like to accompany us after all, if we wouldn't mind slowing down enough to take him aboard."

Matt chuckled with relief. He'd been hoping his Lemurian friend would change his mind and come along. "Tell him we can't slow down, but we'll pass as close as we can and he can jump."

"Sir?"

The others chuckled too.

"Never mind. Tell him 'of course' and 'welcome.'"

Sandra went straight to the area of the roofed but otherwise open-air hospital, partitioned from the rest by hanging curtains, or tapestries, woven in bright, cheerful colors. It was the area many considered the "psych ward." She knew Selass, Keje's daughter, was working there, and she wanted to see her. The two had become friends, and the once spoiled, self-centered, and standoffish Selass had changed dramatically over the last few months. She'd become a real asset at the hospital, and her efforts in the psych ward in particular were tireless. Part of that was because she felt genuine concern for the people there. Most Lemurians, with the exception of Aryaalans and B'mbaadans, had never really known war before. They were a peaceful people, ready to defend their homes and families, but utterly unaccustomed to the horrors they'd seen and been forced to endure. Many of her patients had terrible physical wounds, sustained in the recent fighting, and she had to help them learn to cope with that. Others had been just as seriously wounded in the mind. The worst of these was a small, dwindling group of "survivors" they'd rescued from the first Grik ship they'd captured, the one that became *Revenge* and was later destroyed in battle. That was when they realized just how terrible their enemy truly was when they discovered that, to the Grik, anyone not allied with them was nothing but prey to be devoured, and when prey was captured, they kept them as living provisions. The survivors they'd found chained in the Grik ship's hold not only understood this, but they'd seen many others, in some cases their very families, butchered alive and prepared for Grik cook pots. Selass's own mate, Saak-Fas, was one who'd seen it all.

He'd been knocked unconscious and carried aboard the one Grik ship that escaped destruction when *Walker* first came to the People's aid. No one knew what became of him at the time; it was assumed he was lost overboard with so many others, and devoured by the insatiable fish. Not so. Somehow he'd been captured and survived for months in first one hold, then another, and he'd seen . . . terrible things. He was quite mad when finally rescued. In the meantime, considering him dead, Selass finally realized she'd been wrong to take him to mate in the first place, and developed a real affection for Chack-Sab-At, who'd hopelessly wooed her before she made her choice. At the time, she hadn't thought much of the young wing runner, but since then, Chack had become a noted warrior and a true leader. When she made her feelings known to him, he'd promised to give an answer after the battle for the ship. Instead, he'd returned to her with her long-lost mate. It was a crushing, emotional scene, and Sandra felt terribly sorry for Selass. Since then, Chack seemed to have fallen for the exotically beautiful B'mbaadan queen, Safir Maraan, but Selass's feelings for him were undiminished. Added to that was the fact that her mate still lived and she could never leave him in his current state. It was a terrible hardship for Selass to bear: unrequited love for someone increasingly beyond her grasp, mixed with terrible guilt that she had those feelings while her legitimate mate still lived.

Even so, it might not have been so tragic, but Saak-Fas wouldn't even speak to her, no matter how hard she tried to elicit some response. He wouldn't speak to anyone. He was recovered, physically, from his ordeal, and almost feverish daily exercise had left him in better shape than he'd ever been. Sandra doubted he knew about his mate's inner turmoil, so that probably wasn't the reason for his behavior. When his old friends from *Big Sal* visited, he said nothing at all, and showed no interest in life aboard his old home. He cared nothing about reports of the war, and wouldn't even acknowledge the existence of others who'd been through the same ordeal as he. Worst of all, no matter what she said or did, when Selass spent time with him each day, he acted as though she weren't even there. The torment Selass felt was a palpable thing, and it wrenched Sandra to her core.

Sandra nodded and smiled at Pam Cross, who led a small procession of medical recruits through the fabric opening, showing them around. She knew Pam had issues of her own. It wasn't much of a secret anymore that she and Dennis Silva had a "thing," and she couldn't help but wonder how that worked. It was even less a secret that Silva and Chack's sister, Risa, had a "thing" of some sort going on as well, and as much as Sandra hoped it was a joke, with Silva there was no way of knowing. She shuddered and hoped Pam knew. She had to, didn't she? Pam's "thing" with Silva was proof, wasn't it? She shook her head and went to stand beside Selass, where the Lemurian female was watching Saak-Fas do an unending series of push-ups.

"Good morning, Selass," she said softly, the sorrow of the scene wrenching her anew.

For a moment Selass said nothing, but just sat cross-legged, watching the almost mechanical laboring of her mate. Finally, she sighed. "Good morning." Her face, as usual, betrayed no emotion, but her tone was ironic, desolate. "Have they left?" she asked, referring to *Walker*, and more specifically Chack and Matt. Chack was accompanying the mission as commander of a company of the First Marines. She was also well aware of Sandra's affection for Captain Reddy.

"Yes."

For a while, both were silent. The only sounds were Saak-Fas's heavy breathing, the rain on the dense canvas overhead, and the tormented moans of others in the segregated sections of the ward.

"He spoke," Selass said at last.

Sandra rushed to her side. "That's wonderful!" Perhaps some of Selass's misery might be relieved. "What did he say?"

"He did not speak to me." The ironic tone remained, but Selass's voice broke with emotion, and tears welled in her large, amber eyes. "He merely made an announcement, as if it mattered little to him whether anyone heard. As if I were . . . anybody."

For a breath, Sandra was speechless, appalled by Saak-Fas's apparent cruelty. "Well . . . what did he say?" she managed at last.

"He is leaving the ward. He is entirely well and strong, and ready to resume his missions."

"Missions?" Sandra was taken aback.

"Yes. While he was ... in captivity ... he swore an oath much like Adar's: if somehow he was spared, he would never rest until he destroyed as many Grik as he possibly could. No consideration would be allowed to compete with that goal: no distraction, no emotion, no thought. Not even me. No other obligation binds him now, not even to his Home. He has decided the best way to accomplish his missions is to join your Navy." She looked at Sandra. "To join *Mahan*'s crew."

"What if we don't release him? He's still clearly unwell. His mental state—"

Selass interrupted her. "Release him?" She gestured at their surroundings. "How could we prevent him from leaving? We cannot guard him; nor should we. We have too few to do too much already. Besides, I think it would be wrong. He knows what he is doing and why. It ... hurts, but I believe I know why too."

Sandra stubbornly set her jaw. "Well, whatever *his* intentions are, I believe Lieutenant Ellis would have the final say. Saak-Fas might sneak out of here, but he certainly can't sneak aboard *Mahan* and remain there if I don't want him to. I'll have a word with Jim. ..."

Selass rose and faced her. Behind her, Saak-Fas continued his workout, heedless of their words. "Do not," she pleaded. "He must go. I have lost him already to his oath and what the Grik did to him. He exists only for revenge, and if I ever cared for him at all, I cannot stand in his way. He *will* perform his missions. At least this way it might be of some help, have some meaning."

Sandra slowly nodded, and tears stung her own eyes. "Very well. But you keep saying 'missions,' plural. What other mission does he have, and why *Mahan*?"

Selass sighed and averted her gaze. "He wants *Mahan* because, in the fight to come, he believes she will give him his best opportunity to fulfill *all* his goals: to kill many of our enemies ... and to die."

The following morning was as great a contrast to the previous as was possible at their current latitude. The sky was utterly cloudless, and for once there wasn't even the usual morning haze. To starboard, the violet sea sparkled with gentle whitecaps, stirred by a freshening breeze, and to port, the Borneo coast loomed sharp and green, bordered by creamy blue shoals. Alongside, adolescent graw-fish leaped and capered like dolphins, effortlessly keeping pace with the ship, the sun causing their new wings to flash with color. In the distance, near shore, bright lizard birds swooped and circled above a churning school of flasher fish that had cornered their prey against the shallows. They'd learned it was only in the mornings and evenings that "flashies" congregated in shallow water in such horrifying numbers—of course, there were other things. . . . Occasionally the flying lizards tried to snatch some floating morsel. Often they were snatched themselves, by the voracious flashies below the surface.

Spanky McFarlane stifled a shudder at the sight. He hated flashies passionately, and wondered if the things were somehow smart enough to school together just to draw the fliers down. He wouldn't put it past them. They always seemed to figure out ways around every defense they'd used to put men in the water to perform repairs. They hadn't lost anyone during those efforts, luckily, but there'd been plenty of injuries, mostly caused by blows delivered by the flashies' bony heads. God, how he wanted a dry dock!

Reaching in his pocket, he removed a pouch and took a handful of yellowish brown leaves. Stuffing them in his mouth, he began to chew. For the first few minutes he grimaced at the initial foul taste, but once he got past the nasty, waxy coating on the leaves, a flavor like actual tobacco began to emerge. They'd decided the stuff really was tobacco, of a sort, and that had caused jubilation among the crew. It was clearly laced with enough nicotine to satisfy anyone, and was now almost universally used, even by some of the 'Cats, who'd never habitually imbibed. The only bad thing was, no matter what they tried, it simply couldn't be smoked. It probably had something to do with the coating, but whatever the cause, experimenters always became violently ill when they tried to light up. Maybe they'd solve the problem, maybe not, but chewing it was better than nothing.

Spanky stood between the vegetable locker and the empty number two torpedo mount on the port side of the number three funnel, listening to the sounds of the ship. Occasionally he took a few steps and listened some more. It was a habit he'd formed in his early days aboard *Walker*, and it had stuck: trying to discover problems or impending problems by simple sound and feel. It was harder now, because after all the damage, repairs, and jury rigs, nothing sounded "right" anymore, but he was constantly trying to learn which new sounds were okay and which weren't. He'd already stood over the number two boiler, and was working his way aft. After he "listened" to the engines from topside, he'd go below and do the same thing, working his way forward. He figured if anything was really wrong, he'd detect it topside first.

He saw Silva on top of the amidships deckhouse gun platform, drilling a mixed human/Lemurian crew on the number three four-inch-50 gun. The long barrel was trained out to sea, and its crew was going through the motions of loading it. Terrifying as they'd be to the trainees, Spanky thought Silva's bellowed epithets were just as inventive and amusing as usual. In fact, any casual observer wouldn't have noticed any change at all in the new (acting) chief gunner's mate—his recent run-in with the captain over the now epic "Super Lizard Safari" being ample proof he was the same old Silva.

Spanky knew better. He also knew that the public dressing-down Dennis got over the incident was a sham for the crew. The captain was just as glad as anyone that the monster that got Tony was dead, and the killing had been good for overall morale. Spanky also suspected the captain knew Silva—and Stites—had done it for that exact reason as much as any other, and not just as the usual stupid stunt it would once have been written off as. The proof was that, for once, Silva hadn't been reduced in grade for his "stunt." His only punishment at all, in fact, had been restriction to the ship for the duration of their mission. (Like he would really want to go anywhere.) Besides, the last thing they needed, even changed as he was, was Silva on the loose in Manila during diplomatic negotiations.

Apparently, the only thing Captain Reddy was really mad about was that they'd risked Courtney Bradford. Of course, there'd been an element of relief associated with that as well. Bradford had been driving them all nuts with his constant demands to study stuff. Now he had a fresh (albeit shot to pieces) super lizard skull to gawk at and display, and an entertaining, ever-expanding story of heroism and adventure to go along with it. Maybe now there'd be a short respite.

After "feeling" the aft engine room, Spanky moved to the rail and spit a long, yellowish stream in their wake. After a final, wistful survey of the beautiful day he probably wouldn't see again, he dropped down the companionway into the engineering spaces below. The noise of the giant turbines quickly grew louder as he descended, and he was immediately faced with a shouted altercation between the new (acting) chief machinist's mate, Dean Laney, and one of the 'Cat Marines.

"What the hell's going on here?" he bellowed. Despite his diminutive frame and years of smoking, there was nothing wrong with his lungs. Laney, a slightly shorter, less depraved, but also less bold and imaginative "snipe" version of Silva, glared down at him through beaded sweat and bulging eyes. The Lemurian Marine came to attention and merely stood, staring straight ahead. He was short, like most 'Cats, but heavily muscled. Around his waist was the dark blue kilt that had evolved as the unofficial Marine uniform. Three thin red stripes around the hem made him a sergeant, and to gain that rank he had to be a veteran of savage fighting. That was the only kind of fighting there was in this terrible war. His apelike feet were shod with thick leather soles held on by crisscrossing straps wound up to his knees. In battle he'd wear bronze greaves, breastplate, and helmet, and carry a short stabbing sword, bow, and spear.

"This goddamn monkey wants some of my guys to go topside and help sort out their mess, like we ain't got enough to do down here!" Laney complained. He watched Spanky's brows knit together as he furiously chewed his quid. "Sir," he appended.

"I told you last night we'd have to help," Spanky growled. "Our guys left pieces of the rig scattered around the deck like tinker toys. Half the deck-apes aren't even Navy; they're Chack's Marines."

Technically, the Marines weren't Chack's; they were from the First Marine Regiment—some of whom were armed with the fortunate windfall of Krag rifles. They'd become as deadly with the things as their limited practice would allow, but most had seen little action in the war so far. Aboard ship, however, Chack had returned to his old duties as bosun's mate to the 'Cats, using the Marines as crew.

"But there's only so much even he can do," Spanky continued. "Hell, most of his Marines are Baalkpans—land folk. Can't even tie a knot. Even the ones from Homes might as well have spent their lives on battlewagons or flattops. They aren't used to the way the old gal rolls and pitches and they're pukin' their guts out." His tone softened slightly, and a trace of amusement crept into it. "I know you're just guarding your turf, and Chief Donaghey left mighty big shoes to fill in that regard, but you have to bend a little."

Laney looked unconvinced. "All right, Spanky. I hear you. But we're covered in shit down here. After all the repairs, this is like her sea trials all over again. Everything needs adjusting, and the feed-water pump on number three don't sound right. Gauges are all over the place, and we're makin' smoke!"

McFarlane nodded. "All but number two. When the new firemen are off duty, have them go watch the Mice for a while. Maybe they'll learn something."

Laney rolled his eyes. "Those kooks? Besides, they're some of the ones this monkey Marine wants. Says they built the rig in the first place, so they know what needs to go ashore first, and how it ought to be stowed."

Spanky's tone sharpened once again. "Yeah, they built the rig. They found the oil we're burning too, if you'll recall. And they're also kooks. But they're my kooks—and yours now, too—aside from being the best boilermen in the firerooms, so you'd better figure out how to handle them. We need those squirrelly little guys. Use them. They can't teach with words worth a damn, but the new guys, the 'Cats, can learn by example. *Make* 'em watch them." He turned to the Marine. "You can run along now. I'll send them up myself."

When the 'Cat was gone, Spanky turned back to Laney. "Listen," he said, "you're doing a good job, but you need to get along better with the apes—I don't care if they're human or 'Cats. The bosun's already casually referred to you as an asshole in my presence, and I'd take that as a powerful hint if I were you. You don't want him on your bad side." Laney gulped. There was no question about that. "The upper and lower deck rivalry exists for a purpose," Spanky continued. "It spurs productivity and even camaraderie in a way. Besides, it's fun. But don't take it too seriously or let it go too far. Never lose sight of the fact we're all on the same side." He paused. "And *don't* call 'em monkey Marines anymore. They don't like it, and neither do I. It'll just make you look bad in the eyes of the 'Cats in our own division. Don't forget some of them—the best ones—were Marines before they were snipes. Clear?"

"Clear," Laney grumbled.

"Good. Now see if you can sort out the feed water problem, and let me know what's up." He paused. "How many of our guys did he say Chack wants?"

"Half a dozen or so."

Spanky nodded. "Well, just keep working. I'll pick 'em out as I move forward."

With that, McFarlane eased past the sweating men and panting 'Cats and worked his way forward through the condensation-dripping maze of pipes and roaring machinery. The scene in the forward engine room was much the same, and after detailing a couple of guys topside to help Chack, he paused for a few words with the throttlemen. Continuing on, he cycled through the air lock to the aft fireroom. The firerooms had to operate in a pressurized environment to allow constant air and fuel flow so the fires would burn hot and steady. Once inside, he was greeted by yet more activity: men actually working on the feed-water pump, for example, as well as other things he thought were already fixed. He also noted a dramatic increase in temperature. It was probably a hundred and twenty degrees.

Sweat gushed in the hot, humid environment, and he wiped it from his face and flung it aside to join the slimy black slurry coating the plates beneath his feet. The stench was unbelievable. It was the usual combination of bilgewater, sweaty bodies, mildew, fuel oil, and smoke. Added to those was something more like wet dog than anything else he could think of. Ultimately, the sum was greater—and far more nauseating—than the parts. He didn't know how the 'Cats, with their more sensitive noses, could keep their breakfasts down. Number four was offline while repairs were underway, but the 'Cat burner batter on number three stood panting, ready to replace the plate if the fuel tender called for it. The 'Cat looked miserable, and Spanky honestly couldn't see how the furry little guys stood the heat.

When they began accepting Lemurians into the Navy as full-fledged crew members, he'd never dreamed so many would strike for the engineering spaces. It was just too hot and confined. He'd been surprised when he was swamped with applications. 'Cats *loved* machinery, and regardless of the environment, they clambered to be close to the most complicated examples—like the engines and boilers. Some couldn't hack it. Even the ones that stayed, and apparently thrived, shed their fur like mad, and tiny, downy filaments drifted everywhere. Even though they tried to clean it every day, the slurry on the deck and catwalks was tangled with the longer stuff to the point that, from one end of the fireroom to the other, it looked like a clogged shower drain. Every time he entered the firerooms he sneezed, but the 'Cats that stayed were diligent and enthusiastic, and he couldn't have done without them. Maybe some didn't understand everything they were doing, but they didn't always have to, and they treated him like some sort of omniscient wizard.

He listened for a moment, as they expected him to, and occasionally touched a gauge or felt a pipe. It was only his normal routine, but it always left them wondering what mystical significance the act represented. He stifled a grin and nodded friendly greetings before sending a couple of the least occupied above. Passing through the next air lock, he entered the forward fireroom.

"Oh, good God!" he exclaimed, when, looking up, he was immediately greeted by a pair of large, naked, and entirely human-looking breasts (if you could get past the fine, soot gray fur covering them). "How many times do I have to tell you to wear some goddamn clothes? At least a shirt!"

"It too hot!" Tab-At (hence, Tabby to the other Mice) declared. Somehow, her slightly pidgin English also contained a hint of a drawl she'd picked up from the other "original" Mice.

"It's no hotter than usual. You just do that to aggravate me," Spanky complained, knowing it was true. When Tabby first came to the firerooms he'd thrown an absolute fit. To have females of any kind in his engineering spaces went against everything he stood for, from ancient tradition to his personal sense of propriety. He'd even tried to force the issue once by decreeing everyone under his command would perform their duties in full uniform, something never before required. It was a blatant attempt to get her to strike for a different, more comfortable division. All the Lemurian deck-apes, male or female, were required to wear only their kilts, after all. Tabby's allies rose to the challenge, even so far as providing her with trousers—with a hole cut in the seat for her tail—and he realized he was being mocked.

He finally relented for several reasons: First, he recognized that his stance was ridiculous, and even the captain had decreed—surely reluctantly—that full equality of the sexes would be enforced aboard the ship. It was the Lemurian way, and with at least half the crew filled out with 'Cats, they certainly couldn't antagonize their allies. Second, all the snipes suffered under the order, human as well as Lemurian. It *was* too hot for them to work efficiently under such regulations. Third, and perhaps most astonishing to him, Tabby made a damn good "fireman." She was small and agile enough to perform many tasks that were difficult for others; she could scamper through the bilges like, well, an ape. She was probably the best burner batter aboard, and she'd proven herself absolutely fearless. Sometimes she had a little trouble with rough weather—many 'Cats did—but otherwise she was perfectly competent. Finally, she was probably the only 'Cat in his division that fully understood what she was doing and didn't consider him some sort of mechanical mage. That came from her association with the irascible Mice, surely, but even though she'd virtually become one of them, she hadn't lost her sense of humor. She'd gotten his goat, and he respected that. She was supposed to be wearing a T-shirt, however.

He looked around the gloomy compartment, spotting a dingy shirt draped nearby, and knew she must have taken it off deliberately, just now, simply to "get his goat" again. The fur where it should have been was far too clean.

"Shirt. Now."

Grinning, she retrieved the shirt and languorously pulled it over her head.

He rolled his eyes. Spotting the other Mice, Gilbert Yager and Isak Rueben, beyond her, he growled exasperatedly. "Why do you let her do that?" he demanded. "Next time I'm putting her on report, swear to God!"

Frowning grimly, the two men looked at each other. "Do what?"

No single word or phrase was adequate to describe the Mice. "Strange" came closest, but was still almost too specific. By their appearance, Isak and Gilbert might have been brothers. Both were intense, wiry little men with narrow faces and sharp, pointed noses that contributed much to the rodentlike impression they made. They were unfriendly and annoying to just about everyone they came in contact with. They never socialized, and back when there'd been one, they shunned the ship's baseball team. They were quintessential "snipes"—firemen, to be precise—but they took it further than that. Given a choice, they'd never leave the sweltering heat of their beloved firerooms and the boilers they worshiped there. They were painfully insular and just as apparently unimaginative, but Spanky had learned there was more to them than met the eye. Normally their skins were pasty with a belowdecks pallor they worked hard to maintain, but now their exposed skin still bore the angry red-brown tans they'd accumulated while operating the first oil rig outside of Baalkpan. A rig they designed based on a type they were intimately, if ruefully, familiar with, from their years in the oil fields before escaping that hated life and joining the Navy.

They treated Tab-At like a puppy, and she followed them around like one. Since Spanky knew she certainly wasn't, he suspected her association with them was, at least initially, an attempt to learn as much from them as she could. She'd worked with them on the previous rig and considered them enigmatic fonts of wisdom. When they spoke, if nobody understood what they were trying to say, it was because they were too stupid to understand the words. It never occurred to her that much of their irascibility was due to compensation for a profound shyness, and they spoke only monosyllabic words whenever they would serve. Presumably, she knew them better now, but instead of moving on with the knowledge she'd gleaned, she acted more and more like her mentors—except for the shyness. She obviously liked them, although he couldn't imagine why. Their reaction to his obvious question didn't seem feigned, and he couldn't decide whether it was ignorance on their part, or a mental effort to block her full, rounded breasts from their consciousness.

Gilbert peered at him through slitted lids and proceeded to perform another feat he and Isak were very good at: mentally tripping Spanky up with their disjointed stream-of-consciousness thought processes. "We're goin' to set up the spudder someplace else, ain't we?"

"Well . . . of course. That's part of the reason for this trip."

Gilbert looked at Isak significantly. "We know that, but you've come here to tell us *we're* gonna hafta do it!" he accused. "Leave our boilers and toil away onshore, just like last time!"

"Ain't fair!" Isak proclaimed. He held out his tanned, skinny arm like a bloody rag. "Just look at that, what the damn sun did to me! We joined the Navy to burn oil . . . not to keep diggin' it up!"

Spanky glanced at his battered wristwatch, an item he'd always taken for granted, but which was now precious beyond words. A few Lemurian artisans had experimented with large clocks, achieving mixed results. Right now everyone's priorities were elsewhere, and the best potential clock makers were consumed by the necessity of creating the more complicated armaments. If he didn't hurry, he'd be late for the meeting in the wardroom.

"Life isn't fair," he said, "but you do your best. My curse is, I have to put up with you. But right now you're the best oil men we've got, and if that means you keep working on your tans, that's what you'll do. For what it's worth, though, that's *not* what I came to tell you. Right now I want one of you to run topside and show those apes what parts of the rig have to come off first. They want to restow the stuff. There's not much point; we'll be there tomorrow, but just make sure they don't screw anything up. As to the other . . ." He scowled, contemplating. "I'd just as soon you didn't go either. We've got too many green firemen down here, and I need someone to show them what to do. Maybe I can get the captain to let me keep one of you, at least."

He expected an argument over that, something like, "Where one goes, we all go," but there was only silence and calculating expressions.

"Jeez. Well, carry on." With that he strode forward, past the other firemen in the compartment. He chose one more to accompany one of the Mice above and then paused at the huge copper fuel tank taking up most of the space once occupied by the number one boiler. He felt the cool metal and was relieved, as always, that the hellish temperatures didn't seem inclined to heat the fuel inside. All the sloshing around probably helped dissipate the warming effect. He didn't like the idea of all that fuel right here in the fireroom; if they ever had an accident . . . but there was nowhere else to put it, and it was his idea, after all. Oh, well. He patted the tank and went through the forward air lock.

"I swear, Tabby, how come ye're always waggin' yer boobs at the chief?" asked Gilbert after Spanky was gone. "You know it drives him nuts. Just havin' wimmin aboard at all is enough to cause him fits—and then you do that!"

"Yeah," agreed Isak, "ain't ever'body in the Navy as sensitive as us two."

"He needs to laugh," Tabby replied, "and he will, later."

The meeting in the wardroom was also a late breakfast, catered to perfection by Juan. The food was laid out, buffet style, on the wooden countertops on the port side of the compartment spanning the width of the ship. Juan and Ray Mertz, a mess attendant, stood ready with carafes of ice water and coffee. Those eating were seated at a long, green, linoleum-topped table that also served as an operating table when necessary. A bright light hung above it from an adjustable armature allowing it to be lowered over a patient. It was currently raised and stowed, but there was plenty of light, and even a slight breeze through the open portholes on each side. Much of the food looked familiar to the humans, even if the source wasn't. Mounds of scrambled eggs and strips of salty "bacon" tasting much like one would have expected them to—even if the eggs came from leathery, flying reptiles, and the bacon from . . . something else. Biscuits had been baked with the coarse-grained local flour, and pitchers of polta juice were provided for those who cared for it. There was no milk, although there was something that tasted a little like cream with which they could season their ersatz coffee if they chose. Lemurians were mammals, but considered it perverse for adults to drink milk. Understandable, since the only other creatures that might have provided it were decidedly undomesticated.

Juan had worked wonders to lay in the supplies and logistical support necessary to provide the simple, "normal" breakfast. Standard Lemurian morning fare was dry bread, fruit, and fish. It *had* been standard, at least, until Juan Marcos stepped up. Many Navy 'Cats had developed a liking for the powdered eggs and ketchup the American destroyermen ate, but that was long gone now. The refrigerator was stocked with fresh eggs, though, and that would serve until they ran out. Alan Letts was working on several projects to desiccate food—eventually, for longer trips, they'd have to come up with something—but for now they'd laid in a supply of dried fish and fruit for when the fresh stuff ran out. Strangely, they did still have plenty of one type of food they'd stocked so long ago when *Walker* escaped Surabaya: crates of Vienna sausages. The cook, Earl Lanier, still tried to infiltrate the slimy little things into meals on occasion, carefully camouflaged, but the men hated the "scum weenies" with a passion, and always ferreted them out. Even the 'Cats had finally grown to dislike them. Regardless, the fat, irascible cook refused to get rid of them, calling them "survival rations."

After cordial greetings, the officers in the wardroom ate in silence, for the most part. It was the Lemurian way not to discuss matters of importance during a meal, and Matt thought the custom made sense. Instead of talking, he enjoyed his food and looked around the table at his companions. Seated to his left like some reddish brown, cat-faced bear was Keje-Fris-Ar, High Chief of *Salissa* Home—*Big Sal*, as the Americans called her. Matt was glad his friend Keje felt free to make the trip. Like the other Homes in the alliance, Keje's would take its turn guarding the mouth of the bay, but under the command of his cousin, Jarrik-Fas, she didn't really need him for that. Also, he'd finally decided to allow some of the "alterations" Letts and Lieutenant Brister had been harping on, so *Big Sal* would spend much of his absence at the fitting-out pier. Initially reluctant, Keje was now prepared to allow any modifications whatsoever to his Home that would make her more formidable. He'd cast his lot, and that of his people, entirely for the cause of destroying the Grik forever. Matt was grateful not just for the sake of the alliance, but for his own. He'd grown extremely fond of the gruff, wise Lemurian, and had come to rely heavily on Keje's judgment and support.

Keje's sky priest, Adar, sat in the next seat. He was the only sky priest

Matt knew well, and he'd been Keje's childhood friend. With Naga's de-
cline, he had, for all intents and purposes, become High Sky Priest of all
the allied powers, so his presence on the expedition, while chancy, should
help immensely with negotiations. In theory, even among the Maa-ni-los,
every high chief of every Home, whether land-based or seagoing, was a
head of state in his own right, and all enjoyed equal status according to
custom. But Sky Priests were a little different. As High Sky Priest of the
entire alliance, there was no question but that Adar was a little more
"equal" than the others. He hadn't planned it that way, but that was the
way it was, was the way it had to be. His position was fragile, but potentially very powerful. Right now that power was founded on trust. A well-
founded trust, in Matt's opinion. It was Adar who'd have to convince the
Maa-ni-los it was in their best interest to openly join the alliance, and if
anyone could do that with heartfelt arguments, it was Adar. Time would
tell.

If there was a potential weak link in the command staff chain represented on his ship, there was only one. Everyone at the breakfast table had
been tested in a variety of ways and hadn't been found wanting, but seated
to Matt's right, beyond Lieutenant Dowden, was Lieutenant (Brevet Major) Tamatsu Shinya: a fellow destroyerman, but one who'd served the
Japanese Imperial Navy. The compact, dark-haired man had once been an
anonymous enemy on a half-glimpsed ship in an impossibly far-off war.
Unbelievable as it sometimes seemed even now—he was a Jap, for crying
out loud!—Shinya had become a trusted and valuable friend. He'd found
his calling as a commander of infantry, and had served with distinction
in every battle since the Squall brought them together. He was highly regarded by his 'Cat infantry, and even the old Asiatic Fleet destroyermen
had grown to grudgingly accept and respect him. Matt doubted he'd need
his services on this trip, and he'd probably have been more use back
"home" helping prepare defenses, but it was clear he had issues that needed
sorting out. Perhaps the trip might help.

To Shinya's right was the captain of the Second Marines and also one
of *Walker*'s bosun's mates when he was aboard: Chack-Sab-At. Of all the
Lemurians Matt had come to know, Chack was possibly the most remarkable. He'd come aboard *Walker* right after she first met the 'Cats as a kind
of full-immersion exchange student. He'd been a willing, happy addition
to the crew, and as time went by Matt came to realize just how skilled an
ambassador he'd been. He came among the Americans at a time when
they'd just lost a lot of friends and were only beginning to grasp the fact
that something terrible and extraordinary had happened to them. They
were afraid, and a little shocky, and even with their relatively sophisticated

weapons, they'd been vulnerable. They hadn't been vulnerable to the People of *Big Sal*—or the thousands of Grik they helped defend her from—but they were quite vulnerable to their fears. They were on a hair trigger, and none of the People wanted it to go off pointed at them. Matt now knew Keje chose Chack to send over partly because he had just, somewhat unexpectedly, proven himself a warrior of unusual skill, and Keje believed it took a warrior to evaluate warriors. But the main reason was that no other of his people combined the skill of a warrior—newfound as it was—with anything close to Chack's simple, inherent friendliness. He'd been the perfect choice.

Once aboard, Chack had been his normal, inquisitive, gregarious self, and if not all of *Walker*'s crew was smart enough to realize he was at least as smart as they were, nobody considered him any more dangerous or offensive than a pet monkey. The fact that the Americans had already formed something of a protective attachment toward his people, combined with Chack's engaging ministry and a mutual desire for allies in the face of the Grik threat, had resulted in what was probably the most seamless amalgamation of purpose two races had ever experienced. Let alone two entirely different species. Matt wasn't sure anyone else could have done it. *Walker*'s Asiatic Fleet sailors had been worldly, but also extremely insular. Much like Chack's sea folk or "People of the Homes," they'd seen much of the world as they knew it, but wherever they went, their "home" was still USS *Walker*. Even when they were in foreign ports, they went ashore with people they knew, to visit familiar haunts, and do familiar things—often with familiar results. (Chief among these were hangovers and "social" afflictions.)

Walker, and a fair percentage of her people, had been on the China Station so long that any change in the ordinary routine of life was potentially traumatic. The word that reached them in the wee hours of the Philippine morning of December 8, 1941, had been catastrophic. An endless procession of brutal changes proceeded to destroy the world as they knew it, when they were forced to evacuate the Philippines and participate in chaotic, ill-conceived battles against overwhelming forces. The pitiful remains of the outdated Asiatic Fleet withered under the Japanese onslaught like a candle under a blowtorch. Then, during the mad dash to escape the relentless enemy, the greatest change of all occurred: the Squall that swept them . . . here.

Chack had been a calming influence during the difficult time following their arrival, and everyone now knew he had far greater depths than he'd first displayed. Probably deeper than he'd known himself. Events since then had changed the young Lemurian, matured him beyond his years. He wasn't as gregarious as before, was less engaging and carefree than the Chack they'd first come to know. After all the battles and suffering they'd endured together since that first strange day, it was no wonder. Like all of them, he'd lingered in the hellish heat of the cauldron of battle a little longer than might have been wise, and emerged as something different. Harder, maybe. Similar, but not quite the same. Matt recognized the shift, just as he'd once seen it in himself. At the moment, however, any change was hard to see. Chack was grinning and blinking amusement at something Courtney Bradford had said.

Matt took a bite of the ersatz bacon and contemplated the strange Australian for a moment. Just as he'd been genuinely angry at Silva for taking the self-proclaimed "naturalist" super lizard hunting, he'd actually hesitated to bring Bradford on the mission because he was just too damned valuable to risk. Bradford would have none of it. He'd "suffered in silence" long enough, he claimed. How could Captain Reddy, if he possessed a conscience at all, continue to persecute him by refusing him yet another opportunity for discovery? He'd finally threatened to "feed himself to death" if left behind, and ultimately Matt relented. Not because he thought Bradford was actually willing (or able) to carry out his threat, but he knew Bradford would be an asset to the trip. Not only was he a fair diplomat, but he spoke fluent Latin—the liturgical language of the Sky Priests in which their Sacred Scrolls were transcribed. Also, Matt had to admit he liked having someone around to bounce ideas off of who didn't look at everything almost solely from a military perspective. Sandra was the only other person who fit that description, and he couldn't have allowed her to come along. For lots of reasons.

He nodded at Spanky, coming in late and sitting down with a plate of food. The engineer was already sweaty and stained, and his slight tardiness wasn't even worth mentioning. There was bound to be a good reason. He missed the other officers who would normally have joined them, but those still alive had remained in Baalkpan to continue defensive preparations. That left space for a few new faces. Acting Lieutenant and Gunnery Officer Charles "Sonny" Campeti was there for the first time, replacing Lieutenants Greg Garrett and Pruit Barry, who'd have command of the first new construction frigates. Campeti looked a little nervous. He'd always dined with the other chiefs in their own, smaller version of the wardroom. He'd get used to it, Matt predicted. Chief Gray had.

The Bosun was the only noncommissioned officer to join them, but ever since the Squall, his presence had been fairly routine. Besides, he wasn't really just the chief bosun's mate anymore. He was something else, ill-defined, but damned important. Of necessity, promotions had rained down on many of the crew, but to what did you promote the Bosun? Only the most senior officers would dare give him an order, even though the most junior 'Cat ensign technically outranked him. "Promoting" him to ensign, or even lieutenant, would be almost like a demotion, practically speaking. So the Bosun remained the Bosun, but his real status was something akin to Spanky's or Dowden's: one of the captain's right-hand men.

As each officer finished his meal, Juan or Mertz swept the dishes away and refilled the coffee cups that remained. The 'Cats couldn't stand the stuff, but their cups were filled with more water or polta juice. There was still a little tea left, something Lemurians had become fiends for, but it was now reserved for special occasions. After Spanky wolfed down his meal (it was a very late breakfast for him, after all), Matt gently tapped his cup with his spoon to get everyone's attention.

"First," he said, "I have some good news. The morning radio check was successful, and High Chief Nakja-Mur reports the christening of our first new construction frigate. Gentlemen, I give you USS *Donaghey*!" Palms slapped the table all around in satisfaction. Chief Donaghey had been a true hero, sacrificing his life to save his ship. "I've also been informed, although they haven't been launched yet, that the next two frigates will be named after Rick Tolson and Kas-Ra-Ar." The acclaim was even greater than before. Rick and Kas had commanded *Revenge* and had died defending her against overwhelming odds. Ultimately they'd destroyed their ship and all aboard to keep her (and her guns) from falling into enemy hands. Clearly the names were popular choices.

"It's a shame we missed *Donaghey*'s christening, but we should be back in time for the others. I understand *Donaghey* will sail within days, in an attempt to rescue more of Queen Maraan's people from B'mbaado." He glanced at Chack for some reaction, but there was none. Everyone knew he and the B'mbaadan queen were besotted with each other. They also knew that, regardless of risk, she'd accompany the expedition.

"Next, as you know, we should reach Tarakan Island tomorrow morning. The supply ship set out more than a week ago, so she should be waiting for us now. We have much to do there, obviously, but I don't want to linger longer than necessary. We're constrained by time and fuel, so hopefully we can off-load all the equipment and personnel in a single day and be on our way. We still have a long trip ahead of us." The others murmured agreement, and he turned his attention to Shinya. "Chief Gray will be in overall command of the operation. He'll have to coordinate the off-load with Spanky, but once we're gone, he'll be in charge. That being said, have you decided who will command the security force?"

Shinya was silent for a moment, looking at the Bosun. He knew Matt was giving him an out. Of all the crew, Gray had probably maintained his hatred of "Japs" more fiercely than anyone else. In that one respect he seemed almost irrational. Shinya didn't even think it was personal; the man had, after all, once saved his life. But Gray couldn't get over the fact that when they went through the Squall, three months after Pearl Harbor, his son was still listed as missing. The younger Gray had been aboard the USS *Oklahoma*, one of the battleships sunk in the attack. She'd capsized and settled, upside down, to the muddy bottom of the harbor, trapping countless souls aboard. Many had never even known who was attacking them. Even though Shinya hadn't been there, he knew Gray could never forgive him—for being a Jap.

"I will command the security force," he said at last, "if Mr. Gray has no objections." The Bosun only grunted. "Chack will command the Marines remaining aboard the ship."

Matt nodded thoughtfully, noting the tension between the two. It would probably actually be better to leave them both there, he decided, and let them sort things out. He didn't think either would let their animosities interfere with their duties. Besides, if things got out of hand, they were still close enough to Baalkpan for the Bosun to send Shinya home on a supply ship.

"Very well. Fifty Marines will land from the supply ship, and we'll leave twenty of ours behind. That should be more than sufficient to deal with any local menace. I'd highly recommend beginning defensive fortifications, however. Seventy Marines and about a hundred workers from the Sixth Baalkpan might seem a formidable force, but if only one Grik ship should come as far as Tarakan, you'll be outnumbered two to one—and we know the Grik usually operate in threes."

"Of course, Captain Reddy. Defenses will be my first priority."

"Mine too," the Bosun growled.

"Of course. Now, Mr. Bradford, I assume it will be no inconvenience for you to accompany the landing force? Bear in mind your primary duty will be to pinpoint an appropriate place to sink the first well and establish our refinery. Fascinating as I'm sure you'll find them, don't be distracted by every new bug and beetle you come across. I promise you'll have plenty of opportunities to play tourist later on. Just find them a place to drill; then get back aboard."

"I suppose I can delay my explorations for the sake of the war effort," replied Bradford with a rueful grin, "but really, I must protest. Plotting the best spot to drill should not be difficult at all. Tarakan was a veritable island oil well before the war. The Jappos snapped it up right quick, let me tell you!" He glanced at Shinya. "No offense personally, I'm sure! Anyway, the place looked like one great refinery sprouting from the very sea. You could poke a hole in it just about anywhere and find oil, I expect. It's disgraceful how little time you've included in your schedule for scientific discovery."

"Discover a magic twig that, when waved about, will erase the Grik from the world and I shall devote myself to carrying you to unknown shores for the rest of your life," Keje barked, and everyone, even Gray, laughed at that.

"Details, then," said Matt, smiling, and the discussion began in earnest.

Another beautiful morning dawned over the Makassar Strait, and even before Matt could see much beyond the fo'c'sle, he heard a cry overhead from the crow's nest. Moments later the talker repeated the belated report of the lookout.

"Tarakan Island, sir, off the port bow."

Binoculars swung and Matt raised his own to his eyes. It was difficult to tell, but he thought he could discern a vague, bulky outline of black against the darkness. Slowly, as more light gathered around them, the shape became more distinct.

"Well, gentlemen, it seems we've arrived." He looked at Keje, standing beside him. "You've been this way before; does that look like the coastline in your Scrolls? It doesn't much resemble the Tarakan I remember." The last time *Walker* steamed past the island it was dark, but the only thing protruding from it then were brightly lit wells, tank batteries, refineries, and other works of men. The island before them had none of those things, and was blanketed by a dense, opaque jungle. Keje took the binoculars and studied the land.

"Certainly, but I have never been ashore there, so I can tell you nothing of what to expect. People live near, on the mainland, I am told. . . ." Matt knew that, but questioning them would probably be of little use; the graw-fish gatherers made their harvest in the shallow, swampy river at low tide. There were no graw-fish on the island; the water around it was too deep and the currents too turbulent.

"We'll just have to explore it," Matt replied. "That should make Courtney happy. Besides, as American territory, I suppose it's appropriate."

It had been decided, since the island was to be developed primarily for the American Navy, it should be considered an American possession. That would actually make political and administrative matters easier, since it would add no new High Chief to the budding alliance bureaucracy. It could simply be enfolded into what most considered the "Amer-i-caan Naa-vee Clan," which was already growing by leaps and bounds on this new Earth. Some in the alliance had protested the . . . unorthodox nature of this "clan," since it represented multiple ships, and now a land possession as well, but most realized the war required considerable adjustment to the way things had always been. A few, like Keje, and possibly Queen Maraan, were even beginning to envision the far more radical adjustment of combining the alliance into a unified nation. In any event, there were so many willing recruits for the American Navy, they didn't have the ships for them all. Nakja-Mur was trying to help. Just as Matt gave his first "prize" to Nakja-Mur (*Revenge*) so Baalkpan would have a physical presence in the expeditionary force, some of the prizes they'd captured after the escape from Aryaal had gone to the Americans. Even Nakja-Mur's beloved "new construction" ships were being placed under Matt's authority. The combined alliance would eventually have a navy of its own, but in the meantime, the Amer-i-caan Naa-vee was the "academy," the school where their own people learned their craft, as well as the necessary discipline to employ it.

An example of Matt's "prize" Navy became visible south of the island. It was the "supply" ship USS *Felts*, named for Gunner's Mate Tommy Felts, who died saving Captain Reddy's, Keje's, and Chief Gray's lives at the Battle of Aryaal. *Felts* was actually rated a ship-sloop in the new/old way they'd resurrected of defining such things, since she mounted only twenty guns, but despite her original owners she was a beautiful sight. She was on a tack taking her directly into the morning sun, and Matt shielded his eyes against the glare. The water was an almost painfully brilliant blue, and was still touched by the golden glory of the new day. At present it was still somewhat cool as well. It would soon warm up, and at some point there would almost certainly be rain. Even now, in the distance, a vigorous squall pounded an empty patch of sea. He contemplated it for a moment, as he always did, hopelessly unable to prevent himself from wondering what it had been about the Squall that brought them here that had, well . . . brought them here. If they ever entered another with that strange green hue, would it take them back again? Home? He massaged his temples. Would he really want it to?

He shook his head and looked at *Felts*. The former Grik "Indiaman" was now a United States sloop. Her once bloodred hull was painted black, with the exception of the broad white band down her length highlighting the closed black-painted gunports piercing her side. One of Matt's decrees as supreme commander had been, with the exception of "spy" ships that would retain Grik colors, all allied warships (other than the two old destroyers) would be painted in the same scheme that adorned their final sailing cousins on that other Earth long ago. He was glad he'd made that choice. The total difference it made in their appearance went a long way toward divorcing the ships from the terrible creatures who built them, and it was easier to look at them, and live on them, and give them proud names, if their loathsome makers were not so closely associated with them anymore, even by color. And red, the color of blood, was easy to associate with the Grik. Now, in spite of who made her, *Felts* was a heartwarming sight, loping almost playfully along under close-reefed topsails so she wouldn't shoot ahead of the approaching destroyer. Matt could see her barge in the water, coming their way. "Ahead slow," he called to the helmsman. "We'll bring her in our lee as she closes."

The bosun's pipe twittered, and Carpenter's Mate—now Lieutenant (JG)—Sam Clark arrived on deck, followed by his Lemurian sailing master and second in command, Aarin-Bitaak. Clark was from *Mahan*, and had been given *Felts* because of an extensive sailing background. He was raised building boats in his father's shop. Matt, Keje, and Lieutenant Dowden returned his salute.

"Am I glad to see you guys!" Clark exclaimed, then winced and added, "Sirs!" Matt made no comment. He normally didn't discourage familiarity between his officers and himself, but in public, where they now were for all the crew to see, he expected proper behavior. It was as important to morale as it was to discipline. Clark was young and exuberant, and not quite used to being an officer yet. He'd understandably want an assignment like Rick Tolson had had: essentially, harassing the enemy any way he could. He wouldn't enjoy being a freighter, but that was part of the responsibility of command: doing what you were told whether you wanted to or not. Duty was the same for anyone in the Navy, but with command came the added responsibility of inspiring an equally disgruntled crew with the importance of the task. Exuberance must be leavened with introspection, and at least the appearance of calm confidence. Matt suspected Lieutenant Dowden or maybe even the Bosun might slip Clark a word or two before he left.

Clark continued: "We've been tacking back and forth for two days. We tried to anchor, but the tidal race around these islands is something fierce! We had a hard time getting everything ashore."

"I assume you managed?"

"Yes, sir. All baggage and supplies are ashore, and the Marines have established a defensible beachhead." He paused and shook his head. "I have to say, sir, getting the brontosarries ashore was a task I'd sooner not have to repeat." Matt could imagine. Brontosarries were pygmy versions of the dinosaurs they so closely resembled from the fossil record and were indigenous to most of the large regional landmasses. Bradford proposed that one of the reasons their charts were a little off, regarding various coastlines, was that this Earth might be experiencing an ice age of sorts, lowering the sea level. He believed whatever event caused evolution to take such a drastic diversion here was also at work on the planet. Therefore, the seas were not quite so deep as they should be. Perhaps, aeons ago, an even more severe ice age left many of the islands connected in some way. That would explain why brontosarries and other large creatures, clearly unfit for a long swim in such hazardous seas, might be as prolific as they were.

Regardless, the beasts they'd brought were domesticated and "trained"—if such a word could be used regarding a creature with roughly the intelligence of a cow—to provide motive power for the drilling rig. The task of not only transporting them (small as they were, compared to their ancestors they were still twice the size of an Asian elephant) but off-loading them and rafting them ashore must have been harrowing, to say the least. Inexperienced as Clark was, it spoke well of him that he'd accomplished it.

"Very well." Matt grinned wryly. "We'll try not to delay you much longer"—the young lieutenant winced again—"but I'll trouble you for your boats and crew to help us unload as well."

"Aye, aye, Captain Reddy!"

Clark was right about the tide. When it came in, it did so with a mounting fury, and when it ebbed, the drop was equally dramatic. In between, the currents surged and swirled so violently they were forced to moor the ship fore and aft (with plenty of water under her keel) to begin off-loading the large pieces of the rig. This took much longer than Matt had been prepared for, but there was nothing for it. Powered boats and launches (*Walker* had all of *Mahan's* for this trip, while new ones, using the salvaged engines of the old, were built at Baalkpan to replace those that were destroyed) plied back and forth from the beach carrying supplies and personnel, as well as the smaller parts of the rig. The heavier pieces were swayed out, causing the ship to lean noticeably to port, and lowered onto barges and rafts that were then either towed or heaved ashore by the monstrous beasts of burden. The loud bellows of the Bosun and the croaky shouts of the Mice made sure everything was accomplished as quickly and efficiently as possible, and by the afternoon watch, the transfer was finally complete. Matt moved to stand next to Bradford, who leaned on the bridge wing rail, intently studying the island through his binoculars. He was clearly impatient to go ashore.

"Take the Mice, Silva, and a dozen Marines, and find a suitable well site as quickly as you can. Shinya's going to be tied up with the security situation, but I'm sending the Bosun to chivvy you along, so don't go chasing lizards and bugs, clear? Also, the Bosun'll be in charge after we leave, so make sure you mention any *pertinent* observations you make to him."

"Absolutely clear, Captain! I'll impart what wisdom I may ... and obey Mr. Gray's every whim. But are you certain I mustn't remain here to help? I'm sure there's much I could contribute."

"Absolutely positive. Remember, this is just our first stop. We'll be crossing deep water for the first time. Just imagine the strange creatures we may find on our *next* landfall. Besides, we might even see a 'mountain fish' and get to try our experimental defenses!"

"My God! Of course you're right, Captain. I'll certainly be of more use later on. I fear my current excitement must have addled my thoughts."

"Good. For now, though, prepare to go ashore"—he raised a warning finger—"but don't get sidetracked."

"I don't even know why I'm here, goddamn it!" Dennis Silva complained. "I'm still restricted to the ship!" He gestured at the impenetrable jungle around them. "This look like the ship to you, Bosun?"

Chief Gray shook his head, avoiding another branch Silva let spring back toward his face. "It damn sure don't look like Tarakan Island!" he gruffed. "We steamed right by it when we retreated from the Philippines. It had a lot of oil field equipment, some big sheds, and a few palm trees. . . . Hell, I wasn't expecting that, but I didn't expect to hack my way through steel wool neither!" The large group of men and Lemurians were creeping down a well-used game trail. It was, apparently, the only way to move on the densely forested island. To make matters worse, whatever made the trail couldn't have been taller than a cow, and although it was a minor inconvenience to the 'Cats, the constant crouching and hacking with their cutlasses was hell on the destroyermen.

"How much farther?" Gray asked.

Bradford had stopped to consult a compass. Landmarks were, obviously, out of the question. Sweat dripping from his forehead obscured the dial, and he wiped at it with his sweaty shirt and sighed.

"Can't be much farther now, I'm sure. Bloody island's only ten miles long, from tip to tip! We came ashore south-southwest, and the site I wanted was only about two miles inland. We should be there . . . well, now."

Silva looked around. "Why can't we just burn the bastard off?" He was the tallest in the group and was suffering the most. At one point he'd grumblingly suggested they name the place "Spanky Land" after *Walker*'s engineering officer. He didn't say why. They'd been searching for three hours, but the twists and turns the game trail took made it impossible to go straight to the spot Bradford wanted.

"That big ape Silva might actually have a point," grumbled Gray. He kicked the mushy jungle floor. "If we could even get this shit to burn, I'm for trying it. Wait for a day when the wind is right . . ."

"Outrageous!" Bradford declared. "You're contemplating ecological . . . murder! It would be a crime against nature and humanity to raze this island. I've already glimpsed many creatures I've never seen on the mainland! They might exist nowhere else!"

Gray sighed. "If you'd let me finish . . . I wasn't talking about burning off the whole damn place, just part of it. Besides, you can't tell me there's never been a lightning fire here. If we do it—if we *can* do it—we'll be careful."

Somewhat mollified, Courtney considered. "Well, yes, that might work. But you'd have to be very careful indeed."

Silva glanced back at the Bosun and rolled his eyes. "There wasn't nothin' here on the 'old' Tarakan," he said.

"Well . . . of course not, but that's entirely different."

"How's that?"

"Because," Gray remarked cynically, "there was nothin' left for him to ogle before. Now there is." His tone changed. "I'm sorry, Mr. Bradford, but we'll do whatever we have to to get oil outta this rock. If that means burning the whole thing down, we will. We'll try to be careful, but the 'needs of the service,' et cetera, not to mention the needs of our allies and ourselves, must be met. Now, how much farther?"

Bradford sighed. "I suppose this is as good a place as any. The captain was adamant that we be back aboard before nightfall." He glanced absently at his watch, but couldn't see the numbers through his sweat-streaked glasses. He took them off and wiped them vainly on his sweat-soaked shirt.

Suddenly there was a violent commotion to the side of the trail, and something upright, about the size of a large crocodile, lunged from its hiding place and snatched one of the leading 'Cats by the arm. With a shriek of pain and terror, the Lemurian was dragged into the impenetrable gloom.

"Shit!" Silva bolted forward, even as the others backed away in fright. Several were bowled over by his rush. Another scream marked the place the 'Cat disappeared, and he knelt and fired at a dim shape in the darkness. He fired again and again, on semiautomatic, and his efforts were rewarded by a different type of shriek, and muffled, panicky jabbering. On his hands and knees in the damp mulch, he scurried into the tunnel of brush.

"Well, don't just stand there, you useless sons of bitches!" roared the Bosun. He dashed forward, sweeping all the others, including the Mice and Courtney Bradford, along. More shots, muffled now, sounded from within the hole. Gray crouched at the opening as others fanned out behind him.

"Silva!" he shouted. "Silva, goddamn it! Where are you?"

A moment passed, and a final shot reached their ears. "Here!" came a breathless shout, sounding much deeper in the tunnel than they could credit. "I'm comin' out with the 'Cat, but some of you bastards need to come get my 'trophy.' He ain't much, but I want a better look at him!"

"Is your, ah, 'trophy' quite dead?" Bradford inquired anxiously.

"Yep. But this 'Cat ain't, so you'd better have some first aid ready."

Several moments later Silva's back appeared, and he dragged the moaning, bloodied Lemurian clear. He had him by the scruff of the neck and one arm. The other arm had been savagely mauled. Gray directed their two corpsmen to attend to the wounded 'Cat and then regarded Silva.

"What was it?"

"Not sure," Silva panted. The exertion and excitement had caught up with him. "It's dark in there." He gestured at the 'Cat he'd saved. "Lucky I didn't hit the little guy, but I had to shoot. It was draggin' him down another trail back in all that shit. I don't know, but it looked sort of like a midgety super lizard."

"The method of attack would seem consistent," Bradford agreed, with feeling, "but the size difference . . ."

They ceased speculating, knowing soon they'd see the creature for themselves. Several Marines had already ducked into the brushy tunnel. Soon they heard panting, and an occasional chittering curse. Whatever they had was heavier than they would have thought after their fleeting glance.

"My word!" Bradford exclaimed, when they finally dragged the dead creature clear. Once everyone could see it, the Marines backed away and acted eager to cleanse themselves. They quickly stooped and grabbed handfuls of moldy mulch, rubbing it between their palms and fingers.

"Lawsy," muttered Isak Rueben, the first word any of the Mice had spoken since they came ashore. They had all, including Tabby, been too preoccupied with gloom over the prospect of at least one of them remaining on this miserable island. The creature before them, adding its blood to the damp soil, looked like nothing they'd seen before. Certainly there were similarities to several others, but taken as a whole, it was unique. Silva's comparison to a small super lizard wasn't without grounds; it had a long tail and coarse, crocodile-like skin, and its physique was similar, on a smaller scale. But its head was smaller in proportion to its body, and the tooth-bristling jaws were longer and slimmer. Its sightlessly glaring eyes were much bigger too, proportionately, and positioned closer to the top of its head—again like a croc—but it had long, powerful forearms with viciously clawed, grasping fingers. The arms were long enough for it to roam on all fours if it wished, but it could obviously use them for grasping or carrying prey. This last reminded them of the "aboriginal" Grik the destroyermen had encountered on Bali—the ones that got Mack Marvaney. Those creatures weighed about two hundred and fifty pounds. This one was closer to four hundred.

Thunder muttered indistinctly, and rain began pattering the canopy above. It would probably be a while before any made its way down to them.

"Raunchy-lookin' booger," Gilbert Yager agreed with his companion.

"Amazing!" Bradford said. "I walk in the very footsteps of Mr. Darwin himself, except here, every land is a Galapagos!" He gestured at Silva's "trophy," its two-foot purple tongue lolling from between its jaws. "Don't you see? This creature probably is the 'super lizard' of this island, filling the exact same ecological niche." He pointed at the diminutive trail. "Smaller island, smaller prey, smaller predators! We've already theorized the hostile sea must prevent dissemination of species on this Earth to a much greater degree than our own, and we find truly similar fauna only on lands that must—quite recently, geologically speaking—have somehow been in contact. But this . . ." He paused in happy contemplation. "This proves lands with no 'recent' physical contact with others might have evolved even more unimaginable species! Just think what creatures might dwell in America or Europe . . . or Australia!"

"Keje's been to Australia; the 'Cats have land Homes there. And yeah, he says they have some goofy-lookin' critters runnin' around," said the Bosun curiously, "so there might be somethin' to what you say. I never was a 'Darwin man' before, especially when it comes to monkeys and folks, but I've had to . . . adjust my thinkin' a little since we came here. How do you get all that just by lookin' at one dead lizard, though, and what difference does it make?"

"Yeah, and who cares?" grumped Isak.

"Look closely, gentlemen; that creature is clearly not an allosaurus gigantus," Bradford said, insisting on his own term for super lizards. "Believe me," he added with feeling, "I *know*!" There were a few chuckles. Even the wounded 'Cat managed a tight grin, while the corpsmen applied the antiseptic paste to his arm and began binding it up. He'd require much more care when they got him to the beach, but the paste was an analgesic as well as an antiseptic, so his pain was under control. "That being said," Bradford continued, "I believe its distant ancestors were. They arrived on this island aeons ago—my ice age theory again!—and when it was separated from the mainland by water, they had to adapt or die. Can you imagine an island this size supporting even one creature as big as the one we took on the pipeline cut near Baalkpan? Of course not. In fact, those that came here must have been smaller to begin with. Over time, they got even smaller, but also evolved other differences to make them more efficient predators within their limited domain. I shouldn't wonder if their metabolisms were slower as well. My point is, besides the scientific interest it inspires, we may not be stuck on a world ruled entirely by the descendants of dinosaurs! On other lands, with different or greater varieties of climates, entirely different creatures—perhaps even mammals—might have risen to the fore . . . and dare I say it? If Mr. Darwin's theories and your own religious teachings are both correct, Mr. Gray, perhaps we might one day find other humans not simply stranded here as we were, but who are indigenous to this world!"

"All that from one dead lizard?" Gray inquired again, with an arched brow and a skeptical tone.

"Well . . . of course, it's a stretch. But I feel quite reanimated by the possibility!"

Ever practical, Silva bit a chaw from a plug of local tobacco. He'd taken to compressing the stuff in the ship's hydraulic press. He kicked the "lizard" in question. "Well, nothin's gonna reanimate this booger!" He stooped to examine the bullet holes. "Took six shots to kill it," he said with the objective air of a professional, "but none of 'em was particularly well aimed. One good shot'll take down a Grik. I expect the same's true with this 'un." He looked at Gray. "They ain't nothin' your boys can't handle. They'll just need to be careful." He glanced toward the sky he couldn't see, then looked at Bradford. "We better reanimate our own asses and get back to the ship before the captain decides he's better off without us after all. If it was just me, I bet he'd already be long gone." He kicked the lizard again, spit on it, and turned back to Gray. "If you want to muck around out here awhile longer, that's fine, but I gotta get Mr. Brain back to the ship. He's gonna want to take his new lizard back to play with," he added resignedly, "so you better give me a detail to drag the damn thing. That just leaves one final question." An evil grin split Silva's face, and he looked at the Mice. "Which one of these squirrely snipes are you gonna keep? You only get one; Spanky's orders, and the captain said so too." He shook his head. "I'd leave all three, except maybe Tabby, and hope they get ate. Tabby's smart enough; we might still straighten her out."

Gray looked at the Mice, standing dejectedly, eyes lowered. "What do you want to do? Flip a coin?"

"There's three of us," Isak objected, "only two sides on a coin. 'Sides"—he glanced fleetingly at his comrades—"we ain't got a coin."

"Tabby's going back to the ship," Gray declared. "She didn't start working with you two until you had the rig set up. Besides, if we have problems, I want one of you with real experience."

"Ain't fair," Isak almost moaned.

"Yah!" Gilbert agreed, spearing Tabby with a suspicious glare, as if she'd somehow cheated. "That cuts our chances in half!"

Gray rolled his eyes and fished in his pocket, producing a tarnished silver dollar. He looked at it with a strange expression. "Only thing I keep it for," he said softly. "Only thing it's good for anymore."

Parting company with *Felts*, *Walker* steamed east, northeast, then almost due north as the sun sank into the Borneo jungle, beyond Tarakan, off the port quarter. Gilbert Yager sat on the gun platform atop the aft deckhouse near the auxiliary conn. Tabby was beside him, sitting in a similar fashion: legs crossed and elbows on her knees. Both stared glumly at the silhouetted island in the middle distance. Gilbert hadn't seen many sunsets in the last few years; he was usually below when they occurred, and he was immune to any aesthetic appreciation of them in any case. The only significance they generally held for him was, after they took place, the firerooms gradually became a little cooler for a while. But this sunset was remarkable to Gilbert in several ways. It marked the close of a day that had seen a profound change in his everyday life, and change was always bad. For the first time, really, since he'd joined the Navy—since he could remember, in fact—Isak Rueben was not within earshot, and he felt an inexplicable . . . emptiness. He also became aware that he wasn't sure he really even liked Isak very much, and that caused him to spend a moment or two engaged in an extremely uncharacteristic activity: introspection.

He was comfortable around Isak—they were brothers, after all, although nobody aboard had any idea. They shared physical similarities, and that was not unremarked upon, but they had different last names, and apparently no one ever came to the obvious conclusion that they had different fathers. He relied on Isak in many ways; he was the "smart" one who prodded him to join the Navy to escape the oil fields in the first place. He was someone to talk to in a world with few such individuals, except maybe Tabby, now. But did he like him? How would their lives have differed if they'd taken separate paths? Had they held each other back by their self-imposed seclusion? Maybe they'd taken Tabby on only as an experiment to see if they could even make friends. If that was the case, all they seemed to have done to her was create a copy of themselves. She'd become almost as acerbic and insular as they were. Maybe he should use this sunset as a break, a dividing line between his old life and a new one, somehow different. He could take his isolation from his brother, brief as it was supposed to be, and see if he could change himself, make a friend, "get out more," as Spanky always suggested. He would try, he determined, without ever deciding whether he liked his brother or not. That realization would probably come when they saw each other again. Still, invigorating as his decision was, he couldn't help feeling a sense of deep foreboding as he stared at the last light of the setting sun. Something was bound to happen; it always did. Change was never good.

"Let's get sumpin' ta eat," he suggested, and Tabby nodded her head. He suddenly wondered what she'd been thinking. Were her thoughts similar to his? He hoped not. It was suddenly important that she, at least, like him. They climbed down the ladder to the main deck and worked their way forward past the covered holes where the numbers three and four torpedo mounts used to be, past the searchlight tower and the aft two funnels, until they stepped under the raised gun platform/roof over the amidships deckhouse and open-air galley.

A short line leaned on the stainless-steel counter under a window, waiting their turn to snatch a sandwich from a dwindling pile on a large tin platter. The group were mostly humans, since they generally preferred sandwiches to Earl Lanier's cooking. The 'Cats were the other way around; they liked his stews and other concoctions. That was understandable, since he made them from animals and vegetables they were familiar with. The way he cooked them and the seasonings he used were still novel, and they enjoyed that too. Most of the humans liked things they were used to, though, and even if the sandwiches tasted a little strange, they were still sandwiches. As they approached the window, they heard Lanier heaping abuse on those he was serving.

". . . wouldn't have to build so many goddamn sammiches if you bastards'd eat real food!"

"You ain't cooked real food since you was in the Navy!" retorted Paul Stites.

"Why don't you fry me up one of your fishes?" taunted another man. Lanier was known to fish over the side when the occasion permitted, because he was deeply devoted to fish—and he couldn't stand to eat the other stuff he cooked either. Some of his fishing exploits had become legendary, and a few of the creatures he'd brought from the depths had even provoked desperate gunfire.

"Be a cold day . . . here . . . before I waste one of my beauties on you ungrateful turds. You wanna eat fish? Catch 'em yourselves and cook 'em on the boiler burners!"

Tabby reached the platter next, behind the laughing destroyermen, and took a sandwich. Gilbert snagged another, then paused. Isak was the one who usually instigated conversation, but he thought he'd give it a try. He leaned in the window and saw Lanier's massive shape within, sitting on a creaky wooden chair, while Ray Mertz and a black-and-white 'Cat Earl called "Pepper" assembled another platter of sandwiches.

"Ah, how's repairs to the Coke machine goin', Earl?" Gilbert inquired, expecting a diatribe. He was surprised when Lanier's face brightened from its customary glower.

"Purty good." He gestured beyond the bulkhead Yager leaned on, and the fireman turned to look at a bench behind him upon which the treasured Coke machine had lain in state ever since it was killed in action against the Japanese. Lanier had clearly been working on it, and many of its internal parts were restored. There hadn't been any Cokes for months, even before it was destroyed, but the crew had taken perverse comfort from the fact that, no matter how bad things got, the Coke machine still worked. When splinters from a Japanese shell eviscerated it during their final torpedo attack on *Amagi*, after *Nerracca* was destroyed, the crew took its loss disproportionately hard.

"Compressor's back in, and most of the lines are patched. Won't be long before I try some ammonia in her. Cross your fingers!"

"Will do, Earl," Gilbert said fervently, and stepped away, still looking at the battered remnant of another world. "It'd be a fine thing if it was workin' again," he almost whispered.

"Why?" asked Tabby around a mouthful of sandwich, her long whiskers festooned with crumbs. "You say ain't no Cokes. I never had me no Cokes. Why fix thing to keep something cold . . . there ain't none of?"

"We could use it to cool other stuff," Gilbert defended. "Besides . . ." He thought of comparing it to a pet, but Lemurians thought the very idea of keeping pets was silly—for good reason. There weren't many animals on this world that would make suitable—or survivable—pets. Much as they treasured their Homes, on land or sea, they didn't seem particularly sentimental over inanimate objects, either. They did take trophies, though. "Think of it like a necklace of Grik claws. When the Japs busted it, it was like the string on the necklace broke and you couldn't wear it no more. Fixin' the Coke machine is like fixin' the string." He knew it wasn't a very good comparison—"analogy" was a word he'd never encountered—but it seemed to suffice, and Tabby nodded apparent understanding.

"I see. You captured Coke machine from God-daam Jaaps?"

Gilbert closed his eyes and shook his head. He was about to correct her when he was interrupted.

"There you are, you little twerps!"

He looked up and saw Laney standing before him, hands on hips, a grossly oversize affectation of Spanky's authoritative pose.

"What do you think yer doin'? Both of you was supposed to be on watch!"

"We been ashore, Laney," Gilbert grated. "You know, with the *shore* party."

Laney's face clouded. "That don't cut no ice with me. I don't care if you been 'rasslin' sea monsters, you'll stand your watches when you're told! And that's 'Chief' Laney to you slacking malingerers!"

"We ain't lingerin'; we just got here. We's eatin' and movin' along. Earl didn't yell at us for lingerin'."

"Just . . . get your asses down to the aft fireroom, and get that goose-pull sorted out. Most of them 'Cats can't tell fuel oil from bilgewater. And check on that damn feed-water pump! It's still makin' screwy noises!"

"All right, Laney, quit yer fussin'. We'll be along." Gilbert sighed and began wolfing his sandwich down. Laney stood a moment, still cloudy, then moved away. Gilbert couldn't help but compare his tyrannical attitude to poor old Chief Donaghey's. Donaghey had been a professional who inspired proper behavior and diligence by example, as well as an inherent ability to lead. He didn't lord it over the snipes in his division, and he was usually as grimy as they were because he worked alongside them. He'd been in the Asiatic Fleet a lot longer than Laney too. Volunteered for it. Even had a Filipino wife . . . back there. Everyone knew his worth, even the captain, and when he was killed saving the ship from an improvised mine, Captain Reddy was prepared to risk the very alliance to avenge him.

Now they had Laney.

"Like I've said, change is always bad," he muttered.

Matt paced slowly between the starboard bridge wing and his chair, bolted to the right side of the forward pilothouse bulkhead. It was how he spent the majority of his time on the bridge, particularly over the last six days. He believed the smudge of land he'd seen off the starboard bow was the poignantly familiar Dumagasa Point, on the western peninsula of Mindanao; the sextant said it was, so did the scriggly lines on the Plexiglas over the chart, but it didn't look quite the same as he remembered it. Funny. He'd been to Surabaya—now Aryaal—and Balikpapan—now Baalkpan— and they bore no resemblance whatsoever to the places he'd known, but somehow the only slightly different promontory they'd passed filled him with a new sense of loss. Perhaps because they were entering what had once been considered *Walker*'s "home" waters.

Ahead lay the Philippines—which he'd never even liked. The place was too sudden and too big a change from his native Texas, where he'd returned after being discharged during a force reduction frenzy. Then, when the worldwide threat loomed ever larger, he'd been snatched back up by the Navy and immediately sent to the, to him, already alien land. The Philippines, at least the parts frequented by Navy ships, had been a den of iniquity paralleled only by those parts of China the Navy had even then been evacuating. The short, brown people jabbered in Tagalog, or a version of Spanish he could barely comprehend. The military situation was clearly unequal to the growing Japanese threat, and those in charge didn't seem to care, or tried to pretend the threat didn't exist. When hostilities commenced, the incompetent, almost slapstick response would have been hilarious if it hadn't been so tragic. The litany of mistakes that rendered the islands indefensible was without end, and was itself indefensible. It still made him sick to remember how the formidable airpower gathered there, which alone could have made such a huge difference, had been so criminally squandered.

He had to remind himself that many of the crew felt quite differently. To some, the Philippines had been paradise. The waterfront had been a place they could find anything their hearts desired, where they could slake any thirst or lust if they chose, or set themselves up almost like gentlemen on their comparatively munificent wages. Of course, quite a few knew the islands far better than he, and spent their time away from the waterfront, where the atmosphere of iniquity prevailed. In the suburbs or the country, they could find virtuous women and homes where they could settle down and forget the stress of their duty. He wondered how their approach might affect the men who'd loved it there, had expected to retire there and spend the rest of their lives with women they loved. Women who weren't there anymore.

During the last six days, counting the time they'd lingered at Tarakan, *Walker* had left her new "home waters" of the Makassar Strait, and entered the Celebes Sea. Their average speed was reduced, by necessity, from the almost twenty knots they were gratified to learn their ship could still make on two boilers, to less than ten, and finally to the excruciatingly slow pace of six knots. They'd picked their way through the tangled, hazardous islands off the northeast coast of Borneo, before tentatively beginning their island-hugging journey through what the Americans still called the Sulu Archipelago. They had finally, that morning, increased speed back to fifteen knots, but would likely have to slow again. The sea was shallower than it should be, and they couldn't entirely trust their old charts anymore. Six long, torturous days, and according to the landmarks, and Keje's and Dowden's calculations, they were only about halfway to their destination.

He rubbed his face and wished Juan would hurry with the coffee he'd promised.

This tedious, circuitous route was intended to allow them to avoid the abyssal depths of the Celebes and Sulu seas—and the monstrous creatures that dwelt there. Among those they were trying to avoid was one so huge it actually posed a significant threat to ships as large as Lemurian Homes. "Mountain fish" they were called by some, or "island fish" by others. Whichever it was, it made no difference. The name was not idle exaggeration. Matt had never seen one, nor had anyone who'd been aboard *Walker* since the Squall. Jim Ellis and the crew of *Mahan* swore they'd been *chased* by one when that ship attempted to cross to Ceylon while under the deluded command of the now lost Air Corps captain named Kaufman. *Mahan* was badly damaged at the time, and could barely make fifteen knots. Ellis still insisted the fish nearly got them, and was convinced only the shoaling water discouraged it. Impossibly big *and* fast. The Lemurians were just as insistent that if the thing had indeed caught *Mahan*, if it was mature, it could certainly have seriously damaged or even destroyed the three-hundred-foot destroyer—iron hull or not.

They had a few "surprises" if they met a mountain fish on this trip, but Captain Reddy hoped they wouldn't be needed. Discovering whether they worked was important, particularly in the long term, but making it to Manila and securing an alliance was of first importance, and they couldn't risk damage to the ship before that was achieved. Bradford was disappointed, and Matt was anxious to complete their mission, but so far the daily radio transmissions left them reassured that the Grik remained quiescent, content to consolidate their hold on Aryaal and make repairs to the damaged Japanese battle cruiser. USS *Donaghey* had begun her maiden voyage—another trip to take more of Queen Maraan's people off B'mbaado—and maybe she'd have something to report in a week or so. In the meantime, there seemed no reason to rush, so they chose the safest, most conservative course that left them least exposed to the giant fish.

Fortunately, the things were pretty serious about avoiding shallow water, "shallow" being anything under three hundred feet or so. The Makassar Strait was considerably deeper than that, but the 'Cats believed the hundred-mile width of the strait was too confining for the monsters. Usually. They were known to haunt the deep water of the Celebes and Sulu seas, however. They cruised along with their mouths open wide, much like the blue whales Matt was familiar with that constantly ingested swarms of krill to sustain their tremendous bodies. Mountain fish were similar in principle, except the "krill" they consumed was anything else that swam in the sea, up to and including the huge plesiosaurs the

Lemurians called "gri-kakka." Matt had seen gri-kakka as large as sperm whales.

For obvious reasons there weren't many mountain fish, and the estimated half dozen or so that could sustain themselves in a body of water the size of the Celebes Sea were highly territorial. They didn't migrate, as far as anyone could tell, which meant they must not have to eat all the time, because the majority of their prey did move from place to place. Regardless of the hopefully effective "surprises" *Walker* had in store for the immense creatures, Matt was perfectly content to leave them in peace as long as they extended the same courtesy to his ship.

Juan finally arrived with his coffee, and he took the cup with gratitude. Vile as the stuff was, it might help keep him awake. In spite of what Juan might think, he hadn't been sleeping well. There'd been no recurrence of the old dream that once eluded him so, not since *Nerracca*'s destruction, but it had been replaced by others, ones he remembered when they woke him. The difference, he now knew, between the old dream and the ones that plagued him now was significant. Before, he'd been tormented by a sense of loss and failure—guilt, almost, that they'd survived that long-ago flight from the Japanese juggernaut when their consorts, *Exeter*, *Encounter*, and *Pope*, were all rubbed out by the relentless enemy. That they could do nothing to help, not even slow to pick up survivors, haunted him still. But the destruction of *Nerracca* and the thousands aboard her put that previous loss in perspective. They'd rescued some survivors from *Nerracca*, but only a tithe, and the hopelessness of saving more and the risk of what little they'd done in the face of *Amagi*'s guns finally galvanized his subconscious agony with a burning hatred for their foes, old and new: the Grik, and the Japanese allied with them.

He dreamed of frantic orders and desperate attempts to save all they could, of bright, distant muzzle flashes and towering geysers of spume. Blood-streaked bodies and mangled flesh aboard his own ship, where some of the enemy's fury found its mark, a swirling typhoon of raging flames consuming the gallant Home as shells continued to fall—these were the dreams that tormented him now, but they didn't leave him weak; they goaded him to revenge. A revenge that would be complete only when the Grik were exterminated forever, and *Amagi* lay broken on the bottom of the sea.

His thoughts must have been evident on his face, because a familiar, gruff voice interrupted his reverie.

"It's an important mission," Keje said. He and Adar had approached unnoticed. They were both given the privileges of officers aboard his ship, and hadn't asked permission to come on the bridge.

"I know. And it's a good idea. We're going to need all the help we can get to beat the lizards once and for all. I hope we can stir some up." He smiled with little sincerity and lowered his voice so only his Lemurian friends could hear. He knew they were at least as passionate about their task as he. "I guess I'm just a little antsy."

"Antsy," tried Keje. "It means nervous, but not afraid, correct?"

"Sort of."

"Hmm. A new word to add to a new phrase I learned from Mr. Braad-furd today. He just said he came up here to speak to you about his new liz-aard." He wrinkled his nose. "What a stench! Must he dismember his toys so close to the galley? Mr. Laan-ier has threatened his life! In any event, he told us you did not even notice his presence, that you were in a 'brown study,' whatever that might be."

"Is it much like 'antsy'?" Adar asked.

Matt's smile turned genuine. "Maybe a little. I think 'brown study' is more like 'thinking disturbing thoughts.' Add 'antsy' to it, and I guess that's a pretty good description." He sipped his coffee and grimaced. It had grown cold.

"I am 'antsy' as well," Adar confessed. "Reports from home are reassur-ing, yet . . . perhaps too reassuring?"

Matt nodded. "The farther we get from home, the more I think how unlike the Grik it is for them to just sit pat and goof around. Their war-riors might be mindless killing machines, but there's a brain behind them, something that aims them and turns them loose. Those Hij. Just think of the logistics required to support a force their size, to equip it and build the ships to move it." He shook his head. "I just can't shake the feeling that they're up to something."

They finally knew a little about their enemy now, thanks to the charts, logbooks, and other papers they'd captured aboard their various prizes. They'd even taken a few of the enemy alive for a change, although no in-formation had been forthcoming from them. They'd seemed insane, but with no comparisons they couldn't confirm that. Regardless, the prisoners all died within days of being placed in captivity, either from the wounds that let them be captured, or other unknown causes. But some information had been gleaned. They'd discovered before, to their horror, that a lot of Grik formal correspondence was printed in English. Whatever bizarre lan-guage they spoke, English seemed their official or liturgical written lan-guage, much as Latin served the 'Cats. For the Grik, however, English was a captured language they'd probably adopted of necessity to make sense of the information they'd captured with the East Indiaman so long ago. Matt felt a twinge when he thought about how those ancient British mari-ners must have been persuaded to reveal their secrets. Latin was given to the Lemurians willingly, from two other East Indiamen that decided to sail east instead of west, after all three came to this world the same way *Walker* had. They'd apparently used Latin so only approved information could be funneled to the 'Cats, and not just anybody aboard could communicate with them. Fortunately, the westbound ship had been stripped of her guns and powder.

In any event, they still didn't know what drove the Grik to such extremes of barbarity, but they'd learned a little about their social structure from the captured documents. For example, they now knew the average Grik warrior came from a class referred to as Uul, and they possessed primary characteristics strikingly similar to ants or bees. Some were bigger than others, some more skilled at fighting. Some even seemed to have some basic concept of self. All, however, were slavishly devoted to a ruling class called the Hij, who manipulated them and channeled and controlled their instinctual, apparently mindless ferocity. There were different strata of Hij as well. Some were rulers and officers; others were artisans and bureaucrats. Regardless of their position, they constituted what was, for all intents and purposes, an elite aristocracy collectively subject to an obscure godlike emperor figure. Nothing more about their society was known.

The Hij were physically identical to their subjects, but were clearly intelligent and self-aware to a degree frighteningly similar to humans and their allies. They didn't seem terribly imaginative, though, and so far that had proved their greatest weakness.

"We know they plan to attack us at Baalkpan. Isn't that enough?"

Matt looked at Keje and sighed. "I don't think so. I don't *feel* so." He watched the men and 'Cats working on the foredeck under the glowering gaze of Silva and Chack. Both stood side by side, hands on their hips, occasionally trading comments. Silva, in his stained khakis and battered hat, towered above the furry, muscular, brindled 'Cat in the red kilt and white T-shirt. For now, in his bosun's-mate persona, Chack had traded his usual helmet for a white cotton "Dixie cup" hat like most of the enlisted destroyermen wore. Silva, in exasperation, moved to show a group of 'Cats how to run a long shaft with a bristle brush down the muzzle of the number one gun. For a moment he was partially obscured by the patched and dented splinter shield, but then he stepped back, evidently watching his pupils perform the task. He shouted instructions that were swallowed by the wind before they reached the bridge, then nodded. A few moments later the big chief gunner's mate returned to where Chack was standing, Wiping his brow with a rag, he resumed their conversation.

It struck Matt again how harmoniously the two races worked together. Once, not long ago, some of his destroyermen might have objected to sharing their labor, berthing spaces, even the drinking fountain on the side of the huge, ridiculously exposed refrigerator on deck, with another human who just happened to be a different color. Now those same men worked companionably alongside "people" of an entirely different species. He was gratified there'd been so few instances of racism—none at all after the mysterious disappearance of a certain *Mahan* crew member, who'd reportedly been something of a problem—but he couldn't help being amused by the irony. He knew the camaraderie of his integrated crew would be tested, eventually, in the cauldron of combat, and he believed it would withstand the test; humans and Lemurians had fought well together so far. But the coming test seemed so far beyond their capacity. No matter how well they got along, or how well trained they were when the Grik—and *Amagi*!—finally came in force, they were just too few and *Walker* too frail. Strangely, though, he no longer dreaded the inevitable confrontation; he almost welcomed it . . . but he *was* antsy.

Nothing yet, Cap-i-taan," hailed the muted, yowly voice of the Lemurian lookout in the mizzen-top above. Lieutenant Greg Garrett, former gunnery officer of USS *Walker*, now captain of the brand-new sailing frigate USS *Donaghey*, could barely discern the speaker from the predawn gloom, but knew the lookout's eyesight was much better than his own. With watchers at all three mastheads, the little flotilla of refugee-laden barges would undoubtedly be seen as soon as it pushed off from shore. He paced the length of the darkened quarterdeck. The almost entirely Lemurian crew went about their duties professionally, quietly, leaving him room to pace and think. He paused for a moment by the smooth, polished rail and peered intently at the hazy shore. *Donaghey* was hove to, with nothing to do but wait, less than two miles from the treacherous breakers.

The ship was Garrett's first command, and he loved her for that, but he also loved her classic lines and intrinsic beauty. He was highly conscious of the singular honor of being named her first commander. Those given the "prize ships" could never quite get over who made them. The barbaric nature and practices of their previous owners, and the acts performed aboard them, tainted them forever, regardless of how well they were scrubbed. They'd been found adrift, mostly, damaged by *Walker*'s guns during her escape from Aryaal and the battle that cost them *Nerracca*. Boarding parties faced ferocious, if uncoordinated defenders, but some of the Grik "survivors" went into an apparently mindless panic Bradford called "Grik Rout," and simply leaped over the side. No one would ever know for certain how many defenders there'd actually been. Hundreds were slain in the brutal fighting aboard the several ships, but more met their fate in the sea, and the water around the ships had churned as the voracious "flashies" fed. Allied losses had been high, particularly when they fought to rescue any Lemurian "livestock" they found chained in the enemy holds. Just as when they first captured *Revenge*, the sights they saw in those dark, dank abattoirs prevented the ship's new owners from ever being able to love them.

No such stigma clung to USS *Donaghey*, and her people loved her unreservedly. She was larger than the prizes, with a more modern and extreme hull configuration that, combined with her more efficient sail plan, made her considerably faster than the enemy ships. She was a true frigate too, being armed with twenty-eight precious, gleaming guns.

Unfortunately, she was one of only three such ships likely ever to be built. She was considered a transition, a stopgap. Future variants would combine steam and sails and therefore sacrifice some of their purity and grace. But this was war, and one took every advantage one could when the consequence of defeat was extinction.

They'd bloodied the enemy at Aryaal and in the following actions, but if the charts they captured showing the extent of the enemy holdings were to be believed, the Grik could quickly replace their losses. They apparently bred like rabbits, and according to Bradford's theories, their young reached mature lethality in about five years. If the remaining Americans and their allies were to have any chance of survival—not to mention victory—they needed innovation. That was why there were so few humans in Garrett's crew. Combined, the surviving destroyermen from *Walker* and *Mahan* numbered just a little over a hundred and twenty. Forty were still aboard *Walker*, and twenty or so were on *Mahan*. The rest were involved in various projects and training regimens they'd need to build the army and navy they needed to survive. The skills and experience of every last destroyerman had become not only essential, but irreplaceable. Garrett found it ironic at times that the ragtag remnants of the Asiatic Fleet who'd wound up in this place—men once considered by some to be the dregs of the Navy—were now an indispensable, priceless resource. They were the core, the innovators, the trainers of the native force needed to see them through, and there were not nearly enough hands and minds for all the work.

Certainly great work had already been accomplished. They'd transformed the nomadic, insular, and, in some cases, fiercely isolationist Lemurians into seasoned, professional soldiers and sailors. But their ranks had been horribly thinned as well. Recruitment was constant, and hopefully Captain Reddy's diplomatic mission to the land that had been the Philippines would bear fruit. In the meantime, they had to make do with what they had, and there just weren't enough of them. Part of Greg's current assignment was to try to remedy that to some small degree.

When the Grik armada swept down from Singapore and forced the Allied Expeditionary Force to abandon the city of Aryaal, as well as the island of B'mbaado, Aryaal had been thoroughly evacuated, but there'd been little time. Hundreds, perhaps thousands had been left behind on the island, and its queen protector, Safir Maraan, had sworn to get them out. So had the Americans. Therefore, a series of stealthy nighttime missions had been undertaken to rescue as many B'mbaadans as they could from under the very snouts of the Grik. So far there'd been few incidents or encounters, and quite a few refugees had been carried away. The Grik were not yet as thick on the island as they might have been. The cream of a portion of their invasion force had been mauled by *Walker* on its way to Baalkpan. Only about half of their "Grand Swarm" had been diverted to Java, and when the rest were turned back, they became busy repairing *Amagi*, consolidating their gains, and rebuilding the walls and fortifications of the cities the retreating force had destroyed. That meant *Donaghey* "only" had to avoid around two hundred and fifty ships and a hundred and fifty or sixty thousand crazed, ravenous warriors. But again, so far it had been a snap. Over the last couple of months Jim Ellis had made several trips in command of one of the prize ships, and either the Grik were unaware the missions were taking place, or they just didn't care. Their ships seemed content to remain at anchor in Aryaal/B'mbaado Bay, and let the rescuers come and go at will. Perhaps they just didn't know there was still a sizable number of Lemurians clustered on the southeastern shores of B'mbaado. Greg Garrett felt relieved, but also strangely cheated. His new ship was more than a match for any Grik ships yet encountered, and he yearned to strike a blow.

Before the war began, the Grik had no concept of gunpowder, and their artillery was limited to a ballistic device that hurled clay pots full of incendiary substances. "Grik Fire," it was called. Garrett would have loved nothing more than to pound a few Grik ships into floating splinters and send a few hundred of their warriors to the ravenous, waiting jaws of the hungry fish. At the same time, he'd seen enough of war by now to know that once any battle was joined, there was no way to predict what would happen. Every encounter carried a measure of risk, and in this war, surrender wasn't an option. Much as he yearned to lash out against their loathsome enemies, he'd be content with the successful and uneventful completion of his mission.

He paced the quarterdeck again, conscious that he might appear nervous, but he couldn't help himself. In addition to his mission, he'd also been entrusted with the safety of the headstrong Queen Maraan, who'd personally gone ashore to gather her people, and Pete Alden, once a simple sergeant and now the commander of all allied land forces, who'd accompanied her. Safir Maraan could usually take care of herself. She was a charismatic leader and a skilled warrior in her own right, but those were the very qualities that made her too precious to risk. At least, as far as Garrett was concerned. Not to mention that he personally liked her quite a lot, and she was betrothed to his friend Chack-Sab-At. In spite of a clear understanding of her important role, Safir Maraan remained committed to an oath she'd sworn to personally rescue the people she'd left behind, no matter the cost. To her, no role could supersede that of queen protector of B'mbaado.

Pete Alden accompanied her for little good reason Greg could see, besides imposing a measure of vigilance and reason upon her. In military matters she'd acknowledged him as her superior, and he probably hoped he could prevent her from doing anything rash if the rescue met with difficulty. That was how he justified it, anyway. Garrett thought there might be more to it. In spite of being their land force commander, Pete had mostly been on the sidelines of the war so far. He'd participated in the boarding action that captured *Revenge*, but since then he'd been consumed by the necessity of improving Baalkpan's defenses. He'd missed the Battle of Aryaal, and Garrett sensed a supreme unwillingness on the Marine's part to send others into situations he hadn't shared. Going ashore in this instance probably had as much to do with that as anything else. Besides, this mission was their last, and Queen Maraan's great general, Haakar-Faask, would come off with the final refugees and warriors he'd managed to gather, and Pete probably wanted to greet him personally. In any event, there were far more precious eggs in a dangerously exposed basket this morning than Greg Garrett would have liked.

High clouds appeared as wispy pink tendrils in the eastern sky, and the shore party was considerably overdue. Daylight might reveal the solitary ship to searching eyes, and just because the Grik hadn't interfered with previous missions didn't mean that would remain the case.

"They should have returned by now," murmured Taak-Fas. The 'Cat was *Donaghey*'s sailing master, and Garrett's second in command. Garrett turned to look at the brown-and-tan-furred officer. As usual, the strikingly feline face bore no expression, but his voice betrayed growing anxiety.

Garrett replied with a quick nod. "She's pulled stunts like this before," he said with a sigh. "Jim—Lieutenant Ellis—said she did it twice when he brought her here. She won't leave anyone behind who's at the appointed rendezvous. I can't blame her, but this waiting sure is nerve-racking."

"Why can't the refugees just wait for us on the beach, and meet us when the shore party goes in for them?" The question came from Russ

Chapelle, former Torpedoman First Class from *Mahan*, and now *Donaghey*'s gunnery officer, or master gunner. He'd stepped up to join the conversation.

Taak-Fas shook his head. "Grik scouts might see them while they wait for us. Also, since our ships look similar to the enemy's, even painted differently, it might be difficult to persuade some civilian refugees to come out if we didn't meet them at an inland rendezvous."

"On deck," came a sudden cry from above. "Three barges in the surf."

Russ grinned with relief. "Well. All that good worryin' wasted."

It was much lighter now. Garrett raised his binoculars and studied the three wide-beamed boats laboring through the breaking waves. They were packed to overflowing with Lemurians of every color. Most looked thin and haggard. *Understandable*, he mused grimly, *after all they've had to endure.* He focused the binoculars on a figure standing in the bow of the center barge, and could just make out the black-furred form of Queen Maraan, resplendent in her silver breastplate and helmet. Alden's distinctive, imposing form was beside her, as was a 'Cat wearing battered armor over a stained leather smock that stood almost as tall as the Marine. "It's about time," he grumped. "Have the boarding nets rigged, and prepare to bring them aboard. As soon as they have been, we'll make sail. Shape a course for Baalkpan." He paused and grinned at his subordinates. "We've been goofing around here long enough."

Just then, another cry came from the masthead.

"Sail! Two sails . . . Three!"

"Where away?" Garrett shouted. For a moment the lookout fumbled with the words. Most of *Donaghey*'s crew could speak at least a little English by now, but sometimes the nautical terms of the Americans were confusing. The ones pertaining exclusively to square-rigged ships were still awkward even for Greg. He'd had little sailing experience back home, and competent as he'd forced himself to become, most of his knowledge of sailing terms, practices, and commands came from an old book entitled *A Manual for Young Sea Officers in the Service of Her Majesty's Navy.* The book, like so many others they'd found of use, was a legacy of *Walker*'s long-dead surgeon, Doc Stevens, and his eclectic library. It was authored by a retired British admiral in the 1870s, during the transition to steam-powered warships that still used sails as well as engines.

"Port . . . ? Port bow."

Garrett redirected his binoculars and thought he saw something against the purple horizon, but wasn't sure. The lookout was certain, however, and he trusted the 'Cat. He glanced aloft at the floating pennant and turned until the wind blew directly in his face. "Not good," he said aloud to himself. "They have the wind in their favor."

"So what?" Chapelle shrugged. "What are they gonna do? If they get too close we'll blow the hell out of them."

Garrett spared him a glance. "If they get here before the boats do, they could stop us from loading the refugees. They might even attack the boats themselves."

Chapelle's eyebrows rose. "You want me to get ready for them?"

"By all means. Clear for action and sound general quarters."

A rapid, rhythmic gonging reverberated through the ship as the general alarm bell was struck. The tense mood of anticipation clutching the crew since before dawn was shattered by frenzied but purposeful activity. The decks were sanded, and overhead netting was rigged to protect against falling debris. Buckets with ropes attached were dropped over the side and hauled back aboard, filled with seawater. These were distributed around the deck and sent up to the tops to defend against enemy firebombs. Guns were loaded and run out, and soon the smell of smoldering slow match reached Garrett's nose. Marines lined the quarterdeck rail with their bows, and the few armed with Krag rifles scampered into the tops, prepared to pick off the enemy officers. *Donaghey*'s well-drilled crew prepared for battle very quickly, but by the time they were finished, the enemy was clear to see from deck, and the brightening sun shone upon the leaning pyramids of canvas.

Chapelle rejoined Garrett on the quarterdeck. "Taking their time," he observed, referring to the barges still laboring against the offshore swells. Dripping oars flashed in the morning sun, and Garrett glassed the figure with the flowing black cape and silver armor. She was staring in the direction of the approaching ships.

"They're coming as fast as they can," Garrett said.

Taak-Fas gauged the distance. "They will not reach us much before the enemy, if they do at all." He sounded worried.

"Yeah. This could get tricky," Garrett agreed. "If it looks like they aren't going to make it, we'll secure the boarding nets. I don't want to make a present of them for the Grik." He turned and saw the shocked expression on Chapelle's face. "No, we won't abandon them! We'll stand toward the enemy and destroy them, then come back for our people." Garrett shook his head and turned his back on his gunnery officer. The former *Mahan* torpedoman didn't know him very well, but it irked him that the man thought it even possible he might leave anyone at the "mercy" of the Grik. Let alone anyone as important as Queen Maraan and Pete Alden.

"Damn lizards are really flyin'," Chapelle muttered a few moments later. "They must know what we're up to. Afraid we're going to steal their 'rations,' I guess." He spit a yellowish stream of the local tobacco juice over the side.

Garrett nodded, but didn't take his eyes off the approaching ships. Something wasn't right. The Grik were notorious for their single-minded aggressiveness. The all-out frontal assault, regardless of losses, had seemed to be the only military tactic they knew before and during the Battle of Aryaal. Since then, however, whenever they encountered an Allied ship, they'd demonstrated an uncharacteristic caution and respect. Garrett suspected they were capable of learning from their mistakes, and believed the Hij commanders of the Grik fleet had figured out that tangling with artillery-armed allied ships without overwhelming numbers was pointless. Up till now his suspicions had been confirmed, but the three Grik vessels approaching from the northwest were really cracking on. They were coming on in the "same old way," and he couldn't help but wonder why.

He carefully studied the laboring boats. The oarsmen had redoubled their efforts when they saw the Grik, but their progress against the wind and current was excruciatingly slow. He yearned to move *Donaghey* closer in, but the shoals here were treacherous, and, deprived of engines, he'd already gained a healthy respect for a lee shore. Totally at the mercy of the wind, *Donaghey* might be driven aground. He refocused on the enemy. Chapelle was right: they were flying. With another last look at the boats, he lowered the binoculars to his chest.

"They're not going to make it," he stated flatly. "Secure the nets and signal Her ... Highness ... and Sergeant—I mean *General* Alden that we'll return to pick them up as soon as we've dealt with the enemy."

"Aye, sir," Taak-Fas replied with a frown. Unease over the brazen Grik advance was affecting him too, but it didn't show in his voice when he relayed Garrett's order at the top of his lungs. Chapelle spit again, and his lips formed an ironic grin, slightly distorted by the chaw in his cheek.

"I'm afraid we're gonna get our brand-new ship all scratched up, Skipper."

Safir Maraan, queen protector of the People of B'mbaado, representative to the Allied Council and general in what she liked to think of as the Allied Army of Liberation, watched with dread as the three Grik warships slanted swiftly down toward *Donaghey*. Quietly she urged the exhausted oarsmen to even greater effort. A few civilian refugees wailed with fright, but the sailors, warriors, and Marines at the oars made no complaint. They merely reached down and somehow grasped the final measure of their flagging reserve of strength. The gunwales creaked and timbers groaned as the panting Lemurians heaved against the disorganized swells.

"A signal from *Donaghey*," observed Haakar-Faask, captain of Safir's personal guard of six hundred, sometimes called the "Orphan Queen's

Own," and general of the army of B'mbaado, who stood beside her in the front of the boat. He rolled his massive, muscled shoulders and regarded Pete with a steady gaze. "What does it say?"

Pete Alden scratched his bristly black beard and stared, his eyes shaded by his battered, faded fatigue cover. "They mean to engage the enemy and return for us."

Safir responded with a curt blink of her wide, silver-gray eyes. "I have learned the Amer-i-caan signals, Captain," she said, addressing Faask by his Guard rank, which in both their estimations was superior and more intimate than his other. "Allow the rowers to rest, but let us try to maintain our position."

"As you command, Queen Protector," Faask replied in a pious tone that made her snort.

"Now he obeys me," she said aside to Pete. "He was insubordinate enough on earlier missions, when I ordered him to come out to the ship."

Haakar-Faask had been her personal protector since the day she was born, and he often behaved more like a long-suffering elder brother, or even father, than she would have liked. Often. She loved him as she would have her father or brother if they'd lived, but sometimes his obsessive protectiveness could be infuriating. She'd left him behind—ordered him to stay—to gather and organize the people they'd been forced to abandon during the hurried evacuation of their homeland, and she'd been torn by anguish and missed him terribly. Compared to his former mighty self, he was weak and malnourished like the other refugees, but in spite of her efforts to protect him for a change, he'd immediately resumed his former role. She glanced at his still-powerful form and realized for the first time, with a quick stab of grief, that not only had he suffered from deprivation in the months since the evacuation, he was getting old.

"As I *command*," she said with a false, triumphant grin, stressing the word.

Haakar-Faask regarded her with an innocent stare. "I have seen the Amer-i-caans fight," he said. He'd been there when *Walker* savaged the first Grik invasion fleet that tried to conquer Aryaal. "But that new ship, it is not made of iron like the other." He glanced at Alden. "There is no question of valor, but one against three is questionable odds. Should we not return to shore? We might be forced to hide or disperse if the Grik are victorious. They will search for us."

"They will not be victorious, Captain," Safir replied before Pete had a chance. Her grin had become predatory. She watched while *Donaghey*'s sails filled, and she heeled sharply to starboard, slanting away from the waiting boats. To the unknowing eye, it looked as though the ship were abandoning them, leaving nothing between them and the Grik. Cries of alarm arose from the boats, and she understood her people's fear, even though she knew it was unfounded. She was no sailor, but she knew the ship would soon tack back across in front of the approaching enemy. Garrett was trying to force the battle farther away from the boats and the shore, where his ship would have better maneuverability and more water beneath her keel.

"Do not fear," she cried out as soothingly as she could. "They will not leave us."

Long moments passed while the Grik grew closer and *Donaghey* became more distant. Even to her it was a terrifying sight. Just as the first sense of doubt touched her soul however, she saw *Donaghey*'s aspect change, and she was filled with exhilaration when the tall ship came about and began a headlong rush toward the enemy. A cheer rose up.

"Now you will see something!" she promised.

The sun crept ever upward and the day grew hot as the four ships came together. From their current angle it looked like all were heading straight for her, but Safir could see the distance between the one and the three dwindling rapidly. *Donaghey* would soon "cross their tee," as she'd heard the maneuver called. She would destroy the Grik, and the refugees would remember the long morning they'd spent in the boats as a stirring adventure: an exciting, reaffirming proof that the hardships they'd endured hadn't been for nothing, and most of all, in spite of everything, victory might someday be achieved. She watched with growing inspiration as a large battle flag, the one with the stars, blue field, and curious red stripes, unfurled at *Donaghey*'s masthead and streamed to leeward. She'd heard Captain Reddy tell a tale about a battle on the world the Americans came from when a ship called *Exeter* defiantly flew a giant flag in the face of certain destruction. Matt had clearly been moved by the act, just as Safir Maraan was now. The flag of the Americans had become a powerful symbol to her: in some ways an even more powerful symbol than the nine trees and one gold star on the stainless field now representing the alliance facing the Grik. It was a symbol of hope and defiance in the face of overwhelming odds. Even despite their setbacks, it had become a symbol of victory.

She knew the flag meant much the same to *Donaghey*'s crew, though there were few human Americans aboard her. Her people were land folk; descendants of that great, prehistoric nautical exodus that had carried her race from their ancestral home and deposited them here. The Grik had been the ancient enemy from which her people fled. Rejecting a seafaring life, they estranged themselves from the majority of their species. They became isolationist, feudal. Warlike as they were, compared to sea folk they'd been vulnerable to the first major Grik incursion.

Among sea folk, each of their huge, island-size ships were nations unto themselves, and their leaders enjoyed coequal status as High Chiefs among their peers. With the coming of the war, and the Grik Grand Swarm, changes to this age-old system began to evolve. The alliance now included not only sea folk, but land folk as well, and a collective, coordinating leadership was required. Captain Reddy was supreme commander, but Nakja-Mur, High Chief of Baalkpan, had become the civic leader of the alliance by default, since his was the "nation" hosting the other chiefs: Baalkpan was also the center of all their collective industry. Safir was beginning to see the advantages of the formation of a true, formal alliance. Not one of expedience only, but one evolving to unite all willing Lemurians beneath the Banner of the Trees into a strong political union such as the Amer-i-caans claimed to spring from.

The one gold star on the stainless banner represented the Americans. It was placed in the center not to show dominance, but to symbolize that they were the organizing force, the glue holding all together during these early, terrible, trying times. Also, unlike the golden trees surrounding it, the star now represented more than the single city-state personified by a single ship. Matt continued to insist the star didn't represent him and his surviving destroyermen, or even just his tiny but growing fleet; it represented the United States Navy in particular, and that vaguely understood nation his navy defended in general. He wanted it clear that, wherever it was, his "America" was part of this alliance. Every Lemurian joining an "American" crew became a member of the United States Navy, and swore to defend an even more vaguely understood Constitution. Captain Reddy insisted on that too. Therefore, wherever they came from, and for however long they served, any Lemurian who swore the oath became a "Navy man" and was considered by all to be an Amer-i-caan for as long as they kept that oath, and followed the Americans' strict rules.

Nothing like those rules—or "regulations," as they were called—had ever occurred to any Lemurian, anywhere. People did as their leaders specifically instructed them, of course, but otherwise they did as they pleased. Even in the more socially stratified lands of B'mbaado and Aryaal, behavior was not regulated by written rules or laws, but by decrees generally favoring those, like herself, who made them. She'd never imagined so many of her people would willingly submit to the level of discipline demanded by the Americans. To her surprise, as many of her people volunteered for the "Amer-i-caan Naa-vee" as did for the B'mbaadan infantry regiments forming in Baalkpan—even though those were now held to the same high disciplinary standards by General Alden. Most were turned away from the Navy because they just didn't have the ships, but it was something to consider. The American Navy had become a tight, close-knit clan of elite professionals that watched out for their own, no matter what they looked like. Safir wasn't sure if that was a good thing or not, although she tended to believe it was, and she suddenly wondered if it might not be the strict regulations themselves that made the difference. Not only did they enforce discipline; they also enforced the rights of those subject to it. It was a concept she'd been giving much thought. In any event, as far as she or anyone else was now concerned, the streaming flag showed that everyone aboard *Donaghey*—human or Lemurian—was "Amer-i-caan."

The ships converged rapidly now, their hulls and towering canvas contrasting sharply against the dark, cerulean sea. The American ship was bigger than the others, and clearly faster. It was a stirringly beautiful scene, in a way, that would soon be more beautiful still, when *Donaghey* began her destructive work.

"Just a few moments more," she breathed.

"Son of a *bitch*!" shouted Chapelle when the side of the nearest Grik ship disappeared behind a heavy cloud of white smoke. He'd been reminding his gunners to aim for the enemy's rigging when somebody pointed at the curious squares spaced evenly along the sides of the enemy ships. Squares just like *Donaghey*'s. Even as he stared, stunned, the squares opened and the snouts of crude cannons poked through. Too quickly for accuracy, a broadside—a *cannon* broadside—erupted from the enemy ship.

The angle was terrible. The Grik commander must have decided it was a matter of "use it or lose it" and given the order to fire, even though few guns would bear. As it was, not a single ball struck *Donaghey*, but the surprise caused by the sudden realization that they'd lost their only material advantage over the enemy was almost as damaging as an effective broadside would have been. As the distance closed, and *Donaghey* prepared to cross the bow of the ship that had just fired at them, all the gunners on the starboard side merely stood, transfixed by what they'd seen. Chapelle glanced at the quarterdeck and saw the shocked expression even extended to the captain's face, and he knew there was no time.

"What the *hell* are you doing?" he bellowed, in a voice carrying the length of the ship. He ran forward, yelling as he went, "Starboard battery! At my command! Fire as they bear!" Reaching the foremost gun under the fo'c'sle on the starboard side, he elbowed the Lemurian gunner aside and peered through the gunport, sighting along the top of the barrel. A moment more and it would be pointing at the enemy ship. All thought of finesse, and firing at a specific point, was gone. They had to get this first broadside off as quickly as they could, as effectively as they could, and break the shock that had seized the ship. Stepping back, Chapelle looked at the 'Cat gunner.

"Get hold of yourself," he growled. "So they've got guns. So what? They don't know how to use them, do they?" The gunner jerked a nod. Chapelle glanced through the port again. "Fire!"

The refugees in the boats cheered lustily when the first blossoms of smoke appeared. Safir had told them what to expect, and they probably thought the stabbing flames and smoke were the result of *Donaghey*'s fire. But in the front of the barge where she, Alden, and Haakar-Faask stood, there was silence. The queen clutched her protector's arm, and her blood felt like ice.

"Holy shit." Pete gasped.

"Should we return to shore?" Faask asked her quietly.

"Not yet."

"No, not yet," Alden agreed grimly. "We need to see this."

One by one, *Donaghey*'s guns replied to the unexpected barrage, as Russ Chapelle raced down the line, exhorting the gun's crews to do their duty. With each resounding crash it seemed the effect of the enemy surprise lifted a little more. By the time he reached the last gun under the quarter-deck, he believed the crisis was past. All the crew were veterans of fierce fighting, and many, survivors of *Nerracca* or transferees from *Walker*, had even been on the receiving end of *Amagi*'s mighty salvos. The constant drill and discipline they'd learned also helped them recover, and soon they were firing with the same skill and dedication they showed during the daily exercises. Guardedly satisfied, Russ mopped his brow and left the gun divisions under the direction of the officer trainees, or midshipmen, commanding them and ascended to the quarterdeck. Garrett was standing near the wheel, glassing the results of their fire on the first Grik ship. Chapelle was hard-pressed to see through the smoke, but it looked like they'd done little damage. A few shot holes in her sails, maybe. He shook his head.

"Sorry about that, Skipper," he said, joining *Donaghey*'s commander.

"Nothing to be sorry about. It shook everybody up. Me too. My God . . . *Guns*!" He lowered his voice. "Thanks."

"What for?"

Garrett's lips formed a small smile; then he gestured at the enemy ships. They were about to cross the second ship's bow. The starboard battery of the first—they seemed to have only five or six guns to a side—fired another ineffectual broadside that did little more than churn the sea in their wake, but the gunports were open on the ship they approached.

"At least their gunnery isn't very good," Chapelle observed. Just then, a rolling broadside erupted from the next ship in line. Like the first, the angle was poor, but the range was much closer, and they felt an unmistakable shudder beneath their feet when a couple of shots struck home. A high-pitched, keening wail arose from forward.

"They're learning fast," said Garrett grimly. He turned to his second in command. "As soon as we rake the third ship, we'll come about and do it again. Make sure we keep our distance. If we foul one of them, the others will gang up on us and board"—he paused—"and their crews are a lot bigger than ours." He didn't need to remind them what would happen if they were overwhelmed. A quick death, at best. He glanced astern at the distant, bobbing barges. "We have to win this, and we have to do it quickly." He looked at Chapelle. "I want you to hammer those ships if you have to aim every gun yourself." Russ nodded and raced back down the ladder. Garrett watched him go and then shook his head at Taak-Fas. "A hell of a thing," he said in frustration.

The cheering in the boats had stopped when it became obvious that all the ships were using cannons—something their queen assured them only the alliance possessed. They watched in quiet awe as the single ship opposed the three, and nimbly maneuvered to cross their vulnerable bows again. The deep, throbbing boom of gunfire reached them from across the water, and white smoke gushed downwind. A small cheer was raised when a Grik mast tottered forward, taking the top of the next one in line. The ship quickly slewed, beam-on to the wind, as the fallen mass of timber and sails dragged it around. As though a preplanned maneuver, the newly presented broadside thundered out and *Donaghey* visibly shivered from the impact. Splashes from debris and shot fell all around her, but she appeared little damaged, and punished her tormentor in response. For a long while, it seemed, while *Donaghey* gathered way, she lingered near the bow of the closest enemy ship, and a furious exchange of gunfire ensued. Two of the Grik were now firing at *Donaghey* while she concentrated all her efforts on the one helpless to respond. Even from the distant, pitching boat, Safir saw that the enemy was beginning to hurt Garrett's ship, and she shrank from the thought of what he and his crew were enduring. The choking smoke, the noise, the flying splinters and metal that could tear their bodies apart. But she knew what he was doing. He was trying to destroy the enemy by concentrating all his fire on one at a time, and it was working. By now, the closest Grik was a battered wreck. Only her mainmast still stood, and flailing lines and fallen spars hopelessly snarled the yards. *Donaghey* edged past, beginning to play her guns upon the next in line.

Suddenly black smoke gushed from the derelict, and almost immediately the people in the boats saw orange flames leaping from her forward gunports. They cheered. All three of the other ships—both Grik and alliance—immediately steered away from the one that was afire. The Grik in the center of the line was too eager to get at *Donaghey*, however, and had closed the distance too much. When she tried to turn, her mizzen rigging fouled the shrouds of her burning sister, and they collided and twisted together in a flaming embrace. White smoke vomited skyward, mixed with black, and clouds of burning canvas and ash drifted downwind, some coming to rest on *Donaghey*, as she tried to gain some distance.

A brilliant flash of light followed by a tremendous thunderclap explosion tore across the wave tops at the drifting boats, now less than four miles away. Only the hands of her devoted protector prevented Queen Maraan from falling into the sea. When she regained her balance and looked again, at first all she saw was a monstrous fog bank of dirty smoke and thousands of splashes, large and small, covering an area of several square miles. A few even came uncomfortably close to the boats. As the smoke gradually dispersed, she finally caught sight of the two remaining ships.

Both had been horribly mauled by the massive explosion. *Donaghey*'s sails were a tattered, flailing mess, and her mizzenmast had fallen against the main, fouling its yards and creating a jumble of tangled rigging. She was listing to starboard, and her stern looked like a mountain fish had taken a bite out of it. The Grik still had all her masts, but her sails were shredded to the point of uselessness.

"We must return to shore," she said, her voice wooden.

"But . . ." Faask began to object, but Safir shook her head.

"Cap-i-taan Gaar-ett cannot concern himself with us now. He will be hard-pressed to save his ship. We are land folk, but I can tell which way the wind is blowing. If *Donaghey* is very fortunate, she will be carried around the point. Perhaps she can make repairs and return for us then. If she does not clear the point, she will be wrecked, and there is nothing we can do to stop that."

For a long moment she watched the stricken ships drifting downwind. Occasionally a puff of smoke heralded the report of a gun from one ship or the other as they continued to fire whenever they could. She thought she could even hear the shrieks of the wounded and shouted commands over the intervening distance, but that was probably just her imagination. Whatever happened to *Donaghey* now, she'd have to see to her own survival, just as Safir Maraan had to see to the survival of those who depended on her. If *Donaghey* couldn't return, she knew it would become far more difficult to rescue them. With the Grik guarding the approaches with cannons on their ships, no single ship would dare make the attempt.

Without the explosion that crippled her, she believed *Donaghey* could have defeated all three Grik vessels armed with cannons. The enemy had clearly not known how best to employ their new weapons. But they were learning, and with their limitless numbers, they were unlikely to be so amateurish and unprepared again. Next time there might be a dozen ships sent to do what three had done today.

Safir sent a prayer to the Sun that *Donaghey*—and her friend Garrett— could escape or defeat the remaining Grik ship, and quickly mend her wounds. Perhaps then she might return for them before the enemy did. The thought of Garrett sent a chill down her spine, because it reminded her of someone else. If *Donaghey* survived but couldn't come back, Safir would be stranded with the rest of the refugees the alliance may no longer have the power to rescue. What would Chack think? What would he *do*? Chack had accompanied Captain Reddy on the expedition to Manila, but with the magic of the Americans' radio, he'd know what happened as soon as *Donaghey* made port. With the sudden thought of her beloved, a shiver of sadness and fear crept deep into her bones.

"To the shore," she repeated in a voice she didn't recognize.

An hour after the explosion, the surviving Grik ship was worse off than she'd appeared at first. None of her masts had fallen, but all her sails were rags, and so far no replacements had been sent aloft. Her deck was like an anthill, stirred with a stick, choked with her surviving warriors. They seemed to have no direction, no guidance at all, and all they appeared able to manage was to rush about and roar with frustrated rage as the wind and current swept them ever closer to the breakers. At least *Donaghey* could still make steerageway, and she'd continued to claw away from the menacing shore until the two ships exchanged their relative positions. The cannonade never completely ceased, but it became sporadic and ineffective. Occasionally the Grik ship commenced a spirited fire, but as often as not the guns weren't even pointed in *Donaghey*'s direction. It was bizarre. The only explanation was perhaps her Hij officers had been killed, and no one remained to tell the Uul warriors what to do. Once it was clear they had little to fear from the enemy, most of *Donaghey*'s crew ignored the Grik and focused on saving their ship. The Grik was inshore now, and headed straight for the shoals and booming surf of the protruding point.

Garrett sat on one of the quarterdeck gun carriages, mopping his face with his hat and grimacing with pain while the Lemurian surgeon bound his wound. A large splinter had been imbedded in his thigh, and the waves of agony caused by its removal were only now beginning to subside. All around him was chaos like he'd never known. Shattered timbers and shredded sailcloth festooned the deck, and seemingly thousands of frayed and ragged lines created a nightmare web of destruction. He'd seen his share of naval combat in the last year, first against the Japanese, then against the

Grik—and Japanese. But he'd always been on *Walker* when the fighting took place. He knew war was terrible, terrifying, and bloody—sometimes catastrophically so—and naval warfare could seem particularly over-whelming. Even so, he'd believed he was ready for a command of his own. Now he wasn't so sure.

He'd trained to become a destroyerman in . . . well, yes, a compara-tively modern navy. He was a good gunnery officer, and managing his new ship's weaponry wasn't so different from firing *Walker*'s in local con-trol. He could navigate and stand a watch, and he wasn't afraid to fight. Thanks to the old admiral's manual, he'd even learned to handle *Dona-ghey* in a fairly competent fashion. But this type of warfare—gone for the most part for a hundred years on his own world—was completely differ-ent from what he'd been prepared for. The stakes were the same, and so was the objective: destroy the enemy before he could destroy you. The re-sults were apparently the same as well: shredded bodies, blood-splashed decks, and a stunned sense of unreality. But the *way* it happened and the pace of it all were what so disconcerted him. (He hadn't suspected splinters would be such a menace, for example.) He knew even the twenty-five-year-old destroyer he was accustomed to was far more complex, but somehow, on a sailing ship the complexity was much more apparent—particularly when it had been so horribly brutalized.

Even now, with a pause in the action, the air was filled with screams and shouts, grinding timbers, and chopping axes. The occasional gun roared, when enough debris was cleared to allow it to fire at the equally bat-tered enemy. But above all the unfamiliar sounds of this new/old type of war, there was a deafening silence. A silence of absence. Instead of the com-forting roar of the blower, and the grinding, rasping, high-pitched wheeze of the turbines, there was only the capricious wind. A wind that would drive them onto the deadly shoals as well if they couldn't quickly bend it to their will.

"Cease firing," he ground out through clenched teeth, when Chapelle approached to report. The blond torpedoman didn't seem injured, but his shirt was torn and spattered with blood.

"I just did, Skipper," he replied. "I figured the little guys had practiced enough for one day." He shrugged. "Besides, Taak took my crews and put them to work clearing debris."

Garrett nodded and struggled to rise and gaze over the nearby bul-wark. The Grik was beginning to wallow, beamon to the inshore swells.

"It won't be long before she strikes. How about the refugee barges?"

"Safely ashore," Chapelle confirmed. "I almost wish they'd stuck it out. If we get things squared away, we might be back for them in a couple of hours."

Garrett shook his head. "It was the right call for her to make. It'll be evening, at least, before we can beat back around the point—if we make it around the point." Garrett was gauging the angles as he spoke, studying the wind direction and the shore. "As hot as it is, they'd have been really suffering by then."

"We'll weather the point," Chapelle assured him, "but you're probably right. It sure is hard to get used to not having engines."

"I was just thinking that myself. It's tough getting used to a lot of things here," Garrett muttered.

Chapelle frowned. "Hey, Skipper, don't beat yourself up. You did okay." He gestured at the now clearly doomed Grik. It was rolling so violently, the masts must soon fall. With a distant, muted "crack," the main snapped off at the deck and collapsed into the churning sea even as they watched. Moments later the other masts went down as well, and all that remained was a wallowing, helpless hulk. Try as he might, Garrett could summon no compassion for the horrible creatures he knew had only moments to live.

"One against three . . . Three down and us still up. Not a bad showin', if you ask me." Chapelle chewed philosophically. "Sure, we're beat up"—he grinned—"and our brand-new ship got scratched a bit, but that's mostly because those two blew up in our face. Their guns weren't doing much harm. A few weeks in the yard, a little paint here and there, and she'll be good as new."

"Not good enough," Garrett growled. "Not nearly good enough. A few weeks sounds about right, but it'll take more than a little paint. For now, *Donaghey*'s out of the war. They have the ships to trade three to one; we don't. And . . . Damn it, Russ, they have *guns* now! Where'd they get them? How many do they have, and how fast can they make them? Damn it! Our one big advantage . . . shot!" He grimaced belatedly at the pun. "Yeah, they used them stupidly, but we can't count on that next time. We aren't exactly professionals at this kind of war either, you know."

Chapelle looked uncomfortable. "Not much doubt where they got them," he muttered darkly. "Those Jap bastards showed them how to make 'em."

Taak-Fas trotted up, weaving his way through the debris on deck. He had something in his hand.

"Cap-i-taan, we are almost ready to cut the final lines and let the mizzen fall over the side." He grinned. "You might want to be somewhere else when that happens."

"Of course."

Chapelle and the surgeon helped Garrett to his feet. One of the surgeon's assistants, covered with blood, arrived to help. Garrett shooed him away, and with a grateful nod the 'Cat raced back to whatever operation he'd been summoned from.

"As soon as it goes over," Taak-Fas continued, "the fore and main will draw much better. We'll be okay." He sounded relieved, and Garrett was too. He was also glad he had such a capable, levelheaded exec. Excited, chittering voices drew his attention back to the Grik ship. She was among the breakers now. Suddenly she heeled sharply over and performed a drunken, jerky pirouette. Waves broke over her deck, and struggling forms disappeared over the side. Garrett briefly wondered if they'd drown before the voracious "flashies" tore them apart. He still felt no pity, but was again struck by how much more inhospitable this world's seas were than those he remembered. And it could've just as easily been him and his crew dying in the surf. He shuddered.

"Let me get out of the way so we can take that mast down," he said. "Otherwise, we'll be joining them." He stopped. "What have you got there, Taak? In your hand?"

Taak-Fas raised the object and studied it curiously. "A Grik cannonball," he said. "It was rolling loose on the deck. It is about the same size as ours, and weighs much the same, I think, but it is clearly different. Here." He handed it over. "I have duties, and you must allow the surgeon to properly dress your wound. I assure you, Cap-i-taan, I can somehow manage for the short time that will take."

Garrett took the ball and laughed. Taak was right. The repairs were under control, and he was just getting in the way. Taak spoke to the surgeon in his own language; then he and Chapelle assisted Garrett down the companionway. Once they reached the wardroom, they eased him into a chair, where he sat and waited while others with more serious wounds were tended. He'd insisted as soon as he saw them. Some of the wounds were utterly ghastly: mangled limbs and terrible gashes—mostly caused by splinters, he again realized. His ship was in capable hands and his leg would keep. He looked at the ball he'd laid in his lap.

The cannons they'd helped the Lemurians create were bronze. There was plenty of copper and tin all over this region that had once been the Dutch East Indies. Iron was harder to come by and harder still to work. They desperately needed iron to make structural repairs to *Walker* and *Mahan*, and implement many of their other plans. In the short term, though, it didn't seem critical. Bronze was actually better than iron for smoothbore cannons. The elongation was better and the quality control not as critical. They made their cannonballs of copper, which flew just fine. But without a steady source of iron, and the ability to smelt and forge it in quantity, there was only so far they could go, industrially speaking. Even with their limitations, Garrett had thought they would enjoy a significant advantage over the enemy for some time to come. At least until today. As he contemplated the projectile in his lap, it suddenly dawned on him with a sickening sense of dread that the Grik had not only caught them technologically, but taken a leaping bound ahead. The ball in his lap was iron. *They're making cannonballs of iron*, he thought numbly. His thoughts immediately rearranged themselves. *They have so much iron they can* waste *it on cannonballs!*

"My God."

Hisashi Kurokawa, captain of His Imperial Majesty's battle cruiser *Amagi*, paced nervously back and forth in the gloomy anteroom of the Imperial Regent's palace. The regent, an imposing Grik named Tsalka, was not present, nor had he been since shortly after the disappointing setback delivered to the Grand Swarm in general, and *Amagi* in particular, by the "Tree Prey" and their American allies. He'd returned to Ceylon, where he presumably awaited either death for his failure, or a requested audience with the Celestial Mother, the Supreme Empress of all the Grik Herself, on the distant island of Madagascar where the Imperial Palace stood.

Kurokawa doubted he'd ever see Tsalka again. The regent would either be killed out of hand, or executed (hopefully eaten alive) after his audience with the empress. Even though he'd essentially been only a "passenger" aboard the Grand Swarm's flagship, and not in actual command, he'd been the highest-ranking Grik in the region. Intolerance for failure was one trait the Grik shared with the Japanese, and if the one punished was not actually responsible for the failure, it was the example that was important. Even if he wasn't killed, there was a very good chance he wouldn't survive the trip to Madagascar. Voyages across the deep water of the Indian Ocean were notoriously hazardous. Apparently, the deeper the water, the larger the predators grew. Large enough to *eat* ships such as the regent would travel in. The thought warmed Kurokawa slightly. He patently loathed Tsalka—and all things Grik, in fact—even though only Tsalka's forbearance had prevented him and all his surviving crew from being eaten in the aftermath of the "setback." Kurokawa felt little gratitude, however, since one in ten of the Japanese survivors—almost sixty men—had gone to the butchers and feasting fires of their "allies." It was nothing personal, he was assured, simply tradition. The hunter that drops his spear when the prey is brought to bay is always eaten in its stead, and the American torpedo that nearly sank his ship certainly made him drop the Grik's mightiest spear.

Kurokawa had been indignant, but since he felt no real allegiance to his men either, he'd shed no tears for those who died. They were cowards and traitors all. Particularly his executive officer, Commander Sato Okada, who constantly questioned his decision to make alliance with the Grik, and would even make an accommodation with the Americans, he suspected, if he could. He'd grown far too close to their American prisoner of late. But Okada was not unique; his entire crew had betrayed him and the Emperor with their failure. After the strange storm that brought them here, *Amagi* had been the most powerful ship in the world. He'd believed it was only a matter of time before he could use her might to gain a position of power over the Grik. The Grik were loathsome creatures, but clearly the dominant species. Once he rose in their esteem, he could co-opt, or even supplant their ridiculous "Celestial Mother" and eventually rule this world himself—all in the name of Emperor Hirohito, of course.

Amagi's worthless crew had thwarted his ambition, at least temporarily. They'd allowed the mightiest ship this world had ever seen to be grievously wounded by an insignificant American destroyer, a ship so poorly armed and obsolete even the Americans had considered her class as expendable as napkins before the war. Therefore, Kurokawa cared nothing for the welfare of his crew, except insofar as their training and experience enhanced his own value and prestige. He couldn't use them to further his aims if they were dead. He raged to admit it, but he himself would have little importance to the Grik without the skill and knowledge he commanded through his surviving crew. He therefore did his best to keep them alive and relatively comfortable.

Besides, the main reason Tsalka hadn't killed them all was that another Grik, General Esshk, had intervened. Not immune to blame himself, it was he who prevailed with the argument that the Japanese and their mighty, wounded ship might be of use. Perhaps even essential to the ultimate success of the Swarm. Esshk made Tsalka realize the old ways of war, the Great Hunt that exterminated their prey almost as sport, might not succeed against the rediscovered Tree Prey, who'd escaped the conquest of Madagascar itself countless generations before. They'd grown much more formidable than the ancient histories described.

Kurokawa had learned that when the Grik first encountered the Tree Prey, as they were called, they'd posed no more of a challenge than any other predatory species the Grik had exterminated. They usually hid in trees, of all things, and when they fought, they did so ineffectually. But unlike any other prey the Grik had hunted, the Tree Prey somehow escaped. In desperation they'd built great ships from the dense forests of their home and braved the deadly sea the Grik couldn't cross. Not until merely a couple of hundred years before had the Grik been given the gift of a seagoing ship to copy for themselves. A strange race of tail-less prey—not unlike the present Japanese, Esshk inferred—arrived in a three-masted ship with a sturdy, ingeniously planked hull. No one knew where they came from, and it really didn't matter. The prey was devoured, but the ship and technical language required to make her was copied. Educated Hij among the Grik learned to write and cipher in the strange, captured tongue, even if they couldn't form the words to speak it. More and more ships were built along the lines the captured drafts referred to as "East Indiamen." The Grik now had a fleet with which to expand their empire— although progress was slow. Even the much-improved ships the "English" prey brought were not proof against the largest denizens of the terrible sea.

It all made sense to Kurokawa. He suspected an East Indiaman had been swept to this world a few centuries before, just as *Amagi* had. Inexplicably, it was unarmed. He didn't understand that at all. Historically, British East Indiamen usually carried an impressive armament for protection against pirates, and even belligerent warships. Perhaps those long-ago Englishmen already knew something about the Grik before they were captured, and feared what would happen if "modern" weapons fell into their hands. Maybe they heaved them over the side? If so, what had they thought they were protecting? Regardless, there were no cannons aboard when the Grik took the ship. Otherwise they'd already have them and they wouldn't have come as such a devastating surprise when the hated Americans recently introduced the technology.

Kurokawa seethed. Oh, how he hated the Americans! They were responsible for his being here in the first place, instead of back where he belonged, riding the tide of Japanese victory across the Pacific. Perhaps the war was already won? The long-respected American Navy had proven ineffective, and had been unable to muster much of a defense after the devastating attack on Pearl Harbor. Nearly a year had passed since the bizarre green Squall transported him here. At the rate they'd been going, the Japanese Imperial Navy might have dictated terms to the United States from within San Francisco Bay by now. That was where he ought to be: covered in glory and recognized for his brilliance. Not here in this barbaric, perverted caricature world, where the emperor—*his* emperor— did not reign. The Americans were the cause of all that, and someday he'd have his revenge.

His value had been recognized by General Esshk, at least. The general was acting as forward vice regent in Tsalka's stead, and his quarters were in the palace of the former king of Aryaal. Even Kurokawa had to admit the palace was an impressive edifice. It was constructed of white marble, and the spired towers and spacious, arched balconies gave it a medieval Eastern European flair. It was even more striking, since it was the only building still standing within the walls surrounding the conquered city. Aryaal was "conquered" only in the sense that it no longer belonged to the enemy. The first attempt to take it failed catastrophically, and it finally came into Grik hands as a burned-out, abandoned wasteland. All except the palace that somehow escaped the inferno. Briefly, he wondered why.

Kurokawa knew the Americans had to be responsible for the scorched-earth policy that greeted the invaders when they reached the city, as well as the neighboring island of B'mbaado. He doubted their primitive lackeys were sophisticated enough to think of the strategy on their own. With the inhabitants gone, and nothing left but the palace, there was no food, no supplies. There wasn't even shelter from the terrible storms that some-times slashed at the exposed coastal city. The Americans had managed to sour even the seizure of Aryaal, which was the one small victory the Grik had achieved. Everything they needed had to be brought by ship, putting even further strain on available resources and indefinitely delaying the buildup they'd need before renewing the offensive. Only by renewing the offensive could he prove his worth, and only by proving his worth could he renew his broken scheme for power. Captain Kurokawa continued to brood and pace.

The tapestry separating the anteroom from the audience chamber parted to reveal the terrifying form of a Grik. It looked like a bipedal lizard, except it had short, feathery fur instead of scales. Its snout and tail were shorter, proportionately, than one would have expected from a lizard, but the tightly spaced, razor-sharp teeth packing the short snout left the fiercest shark wanting. Empty, remorseless, sharklike eyes regarded Kurokawa in silence for a moment before the creature spoke.

"The vice regent will see you now."

The voice came as a series of hisses and clicks, but Kurokawa had learned to understand the words even if he couldn't speak them. Much of the meaning came from subtle sounds requiring a foot-long tongue and two-inch pointed teeth. By now a few Grik had also learned to understand English, although it was apparently even more impossible for them to speak. Most Hij could read written English. It was their technical language, and that was how Kurokawa first communicated with them: writing notes back and forth. But that was no longer necessary, and he could converse fairly normally, with Esshk, at least.

In the Japanese Navy he'd risen in, it was required that all bridge officers know and speak English, since most of the maneuvering commands were made in that language. He knew the tradition began at the turn of the century, when Japan purchased her first modern battleships from Great Britain. Even more were acquired during the Great War, when the two countries were actually allies against Germany. Since everything on the ships was written in English—the instruction manuals were in English, and most of the instructors and advisors spoke only English—Kurokawa and his peers were forced to speak English as well. The Japanese Navy was an infant in need of traditions, and speaking English on the bridge became one. He was glad that was one tradition quickly fading back home, even if he made use of it now.

Controlling a shudder, he bowed stiffly to the gruesome messenger, straightened his tunic, and marched quickly into the vice regent's audience chamber.

General Esshk, complete with plumed helmet, scarlet cape, and shiny plate armor protecting his chest, looked for all the world like a sinister, reptilian gargoyle dressed as a Roman tribune. Mighty muscles rippled beneath his downy skin, and he carried himself as fully erect as his alien physique allowed. Even slightly hunched, he towered over the Japanese officer. Kurokawa knew that, before the recent setback, Esshk had been a favorite among the Grik elite. He was considered their greatest living general, and was actually a sibling, of sorts, of the empress. He also had an unusual reputation: he was deemed something of a philosopher. Kurokawa knew that really meant he had a keen and inquisitive mind. He was unusually open to new ideas and innovations, and seemed less entrenched in the instinctual behavior patterns and responses he'd seen in other Grik, even Hij. That was both an advantage and disadvantage, depending on the circumstances, since it made Esshk both easier and more difficult to manipulate. When working with the general, the supreme question always was, Who was manipulating whom?

Esshk noticed his arrival, and motioned another Grik he'd been speaking with to leave. He hissed a pleasant greeting.

"Ah! Captain Kurokawa! I trust you are well?"

Kurokawa bowed deeply. Visitors were expected to prostrate themselves, but he simply would not. A formal bow was as much as he was willing to compromise. Strangely, Esshk never insisted he do more.

"Well enough, Your Excellency. I do grow anxious."

"Anxious to resume the hunt? Good. That is why I summoned you here."

"There is news?"

"Actually, yes. Several days ago I dispatched three of our newly armed ships"—he bowed his head appreciatively toward Kurokawa—"to patrol the eastern approaches to the neighboring island. I hoped they might encounter one of the ships of the prey that sometimes visit the vicinity. They did."

Kurokawa contained a surge of annoyance. He'd often counseled Esshk to conceal the fact that they were arming Grik ships with guns, and to reveal the surprise only when they had sufficient numbers for a decisive blow. He was constantly amazed that a race whose only military tactic was a full frontal assault with overwhelming numbers had such difficulty understanding the principle of mass. It was an old argument by now, however, and one he had no hope of winning. Besides, perhaps the sortie had been successful. Esshk certainly seemed in a good mood.

"I take it the enemy ship was destroyed?" he ventured.

"Unfortunately not, but it was severely damaged. I congratulate you on your perseverance in training the crews to use their new weapons effectively." Esshk seemed to consider. "Perhaps even more such training is in order."

Kurokawa sighed. He did not, of course, perform any of the training duties himself. That, and other things, was what certain members of his crew were for. He'd heard, however, that teaching the semisentient Uul to do anything beyond hack at their opponents with swords was like forcing water to run uphill. He'd speak to those responsible for the training and see what more could be done.

"Perhaps. With respect, what kind of damage . . . did our . . . forces sustain?"

Esshk waved a clawed hand. "Total. All three ships were destroyed. An explosion of the black dirt that burns destroyed two. It seems a fire began." He jerked his snout upward in a gesture Kurokawa had come to equate with a shrug. "The other suffered damage to its sails and went ashore. The ship of the prey was also damaged, but managed to avoid running aground as well. It was, in fact, attempting to return to the scene when our other three ships with cannons arrived and drove it away. Perhaps they were trying to rescue some of their people left behind on the island?" He paused, considering. "I would not have thought it possible, but . . ." He looked at Kurokawa with what might have been respect.

"If I had not given the . . . unusual . . . command that some effort be made to rescue doomed crews, we would not now know what transpired in the fight, or how well the new cannons worked. As it was, almost a dozen Uul were saved from the grounded wreck. Perhaps the prey are doing the same? Trying to learn what has happened here since they left?" Esshk paused and jerked his head again. "As a further gesture, an experiment, if you will, to test the possibility you might be right yet again, I have not ordered the survivors destroyed. They were defeated, but they were not, after all, made prey. It was the ground upon which they stood that fled, not they. We will let them pass their experience to others and see what may transpire."

Kurokawa was surprised. He'd often tried to explain to Esshk how wasteful it was to kill defeated troops. All of them, anyway. Sometimes it was necessary. The Grik were perfect physical predators. Even the Uul were born with such strength and such an awesome array of personal weaponry, no creature he'd ever heard of could hope to match one unarmed. They were like cheetahs, and every other species, including man, were sheep compared to them. But with the exception of the curiously elevated Hij, the physical gifts of the Grik were balanced by some rather peculiar and apparently instinctual behavior patterns. Chief among these was a total—indeed, pathological—inability to understand the concept of defense. They comprehended only attack. Like a cheetah attacking a lamb, feeble attempts by the lamb to escape, or even defend itself, only made the cheetah attack more aggressively. As long as it was attacking, it was winning, no matter what injury it had sustained. But if the attack were ever blunted or hurled back . . . the cheetah that ran from a lamb could never be a cheetah again.

Something happened to the Grik that ran away. Something sprouted within their primitive, retarded brains, and there was not the slightest hint of its existence until the instant it took place. Kurokawa saw it after the Battle of Aryaal, when dozens of ravaged ships limped back to Singapore. They'd been advancing with the Grand Swarm, and he'd seen hundreds of Grik destroyed by their own comrades in what seemed, at the time, a mindless frenzy of wild butchery. Since then he'd given the phenomenon considerable thought and believed he knew what triggered the sudden, primordial, all-consuming urge in defeated Grik—those "made prey"—to flee, and never find it within themselves even to look back. It was panic, fear, the sudden realization that they'd encountered a predator greater than themselves. Just as the Grik attacked as a mob, they were capable of panicking as a mob if things went against them. It was a contagious thing that had to be snuffed out at once.

Kurokawa had tried to explain to Esshk that sometimes defeat in itself was not always the same as being made prey. Sometimes the heart was still willing, even when the ship beneath it could not carry on, for example. Warriors . . . removed from the hunt in such a way might not always be unfit to rejoin it. He'd used this argument, in part, because that was what happened to him when *Amagi* was torpedoed on the way to Baalkpan, and he wanted to establish firmly in General Esshk's mind that Hisashi Kurokawa had *not* been made prey. It was a selfish gesture, but practical as well.

If, when they inevitably resumed the offensive against the Tree Prey—and Americans!—they continued to kill or abandon their trained crews simply because their ship was sinking, they'd lose valuable resources and delay their ultimate victory. It seemed Esshk was willing to give it a try.

Kurokawa reflected momentarily while General Esshk regarded him with his intense reptilian eyes. Finally he spoke. "But the prey escaped the other three?"

"Regrettably."

"The Americans . . . The prey will now know we've matched their advantage. That knowledge might be costly."

"Perhaps. But they cannot know to what extent we have surpassed them."

"Surpassed them?" Kurokawa inquired.

"Indeed. The factories your workers established in Ceylon are performing wonders. Again, you were right when you suggested they be treated differently from other Uul. They thrive with better treatment and are industrious. You Japanese never cease to amaze me! So frail, yet so useful. And to think Tsalka wasted so many of you on his table! I am sure he has certainly changed his mind!"

"If he lives," muttered Kurokawa bitterly.

"He does. Word arrived today. That is one reason I summoned you: to tell you he not only lives, but basks in the glow of the Celestial Mother's favor. The fast ship he sent to request an audience with Her returned with Her benevolent blessings for our strategy, and instructions that he continue as your patron. She extols the virtues of the Japanese helpers of the Hunt! Just think on it, the Celestial Mother Herself knows you exist! It is a great honor!"

"Indeed," Kurokawa hedged.

"Soon all the Grik will share the benefits of these glorious cannons of yours. By the next time the moon passes into darkness, ten more ships will arrive from Ceylon, each already armed. In their holds will be more than two hundred guns—enough to arm ten of the ships we already have! A moon after that a like number will arrive, and Tsalka will accompany them at the head of another grand fleet to add to the Swarm. With your *Amagi* and over forty ships armed with cannons, and hundreds of conventional ships filled to overflowing with hundreds of thousands of Uul, the prey can do nothing to stop us! That is when we will strike!"

"A month and a half. So soon?"

Esshk peered closely at the Japanese officer. "I do not understand your face. You seem pleased, yet wary. What troubles you? Surely you do not doubt our fleet will easily sweep the prey from the sea?"

"I do not. They have few ships, and even though the large ones are formidable, they cannot maneuver. The only thing concerning me at all is the iron ship, the American destroyer. Its guns have much greater range than ours."

"*Amagi* will concentrate on the American iron ship. Surely its guns cannot outrange yours?"

"Of course not . . . I . . . I only hope *Amagi* will be ready."

Esshk's eyes narrowed slightly. "Will it?"

Right then Hisashi Kurokawa knew his very existence depended upon his next words. He contemplated the progress of his ship's "refit" so far and almost shivered in horror. The project was the most ghastly thing he'd ever seen. There was no dry dock in Aryaal, not on this Earth, as far as he knew, but somehow they'd had to get at *Amagi*'s underwater damage. After much discussion with Esshk and what passed for Hij engineers, they'd settled on a cofferdam. At low tide, weighted down by the bodies of thousands of Grik, they'd run his ship aground in the silty mouth of the river below the fire-blackened walls of Aryaal. There, a massive pile driver encircled *Amagi* with titanic beams dragged for miles through the almost impenetrable jungle beyond the plain still littered with bones from the battle fought upon it. When the framework was complete, Kurokawa's own engineers began devising ways to plank it up. Heavy, prefabricated sections were prepared and lowered into place with the ship's cranes, but they couldn't decide how to secure them to the pilings. The answer was simple: Uul warriors were ordered to jump in the water and do it by hand.

Kurokawa still lived aboard his ship, so he was there to see. As much as he hated the Grik, he was sickened by the sight. Uul by the hundreds, each covered in armor and holding a length of line, shrieked a battle cry and leaped into the water. The armor carried them down—it would be a one-way trip—and protected them slightly from the silvery fish that arrowed in from the bay at the sound of splashes. If they were lucky, they sometimes managed to tie their line before being torn to shreds. Slowly at first, but quickly growing to a nauseating pink, white, silvery roil, the water began to churn. Pieces of bodies and buoyant debris rose to the surface, only to be snatched down by ravening, gaping jaws. On command, hundreds more leaped to their doom, each clasping his piece of line. Most of the Japanese sailors couldn't watch, but Kurokawa stared, transfixed, as much amazed as horrified. Such obedience!

The second wave probably didn't fare as well as the first, but when the third command was given, the boiling water had simmered down. Perhaps the fish were sated? This time a few Grik wouldn't go. It finally occurred to their primitive minds that if they did, they wouldn't come back up. Instead of refusing or attempting to flee, however, they turned on their comrades in a wild attack. All were disarmed, but no Grik was ever truly without weapons, and they used their terrible teeth and claws on those around them. They were quickly subdued, killed, and thrown in the water, but after that first incident, there was an ever-growing number that had to be "destroyed." During this entire procedure, *Amagi*'s pumps were at work, using steam from her few remaining boilers. Finally, Kurokawa noticed that the water level inside the cofferdam was slightly lower than that outside, and he suggested a halt to further wastage of warriors.

The cofferdam was built, and within a week they began repairing his ship's underwater rents, but at such an appalling cost! Surely thousands had died. He'd learned a valuable lesson that day, besides the crystallization of his theory regarding how panic affected the Grik. He'd learned that to the Hij, all other creatures were simply tools, no matter what they said about the Uul being their "children." Life had no value beyond how useful a tool it might be. *Amagi* was just a tool . . . and so was he.

Meeting General Esshk's gaze, he finally nodded. "She can't be finished that quickly. There is still much damage to her engines and boilers, so she won't be as fast as she once was, but she'll be ready for battle."

Esshk seemed to relax, and Kurokawa did too—slightly.

"Excellent," Esshk said. "So now we may turn to another subject: the American flying machine, their 'flying boat,' you called it."

Kurokawa's cheeks burned. During the campaign against Aryaal and the abortive thrust toward Baalkpan, the damned Americans had unveiled a dilapidated PBY Catalina. His inability to prove he'd destroyed the plane still rankled. Aside from its value for reconnaissance purposes, the plane had caused a lot of damage, and the fact that it could fly higher than *Amagi* could engage it damaged his prestige.

"It must have been destroyed," he said. "I sent one of my own aircraft, an observation plane, to engage it. Since then, it has not been seen."

"But your 'observation plane' never returned, so we cannot know for certain. Perhaps they destroyed each other, as you speculated, or perhaps your plane was destroyed and theirs only damaged. If so, perhaps they do not have the . . . capacity, I think you said, to repair it. But perhaps there is nothing wrong with it, and they hold it back only until it can do the most harm. I cannot tell you how disconcerting that machine was to our Uul."

The plane, armed only with machine guns, caused an amazing amount of damage that couldn't be defended against, and the psychological effect had been profound. A shocking number of Uul turned prey merely at the sight of the thing.

"If you're still concerned about it, it's only prudent to attempt to discover its disposition," Kurokawa said, a little heatedly.

"Then do so."

"How?"

Esshk hissed exasperation, and Kurokawa knew then that the Grik general had boxed him in. It was suddenly clear who was manipulating this conversation. "Your precious aircraft, of course."

Amagi had only one observation floatplane left. One was lost chasing the PBY, and the others were destroyed, ironically, when a Japanese dive-bomber crashed into them during *Amagi*'s first encounter with the two American destroyers that somehow resulted in their exile to this place. That the plane crashed into his ship because one of the destroyers shot it down only added to his hatred. All that remained was a single Nakajima Type 95 biplane. It was old-fashioned, slow, and short ranged. Kurokawa had offloaded it before his ship began repairs. He hadn't considered it necessary to the success of the upcoming campaign, and meant to leave it behind because he didn't want to risk losing it. If he was right and the PBY was truly gone, his was the only airplane in the world. It could so easily be damaged or destroyed by a lucky shell or bullet while sitting exposed on its catapult. Also, fire had always been a big part of the way Grik made war—a sometimes indiscriminate use of fire—and the plane, and the limited fuel he had for it, was an increased hazard to his ship.

The plane had languished, floating peacefully at the dock ever since, under guard by its flight and support crew and a much larger contingent of Grik. Esshk said the guard was to protect the plane, but Kurokawa knew it was really there to prevent it from flying away. Given the treachery of his crew, that was something Kurokawa himself was a little concerned the pilot might try. He'd given strict orders that the plane be properly maintained, but the crew was not to even start the engine. He didn't want them to waste a single gallon of the precious aviation fuel—or give their captors the slightest excuse to harm the irreplaceable pilot and plane.

So far, he'd resisted every "request" by Esshk to use the plane. It was his "ace in the hole," as the Americans would say. At his orders, the Japanese sailors had cooperated with the Grik in every way. They'd given them as much technology as their primitive industrial base could exploit. He supposed that had brought them up to the seventeenth century, militarily speaking, at least as far as weaponry was concerned. But the plane represented his greatest example of truly modern technology. It was proof that, no matter how far the Grik progressed, they could never hope to match the magical powers Kurokawa possessed, and most amazing of all to the Grik was the power of flight. He was certain the PBY had been destroyed or seriously damaged. He'd even ordered the pilot of the other Type 95 to ram it if he had to, to return with his shield or on it, or his flight crew would be executed. With that threat to motivate him, Kurokawa was positive the pilot must have resorted to the final option, since he never returned, but neither had the PBY. Ultimately, whether or not the flying boat actually crashed was immaterial; he was certain it would never fly again. There was simply no way to repair it—just as there was no way to repair his own last plane if it was damaged. He therefore basked in the reflected glow of its importance while hoping he'd never have to actually use it. His reluctance was the source of growing strain between Esshk and himself.

The Grik couldn't use the plane themselves, so taking it was pointless. Even if they could be taught to fly, they couldn't physically sit in the cockpit because of their heavily muscled tails. In all the world, only the Japanese hunters controlled the miracle of flight, and that was how Kurokawa intended it to remain.

Esshk pressed him this time. "Is your plane truly so fragile it will ruin it to use it once? If that is the case, what good is it?"

Kurokawa recognized the threat in the question. In other words, what good was he?

"It is quite sturdy, Your Excellency, but we have little fuel. Also, as I've said, if it's damaged, it cannot be repaired. We haven't the tools or materials."

"The prey flew their airplane all over the place. They must have plenty of fuel. We will capture it, and you will have more than you need. As to the other, I still do not understand. They are machines, are they not? Machines created by your folk. Surely they know how to make more. I tire of your obstructionism. You must use it! The sword that remains at the belt is of no use in the hunt."

"But the materials! I tell you we cannot repair it if it is damaged. We should wait to use it at the proper time—when it might tip the scale."

"Materials!" Esshk snarled, and Kurokawa realized he'd objected too long. He knew the conviviality Esshk greeted him with was only an act. The general began to pace, and Kurokawa remained rigidly at attention, staring straight ahead. "You mean metal? We make metal for you by the shipload! Do not toy with me!"

"I do not, Your Excellency! As I've told you, the metal we need to build more planes is called aluminum. It is . . . magical, and can be made only in the world from which we came. It is strong, like iron, but much lighter. No aircraft made of iron could ever fly."

"Then make them of something else!" Esshk raged in frustration. "You keep telling me we need to know what we face before we attack. Your aircraft is the only way to discover that and yet you refuse to use it!" Esshk glared menacingly at Kurokawa. "Reconcile this contradiction at once!"

Kurokawa stared at Esshk, his mouth open slightly. Peripherally, he was terrified of the general's behavior, but his mind fastened onto something Esshk said. *Of course!*

"General," he said calmly, "we will use the plane, and if you give me free rein, I'll make more for you. They won't be as strong, or nearly as fast, but I'll make airplanes even Grik can fly! But I warn you, it will take time. It will take more time even than the modern ships I promised, since that's what we've already begun. But I can do it for you, and because you have been such a friend, I will. But in return, you must do something for me."

Esshk's eyes widened and his nostrils flared with indignation. Then, slowly, his terrible jaws moved to form an expression Kurokawa hoped was a grin.

"A bargain? How interesting! I wonder what it is you could possibly want?" He seemed contemplative for a time, but finally waved the matter aside. "We shall see, shall we not? My power to grant a boon depends on our success, after all. In the meantime, we must concentrate on the matter at hand. You will provide me with a list of requirements to ensure your plane has the 'legs' to reach its destination and return. We must time the mission carefully, since we will open the final campaign in no more than a moon and a half. All must be in readiness by the time Tsalka returns. You will need ships placed at intervals for refueling, of course. I will order them to scout far forward after that mission is complete, to ensure the prey has no further surprises for us. Ideally, they will rendezvous with the Swarm before the assault begins." He waved a clawed hand vaguely toward the curtain. "Leave me now, and begin your calculations."

"Of course, Your Excellency," Kurokawa said with outward calm, but inwardly he seethed. "One further question, if I may?"

Esshk nodded. "Oh, very well."

"What of the enemy holdouts on B'mbaado? Will you take them seriously now? It seems to me they have evaded us too long. It's possible, if they're rescued, they might report our progress: the gathering Swarm, the pace of repairs to my ship, for example."

"Fear not. I have suffered their existence for my own purpose: to see what efforts the prey might expend to rescue them. I admit you were right, and I am surprised. I should have destroyed them sooner. But perhaps any information they have taken away has been to our advantage?"

"How so?"

"If they are spying on us, and not just huddling together on the farthest reaches of the island, then they will have seen the might we will bring against them—and more is still to come. Let them infect others with that knowledge. That terror. As for the remainder?" He sighed. "I will dispatch one of the newly arrived drafts to dispose of them. They are jungle warriors from the home province. They will make short work of them, and we shall feast upon their leaders!"

Kurokawa's stomach turned at the thought of enduring another such "dinner," but he bowed.

"Of course, Your Excellency."

Muffled machinery noises still reverberated throughout the ship, and the steel still hummed with life, but there'd been no throbbing roar from the engines for some time, and even the slight, almost imperceptible motion of so large a vessel riding at anchor was stilled. Deep within *Amagi*'s bowels, Captain David Kaufman, United States Army Air Corps, noticed the difference, but didn't understand the significance. He didn't understand the significance of much of anything anymore. He tried to do a single push-up on the cool deck plating, but just didn't have the strength. Straining as hard as he could, he couldn't raise himself from the dank, grimy floor of his cell. His jailors fed him once a day, but it was never enough, and his once powerful frame had diminished to a shadow of its former self. Tears pooled beneath his face, and he rolled onto his back, trying to control the sobs that came so frequently now. Above him dangled the single bulb that stayed on day and night. It was one small favor the Japanese officer had granted, and it was probably the only thing that retrieved him from the bottomless chasm of insanity. At least, he thought it had. He still had . . . spells, but today he could at least remember his name, and he willed that knowledge to be enough to cheer him just a bit.

The officer had granted other favors as well, when he could, and Kaufman got the impression he did so with the utmost care. A small stack of magazines was arranged carefully in the corner, opposite his slop bucket, and a couple were even in English. He didn't know how many times he'd read them—hundreds, probably. He'd memorized every word. He read the other ones too, and he'd slowly learned a smattering of written Japanese by putting the pictures in context with the curious symbols beside them. He didn't have any idea what the words sounded like, but he knew what many of the characters meant.

He rose slowly, painfully to his knees, and scooted to the overturned bucket that served as his only chair in the small, barren compartment. Easing onto it, he sat and stared at the glowing bulb for a while. It was how he passed much of his time, focusing on the bright filament until he could see it wherever he looked. His face began to twitch uncontrollably, and he tried to still the muscles and nerves by twisting his tangled beard. It never worked, but he always tried. He couldn't remember how long it had been doing that; it always started within a few minutes of his awakening from his constant, hideous dreams. Dreams of blood and screaming death, and reptilian creatures devouring people he was somehow responsible for. He couldn't remember why. He had no idea how long he'd been a prisoner of the Japanese either, but at least they hadn't eaten him.

The latch on the compartment hatch clanked, and his heart began to race. With a joy he could barely contain, he saw the Japanese officer who'd been so kind to him. How long had it been since his last visit? Months? It didn't matter. He'd feared the creatures had eaten him, but here he was, alive! The treasured face contorted into a grimace of distaste, probably at the smell in the compartment, but honestly, Kaufman didn't notice it anymore. He felt tears sting his eyes; he couldn't help it.

"Captain Kaufman?" The greeting came almost as a question, as though the officer didn't recognize him.

"Oh, ah, yes! It's me!" he croaked. It seemed strange to speak after so long, and it was pleasant to have someone confirm he was who he thought he was.

"You have not been eating!" the officer accused. Kaufman's face contorted into a grimace of contrition. He understood how the officer might think that, since he'd lost so much weight.

"But I have!" he insisted fervently. "I eat everything they bring me! Everything, I swear!"

The officer's eyes narrowed. "Then clearly my orders have been disregarded. You have my most abject apologies. I gave orders that you be fed properly. It seems that word is subject to interpretation. I will make its definition clear."

Kaufman stared at him for a long moment, mouth agape, revealing cracked, blackened teeth. "More food would be nice," he finally agreed softly, trying not to make it sound like a complaint.

"You will have it," the officer promised; then he too hesitated a moment. "I must also apologize for not visiting you more often, to see to your needs. I . . . am ashamed you have been treated so poorly by my countrymen. Necessity forced me to stay away, however. My commander has noticed my attention toward you and does not approve. He has threatened several times to return you to those despicable creatures we got you from. He does not believe you still have value as a source of information."

Kaufman felt a surge of panic. One thing he remembered very well was his terror of the Grik. But what could he say? His mouth formed a protest, but he ultimately only lowered his head. "He's right," he mumbled. "I don't know anything more than I've already told you. I guess my 'usefulness' is over." As soon as he spoke, he was shocked and terrified by his admission, yet strangely liberated as well. One way or another, perhaps his suffering might soon end. He raised his head and rested his twitching gaze on the Japanese officer. "So that's that, I guess," he said, and began to tremble. "The Grik can eat me, but I'll be free."

"Perhaps 'that' is not 'that.' Certainly not if I can prevent it, and there might yet be something you can do."

Kaufman looked confused. "I already told you I don't know anything else!"

In fact, he didn't. He'd told the Japanese officer everything he could remember, and even though he still felt a vague sense of shame, he'd left nothing out. Subconsciously he knew it was wrong somehow to do so, but he couldn't remember why. He couldn't even remember what he'd told them now, only that it had, indeed, been everything.

"That's not what I meant," the officer assured him. "Do you remember, some time ago, I asked if you would be willing to signal your old friends with a transmitter?"

Kaufman looked around as though searching for something, his expression desperate. "I . . . I think I remember you asking that, but . . . I don't know who you mean. All my friends are dead . . . but you." His gaze continued to wander. "Dead."

Commander Sato Okada's expression tensed, and he did feel a surge of shame. And hopelessness. Kaufman had clearly entered into a deep psychosis, and he didn't know if he could bring him out of it. The months of solitary confinement, sensory deprivation, and malnutrition had taken their toll. Okada had said he wasn't responsible for the ill treatment, but he knew he was. He'd given orders that the prisoner be properly treated, but what was proper? Japan was not a signatory to the Geneva Accords regarding the treatment of prisoners of war. Japanese troops and sailors were taught that surrender was unacceptable, dishonorable. Lacking detailed instructions, the ratings assigned to "care" for Kaufman would treat him as they expected to be treated in his place. He should have been more specific, and found a way to check on him more often. Now it might be too late. Okada remembered the details of Kaufman's capture and knew he hadn't surrendered; he'd been overwhelmed, so the initial dishonor was not his. Since then he'd been subjected to horrific brutality, not only at the hands of the Grik, but the Japanese as well. He eventually did surrender information, but not until his soul—and apparently his mind—had been taken from him. Okada realized he must somehow bring the aviator back from the abyss, save him from the madness he took refuge in. He was no traitor, but he'd finally decided he must risk everything to contact the Americans before it was too late. Warn them, somehow.

The Grik were evil incarnate, and *Amagi's* captain had embraced them for reasons of his own. Even if Okada could supplant Kurokawa, *Amagi* was in the power of the Grik, surrounded, watched. At the first sign of treachery, their reptilian masters would swarm them under. The Grik dreamed of a world dominated entirely by their evil, clutched in their wicked claws. Kurokawa was blinded by his own ambitions and his obsession for revenge. He didn't realize he was but a rat taunting a mighty serpent that might make use of him for a time, but would devour him in the end. For the human race, Japanese or American, the Tree Folk, or any other sentient species inhabiting this Earth to have any hope for survival, *Amagi* and the American destroyer must find a way to work together. Any other course of action was itself madness.

But in order to plan any concerted action, he needed Kaufman's help. He cleared his throat. "Recounting your experiences might be painful," he said gently, "but we must. I will start at the beginning, as I know it."

G oddamn you, Silva!" Chief Laney snarled as he approached. "What do you mean by takin' over my machine shop without even a 'by your leave'? We were workin' on critical repairs! Even you should've been able to tell the lathe and little mill were in use; they were both set up! Hell, the setup took half a day!"

Silva turned to him with a beatific smile. He'd been leaning on the starboard rail on the welldeck, just aft of the bridge, staring thoughtfully at Mindoro—or at least what had *been* Mindoro. They were in the Philippines proper now, steaming north through the east passage of Mindoro Strait. Their old stomping grounds. In fact, Dennis suspected the distant promontory ahead should have been the mouth of Paluan Bay, but he wasn't sure, because nothing really looked the same. It took him a while to figure out what the main difference was. There were no people, no fishing villages lining the shore, and very few boats. The few they'd seen were like the other Lemurian feluccas they'd grown accustomed to, but they hugged the shallows and kept their distance from the strange, smoking ship. Several days before, they'd overhauled and spoken one of the massive Homes they knew, returning empty to Manila for more supplies. He hoped it would be full of troops when it turned back to Baalkpan.

If they were where he thought they were, they'd spot Lubang Island before nightfall, and their voyage would be nearly complete. A lot of the men had grown quiet and somber as they neared their old "home," and even he wasn't immune to a certain nostalgic sense of loss. He had, in fact, been thinking a little morosely of several young ladies in particular who'd have been glad to see him very soon in the old Cavite they'd left behind, and so, when Laney stomped up, offering an outlet for his frustrations, it actually cheered him up.

"That's 'Chief' Silva to you, Laney, you frumpy little turd." He tugged on the visored hat he now wore for emphasis. For some inexplicable reason, the Bosun had given it to him, and it wasn't even his oldest, most beat-up one, either. He just said if Silva was going to be a chief, he had to look like one. Laney wore one of Donaghey's old hats, and despite the fact that he was larger than the late engineer, it was too big, and only his ears and eyebrows held it up. Otherwise, no one else aboard would have called Laney "little," though. He was only slightly shorter than Silva, and a comment like that would once have started a fairly equal fight. Now, both were conscious of the limitations placed on them by the new hats they wore. All the same, Laney suddenly remembered another time, and he was glad they were standing by the solid rail instead of the safety chains.

"It ain't *your* machine shop, neither," Silva added. "I swear, you've got mighty uppity of late. One of your 'Cats even wants to strike for the deck." He shook his head. "Shows good sense if you ask me, but Spanky and Donaghey never ran anybody off. You always was a asshole, but you've got even worse since they gave you that hat."

"Who is it?" Laney growled. "We'll see about that!"

"Ain't gonna tell you. He don't want ordnance anyway. Ask the Bosun when we pick him up."

Laney hesitated. He couldn't afford to lose anybody, but he also couldn't go crawling to the Bosun. "Well, what about the machine shop?" he demanded. "Spanky's gonna shit worm gears when I don't deliver them parts!"

Silva laughed. "I cleared it with Spanky before we started. Besides, he said you got scads of spare pressure couplings by now; you're just doin' busywork."

"Well . . . the second reduction pinion off the low-pressure turbine is thrashed—goddamn lube oil we're getting ain't up to spec—and we gotta turn a new one. 'Sides, what are you doin' in there, makin' mop handles?"

"Matter of fact, we broke the firin' pin on number three this mornin'—all the practicin' I've had the fellas doin'—and we figured we'd make another one." He scratched his beard. "Funny, but without a firin' pin, we can't make the big, scary bullets go out the other end. I told Stites to make a dozen while he was at it. There's a fair chance we'll break another one."

"What about my pinion?"

"You gonna put it in while we're underway? That'd be a rodeo! You're a crummy machinist anyway; I don't care what your rating is. Hell, Juan's a better lathe man than you; so's the Jap. You'd be just as well using a mop handle as anything you'd turn out."

Chack was listening to the conversation with amusement a few steps away. It went on a little longer, but finally Laney stormed aft, grumbling with every step. Chack drifted over and replaced him at the rail and caught Silva chuckling.

"I swear, if he found a roach floatin' in his coffee cup, he'd turn it into a mountain fish by the time he got done yellin' at the mess attendant."

Mountain fish had dominated just about everyone's conversation the last two days. They'd finally seen one of the things—a young one, Chack assured them—lazing on the surface, taking the sun. Silva had always suspected people exaggerated their size, but now he knew they hadn't. Everyone got a good, long look through the binoculars that made the rounds, while the captain gave the creature a wide berth. It was enormous! The part they saw, just a dark hump in the distance, and a small fraction of the monster's total size, was half as long as the ship. It blew like a whale, and occasional waterspouts geysered a hundred feet in the air. Everyone was excited to see the mythical creature at last, but no one was sorry to watch it disappear astern, either. Since then, they'd spotted a couple of truly huge gri-kakka, bigger than any they'd seen before, that were as dangerous to the ship as an iceberg or torpedo, but even giant plesiosaurs paled to insignificance compared to the mountain fish they'd seen.

"Perhaps he is high-strung," Chack suggested, referring to Laney. "I've heard Mr. McFarlane say so."

Silva laughed out loud. "High-strung, and fit to snap a string, I'd say. If he's a chief engineer, I'm a Chinese fighter pilot."

They stood in companionable silence for a while, the foaming sea sluicing by beneath them. They were friends again, although there was still a measure of friction. Not enough to bring them to blows; they'd already discovered, despite Silva's height advantage, Chack's extraordinary strength—he'd spent most of his life as a wing runner or sail trimmer on *Big Sal*, after all—made them a remarkably even match, and their one altercation had left both of them uneager for a rematch. Besides, Chack was no longer certain he was mad at Silva anymore. Most of his anger had resulted from Silva's and his sister Risa's boisterously public "marriage." He felt at the time they'd done it to "get even," or humiliate him for a prank he'd pulled on Silva. He'd since learned that Silva was a *professional* prankster, who enjoyed it when somebody "got" him, but he didn't "get even." His retaliation usually consisted of gross, sometimes even dangerous escalation.

Just about everyone believed the "marriage" was a joke, but Chack still wasn't certain. Sure, Silva and Risa might have carried on so at first, just to get his goat, but since then, in several situations, he'd sensed genuine respect and affection between them. He still found the idea that they might be engaging in *sexual* relations repugnant, but he supposed if they truly did consider themselves mated, then Risa's fate could have been worse. She was a far better warrior than most males he knew, and that, as well as her own rather twisted sense of humor, had left her with few prospects for a fulfilling relationship with a male she could enjoy and respect. Silva seemed to fit that role, and even if such a match would never result in young-lings—he shuddered—it might result in happiness, and he was prepared to accept that.

It was time to clear the air, though. His people had few sexual conven-tions, and most everyone, even Keje and Nakja-Mur, had been amused, at worst, over the possible relationship. But Chack knew the Americans were much less understanding. They liked his people a lot—more than many of their "own." They were at war with the Japanese, after all. But he'd learned an old quip: "I've got nothing against them; I just wouldn't want my daughter to marry one." He expected it was used in jest, at least when he was in earshot, but the phrase struck home. Besides, there was Silva's al-leged affair with the American nurse, Pam Cross, to consider. His people were not necessarily strict monogamists, but he knew Americans could be. Monogamy was, in fact, the norm among them. He worried that, if Silva and his sister were truly mated, Nurse Cross might try to supplant her, and he didn't want Risa hurt. He cleared his throat.

"We should speak," he said at last.

"Shoot."

"About you and Risa, and about your intentions regarding her. We must speak seriously about this at last."

"Sure."

Chack blinked annoyance, and his tail swished rapidly behind him. "I am about to muster the Marines for exercises, so I don't have a great deal of time. Will you just answer my question?"

"You ain't asked one yet."

"As hard as I've worked to master your language, you've surpassed me at being obtuse!" Chack growled.

Silva grinned, but turned to look closely down at him, and his eyes betrayed what might have been an inner sadness. "I like Risa a lot. She's a swell gal. She's a hoot, and she makes me laugh. I wish she was along with us instead of back in Baalkpan on *Big Sal*. She's the only dame . . . uh, female I could ever just let loose with, be myself, talk. I figure if things was different, she'd be about the perfect dame for me to settle down with." He paused, still looking at Chack, and was amused by the indignant blinking he saw. "Now, ain't that somethin'! All this time you've been mad at me be-cause you thought I wasn't good enough for her; now you're mad because you think I just said she ain't good enough for me! Fact is, like I said, we're just about right for each other, even if she is a 'Cat. Trouble is, we're *too* much alike, and neither of us is ready for a rockin' chair." He laughed at Chack's puzzled expression. "You still got some work to do on our language. I mean neither of us is ready to settle down. Do I love her?" He stared back over the rail at some distant point, and when he spoke again his voice was soft, barely audible over the blower, the whoosh of hot gases rising from the funnels, and the curling, splashing wake alongside.

"Once upon a time, the only feelings I had were happy, hungry, horny, and mad. Usually they got all mixed-up. I'd get mad at a fella, we'd get in a fight, and I'd be happy. After it was over I'd wind up hungry, and probably horny too. Or I'd be happy 'cause I wasn't hungry. . . . You get the idea. Anyway, I had a buddy once, Mack Marvaney, who got killed by them island Griks on Bali before we met y'all, and all of a sudden I found out I had another feelin': sad.

"I don't much remember my folks; they both died when I was a sprout—about three, I guess. En-floo-en-za. It was all over the place, but Daddy might've brought it back from France." He shrugged. "I went to live with my uncle Bob, and he worked me and whupped me like a mule from then on. Got even worse after the Crash, and I had to scrape for everything we ate. He'd bring a little money home now and then, makin' 'shine, but he drank as much as he made, and one day he took a harness strap to me and I killed him with a grubbin' hoe." His jaw clenched tight. "Never felt sad about that. Anyway, I wandered around for a few years, doin' things I ain't much proud of, mostly, and when I turned sixteen I lied about my age and joined the Navy." He looked at Chack. "Now you know more about me than anyone alive . . .'cept Risa.

"I never knew what 'love' was, or 'sad' or 'safe,' or really 'happy' either, but now I guess I do." He suddenly slapped Chack on the back hard enough to take his breath. "I love you like the brother I never had, and Stites and Rodriguez, Mertz, Kutas, even Juan and all the others, 'cept maybe Laney. He's a jerk. The Mice—and Bradford!—are like the freak cousins nobody ever talks about, but I even love them too. The skipper's not that much older'n me, but him or the Bosun are the closest thing to a real dad I ever had, 'cause they keep me in line without a harness strap, and they do it for my own good." His mighty fist pounded the rail. "And I love this damned old ship that's as old as I am. She's the only real home I've ever had. She leaks, she squeaks, hell, sometimes she coughs and gags. She prob'ly couldn't hold her own in a stand-up fight against a rowboat full of Boy Scouts with BB guns, but she's my goddamn home!"

Silva quickly turned away and jabbed his fingers in his eyes, rubbing vigorously. "Damn soot!" he mumbled huskily. "Snipes must've blown tubes on one of the boilers." After a while, he turned to face Chack again with a mysterious dampness around his eyes. He made a production of pulling a pouch from his pocket and biting off a chew. Finally, when the quid was properly formed in his cheek, he spoke again.

"You wanna know if me and Risa have wrassled and romped around, and had a little fun; that's none of your damn business. Do I love her? Sure I do, and I wouldn't do anything to hurt her. She's my pal. Will I tear your heart out and eat it if you spill any of what I just told you? You can bet your life on it, brother or not."

Captain Reddy was watching the two from the perspective of the open deck behind the pilothouse. He grunted. He was glad to see that, whatever accord Chack and Silva had reached, at least they'd made up. He needed them too badly, and their strained relationship had been felt throughout the ship. Turning, he rejoined Keje, Bradford, and Adar, where they were discussing Maa-ni-la protocol on the starboard bridge wing. There wasn't that much to discuss; it was roughly the same as Baalkpan—the two land homes were related, after all—and they'd already been over it a dozen times. There'd be the initial "request to come aboard" that was a holdover from the seafaring tradition all 'Cats shared and most still adhered to, but Matt, as "High Chief" of *Walker*, must make the request this time himself. A lot would depend on how he was received by Saan-Kakja, Maa-ni-la's High Chief. *Walker* was a very small "Home," after all, and despite Matt's position, and what he represented within the Alliance, Sasn-Kakja might not recognize him as a High Chief. Nobody wanted to set the precedent that every captain of every fishing boat or trader had the same status as the leaders of the great Homes of the sea and land. Even if he was accepted, however, it'd be up to Keje or Adar to do most of the talking. Matt's Lemurian was improving, but it wasn't up to the task of serious negotiations. Sasn-Kakja was a new High Chief and an unknown, but it was a safe bet he knew no English, and Matt might as well recite nursery rhymes when he spoke. Keje and Adar already knew what to say.

He glanced at his watch and compared it to the clock on the bulkhead. It was almost time for the watch change, and he'd soon relieve Dowden, who currently had the deck.

"One thing I can't stress enough," he reminded, interrupting the 'Cats and the naturalist, "is that you immediately try to learn as much as you can about the reports of an 'iron fish.' If it's a submarine, as I suspect, I need to know as much as possible about what it looked like and where it was most recently sighted. I understand it hasn't been seen for months. It'd undoubtedly be out of fuel by now, so we'll have to base our search on its last reported position, investigate the closest islands and so forth. Hopefully, we can begin that process while your discussions are still underway, if they drag out too long. We really need to find that boat. It could make all the difference."

"What makes you so sure it *is* a submarine, Captain?" Bradford asked. "Who knows what creatures lurk in these mysterious seas? And even if it is one, what if it's an enemy vessel? The Japanese on *Amagi* have shown no inclination to aid us, certainly!"

"C'mon, Courtney! An *iron fish*? And the stories tell how strange, tail-less creatures went inside it before it swam beneath the sea! As for it being one of ours, it only makes sense. We had lots of boats in the area, more than the Japs. They might've even been enough to make a difference, but their torpedoes weren't working either. If it weren't for our crummy MK-14 and -15 torpedoes, we might've even *stopped* the Japs." His voice had begun to rise, and he stopped himself and took a deep, calming breath. "If a sub was in the vicinity of the Squall, like the PBY was, it could have been swept here just like us. Unlike us, they might've made for the Philippines, looking for a familiar face. Last we heard, we still had Corregidor, and subs were getting in and out. If they poked their scope up at Surabaya—I mean Aryaal—and saw what's there now, the next place they'd check, their only hope really, would be the Philippines. If it was a Jap sub . . . I really don't know where it would head, probably not the Philippines, though. Maybe Singapore. They've got some really big, long-range boats; they might've even tried to make Japan."

Adar shuddered. "How big would this 'sub-maa-rine' be, if it was Amer-i-caan?"

"Depends on the class; either about the same length as *Walker*, or three-quarters as long."

"Just imagine," Adar gasped, "cruising beneath the sea, and in something that small!"

Matt nodded grimly. "You bet. I always thought submariners were nuts, and that was before there were fish big enough to eat the whole bloody boat. God, I hope that's not what's happened to her!"

"You've mentioned before how . . . aad-vaan-tage-ous . . . it would be to find this amazing vessel, but despite the happy prospect of finding more Amer-i-caans, what good would it be? You have already recognized the terrible dangers of operating it, particularly underwater. I'm sure, if they live, the same dangers have occurred to its crew."

Matt nodded. "Sure, but the danger would be much less within the confines of the Makassar Strait, or Baalkpan Bay itself, and didn't you already hear me say it might have torpedoes aboard? We only have one left, and we know why they weren't working now. She might be our ultimate surprise against *Amagi*."

"I should think securing more troops than the few Saan-Kakja has already sent would be our highest priority, not finding a submarine that may or may not exist," Bradford opined.

"Probably, but that'll be largely Adar and Keje's job. If we can manage both, however—" He was interrupted by the clanging bell that signaled the watch change. "Let's just hope we can manage at least one or the other."

They could have made Manila before sunup, in the wee hours of the morning, but Matt didn't want to sneak in; he wanted to be seen. He also wanted to see the city in the light of day, gauge the reaction of its people to their arrival. Most would know what it meant, and why they were there; refugees had been crowding into Manila for months. He hoped the sight of his ship, newly painted with most of her visible damage repaired, would inspire confidence in their cause. She'd made quite a sensation the first time she steamed into Baalkpan Bay, after all. So they loitered in the mouth of Manila Bay in the dark, while swarms of fishing boats hurried past her for the morning catch. Most never saw her, or if they did they paid no heed, since her arrival wasn't a surprise. The mission had been announced over a month ago, plenty of time for even one of the lumbering Homes to bring the news. A few boats stopped, their people staring at her with their uncanny vision, but none stopped to chat. Matt wondered if that was good or bad. A few coastal traders came out with the sun, scudding before the brisk morning breeze, but they immediately went on their way. Matt cleared his throat.

"Very well. Mr. Kutas, I have the deck and the conn," he said, much to the chief quartermaster's relief. Kutas had rarely conned the ship in confined waters. "Relieve Reynolds on the helm and take us in. Carefully and politely, though, if you please." It was Reynolds's turn to gulp with relief. The young seaman had only recently been rated capable of standing a helmsman's watch.

"Aye, aye, Captain," Kutas replied. "You have the deck and the conn." He turned to Reynolds. "I relieve you, sir." Reynolds gratefully stepped aside and unobtrusively relieved the talker of his headset. The 'Cat, just as glad, scampered up the ladder with a pair of binoculars to add his eyes to the already numerous lookouts. Manila Bay was reputed to be the busiest waterway in the known world, and the last thing they needed with everyone watching was to collide with anything, even a rowboat.

They entered the bay much as they always had so many times before, back on their own world before the Japanese drove them out. They steamed up the Boca Grande between Caballo Island and the El Frailes. Just beyond Caballo—startlingly barren of the familiar Fort Hughes—was the imposing form of Corregidor. Unlike the Corregidor they remembered, there'd been no fortifications upon this one until recently. Now a great stone works was under construction. Through his binoculars, Matt saw the two heavy thirty-two-pounders Baalkpan had sent Saan-Kakja as gifts, brooding through embrasures in the hastily built walls. Interestingly, they'd been joined by several more, and he realized the Manilos were now making cannons of their own. No reason they shouldn't, once they understood the concept; their industry was certainly up to the task. It still left him feeling odd. In the past, the gift of artillery to native peoples had often been a double-edged sword.

He felt like they should salute the fort in some fashion, but the Maa-nilos had no flag, and he wasn't about to fire a gun. They'd had few blanks, and those were given over to Bernard Sandison with all their empty shells, so he could reload them with the experimental solid copper projectiles and black powder. He settled for having their own flag dipped. Perhaps they'd understand the courtesy. He gave the order in a hushed tone, however. Even he wasn't immune to the strange emotions sweeping the men around him at the sight of the familiar, but alien landmarks.

Beyond Corregidor was the Bataan Peninsula, and there was even a small town, of sorts, where Mariveles ought to be. In the distance, barely visible in the early morning haze, stood the poignantly familiar Mariveles Mountains.

"Recommend course zero, four, five degrees," Kutas said, glancing at the compass and breaking the spell that had fallen upon the Americans in the pilothouse. Juan had appeared unnoticed, carrying a tray of mugs and a coffee urn, and when Matt glanced his way he saw unashamed tears streaking the little Filipino's face as he gazed about.

He coughed. "Thanks, Juan. I was just thinking some of your coffee would taste pretty good right now." A brittle smile appeared on the steward's face, and he circulated through the cramped pilothouse, filling the mugs taken from his tray by the watch standers. For once, none were left behind. Sensitive to the gesture, he bowed slightly.

"I will bring sandwiches, if you please, Cap-tan," he managed huskily. "It has been a long night . . . for all of us."

"Thanks, Juan. Please do." When the Filipino left the bridge, there was an almost audible general sigh, as nearly everyone realized that no matter how hard it was for them, entering *this* Manila Bay must be a waking nightmare for Juan. Looking around, Keje sensed the tension.

"What is the matter?" he quietly asked. "This is our goal, our destination. All should be glad we have arrived."

"In that sense, I guess we're glad," Matt answered, "but where we came from, this was our . . . base, before the war against the Japs. I've told you before, I was here for several months, but others were here for years. They considered it home. What you may not know is, for Juan, it *was* home. He was born here . . . there . . . whatever. We all understand the places we came from are lost to us, probably forever, but to see it with our own eyes . . . I try not to think how I'd react to see the place that should be my home near Stephenville, Texas—a place on the far side of the Earth—but I can't always help it, and neither can anyone else."

Keje refrained from pointing out the impossibility of anyone living on the far side of the Earth. He suspected Captain Reddy meant it metaphorically. Regardless, the point was clear. "You have my deepest sympathies. I cannot imagine how you feel. I only hope time and good friendship can help ease the pain."

They steamed northeast at a leisurely and courteous—but awe inspiring to the natives—twelve knots against the prevailing wind, and the closer they got to Cavite and Manila, the more surface craft they met. Most were the ubiquitous feluccas: fore-and-aft-rigged boats, large and small, that seemed universally known and used among all Lemurians they'd met, even the Aryaalans and B'mbaadans. Matt often wondered about that. Compared to the massive Homes, the smaller craft boasted a more sophisticated rig: a large lateen-rigged triangular sail on a relatively short mast with a fore staysail, or jib, allowing them to sail much closer to the wind than even the Grik square-riggers could accomplish. Of course, they couldn't sail *with* the wind as efficiently. . . . It suddenly struck him the rig might be yet another legacy of those long-ago East Indiamen. Their small boats and launches might have carried a similar sail plan. Of course, not all Lemurian feluccas were open boats. Most had at least one deck, and sometimes two, and he'd seen several over a hundred feet long, really not feluccas at all. Kind of a cross between a felucca and a caravel. He shrugged inwardly. It didn't really matter. He was more interested in the generally positive reception they were receiving.

He'd half feared they'd be met with stony glares. Manila was where most of their own "runaways" had fled, convinced the arrival of the Americans and their iron ship had started the war with the Grik in the first place. There was nothing he could say to that. Doubtless there were people back home who thought Pearl Harbor was America's fault, but most were more sensible. The same seemed true of the majority of Lemurians, thank God. Those in the boats they passed weren't exactly cheering and throwing flowers, but they appeared friendly, and even somewhat glad to see them. They were certainly fascinated by the ship they'd no doubt heard so much about. Some of the more daring captains of what must have been primarily pleasure craft even tried to pace them. It was impossible, of course; no sailing vessel could steer directly into the wind, and even their tight tacking maneuvers soon left them behind, but many of *Walker*'s human and 'Cat destroyermen lined the rails and cheered their efforts. It was a relief in more ways than one. There was no overt hostility associated with their arrival and the request that arrival implied, and it took the men's minds off the gloomy thoughts that had filled them.

They reduced speed to ten knots, then eight, and finally five as the bay grew ever more crowded, and they picked their way carefully through the capering boats. Matt had been warned how busy Manila was, but he hadn't truly credited it until now. Baalkpan was a major city, but essentially compact, having been hacked out of the hostile wilderness around it. Evidently Manila was a far more sprawling and populous place. Homes and small docks began to appear ten miles short of Cavite, and the shore grew more densely populated the closer they got to the peninsula that had once been the center of America's Asiatic naval power on that other world. It was a natural place for similar activity here, and a massive shipyard and repair facility dominated it even more thoroughly than they remembered. The tripod masts of a dozen seagoing Homes jutted from the yards and Bacoor Bay beyond, and more of the massive vessels were moored before Maa-ni-la.

When *Walker* first steamed into Baalkpan Bay almost a year ago, her people were impressed by the size and vitality, the riot of color, and the architectural wonder and singularity of the place. Even the more familiar, almost medieval appearance of Aryaal, with its walls and spires and arches, had not been as impressive. But Baalkpan was positively provincial compared to Maa-ni-la. When Matt asked Nakja-Mur what differences to expect, he'd been told Maa-ni-la was "a little bigger," but he now saw that had been a significant understatement. The closer they came, the more clearly he grasped that *everything* was bigger here. The exotically eastern, pagodalike structures were virtual skyscrapers in comparison, and the docks were proportionately massive. The Bosun once compared Baalkpan to Chefoo, but if that was the case, Manila was Shanghai, or some alien, chaotic, eastern-flavored Manhattan. There was no Empire State Building, of course, nothing even close to that, but everything was taller, more tightly packed, and far more densely populated than Baalkpan when they first saw it. The only thing less impressive was the massive Galla tree growing up in the center of the city. Presumably encompassed by Saan-Kakja's Great Hall, the tree wasn't as tall as the one in Baalkpan, but then again, Maa-ni-la was a younger city, closer to the shifting center of trade and commerce. There were land homes on northern Borneo now, and even in Japan. If the water was deeper and more dangerous, its coastal bounty was richer. Homes were rarely bothered by mountain fish, except for certain times of year, so they increasingly dared the deeper seas, and a place was required to build them, supply them, and trade for the rich gri-kakka oil they rendered. So even though Baalkpan prospered and enjoyed much influence, Maa-ni-la not only prospered, but grew.

Walker backed engines and shuddered to a stop two hundred yards short of the main wharf Keje directed them to. With a great rattling, booming crash, her anchor splashed into the water and fell to the bottom of the bay. Just like the first time they visited Baalkpan, Matt wouldn't tie her to the dock until invited to do so.

"All engines stop," he commanded. "Maintain standard pressure on numbers two and three, and hoist out the launch. Make sure the shore party wears their new whites."

With Baalkpan's impressive textile capacity, they'd made new uniforms principally for this mission. They were remarkably good copies, even though they were hand-sewn, and no Lemurian had ever made anything like trousers before. It took a while to get used to the feel of the strange, itchy material. It wasn't really cotton, and certainly wasn't wool. More like linen, and Matt honestly didn't have any idea what it was made of, although he was sure Courtney Bradford could go on about the process for hours. He relinquished the deck to Larry Dowden and started for his stateroom to change into his own new uniform when he had a thought. When they first entered Nakja-Mur's Great Hall, they'd carried sidearms, and the more recognizable Navy cutlasses, pattern of 1918, thinking their version of commonplace weapons might make their hosts feel more at ease. Matt had worn his now battered and ironically much-used academy sword. That resulted in a delicate social situation when he'd given the "sign of the empty hand"—essentially a wave—when his hand wasn't metaphorically empty. He'd learned the sign was customarily given only when visitors arrived unarmed. That left him with a dilemma. He knew they should have little to fear, even in the massive, sprawling city they were about to enter, but they'd suffered treachery before, and he wouldn't take any chances.

"Sidearms and cutlasses for the diplomatic mission," he said, then held up his hand before Keje could protest. "Thompsons for the detail to stay with the boat."

"Aye, sir," Larry replied, somewhat triumphantly. He'd argued strenuously that the shore party must be armed, against Adar's equally adamant disagreement. Matt turned to Keje.

"We know not everybody's on our side," he said, explaining his decision to an equal as he wouldn't have done to anyone else, "and not all the 'pacifists' are nonviolent either. I won't risk anybody in a city that large, and with that many people, on faith alone. I'll compromise to the extent that we'll leave our weapons with another guard detail before we ascend to the Great Hall. Fair?" After brief consideration, Keje nodded with a grin.

"Fair. Baalkpan has never known real crime, but in a place like this?" He waved generally toward the city. "I have rarely been here, and not at all recently. Since my last visit, the place has 'boomed,' I believe you would say. Adar will object, of course, but it is unreasonable to assume there is no risk at all. Besides, some of the more subversive elements have gravitated here, and I personally would feel much better with my scota at my side. I think leaving our weapons under guard is a fine compromise between trust and prudence."

Matt grinned back. "I'm glad you approve. Should we tell Adar the plan, or let him stew?"

In the event, they had no difficulty reaching the Great Hall. Saan-Kakja had provided an escort that led them through the teeming multitudes, swirling smells, and riotous colors of the dockside bazaar. There were ten of them, besides the four they'd left with the launch. Captain Reddy, Keje, Adar, and Courtney Bradford constituted the diplomatic mission, and Chack and Dennis Silva would ascend with them to the hall as guards of honor. Matt was dubious about including Silva, but he and Chack were the most visibly formidable representatives of their respective species aboard the ship. Three of Chack's Marines, resplendent in their blue kilts and polished armor, would guard their weapons under the command of the Marine captain, Graana-Fas, who was the son of Jarrik-Fas, Keje's cousin and personal armsman he'd left commanding *Salissa*.

Their escort consisted of two dozen 'Cats in Saan-Kakja's livery: yellow-and-black-checked kilts, burnished silver-plated breastplates, and platter-like helmets that looked like deeper copies of the Americans', but with cutouts for the ears. A yellowish plume of something feathery flowed down their backs from a clasp on top of their headgear. Short, stabbing swords swung from their hips, again much like those the Americans introduced, which completed the martial ensemble and added a businesslike touch to their colorful garb. The curious crowd parted before them, though no command to do so was audible over the tumult, and they marched purposefully through the bustling shoppers, tradesmen hawking their wares, alien smells of cooking food, and naked younglings skittering about on all fours. The pulse of the city was vibrant and powerful, though hectic beyond belief. Much like Baalkpan, most of the commerce took place in the open air beneath colorful awnings and tapestries, but there seemed no order to it. In Baalkpan, the various services were clumped more or less together, so it was easier to find what one wanted. Here, there was no apparent attempt at any such organization, and the result was a kaleidoscope of sounds and smells and unintelligible voices that assaulted the senses from the time they left the boat until they drew to a halt at the base of the great Galla tree near the center of the city.

Like Baalkpan, the area immediately around the tree, and the Great Hall encompassing its base, was open and free of structures, permitting a park- or gardenlike effect. The area around Nakja-Mur's hall had long since been churned up by drilling troops, its original beauty sacrificed to the imperative of training an army on the only open ground available. Since then, larger parade grounds and drill fields had been established beyond the new defensive works and hastily cleared jungle, but the original effect was similar enough to inspire a sense of déjà vu. The similarity ended there, however, for the process of greeting was significantly and unexpectedly different.

Nakja-Mur had welcomed them from an opening in his elevated hall, in time-honored fashion, as if they'd approached his "ship" in an open boat. Judging by the finery of the reception committee at the base of the tree, Saan-Kakja would meet them on level ground—an honor, possibly, but something they hadn't foreseen.

Matt stared at the berobed phalanx, and tried to figure out which was the High Chief. The High Sky Priest was simple enough to identify; he was dressed exactly like Adar: younger, skinnier, and not as tall, but with the same silvery gray fur, barely revealed by the closely held purple cape flecked with silver stars. Perhaps Saan-Kakja was one of the beings standing near him? Sotto voce inquiries of Adar and Keje revealed nothing, since Saan-Kakja had risen since their last visit, and the old High Chief had been childless then. An awkward dilemma.

Decisively, Matt unbuckled his sword and pistol belt and thrust it at Silva before striding forward and holding his right hand aloft, palm forward.

"I'm Captain Matthew Reddy, High Chief of *Walker*, *Mahan*, and other units of the United States Navy, as well as Tarakan Island. I come to you in peace and friendship, representing all the allied Homes united under the Banner of the Trees, against the vicious onslaught of our Ancient Enemy, the Grik. As supreme commander, by acclamation, of the alliance, I've been granted plenipotentiary powers, and would treat with the High Chief of this Home. Do I have permission to come aboard?"

Adar nodded approval at Captain Reddy's words and interpreted what he said. For a brief, awkward moment they waited, but there was no response; then the short sky priest took a step forward as if preparing to address them. Before he could speak, however, he was jostled aside by an even smaller form that strode directly up to Captain Reddy. The Lemurian was robed as the others in the same yellow and black, but the black hem was magnificently embroidered with gold thread and sparkling, polished sequins of shell. A fringe of glittering golden cones chinked dully with every step. A matching sash, complete with cones, coiled around a wasp-thin waist, and a gold gorget, intricately chased and engraved, swayed from a ropelike chain. On its head, the Lemurian wore a magnificently engraved helmet, also of gold, reminiscent of the ancient Spartans except for the feathery yellow plume. Large hinged cheek guards and a rigid nosepiece obscured the face entirely except for a pair of brightly inquisitive but astonishing eyes. They were yellow, which was not uncommon for 'Cats, but they looked like ripe lemons sliced across their axes, and dark, almost black lines radiated outward from bottomless black pupils. A small hand rose up, palm outward, in an openhanded gesture.

"I am Saan-Kakja, High Chief of Maa-ni-la, and all the Fil-pin lands," came a small muffled voice from within the helmet. "I greet you, Cap-i-taan Reddy, High Chief and supreme commander of the allied Homes." With that, while Adar translated, another hand joined the first, and together they removed the helmet. Behind it was the fine-boned, dark-furred face of a Lemurian female of an age barely eligible to mate.

Matt was surprised. He'd suspected a youngster simply because of their host's size. But even though he'd learned to accept that Lemurians made no distinction between the sexes regarding occupation—one of the seagoing members of the alliance, *Humfra-Dar*, had a female High Chief, after all—he'd never even considered the possibility something the size of the entire Philippines might be ruled by one. Stupid. Even in human history, there'd often been powerful women, sometimes supremely powerful. He hoped with a twinge of embarrassment that he hadn't blinked surprise; he knew how to do that, at least, and he'd caught himself mimicking the Lemurian "expressions" more and more. He had to continue suppressing the reaction, because even though Saan-Kakja had never seen a human before in her life, young as she was, he detected no surprise, shock, distaste or . . . anything that might offend. Of course, she'd had that helmet to hide behind during her initial reaction, he consoled himself.

"Please do come aboard," she continued. "I have heard a great deal about you and your amazing, gallant ship, and how you came from some incomprehensibly distant place to defend our people against unspeakable evil."

"Thank you," Matt replied gravely in her own tongue. That much he could manage.

She turned slightly and nodded respectfully to Adar first, then Keje—yet another departure from protocol, since Keje was, after all, another head of state. But while Adar's status might have grown ambiguous—there'd never been a Sky Priest who, in effect, represented multiple Homes—it was certainly real, and perhaps even groundbreaking in importance. "High Sky Priest Adar, your reputation as a scholar is well remembered here, as is your knowledge of the pathways of this world and the next. I know of your oath to destroy the Grik forever, and I crave your counsel. . . ." She paused, and it seemed she'd left something unsaid, but then she continued. "Keje-Fris-Ar, you have long been renowned as a master mariner. Now you are a great warrior. I am honored to be in your presence once more, though I do not expect you to remember our last meeting." Her eyes flicked across Bradford, then lingered on Silva and Chack. Especially Chack. They rested on Matt once more. "Do come aboard, and welcome. I would prefer to celebrate your arrival in the traditional way, but the times we live in do not countenance ordinary pleasures, it seems. We have much to discuss and"—she blinked apology, while at the same time the posture of her ears conveyed intense frustration—"little time."

The entire sky was a leaden, dreary gray, unusual for midmorning over Baalkpan Bay. It seemed to radiate no malicious intent to become truly stormy, but there'd definitely be rain and lots of it. (Brevet) Captain Benjamin Mallory stalked back and forth on the beach, his arm still in a sling, watching while the huge but horribly battered PBY flying boat slowly rolled, landing gear extended, back into the sea.

"He looks like a worried mama cat whose kittens are climbing a tree for the first time," Jim Ellis said aside to Alan Letts. Both had come to observe the launching, and they'd escorted Sandra Tucker, who'd decided to join them at the last minute—probably to make sure Mallory didn't strain any of his wounds. It was a good thing too. He clearly felt inhibited by her presence. Letts chuckled, and so did Sandra, although the nurse's laugh seemed fragile, exhausted. Letts looked at her. She'd come straight from the hospital, where she'd been working quite late or quite early, training ever more nurses and corpsmen for the looming showdown, or tending personally to a hurt beyond her students' abilities. Her long, sandy-brown hair was swept back in a girlish ponytail that belied her twenty-eight years and extreme professional competence. It accented her pretty face and slender neck, but it did make her look younger than she was. Younger and more vulnerable.

Alan Letts liked and admired her, as did everyone, human and Lemurian, but he always felt a little guilty when she was near. He was morally certain he'd married Karen Theimer because he loved her, and not, as some whispered, to snatch up one of the only "dames" known to exist. He *knew* he loved her, and they were happy together, but his very happiness inspired much of his guilt. He couldn't help thinking it wasn't right for him to be happy when so many of the men were so miserable. It had strained his relationship with the men, just as he'd expected, and Sandra and Captain Reddy predicted. As Captain Reddy's chief of staff, he was obeyed, but he'd lost a measure of moral authority, he thought. On the other hand, everyone knew Sandra and the captain were nuts about each other—*Walker*'s crew had probably known it before they had. Even so, they'd tried to hide their attraction out of respect for the feelings of the crew, and they'd never once acted on that attraction beyond a rare stolen kiss they thought no one could see. They'd both already been held in high esteem, but their poignant sacrifice endeared them to the crew even more. It was obvious their love continued to grow, and each was very much a reservoir for the other's strength, but still they didn't marry or "shack up," as the scuttlebutt said Silva and Pam Cross had sometimes done—not to mention Silva's "other" affair! They did nothing any of the surviving destroyermen from *Walker* and *Mahan* couldn't do. The men called them dopes and rolled their eyes in exasperation . . . and loved them for it. It was ongoing, positive proof the skipper wouldn't rest until he fulfilled his promise to find the other humans he believed must exist in this twisted, messed-up world. Alan Letts was in awe of their willpower, and amazed by their self-sacrificing, almost tragic nobility. It was like two star-crossed lovers from a John Ford western had found themselves in a Cecil B. DeMille epic—complete with a cast of thousands, monsters, and freak weather events. And every time he saw the sad, melancholy look on Sandra Tucker's face, he felt like a heel.

"What's the matter?" she asked, apparently noticing his expression.

He smiled. "Nothing. Just woolgathering. Hoping they patched all the holes and the damn thing doesn't sink." Mallory sent him a scorching look.

The plane was in the water now, fully buoyant and straining against the taglines attached to each wing and held by forty 'Cats apiece. The current here could be fierce when the tide was ebbing. Another hundred were sitting back, awaiting the order to drag the plane back up the ramp. This was merely a flotation test to see if they had, indeed, patched all the bullet holes. A lot of other repairs had been "completed" as well. The fuel tanks were patched and the wings repaired. The jagged section of the port wing had been trimmed and faired where a four-foot section had been torn completely off when the Japanese scout plane rammed them. Fortunately, the float was down at the time and hadn't been carried away, but now it was secured forever in a lowered position, as was the starboard float. Ben had decided to go ahead and cut off a corresponding length from the other wing to trim the plane and provide enough aluminum for repairs. The plane would lose some lift—and a lot of speed from the additional constant drag—but it was the best compromise he could make. Maneuverability would suffer as well, since they'd been forced to construct new, slightly abbreviated ailerons from the local, almost indestructible Borneo bamboo covered with "linen" and heavily doped.

They hadn't been able to come up with a replacement for the shattered Plexiglas yet, either for the cockpit or the observation blisters, but they were still kicking around a few ideas. Beyond that, the plane was patched and dented, and the once proud blue paint had faded and oxidized to a general blotchy gray, but Mallory said it would fly—once he and Jis-Tikkar finished with the starboard engine. Even now, the plane floated with a decided list to port, the float almost underwater, because the place where the starboard engine should be was just a tangle of mounts, hoses, and lines, covered with a bright green tarp.

"How's she doing?" Mallory bellowed, and Ensign Palmer—formerly signalman second—poked his head out of the cockpit.

"There's a few leaks . . ." he hedged.

"How bad?"

"Just a second, Tikker's checking them now." Moments later, a sable-colored 'Cat with a polished brass cartridge case thrust through a neat hole in his right ear appeared. Sandra put a hand over her mouth and giggled as he conferred with Palmer.

"Yeah," Mallory said aside to her with a grin, "little booger doesn't want anyone to forget his 'noble wound.' I wish I had a medal for him, but I guess that'll do." He shook his head. "I still can't believe the two of them flew that plane back here after I passed out. Especially in the shape it was."

"He'll get a medal one of these days," Ellis assured him, "and he's already been made an ensign." He laughed. "Of course, he's not in the Army Air Corps. The Navy'll get to claim the first commissioned Lemurian aviator!"

Palmer shouted at them: "She's doing okay, mostly, but leaking pretty fast in a couple places. We'd better drag her out!"

Ben nodded and gave the command. A moment later the inactive 'Cats on the beach joined the others on the taglines. With a shout from a Guard NCO, they heaved in unison. He grunted. "We'll have an Air Corps someday. We have to. Even when we get *that* back in the air"—he gestured at the plane—"it won't last long."

Letts nodded grimly. "Airpower's the key; the Japs taught us that. But for now we have to concentrate on the Navy, I'm afraid. And, of course, there's the problem with engines—speaking of which . . . ?"

"We'll get it running," Mallory promised. "It's going to be rough as hell and sound like shit, but we'll get it running."

"How?" Sandra asked. They all looked at the savaged motor, hanging from a bamboo tripod nearby under an awning. Beyond was the "radio shack," a simple, sturdy, waterproof shelter erected to house the radio they'd temporarily removed from the plane—just in case it *did* sink. The PBY's starboard motor was surrounded by benches covered with tools and ruined engine parts.

Ben shrugged. "It's almost back together. We had to take it completely apart." He nodded at Alan. "Mister Letts really came through again with that weird corklike stuff!" Ellis nodded, and Letts shifted uncomfortably before he replied.

"Yeah, well, Bradford discovered it. Some sort of tree growing in the northwestern marshes where all those tar pits are. The trees draw the stuff up in their roots and deposit it in the lower, outer layers of their trunks. They creosote themselves! Bradford says it protects them from insects."

"Whatever," Ben muttered. "Spanky said it's the best gasket material he's ever had his hands on, and you're the one who figured out the application."

Jim nodded thoughtfully, looking at Letts. "He's turned out pretty good, hasn't he?"

"Yeah," agreed Mallory, his tone turning wistful. "Married life seems to agree with him."

"So it would seem."

There was an awkward silence, but Mallory broke it before it stretched out. "Anyway, we had to take it apart so we could get at the connecting rods on the crank and take the two bad pistons out. Only one was really junked, but we lost two jugs."

Sandra smiled patiently. "And what does that mean?"

"Well . . . see those round, knobby things sticking out of the main part? The things with . . . ribs on them?"

"The cylinders?" Sandra asked. "Cylinders are jugs?"

"Uh . . . yeah." Ben smiled with relief. At least she understood that much. "Two of them we can't do anything about; they took too much of a beating. One was even shot through. We just can't fix them now. Maybe someday. Anyway, we've pulled the pistons and rods, and we're just going to plug the holes. Like I said, it'll run pretty rough, and it'll lose a lot of horsepower, but it'll run."

Ellis winced. "I guess if there's nothing else for it . . ."

"'Fraid not."

They heard a deep, dull thump of cannon far across the bay, and turned toward the sound. Another gun followed the first, then another. A square-rigged ship, the new frigate *Donaghey*, by the distant, fuzzy look of her, had finally returned from her rescue mission and was saluting the Tree Flag of the Alliance, fluttering above the ramparts of Fort Atkinson at the mouth of the bay. The fort returned the salute, but a few minutes after the last guns fell silent, a red rocket soared into the sky and popped above the fort.

"What the hell?" Ellis breathed. A red rocket from the fort was the signal for alarm. A moment later two green rockets exploded in the air. "Okay," he said. "That's a little less terrifying. The ship must be flying a signal we can't see yet, and whoever's on duty at the fort decided we needed a heads-up."

Mallory looked at him curiously. "I know what the red rocket means, but I must've missed the green rocket briefing."

"There wasn't one," Letts told him. "Jim, Riggs, and I just worked the signal out a couple days ago." He gestured at the plane, then vaguely all around. "We've all been a little preoccupied. The new system's on the roster at the fort, but not here yet."

"What's it mean?"

"One red means alarm, like always, but it's also an urgent attention getter now, too. The first green rocket after a red means 'important information.'"

"What's a second green one mean?"

"Immediate, command staff level. Basically what we just saw was somebody sending a message that says: 'Wake up! We've got important, deep-shit information. We don't have time to tell it twice, so get everybody who can do something about anything in one place right now. Damn it.'"

Ben's eyes were wide. "Those three little rockets said all that?"

"Yeah."

Mahan's general alarm began to sound, its thrumming, gonging blare somewhat muffled by the humidity and a light mist that had begun to fall, even though the ship was moored less than three hundred yards away. The sound was instantly recognizable, however.

"What the hell now?" Letts demanded. Jim Ellis was already sprinting for his ship. In the distance, also muffled, they suddenly heard an engine. An airplane engine. Ben looked frantically around at the darkening sky, his eyes suddenly focusing on an object to westward.

"This is something else!" The straining Lemurians had the plane about halfway out of the water, and he ran toward them, sling flapping empty at his side. "Get it out! Get it out! Get my plane out of the goddamn water!" He grabbed one of the lines himself, insensitive to the pain. Ed and Tikker leaped down from the cockpit and joined him. "Heave!"

"What is it?" Sandra asked Alan, still standing beside her. He wasn't wearing binoculars and his eyes were straining hard. He suddenly remembered the description of the plane that attacked the PBY, and the indistinct form didn't snap into focus, but he knew what it was: a biplane with floats.

"Oh, God!"

"What?"

Letts snatched her arm hard and tugged her toward a covered gun emplacement some distance away. "C'mon!"

"But why are we going that way? The plane, the ship . . ."

"Right! They're what it's after! I'm not telling Captain Reddy I let you stand here and catch a Jap bomb!" Sandra was torn. She knew she'd be needed here if the plane inflicted any damage, but if she were dead . . . She made up her mind, and in an instant she was running beside Alan as fast as she could, the engine sound growing louder by the moment.

"Run!" Letts gasped, as the two machine guns on the starboard side of the ship opened up. Many Lemurians were just standing and staring, and Letts and Sandra screamed at them to take cover. They made it under the bombproof and turned to look just as the plane roared over the moored destroyer. Plumes of spray were subsiding where the plane's bullets had struck the water, and a dark object was falling toward the ship. A huge geyser erupted just short of *Mahan*, and the harbor resonated with a thunderclap roar. The plane pulled up, poorly aimed tracers chasing it, and banked hard left, to the north. All they could do was watch while it slowly turned and steadied for another pass, this time clearly intending to strafe and bomb the ship from aft forward. Bullets kicked up white bushes of spray, and *whrang*ed off the steel of the motionless ship. There were a few screams. *Mahan* seemed helpless, but at the last instant the plane staggered slightly, perhaps from a hit, and steadied on a different course: toward the PBY and ultimately directly at Sandra, Letts, and the others who'd taken refuge with them.

"Get down," Letts shouted, but he couldn't bring himself to follow his own advice. His normally fair, freckled face was pale and drawn. Angry flashes sparkled above the cowling of the oncoming plane, and clouds of sand erupted among the people heaving on the taglines. A few Marines were shooting back with Krags, to no apparent effect, and several of the laborers pitched to the ground. Another dark object detached itself as the plane bored in, seemingly destined to land right atop the helpless flying boat. Again, miraculously, the bomb fell short, detonating close to the trees beyond the plane, and sending a greasy brown plume of smoke high in the air, along with shards of trees, timbers, and other debris that rained down on the plane and the detail still straining against its weight. A massive secondary explosion sent a roiling, orange ball of fire into the sky, consuming the barrels of ready gasoline they'd stored nearby, and more flaming debris clattered down, almost to the bombproof. Still firing its single, forward machine gun, the plane sent a fusillade into the defensive position, and bullets thunked into the heavy timbers and whirred away, showering them with splinters. Sandra clutched the dirt and burrowed even lower as the float-plane thundered overhead and pulled up, heading toward the city.

"No more bombs," Letts surmised, then coughed. "Probably going to make a leisurely recon of our defenses and just fly away. Damn-all we can do about it." Sandra looked up at him and saw he wasn't injured, just coughing on the dust and gathering smoke in the air. Others around them were standing now too, but all she saw were a few superficial splinter wounds.

"Will it come back?" she asked, rising beside him.

"I don't think so."

In an instant she was running back toward the plane and the pall of smoke and licking flames beyond. "Get some medical help down here!" she shouted, and was gone.

"Avast heaving," Mallory wheezed, wondering blearily why he'd used a nautical term even as he did it. 'Cats collapsed to the ground, gasping and coughing as they breathed the black and gray particles drifting down from the dense smoke above. It was raining now; soon it would become a torrent. His shoulder was killing him, and he absently began trying to stuff his arm back in the sling. There were moans among the workers too, but he couldn't tell the wounded from the exhausted through the burning tears filling his eyes. Ed Palmer appeared, dirty and bleeding from a cut on his brow. The ensign leaned over and put his hands on his knees when a coughing spasm took him.

"Where's Tikker?" Ben demanded. Ed gestured toward the engine, still swaying gently beneath its tripod. It seemed okay, but the awning was gone. Tikker and a dozen other 'Cats were throwing shovelfuls of sand on the burning gasoline, dangerously close to their workbenches.

"The plane?"

Ed's fit finally passed, and he spit a gobbet of dark phlegm. "We saved her, I think. A few more holes from bomb fragments, maybe." He shook his head wearily. "Nothing we can't patch. Might've sunk her if she'd still been in the water, though, and it'd have been a bitch to drag her out then." Mallory nodded. Just then Sandra Tucker joined them, breathing hard and beginning to cough as well.

"How many hurt?" she managed. Mallory gestured at the prostrate forms. "Damned if I know. Hey, you monkeys!" he shouted. "Off your asses! Anybody that ain't dead, fall in!" The workers struggled to their feet, still coughing and gasping, leaving several on the ground who were either too badly wounded or would never rise again. Sandra surveyed the scene.

"Get some first aid started here!" she instructed. "Corpsmen are on the way." With that she hurried into the smoke, closer to where the second bomb had struck, knowing there'd be more injured there. They couldn't see *Mahan* through the smoke, but her general alarm was still echoing across the water.

Mallory sighed and pointed at a group of five guardsmen who seemed relatively fit. "Well, don't just stand there; go with her! The rest of you goons check your buddies." He glanced at Ed and saw him staring at the fire as though stricken.

"God a'mighty," Ed whispered numbly.

"What now?"

Ed pointed at the fire, then fell to his knees in the sand in apparent desolation.

"What?"

"The radio shack," he whispered. "It's . . . gone."

All the top military and administrative personnel in Baalkpan had gathered in Nakja-Mur's Great Hall, summoned by the rockets—when word got around what they meant—and the attack, of course. Heavy rain still pounded the ceiling high above, and there was a cool, damp, but refreshing draft in the place. Combined with the general gloom of the few guttering lamps, the drab evening light from the open shutters, and the events of the day, however, the comparative cool served little to temper the prevailing sense of anxiety. Old Naga might have helped; part of the High Sky Priest's job was to administer to the spiritual needs of his flock, but all he did was sit by himself, chanting a nonsensical lamentation. It was inappropriate for any other Sky Priest or acolyte to speak without invitation while Naga was present. Adar could have—he'd practically been designated Naga's successor—but Adar wasn't there.

All the "battle line" commanders were there, the High Chiefs of the few seagoing Homes of the alliance. Jarrik-Fas represented *Salissa* in Keje's stead. Lord Muln Rolak commanded the third-largest infantry force, that of the displaced Aryaalans, but with Alden and Queen Maraan missing, and everyone else away, Rolak was the senior general. He couldn't hold still. Safir Maraan had been queen of his people's bitterest foe, and Aryaal had been at war with B'mbaado before the Grik came. Since then, however, he'd developed an intense fondness for the Orphan Queen. He thought of her almost as a granddaughter now—but more than that, as well. They'd fought side by side in the fiercest battle the world had ever known, and he couldn't bear the thought that she might have fallen into enemy hands. So he paced.

Commander Ellis had just arrived, soaked to the bone, his uniform badly stained from many hours overseeing repairs to the damage the near miss had caused his ship. He looked exhausted. He joined Ben Mallory and Ed Palmer, as well as Lieutenant Riggs and Lieutenant Commander Brister, who'd just arrived from Fort Atkinson. Alan Letts and Lieutenant Bernard Sandison, *Walker's* torpedo officer, currently serving as the ordnance officer of the alliance, were standing beside Nakja-Mur's throne of cushions where the High Chief of Baalkpan reclined, eyes darting pensively at the uproar caused by the conversations of his other advisors. None of the "principals" had spoken yet; they were waiting for another to arrive.

When Lieutenant Greg Garrett limped in, leaning on a crutch, attended by Sandra Tucker, Karen Theimer, and Keje's daughter, Selass, he was freshly shaven, and his uniform, while damp, was as crisp as he could make it, given the dingy spots where soot, powder fouling, and blood had been scrubbed away. His narrow, handsome face was pale and drawn, and he looked . . . miserable. Letts had ordered him to stop by the hospital for a checkup before appearing in person. The gist of his story was in the report he'd already submitted by courier as soon as he dropped anchor, however: a report that had spread like wildfire. Letts and Ellis crossed to him, assuring him by their solicitude that they didn't blame him for what happened, but it was clear that, no matter what they said, he blamed himself.

Nakja-Mur didn't stir from his seat. He felt no bitterness toward the young officer, nor did he blame him in any way, but so many new worries had been added to his endless list that day, he didn't trust himself to stand. Besides, ever since battered *Donaghey* entered the bay on a weak, sodden breeze, and the rockets soared into the sky—and then they heard the report of the explosions down at the shipyard and *saw* the Japanese plane soaring unimpeded over his city—he'd felt a strange tightening in his chest. Now they had some hard choices to make, choices that might lead to disaster. As much as he trusted his current human and Lemurian advisors—his friends, he felt—none of the "steadier heads"—Captain Reddy, Keje, Adar, Alden, even Chief Gray and the Japanese officer, Shinya, the ones who'd always been there for him in the past—were there. Oh, what a terrible stroke of ill luck! He almost wished the Japanese bomb had struck the ship or the plane instead of the priceless radio!

"Is the raa-di-o truly beyond repair?" he asked almost plaintively, silencing the hubbub around them.

"I'm afraid so," Palmer replied woodenly. "Everything's gone, even the batteries."

"We lost nineteen people too," Sandra added harshly, putting things in perspective. "And it could have been a lot worse."

Nakja-Mur nodded to her, acknowledging the hit. He visibly straightened himself. Now was not the time to wallow in self-pity. He had to set an example. "Of course. While I grieve for the families of the lost, I am grateful it was not worse. I only needed to hear the words myself. In the 'bigger picture,' as Captain Reddy would say, the loss of the raa-di-o is surely a straa-tee-jik setback."

"So where does that leave us?" Letts asked remorselessly. "I'll sum it up. Two of our most important leaders are marooned, at best, behind enemy lines. . . ." Garrett flinched, and Alan looked at him apologetically. "It's not your fault, Greg; it's theirs. Damned silly heroics. Besides, you handled your ship superbly, not only in battle, but by getting her back here so quickly in the shape she's in, with such important information. My God, Grik with cannon! But the fact remains, we've left some very important people behind. If we can't get Queen Maraan out, at the very least it'll clobber the morale of her subjects here—who, I might add, constitute over a quarter of our combined army."

"Getting her out is the very first thing we must contemplate!" Rolak demanded hotly, still pacing back and forth.

"I agree. But we've got to figure out how, and we've got some other angles to consider. First, though, *how*." He turned back to Garrett. "What shape's *Donaghey* in?"

"Not good," Garrett admitted grudgingly. "Her stern was battered in by the explosion, and besides the loss of her mizzen, her top hamper's a mess. We repaired a lot, and jury-rigged more, but it'll take several days, at least, of intensive effort by the yard to accomplish the bare essentials—such as replacing the mast and stopping all her leaks."

Letts nodded somberly. "The next two frigates are nearing completion, but neither is ready for sea. The yard manager says he needs another week—and repairs to *Donaghey*'ll set that back. The rest of the 'fleet' of captured Grik ships is either still undergoing alteration and arming, or is scattered all over the place. Only *Felts* is in port, taking on more supplies for the Tarakan expedition. The Homes of the battle line are certainly powerful enough to face however many cannon-armed ships the Grik might have so far, but they're just too slow."

Nakja-Mur listened while Letts spoke, and honestly wondered if anything they did at this point would make any difference. But they had to do something. He heard the American discussing all the possibilities and discarding them in turn, just as he already had in his mind. There really was only one choice, but he waited diplomatically until the others came to the same conclusion.

"We'll have to use *Mahan*." Ellis sighed at last.

Sandra pounced. "Two things wrong with that," she said. "First, can she even do it? What kind of damage did she sustain today?"

"Two dead, and seven wounded by machine-gun fire." Ellis looked at Selass. "Saak-Fas was one of the wounded, but only lightly," he added with compassion. "He's already returned to duty. Damage to the ship consists of a few sprung plates from the near miss. Maybe some cracked firebricks in the number two boiler. We've already shored up the plates and welded them, and shut down number two. If the bricks are damaged, we'll have them replaced and be ready to steam by morning. We can take on fuel and supplies and be underway by the morning after that, I believe."

"You've still only got one propeller," Sandra pointed out. That was true. They'd tried to cast another to replace the one *Walker* had "commandeered," but the first attempt had been hopelessly out of balance. They were working on another, but it would be some time before they were even ready to pour it.

"That's right," Ellis agreed, "but *Mahan*'s still faster than anything she'll meet, by a long shot."

"Maybe, but there's still the other consideration: Matt... Captain Reddy left strict orders that *Mahan* not do anything remotely like you're considering. He has a *plan* for the defense of this place, when the time comes, and that plan not only includes *Mahan*; she's essential to its success. Despite the imperative that the enemy never suspects she even exists!"

Rolak slapped his sword sheath in frustration. "Captain Reddy is not *here*, my lady. I am bound to obey his orders more closely than anyone. He holds my life, my very honor, in his grasp, and can do with it what he will. But he is not here, and we must deal with this situation in his stead. Knowing him as I do, I am positive he would bless this course since it is our only option—and it is a thing that must be done. Knowing him as *you* do, I am equally positive you must agree."

Sandra slowly wilted under Rolak's intense gaze, and finally she nodded. "You're right, of course." She sighed. "I only wish we could tell him. It'll be days before he starts to wonder why we haven't made our daily comm check. Even then he won't worry, not for a while. We've missed it before due to bad weather or atmospherics." She looked at Riggs and he nodded confirmation.

"She's right," he said. "And even when he does start to wonder, he won't have any reason to be alarmed. Everything was fine when we made our last report, and he knows we'd have days of warning, at least, if the Grik were on the move. He'll just think the radio's busted"—he snorted—"which it is. But that might not mean we can't get in touch with him." The hall grew silent, and he had everyone's attention. "As you know, Radioman Clancy is with *Walker*, but he, Ed, and I have been working on simple crystal receivers. There's not much to them, really, and we've got all the stuff we need to make a few. We located some galena for the crystals, which is good, but we could have done it by mixing powdered sulfur with lead. They're passive receivers and don't even require batteries. Just a little copper wire and a headset—or we might even try building some simple speakers. That won't help us right now, although they'll come in handy, but I think we can put together a simple spark-gap transmitter that might reach the captain. We'll need stuff: lots of wire, for example, and power, of course. *Mohan*'s generator would do nicely, but since she won't be here . . . I think we can make some wet-cell batteries. Lead acid. I'm pretty sure we can do it, and it shouldn't take much time."

"How much time?" Letts asked.

"We should have done it already," Riggs admitted. "We've all just been so busy, and we *had* a good radio. . . . I've been so occupied building the semaphore towers and training the operators. . . ." He shook his head. "No excuse. A week or so, I guess. We'll have to make everything from scratch."

Letts looked at Nakja-Mur. "Highest priority," he said. "Use whoever and whatever you need."

"So I guess it's settled, then," Ellis said, rubbing his scalp. "We go. What have you got for me, Bernie?"

The dark-haired torpedo officer's eyebrows rose, and he took a deep breath. "Not as much as I'd like. We've got twenty of the new projectiles cast, turned, and loaded in shells for the four inch-fifties, but we're just now gearing up to manufacture the primers, so that's it. The primers have been the hardest part, actually. Up till now we've had to make them one at a time, with a swage, and a stamp to make the anvil—not to mention some very dangerous experimentation with fulminate of mercury. We've got that sorted out now, but it'll be another three or four days before I can get you more." Ellis was shaking his head. "I know, too late. But . . . at least you'll have a few to test . . . if you need them. Remember, though, they're just solid copper bolts, no explosive, and they're loaded with black powder, so the fire control computer won't help you. I was hoping for guncotton by now—we've got all the recipes and procedures—but it's tricky stuff, and we haven't finished making the things to make it with, if you know what I mean. The reloads should work fine against wooden ships in local control, though. They ought to shoot through and through. Sorry, that's all I've got. Obviously we've been working on other stuff, but nothing's ready yet."

"What about the torpedo? Should I take it?" The only torpedo they had left, between *Walker* and *Mahan*, was an old MK-10 submarine torpedo Bernie had salvaged from a shack in bombed-out Surabaya before they abandoned it in their own world. He'd thought it was damaged somehow, since it was with others that were condemned. After exhaustive inspection, he'd determined there was nothing wrong with it after all.

"No," Letts decided. "The captain has plans for that fish. We have no real reason to suspect *Amagi*'s ready to move, and that's the only thing you'd have any business shooting it at. Besides, it might get damaged. The torpedo stays here." Ellis nodded agreement, and Letts looked around at the others. "So I guess it's settled then—except for the other 'angles' I mentioned at the start."

"Like what?"

"Like that plane didn't get here by itself," Mallory interrupted with absolute certainty. "It was a 'Dave,' just like the one we tangled with, and it doesn't have the legs to make a trip all the way from Aryaal and back. They must have rendezvoused with at least one, and probably two ships, to refuel on the way. They'll still be out there, and I bet they're the armed ones that showed up when Greg tried to go back for Pete and the queen."

"Grik always travel in threes," Ellis said, pondering. "Maybe we can catch them and destroy them on the way back to Aryaal. Maybe even get the plane, if it was damaged."

"That would be ideal," agreed Letts, "because otherwise they're going to know all about our defensive arrangements. Maybe they'll think they got the plane and the ship, which might be good, but maybe they won't. Regardless, they'll have a good idea what they'll face when they come."

"I fear the events of the last week, the attack on *Donaghey*, and the destructive scout mission, proves they will come soon. Sooner than we planned," Nakja-Mur interjected. "Why else should they do those things now? Why not wait until they are ready—unless they already are?"

"Well, we need to know that too," Letts agreed. He looked at Ben. "How soon can you fly?"

Ben was exhausted and hurting, and his brain wasn't working right, so it took him longer than usual to form a reply. "Uh, we can have the starboard engine reassembled in a day. Another day or two to install it and check it out . . . No sense putting the cowl back on; shredded as it is, it'll drag worse than the motor." He fell silent again, contemplating. Finally he sighed. "Three days, if we have plenty of help and everything works. We still need something for a windscreen, though." He looked speculatively at Ellis. "Maybe some of *Mahan*'s spare window glass?"

"Very well," said Letts, realizing he was treading on another of Captain Reddy's orders: never fly the plane without established communications. Nothing for it. "Top priority on that as well. I want you to fly to Aryaal, take a quick look, see what *Amagi* and the Grik fleet are up to, and head straight back. Can you do it?"

Ben shrugged. "It'll probably be the roughest flight of my life, but we should still be able to go higher than they can shoot. Yeah, provided the wings don't fold up on us."

"Then that's what we'll do. In the meantime, *Felts* sails tomorrow, whether Clark's ready or not. He'll warn Tarakan, in case those three Grik ships didn't head back to the barn, and then proceed to Manila. If we can't get a transmitter going, he'll be the quickest way to inform the captain the Grik are up to something." He looked at Nakja-Mur. "Yeah, I feel it too."

Brevet Captain-General Pete Alden and Captain Haakar-Faask lay in the undergrowth near the beach, taking turns with Pete's binoculars and watching Grik warriors disembark from the three ships closest to shore. Those three had no cannons they could see, but they suspected the other three, keeping station to seaward, did. The tactic was far too methodical and sensible for Alden's taste. He looked at Faask and arched an eyebrow. Faask almost snorted a laugh—he found the face moving of the humans hilarious—but he understood the gesture, even if he had little English. Fortunately, Alden had picked up a functional 'Cat vocabulary by now. "I think they're through messing around with us," was a rough translation of what he said.

Two weeks had passed since he and Queen Maraan were marooned with the rest of the refugees, long enough for the three Grik ships that drove *Donaghey* away to return to Aryaal with news of the battle, prepare this expedition, and return. It was also past long enough for *Donaghey* to make it to Baalkpan, damaged as she was, and another relief force to be dispatched. The problem was, with the allied navy scattered from here to the Philippines, could they even scrape together a force large enough to come to their aid?

He had no doubt that, eventually, help would come. If nothing else, Garrett would return as soon as his ship was repaired, but that might be a while. In the meantime, the better part of a thousand Grik warriors were about to start beating the brush for the less than three hundred souls left in Faask's and his care, mostly males by now at least, but mostly civilians too. Less than a hundred had ever borne arms, but ever since he'd been left behind, Faask had been training all the refugees, females and younglings included, for just this eventuality. Fortunately, most of the latter had already been rescued. There were still a few, those who wouldn't leave their mates, or females who'd been separated from their younglings and still hoped against hope they might turn up. A few elders had remained as well, too old and frail to wield a sword or spear, but who wouldn't leave until everyone else was rescued. Many were ill, due to either malnutrition or exhaustion. That left Alden's "effectives" at just over two hundred.

His scouts had discovered a force of two thousand or more closing from the west-northwest, pushing them back from observation points overlooking the bay they'd used to such good effect, and now this blocking force was landing in their "rear," cutting off their egress to the sea.

"We better get back to the rally point and tell the queen what we've seen," he said. Motioning a pair of pickets to maintain their positions and keep tabs on the enemy advance as long as they could, Alden and Faask slithered down the embankment and hurried off through the jungle.

Queen Maraan awaited them, anxious for their news. "Is it true?" she hissed. Pete and Haakar-Faask both nodded, and her eyes turned to slits. "What will we do?"

"We must keep you safe, Your Majesty," Faask replied.

"How? Would you have me slink off into the jungle, dig a hole, and crawl into it?" She gestured around at the refugees, huddled under make-shift shelters against the rain that had begun to fall. "What of them?"

"With respect, Majesty—" Faask began.

"No! I will not skulk around, leaving my people to be slaughtered!" She stared levelly at Alden and Faask. "We will fight! All of us! You two are probably the greatest generals this world has ever known. In different ways, perhaps, since you come from different backgrounds, but that should give us an insurmountable advantage, not a disadvantage. Surely, between you, you can devise a plan that will, if not give us victory, at least deny it to them! All we need is time, my friends. Our allies will not abandon us." She grinned. "We are too important, are we not?"

"But they are simply too many!" Faask protested. "They outnumber us fifteen to one!"

Alden scratched his beard. "Yeah," he agreed, "if they were all in one place, that would be true." He knelt to the soggy ground and swept the leaves and brush away, revealing a bare spot of damp earth. The rain was already tapering off—another short squall—and he selected a small, pointed stick. After he scratched a rough outline of the island, he drew a line across the top. "This is the main Grik force. There're many of them, but they're stretched across the entire width of the island. If we mass our forces here"—he pointed to the south—"we can strike their right flank and probably have numerical superiority, at least locally. We hit 'em like maniacs and break through into their rear. Even against a 'normal' enemy, that'd leave them dangerously exposed. With any luck, they'll go nuts—like we've seen them do before—and we roll up their flank, killing as we go." He grinned. "We might even set the whole army to flight, but probably not. Sooner or later our guys'll get tired and the attack'll run out of steam. That's when they'll hit back."

"I agree so far," Faask said, "but what good will that do? It will be a glorious end, but it will not protect the queen."

"Sure it will, because we don't let our 'army' run out of steam. We pull back to here"—he pointed again with his stick—"where we take a breather while the Grik center turns to attack us on their right. Where we *were*. When they do that, we hit 'em again, on their new *left* flank!"

Faask was silent for a moment, studying the impressions in the dirt. "But that's . . . brilliant!"

Pete grinned. "Of course it is! We just have to make sure our coordination works like clockwork, and we have signals that work and are obeyed instantly."

Faask stroked his own beard. Alden was more used to the sea folk, who generally kept their facial fur clipped short, but on the veteran warrior the beard seemed appropriate somehow. "And the tactic should work equally well against the Grik far left, if they have not, as you say, gone 'nuts' already. It would be the greatest, most audacious victory of the age!" He looked at Alden with renewed respect, then frowned. "But what of the blocking force? Our warriors will be exhausted, even if we are successful."

Alden gestured toward the sea. "It'll take them a day to get their shit together. We know where they are, but they don't have a clue about us. They'll figure it out pretty quick, but by then we'll already be headed toward the main force. That ought to confuse them. I figure we'll have a day or so to rest before they catch up, and they'll be at least as spread out as the first bunch by then."

"And we do it again!" Faask shouted triumphantly.

"And then we do it again," Alden confirmed.

Queen Maraan coughed. "All very inspiring, noble generals. I am impressed. I knew you could do it, and it seems an outstanding plan . . . only remember the single greatest lesson I have learned from both of you: no plan may ever be entirely relied upon, once the battle has begun!"

CHAPTER 7

W arm sunlight filtered through the delicately woven curtains draped across the doorway to the balcony, and Matthew Reddy opened his eyes and blinked. He'd slept late again, he realized with chagrin. That was two days in a row. All his life he'd risen with the sun—or before—but lately . . . He shook his head and rubbed his eyes. Rolling off the great, mushy cushion that served as a mattress, he stood and walked to a water basin on a table near the door. He submerged his face for the count of ten, then rubbed it briskly with his hands. Rinsing, he parted the annoyingly long hair and combed it from left to right across his scalp, and looked intently into the polished silver mirror above the basin.

"Starting to look like a hobo," he growled, remembering the ones he used to see wandering around the stockyard train station when he was a kid. "Acting like one too. Waking up when I feel like it—damn, I bet it's nearly oh eight hundred!" He glanced at his watch: 0750. He frowned, shaking his head, then looked at the mirror again. His hair was halfway down his ears, and starting to curl a little against his collar in the back. It also had a little gray in it all of a sudden. The stubble on his face seemed as much salt as pepper, and he was only thirty-three. He needed to hit Juan up for a haircut, he thought with a grimace, but then, with a twinge of satisfaction, he remembered he still controlled his razor, at least.

He shaved as carefully as he could. Most of his old Asiatic Fleet destroyermen had long since ceased shaving. He wouldn't force them to, with razors so scarce. The main reason he still did it himself was that the men expected it. He'd kept his face clean shaven, to the best of his ability, throughout all the trials they'd come through together, and even though it was a little thing after all, sometimes it was the little things that made all the difference in the end. It was a symbol of continuity they all could cling to, even him. It was a stubborn statement that not everything they knew before the Squall was lost forever. The skipper still shaved his face. He had to admit it was a rather pathetic affectation, but they'd lost almost everything else.

Stepping to the little closet, he selected one of his new uniforms and put it on. As always, it took a few moments to get used to the itch. He didn't mind. The new uniforms were amazingly well made, and he thought it important that all his people, human and Lemurian, continue to wear the uniform of the navy they were part of: a uniform they were accustomed to, and associated with their duty. The battered shoes and hat contrasted with his new clothes, but there was nothing he could do about that. Finally he buckled the belt supporting his holstered M-1911 .45 automatic, and his hard-used academy dress sword. The sword was polished and well cared for, but the sweat-stained grip and notched blade attested to far more service than he'd ever imagined it would see when he purchased it for his graduation.

Belatedly prepared to face the day, he stepped onto the balcony. The apartment shared by the small allied diplomatic mission to the Maa-ni-los occupied an entire level of the Great Hall, and the balcony went all the way around it like a giant wraparound porch. Despite the hall's robust construction and the massive trunk of the Galla tree that anchored it, as high as he was above the ground, there was still an almost imperceptible sense of motion. Unfortunately, the motion of the diplomacy they'd been engaged in was almost imperceptible as well, scandalously so, according to Keje and Adar. Ever since that first unusual, hopeful meeting with Saan-Kakja, when there'd seemed to be such commonality and unity of purpose, the Maa-ni-lo High Chief had been kept away from them by officious underlings under the pretext of "propriety." That was a bunch of crap, according to Matt's Lemurian friends.

Propriety had nothing to do with it, they said; factional politics was to blame. Both felt grievously insulted, not only for themselves, but for him. Matt was willing to put up with much; they needed the Maa-ni-los' help too badly, and as long as there was any hope at all, he'd wait a little longer. But it wasn't easy. There was so much to do, both back "home" in Baalkpan and otherwise, that he couldn't shake the frustration gnawing him. He'd grown so used to the constant stress of his position, the combat and preparation for it, that to become essentially a tourist on vacation was about to drive him nuts. He had nothing critical to do, and he was too keyed up to relax.

As he'd been every morning for the five days they'd been in Manila, he was greeted by the awesome sight of the vibrant, chaotic, prosperous city. The sights, sounds, colors, and smells blended together to mount an overwhelming assault on his senses. Much like Baalkpan's, the morning activity was centered around the waterfront, where vendors hawked the early catch, but there was more native industry than he was used to as well. More than Baalkpan boasted before he and his people arrived, at least—back before the war became all-consuming. Open-air ropewalks were laid out between the great chandlery buildings, where hot, smoky pitch was daubed on heavy new cable, destined for hawsers or stays aboard the massive ships. Sailmakers toiled under awnings, sewing bolts of fabric together with quick, deft stitches. A singsong, chittering chantey reached his ears on the same breeze that carried smells of savory cooking, boiling pitch, and animal excrement. Less intense, but far more familiar, was the waterlogged, rotting-wood, fishy-salty aroma of any harbor and the sea.

Much of the excrement came from a species of stunted, domesticated brontosaurus, similar to those they knew from other places. Some came from the myriad packs of shrieking younglings scampering heedlessly—and apparently unheeded—about, who'd not yet become shackled to the remarkably refined running-water privies that allowed life to flourish in the densely populated city. The privies were not so different from those aboard *Walker*—water rushing under a hole with a board across it—but unlike in early human cities with similar arrangements, the soiled water passed through mounded ducts, like road-level sewers, instead of open-air gutters. It did, ultimately, find its way into the bay, but the scavenging fish and other creatures were more prolific, and far less picky, than those on that other Earth.

Some of the indiscriminate heaps were deposited by creatures he'd never seen before. One looked a little like a brontosaurus from a distance, although it was smaller, and had a shorter—if beefier and more muscular—neck, and a much shorter tail. The head was larger, with short, palmated antlers. It was also covered with fur—real fur—and Bradford excitedly insisted the things were herbivorous marsupials, of all things. Matt wondered why no one ever imported them to Baalkpan; they were obviously more sensible draft animals than the ubiquitous brontosaurus. Probably smarter and more biddable as well, from what he'd seen. He found himself wishing for some to pull his light artillery pieces. Perhaps they could even be ridden, although he hadn't seen anyone doing it. They were called "Paalkas," but Silva had immediately dubbed them "pack-mooses."

There was an animal the Maa-ni-los did ride, but he'd seen only a couple. They looked like long-legged crocodiles that ran on all fours, as they should, but their legs were shaped more like a dog's. They ran like dogs too, and the only time he'd seen them, they bore troops in Saan-Kakja's livery on some apparent errand. The crowds gave them a wide berth, and Matt noticed their jaws were always strapped and buckled tightly shut. The 'Cats called them one thing, he couldn't remember, and Courtney Bradford had made up another name he couldn't pronounce. Whatever they were, he'd have to find out more about them.

It was all very fascinating, but profoundly frustrating as well. Strangely, he liked this Manila a lot better than the old, in a way, but he was becoming almost frantically anxious to complete his mission and get back. He missed Sandra terribly—missed everybody—and there was still the iron fish to consider. Each day they spent here, dithering over details and placating the endless stream of dignitaries and counselors, was one less they could spend looking for it. And another thing was troubling him too: they hadn't heard a peep out of Baalkpan in days.

"Mornin', Skipper."

Matt noticed that Silva had joined him during his reverie. The big gunner's mate had no official standing as far as the diplomatic mission went, other than that he had, somewhere along the line, taken personal responsibility for Captain Reddy's welfare. He'd stepped into Chief Gray's self-appointed role as Matt's senior armsman, and he commanded a detail of enlisted humans and Lemurians who'd volunteered for the duty—knowing full well that the man they were bound to protect didn't always make it easy. Like that of Juan Marcos, their job had just . . . evolved. Unlike Juan, the "Captain's Guard" had become an official posting at the urging of Keje and Adar. Silva knew the job was Gray's whenever he was able to resume it, but he'd have been protecting the captain anyway, and he'd been making a real effort to behave. His restriction to the ship had been only provisionally lifted, and if he was stuck on the ship, he couldn't do his job. Matt was beginning to suspect Silva was the sort of person who rose to meet expectations. All his life he'd been expected to be a screwup—so he was. Now everyone, himself included, expected more, and so far he'd delivered. Matt harbored no illusions that Silva had completely reformed; the best-trained, most trusted dog still crapped on the floor now and then, but if Matt needed a guard dog, Silva was the best he could ask for, absent Gray.

"Morning, Silva. Anything on the horn?"

Dennis shook his head. "Just came from the ship," he said, and Matt noticed the big man already had sweat circles under his arms. "Still no word. Clancy says it's not on our end. There just ain't anything to receive." He saw the captain's worried frown. "No big deal, Skipper; it's prob'ly nothin'. Last report, everything was fine. Besides, you know what a klutz that Palmer is; he prob'ly popped a tube with a wrench, or maybe the damn airplane sank. Lieutenant Riggs'll get it sorted out, or he'll make a whole new bloody set."

"I know. It's just . . . Everything was fine before Pearl Harbor too," Matt said, immediately regretting the display of uncertainty. Silva had no response to that. "Well," he said, clearing his throat and straightening, "let's see what kind of Kabuki dance the 'Cats have ready for us today. Besides, it's breakfast time." He paused, suddenly decisive. "Run back down to the ship, or send somebody, and inform Mr. Dowden to make preparations for getting underway. The Maa-ni-los are going to help us or not. Hanging around and pestering them probably won't make any difference. It's really Saan-Kakja's decision, anyway. But I've had just about enough, and one way or another, this is our last day here."

"Aye, aye, Skipper," Silva replied with his usual unnerving lopsided grin.

Breakfast was a lavish, quiet affair, but Matt immediately got the impression that, today, things would proceed differently. Perhaps word had slipped that *Walker*'s people were fed up and about to leave. Matt suspected Silva of the leak, but maybe that was best. As badly as they needed the Maa-ni-los, the Maa-ni-los needed them too, and if that was what it took to get the ball rolling, so be it. He was seated at one end of a long table, a position of prestige, and at the other end, in a place of equal honor, was Saan-Kakja. It was the first time he'd seen her since their arrival. All the negotiations had been conducted by underlings. Now, few of those underlings were present and Matt expected, as a result, things would move more swiftly. One way or the other.

Saan-Kakja sat on her stool across from him, locked in a posture of tense precision, lifting careful spoonfuls of fluffy yellow eggs to her mouth. Her short, silken, gray-black fur was carefully groomed, and glowed with the luster of healthy youth. Around her neck hung the golden gorget of her office, and occasionally her short, delicate fingers strayed between her small breasts and absently stroked the metal. It dawned on Matt, despite her noteworthy greeting, that she might not yet be comfortable in her exalted role, and he felt his heart go out to her. They'd learned a few things about her through back channels during the negotiations, and what they knew explained a great deal—particularly about her behavior. She really didn't know how to proceed, and she'd delegated much to her High Sky Priest, who Adar thought was a "jerk," to use a charitable translation. Her father had been Saanga-Kakja, which explained a little of the initial confusion. Keje and Adar had known him long ago, but not as High Chief. They'd hoped to be dealing with a person they knew. A widower like Keje, he died mere months earlier of a long illness. All his older offspring, from another, previously deceased mate, had already moved on: one as High Chief of a newly built, seagoing Home, and two others who'd established land Homes on the southern Fil-pin Islands. All that remained to assume the mantle of leadership was Saan-Kakja, the young child of his young, much adored, and deeply lamented second, and final, mate. Some believed he actually died of sorrow, since he joined his beloved in the Heavens such a short time after her passing.

Regardless, he'd left his daughter—at the tender age of fourteen—ill-prepared to rule, and her understandably tentative approach, and willing-ness to delegate, undermined her authority. Lemurians matured much quicker than humans, but she was still considered a youngling even by her own people. She'd been through a lot, and was clearly aware she had a lot to live up to, but based on his first meeting with her and looking at her now, Matt suspected she'd do all right if she had the right kind of help and support. Safir Maraan had risen at a younger age, and look how she'd turned out. Of course, the cultures were different, and she'd always had Haakar-Faask to back her up. Apparently there was no Haakar-Faask for Saan-Kakja. There was only her Sky Priest.

The Sky Priest in question sat on Saan-Kakja's left. He was called Mek-snaak, and despite Adar's opinion, Matt didn't really know what to think of him. He seemed dour and suspicious, and couldn't have been more dif-ferent from Adar. Adar was seated in his customary place beside Keje, even though he was Sky Priest to more than just a single Home. His example and personality—not to mention his early recognition of the greater threat—had done much to smooth the waters between the Americans and the various factions that ultimately formed the alliance. He'd shamelessly waved the bloody shirt of *Revenge*, the allies' first "prize ship." Her loss, and the loss of her integrated crew in a struggle against impossible odds, had provided a shining example of honor and sacrifice to the technically amalgamated, but increasingly Lemurian, "U.S. Navy." The two species had both been somewhat ethnocentric when they met, but even given their mutual need for allies, there'd been surprisingly little friction. Maybe they were so physically different, there was no real basis for racial resent-ment. Each looked equally "funny" to the other, but each had recognizable strengths the other lacked. The battle resulting in the loss of *Revenge* set the ultimate precedent of coequal status among the two species, and began a growing tradition of "equal glory or a shared death." Matt reminded himself the Maa-ni-los were not yet part of any such tradition.

He cornered the last of his eggs between his spoon and a strip of fish, and when he ate them both he realized the others had mostly finished. He cleared his throat. Recognizing the gesture, Saan-Kakja laid aside her own single utensil, an instrument like a broad-bladed, concave knife that also served as a kind of spoon or scoop. It was gold, like so many other Maa-ni-lo devices. Matt hadn't seen as much gold in his life, certainly not among other Lemurians, as he had in the last few days. The thing was, it didn't seem to have any value other than that it didn't tarnish and it was pretty. The High Chief . . . tess?—absurd, they didn't think like that. Their word, U-Amaki, transcended gender. The High Chief dabbed daintily at her mouth with an embroidered napkin and sat even straighter, if possible.

"Cap-i-taan Reddy," she began. "I must begin by begging you to forgive me for neglecting you so inexcusably." Meksnaak blinked furiously and opened his mouth to speak, but she darted a look in his direction that Matt couldn't read, and his jaws clamped shut. "I have wasted much of your time," she continued, "and I fear in doing so, I have squandered valuable time we may all remember with wistful regret." Matt waited patiently for a full translation, even though he got the gist of what she said. "You come here seeking alliance against the threat posed by our Ancient Enemy, an enemy as implacable and relentless as the very sea. It may be deceptively calm for a time"—she looked back at Meksnaak—"but eventually, inevitably, the Strakka strikes with unbound fury. I am . . . a young High Chief who has seen little of life, and learned even less of what is expected of me, so I was persuaded to delegate the task of treating with you on this subject." Her voice became hard. "That was a mistake. It was rude and irresponsible, and I apologize." She blinked sincere regret and lowered her head. When she looked up at Matt, her remarkable eyes were gleaming.

"I have heard much about your adventures and battles against the scourge from the west, and I am inspired. I allowed myself to be convinced, however, that my excitement was that of an emotional youngling, and here we are safe from attack. Better to stay uninvolved—beyond learning as much from you as we can, and helping you in small, safe, material ways. There are . . . factions in Maa-ni-la that thrive on contention and intrigue, and are obsessed with their own petty concerns. They counsel that we let you, Baalkpan, and the other allied Homes stand alone against the Grik, while we remain safely uninvolved. We are prosperous, happy, stable, and untouched by the distant threat. Even if Baalkpan falls, the Grik will be content to remain far away, and in the meantime our trade, industry, and prosperity will flourish even more." Her ears flattened with contempt. "Of course, there are also the ones you call 'runaways,' who counsel that, even if the Grik do someday come here, we can flee once more as we did in the ancient tales of the Scrolls; that we have grown too comfortable, too fixed in place, too reliant upon the land."

Matt nodded. Those were the same arguments he and Nakja-Mur had faced when they first suggested defiance. Most people on the seagoing

Homes couldn't comprehend their cousins' attachment to *places*, or understand their unwillingness to leave them. Keje did, and so did the other members of the alliance. They knew there'd be no escape this time. The world was a smaller place, and now the Grik had oceangoing ships of their own, albeit tiny in comparison; they had so many, the terrible sea was no longer the protector it had been. It was like the old scorpion and tarantula in the jar. The tarantula wasn't well equipped to cope with the scorpion, but sooner or later he had to deal with his deadly, aggressive adversary, because he couldn't avoid him forever, and there just wasn't anyplace else to go. It was always a toss-up who'd win.

"I understand you grow impatient," Saan-Kakja resumed, "and I do not blame you. Your most powerful ship is here, and you languish in comfort and are free from want, but all the while the enemy may be massing against you. You are frustrated by our intransigence, and don't understand our hesitation to join you." She shook her head. "Honestly, I am as frustrated as you, and my patience is possibly even less. I do know what causes it, however. My people are comfortable and free from want. That is a condition any good ruler desires, but there are times, such as this, that that very condition makes it difficult for such a ruler to convince those comfortable people they must put that aside and face the unpleasant reality of the harsher world beyond their sight." She sighed and turned again to Meksnaak.

"What of the proposal I put before the counsel? That we join the alliance to destroy the Grik threat forever, and send whatever we may in the way of troops and supplies to their aid?"

Meksnaak shifted uncomfortably. "My dear, it is . . . unwise to reveal our private discussions in the presence of strangers—particularly when those discussions involve them." He hastily turned to Captain Reddy with a glare. "No such decision has been taken!"

"The decision has been taken by me," Saan-Kakja retorted.

Meksnaak shook his head sadly. "You are powerful, High Chief, and your *opinions* have great weight, but even you cannot engage us in full-scale war on your own authority. The clan chiefs must speak."

"Then let them speak! So far, none has done any speaking but you and other members of the counsel who represent those with the most to gain by inactivity!"

"There are legitimate objections," Meksnaak insisted, "not only to going to war, but to any association with these Amer-i-caan . . . heretics!" He blinked outrage at the thought of the Americans' Scrolls. He'd never seen them, but he'd been assured they were . . . extraordinary. His initial concern that their existence represented heresy was not dispelled when Adar told him with glowing eyes that the American Scrolls almost perfectly mirrored their own, except they were even more precise! Meksnaak accepted that. Adar was a Sky Priest of extensive renown, and Meksnaak was willing to take his word in that respect. But the knowledge did not make him admire the Americans, or soothe his concerns about their spiritually corrosive behavior. If anything, it made him resent and fear them even more. If their Scrolls were so much more precise than those of the People, they must be holy indeed. Could they even be the very originals from which all others were copied long ago? Scrolls formed under the hand of the Great Prophet Siska-Ta herself? And what of the rumors that the Americans possessed Scrolls no one else had ever seen? Scrolls depicting mysterious lands far beyond the world known by the People? And Adar assured him they displayed their precious Scrolls in the open, for any and all to see—even to *handle*! How could the Americans be so careless and . . . irresponsible? Incredible. He'd asked the question of Adar during one of their meetings, and was shocked that one so highly regarded could harbor such liberal views.

"I was as troubled as you, at first," Adar had confessed, "but that is because I had grown set in my ways, ossified and concerned about a diminution of my precious prerogatives. After much consideration, I changed my mind. Are the Scrolls to be kept secret, and viewed only by those such as we? Surely the great Siska-Ta never intended that; otherwise why write them at all? It was her goal to teach, to enlighten, to share the knowledge of the past and the heavens and the pathways of the sea and sky—not create an exclusive club reserved for only a select few!"

Now Adar stood and spoke with heat. "They are *not* heretics; I told you that already! They have different beliefs, surely, but they do not seek to trample or transgress upon our own! And regardless of their differences, the very Scrolls you would use as examples of their heresy prove we share more similarities of thought than differences, and *they*, at least, gladly aid us against our Ancient Enemy!"

"An enemy made stronger with the aid of others of their kind!" Meksnaak retorted.

Adar took a strained breath. "Perhaps their enemy does collude with ours, but they didn't know that when they joined us, and it has not altered their commitment. That you, a Sky Priest, would counsel inaction during our current, collective crisis, when our race faces extinction at the very hands that drove us from our sacred, ancient home—as described in the same Scrolls you profess to revere—makes me question *your* commitment!"

Meksnaak sputtered for a moment, then spat: "*Ser-vaabo fidem summo studio!*"

"*Suspendens omnia naa-so! Usus est ty-raannus, usus te plura doce-bit!*" Adar replied scornfully. "*Cucullus non facit monachum. Cul-paam maiorum posteri luunt!*"

"*Gratis dictum. Honos haa-bet onus, maag-naavis est conscientiae.*"

"Oh, Lord." Bradford sighed. "I do hate it when they do that!"

"What're they saying?" Matt demanded.

"Let me see, I've brushed up my Latin a bit of late, from necessity, but their pronunciation is quite bizarre. Hmm. Well, as you know, Latin is somewhat difficult to translate literally even when spoken well—which makes the Lemurian capacity for it doubly fascinating, since they are so literal-minded! Their own language . . ."

"Courtney?"

"Umm? Well, it seems their Meksnaak has said he only keeps the faith, while Adar says he's shackled by it, and his people will pay the consequences. Meksnaak says that's ridiculous, and he has an obligation to his people."

The argument continued.

"*Medium tenuere be-aati,*" Adar scoffed sarcastically, "*mihi cura futuri. Quousque tandem abutere paa-tientia nostra? Recovate aa-nimos! Aude saa-pere. Stant belli causa, belli lethaale . . . belli internecinum. Timor mortis morte peior!*"

"Oh, dear," Bradford said with real alarm.

"What?"

"Adar has admonished Meksnaak to remember the cause of the war . . . and I think he called him a coward!"

Matt coughed politely before Meksnaak could respond. "We consider it rude to carry on in a language others can't understand." He glanced at Saan-Kakja, and she nodded. Adar resumed his seat with a huff, and Meksnaak blinked insincere apology. Courtney Bradford couldn't entirely stifle a sigh of relief, and Meksnaak's eyes narrowed irritably.

"If the . . . plodding pace of our discussions is so unsatisfactory, you can always go aboard that . . . smoking iron abomination of yours, and leave us as we were."

Bradford leaned back in his chair and arched an eyebrow. Now Matt began to rise, his face red with indignation.

"Meksnaak . . ." began Saan-Kakja.

"No. With respect, child, I grow weary of the constant complaining of these . . . foreigners. Maa-ni-la has prospered in peace for over eighty years, and will be doing so long after our spirits have gone above. If you ask my opinion, I tell you we neglect our own people's interest by even contemplating the risky adventure these . . . others . . . propose. And honestly, this extraordinary meeting and the pointless haste in which it was convened is . . . unseemly." Meksnaak glared at Bradford, but continued to speak to his High Chief. "I remind you, child, my friend, your father, did not rush to war when first he heard of this unlikely threat!"

There was an uncomfortable silence, and all eyes turned to the young, smallish . . . well, girl. That was the only word that really seemed to fit, as far as the humans were concerned. But Matt could only wonder if he was the only one that saw the wide, striated eyes suddenly become pools of molten iron. When she spoke, however, her voice was under firm control.

"My lord Meksnaak, I know you were my father's friend, as well as his most trusted advisor. That is, after all, one of the primary duties of all Sky Priests to their chief. I honor you for that service and friendship." She slowly turned her head to look at the older Lemurian, and Meksnaak must have seen the same thing Matt had, because he visibly blanched. "I am High Chief of Maa-ni-la now, by acclamation as well as birth. I am my father's daughter. Although I do not doubt your devotion to my father, I begin to doubt your wisdom. I say this not to hurt you, but because you will not *see*. You and I cannot know what it was like for our guests to face the Ancient Enemy, the terror of all our nightmares. Neither of us can fully understand what that is like. But because I love my people and yearn for them to be forever safe and free, I fairly chafe to go myself to the aid of our western friends. I *yearn* to send them aid, because only then can we harry the Grik vermin from the sea, and ultimately from our dreams and our ancient home as well!"

For just a moment Meksnaak held her gaze, but then came the long, slow blink of abject apology. "You shame me, child."

"No. You shame *me* with your impolite behavior." Her hand swept outward in a gesture encompassing all those seated at the table. "You have been impolite to my guests and to me. I am no mere youngling to be dismissed at the table of adults, any more than . . ." She paused, and her mesmerizing eyes fell upon Chack. "Any more than the noble Chack-Sab-At, of whose exploits I have heard so much! He is little older than I, yet he has faced our enemies many times. Tell me, Master Sab-At, are you a youngling?"

Chack, uncomfortable with being forced to speak under the circumstances, glanced at Captain Reddy and saw his confident nod of approval. He stood with as much dignity as he could muster.

"I have seen my former Home, *Salissa*, ravaged by the Grik, and I fought them with all my might, though I was not yet a warrior. I joined the Amer-i-caan clan and learned not only to fight more efficiently, but also to lead. I have participated in five boarding actions now. . . ." He paused and regarded Meksnaak. "I truly cannot convey how horrific that can be. If you saw the aftermath of such a thing only once, you would not doubt our cause. The Grik carry our people as cargo . . . live provisions aboard their ships. . . ." His tail swished impatiently, and he shook his head. "I was in the great Battle of Aryaal, where we slaughtered twenty thousands of our foes and lost many of our own. It was after that we came to know that, no matter how many we killed, it was but a tithe against their total strength. I saw *Amagi* pound *Nerracca* into a sinking inferno. We rescued as many as we could—hundreds—but thousands were left to burn or drown or be taken by the fish." For a moment he closed his haunted eyes while he spoke, and no one doubted he was seeing again the events of that terrible night. "I saw Tassana, daughter of *Nerracca's* High Chief, younger even than you, Saan-Kakja, help cut the tow cable that connected her helpless, sinking Home to the wounded Amer-i-caan destroyer trying to drag her to safety. She did it because her father knew Captain Reddy, and feared he might wait too long, hoping to rescue more. As it was, damaged and leaking, *Walker* nearly sank under the sheer weight of the survivors she managed to save."

Not a word was uttered in the chamber while he stood silent, contemplating his next words. "I was a youngling before all this started, if not in years, then certainly in experience. Now I am a bosun's mate, a captain of Marines, and I guard some of the most important leaders of our alliance." He stared hard at Meksnaak. "Do you dare call me a youngling, or offer further insult to those I protect?"

Saan-Kakja took a breath and realized she'd been holding it. She looked around the table, surprised how much Chack's words had changed her perceptions of the people there. Particularly the Amer-i-caans. She'd heard the tales, of course, but they'd been told dispassionately. To hear Chack tell them, in his own words, made them real. She pierced her Sky Priest with another molten stare.

Meksnaak's apologetic blinking was constant now and, from what Matt had learned of Lemurian expression, sincere. He even felt a little embarrassed for the Sky Priest, but he also knew Saan-Kakja needed to get this sorted out. He thought she had. She and Chack had. The new High Chief of Manila might be young, but she was no "youngling." Not anymore. She finally spoke again, and when she did her voice had lost much of its fury.

"You may one day earn the right to be rude to me, Meksnaak, but you will never be rude to my friends again. They have earned our respect and gratitude. Besides, none of us have the luxury of being rude to *anyone* who will help us in this fight. Yes, we need their help as much as they need ours. This is our war too. The Grik have come as if our most horrible dreams have been made flesh, and they come to devour us all! Our only hope is to destroy them first, and we must have friends to do it. How can we expect to make those friends when we can't even be polite at the breakfast table?"

"Hear, hear!" Bradford said, banging his coffee cup on the table for emphasis. It wasn't quite empty, and much of the remains wound up on his sleeve. "Saan-Kakja for queen, I say!" He looked at the suddenly wary Sky Priest. "She certainly settled our hash! I suppose we'll have to keep our little arguments more private from now on." Meksnaak hadn't had much contact with humans, but he'd learned a nod was still a nod. He nodded now and forced a small smile.

"If that is the will of my chief," he said quietly.

"Surely she can't object to a little debate between two scientific beings, though?" He arched his eyebrows once again, and Saan-Kakja couldn't restrain a giggle. Like the cats—and lemurs for that matter—they so closely resembled, Lemurians had an extraordinarily limited range of facial expression. They were *very* expressive, through eye blinks, ear positions, and body posture, and their tails added an emphasis to their emotions and attitudes that humans couldn't hope to match. A grin was a grin and a frown was a frown, but other than that their faces hardly moved at all. Humans, on the other hand, used comparatively little body language, and it took quite a while for Lemurians to understand that much of the true meaning behind their words was conveyed by a bewildering array of inimitable facial contortions. Courtney Bradford had discovered early on that 'Cats sometimes found these contortions amusing. Particularly when wildly exaggerated. He made good use of that knowledge now, bouncing his bushy eyebrows up and down like a pair of spastic caterpillars. Even Meksnaak couldn't resist, and he suddenly broke into a grin after an explosive snort. Bradford looked at Chack, who'd resumed his seat, but was now barely able to stay on his stool. His eyes were clenched shut, and he was making a kind of high-pitched, hacking sound.

"What?" demanded Bradford in a voice of purest innocence. A moment before there'd been a dangerous tension in the room. Now . . . there wasn't. Matt congratulated himself again for bringing the Australian along.

"Mr. Bradford," he said, shaking his head with a grin, "I think you've made your point." He nodded respectfully at Chack. "As has our captain of Marines. Now . . ." He looked at Saan-Kakja, who was gaining control of herself. "With your permission, perhaps we might proceed?"

"Of course."

Walker steamed southwest under a cloudless, hazy sky through the treacherous waters of the Visayan Sea. Lookouts were on constant alert for shoaling water and the little islets sprinkled about. Through Adar they'd acquired copies of Lemurian Scrolls for this portion of the trip, and Mek-snaak was partially mollified to discover that, regardless of the detail American Scrolls possessed, they depicted a slightly different world, where conditions weren't entirely the same. He'd also pinpointed the area, west of wild, largely unexplored Mindanao, where fishing boats of the southern clan colonies last reported the "iron fish."

They departed Manila with Saan-Kakja's promise her personal Guard of a thousand troops would depart immediately aboard one of the "supply" Homes bound for Baalkpan. Chack's Marine lieutenant remained behind to give rudimentary training to the levy, before taking ship with the Guard, whom he'd train as much as possible on the way. More would follow. It wasn't as much or as quickly as Matt had hoped, but it was more than he'd begun to fear they'd get. As it was, they still had a few days left of the time he'd allocated for looking for the submarine, even if he'd begun to begrudge it. They still hadn't heard anything from Baalkpan, and they had to assume, at the very least, that the radio was out. He didn't want to think about other possibilities, no matter how far-fetched or unlikely.

Those possibilities were beginning to affect the crew, however, and Chack was becoming openly worried about Queen Maraan. Somehow he sensed she'd done something foolish, and he couldn't get the conviction out of his head. Matt tried to soothe his nerves (and his own) by assuring him the problem was probably just some glitch with the radio—yet another piece of equipment they'd relied so heavily upon had let them down. Regardless, he was anxious to complete their quick sweep and head for home.

They saw plenty of gri-kakka, and even hit one again. This specimen wasn't nearly as large as the plesiosaur they struck in the Java Sea, so there was no damage. The coloration was peculiar, however, and Mr. Bradford's insistent demands obliged them to heave to briefly and compare the dead creature to others they'd seen. He didn't have much time. Being back in relatively shallow water, the flashies made an immediate appearance, drawn by the blood, and soon the water churned with such violence he was forced to abandon his investigation. In the short time he had to study it, though, he documented a few distinct variations.

Land was never entirely out of sight, and strange, flying creatures dogged them constantly, swooping among the signal halyards and roosting on the number one funnel and generally shitting all over the ship. Chack had a constant detail plying hoses and mops, but it made little difference. Most of the creatures were familiar variations of the lizard birds they were used to, even if the colors were generally different. Some "birds" looked like actual birds, with real feathers, and they shrieked and cawed right among the others. On the amidships gun platform, Silva was pitching small morsels in the air, and the off-duty crew were betting on which creatures would slaughter the others to get them.

Matt was leaning on the bridge wing rail with Spanky and Keje, watching the entertainment, and was surprised to see Gilbert and Tabby participating. He raised an eyebrow at the engineer.

Spanky shrugged. "They've been getting out more," he confirmed. "Weird. It's like we had three trees growing off the same root, and when we cut one down, the other two took off." He shook his head. "I wonder how Isak's doin'. I know it sounds selfish, but I hope they all get along when we get them back together." He grinned. "They still do their jobs, but I don't get as much extra work out of them as I used to, what with them hanging around in the firerooms off watch."

Matt saw Silva stiffen suddenly, his predatory eye fixed like a cougar on its prey. He shoved his way forward through his bewildered audience, scooping the large, slimy quid of "tobacco" from his cheek. Pausing by the rail next to the ladder, he waited for his chance. Below him, Chack and a couple Marine "deck apes" were working their way aft. Chack was grousing loudly about something, probably all the "bird" crap. Like a bombardier, Silva took careful aim at his objective and, when he judged the moment was right, released his payload. It struck the deck directly in front of Chack with a resounding, viscous *splap*, and the 'Cat quickly looked skyward, searching for whatever creature was capable of creating such prodigious droppings. Instead of an unprecedentedly large flying reptile, however, his eyes fastened onto Silva's bearded face, leering happily amid the sound of raucous laughter.

"Oh, Lord." Spanky sighed.

Matt's first instinct was to shout a reprimand. Instead he stifled the impulse and laughed. He caught Spanky's questioning, almost indignant look. "Oh, don't worry; he'll clean it up. He's become 'responsible'! I'm just glad to see his practical jokes have moderated with his increase in rank."

Spanky shook his head. "But have Chack's?" he wondered aloud.

Lieutenant Dowden joined them with a smirk. "You know, right now we've got half the deck division spraying bird crap off the ship, while the other half is encouraging the damn things to squirt more on it." He shook his head when the others laughed.

"Is this a . . . met-a-for? A metaphor for human behavior?" Keje asked, and joined in when the laughter redoubled. In spite of their worries about the radio, everyone felt a certain lightness now that the greater part of their mission had been achieved. Baalkpan would be reinforced. It would take a while, but they should have the time.

"Maybe so," Matt conceded, "but there're plenty of 'Cats doing it too. Maybe we're too much alike for our own good." He sobered and looked at Spanky. "How's our fuel holding up?"

"Okay, so far. We made a slower run out than planned, so we saved a little there. We're kind of pouring it on for this little side trip, holding twenty knots, but we'll have to slow down again in the Canigao Channel. We'll be taking the Surigao Strait in the dark, so we ought to keep it slow. . . . Plenty of fuel for a return trip like the one we came out on. Where are we looking first for this sub?"

Matt stepped around the charthouse and stared down at the copied Lemurian Scrolls rolled out under the Plexiglas on the chart table. The others joined him there. "Last reliable reports have it in this vicinity," he said, pointing at Davao Gulf and circling his finger south of Mindanao. "Fishing boats from Saaran-gaani—used to be General Santos, where one of Saan-Kakja's brothers set up house—saw it pretty often for a week or two, from the reports Meksnaak finally coughed up, but nobody's seen it for a year now, which would be about right." Matt frowned. "I know Meksnaak finally made all nice, but I still don't know about that guy. I'm pretty sure he's still convinced it's a sea monster of some sort. Anyway, given that it must have gone through the same Squall we did, and the fuel it must've had, it couldn't have made it much farther than that. By the time they made it here, they must have realized something was seriously out of whack." His finger traced the western coastline of Mindanao, paused at the bay where Mati should be, considering, then swept around Cape San Agustin and into Davao Gulf. "If it was anywhere near Saaran-gaani, or beached on the coast anywhere along here, Saan-Kakja's brother would know about it. We'll look, of course, especially in that bay, but I don't think we'll find it there. No one's reported it, and I understand the local wildlife is even more extreme than usual. If they tried to land along there, I bet they didn't stay."

"Maybe it's just gone, Skipper," Dowden said. "Sunk."

"Maybe . . ."

"Where, then?" Keje asked.

Matt's finger roamed south about a hundred and fifty miles to Talaud Island and drew a circle, encompassing the tiny islands around it. "Here, I think, if they had the fuel. These islands are . . . were Dutch. Maybe they hoped to find *somebody* home."

Keje studied the chart. "Deep water. Deep water all around."

"Yeah. Nobody in their right mind would go monkeying around down there. No reason to, besides. Dangerous water and nothing to catch. If they're there, they could've easily gone a year without anybody noticing." He looked at Keje and their eyes met.

"I have seen those islands," Keje said softly, "many years ago. I did not go ashore—that was not our purpose—but the land on the big island, this Taa-laud, is lush, and could sustain them if they were not eaten by predators—and if they made it across the deep waters in the first place. The island is also founded upon a burning mountain, a 'vol-caano' that rarely sleeps. I have heard the earth moves often, and the very sea sometimes behaves strangely."

Matt straightened, decision made. "We'll work south along the coast of Mindanao, checking every nook and cranny, but then, if we haven't found it, we'll cross to Talaud."

"What if it's not there either, Skipper?" Spanky asked.

Matt shrugged. "We go home."

I t was overcast, but not raining this time when Sandra waved good-bye to yet another destroyer. Now *Mahan* was steaming toward the mouth of the bay, looking just like *Walker* from a distance, and fingers of dread clutched Sandra's heart. *Mahan* was following in the wake of a pair of fast feluccas that had departed the night before. They'd serve as scouts at first, then transports if the need arose. Nobody really knew how many people remained on B'mbaado—trapped now behind enemy lines.

Selass was with her, come to say farewell to her mate, Saak-Fas. He'd been leaning on the rail, staring, as the ship moved away, but if he saw her in the throng he made no sign. Now the ship had almost vanished against the dreary, light gray sky. They saw a wisp of smoke, a sense of ghostly movement. Otherwise all that marked her passage was a flicker of color at her masthead as the Stars and Stripes streamed aft in the sultry air, stirred only by the ship's motion. Sandra watched the flag slowly fade with mixed emotions, an elusive memory of something Matt once told her rising to the surface. Something he'd seen a doomed British destroyer do in the face of impossible odds, and then *Exeter* did the same thing before her final battle. She strained to remember, sure it was important.

"Do you think they will return?" Selass asked quietly.

"They must. We'll need them desperately when *Walker* returns."

"I meant *Walker*," Selass almost whispered. "I feel so guilty. I find myself almost hoping *Mahan* will fail. That would mean the end of Queen Maraan, but then I might have a chance when Chack returns. It would also probably mean the end of Saak-Fas as well." She paused, then almost pleaded, "But that is what he wants, is it not?"

"I suspect so," Sandra replied, saddened for her tragic friend, though not shocked that her thoughts had taken such a turn. "If that's the case, if he truly wants to die, he'll likely get his chance." She sighed. "Jim Ellis is a good man and an excellent officer, but I'm not sure he should be commanding this mission. He still blames himself for losing *Mahan* when Kaufman shot him and took command. He thinks his ship's honor is stained—*his* honor too. He feels he has something to prove. Nobody like that should ever command a mission like this, with so much at stake. I know Jim, and trust him, but I can't shake the fear that he'll take chances with himself and his ship, hoping to remove that stain, when his most important objective is to get himself and his ship back in one piece."

She lowered her head in thought as they walked back through the bazaar in the direction of the hospital. They entered the textile section, where colorful tapestries and fine fabrics swayed gently in the light air. A matronly Lemurian female, with hard-used, pendulous breasts, was perched on a high stool, embroidering a smock with an ornate design, and Sandra paused to admire the work. Then it hit her.

"Excuse me," she said excitedly. "Your embroidery is beautiful, but do you also sew fabric together?"

"Of course! What a silly question . . ." The female grunted rudely, then looked up and hastily added, "Esteemed healer!" She stood and bowed low. "My apologies! Indeed, I must first make these garments before I embroider them."

"Excellent! I know you're busy, but could I commission you to make something for me?"

"For you, anything! You healed one of my daughters, badly wounded at Aryaal. Nothing will take precedence. I will begin work today! What would the esteemed healer have me make?"

Sandra took her precious notebook and pen from her shirt pocket and began to draw. Curious passersby stopped to stare, and it occurred to Sandra that she'd probably doubled the old seamstress's business by choosing her. She displayed the sketch and said how big she wanted the finished product.

"I have seen that before," the matron said. "Everyone has. Certainly I can make it, but so large?" Sandra nodded emphatically. Then, thinking of the female's embroidery skills, and her own Virginia heritage, she scribbled some more on the drawing. "And I want that on it too."

Tarakan Island had changed dramatically. Chief Gray had finally taken Silva's advice and burned half of it off. They took extreme care to make sure the prevailing winds confined the blaze to only half the island; still, Gray knew Bradford would be livid. There'd been nothing for it, though.

The dense foliage simply couldn't be cleared in the time they had, and the priority, after all, was the well. Besides, it was a dangerous place. They'd lost two more 'Cats surveying the site—killed this time—and the Bosun wouldn't sacrifice another life for every tree on the island. Even so, he'd been surprised how well the place burned. He hadn't even been sure they could light the wet, waxy undergrowth, and when it went up like kerosene-soaked wood, it was a scramble to contain the blaze and get everyone clear. They even had a battle on their hands, of sorts, down on the beach, when swarms of wildly unlikely creatures stampeded from the forest. Fortunately, Shinya had already begun defensive positions, and a lot of the fleeing beasts simply leaped the entrenchments the workers and Marines scrambled into. Some of the terror-maddened creatures wanted to fight, though, and some of his people suffered a few injuries—none serious, fortunately, but they were well supplied with meat for a couple days before it began to spoil.

Work on the well proceeded rapidly after that, surrounded by a surrealistic landscape of fire-blackened stumps and a jumble of fallen trees. At least the workers were no longer in peril from predators, although nighttime brought a variety of scavengers anxious to pick the cooked victims clean. Soon even they lost interest, and before long one could walk from the beach to the well at any time of the day or night in relative safety.

Shinya and Gray had a falling-out over the burn, but not for environmental reasons. Shinya wanted to leave a belt of jungle as a fallback defensive position. Gray even tried to arrange it, but the fire took off quicker than anyone expected. Angry, Shinya accused Gray of deliberately disregarding his advice, and, just as angry, Gray told him to go to hell. They coexisted even more uneasily than usual after that, and each concentrated on his own area of responsibility. As a result, both probably did a better, quicker job than they would have otherwise, but they drove their work crews unmercifully. By the time Isak brought in the well, everyone was exhausted.

The upside was, that left little strenuous labor for anyone to do. The storage tanks were erected and emplaced, and a pipeline had already been run to where the new refinery would be once *Felts* returned with the equipment. Shinya had overseen the construction of impressive works down at the beach, with multilayered defenses anchored on the impenetrable jungle on one flank, and a rocky mole extending into the sea on the other. The storage tanks were just outside the secondary defensive perimeter, but the wellhead was protected.

Gray sat on the edge of his cot under a makeshift shelter the Marines erected. It was a sturdy affair and would probably survive a moderate blow. It wasn't big, but at least he had it to himself. All the workers and Marines shared similar structures with ten or more. He heard a loud *crack* and glanced up from the journal he was keeping, pen poised over the paper. He had a good view of the beach, and experienced a nostalgic moment when he realized it looked just like any other island beach he'd seen—like those in the Keys where he took the Boy fishing when he was on leave—before his wife got fed up and took the Boy away. He hadn't seen him more than half a dozen times after that, so he'd been shocked to run into him, all grown up, in a bar in Cavite. The Boy was in destroyers then too, but he'd received a transfer. They had a few beers, talked about things, and then went to the beach and fished until the sun came up. The next day, the Boy shouldered his seabag and boarded an oiler bound for Pearl. From there he'd hitch another ride to the States and spend a few days with his mother before joining his new ship: the USS *Oklahoma*.

When things started getting hot with the Japs, the Pacific Fleet—and *Oklahoma*—moved to Pearl. Gray had been planning on taking some leave to get together with the Boy, but a little over a year ago now, on December 7 . . . The letter he got said the Boy was "missing and presumed lost." He figured his ex got one just like it, but he never wrote to find out. There wasn't any point. He closed his eyes and rubbed his face.

There was another *crack* and he focused on the cause. Down by the water a group of 'Cats was gathered around a man, and Gray did a double take. He snorted with amazement. He'd seen dinosaurs, monkey-cats, flying lizards, and Grik, but nothing rivaled this: Isak Rueben was teaching the 'Cats how to swing a baseball bat. Gray was shocked that he even knew how. The Mice had always scorned the ship's team, back when there was one, and never even watched the games. While Gray stared, Isak tossed another of the softball-size, inedible nuts they'd discovered on the island into the air, and with a confident flourish twirled the bat and whacked the nut far out over the water. It disappeared with a splash, lost in the sound of the surf.

"I'll be damned," he muttered, a grin creeping across his face. It vanished an instant later when he heard the insistent clanging of the general alarm bell. The bell was little more than a hollow bronze pipe, but its sound carried amazingly well when it was vigorously struck. There was only one reason for anyone to do that. Tamatsu Shinya appeared in the entrance to his hut, breathing hard, almost coming to attention.

"We have visitors," he said, very formally.

Shinya and Gray stood on the beach surrounded by their "staff," consisting of two Lemurian Marine captains, their four lieutenants, and a Guard captain in charge of the project company. His lieutenants were organizing his workers into squads and arming them, while the Marine NCOs directed their troops into their fighting positions. Signalman "Mikey" Monk, from

Mahan, and Shipfitter Stanley "Dobbin" Dobson from *Walker*, were also there, and, for some reason, so was Isak. Gray lowered his binoculars and grudgingly handed them to Shinya.

"Three Grik ships—you can just see the red of their hulls—working up from the south. There's another sail, southwest and farther away, but coming up fast. She's got a better wind."

"You reckon it might be *Felts*?" Isak asked, uncharacteristically curious. "She's due back."

"Could be," Gray answered. "Whoever it is, they're by theirself. If she's ours, maybe she'll get here in time to intercept those Grik bastards." He grinned wickedly. "I wonder how they'll like her guns."

A blue-kilted staff sergeant scampered up and saluted. "The Marines are in place, sirs." His tail twitched. "The Guards soon will be. I sent first squad, second platoon, to help them get sorted out." The Guard captain bristled, but said nothing.

"Very well," Shinya replied. "Once they're in position, have them stand easy. It will be a while before the enemy arrives. Make sure there is plenty of water and the ammunition is distributed."

The ammunition was mainly arrows and crossbow bolts, although some of the NCOs had Krags. There were also the two field guns they'd brought ashore, six-pounders, now emplaced halfway from the center to each flank, where they could sweep all approaches.

For the better part of the morning, the group stood rooted, watching the approaching ships. A single, towering cloud appeared and lashed the sea with a vicious squall before vanishing entirely. The Grik ships continued their relentless advance. So did the other "sail," and before long they saw the white stripe between her gunports. *Felts*.

"This ought to be a pretty good show," Gray surmised, and indeed, he was right. *Felts* slanted down, Stars and Stripes streaming to leeward, and crossed the bows of the tightly packed enemy squadron. A single, billowing white cloud erupted along her side, and long moments later a dull thumping sound reached them over the surf.

"Give 'em hell, Mr. Clark!" Mikey growled.

They couldn't see the effect, if any, of the initial broadside, but *Felts* wore around and punished the enemy with her portside guns. They saw splashes of debris, and a mast toppled into the sea. Cheers erupted behind them. The Grik squadron's precise formation fell into disarray, and two of the ships slewed around, beam-on to their attacker. Then, with disbelieving eyes, those on the beach watched sporadic puffs of white smoke gush from the sides of the red-hulled ships.

"Holy *shit*!"

Round shot kicked up splashes, skipping across the wave tops in the general direction of the beach, and a few of the staff cringed involuntarily.

"Holy shit," Dobbin murmured again. "Where'd they get *cannons*?"

"Same place we did, idiot," Gray growled more fiercely than he intended. "The bastards made 'em."

Felts didn't wear this time; instinctively Clark must have known it would expose his vulnerable stern. Instead, the sloop hove to and held her ground, pounding away at the enemy.

"Gonna be a better show than we thought," Gray said ironically.

Felts's gunnery was far better, and she hacked away at the red ships. She finally fell away before the wind, to keep the Grik at arm's length, and took a pounding then, but when the now crippled squadron re-formed for the advance, she hove to once more and raked them again and again. The damage she inflicted was exponentially greater this time. Rigging and stays, weakened by the previous fire, parted, and shattered masts teetered and fell, taking others, less damaged, with them. One enemy ship was a wallowing, dismasted wreck, and the other two weren't much better, but their gunnery was improving at the point-blank range of the duel, and *Felts* was suffering too. Over the next hour they watched while the battle raged on the sea, and *Felts* maintained the same tactics: pouring withering fire into her foes until they got too close, then gaining some distance again. The dismasted, sinking Grik ship fell far behind, but the remaining two learned to present their own broadside whenever *Felts* moved away. It was difficult for them, since they could barely maneuver, but the American ship had finally lost her foremast and maintop as well.

"Mr. Clark is fighting his ship well," Shinya observed politely.

"He's a brawler," Gray conceded, "but he's fighting stupid. *Felts* is faster and more maneuverable, and her gunnery's obviously better. He should be taking advantage of that. He's gotten sucked into a slugging match, and that's the Grik's kind of fight." The ships were close enough now that there was only the slightest pause before they heard the sound of the guns. The tearing-canvas shriek of shot passing nearby was more frequent too, but the staff no longer flinched. "He needs to get out from between us and them. The tide's out, and he'll run out of water pretty soon." Sure enough, while they watched, *Felts* heeled slightly, righted herself, then heeled sharply over as she went hard aground, beam-on to the advancing swells and the enemy.

"Dumb ass. Give the kid a ship and what does he do?" He shook his head. "Mr. Shinya, get a platoon of Marines into the boats and pull for *Felts*. Those Grik bastards draw more water and they'll be aground too, I expect, but they'll send boarders. I doubt they'll fool with us while they've got the ship right in front of them. We have to keep them off her at all costs."

Shinya saluted. "Very well." He looked at the commander of First Platoon. "With me."

Even aground, *Felts* kept up a withering fire, but the Grik remorselessly advanced. Inevitably, they too struck, and then it became a race to see whether the Marines or the enemy boarders reached *Felts* first. Another of the Grik ships, holed repeatedly, filled and heeled over on her side in the shallow water. Most of her crew were already in the boats, however, and *Felts*'s guns churned the sea with canister, splintering boats and scything down their crews. Before long, though, they were under her guns. At their upward angle they just couldn't be depressed far enough, and when they gained her side they swarmed up and over the bulwarks. They were met by a withering fusillade of arrows and more canister from the guns that were loaded and waiting. Mangled bodies rained into the sea, and the "flashies" quickly went to work, thrashing the water beside the ship into a white, pink-tinged froth.

The Marines pulled as hard as they could, oars dipping and straining, with Shinya in the foremost boat, waving his modified cutlass and exhorting his troops to greater effort. They almost made it. They would have made it, Gray thought bitterly as he watched. The fighting was dying down, the first onslaught repulsed, when *Felts*'s own boats dropped to the water, and her crew, wounded and hale, scrambled into them. Dense smoke poured from the bowels of the grounded ship, and soon flames were licking up her masts.

"Goddamn it!" Gray seethed. "That better have been an accident, or I'll have that useless bastard shot!"

Shinya paused his advance, resting his Marines while the abandoning crew joined him. Then, at a more leisurely pace, the flotilla of boats returned to shore. Behind them, *Felts* became fully involved, flames soaring high into the sky, still-loaded guns occasionally booming from within the inferno. The mainmast toppled amid a cloud of gray smoke and swirling sparks, about the time the first boats nudged ashore through the gentle surf. Guardsmen sprang forward to assist the wounded, and Marines and uninjured sailors mingled on the beach, sorting themselves out, while Shinya escorted Lieutenant Clark before Gray and his impatient staff.

Clark's uniform was stained and bloody, and his hair and face were scorched. He'd clearly been the last to leave his ship. His cutlass was in its sheath, blood trickling down the side where it scraped from the blade when he thrust it in. He drew himself up before Gray and saluted. If either was struck by the irony of an officer saluting a noncom, neither commented on it; there was no question who was in charge.

"What happened?" Gray snapped.

"Why, well, we fought a hell of a fight!" Clark retorted after a brief hesitation, clearly surprised by Gray's tone. "The bastards had cannons! We knew it was possible, of course, but we didn't really expect it."

"What do you mean, you knew it was possible?"

"That's right," Clark replied, "you couldn't know." He quickly outlined recent events while Gray stood, listening with growing rage.

"Let me get this straight," Gray said at last. "Queen Maraan, Pete, and who knows who else are stranded behind enemy lines, *Donaghey's* laid up, the rest of the new construction's not ready for sea, *Mahan's* gone—against orders—to rescue the queen, the goddamn Griks are gettin' frisky and they have *cannons* now, the radio's busted so we can't even tell the captain"— he gestured out at the inferno—"and you just burned our only way home! You better convince me real fast why I shouldn't have your sorry ass shot!"

Clark shook his head in astonishment. "Mr. Gray, there were *three* of them! We whittled them down to one, killed most of the boarding party they sent against us, but another was forming from the other, mostly undamaged ship. There was no way we could repel another attack."

"The Marines were almost there!"

"Yes, sir, and maybe that would've helped, but I didn't see any point losing more lives over a wrecked ship."

"Was she wrecked?"

"She was hard aground!"

"Sunk? Leaking bad?"

"Well, not really, but . . ."

"But the goddamn tide's out! We could've held her until it came back in and refloated her!"

"But . . ." Agonized realization dawned across Clark's blistered face. "Oh my God."

"Yep. You screwed up by the numbers in each and every category. We bett—"

Isak poked him in the ribs with his elbow. "Griks is comin'," he said, motioning out to sea. Gray looked past the burning ship at the mass of approaching boats.

"We better get ready," he growled. "Mr. Shinya?"

"Sir?"

"See to our defenses. Arm the sailors if they lost their weapons, and if we have anything extra." He looked back at Clark. "If they're true to form, there'll be six or seven hundred of 'em. With your boys, we'll have about two hundred and fifty. Looks like this'll be the Grik's kind of battle too."

"At 'em, boys!" Alden bellowed as he dropped his shield and sprinted into the clearing from the cover of the dense forest. Others surged forward to join him: dozens, then nearly a hundred. Fortunately most didn't follow his exuberant, somewhat irresponsible example by throwing their own shields aside. The disorganized Grik line was caught completely by surprise. This time an even larger number turned on their fellows and began hacking away. Some even dropped their weapons and simply ran—something Pete had never seen. Quite enough Grik to satisfy him reacted in a more predictable fashion: they charged to meet the attack.

He emptied his Springfield into the mass, then slashed with the bayonet at its muzzle. Knocking a sword aside, he skewered what appeared to be an "officer," if Grik infantry had such things. The "troops" under his command maintained a relatively cohesive front when they slammed into the enemy with their handmade shields and spears of sharpened wood. Enough of them, Alden's personal guard and B'mbaadan warriors, had real spears to do most of the killing, while those on the flanks funneled the enemy toward them. There came a crash from the center when the disorganized remnants of the Grik mob slammed into the interlocked shields and those shields pushed back. Spears bristled and jabbed, and Pete's little army fought with everything they had, from swords to garden tools. Some of these Grik had no weapons either, the earlier surprise sweeping them away before they had a chance to grab them, but even disarmed, the Grik were deadly with their terrible claws and teeth. Therefore, brief as it was, the fight was still unimaginably fierce. Finally, all the Grik that charged the line were dead or writhing on the ground, with the exception of a trickle that ultimately ran away as well. Gasping after the sharp fight and aching after the long morning of exertion, Pete took a drink from his canteen.

The sun hadn't been up long, but the battle had raged since before dawn. With their amazing eyesight, Lemurians could see fine in the dark, where apparently their enemy couldn't. The Grik had no "taboos" or anything against fighting at night, but they weren't very good at it. The local 'Cats preferred not to either, for religious reasons. Therefore, aside from his huge numerical superiority, it must've never even occurred to the Grik commander he might be in danger even as he slept. The sight of the enemy army asleep, totally off guard, was too much of a temptation, and Pete kicked off the attack ahead of schedule.

The killing had been almost wanton, and those that survived the initial onslaught broke and ran in all directions. Pursuit was unthinkable, though, and Alden gathered his force and withdrew to his secondary position. The enemy reacted quickly, sending reinforcements against the thrust. Like most highly specialized predators, however, Grik seemed to key on motion even in the daylight, so they were completely surprised again when they ran right into Haakar-Faask's force that Pete's had retired behind.

Savaged again by the stalwart B'mbaadan general, the Grik reeled back in the direction of their own lines. That was when Alden's rested troops struck them again on the flank. It appeared this element of the Grik advance, at least, was shattered beyond reclamation.

Alden wiped his bayonet on his pants leg and snapped it back on his rifle. Taking another long drink, keen eyes glancing all around, he spit and began thumbing slender .30-06 rounds back into his empty magazine. He was already out of stripper clips, and had only the dozen or so loose rounds in his pocket.

"All right," he said, closing the bolt, "let's pull back. Easy does it; don't get split up in the woods. We'll re-form with General Faask, and see what kind of hornet's nest we've stirred up. Stretcher bearers, get our wounded out of here."

The wounded would be carried back to the "reserve" commanded by the Orphan Queen, whose primary responsibility was guarding the younglings and noncombatants.

He glanced at the sun, now clear of the treetops overhead. "It's gonna be a long day."

"So this is your 'surprise' for the mountain fish," Keje observed.

"One of them," Matt confirmed. "At least, I hope so. Took Sonarman Brooks long enough to get it working again, even though we had all the parts." He shrugged. "We just never saw any point in it at first. It's meant to find submarines underwater, and we had no reason to suspect we'd need it against any of those. I've heard active sonar plays hell with whales back home—our version of mountain fish, even if they're a lot smaller—so maybe it'll kick these big bastards in the head too."

"Why are we going"—Keje grinned—"so slow? I thought you wanted to cross to Taa-laud as fast as possible."

"I do, but I want to see if this works. We can't get a return at anything much over fifteen knots. If we can get a return, Brooks ought to be able to tell us what effect it has on the big devils by how they react to it."

They waited for the better part of an hour, crowded in the charthouse behind the nervous sonarman's chair, while he listened intently through his headset. The constant, eerie pinging continued uninterrupted.

"Contact!" Brooks suddenly shouted, unaware his voice was so loud. "Bearing one nine five! Probable sub . . . probable mountain fish! Range fifteen hundred yards, down Doppler. Wait! Return is narrowing. Either he's turning toward us, or away."

Matt leaned out the hatch and caught the talker's eye. "Sound general quarters," he said calmly.

Knowing the cause, the talker gulped. "General quarters, aye!"

During *Walker*'s refit, much was repaired, but somehow they'd over-looked her ill-sounding general alarm. There'd been no emergency aboard since they began the mission, but daily exercises—something Matt insisted on—still took their toll. The musical, insistent *gong! gong! gong!* had gradu-ally been replaced by something more like a loose guitar string being bru-tally plucked. The alarm was still referred to as "Gee-Kyoo" by the crew, but the act of setting it off had become: "Somebody up there's (on the bridge) stompin' on a duck." Abused duck or not, the alarm still had the desired effect, and within seconds reports started coming in. Finally, the talker looked at the captain.

"All stations report manned and ready, Captain."

"Very well." Matt looked back in the charthouse. "Well?"

"He's moving away, Skipper! First he was running straight away; now he's on a bearing of two one oh, and picking up speed!"

"Let's hope the neighborhood just got too noisy for him."

"Captain," shouted the talker, "lookout reports 'something' surfacing astern!"

He looked aft, but couldn't see past the amidships deckhouse, so he scrambled up to the fire control platform. "Mr. Campeti," he acknowledged as the new gunnery officer directed his gaze, and Matt raised his binocu-lars. It was a mountain fish, all right, a different one. It had risen directly astern, and was giving chase. Matt suddenly realized this "surprise" had one small weakness: *Walker*'s sonar was directed primarily forward.

He'd known, intellectually, that mountain fish were big; he'd been told so often enough. But to actually *see* one this close! *Jesus*, he thought, *the damn thing's* huge. *Now I know what it feels like to be a grasshopper in a stock tank full of bass!* "All ahead flank!" he shouted, knowing the order would be passed along. "Mr. Campeti, have the number four gun com-mence firing in local control! Stand by to roll depth charges!" It looked like they'd get to try all their "surprises" today. It would be a few minutes be-fore they accelerated to their maximum speed. In the meantime, the thing was gaining on them! "Set your depth at fifty feet!" Any shallower and they ran a serious risk of damaging the ship.

"Depth charges report set at fifty feet,'" Campeti reported a moment later. "Ready to roll at your command!"

Silva was on the aft deckhouse, watching, while the crew of number four made ready. His new exalted status was liberating in a way; he wasn't a gun captain anymore, so he could pretty much pick where he wanted to be dur-ing general quarters, but it also left him feeling like he had nothing to do at times. Lieutenant Dowden, a few feet distant, probably felt the same way,

manning the auxiliary conn. It was his duty to conn the ship if the bridge
or its personnel were disabled. In the meantime, he didn't have anything to
do either, except watch the god-awful, humongous fish come swimming
up their skirt. All they could really see was an enormous, rounded hump,
pushing displaced water like a rogue tsunami. Occasionally it blew a mist
of atomized water high in the air from an indistinct hole that closed immediately after. Its massive flukes, or tail, or whatever drove it, never broke
the surface, and it did look for all the world like a big, rounded, barnacle-
encrusted . . . island, chasing them to beat sixty. The stern crouched down
suddenly, and Silva felt the ship accelerate, but the damn thing was fast!
Realistically he couldn't imagine the fish maintaining its nearly twenty-
knot surge for any length of time, but realistically it shouldn't exist at all.
He wasn't sure they'd get clear in time.

"Commence firing!" shouted the talker beside the gun, and an instant
later the pointer stomped the trigger pedal. There was an earsplitting *boom!*
and the gun jumped back, vomiting its empty shell to clang on the deck.
Another shell went in and the breech slammed shut, while a 'Cat ordnance
striker chased the empty shell with outstretched gloves, trying to catch it
before it went over the side, and keep an eye on the approaching horror at
the same time. *Boom!* The breech clanked open, spilling another empty,
and the shell man slammed another home. *Boom!* Three high-explosive
four-inch shells disappeared into what had to be the thing's head and detonated with enough force to scatter gobbets of flesh hundreds of yards. A
massive, gaping wound as big as a car had appeared where the shells
struck home, and the wave it pushed had taken a pinkish tinge from blood
coursing down. Suddenly, much closer than they expected—less than a
hundred yards astern—another hump rose up, clearing the water and exposing monstrous ivory teeth. The thing emitted a roar like a hundred
whales being electrocuted, and surged in for the kill. They hadn't been
shooting at its head at all!

"Out of the way, goddamn it!" Silva shouted, yanking the 'Cat pointer
out of his chair and sending him sprawling on the deck. He jumped on the
metal seat and looked through the eyepiece in front of him. He barely
heard the shouted, "Roll two!" command and the muted splash of the
depth charges. "Clear!" he roared, making sure no one was behind him,
and he pressed the firing pedal with the cross-hairs centered far back in
the roof of the creature's mouth. *Boom!* The overpressure of the gun's report was like a lover's embrace. "Load!"

The water beneath the monster's upper jaw spalled suddenly, and two
enormous spumes of water obscured their vision. There was a sense of
massive motion, and then what seemed like tons of seawater deluged the

men and 'Cats on the stern of the ship. Silva wiped his eyes and searched frantically for the target. For an instant he felt disoriented, and started to yell at the trainer, thinking he'd spun the gun out to one side. But wait, there were the depth charge racks right below him. He stared again, squinting, and realized it was true: the monster was gone. All that remained as *Walker* continued to accelerate away was a giant field of churning bubbles, harsh against the cerulean sea, and in its midst, like an oil slick, an expanding stain of black-red blood.

"Goddamn!" Silva whooped, joining the cheers around him. "I sunk him!"

Lighting a third boiler, and keeping a steady twenty-five knots, *Walker* managed to outrun anything her sonar didn't scare away for the remainder of the transit. By midafternoon, Talaud Island was drawing near, as well as a group of smaller islands off the port bow, and Matt finally gave the order to reduce speed as the water shoaled rapidly closer to land.

"Which way, Skipper?" Dowden asked. They'd raised the island on its northeastern coast, and there was nowhere immediately apparent even a small boat—much less a submarine—might find shelter. Now they must decide whether to steam west, then south, to inspect the rest of the northern part of the island, then its western flank, or explore the eastern flank first. Matt glanced at Bradford, leaning on the rail, "his" binoculars glued to his eyes, oblivious to the question. He'd been morose when they'd been forced to injure and possibly kill one of the enormous mountain fish, and scandalized that he hadn't been able to at least view its corpse—if there'd been one. Now his earlier petulance was gone, as he prepared for yet more fantastic discoveries. This would be the first time they'd visited a landmass far enough from any other and surrounded by deep and hostile enough waters that there'd have been little, if any, dissemination of land-dwelling species. He was excited by what he'd seen so far, even from a distance, and occasional happy chortles escaped him.

There were plenty of "birds." Already they'd begun littering the deck again—and actual birds seemed to predominate. Bradford believed that, even if they weren't as fiercely armed as their leathery competitors, they were lighter and probably had a longer range. Therefore, more species of feathered birds might make it to this isolated place to diversify and thrive. Perhaps the ones they saw before were even migrants from here? There were still plenty of lizard birds, but not in comparison, and most were larger than their northern cousins. In any event, Bradford was in no position to offer constructive opinions regarding which direction to go. He didn't care.

Matt conferred quietly with Keje, and finally nodded in agreement.

"We'll explore the western flank first, Mr. Dowden. If we don't find them there, or in the south or east, we'll be in position to check out the smaller islands over there"—he gestured—"before heading home."

"But . . . Captain, there're still lots of other places they could be."

"Possibly, but we don't have time to look. It's time we headed back, regardless." He paused a moment, considering. "Have Mr. McFarlane secure a boiler of his choice. We'll reduce speed to one-third, but let's keep a close sonar watch, shall we? Helmsman, make your course two six zero, if you please."

"Aye, sir, making my course two six zero."

For the remainder of the day they cruised sedately on a calm, gently rolling sea. They saw nothing in the north and when they turned south it looked like more of the same at first: dense, impenetrable jungle growing right down to and beyond the shore, by means of a mangrove-type root system. It was unlike anything Matt had ever seen on such a large and isolated island, and always, in the distance, a large volcano loomed menacingly from the jungle mists enshrouding its flanks. Jets of smoke or steam curled from vents in its side. Eventually they began to notice irregularities in the shoreline, and they slowed to a crawl so they could glass them more carefully. Still, no true inlet was apparent, or even a beach. There was no sign of life at all, in fact, besides the ever-present, swooping, defecating birds. Even Courtney began losing interest by the time the sun edged toward the horizon.

"I say, Captain Reddy, shouldn't we speed up? Hurry along, as it were? Surely the eastern side of the island is more hospitable and, well, easier to land upon."

"We can't know that, and we're only looking once. If we 'speed up' we might miss something. It'll soon be dark anyway, and we'll have to anchor. I want to do it in the shallowest water possible, and right now there's less water under our keel than we've had all day." Making up his mind, he spoke to the talker. "Pass the word for Chack; have him call the special sea and anchor detail. This is as good a place as any."

Lightning lit the night, slashing the sea in all directions, but there was little thunder, and the wind and sea remained calm and placid. It was an almost surrealistic spectacle, and nobody got much sleep. Earl Lanier went fishing—as was his custom whenever the ship was at rest. For once he didn't whistle tunelessly or snap at others standing by the rail, watching the silent display. He didn't catch anything either. Every time he lowered a hook, something immediately snapped his line. What's more, things in the water evidently began associating the bait with the ship, and an unnerving bumping and . . . sliding . . . commenced against the hull. Campeti had the watch and ordered Lanier to hang it up before whatever was down there got any friskier. For once, Earl didn't argue.

Before dawn, the anchor detail sprayed the heavy links with water as the chain came aboard, booming and rattling into the locker below. The crew stood to their battle stations as they did every morning when the ship was most vulnerable to observation, silhouetted against the graying sky. The practice had even taken on a more conventional feel. They knew they were looking for a submarine, and conventional wisdom said it was American. But they didn't *know* it was American. Besides, even if it was, and even if it was out there, it might not know *they* were Americans, and after a year on this God's nightmare of a world, it might have an itchy trigger finger.

In the pilothouse, holding his steaming "Captain's" mug, Matt didn't try to lighten the fresh tension around him. He knew there was almost no chance the iron fish would even be at sea, much less stalking them, but after the tiring night they'd passed, heightened awareness was a good thing. He gulped Juan's coffee and didn't even grimace. Bradford clomped up the ladder behind him, yawning loudly, followed by Adar and Keje. One way or another today would solve the mystery, at least so far as it was in their power to solve it, and they'd either find the elusive submarine on Talaud's eastern flank or the little islands to the northeast, or they'd turn for home. Either way, everyone was anxious to get about it. The sense of "something's not right" at Baalkpan had become a palpable thing, and every day they remained away added an exponential layer of anxiety. Even Bradford seemed resigned when Matt told him that unless they saw some evidence of the submarine, there'd be no excursion ashore.

"Anchor's aweigh, Captain," Dowden reported quietly in response to the shrill call of the bosun's pipe on the foc's'le. Matt nodded. He'd been wondering how 'Cats could toot on a bosun's pipe when they couldn't make a sound with a bugle. They'd learned at the Battle of Aryaal that they needed something like bugle calls to pass commands on the battlefield. Maybe they could adapt something like a giant bosun's call. Use whistles or something? He shook his head. He'd have to ask someone. All he could make a bugle do was fart.

"Very well. All ahead slow; make your course zero seven five. Extra lookouts to port."

When they rounded the island's southern tip and headed north, they began to discover beaches. Visibility was excellent, and the rising sun penetrated the shadows of the suddenly less dense forest, and they caught glimpses of a few animals here and there. Most, beach scavengers probably, scampered quickly under cover at the sight of them, but one creature the size and shape of a rhino-pig, but with a powerful neck as long as its body and a head like a moose—with tusks—stared insolently at them as they passed. It occasionally even rushed the surf, as if warning them away.

"Oh! You're a nasty fellow, aren't you!" Courtney giggled happily. "Oof! Oof! Orrrrr!" There were chuckles in the pilothouse, and Matt stifled a grin.

By late morning the distant humps of the small islands to the northeast appeared through the haze, and everyone knew they were about out of luck. There'd been a couple of promising lagoons, but they turned out to be little more than crescents eroded into the island by the marching sea, and they could see clearly to their termination. Another such lagoon, or the point at the mouth of one, was coming up, and all were grimly certain it was their final chance. They'd almost reached the point where they'd initially turned west.

"Captain," called Reynolds, "lookout reports this one's deeper than the others. Maybe better protected."

"Very well. We'll stick our nose in and take a look. Pass the word for the lead line. Dead slow when we round the point, consistent with the current, of course."

They passed the point and *Walker* slowed, Norman Kutas inching the big wheel ever so slightly to bring the bow around. The long swells pushed them toward the cove, and a series of constant adjustments were required.

"It *is* a deep inlet" Reynolds confirmed, passing the lookout's observations. "Surf's a little gentler inside."

"What's our depth?" Matt asked.

"Seven fathoms, coming up fast."

Reynolds looked up, eyes wide, and holding his earphone tight against his head as if not sure he'd heard correctly. "Uh, Captain, lookout says—I mean reports . . . there's something on the beach, high on the beach, twenty degrees off the starboard bow. It looks sort of like the pictures you showed them."

There was a rush to the bridge wing.

"Five fathoms!"

"Left full rudder," Matt commanded, "port engine ahead two-thirds, starboard back two-thirds!" *Walker* eased to a stop and the stern began swinging right. The ship pitched uncomfortably on the rollers for a moment, then began to roll. "Drop anchor. Mr. Dowden? How's the tide?"

"Low ebb, sir, about to turn."

"Very well. Leadsman to the stern. Prepare the launch." Only then did Matt go to the bridge wing, shouldering his way through the onlookers, and raise his own binoculars.

"I'll be damned," he said with a sinking heart. "Jesus, there she is . . ."

He lowered the binoculars, but continued to stare. One of his questions had been answered. The stern continued coming around until *Walker* rode at anchor, pitching against the incoming sea.

"Stern lead reports three fathoms."

Matt raised his glasses again and studied the object of their search, the object of so many secret hopes. "Well," he said, his voice neutral, "stand by to lower the launch. Have Silva prepare a full weapons load for a shore party of twelve. Food, water, and medical supplies as well, in case there're survivors." He sighed. "As for the sub, we won't be getting her off *that*. Not this trip, anyway."

They took "Scott's" barge, named after the dead coxswain. It was the biggest, and still the best maintained. Besides Matt (Lieutenant Dowden hadn't even tried to talk him out of going this time), the barge carried Bradford, Adar, Keje, Spanky, and Gilbert Yager. Also aboard were Chack, Silva, Stites, and three Marines. Stites did a creditable job as coxswain as he conned the burbling boat through the rollers into the calmer water protected by the northern point of the lagoon. They were so fixated on the beached submarine, they hardly noticed the flashies bumping the hull with their bony heads, and the closer they came to shore, the more disheartened they became.

The submarine wasn't only beached; she was high and dry. Even the incoming tide wouldn't float her. It would barely reach her. It would've taken a severe storm indeed to leave her that high on the beach, and there was absolutely nothing they could do with the time and manpower available to get her off—not that there seemed much point. She lay at thirty degrees, keel toward the sea, and rust streaks ran from her cracked, peeling, faded gray paint. It was an old S-Boat, as Matt suspected all along. There'd been quite a few of the obsolete submarines attached to the Asiatic Fleet, and this one was clearly a *Holland* class, based on its unique stern configuration and distinctive sow-belly shape. Matt quickly reviewed what he knew about *Holland* boats in his mind: a little over 200 feet long with 20-foot beam, somewhere around a thousand tons, with two diesels and electric motors. Top speed of fourteen or fifteen knots on the surface. Four torpedo tubes, a four-inch-fifty deck gun—just like *Walker*'s main battery.

"S-19," Spanky announced when the weather-ravaged numbers on her hull finally came in view. They couldn't see the larger numbers on her conning tower at the angle she lay. "I know that boat," he continued. "She was trying to clear Surabaya the same time we were. Having trouble with one of her diesels or something, and awaiting special orders. Battery trouble too, if I remember right. I talked to her chief, and he was run pretty ragged."

"We all were," Matt reminded him.

"True, but that boat's even older than *Walker* and *Mahan*. And to think fellas would go *underwater* in it. Gives me the heebie-jeebies." Another detail about S-Boats came to Matt's mind as the barge scrunched onto the sandy beach and the shore party scrambled ashore: they had a crew of about forty officers and men. So far they'd seen no sign of them.

Stites and one of the Marines secured a line from the barge to the submarine's port propeller shaft, and joined the others fanning out to inspect the environs. The Marines and Bradford had their Krags, and Silva and Stites both carried BARs. Matt and Keje were the only ones with Springfields, and Adar wasn't armed at all—beyond a short sword at his side. Keje had become quite a marksman, but Adar wasn't any kind of fighter. Heavens knew he wished he was, but he thought he'd be more dangerous to his friends than to an enemy with the powerful American weapons. He didn't mind the little sword, because he could use it to hack brush—and he probably couldn't hurt anyone with it but himself.

"There are many tracks in the sand," Chack observed, and Bradford and Silva stooped to examine the impressions.

"Indeed there are!" Bradford exclaimed. "Some quite unique! I've never seen them before." He pointed. "Here's one that might have been made by one of those unpleasant buggers we saw earlier today!"

"I'm more interested in human tracks," Matt replied, also stooping, "like these." There was a large, well-beaten path leading from the submarine into the jungle. The tracks ran both ways, and some were relatively fresh. One very distinct set of tracks left him puzzled, however; the impressions were human, but only about half the size of the others.

"Jumpin' Jesus!" Silva exclaimed. "There's Grik tracks if I ever saw 'em! Lookie here, Skipper!" Matt hurried to where Silva stood, swatting sand off his knees.

"You're right," he confirmed darkly. "Everyone, there's definitely Grik on this island, so keep your eyes peeled." He stared at the trail leading from the submarine for a moment, then looked at the source. "I'd rather we all stuck together, but I'd also rather we didn't waste any time. Spanky, Yager, and I will inspect the submarine, see if there's anything we can salvage immediately. Maybe we can at least dig up some more four-inch-fifty ammunition. Stites'll remain topside on the sub as security while we go inside. Chack, you and Silva lead everyone else up the trail and search for survivors. Keep an eye on Mr. Bradford." He looked at Adar and Keje. "Would the two of you prefer to stay or go?"

Both Lemurians looked dubiously at the sharply leaning submarine.

"Fascinating as it might be to crawl inside that . . . contraption," Keje hedged, "for myself, I would prefer to stay in the open."

"I as well," Adar agreed fervently.

"Suit yourselves. Can't say I blame you. I'm not wearing dolphins for a reason."

A cargo net hung from the shoreward side of the submarine, and they scrambled up without much difficulty. The deck was a little rough to stand on, since there were few stanchions, and S-Boat decks were notoriously slender to begin with. Only the area around the gun was very wide, where it swelled abruptly to give the gun crew footing when it was traversed. Matt eyed the gun greedily. If they couldn't salvage the sub, he at least wanted that gun someday, and it looked more and more like he'd have it. Onboard, the sub looked even worse. The wooden strakes were rotting and a few had collapsed. They had to be careful not to fall through to the pressure hull below. One of the periscopes was badly bent, and the hull plating was washboarded like one would expect after a severe depth-charging. They climbed up to the conning tower hatch, and Spanky undogged it easily enough. He stuck his hand out to Gilbert, who fished in a pack and produced a pair of battle lanterns. Spanky briefly shone one down the hatch, and then slid down the ladder. Matt followed him, and Gilbert brought up the rear.

"Stinks in here," Gilbert said, joining the others in the cramped compartment. "Ow." He'd jabbed himself with something. Matt had been aboard submarines before, and knew they weren't made for people as tall as he was. He had to crouch everywhere he went, and there was always something, a valve handle or pipe or who knew what, waiting to conk his head or poke his ribs. With only the light of the battle lanterns, it was even worse.

"Ow," he echoed.

"Always stinks in a pigboat," Spanky said. "That's why they call 'em that."

"There's something else," Matt said.

"Yeah," answered Spanky, "smells a little gassy." He cocked his head. "A little smoky too."

They descended another ladder to the control room. There was slightly more space, but the protuberances were even more aggressive, particularly at the angle the boat lay. Spanky shone his light at something.

"I wonder," he murmured, and flipped a switch. Much to their surprise, an eerie red light flickered to life, glowing dully in the compartment. "Night-light," he explained. "So there's a little juice, anyway."

"Which way?" Matt asked the engineer, leaving the decision to him. It was stiflingly hot, and he knew they couldn't stay below long. "Forward or aft?"

"Torpedoes would be forward, engines aft. What's our priority?"

"Torpedoes."

"Ain't as thick as most jungles I've vacationed in lately," Silva noted, swiping at a vine with his cutlass as the group of eight marched inland.

"This side of the island is more exposed to extreme weather," Bradford explained. "Saplings are often swept away before they take root, I should think."

"Mmm."

There were still areas that were quite dense, but occasionally the trail opened into clearings, of a sort, where strange pine/palmlike trees stood tall with little undergrowth. Whenever they came to such a place, Silva covered Chack and his Marines while they split up and scouted ahead, in case someone or something intended to use it for the excellent purpose of laying an ambush. Super lizards weren't the only creatures that knew clearings were well suited for that. When the Marines were satisfied no threat existed, the party moved on. Currently the trail was clear, but the foliage was dense on either side. Up ahead another clearing opened, however. Silva advanced slowly, BAR at his shoulder. When he reached the edge of the opening, he'd scan it for obvious threats before the Marines cast ahead once more.

"Leapin' lizards!" he hissed. Standing in the center of the clearing, about thirty yards away, was a Grik. It was broadside-on, motionless, nose sniffing the air. The light filtering from the canopy above made it a perfect target. Even as Silva's finger automatically tightened on the trigger, his subconscious mind noticed several startling things: the Grik was an entirely different color from any he'd seen, kind of a stripey, orange-ish-black—like a tiger—and its tail seemed longer. It wore no armor, only a ridiculous, uselessly oriented leather breechcloth. A pouch hung at its side. The most outlandish thing about it, however, had only an instant to register before Silva's instinctual reaction to shoot it fully manifested itself. Maybe the subconscious realization threw his aim, or maybe he sensed something creeping up on *him* even as he fired. Whatever the reason, he knew the shot was bad even as the deafening bark of the BAR shattered the silence of the forest and a number of things struck him at once.

First, something *was* creeping up on him—rushing, in fact. The second thing to strike him was a club of some kind, moldy-soft on the outside, but with a core as dense as iron. Third, even as he staggered from the blow and heard high-pitched shrieks accompanying it, his subconscious mind screamed out the shocking detail he'd half missed about the Grik: it was carrying a musket.

He fell to the ground, too stunned even to defend himself, much less strike back. For a moment he had no idea what was on top of him, shrilly shrieking and landing blow after blow. As his head cleared from the initial strike, he realized whatever had "ahold" of him wasn't very big, it wasn't eating him, and the incessant blows didn't really hurt. He also understood the hysterical screaming—as well as the hysterical, chittering laughter accompanying it. He opened his eyes. There, straddling his chest, was a nymph-size fury, jade eyes wide with rage, lips skinned back from perfect, if yellowed teeth, long, wildly disheveled hair revealing glimpses of the golden radiance beneath the filth.

"Oh, you monster! Vile, loathsome, horrible beast!" it ranted, still pounding him with little fists.

"Goddamn it, fellas! It's a *girl!*" Silva almost squeaked, to a fresh round of laughter.

"Don't you use such language in front of *me,* you filthy murderer! You . . . you *bastard!*" The blows resumed with renewed fury.

"Get this wildcat offa me! Chack, you little turd!" Silva yelped, but Chack couldn't move; he could barely breathe. He was paralyzed by the sight of a clearly human youngling beating the stuffing out of the mighty Dennis Silva. Silva finally resorted to simply immobilizing the girl in a tight embrace. She struggled mightily, but there was no escape. Finally her shouts became desolate sobs.

"Listen . . . girlie . . . I ain't gonna hurt you none—nobody is—but you gotta leave off whuppin' on me, see? It ain't polite."

Courtney Bradford shook off the shock of the moment and raised a restraining hand to Chack's Marines. Keje and Adar weren't laughing. They'd instantly realized the possible significance of their discovery.

"Chack!" Keje rumbled. "If you cannot control yourself, or your Maareens, I will do it for you!" Keje might no longer be Chack's personal High Chief, but the young Lemurian still respected him tremendously. Chastened, he and the three Marines sobered.

Bradford knelt down. "There, there, child. Please do compose yourself," he said gently. The small girl was filthy, and dressed in rags. Clearly she'd suffered a terrible ordeal. Perhaps she was unhinged. What else might motivate her to attack Silva that way?

"Yeah," Silva grated as softly as he could. "If you'll cut it out, I'll turn you loose." The grimy, tear-streaked face nodded, and Dennis let her go. Instantly she scrambled to her feet, and bolted toward the Grik on the ground. Silva jumped up, snagging his rifle. "Shit, girlie," he yelled, "are you nuts? The damn thing might still be alive!"

"I certainly hope he is, for your sake, you vicious, murdering villain!"

the girl shouted back. Unable to shoot even if it was, with the girl in the way, Silva ran after her. So did the others. When they arrived at her side they were in for another shock. The girl had collapsed, sobbing, beside the writhing Grik. It moaned piteously and she stroked it with the utmost tenderness.

"Lawrence!" she cried tearfully. "Oh, Lawrence, you mustn't die!"

The evil jaws opened slightly, and a long, purplish tongue moved inside them. "Hurts!" it said. The humans and Lemurians looked on, stunned.

"It spoke!" jibbered Bradford.

"Of course he spoke, you silly man! This is Lawrence," she snarled, "my friend!" Looking up, she seemed to notice for the first time that they weren't all humans, and her eyes went wide again, but with something besides rage. "My God!" she said, hushed. "You are not all people!"

Adar hesitantly stepped forward and bowed to the girl. If he was affected by the bizarre irony, he managed to conceal it. That must have taken considerable effort, since few loathed the Grik as much as he. "I am Adar, High Sky Priest of *Salissa* Home, and currently Steward of the Faith to the various members of the alliance under the Banner of the Trees. We are indeed 'people,' just a little different. Where we come from, creatures such as your 'Lawrence' are vicious predators, intent on exterminating us. Our Amer-i-caan friends have explained their concept of 'pets,' however, and though I consider it foolhardy and . . . astonishing . . . you have chosen such as this as your own, I . . ." He started to say he was sorry, but simply couldn't manage it. "We would not have harmed it had we known," he concluded gently, but with little conviction.

"Lawrence isn't my pet, you furry imbecile! He's my friend!"

"Rend!" confirmed the Grik with a gasp.

Adar tried to reply, but ultimately he could only blink.

"Goodness gracious!" Bradford breathed, then cleared his throat. "My dear, I'm Courtney Bradford, and these are my friends." The girl looked at him, zeroing in on his accent, strangely similar to her own. "If you guarantee your . . . friend's . . . good behavior, I think we may repair him. He's most fortunate, actually. Mr. Silva's usually a remarkably good shot. You cannot know how glad I am his aim strayed just this once! We have a doctor, of sorts, aboard our ship. . . ."

"Ship?"

The word came from behind them, and Silva and the Marines whirled to see a variety of weapons pointed in their direction. They'd been so focused on the girl and the Grik, they'd never sensed the strangers' approach. Most of the weapons were Thompson submachine guns, or 1911 Colts, and they were held by men dressed in remnants of garments once issued by the United States Navy. One man, dark skinned, with a huge mustache drooping over his beard, held a sawed-off musket in his one hand like a pistol. It was he who'd spoken.

"S-19?" Silva challenged.

One of the apparent Navy men lowered his Thompson slightly. He was short, with a scruffy red beard and long, thinning hair poking from under a battered chief's hat. "I really am in hell," he muttered, "and here's the devil himself!"

"In the flesh," Silva said absently, staring hard at the speaker. "Billy Flynn! It *is* you, you redheaded Irish ape! You owe me seventeen dollars!" The tension evaporated, and all the weapons were lowered except the musket/pistol held by the dark, mustachioed man. Silva regarded him appraisingly, recognizing a fellow predator. He nodded slightly before returning his attention to the others. "Who's with you, Billy?" he asked, then added for his companions' sake: "Billy's the sub's chief of the boat—sort of like the bosun, in a slimy pigboat sort of way."

"We've lost some guys," Billy acknowledged, "but we've preserved most of our passengers." He nodded at the girl, the Grik, and the one-armed man. "Picked up a couple too," he added enigmatically. Then his fierce visage disintegrated into an expression of open joy. "I never thought I'd say this, but damn, am I glad to see you!"

"You know this guy, Chief?" one of the others asked.

"You could say that." He paused, gesturing at the Lemurians. "What's with the monkeys? You friends of theirs?"

"Yeah," Silva answered, a hint of threat in his voice, "good friends. Why?"

"We ran into one of their ships once. Great big bastard. Damn thing launched giant spears at us!"

Silva laughed. "That's how we knew you were here! They thought you was a metal fish! Don't take it personal; I'm sure you know there's bigger fish than yours in *this* sea!"

Billy's expression became grim again. "Tell me."

"Tell *me*," insisted the dark-haired man, still holding the gun, "about your ship!"

Silva bristled, then slowly grinned. "USS *Walker*, DD-163, at your service!"

Mahan stood off the B'mbaado coast, numbers one and three guns covering the beach, in the general vicinity of where *Donaghey* had fought her battle with the three Grik ships. Now another enemy ship was aground, burning fiercely, and two more were on the bottom of the Java Sea. There hadn't been a fight, really, merely an execution, and they didn't even know if the ships had been armed, since *Mahan* destroyed them well beyond their own possible range. The telltale column of smoke from the burning ship was regrettable, but it wasn't like they could put it out now.

Jim Ellis was on the port bridge wing, watching a small boat approach. Four adult 'Cats were at the oars, and a number of younglings filled it to overflowing.

"Lower the whaleboat," he ordered. "Tow them in. We don't have all day."

Shortly, both boats were alongside, and willing hands helped the younglings to the deck. One of the adults raced to the bridge, accompanied by Lieutenant Steele.

"What's up, Frankie?" Jim asked when they arrived. Steele waved at his companion, who spoke English. He was one of the Marines who'd gone ashore with Pete.

"Cap-i-taan Ellis, Gener-aal Aalden sends his compliments. Our scout saw your approach and reported your presence."

"What's the situation?"

"Complicated and desperate," the 'Cat conceded, but there was pride in his tone. "Gener-aals Aalden and Faask defeated a large enemy force advancing from the city, but we took many casualties. They then turned on the force those ships landed"—he gestured at the burning wreck—"and struck their left flank, cutting a gap to this beach. Even now, Queen Maraan leads the wounded and noncombatants here. We have the boats of the Grik landing force, but if you can tow them out as you did us, it would help."

Ellis nodded. "Of course, but what of General Alden?"

"His force now numbers little more than a hundred. He is 'rolling up' the enemy flank—a tactic that has worked very well—but he is . . . significantly outnumbered. When the enemy stiffens its spine, he will try to hold them long enough to complete the queen's evacuation. The difficulty is, besides the numbers before him, it would seem the force approaching from the city has been reconstituted and reinforced. It will soon flank him in turn."

Ellis looked thoughtfully at the shore. The battle couldn't be far away, though he couldn't hear anything. That was still so weird!

"How long before the second force arrives?" he asked.

"An hour. Perhaps two."

"Very well." He looked at Frankie. "Here's what we'll do. You stay here, and be ready to support us with gunfire." Steele tried to protest, but Ellis continued talking. "Keep an eye out for more ships too. I'll take a company of the First Marines ashore"—he nodded at the Lemurian—"if this gentleman will be kind enough to lead us. We should be able to hammer the enemy hard enough to let Pete break contact; then it'll be hell-for-leather back to the boats." He frowned. "That means you'll have to have all the queen's people aboard, and the boats back ashore, before we need them."

"It's gonna be tight," Frankie observed.

"Sure, but . . ." Jim's eyes got a faraway, haunted look. "It'll give us . . . and *Mahan* . . . a chance to do something right for a change."

Boats plied back and forth, carrying survivors and salvaged equipment to *Walker* from the beach, while Matt listened to Silva's and Chack's reports and spoke to S-19's chief. More Marines guarded the perimeter. Even if the girl's strange pet was the only Grik on the island, there were plenty of other dangerous animals. Bradford, Keje, and Adar were still present, as was the strange one-armed man, and Matt certainly had a few questions for him, but he wanted to hear Flynn's story first. Work proceeded under Spanky's supervision while they talked. There was little heavy equipment they could take from the sub; it just wouldn't fit through a hatch. Besides, they couldn't disable it further if they hoped to salvage it later—something Matt still hoped to do. She wouldn't need her ammunition, though, and they'd discovered close to a hundred four-inch-fifty rounds.

To Matt's bitter disappointment, there'd been no torpedoes. S-19 carried only two when she left Surabaya—there just hadn't been any there, as Matt well knew—so that still left only the single MK-10 they'd scrounged. Besides, the sub had needed space for her "cargo," and couldn't have carried many more torpedoes anyway. She'd fired the two she had at a Japanese transport that blundered across her path and even got a hit, Billy claimed, but they got worked over by the transport's "tin can" escort for their trouble. That was when their problems began. The sledgehammer blows of the depth charges cracked a battery and popped a bulb, causing an explosion in the forward battery compartment. The forward crew and officers' berths—as well as the radio room—were incinerated. They shut the hatches to the torpedo room (S-19 had only one, forward) and the control room, but six men died, either burned or suffocated by chlorine gas, created by seawater flooding the damaged batteries.

Their "cargo," twenty children—mostly of diplomats and highly placed executives, as well as four nannies and a nun who'd been sent to care for them—spent several terrifying hours isolated in the torpedo room while S-19 lay on the bottom of the Java Sea, a hundred feet below her test depth. Finally, the Japanese destroyer lost interest. Pressurizing the half-flooded compartment, S-19 slowly rose to the surface after dark to vent the gas and pump out the water. Still trying to reach Fremantle (and avoid enemy planes), they barely managed to submerge the following day. That was when they heard the thrashing screws and heavy detonations of *Walker* and *Mahan*'s battle with *Amagi*. They had no idea what was going on, of course—the search periscope had been damaged by the depth charges—but that must have been what they heard, because soon after that their screws ran away and they shut the motors down. Unlike the two American destroyers' traumatic experience on the surface, that was the only effect of the Squall they felt.

Of her crew of forty-two officers and men, only twenty-six remained—and none were senior officers. The highest-ranking crewman was an ensign, who'd wisely deferred command to the more experienced chief of the boat. The rest were killed during her various attempts to land in different places, or by the local predators over the last year.

Matt could only imagine what it must have been like. He and his people had figured out pretty quickly that things were out of whack, and they'd also made some friends. S-19's people had spent the last year living on the edge, never really knowing what had happened. Except for the moment when the screws ran away, there hadn't even been a "transition event" to blame. They just went underwater on one world and came up on another. Their first idea that that might be the case came when they met fish as big as their boat. Matt shuddered. *Walker* wasn't much bigger than the sub, but she was higher out of the water and a hell of a lot faster. It didn't *feel* as much like swimming with the sharks.

"My dear Mr. Flynn," Bradford puffed, wiping sweat with his sleeve, "a dreadful adventure indeed." He peered at the one-armed man. "But who might you be, and the young lady, of course, and where did you find her fascinating . . . friend? We've tried to capture them before, you know, but . . ." He shrugged. "They simply won't surrender, you see."

The man saw them all staring at him, expecting answers. Matt noticed even Flynn appeared curious. Why would that be?

"I'm O'Casey," he said at last. "Sean O'Casey." He paused, considering, glancing at the destroyer riding at anchor in the mouth of the lagoon. "The lass's name is . . . Becky. We was shipwrecked an' these . . . fellas was good enough to pick us up. As for her 'friend,' the beastie was a maroon hi'self. We found 'im on a little isle where nothin' could survive." His voice was deep, with a kind of lilting accent that stressed unusual syllables. It was almost as if he spoke a different language, and his awkward insertion of words like "fellas" were substitutes he'd picked up.

"Found 'em floating in an open boat, drifting with the current, when we crossed from Mindanao to here," Flynn supplied. "O'Casey was almost dead. Bad fever from a recently severed arm."

Matt put his hands on his hips. "That tells us who you are, Mr. O'Casey, but not what you are, or where you come from." He looked at Flynn, who shrugged.

"He never would say, Captain. Once he got well, him and the girl sort of kept to themselves. The . . . 'beastie' was friendly enough, even if he's scary as hell, and to be honest, he prob'ly brought in more than his share of game. But the girl never played with the other kids, and O'Casey didn't talk much. Carried his weight, though, even with one arm, and after a while that was all that mattered, you know?"

"I do know, Flynn, but that's changed. It matters a lot—before I let him on my ship." He scrutinized O'Casey. "So far, I've had a better character reference for an animal whose species we're at war with. You're not a shipwreck survivor from our world at all, are you?"

"Of course he is not," Adar said, his face inscrutable, but his ears quivering with excitement. "He is a descendant of the Others, the tail-less beings that came before! The ones who taught the ancient tongue to the Prophet, Siska-Ta, then sailed across the Eastern Sea."

Conscious of Captain Reddy's veiled threat, O'Casey nodded reluctantly. He didn't think for a moment these Americans—more Americans! how much more twisted could the world his ancestors left behind have become?—would leave the girl behind, but there was a distinct possibility they'd leave him, and he wanted to get to know them better despite his need to be circumspect.

"There's old . . . tales of folk such as ye," he admitted to Adar, "an' our founders did pass through yer seas."

"I knew it!" Adar exulted. "As soon as I saw the young-ling! There is so much about our early history we can learn from you! So many missing pieces of the puzzle! Where did you ultimately go?"

"East," he said vaguely. They knew that already. "Some islands. I'll tell ye what I can, but ye must respect the fact that I know as little of ye as ye know of me. I may tell ye more as me knowledge of yer intentions . . . an' capabilities grows."

"Fair enough," Matt conceded. "You can come with us, but I'll expect further revelations." He noticed that Silva's attention had been diverted, and saw the "nannies" climbing aboard one of the boats with the remaining children. He'd spoken to them briefly. One was British but the others were Dutch. All spoke English, as did the nun. The children were about half Dutch and half English, with a young Australian boy thrown in. Dennis had pronounced one of the nannies an "old frump," but the others were young. One was even attractive, as was the young nun. She'd managed to keep her habit fairly well preserved, even her bizarre hat. The women doubled the number of human females they knew about—not counting the children—and even the "frumpy" one would probably be the object of more attention than she'd ever known. He shook his head. He'd have to speak to them again.

The whaleboat was coming back, its coxswain really laying on the coal. It smashed through the marching rollers, throwing spray, until it gained the calmer water and accelerated to the beach. Clancy leaped out and hurried to him, a message form in his hand. He looked a little green after his wild ride, but his expression was grim and purposeful.

"Captain!" he said urgently. "We picked up a faint transmission in the clear! You need to see it right away!"

A tendril of dread crept down Matt's spine as he took the sheet. "Excuse me, gentlemen," he said, walking a few paces away.

THESE SPACES FOR COMM OFFICE ONLY

TIME FILED	MSG CEN No	HOW SENT

MESSAGE
(SUBMIT TO NAVY DEPT. IN DUPLICATE)

No   DATE

TO

TO CAPTAIN REDDY FROM CAPTAIN KAUFMAN X AM CAPTIVE ON JAPANESE BATTLECRUISER AMAGI X MINORITY ELEMENT HERE BELIEVES COOPERATION AGAINST GRIK ESSENTIAL X CANNOT REPEAT CANNOT GUARANTEE COOPERATION X YOU MUST EXPEDITE OR ABANDON WALKER RESCUE MISSION B'MBAADO X GRIK SWARM UNDERWAY X AMAGI ALMOST READY FOR SEA AND WILL FOLLOW WITHIN DAYS X JAPANESE AIR NO THREAT X OB PLANE DAMAGED BOMBING BAALKPAN X ONLY OPPORTUNITY FOR WARNING X DO NOT REPEAT DO NOT RESPOND X SORRY ABOUT MAHAN X TRANSMISSION ENDS

OFFICIAL DESIGNATION OF SENDER	TIME SIGNED

SIGNATURE AND GRADE OF WRITER	*Clancy*

"God*damn* it!" Matt swore. He looked at Silva. "Tell Lieutenant McFarlane our scavenger hunt's over. He's to be in the next boat back to the ship, and I want number three lit off."

"What's up, Skipper?"

"We're out of time."

"Hurry up, damn it!" Ellis shouted as half his surviving, exhausted Marines streamed back through the open ranks of the other half. Close on their heels came whickering arrows and a roaring tide of Grik. They'd fought all day, and the late-afternoon sun glared mercilessly upon them. They'd made the beach at last, and all the refugees were safely aboard ship except Queen Maraan, Haakar-Faask, and the tiny knot of remaining Guardsmen. Pete was still there as well, woozy from fatigue and loss of blood, but he wouldn't leave before the queen and his new friend, Haakar-Faask, and *they* wouldn't leave while anyone else remained. Idiots! Jim was tempted to knock them all on the head and have them carried to the boats.

Mahan's guns opened up, now that they knew exactly where their friends were, and massive concussions burst in the trees beyond the beach, sending shrapnel and blizzards of splinters into the greater mass of Grik infantry. Tracers arced overhead toward the enemy as well, and the weight of the assault began to ease. There were still the berserkers out front, however.

"Second rank, present!" Ellis yelled, voice cracking. *"Fire!"* The volley staggered the enemy, and a cloud of fine sand erupted when dozens of bodies hit the ground. "Fire at will!" he commanded, and the staccato report of thirty-odd Krags competed with the explosions in the trees. He whirled to those he'd come to save, angry at their stubbornness. "The time's come for you to act responsibly! We need to get off this beach, and there're people dying so you can satisfy your 'honor' and be the very last ones! That's not going to happen." He looked at Safir. For the first time since he'd met her, she looked utterly spent. Her garments were torn, and her silver breastplate was tarnished and splashed with blood. "We didn't just come get you because we gave our word not to leave anyone behind; we came because we *need* you!" His gaze slashed Alden, who was covered with blood from many superficial cuts. "*All* of you! This'll have been for nothing if you get your asses killed now!" He pointed where the other Marines were forming in front of the boats. "This isn't just about you; it's not your decision. Winning the war's a lot more important than this pissant little fight!"

Faask whispered urgently to his queen, and finally she jerked a tearful nod. Grabbing Alden's bloody shirt, she pulled him toward the boats, leaving behind Faask and the dozen real warriors he had left. Ellis looked at him, and Faask grinned back.

"You will not leave before the last of your Marines, will you?" Ellis didn't answer, and Haakar-Faask laughed. "You are important too, you know. When you finally enter the boats, someone must keep them away." He drew his sword and looked at the notched, blood-encrusted blade. "To talk of 'winning the war' is very well. It is also true. But I am old, and I have seen my world collapse. I think this 'pissant little fight' will be enough for me."

Jim was the last to climb the rungs to *Mahan*'s deck. He was sick with sorrow at what he'd seen, but also filled with pride. The Orphan Queen's tear-soaked face was the first he saw, and on impulse he embraced her briefly. When he stepped back, he saw her looking at the beach where hundreds of Grik, no longer galled by *Mahan*'s guns, capered gleefully over the scattered corpses. One waved a severed leg above its head, bloody teeth still chewing.

"I'd love to bust those bastards up!" growled number three's gun captain, just above his head on the amidships deckhouse.

"No point," Ellis replied. "Save your ammunition."

A 'Cat signal striker raced up. "Skipper!" he said. "Lookout says sails to the north! Many, many sails!"

Dowden, Campeti, and *Walker*'s other officers were waiting when Matt and the last of the shore party came aboard, already laying plans. The sun lay on the horizon, and the long day was nearly spent. Menacing clouds roiled in the east, and the rollers had a distinct chop. All except O'Casey saluted the colors, but no time was wasted on ceremony. Many of the crew stood watching, wide-eyed.

". . . I *think* we've got the fuel for it, but . . ." Spanky continued, joining Matt on deck. He looked around at the many faces and stopped. Swearing, he shook his head and disappeared down the companionway, bellowing for Laney. Matt's eyes found Dowden's.

"Plot a least-distance, least-time course for Baalkpan, via Tarakan. Consult Spanky and determine our best speed, without getting home completely dry. We might show up in the middle of a battle. Have Clancy transmit 'on our way, *Walker*' over and over. Standard code. Maybe they can hear us, even if we can't hear them."

O'Casey was staring around at the ship, as curious about it as about the sudden activity. He'd been offended when they took his antique weapon away, and resisted giving it up—until Silva and Stites had "insisted." Stites had discovered several more muskets at the castaways' camp, and, never one to abandon any weapon, he'd brought them along. O'Casey wasn't overawed by the ship, exactly, but he did seem amazed. And envious. He stiffened when he heard the word "battle," however. Silva was watching him at the time, and noticed the reaction.

"Aye, aye, sir," Dowden answered. "Uh, Captain, I've taken the liberty of putting the children and their chaperones in the chief's berthing spaces, and moving the chiefs to available officers' and enlisted berths, based on seniority. I've also begun entering S-19's survivors in the books. We'll have to see who fits where best; they're not destroyermen, after all."

"Of course." Matt knew when Dowden was beating around a bush. It was his job to sort out everything he'd reported, and unnecessary for him to report it. "What else?"

"Well, sorry, Skipper, but there's two things, actually. First, the girl with the pet Grik won't berth with the other kids. Says she'll only berth with Mr. O'Casey here, and she won't leave the damn lizard till we have a look at him and promise not to hurt him."

Matt looked at Bradford, still puffing from his climb. "Go have a look. You're our expert on Grik anatomy. Have Jamie give you a hand." He paused. "Silva?"

"Skipper?"

"Go with him. Damn thing may be tame as a puppy, but if it even looks cross-eyed, blow its head off."

"Aye, aye, sir!"

Silva and Bradford clambered down the metal stairs.

"I will accompany them," Adar proclaimed. "I am curious about this 'tame' Grik, but I would get to know the youngling better."

Matt nodded. "Me too. See what you can find out." He looked back at Dowden. "What else?"

"Well, Skipper, it's the nun. Says they all appreciate being rescued, but she'd like to speak with you again. She hopes . . . you won't be so 'rude' next time."

"*Rude?*"

Dowden shrugged, and Matt rolled his eyes.

"Maybe later. Chack?"

"Sir?"

"Assemble your sea and anchor detail, and prepare to pull the hook. We're getting underway."

"Aye, aye, Cap-i-taan."

All that remained were Keje, and *Walker*'s officers. Captain Reddy turned to O'Casey.

"We're about to leave your island resort behind, and I've made good on my part of the deal. We're all going to the pilothouse now. Things are going to be busy while we get underway, but as soon as I have a free moment, you'll be standing right there, ready to pay your passage. I have some questions and you're going to answer them."

"Very well, Captain. I've a few questions of me own, if ye please. Ye say we might be headed fer a battle. Might I ask who you expect to fight?"

Ignoring O'Casey, Matt turned and strode purposely toward the bridge, leaving his surprised entourage hurrying to catch up. Taking the steps two at a time, he arrived in the pilothouse, preceded by his own shouted, "As you were!" Facing the startled OOD, he announced: "I have the deck and the conn. Make all preparations for getting underway." He looked speculatively back at O'Casey, as the one-armed man reached the top of the stairs.

"We're at war with creatures like your young lady's pet, and they're on their way to attack our . . . our home. Maybe a few hundred thousand of 'em. The first thing I want to know is how you made friends with one."

Silva, Courtney, and Adar slid the green wardroom curtain aside. Silva had handed his BAR to Stites, who'd recover the rest of the shore party's arms. All he had was his .45 and cutlass, but the Colt was in his hand. The lizard lay on the wardroom table, moaning as the rolling ship caused him to shift back and forth under the lowered operating light. The girl sat beside him on a chair, petting him reassuringly, and glaring at the new arrivals. Jamie Miller, former pharmacist's mate, and now *Walker*'s surgeon, nervously gathered his instruments and laid them out.

"Critter give you any trouble, Jamie?" Silva gruffed.

"No . . . it's just . . . Shit, Dennis, it's a Grik!"

"Noticed that myself. So what? Ain't you got a hypocritical oath, or somethin'? Patch him up."

"Hippocratic," murmured Bradford, moving raptly toward the creature. The girl stood unsteadily, but hovered protectively near. "We won't hurt him, child, I assure you. You must understand; I've never been this close to a *live* one before that wasn't trying to eat me." The girl jumped at the rush of iron links flooding into the chain locker forward. "There, there," Bradford soothed, "nothing to fear, the racket is quite normal, I'm afraid. Please do sit again, before you fall and hurt yourself. We're old salts, and quite used to this abominable motion."

Silva smirked.

"You said his name is Lawrence?" Bradford continued, ignoring the big man.

The girl nodded. "I named him that," she said.

"And you're Becky? How interesting. Charmed, of course, and very pleased to make your acquaintance."

Soon the ship came alive beneath their feet, and the nauseating pitching motion became more bearable as *Walker* accelerated into the swells. Becky finally sat, but continued glaring at Silva.

"I don't want that evil man in the same room with my poor friend," she insisted. "If Lawrence is to die, I prefer it not be in the presence of his murderer!"

"Now see here, girlie!" Silva protested.

"My name is *not* 'girlie'!"

"Calm yourself, child!" Bradford pleaded. "Mr. Silva cannot leave; he has his orders. Besides, he didn't mean to injure your friend; it was a dreadful misunderstanding!"

"He did too," the girl fumed. "And my name is not 'child' either!"

"Of course, my dear. I apologize." Bradford glanced hurriedly at the wounded Grik. "I think your friend will recover well enough. The wound is painful, certainly, but not fatal, if my memory of his anatomy serves. The bullet passed cleanly through his left pectoral muscle, left to right, and if you allow us, Mr. Miller has some salve that should accelerate the healing process and prevent infection. It will also ease his pain. May he proceed?"

Becky sighed. "Of course, but please hurry!"

Jamie advanced hesitantly with the Lemurian antiseptic, analgesic paste, made from fermented polta fruit, on a wooden spatula. The creature seemed to understand the conversation, as well as Jamie's intent, and lay docile, waiting for him to apply the medicine. Jamie gulped and did so. Within moments the creature's tense, straining muscles began to relax, and it sighed in evident relief.

"Do you feel better now, my dear?" the girl crooned.

"'Etter. Thank you."

"Well . . . good," Silva gruffed, strangely moved. His world had been turned upside down yet again. Here was a Grik, a member of a species so terrible it almost defied comprehension. Yet lying there with a child stroking its brow, it looked almost vulnerable and benign. What was more, not only did it understand what they said, but it could speak. It was even polite! He scratched his beard sheepishly, glancing around. "Sorry I shot you. Maybe there's good Griks and bad Griks, just like good people and Japs."

"I not Grik," it said, almost dreamily now, another effect of the paste. "I Tagranesi, on islands east-south. I lost, like 'riend 'Ecky." Its eyelids fluttered. "I sorry you shoot too."

"He'll sleep now," Bradford assured the girl. "Mr. Miller will bind his wounds."

"Uh . . . I don't want to bug him," Jamie almost sputtered. "Why don't I wait until he *is* asleep?"

Bradford rolled his eyes. "He's quite harmless."

"I wouldn't say that," disputed Silva, then paused. After a moment he dropped his pistol in his holster and buttoned the flap. "But maybe he ain't dangerous, if you know what I mean." He looked at the girl again. "I'm sorry to you too. I never would've figgered it. You want somethin' to eat?"

Becky started to flare at him again, but caught herself and just sat, looking disoriented.

"I . . . I suppose. Yes, thank you . . . Mr. Silva."

Once summoned, Juan brought a tray of sandwiches and bowed. "It is a great pleasure," he said, "to have a young lady as beautiful as you grace our poor, drab ship. It has been too long!" He looked her over. "I will see if I can find more suitable clothes to replace those rags."

Becky paused before taking a bite of one of the steaming sandwiches. "Why . . . thank you. You are very kind."

"De nada," Juan said, and departed.

"Was that Spanish?" the girl asked, shocked.

"Sorta," answered Silva, surprised. If she was one of these "Others" Adar always spoke of, where'd she learn to recognize Spanish? he wondered. "He's Filipino. You know who they are?" Becky didn't answer, but dove into her sandwich. They munched companionably, seated around the unconscious lizard. Everyone was famished, and the stack of sandwiches soon disappeared.

"My dear—" began Adar.

"Young lady . . ." interrupted Bradford.

"Whoa!" said Silva. "Damn, fellas! She just ate. Give her a while." He looked into her large, jade eyes. "You tired?"

"Not especially." She saw the light dimming beyond the porthole. "I suppose I should be; this is the time of day we usually prepared our defenses for the night."

"Mmm," Silva replied. It must have been tough living on that island, fighting off nightly incursions by predators, both by land and from the trees. The shore party hadn't encountered anything dangerous, but Flynn had described some particularly terrifying creatures that dropped on them at night from above. They'd quickly learned to keep to the clearings. "Don't have to do that tonight, doll. Yer safe as can be! How about a evenin' stroll? I'll show you around the ship!" He caught Adar's eye and winked.

"I really shouldn't . . . Mr. O'Casey . . ."

"O'Casey'll be busy talkin' to the skipper till who knows when."

The girl stood and, with a final glance at her sleeping friend, nodded. "Very well then, if it isn't any trouble. I must admit to an intense curiosity about your ship." She paused. "I must also admit I misjudged you, Mr. Silva. I still dislike you, but perhaps that may pass as well. I apologize for attacking you."

"Good thing you did," Dennis admitted, also looking at her friend. "I *would've* killed him if you hadn't."

"Just so. Very well, then, please do lead the way."

They left the others behind, mouths agape like beached fish, and climbed the companionway to the open deck. Silva described the various features of the ship visible from where they stood: the back of the bridge, the funnels, the amidships deckhouse. He noticed she was particularly interested in the four-inch guns atop it on either side, fascinated by the rifling at their muzzles.

"What are those twisty grooves for? I've seen many cannons, but nothing like them."

Silva blinked, hesitating, then laughed. "Why, they spin the bullets. Makes 'em fly straighter."

"Oh."

Her tone sounded like he'd satisfied a long-burning question. Surely she'd seen the gun on the sub? Maybe she'd never asked the pigboat pukes. O'Casey'd probably told her not to. Silva remembered Flynn telling them she never played with the other kids, and suddenly realized that despite O'Casey, she'd probably been very lonely indeed. They passed under the platform and walked by the galley, ignoring Lanier's strident criticism of his assistants. Standing between the port and starboard torpedo mounts, the small girl got her first look at the passing sea.

"My goodness!" she declared. "This is a very fast ship! How fast can it go?"

"'Bout twice as fast as this, give or take." He looked at her. "How old are you?"

Her eyes never left the surging wake. "I'll soon be ten," she answered absently.

"Lordy. You look six and act twenty!" His tone prevented her from taking offense. "You on that island a whole year with them submariners?"

"Indeed. They picked us up at sea after our ship was destroyed by a leviathan. It was terrifying."

"If 'levy-than' means what I think it does, I know what you mean," he agreed. "Them big boogers scare me to death!"

She glanced at him with a tentative, impish smile. "I cannot imagine you frightened."

"Mmm. Well, I was. A little. Least I sunk one of the bastards!"

She giggled. It was such an unusual, forgotten sound it almost broke his heart.

"Did not! What a villainous liar you are! Besides, I asked you before to control your language."

"Did too!" Dennis insisted, willing away the strange, fluttery sensation in his chest. "With the four mount! Shot him right in the mouth! Course, the depth charges might've helped, but that don't matter." He looked at her. "Besides, you called me a 'bastard.' I figgered I could say it."

She giggled again, and held her hand over her mouth. "I *am* sorry. What would Master Kearley say?" Her expression grew sad. "Poor man. He knew he was doomed, but he saved my life, as did Mr. O'Casey."

"Master Kearley?"

"My tutor. He . . . didn't make it off the ship."

"How long were you adrift?" Dennis asked gently.

"Something over four weeks. I'm not certain. We had plenty of provisions—just two of us in a boat meant for twenty. Still, it was terrifying. There are few silverfish in the deep waters to the east, but there are other things." She shuddered.

Silva took a pouch from his pocket, loosened the string at the top, and removed a plug of yellow-brown leaves. He bit off a wad and worked it for a moment until it formed a bulge in his right cheek. Seeing her watching him, wide-eyed, he graciously offered the pouch. "Chew?" Revolted but intrigued, she shook her head. "Suit yerself," he said, and pulling the string tight, he returned the pouch to his pocket. "Where'd you come up with Lawrence, anyway? Flynn said he was in your boat."

"He was. We found him on an island we landed upon, searching for a place with food and water closer to . . . where our people might search for us. There wasn't any, but he'd been there several days, a castaway as much as we. All he had was a dugout canoe, and no idea which direction to head! His species is not unknown to us, a few meetings on isolated islands southeast of my home somewhere. But I'd never seen one before!"

"Peaceful meetings?" he asked, apparently astonished.

"I believe so, yes."

"I'll swan. Where's home?" Dennis ventured.

She started to answer, then caught herself. "Are you interrogating me?"

"Yep."

Hands on hips, she looked up at him. "How rude! A gentleman never pries into the affairs of a . . . a young lady!"

Silva shrugged, a twisted grin on his face. "I ain't no gentleman, doll. 'Sides, whose rules are those?"

"Why . . . they're society's rules—the rules of civilization."

"Land rules."

"Not just 'land' rules!"

"There's other rules, you know. Sea rules. When somebody rescues castaways, either adrift or ashore, he can ask 'em anything he wants."

The girl became pensive. "Truly?"

"Yep."

"Must one always answer such questions?"

Silva laughed, a deep, booming laugh that drew the attention of those working nearby. "Not always, doll, but it's sorta rude not to."

"Do you have to answer my questions too?"

"No, but I will. I already have, some."

She pointed at Chack, supervising a deck crew lashing covers over the fireroom skylights. Silva was expecting a blow, and it looked like the skipper was too. "What are those creatures?"

" 'Cats. Cat-monkeys, monkey-cats—Bradford calls 'em 'Lemurians,' and I guess that's stuck, but most fellas just call 'em 'Cats. They have another word for theirselves—can't remember it—that means 'People.' They're good folks, too: smart as a whip and twice as strong. Hell, Adar—that's the fella in the wardroom—and Keje are prob'ly the smartest fellas I know. Them and the skipper."

"Skipper?"

"Captain Reddy, to little girls."

"He mentioned a battle, and several times people have acted afraid of poor Lawrence—and you shot him, of course! What is that about?" She seemed genuinely curious, so Silva told her. He wasn't used to talking to kids, especially ones who acted so grown-up, so he didn't pull any punches. When he was finished, she just stared at the wake. They'd moved to the rail while he spoke, and she was leaning on it now. "So you Americans are fighting for the freedom and safety of others, essentially. You yourselves could simply leave, if you wished."

He spit a yellowish stream over the side, and she shuddered. "Well, sure. But where would we go?"

"You could . . ." She stopped herself again, and shook her head. "It makes no difference. You wouldn't leave even if you could. You are engaged in a noble war, a holy war. A war against absolute evil." In a small voice she added, "I think Father would approve . . . almost envy you that." Her face was suddenly stricken. "Oh, Lawrence will be so upset to discover others of his kind behave so!"

"That's okay. There's others no more different from us than he is to Griks, helpin' 'em. Buncha Japs, with a great big battle cruiser. Could eat us alive, like one o' them 'levy-than' things."

"Yet still you stay?"

Silva shrugged. " 'Tween the Japs and Griks, I've lost 'most every friend I ever had. It may be a 'noble holy war' to some, but to me—and the Skipper too, I think—it's plain ol' simple revenge." He was almost shocked out of his wits when he felt her warm, tiny hand crawl into his massive paw.

"You have a new friend now, Mr. Silva, even if you are a disgusting beast. I don't dislike you anymore at all. I have another question, though."

"Shoot," he said, still rattled.

"Why do you call me 'doll'?"

He was silent a moment, watching the lightning off the starboard quarter; then he sighed. "You don't like 'girlie' or 'child,' and you don't look like a 'Becky' to me. . . ." He shrugged. "You look like a doll. A fragile china doll. Dirty, shaggy haired, with raggy clothes, and you need a good washin', but underneath, you're a beautiful china doll." He growled incoherently and shook his head. "Say, while yer all dirty, you wanna see the engines?"

Later, in the wardroom, Silva made his report. He stood as if he didn't notice the deck heaving beneath his feet, and he probably didn't. The ship was pounding through the rising swells of the Celebes Sea at twenty-two knots, and the storm that had stalked them for the last couple days in the east was chasing them now in earnest. It was a godsend, in a way; it kept the monstrous fish from basking in the surface sun, and the lashing sonar chased away those lurking in their path. Their speed outpaced any that rose behind them.

Every officer was present except Campeti, who had the watch. Flynn and his nominal superior, Ensign Laumer, sat beside the captain. Adar, Keje, Bradford, and Chack were also there, as were a couple of Chack's senior Marines. Silva felt awkward being the center of attention in such a . . . respectable way . . . and also felt uneasy recounting his conversation with the girl, as if he were betraying her confidence. Still, despite the girl's obvious attempts to conceal certain things, he'd gathered a lot of information the captain needed.

"We already knew their ship was wrecked by a mountain fish," he began, "an' they were the only survivors. Girl had a tutor named Curly er somethin' who didn't make it, so I figger she's sorta 'somebody.' I thought that anyway 'cause of her name. She just don't seem like a 'Becky' to me. That might be a nickname, er part of her real name, but I don't think she's used to goin' by it."

"I got that impression too," Matt murmured thoughtfully. "Please continue."

"Yes, sir. Anyway, she said they'd drifted on the current four or five weeks from the 'deep water to the east' and went ashore on an island close to their own shipping lanes. They had to leave 'cause there wasn't no food er water, but that's where they picked up their lizard. She'd never seen one, but knew about 'em. Said they came from islands to the southeast of her home, and there'd been contact with the critters before. She also didn't seem to think it unusual for it to be friendly. Said her friend'd be upset how vicious 'our' Griks are."

"Good God!" Bradford exclaimed. "If there was no food or water on the island, why was the creature there, and how did it survive?"

"'Marooned' too. Showed up on a dugout canoe."

Adar and Keje exchanged significant glances, and Bradford sputtered: "By canoe on such a sea! But that certainly explains much. I've often wondered why the 'aboriginal' Grik seem so prolific from one land to another, when other creatures don't. I've studied our sleeping guest, and though there's no question he's the same *species* as our enemy, he's clearly an entirely different *race*—as different as Europeans from Polynesians! Perhaps his race evolved a different sociology—less violent! Oh, I can't wait to speak to him!"

Silva shrugged. "Could be. Maybe we could raise a regiment: Comp'ny A, First Stripey Lizards!"

Matt scowled, looking at Adar's disgusted blinking. "Mr. Silva . . ."

"Oh. Yes, sir. I picked up some technical things too. Granted, she's only ten, but she was very int'rested in our guns and engines. Not shocked, she *knew* what they were, just amazed by what they could do."

Matt nodded. "I got the same sense from O'Casey, though I admit you picked up more information than I did. How'd you do it?"

Dennis grinned. "She's a kid, Skipper. So am I. Just a great big kid."

Matt sipped his coffee and rubbed his chin. "Well, between us, we learned a lot. Almost as much from what they didn't say as what they did. They obviously don't want us to know where they're from. Normal reluctance to reveal too much before they get to know us, or societal paranoia?" He paused. "Either way, they're from the east. Adar suspected as much as soon as he saw the girl, and then we learned they weren't part of S-19's 'cargo.' Now we're sure. They're descendants of the 'Others' that passed through here before. Looking at a map, we could probably extrapolate a pretty good estimate of where their home is.

"They know about guns—witness the muskets—although according to Mr. Bradford, they're virtually unchanged from those the original East Indiamen would've carried. The girl said they have artillery as well, even if it's not any more advanced. That tells us something right there. In all this time, they haven't had any reason to improve their weaponry, so they never did. In our own history, flintlocks reigned supreme for two hundred and fifty years, and reached a level of refinement that couldn't be improved upon. Only constant wars with equally well-armed opponents spurred the innovations we made in the last century. So wherever they are, they must be on top of the heap, and there must not be any really dangerous animals. Steam power's something else they must have. Like Silva said, they're impressed by how fast we can go, but not shocked we do it without sails."

He drummed his fingers on the tabletop the Grik-like creature had lain on most of the afternoon. "All fascinating mysteries I look forward to solving, and it's good to know, at long last, that there *are* other humans on this world. Right now, though, we have more pressing concerns." He opened the note he'd received from Clancy and read most of it aloud. They already knew the gist, but each point needed discussion, and he wanted it fresh in their minds. He slapped the table with the message form. "I have no choice but to believe this is genuine. Kaufman's apology at the end, while also probably genuine, is clearly meant to convince us he is who he says he is."

"But how in hell did the bas . . . did he get access to their comm equipment?" Spanky grumbled dubiously.

"With the help of the disaffected 'elements,'" Dowden speculated. "Probably wouldn't be too hard; it's not like they have a lot of folks to talk to. Most likely just a comm watch to see what *we're* saying."

"But what of the rest of it?" Adar demanded heatedly. "This warning to *us*! A warning that the enemy moves, and we must complete or abandon our 'rescue' attempt? How could they know of that?"

"Simple," Matt answered grimly. "Kaufman's not talking to *us*. He thinks he is, because *Mahan*'s disguise has fooled them. For whatever reason, Jim's taken her to B'mbaado."

All those present, except the submariners, knew that was against Matt's direct orders. They also knew that if Jim Ellis went against those orders, there'd been a damn good reason.

"I've felt something was wrong ever since we lost communications. Felt it in my bones," he confessed. "They must've taken out the radio with this bombing the note refers to." He rubbed his eyes. "Damn! We should've headed back two weeks ago!" Glancing at Flynn and Laumer, he allowed a wry smile. "Sorry. I'm damn glad we found you, but we may not have done you any favors."

"I don't understand, Captain," Laumer replied. The lanky ensign was very young, and probably hadn't been out of submarine school for a month before the war started, back home. As S-19's sole surviving officer, he'd shown unusual maturity by letting the more experienced chief take the lead. He clearly wasn't a coward, and Flynn continued to show proper deference and respect even if he was making the decisions. Matt suspected Laumer would shape into a good officer.

"We probably just dragged you out of the frying pan, into the fire. With us." In response to their blank expressions, *Walker*'s people began to explain.

The storm was a bad one, and it lashed them with its fury throughout the night, even though they caught only the edge. By morning the worst had rumbled into the south-southwest to slam against northern Celebes. Tabby had been seasick again, but not debilitated this time. She'd spent most of her life aboard *Salissa*, barely noticing any but the most severe storms, and the first she'd weathered on tiny *Walker*—a Strakka at that—left her unable to do anything but moan and wallow in vomit. She must finally be getting her "sea legs," as Gilbert called them, and this time it hadn't been so bad. She could only shudder at the thought of the misery she'd have endured if the storm hit them full-on, however.

The sky was still gray, the sea still choppy when she and Gilbert went to the galley for a late breakfast. Lanier complained, of course, about "snipes wandering in any old time, whenever they felt like it," to eat, but they paid him no heed. The griping was desultory anyway; Lanier was in a pretty good mood, since the Coke machine had weathered the storm, still chugging away, cooling the empty space inside. Tabby still didn't understand why that was cause for such celebration, but if the irascible cook was happy, the food would be better.

She and Gilbert munched egg sandwiches under the gun platform protecting them from a persistent drizzle and looked around. Something had the crew's attention forward, under the pilothouse deck. They moved over to see what it was, and were stunned to discover a tiger-striped Grik reclined on a mattress pad, with a semicircle of men and 'Cats gathered around. Bradford was there, sitting on a chair, as were Silva, Adar, and several small children.

"Holy smokes," Gilbert said. "A Grik!"

"He's tame," Stites said, hearing him. "Didn't you know he was here?"

"No. We been workin'. Where'd all the scudders come from?"

Stites looked at him. "You need to get out more."

"I been tryin'!" Gilbert replied, almost plaintively.

Stites shrugged. "We took him, the kids, and a couple dozen pigboat pukes off Talaud." He leered. "Got a couple new women too, but, except for some nun, they ain't showed their faces yet. The nun keeps tryin' to pester the skipper."

"You don't say?" Gilbert scratched his ear and pointed at the "Grik." "Bradford gonna di-sect him?"

Stites laughed. "Hell, no! He's friendly as a hungry pup. The Aussie's been talkin' to him just like he was a person. Silva shot him and he's a little sore, but I swear, sometimes you can even understand what he says! Talks a little like one o' you Georgia crackers, though."

"I ain't from Georgia, you damn Yankee!"

Stites shrugged again. "All you snipes sound the same to me."

"What about Spanky? You understand him fine."

"He ain't from Georgia."

Gilbert shook his head. Everyone "on deck" talked weird as far as he was concerned; so much of their language was salted with archaic nautical terms. He was more accustomed to technical and mechanical jargon.

"Laney's a snipe and anybody understand him," Tabby pointed out. "All he do is cuss." They applied their attention to the bizarre conversation taking place in front of them.

"South of the overhead sun!" Bradford gushed. "How exciting! Do you think you could point out your home on a map?"

"What is . . . 'ap'?" the creature replied.

"Oh, dear. Well, a map is like a picture of the world. It shows where places are." The creature looked blank. "Never mind, I'm sure we'll sort it out. Tell me, though, why on earth were you paddling around the open ocean in a canoe?"

"I grow . . . turn into adult. It time I leave nest, show I adult."

"A rite of passage? Face the dangers of the world and prove you're no longer a . . . a child?"

"Essentially. To ha', to take . . ." He struggled for a word. Bradford had learned there was no limit to the creature's vocabulary, but there were some words he simply couldn't say. Anything requiring the use of lips, for example, was impossible. He understood the words; he just couldn't form them. "To ha', to earn right to . . ."

"Mate?" Bradford supplied.

"Yess! 'Ate! I show strength, courage, I return." He looked down. "I never return, now."

Bradford blinked. "Don't be so downcast. Perhaps you will. This dreadful war can't last forever!"

Becky stirred and looked at Bradford. "Perhaps I should explain. Listening to you two hash this out is excruciating! I've had much longer to get to know him." She looked at those gathered around, particularly the other children. "Mr. Silva has told me castaways should answer questions, but must poor Lawrence do it in front of so many superfluous persons?" One of the little girls sat up straight and sniffed. Becky glared at her. "You have always taunted him as a beast! He has no obligation to unburden himself to you!"

"Not me! I think he's fascinating!" exclaimed a scruffy-looking boy in an incongruous upper-crust English accent. Becky rewarded him alone with a small smile.

"You are always so mean!" squealed the haughty girl. All but the boy loudly agreed.

"Children!" protested Bradford. He turned to Silva. "Surely the crew has other duties," he suggested, "and perhaps these children have had enough fresh air?"

"You bet. Move along, fellas, before somebody gives you work. Kiddies, I think Stites'll take you back below."

"But it stinks down there!" a Dutch girl complained.

"Honest sweat," Stites proclaimed piously, "won't hurt you." Amid whining complaints, he shooed the children down the companionway, while the other observers slunk off.

"You mind if we stick here, Dennis? Mr. Bradford?" Gilbert asked.

Becky glanced at them and did a double take. "Good heavens, that one's female!" Silva laughed, and the girl glared at him.

Gilbert was startled, then looked at Tabby. She was wearing a T-shirt at least, but it was soaking wet. "Yeah, well, I guess."

"There are many others aboard, my dear," Bradford said. "Our allies have unusual mores. Please think nothing of it."

"Think nothing of it . . . ?" Becky shook her head. "Unusual indeed. I thought I'd noticed a couple on deck wearing nothing but kilts, but believed I'd imagined it."

"Can we stay?" Gilbert persisted. "We been in the fire room and ain't seen ya'll yet."

"Very well," Becky replied, still shaking her head and looking at Tabby. "Let me see, as best I understand it, Lawrence's people are quite wild when they hatch—from eggs, you know—and run loose on an island near their home until they reach a certain level of maturity. Not age, necessarily, but a level of self-awareness. They are guided and taught by adults the whole time, but there is little supervision. Just enough to keep them from reverting to savagery. When they do become self-aware, the instruction becomes more intense until, ultimately, they are judged fit to enter society. They demonstrate their ability to reason and use tools by building their own boat in which to return, but they must do so by way of a more distant island, where they must face a final test of courage and resourcefulness. Poor Lawrence completed his test, but a storm took him far from his return course. When we found him, he was dying of thirst and hunger."

"What was the final test?" Courtney asked.

"He won't speak of it. To do so with others who haven't completed it is forbidden."

"I see. Hmm. Fascinating . . . and informative. I have just a few more questions. Obviously Lawrence's species, like the Grik and, well, us, I suppose, are predators. I assume they hunt?"

Becky looked at Lawrence, who said, "O' course."

Bradford blinked. "Oh, please do forgive me; I'm afraid I've fallen into talking as if you're not here."

"It's all right," Lawrence assured him. " 'Ecky?"

The girl frowned. "Well, of course. As you say, his people are predators.

They hunt, but they also raise domestic livestock of sorts, though we've never discussed what kind."

"Fascinating!" Bradford beamed. "But I hoped he might describe *how* his people hunt."

Becky seemed troubled by the line of questioning. "Well, he's spoken of a vague understanding of how his culture allocates labor—you must remember he had not yet joined 'society' as it were—and did not yet know his place within it. But evidently there are different castes among his people; some are herders, some hunters, others are artisans—boatbuilders and the like."

"But he received some small instruction in the basics of each of these?"

"Yes."

"So, how was he taught to hunt?"

"Cooperatively. Much like our own people would, if they had to for survival, and weren't just 'sport shooting.'"

"Are there other predators his people must compete with?"

Becky looked blank, and Lawrence answered for her: "Yes. Shiksaks. Dangerous, scary creatures. They take our li'stock. O'ten kill Tagranesi. Tagranesi hunt. Lots hunters against single Shiksak; Shiksak hard to kill. Shiksaks go sea and land. Thrice size Tagranesi."

"Indeed? Tell me, Lawrence, do your people ever hunt these creatures for sport?"

Lawrence managed an expression of surprise. "S'ort? Insane?"

"Hmm. Sounds as though it would be, yet you can never be entirely rid of them if they're amphibious. And so large! I'd love to see one!"

Lawrence shook his head. "See alone, you die."

Bradford's eyebrows furrowed. "So you do understand theoretical situations then. Marvelous! Tell me, if one of these 'Shiksaks' were making a nuisance of himself and your hunters went after him—had him cornered—and another 'Shiksak' suddenly attacked without warning, by surprise, what would they do?"

"Not . . . can't occur. Shiksaks hate each other. Not hunt together."

"Glad to hear it, but what if they did?"

Lawrence blinked, clearly contemplating the possibility. "Hunters scared?" he finally answered. "Run a'ay."

Bradford realized he'd been leaning forward, anticipating the answer. When it came, he eased back with a sigh. "Quite understandable. Very well. I have only one more question: are your people violent at all? I mean, do they fight others of their kind . . . or any other sentient species, perhaps?"

Lawrence turned to Becky. This was a subject they must have discussed.

"They sometimes fight invaders from other islands," she confessed guardedly. "They do not attack others."

"When they fight, do they ever . . . eat their enemies?"

"No!" interrupted Lawrence. "Disgusting thought! Never eat others . . ."

"They never *eat* other intelligent beings!" Becky finished for him. "What a revolting and insulting question! I might ask the same of you!"

Bradford breathed. "I apologize. We and our allies do not, of course, do such things, but"—he pointed at Lawrence—"the others of his kind, whom we fight, most certainly do. They even eat each other. It was a question I had to ask." He stood. "Now, if you'll excuse me, I must tinker with my journal, write a few things down, you see."

hief Bosun's Mate Fitzhugh Gray sat on a charred stump—about all that remained of his quarters. His face was soot blackened, streaked with sweat, and spattered with blood. His new uniform was destroyed, and it hung on him in rags. A bandage encircled his wrist, and the viscous purple of the Lemurian paste oozed from underneath it. The usual westerly breeze had stalled, as if deciding whether to come around out of the east, and smoke hung over the island like a pall. So did the stench. Their Lemurian dead were already gathered for their pyre, but there was nothing left to burn them with. A few colonists from the mainland, graw-fishers, had sailed out last night and, after viewing the scene with a horror beyond their isolated experience, solemnly promised to return with wood.

Three American dead were buried early that morning, Lieutenant Clark among them. Gray felt responsible for that. He'd severely reprimanded the young lieutenant, and he'd deserved it, but maybe he'd been too severe? As if to atone, Clark had put himself forward in the terrible fighting, and it cost him his life. All young officers make mistakes, and Clark's had been a doozy, but he'd had the makings of a good commander. He'd just been too young and inexperienced for the position he'd held, and then been too immature to accept his mistake and learn from it. The other two humans had died fighting as well, but they hadn't practically courted death as Clark had done. Now three lonely graves, and a marker for the Lemurian dead, would forever bear witness to the price they'd paid for this place.

Hundreds of Grik still lay where they'd fallen, covered with buzzing insects and strange-looking crabs. They didn't know what to do with them; they couldn't just throw them in the surf. Flashies didn't come that shallow, and they'd just wash up again. The surviving Marines and Guardsmen were too exhausted to bury them, though. Maybe when they'd rested a bit, they could heap them on the barges and tow them to deeper water. It would take a lot of trips. . . .

A few days earlier it would have seemed very strange if Gray and Shinya even said "good morning." Now, when the equally bedraggled Japanese officer sat heavily beside him and offered his canteen, Gray nodded his thanks.

"Mr. Bradford will scold us cruelly," Shinya said softly. Gray grunted and took a sip. The island's jungle was gone now, all of it. He wasn't even sure what had set the fire, but there'd been no stopping it this time, not in the midst of battle. He hacked hoarsely and spit dark phlegm.

"I guess he shoulda taken specimens while he was here after all," Gray deadpanned.

In reality, most of the island's species would survive; enough escaped the conflagration to the beach to ensure that. It wouldn't take long for foliage to return with almost daily rains. The herbivores would take a serious hit, and when they grew scarce the carnivores would too, but enough would survive. Lightning, if nothing else, had surely burned the island before. The important thing was that the well was mostly intact, even after being struck by a few round shot, and Isak and his crew were repairing it. Also, somehow, the Stars and Stripes still floated above the island on a makeshift spar, salvaged from the mostly intact Grik ship beached in the shallows. Rooting the last enemies out of it was how they lost Clark.

The Battle for Tarakan had been a desperate, grisly affair. For the first time Lemurians had stood under a terrifying, if mostly ineffectual bombardment. Then the enemy swarmed ashore. They'd been outnumbered at least three to one, and the fighting had been almost as bad as Gray remembered on the plain below Aryaal's walls. Almost. This time they'd had prepared defenses and trenches, making it possible to reinforce weak spots. Still, it had been bad, and their own losses were nearly thirty percent. Nothing compared to the Grik, whose losses were total, but that didn't matter at all like it might if they'd been fighting a human foe . . . or any foe that deserved the slightest speck of compassion. When the attacking force was destroyed, the exhausted Marines mounted an assault of their own on the ship in hopes of taking it intact, and predictably, as before, the cornered Grik fought like fiends. But the stranded ship was flooded, and all they'd accomplished was the capture of some Grik armaments.

"Their cannons are incredibly crude," observed Shinya, as if reading his thoughts. "The bores are rough, and so is the shot. No wonder so many burst when fired."

"Yeah, and they're made from crummy iron too. But it is iron, damn it. We sure need to be working on that."

Shinya nodded, then spoke reflectively: "They relied heavily on those guns. We've given them an appreciation of artillery, at least. I believe they expected theirs to perform as well as ours. That might have made the difference. There were far more of us waiting to greet them than they expected."

Gray matched Shinya's predatory grin. Both men had fought hard, and the battle *had* been desperate; hand-to-hand at times. More than once each had now saved the other's life. They'd both been through the crucible of Aryaal, but they hadn't been back-to-back then. They might never be friends, but they'd finally developed a bond of respect, trust, and shared commitment that could form only in battle. For the first time since they met, there, amid the detritus of bitter strife, they felt . . . comfortable with each other.

The general alarm began sounding again, and Gray saw Shinya close his eyes briefly before rising.

"First Marines," he yelled, "stand to!"

Gray painfully rose to join him while exhausted, bandaged 'Cats shuffled into formation as quickly as they could. "What the hell now," he growled, looking at the distant 'Cat atop the makeshift tower.

A runner sprinted to them, gasping. "More sails," he reported breathlessly, "in the north."

"North?! How many?" Gray demanded.

"Four, sir."

"Well, that tears it," Gray spat disgustedly.

"Perhaps not," Shinya observed. "Our one major advantage over the Grik is their tactical inflexibility. Their strategy can be cunning, but they seem unwilling to change basic procedures. Four, did you say?" The runner nodded. "Most unusual. The Grik usually come in multiples of three—I have no idea why; ancient hunting traditions, perhaps? Regardless, with few exceptions, we've always seen them in groups of three, or in their hundreds. Four seems atypical."

Gray looked at him thoughtfully. "Maybe. I hope so. One way or the other, we'll know before long."

"I'll be goddamned," Gray murmured. The four ships approached rapidly, the fitful breeze giving way to a stiff easterly, but they'd been coming up fast already. Columns of gray-black smoke pouring from tall funnels between their masts explained how. That alone was sufficient proof they weren't Grik, or if they were, the war was already lost. They were long and black with sleek clipper bows, and Gray had seen others just like them as a kid: old then, and obsolete, but occasionally still in use. They were transitional ships, much like the next generation the Americans planned, relying on both sail and steam, and paddle wheels churned the water at their sides. What attracted his attention more than anything, however, were the flags at their mastheads. He wasn't a historian like the skipper, or a knowledge nut like Courtney, but he'd heard enough of their conversations with their 'Cat allies about the "tail-less ones" of old or "the Others who came before" to catch some details now and then. One such detail had been what flag the ancient East India Company visitors would have flown. That was how he knew what he was looking at now: a flag with red and white stripes, strangely similar to his own, but with the familiar Union Jack where forty-eight stars ought to be. "I'll be goddamned," he repeated.

"Friends of yours?" a Marine lieutenant asked hopefully.

"No," Gray said absently, "never seen 'em before."

The ships hove to while they watched, and the largest lowered a boat into the sea. It was filled with red-coated soldiers, and some others in white coats. Probably officers. "No," he repeated, "but let's see if we can keep them off our list of enemies. Spruce up your Marines and form a detail, about a dozen or so, that don't look too scruffy and worn-out." He looked meaningfully at Shinya. "Have the rest return to their fighting positions and stand easy, but no goofing around. We'll meet our 'guests' on the beach."

The reception awaiting the boat was as smart as possible under the circumstances. The lieutenant and Shinya chose the hardest, most powerful-looking 'Cats, wearing the fewest bandages, and whose blue kilts were the most easily cleaned. They stood on the beach in two ranks of ten (Shinya expanded Gray's request just slightly), Krags at port arms, bayonets cleaned, fixed, and gleaming in the sunlight. When the boat rasped ashore, the redcoats stowed oars and leaped into the surf, dragging it farther until the bow was mostly out of the water. Their red coats had yellow trim and looked like something out of a Revolutionary War movie, but their hats were white-painted canvas tricorns, and they wore short white breeches and sandals that seemed infinitely practical under the circumstances, and contrasted sharply with their sun-bronzed legs. Finishing with the boat, they grabbed *muskets*, and assembled to either side of their craft on the beach, facing the Lemurian Marines, muskets held awkwardly high on their shoulders. The "white-coats" picked their way gingerly forward, and exited the boat onto the damp sand below. Their coats and breeches looked like heavy white canvas, lightly stained and yellowed, with bright yellow double-breasted facings, collars, and cuffs. Gold braid bordered the yellow to varying degrees, and adorned the black, low-crowned, sha-kolike hats they wore.

The man with the most braid also had a gold epaulet on each shoulder, and sported a large, sun-bleached, blond mustache, braided at the tips. His well-tanned face wore a calm, curious expression as he gazed at the Marines, the Grik corpses, and the expanse of the fire-blackened island. There was no question he recognized the aftermath of a fiercely contested fight, and he stared curiously at the now proudly streaming Stars and Stripes for a long time before resting his penetrating eyes on Gray and Shinya. An awkward moment ensued.

"So, who's in charge here, then?" he asked, vaguely condescending, in strangely accented English.

"I am," Gray answered, stepping forward. "Chief Bosun's Mate Fitzhugh Gray, United States Navy." He gestured at Shinya. "And this is my second in command, Lieutenant Tamatsu Shinya, late of the Jap Navy, and currently brevet major commanding these Marines. Who are you?"

If the man was confused by the contradictory ranks he'd been presented, or Gray's brusque manner, he took it in stride. "Captain—well, Commodore, actually—Harvey Jenks," he answered, "commanding this squadron, and His Supreme Imperial Governor's frigate *Achilles*. At your service, I'm sure." He added the last with a smirk.

Even as Gray felt his temper rise, he wondered briefly how many wars had been started by such a simple facial expression. "Pleased to meetcha," he said as amiably as possible. *Control!* his subconscious insisted.

A thought seemed to dawn across the stranger's face. "You must be the 'Amer-i-caans' we've heard about! Where is your astonishing ship?" Jenks glanced around again at the wounded, the dead, the distant drilling rig, and finally the stranded Grik ship. "I certainly hope that's not it."

"Americans," Gray corrected, "most of us. Some of the 'Cat Guards are allies, and Shinya's a Jap. Our ship's not here." He nodded at the Grik Indiaman. "That and two others brought our enemies, the Grik, and we killed them." He paused, examining Jenks. "How'd you hear about us? And for that matter, where're you from? We haven't heard doodly about you."

"We have sources," Jenks explained vaguely, looking at the flag once more. His face and tone reflected growing incredulity. "And we spoke one of your Philippine allies' amazing, massive ships a few days past. Fascinating vessels! Dreadfully slow, however. Once we introduced ourselves, they described your predicament. The ship bears reinforcements for your city of Baalkpan, I believe. I hope they arrive in time to aid you." He paused, shaking his head with a little snort. "Pardon me, but that *is* a flag up there, is it not?"

"It's a flag," Gray replied through clenched teeth. "Have you come to aid us?" he asked as neutrally as possible.

"'Fraid not. We're engaged in a rescue mission: searching for survivors from one of our passenger ships that went missing. They may have been swept this direction on the current, if any did, in fact, survive. Other elements of our navy are searching elsewhere even now. We were told your iron-hulled steamer was on a similar mission, to find other 'Americans,' and we hoped they might have rescued our castaways."

"You're welcome to hang around and ask, when she gets here," Gray replied, "but we ain't seen anybody. 'Sides, you still haven't told me where you come from and why we haven't heard of *you*."

"That's simple enough. The location of our homeland is none of your business; I'm sure you understand. As to why you haven't heard of us, I doubt that's entirely true. I admit there has been little recent contact, but the Ape Folk we met had a rather . . . flattering historical recollection of an earlier visit by my people. Gratifying, indeed, to be remembered so fondly and reverentially, don't you agree? Now, although my government has historic claims to all this region, we have not exercised control for quite some time. There are traditional and pragmatic reasons for that, but suffice to say we have no aims here, and pose no threat to you or your 'alliance.' We welcome its existence, in fact, as a more powerful buffer than the simple fragmented tribesmen that once stood between us and the western menace—against which you, sadly, must contend."

"You haven't come around for, what, two hundred years? And now here you are, out of the blue. The people you're looking for must be pretty important."

"That also is none of your concern," Jenks replied tightly. "We wish only to retrieve them, if, again, any have survived."

Gray was already smoldering over the man's apparent derision toward his flag, and his evasion and superior attitude only fanned the embers. "Fine," he snapped. "You do that. Like I said, you can wait for our 'iron-hulled steamer' here, or look for her where she is, which is the Philippines, last we heard. But for the record, you should show a little more respect for the flags around here, because you got *no* claim to anything here now. Look for your 'castaways,' and if you find our ship, USS *Walker*, and go aboard, you damn sure better salute that flag"—he gestured at the streaming bunting behind him—"because she flies the very same one. If you act like you have here, Captain Reddy's liable to scatter fragments of your puny little fleet all over the sea. He ain't as sensitive and forgivin' as me about such things."

Jenks's mustache worked as his jaw clenched tight.

"And another thing," Gray growled. "If you hang around here, you best watch yourselves, because if you're not here to help us, you won't get any help in return. There's a shit-storm of a fight coming against those things"—he waved at the Grik bodies—"that'll make this look like a picnic spat. You don't want to get caught in the middle of it."

Jenks took a step back, his surprised expression clouding to anger. "Is that a threat, sir?"

"No. Just fact. And a word of advice," Gray said, looking at the Marines. "These ain't 'Ape Folk,' or the simple 'tribesmen' your granddaddys abandoned to fend for themselves against a threat they knew would come someday."

Jenks stroked his mustache and regarded Gray more carefully. The contradictory ranks *had* confused him, and the mostly white-haired, powerfully muscled man in torn, bloodstained khakis and a battered, floppy hat must have significantly greater status among these . . . Americans than boatswains did in his own navy. Amer-i-caans—Americans! Colonials from the far side of the world! Ridiculous! He hadn't put it together before. And what were these "United States" the man referred to? Still, he clearly spoke a warped version of English. Could it be the sacred Mother Country on that distant, long-ago world had allowed her squabbling American colonies to pretend they were a nation? Impossible, yet . . . evidently true. He considered himself something of a historian, and he'd always been fascinated by the histories of the pre-Passage world their founders left behind. Yes, he could see a parallel between how his own empire had abandoned this region of savages and how that other empire might have done the same. Might that not have made the "simple" American "tribesmen" into something more formidable one day? He wondered briefly if it might be better to destroy this "buffer" than leave it in place.

"Very well, then. I can see we shall be the *best* of friends. I take my leave and wish you joy in tidying up after your 'spat.'" Captain Jenks tossed a casual salute at the flag and turned back to his boat.

Long after the oars began propelling the boat back through the surf to *Achilles*, Gray stood trembling with rage.

"Well," said Shinya at last, "that is just how I would have recommended keeping them off our 'enemies' list. Perhaps we can cement our friendship with some parting gifts. Some round shot, perhaps?" Gray thought he was mocking him until he saw Shinya's deadly serious expression.

Captain Reddy wiped sweat from his eyebrows with his sleeve and took a long gulp of cool water. Juan had brought a carafe to the bridge, filled from the refrigerated scuttlebutt on the side of the big refrigerator on deck. It was unbearably hot, and ever since the wind came around out of the east, there was only the slightest apparent breeze—even as they charged west through the Celebes Sea at twenty-five knots. Keje and Adar stood beside him on the bridge wing, panting like dogs, and Bradford fanned himself manically with his ridiculous sombrero. Flynn was with them, newly shaved face and close-cropped hair exposing already sunburned bright pink skin. With the dark tan around his eyes, he looked like a raccoon. They'd been talking about Bradford's interview with their Grik-like guest, and comparing what he'd learned with what they knew of their enemies. There were a few similar behavior patterns that seemed to support their theories about the Grik—behavior they hoped to exploit—but there were a lot of differences too. One glaring difference was currently on display.

They were watching Silva, Becky, and Lawrence on the amidships deckhouse, playing with the number two gun. Men and 'Cats stood around watching, but the trio didn't seem to notice. Becky was in the pointer's seat, spinning the wheel that elevated the muzzle, while Lawrence, who couldn't sit like a human, stood to the right of the gun, gleefully spinning the trainer's wheel, moving the gun from side to side. His wound had to hurt, but you couldn't tell to look at him. Silva was pointing at a low cloud far abeam, giving them a target.

"Amazing!" Courtney gasped, stilling his frenzied fanning for a moment. "I declare, Captain Reddy, what a fascinating sight. And your man Silva reveals new depths all the time!"

"He does, doesn't he?" Matt agreed absently. He blinked. "Put something to kill in front of that gun and he'll revert quick enough, I expect."

"As will we all," Keje agreed, and Matt could only nod. The mission had been a success, as long as the promised troops arrived in time. They'd even found the submarine. But the avalanche was loose, and he was beginning to feel the old pull, the impatient, almost yearning for the "game" to begin. If they believed Kaufman's cryptic message—and they had no choice—they'd beat the advance elements of the Grik swarm to Baalkpan by mere days. Perhaps longer if this wind held. Once again he'd be back at the center of the maelstrom with every life he held precious under his command: his responsibility, and there'd be little time for contemplation, only quick, decisive action. Time would compress to the size of an egg, and frenzied activity, chaos, and terror would prevail both inside and out, all trying to crack the egg at unpredictable points. Within the egg were his people, his friends, his love—maybe even the future of civilization on this twisted world. Outside was *Amagi* and the Grik, and all the horrors the shell must protect against, and it was fragile, fragile. In many ways *Walker* represented that shell: old and frail and held together by imagination, but she was just the outer, rusty layer. Without her destroyermen to reinforce her, to give her strength with their bodies, their character, and courage, she was nothing. With her crew she was a living thing, weak perhaps, but game and ready to do what had to be done, and for that she needed a mind. Captain Reddy was that mind, and he was fully aware of the responsibilities and implications. It was a heavy burden. He feared, ultimately, that the primary part of the shell was himself, and he'd made too many mistakes that cost too many lives to be confident he'd keep it intact. He feared and dreaded the great test to come, even as he planned for it, prepared his crew with more frequent drills, and tried to prepare himself. He loathed himself as well, because even greater than the dread was the craving. His hatred of the Grik and their Japanese helpers was so intense he could barely wait to get at them. He'd have to guard against impetuous impulses.

He missed Sandra more than he could say. He missed her face, her insight, her soft voice, her touch . . . and the steadying influence those things had over him. The trip had been a welcome rest, and he'd been able to step back, for a time, from the War and all the stress and urgency that went with it. For a while he was just a ship's captain, a destroyerman once again. But soon the trip—the escape—would end, and he grew increasingly anxious. He knew he'd "revert" just as quickly as Silva, and he needed Sandra's influence to make sure he didn't screw it up.

"That beats all," Dowden said, joining them on the cramped wing. "When that girl came aboard, she would've killed Silva with a bar of soap. Now they're best friends." He paused, seemingly at a loss for words. "And the Grik too."

"Tagranesi," Bradford corrected, flapping his hat again.

"Whatever. Anyway, all the other kiddos stick with their elusive nannies, who act like the ship's full of pirates ready to ravish them on sight. . . ."

"It is," Kutas muttered bleakly from the wheel.

Dowden spared him a glare. "But she sticks to him like glue whenever O'Casey lets her out of his sight. Where is he, anyway?"

"With Chack and Spanky in engineering," Matt answered. "He might be helpful when we build our own reciprocating steam engines. He knows how his people do it, and since turbines are out of the question for the foreseeable future . . ." He shrugged.

"He does seem to know much," Adar conceded sourly. "Apparently he is an engineer, a sailor, a soldier . . . he speaks of his experiences, but only vaguely, and according to Silva the girl doesn't know much about him either. Almost as if he hides himself from her as much as us."

Matt looked at the Sky Priest thoughtfully. "You may have hit on something," he said. "I need another little talk with Mr. O'Casey, it would seem."

They raised Tarakan late that afternoon, and thought at first they were mistaken; it bore no resemblance to the tropical jungle isle they'd left behind a few weeks before. What remained was a barren, blackened tangle of charred trees and brush, with a heavy pall of gray smoke still rising above. Only the flag and the ragged, cheering people on the beach convinced them it was the right place. Not long after they hove to and let fall the anchor, Gray was clambering up the side from a boat. He was grinning when he saluted the colors and turned to salute Matt.

"Permission to come aboard, Skipper?"

"Granted! God, what happened here?" Others climbed aboard while Gray told his tale. All were covered in soot and dried blood, and several were bandaged, including Shinya and Isak Rueben, who stood blinking with his arm in a sling. Matt glanced at each appraisingly, returning their salutes, but continued listening to Gray. His eyes moved to *Felts's* blackened timbers, protruding from the sea, and on to the stranded Grik ship. Flynn, Laumer, and O'Casey were staring at the aftermath of battle with almost identical expressions of concern and calculation, but he suspected the thoughts behind their eyes were somewhat different. He looked back at Gray. "Sounds like you had a tough fight, Boats," he concluded. "What was the bill?"

"Not too bad, considering they had cannons. Good thing their gunnery's not up to par. Otherwise, they just came on in 'the same old way.' Our casualties were about thirty percent, which sounds pretty bad, but most of the wounded'll make it."

"*Cannons?!*" Bradford gasped incredulously.

"Oh." Gray shook his head and blinked. He was clearly exhausted, and honestly, as hard as it was to remember sometimes, he wasn't a young man anymore. "I guess I left that part out."

Shinya continued the report. "Yes, Captain Reddy, they had cannons. Naval guns, much like those we equipped *Revenge*, *Felts*, and the other prizes with. Not as good as our new construction; not even as good as our first attempts, really, since theirs were not only crudely formed, but poorly bored, and made of what Mr. Gray called 'crummy iron,' prone to burst."

"Still . . ." Matt murmured, contemplating the implications.

"Yes, 'still,'" Shinya agreed. "How many do they have, how many of their ships have them, and how will this affect our defensive plans?" he said, stating the obvious questions. "There's another matter we must report," he added. "This morning we had some curious visitors."

"Oh?"

"Indeed. Human, singularly rude. Spoke English with a strange accent." Matt's eyes leaped to O'Casey, but aside from a sudden tenseness, he made no response. "They had four armed sailing steamers, and claimed to be on a 'rescue mission.'" The surprised reaction of those nearby was matched by those from the island when Silva pushed his way through the crowd with a small girl perched on his shoulders. Following close behind, like a devoted pet, was an unusually colored, bandaged Grik. Shinya stepped back, and Gray snarled, going for his cutlass.

"As you were!" Matt said, his calm, firm voice having greater effect than any shout. He glared at a grinning Silva, who'd probably timed his approach for maximum shock effect. "Don't be alarmed, gentlemen. May I present"—he paused—"Miss 'Becky,'" he continued with a trace of irony, "and her friend Lawrence." He pointed at the rail beside Flynn. "And that's Mr. O'Casey, another acquaintance of hers. You may notice when you speak to them, they have unusual accents as well."

"I'll be damned," grumbled Gray. "That bastard Captain Jenks said they were looking for shipwreck survivors. I guess you found them." He glanced around and saw other unfamiliar faces. "And the sub too." He spotted Flynn, whom he knew, and nodded.

"Jenks!" squealed the girl.

"You know him?" Matt demanded. The contrast between Becky's reaction and O'Casey's couldn't have been greater. The girl was animated with happiness, while the one-armed man slumped, in apparent dejection, against the rail.

"Oh, yes! He's a famous naval captain and explorer! Did you hear, Mr. O'Casey? We are rescued!"

"He's also a asshole!" Gray barked.

"Yes, he is!" The girl giggled. "But a very good one. Don't you see?" She patted Silva energetically on the head. "With his help, you should have no trouble with these terrible, vicious Griks of yours!"

Matt looked at Gray, who shook his head. "He's a asshole, Skipper, beggin' your pardon. He's lookin' for *them*. He ain't here to help us, and he won't—not that he'd make much difference. His ships are wooden-hulled paddle wheelers. Probably mount good guns, but they ain't worth more than four or five of the enemy each. Twenty Grik ships won't make a difference one way or the other."

"It might if that's all they have guns on, and they might be worth a lot more that aren't armed."

"Don't matter," Gray snorted. "He won't help."

"Certainly not now," Shinya added wryly.

Matt glared at them both. "What did you do?" he demanded.

"Nothin', Skipper, honest! Like I said, he's a asshole." Gray shrugged. "Maybe we were kinda assholes too, but he was one first!"

Eyes clenched shut, Matt shook his head. "Are we at war with them?" he ground out.

"I don't think so," Gray answered honestly, "but he carried on about how all this area was theirs, but it was okay if we squatted here as a 'buffer' against the Grik and such . . . then he was a jerk about our flag, and I got kind of riled."

The girl's expression of glee had turned to confusion, as if she couldn't understand their doubts about Jenks. "I'm not sure whether it will be up to Captain Jenks whether he helps or not," she said cryptically, then turned to Gray. "He's headed for Baalkpan?"

The Bosun glanced at the captain, then faced the strange girl. "Not necessarily. Said they passed a 'Cat Home out of the Philippines loaded with troops. That's who told them where to look."

"Well, that's good news about the troops," Matt mused. "No reason they shouldn't have told him, either, and it might work to our advantage."

"I, uh, doubt it, Skipper," Gray interjected. "Like I said, Jenks has no intention of helpin' us, and when he asked where you were, I told him the Philippines—which I thought you were. Last we saw, his squadron was headed northeast along the coast. You coming in from almost due east, it's no wonder you missed 'em."

Matt shook his head and glanced at the setting sun, perhaps lamenting a lost opportunity. Finally he took a deep breath. "Listen, we'll bring you up to speed, but right now all you need to know is that the Grik are coming. I want all your people aboard and us underway by dark. Leave the tools, equipment, and brontosarries behind. When this is over, we'll come back and finish the job . . . or we won't."

Chack bellowed commands, and his whistle whirred insistently. *Walker's* borrowed boats went over the side and prepared to run for shore. Signal flags fluttered up the halyards, and rapid preparations commenced on the beach. Amid all this activity, Isak Rueben stared at Gilbert and Tabby—staring back.

"You hurt bad?" Gilbert finally asked.

Isak flapped his arm. "Naw. Nary a scratch in the fightin'. Stayed out of it, mostly. I ain't no good with no sword, an' I loaned my rifle to Clark. He got killed, though. I got this while I was dumpin' a load. Grabbed a burnt tree, squatted back, an' snap! Tree broke, an' I fell an' poked myself on another one. Think they'll gimme a medal?"

Gilbert shook his head with a concentrated frown, just as he always had, but his time without Isak had wrought subtle changes. Where before, the dry banter might continue endlessly, neither of them truly recognizing the humor, this time something in Gilbert's expression cracked. Tabby watched with blinking eyes as the crack turned into a grin, and something like an indignant skuggik's call escaped his lips.

"You laughin' at me?" Isak asked, astonished, while Gilbert's unaccustomed sounds became a recognizable cackle.

"Yeah . . . I am!" Gilbert replied, and he and Tabby both exploded into uncontrolled hilarity. Isak shook his head, eyes wide. For a moment he wondered if his friends had been filching torpedo alcohol, but the way they were laughing, barely able to breathe . . . he saw the stunned expressions or blinking of those standing near, and the absurdity of it all: his wound, his and Gilbert's seclusion, the stagnant, cloistered life they'd led, struck him like a blow. He'd enjoyed being off the ship and doing something else for a change. He'd even made a few friends, sort of. Evidently the separation had been good for them all. Without really realizing it, at some point he'd begun laughing too. Tears streaked his face as he gave himself over to whatever possessed the others, and he didn't know if they were tears of mirth or despair.

Seaman Fred Reynolds sat on the uncomfortable chair in *Walker's* radio room. He had the midwatch radio watch until 0400, and was almost out of his mind with boredom. The earphones emitted only a steady, uninterrupted hum as he monitored the guard frequency listening for . . . nothing. Something was obviously wrong with the PBY's transmitter in Baalkpan. Clancy said it might have been bombed! But the captain had decreed that somebody continue to monitor their own receivers, just in case, and tap out, "We are coming," at least four times every watch. Clancy was the only radioman aboard and couldn't do it all the time, so the tedious chore fell to just about everyone on a rotation basis.

Reynolds had lied to join the Navy—twice, actually. He'd known no one would believe he was eighteen, so he claimed to be seventeen and forged his parents' permission. He'd still been surprised his stunt was successful, since he'd been only fifteen at the time, and probably looked twelve. Now, actually seventeen at last, he was probably the only human on *Walker* still listed as "seaman," since he hadn't struck for anything. He just couldn't decide. He'd become a good bridge talker, and he liked that okay, but anybody was supposed to be able to do that. The exec said he'd probably be an ensign soon, if he'd just pick something and learn to do it well. He'd thought about striking for ordnance, but he wasn't very big. Any thought he'd had about striking for radioman or signalman was losing its appeal. Maybe navigation? It was time to make a decision.

He leaned back in the chair, considering, his eyes sweeping across the clock on the bulkhead. It was time. Sighing, he shifted forward and tapped out the string of memorized dots and dashes. He began to lean back again when he almost lost his eardrums to the intensity of the unexpected reply. Tossing the headset down, he dashed through the hatch to get Clancy.

Matt stared at the vague shape of the message form in his hand with mingled relief and concern. Keje arrived on the bridge, followed by Adar and Shinya. Dowden brought up the rear, escorting a still-drowsy O'Casey. The dim red light in the pilothouse provided barely enough illumination for the watch to move about, and the starboard wing where Matt waited was almost totally dark, a heavy overcast blotting out the stars. "We've finally heard from Baalkpan," he announced without preamble, with a touch of irony. They'd be there in a few hours.

"That is good news," Adar said.

"Very good," Matt agreed. "Mr. Riggs constructed a broadband spark-gap transmitter pretty quickly evidently, but he couldn't power it. The batteries are going to take longer than he thought. Trouble making sulfuric acid. Anyway, *Mahan* finally came crawling in yesterday, and they used her generators."

They didn't like the sound of that. "What happened to her, and why did Mr. Ellis disobey you?" asked Keje.

Matt told them about *Donaghey*'s fight, and how Queen Maraan and Pete Alden got left behind. It all made sense now; with *Donaghey* under repair, and the other frigates incomplete, *Mahan* was the only ship that could have pulled off the rescue against cannon-armed Grik. But it had been a terrible risk. It hadn't gone all her way, either. Baalkpan already knew the Grik were coming; *Mahan* had run the gauntlet of their fleet. She'd expended most of her remaining ammunition and destroyed as many of their cannon-armed ships as she could, but she'd been severely punished in return. Matt had it on good authority now: the crude Grik shot could indeed punch through his old ships' rusty sides at point-blank range.

"Was she badly damaged?"

"She had some casualties—hard not to, as packed as she was, and she lost a boiler. Good thing the wind's in the enemy's teeth, or they might've caught her."

"And Queen Maraan? Aal-den?" Adar asked urgently.

"Safe. They lost Haakar-Faask, it seems, but no details."

"Most unfortunate," Keje rumbled. "I did not know him well, but he had great honor. I trust his end was noteworthy." He hesitated. "Have you told Chack?"

Keje approved of Chack and Safir Maraan's relationship, but he also wanted happiness for his daughter, Selass. It was a tough situation, but one Selass had brought on herself, as far as he was concerned.

"Yeah, I expect he's in the fire rooms now, pestering them to step on it."

"What of *Amagi*?" Shinya asked, carefully neutral.

Matt looked at the Japanese officer. Shinya had been given considerable time to resolve his inner turmoil concerning *Amagi*, maybe too much time. Now he must quickly decide where he stood. The luxury of time for contemplation was over for all of them. Matt felt a pang of guilt, however. He'd read only *most* of Kaufman's message to his assembled officers, and suggested Kaufman might have subverted a single sailor to let him send it—which might be the case. He'd deliberately withheld the possibility that there might be widespread contention aboard the Japanese ship. It would only make the issue more difficult for Shinya, and if *Amagi* attacked anyway, it wouldn't make any difference.

"Jim didn't see her, so she hadn't sailed with the enemy vanguard, at least."

"Oh four hundred, Skipper," Dowden interrupted.

"Very well. Sound general quarters."

The alarm reverberated through the ship, and the relative peace was shattered by frantic activity. Most of the crew was already up, anticipating the daily ritual and eating breakfast, so there was literally no delay before Campeti and his fire-control team scampered up the ladder behind them, and Silva—and now the Bosun too—began loudly exhorting their divisions. Even in the dim light, Matt saw that O'Casey was impressed by the discipline.

"That leaves us with you, Mr. Sean O'Casey ... if that's really your name. You didn't seem as pleased by the prospect of 'rescue' as the young lady did. Is there some reason you don't want this Jenks to find you?"

"Ye ... might say that."

"Well. The last thing we want right now is war with your people—the war we already have is quite sufficient! But if Jenks is as big a jerk as the Bosun says, we're liable to have one if you don't tell me what I want to know. They're obviously looking for you, or more probably the girl, and they've gone to extraordinary lengths to do so. Each of those 'rescue' ships might have suffered the same fate as yours. That's a hell of a risk to take on such slim odds, and I have to know why. Is Jenks a threat? Now, you may not believe it, but this single ship, battered as she is, could slaughter his entire squadron without working up a sweat." He glanced at the others and shook the message form. "Hell, according to this, *Donaghey*'s repairs are complete and the new frigates *Kas-Ra-Ar* and *Tolson* will join her and the guard ship, *Big Sal*, currently on duty." Keje formed a predatory grin. If plans had gone apace, his Home, *Salissa*, had become even more formidable during their absence. "Jenks can hurt my frigates, and it'd probably be a hell of a fight, but based on Gray's estimates I'm confident they can take him. So, do I send those frigates after him, or keep them here, where we really need them?"

O'Casey slumped. "All right. I may be on the run, but I'm no traitor—although Captain Jenks might disagree. I've told ye nothing of the location of our homeland, an' won't, because that's been pounded into us since birth: safety from secrecy. Aye, 'tis a tradition passed down from our ancestors who first came to this world. They knew of the Grik, and the Ape Folk, as they called them, but assumed that eventually the first would conquer the second, an' they didna want anyone knowin' where ta find us. They set a colony on some secluded islands in the middle o' the Pacific, what the Ape Folk—Lemurians—call the Eastern Sea. Over the last two-hundred-odd years, their colony's grown into an empire, the 'Empire of New Britain Isles,' an' now includes many islands, as well as larger lands. It's become prosperous an' powerful but, over time, tyrannical as well. The governor-emperor is a good, kindly man, as have been most of his predecessors, but the company has supplanted the Court of Proprietors an' the Court of Directors to such a degree, he has little power now."

"The 'company'?" Shinya asked.

"Aye, the Honorable New Britain Company," O'Casey answered with a sneer. "They've won their power on fear o' the threats surroundin' us, and kept it by suppressing the lower classes—descendants of lascars and transportees—that gave them power in the first place, in the Court of Directors—like the old House of Commons—who then cemented it in the Court of Proprietors—like the old House of Lords." He paused, a wry smile on his face. "Ye see, I know me pre-Passage history well, though they suppress that too, now. Because I object to the current system, I'm a traitor, a subversive, as far as they're concerned, but in fact, I'm a patriot who supports the governor-emperor wi' all my heart. I'm a soldier, sailor, and an engineer . . . but I also led a wee mutiny, ye see, an' when it was crushed— not enough arms!—I took ship for the western colonies, the 'buffer zone.' I didna think they'd find me there." He paused, apparently considering whether to go on.

"When we were wrecked, I saw the girl! I couldna believe she was aboard! She'd kept to her cabin, I suppose, an' I never, ever knew it. But don't ye see? Savin' the girl proves me word! She's a darlin' creature, an' I like ta think I'd'a tried ta save her regardless, but would a true traitor ha' done so, she bein' who she is?"

The sky was beginning to brighten aft, and there was enough light in the pilothouse to see Captain Reddy blink. "Who is she?" he grated, although he'd already begun to suspect. How much more complicated could their situation become?

O'Casey confirmed his fears. "Why, she's the governor-emperor's daughter, of course!"

Matt took a deep breath. "And this Jenks, he's a 'company' man?"

"Nay, he's Imperial Navy through and through, but he follows orders," O'Casey said.

"Issued by a company-controlled admiralty, I shouldn't wonder,"

Courtney Bradford grumped. Matt hadn't even noticed him join them, and he wondered if he'd heard it all.

"So," Dowden spoke thoughtfully, "is he actually here to rescue her, or to make sure she's gone for good?"

O'Casey shook his head. "I despise the man, but he wouldna harm the child. He may have company wardens aboard he doesna even know of, though. They wouldna miss the chance."

Matt struck the rail in frustration. "Goddamn it, we don't need this right now!"

Bradford looked at him in alarm. "Indeed."

"All stations manned and ready, Captain," Dowden reported quietly.

Matt brooded in silence for a considerable time. Finally he straightened his shoulders and looked them each in the eye. "This stays between us for now, clear? Anybody else we tell only on a 'need to know' basis, and I'll decide who needs to know."

Three distinct pyramids of off-white canvas appeared in the hazy, muggy morning air. An even greater mass of sail signified *Big Sal's* mighty presence, on guard at the mouth of Baalkpan Bay. Home. Beyond, the jungle-choked entrance was broken only by the long southern beach, and the imposing shape of Fort Atkinson overlooking the eastern approach. Hove to in line of battle, the three rakish frigates flew the Stars and Stripes, and Keje's colossal Home anchored the center of the line. However meager it might ultimately be, it was a stirring, impressive sight.

"Thank God!" Bradford exclaimed, echoing everyone's sentiments. "At least we're here in time!"

Matt ordered smoke so everyone would see his ship approaching against the gray day. *Mahan* was out of sight, as ordered, already undergoing repairs. He looked back at O'Casey. "You'd better round up your young charge. I recommend you tell her the whole truth and explain why you're not going with her, if Jenks shows up here." He paused. "I'll give you asylum with us, but you're damn sure going to earn it. And if I find out you've lied to me . . ."

O'Casey nodded sadly. "Thank ye, Captain Reddy."

O'Casey found the girl leaning out over the rail, pointing excitedly at the graceful ships and the massive Home. The big man, Silva, was with her—as he always seemed to be lately—and Lawrence lay coiled on the deck like a dog, head up, sniffing, staring at the other children, and even the women, who'd finally ventured on deck. They were the center of much attention, even dressed in the variety of naval garb they'd taken in exchange for their ragged clothing. All except the young nun. She still wore her battered habit, standing a little apart from the other women, looking about with an impatient, frustrated expression. O'Casey caught her eye and shrugged sympathetically. He knew she was still waiting to speak to Captain Reddy. He nodded at Silva as he approached, then spoke to the girl.

"Young miss, may I have a word?"

"Of course, Mr. O'Casey! I owe you my life!"

He gently steered her away from the others, though he was conscious of Silva's unwavering eye. "Miss . . . Your Highness . . ." he began softly. She looked quickly around, but he made a shushing sound. "No need to fear; no one can hear. Besides, I've told their captain who ye are. No choice . . . for I canna go wi' ye if yer Jenks should come for ye. In fact"—he sighed—"though I hate ta ask ye ta lie yet again, I must beg ye not to reveal my part in yer affairs these past many months."

Tears formed in Becky's eyes. "But . . . *why*? Certainly you'll be knighted, at least, for what you have done. I will see to it!"

"Nay, me dear," O'Casey said. "I'm a wanted man, and I'll certainly be hanged for what I've done." He put his broad hand on her small shoulder. "I've risen against the company, ye see."

She did see, or thought she did, and her eyes went wide. "All this time . . . and you are a traitor?"

"Nay!" he said firmly. "No traitor ta ye or yer father, but perhaps a traitor ta those who subvert ye. Yer father's a good man . . . long ago he was even me friend, but the company's made a stuffed shirt o' him, an' I would change that if I could . . . I tried . . ."

She gasped. "The Mutiny!"

He nodded. "Aye, the Mutiny. It was never against the Empire, er him . . . er you! God knows! It was against the way things have become. We tried ta right a terrible wrong, an' we didna succeed. I'm sorry for that, but not for tryin'."

She still seemed stunned. "So you will stay with these people? Fight with them?"

"Aye. Theirs seems a cause worth fightin' for, after all, an' hopeless as they make it sound, it isna over yet." He lowered his head. "Me last cause is finished, an' there isna any hope a'tall."

"Perhaps," she hedged, still uncertain. "We shall see. In any event, I shall not betray you. If Captain Jenks arrives, I shall tell the entire truth of our ordeal, but at first I shall not reveal you live. Enough?"

He nodded. "Enough, Your Highness. Thank ye."

Silva had drifted over. "What the hell's all this 'Highness' shit?"

Captain Reddy appeared, dressed in his finest, academy sword at his side. "Yes, Mr. Silva," he said quietly, looking at the girl. "You've been associating with royalty all this time, and never even knew it. None of us did." He glanced around. He'd already decided to include Silva in the circle of those who had the "need to know," and he made sure no one else was near enough to hear. "And for now, that's the way it stays. Tell no one. From now on, if, and until her own people collect her, she's your responsibility: yours and Mr. O'Casey's, of course. Her safety's in your hands." He paused. "Highness?" The girl nodded. "Well. Perhaps a proper introduction is in order at last?"

"Becky" cleared her throat. "Rebecca Anne McDonald will suffice, I think," she answered. "As Mr. O'Casey just pointed out, my various titles are rather meaningless anymore. Only one might pertain to the current situation"—she glanced at Silva with a grin—"and I might just trot it out someday, if I get the chance."

Just then she perceived a clattering, rumbling drone unlike anything she'd heard before, growing louder by the moment. She looked up.

"Damn that idiot!" Matt declared. "Who gave him permission to fly?" He paced to the rail and watched the battered PBY approach from the south. It looked decidedly odd with its shortened wings, and the engines sounded like they'd mixed rocks with the oil.

"I can't believe he got it up again," Gray confessed, joining them.

"Ol' Benny's a whiz with gizmos," Silva stated, "an' pretty sharp for an army aviator."

"It's an airplane!" Rebecca squealed excitedly. "Oh, it is, it is! Mr. Flynn told me about them, but I confess I scarcely believed him! Oh, look! Is it going to land upon the sea?"

The Catalina staggered past *Walker*, banked delicately, and flew toward the open sea still separating the destroyer and the picket force. Two hundred yards away it thumped exhaustedly onto the calm sea and wallowed to a stop. Gunning the port engine, the pilot began his approach.

"Oh, look, oh, look!" chanted the girl, almost hopping.

When the plane was within a hundred yards, the pilot—it must be Mallory—turned the plane away from the ship and cut the engines. The ensuing silence seemed almost more intense than the previous racket. A moment passed; then Signals Lieutenant (JG) Palmer appeared on the wing.

Matt spotted Stites leaning on the rail near the whaleboat. "Don't just stand there," he shouted. "Go get him!" He looked at Silva and O'Casey, then glanced at the impatient nun. "Carry on," he said. "I'd better get to the bridge."

"Captain!" shouted the nun, her Dutch accent clear. Grimacing, Matt paused while the woman strode quickly toward him. "Captain, I must protest! I have been asking to speak with you for days!"

"My apologies, uh, sister . . ."

"Sister Audry. I appreciate you rescuing us from our previous . . . circumstances, but now I understand we are steaming directly toward a battle? Have you not thought of the children in my care? Is it possible you will expose them to further risk? I must insist you provide for their safety!"

Matt gritted his teeth. "Lady . . . Sister, I haven't got time for this now, but you have my word those kids'll be as safe as I can make them. If I could drop them, and you, off someplace safe, I would, but there *is* no safe place. I'll do what I can, but for now you must excuse me." He turned and continued on his way, leaving the nun wearing a stormy expression.

Shortly the whaleboat returned, with Palmer standing in the prow. When it came alongside, the signalman scurried up, saluted the flag and Gray, and raced for the pilothouse. "Skipper!" he said with feeling, saluting again. "Am I glad to see you!"

"The feeling's mutual, but what's the meaning of this?" Matt gestured at the plane.

Palmer's face took on a haunted look. "Yeah, well, jeez. Believe me, Skipper, we wouldn't have gone up in that death trap if we didn't have to. It flies, but I think that's only because it hates floating even more." He gathered himself. "Mr. Letts sent us. You were right; the Griks are on the move. They handled *Mahan* pretty rough, but we thought that might've just been a stab at catching her. No go. It looks like the real deal."

"Any sign of *Amagi*?"

"Not with the advance force. Looks like a hundred-plus ships, even after *Mahan* tore 'em up. We might've seen smoke way to the south, but we didn't want to push the old girl, if you know what I mean." Palmer shuddered. "I hate to say it, Captain, but I think it's time we stripped her for the metal."

"Probably right," Matt mused sadly. "We might need her to fly once more, but after that . . ." He shrugged. "How long before the enemy arrives?"

"The wind's against them," Palmer replied, "but by late tomorrow morning, surely."

"Very well. How are the preparations I mentioned to Mr. Sandison proceeding?"

"They haven't started yet, sir. We just now got all *Mahan*'s holes patched. They could commence tonight, but Sandison says we should wait for daylight."

"Quite right," Matt mused. "We'll just have to slow the enemy advance then, won't we?"

"Yes, sir."

Matt turned to Dowden. "We'll go in and off-load nonessential personnel and refuel. We're running on fumes. Signal the 'fleet' . . . prepare for action."

Isak Rueben ran a proprietary hand along a feed pipe in the aft fire room. He stopped at a gauge and tapped it. "So," he said to Gilbert and Tabby, "I guess you managed to keep my babies lit while I was away."

"Sure did," Gilbert answered. "Course, the refit didn't hurt none. Boilers are in better shape than they've been in twenty years. Didn't have to do nothin' but feed 'em oil an' air an' water the whole trip."

"Didn't even need me," Isak muttered.

"Well, it wasn't like the run outta Surabaya, or after our fight with the Japs, but there's always a little somethin'," Gilbert hastened to add.

"Like what?" Isak asked, interest flaring.

"Number two smoke-box uptake is leakin'," Tabby supplied helpfully, "keeps smokin' up for'ard fire room, and tubes in number three is all coked up." She spat on the slimy deck plate. "Damn green snipes is battin' burners too big. Makin' smoke."

"Laney's been real jumpy too," Gilbert added. "Keeps forgettin' there's only been two of us to do all our work, an' his too. An' there you was, takin' yer ease on a tropical island."

"At least you guys didn't have to fight a bunch of Griks! All you did was run around gatherin' up pigboat pukes an' a buncha kids an' dames. An' what's the dope on that pet Grik the deck apes got?" He gestured at Tabby. "Hell, they got the first 'Cat that came aboard. It ain't fair, I tell ya."

Tabby and Gilbert both laughed, and a grin spread across Isak's face; another real one. "Boy, it's sure good to be back, but it was sorta fun too, you know?"

As soon as he saw her, Chack leaped the remaining distance between the ship and the fueling pier and flung himself into Safir Maraan's arms. Wolf whistles from the ship and cheers from the assembled crowd accompanied the feat. The dignified queen showed no restraint on this occasion. Not to be outdone, Silva mimicked the leap (across a much narrower gap) with a wild whoop and a great show of boisterous exertion. Waiting for him were Ensign Pam Cross and Risa-Sab-At, who, as Active Guard training instructor for *Big Sal*'s combined clans, had been ashore helping train the allied armies. There was a collective gasp of expectation as everyone waited to see what would happen. Silva was onstage, poised to commit a blatant act of public misbehavior, and he knew it. Evidently, so did the "girls." With an exaggerated look of alarm, then an even more exaggerated attempt to make a decision between the two, Silva stood on the pier looking from Pam to Risa and back again. Finally he enfolded them both in his powerful arms and raced through the crowd bellowing, "Gangway! Time's a'wastin'!" The crowd erupted with laughter, and there were hoots and catcalls from the ship.

"Secure those lines!" roared Gray over the tumult. "The next man . . .'Cat . . . or I don't care what else, jumps ship is a deserter!"

Dowden shook his head beside Captain Reddy on the port bridge wing. "That crazy bastard! I'll have Silva polishing brass from one end of this ship to the other—with his toothbrush!"

Matt barely heard him. Alone, it seemed, of all *Walker*'s crew, his mood remained unaffected by the stunt. His attention was fixed on a small, slim form, standing a little apart from the others, long, sandy-brown hair unclasped for once, flowing in the stiffening breeze. "Don't bother," he said absently, the words ringing hollow. "I said he could. Everybody needed a laugh."

Dowden chuckled uneasily, then followed his captain's gaze. Lieutenant Tucker wore an anxious, sad smile as she stared back across the impossible gulf the others had simply hopped over, with a sharply focused message of love, welcome, and . . . pain that almost broke his heart. He looked back at Matt. Now he knew why the captain had dressed in his best—and why he wasn't laughing.

Matt stepped briskly back from the rail. Nearby, snugged to the old fitting-out pier, was *Mahan*, looking somewhat the worse for wear. Her crew was waving and calling across the distance, their shouts lost in the wind. A loud *toot-toot* and a jet of steam escaped her forward stack. Her new paint was blotched with rust, and there were patches welded here and there. After her long trip, Matt doubted *Walker* looked much better. He noticed the other destroyer already sported her old number again, 102, and the fresh paint contrasted sharply with that around it. He'd transmitted permission to the request early that morning. The deception didn't matter anymore; with any luck the enemy would never see *Mahan* again, and he was glad *Mahan*'s crew—and Jim Ellis—was proud of her once more.

"Commence refueling at once," Matt commanded. "Off-load our 'passengers' and all nonessential or specified personnel, as well as small arms, ammunition, depth charges—you know the list."

Dowden nodded. "Aye, aye, Captain."

"Maybe, if we have time, we can tear out the other stuff we talked about tomorrow night. In the meantime"—he glanced at his watch, 1310—"try to let as many guys as possible go ashore for an hour or so. We can wait for *Big Sal* to follow us in and tie up, but I want to be underway

by nineteen hundred." He looked around. "Now take over, if you please. I
have someone . . . some people to see."

They gathered for the staff meeting, perhaps the final one, in Nakja-Mur's
Great Hall. Lieutenants Letts, Brister, and Sandison, as well as Lord Rolak
and Queen Maraan, of course, had met Matt on the pier, so he and Sandra
hadn't had a single moment alone. They stood together now, however, and
if they weren't holding hands, they stood close enough for their arms to
touch and make that vital connection: a warm, tingling, electric circuit
both of them needed to draw strength from the other. For now it had to be
enough; neither of them knew what the next few days might hold.

Her Highness, Rebecca McDonald, Sean O'Casey, and Ensign Laumer
stood with them, the first two introduced as shipwrecked survivors of the
fabled earlier "tail-less ones"—which caused quite a stir at first. But old
Naga wasn't there; he hadn't been seen in days. Adar was, but having been
included among those with the need to know, he hadn't resolved the dog-
matic challenges to some fundamental interpretations of the ancient
Scrolls they represented. He'd chosen not to "make a big deal" of their
presence until he sorted things out in his own mind. The specter of bitter
controversy loomed, controversy that might prove distracting at the worst
possible time. There was no telling how—or if—different historical per-
spectives on ancient events might conflict with their own, and if they differed wildly, how might they be reconciled? It was a perplexing problem.
He expected no challenge to the most basic unifying gospel of his people,
however: reverence of the Sacred Heavens. So for now, he'd concentrate
on his sworn task: defeating the Grik. Only with victory would he have
the leisure for theological contemplation, not to mention possible "adjustments" to many of his people's most closely held beliefs.

Ensign Laumer was clearly out of his depth, and it showed in his expression. There just hadn't been enough time for him to grasp all that was
going on. His previous situation had been far enough beyond his experience, but his slowly growing understanding of *this* situation left him overwhelmed. Matt knew the kid wasn't ready to lead his men in battle, but he
knew he'd have to figure out *something* for him to do or he might be ruined. O'Casey was stony-faced, observant, apparently curious about how
he could help. That was what he'd asked the captain, but Matt wasn't sure.
He'd introduced him to Letts and told the lieutenant to figure it out, as
long as O'Casey, Silva, or now—apparently—Sandra was with the girl at
all times.

Sandra became one of Rebecca's "protectors" almost at first sight. Rebecca was a virtual (smaller) twin to the nurse, and each had recognized

herself in the other at once. Both were willful, intelligent, accustomed to getting their way, but profoundly empathic as well. Sandra was impressed by the girl's resilience, her capacity to cope with the hardships she'd endured and remain so self-possessed at such an early age—not to mention her devotion to such bizarre and disparate "friends" as Lawrence and Dennis Silva. When they were first introduced, Rebecca was still seething with revulsion and indignation over Silva's behavior at the pier and Sandra recognized an anger founded on affection at once. She also instantly realized the girl harbored a great secret that wasn't for public discussion.

Rebecca saw in Sandra a mirror image of her mother, but an image— much as she loved her—her mother could never reflect in action. She'd already seen a huge difference between how Lemurians and her own people perceived a female's role, and now she saw a similar stunning difference in the way the "Americans" treated their women. She sensed they were extremely protective of them, which made sense when they were so few, but there was no condescension or disdain, and the protectiveness was of a different sort; it was not of the type extended to property. She'd been immune to that sort herself, considering who she was, but knew it was pervasive among her people. Here, despite their scarcity, women had real power and status—equality—and Sandra Tucker epitomized that equality with her every word, her bearing, and her most casual gesture. Here was a woman like Rebecca had never seen, who, while wholly feminine, demanded and received respect. Not because she'd been born to it, but because she'd earned it.

At the same time, the girl also sensed a sadness, a vulnerability separate from Sandra's professional self, and knew the woman held a great secret of her own. Even Rebecca, a child of ten, quickly realized what it was.

Now she stood, her small hand in Sandra's, eyes wide as she took in the sights, smells, and . . . terrifying momentousness of the proceedings within the Great Hall she was but a spectator to. She missed Lawrence's comforting presence, but knew he'd been left aboard the iron ship for his own protection. The hall was filled with the tension of a looming battle of unimaginable proportions against creatures far too similar to him.

Captain Reddy was talking, describing the voyage they'd returned from. Occasionally Sandra squeezed her hand uncomfortably tight when he spoke of some tense moment. Once she gasped, not sure if it was from pain or because she'd become so caught up in the tale, and Sandra knelt and murmured soft, fervent words of apology. Captain Reddy paused and glanced their way, and in that instant Rebecca caught a glimpse of him she hadn't seen before: a gentle, almost boyishly wistful tenderness, haunted by something lurking beneath a fragile facade. She imagined she sensed a titanic conflict between howling terror and a capacity for unimaginable violence. She blinked, recoiled slightly, and it was gone, leaving only a be-nevolent expression of mild concern.

Matt turned back and resumed, speaking to all, but generally direct-ing his words to Baalkpan's High Chief. Nakja-Mur looked terrible. His once massive arms had seemed actually frail when he wrapped Matt in the usual awkward greeting embrace. "You cannot know," he'd said low, "how glad I am you have returned." His eyes had even been misty. The stress he'd endured the last few weeks had been grueling, and if it hadn't sapped his will, it had wracked his body. Since his greeting, he'd retired to his cushions and spoken little.

"... so," Matt continued, "we'll sortie tonight with the frigates. Try to meet this advance Grik element and bust it up before it gets too close. That'll leave time for Mr. Sandison and *Mahan* to prepare our final sur-prises." He looked at Bernie Sandison. "I can leave you Silva and Chief Gray to supervise the detail. I wish I could leave Campeti, but I'll need him at fire control."

"Thanks, Skipper. I didn't expect Silva or Gray. We'll get the job done."

"What about *Amagi* and the main force?" Pete Alden asked, speaking for the first time. He still looked haggard after his ordeal.

"Day after tomorrow, I expect." Matt shrugged. "That's what Mallory thinks—if that was her smoke he saw. I think it probably was; why else come now at all? All the same, they must've really rushed her repairs to get her to sea this quickly. She's their wild card. Normally she could blast Baalkpan to dust without even entering the bay. Her shells are a lot more effective falling on top of a target than hitting it from the side. If she shoots right at something, she either hits—and trust me, it's a hell of a thump—or misses completely. That's why ships like her usually don't get in too close." He was trying to demonstrate ballistics with his hands as he spoke. "Thing is, if she stands off, she has to see the target herself, which she can't do here, or have forward observers correct her fire. They could stash one on a Grik ship, I suppose, or even send one ashore, if they have radios to spare. But regardless, if they use indirect fire"—his hand described a high arc in the air—"they're still going to miss a lot. My bet is, they won't want to waste the ammunition." He glanced at Sandison, then looked at Nakja-Mur.

"We're almost out of ammunition ourselves," he admitted. "We picked up some from the submarine, and Jim says the copper bolts shoot fine, but have 'limited destructive capability.' In other words, they just punch holes. But they do work, and they're better than nothing. Someday we'll make explosive shells. It'll be a lot harder for the Japs to do that—to make more of their big shells, that'll not only take rifling, but also blow up. Without their explosive force, they're not much more dangerous than our copper bolts. They'll make a bigger hole, but against our defenses here they'll just make bigger holes in the dirt." He grinned crookedly. "And you have to wonder if even the Japs would show the Grik how to make something that might blow a hole in their *own* ship. Regardless, for now, they've *got* to be feeling the pinch—especially after they wasted so many destroying *Nerracca*. They must've thought they had us—that it'd be worth it to go for broke—but it didn't work that way." He paused, remembering that fearful night before continuing. "What I think they'll do is come right up into the bay, use their secondaries as much as they can. That's what we've planned for, and that's what we *need* them to do. Our whole defense relies on it, and I think that's our only chance to kill her." He looked at Keje. "Trouble is, if they do that, the Homes'll be slaughtered."

Keje blinked. "I'd rather avoid the 'slaughter' of my Home," he said dryly.

"Me too," said Matt. "That's why *Big Sal* and the other Homes should leave now. Tonight."

"But we've sworn to fight!" Ramic protested loudly. "I for one have a score to settle! I will not leave!"

"Nor I," said Geran-Eras.

"I'm glad to hear it, but you misunderstand. Your warriors'll fight on land, as they did at Aryaal, but I think the Homes themselves should sail immediately for Sembaakpan, near our new fuel depot at Tarakan. It's a crummy anchorage, but that'll take them out of *Amagi*'s reach. If we faced only the Grik, using the Homes as floating batteries would make sense. We could tear the hell out of them. But if *Amagi* comes in, they won't stand a chance. Second, they could carry away more of the Aryaalan and B'mbaadan younglings *Fristar* and the others didn't wait to take—besides our own recently acquired 'noncombatants.'" He paused, catching sight of Ensign Laumer. The young officer still looked lost. Matt understood how he felt. "Laumer?"

"Sir?"

"I want you and half your submariners to go as well. Continue providing security for our noncombatants. Besides, if we fail here, it'll be up to you to continue the fight, keep helping our friends in technical matters." Laumer straightened, glad to have something to do. Something he *could* do, while he got his feet under him.

"Aye, aye, sir."

Matt turned back to Geran-Eras. "I understand there's a small Baalkpan settlement at Saangku. They may need evacuation as well, if things go poorly here." There were a few thoughtful nods in the crowd. Matt pressed on. "If that happens, then the Homes will serve yet another purpose. If

Baalkpan falls, we'll retreat north through the jungle, and the Homes'll be waiting to take us to safety." He smirked. Everyone knew how dangerous a trek of that distance through the Borneo jungle would be—particularly with the Grik snapping at their heels. Perhaps some would survive. "Not much of a backup plan, but it's better than nothing."

The High Chiefs of the three remaining homes spoke rapidly among themselves. Excited conversations erupted throughout the hall. Matt remained silent, watching, while Keje, Geran, and Ramic made up their minds. Finally they stood ready to speak, and Nakja-Mur touched the gong for quiet.

"Very well," Keje announced. "It's agreed. *Humfra-Dar* and *Aracca* sail immediately for Sembaakpan, with enough people to trim the wings and work the guns, if necessary. The High Chiefs will remain to command their warriors."

Matt nodded reservedly. "Good," he said, "but what about *Big Sal*?"

"*Salissa*, like her sister, *Walker*, will remain here." Keje blinked utmost resolution when he spoke. "That, my brother, is not open to discussion. You conveniently omitted the fact that *Walker* and *Mahan* will face the same 'slaughter' as our Homes. They will not face it alone. *Salissa* will be your floating battery as long as she can."

The hall was silent while everyone considered the implications of Keje's words. Matt didn't know what to say.

"One problem I can see," Ellis interjected, "is their damn observation plane they bombed us with. If it shows up again, it could throw a major wrench in the works. Japs could stand off and pound us—just like you said—and there'd be nothing we could do."

Matt knew Jim wasn't very happy with *Mahan*'s assignment, and his tone actually sounded a little confrontational. Matt glanced at Shinya, then looked his former exec—his friend—in the eye.

"Good point, but I have it on . . . good authority . . . the spotting plane won't be a factor."

"How . . . ?"

"Our radio wasn't busted, remember? We picked up a transmission, in the clear, that the plane was damaged. Must've been right after its attack."

"Well . . . okay, but that's just one example of how easily the plan can get thrown out of whack."

"I thought you liked the plan. If you didn't, why didn't you say something when we were making it?"

"Because I did—*do*—like it!" Jim admitted in frustration. "No, I take that back. I hate the damn plan, but it's probably the best we could come up with under the circumstances. What I disagree with now, that maybe I didn't before, is that the plan leaves *Mahan* out of the fight. By all rights, she ought to have *Walker's* job!"

Matt shook his head. "She's too vulnerable. It'd be suicide. *Amagi* has to *see Walker*, which means she's going to get to shoot at her. With one good boiler and only one screw, *Mahan'd* be a sitting duck."

"*Walker's* not much better off than *Mahan*," Jim insisted stubbornly.

"But she *is* faster," Matt stressed. "And as soon as *Amagi* gets a good look, we're going to make smoke and run like hell. After she sees *Walker* run away, she won't worry about her anymore. That's when *Mahan* does her job. It's an important job, Jim. Besides"—he grinned wryly—"you already changed your number back."

Jim snorted. "All right, Skipper, but next time *Mahan* gets to play target while *Walker* puts the sneak on 'em. Fair's fair. The boys are starting to feel left out—and sort of coddled." Jim chuckled softly, but Matt knew his old exec was more serious than he seemed. The *Mahan*s didn't want to die any more than anyone else, but they did want to do their part. Many still felt tainted by the Kaufman incident, despite their recent success.

"You bet, Jim. Next time."

"I guess it's really come down to this, hasn't it?" Sandra asked bitterly. Everyone looked at her questioningly, surprised by her tone. "You know, 'win or lose, live or die'—probably die even if you win?"

"It's been that way from the start," Matt said gently. "Ever since the Squall. In our old world, maybe it wasn't so black-and-white. I guess you could always surrender—even to the Japs—but that won't work here." He took a breath. "So, yeah, it's down to that, and it's just that simple."

Sandra shivered in the warm hall. She knelt and gathered Rebecca in her arms. "Maybe, but it seems even worse when you joke about it."

Nakja-Mur cleared his throat, and everyone looked at him. "Well," he said, "that's decided, and well-done. I do have a request, if you will permit me, Cap-i-taan Reddy."

"Of course."

"Before you depart, would you share with us again your *not* 'backup' plan?"

*T*salka glared across the water as Kurokawa's launch returned to his ship. "You know, General, I still detest that creature."

General Esshk hissed agreement. "But he is useful. His iron ship is still slowed by damage, he says, but at least it floats evenly now." He hissed amusement, remembering Kurokawa's stormy indignation and fury toward their enemies after they blew another hole in his mighty ship almost four moons ago. "He is also highly motivated," he added cryptically.

"Their iron ship is wondrously powerful," Tsalka agreed. "I will never forget the concussion of its great guns, and the damage it inflicted on the huge ship of the prey. Magnificent!"

"Most impressive," Esshk hedged. He gazed at the lumbering iron monstrosity. Black smoke belched from its middle as it burned the coal that somehow pushed it along. Despite its amazing power, he must not forget that the Tree Prey had friends who could damage it. It was ensconced deep within the protective embrace of the main body of the "Invincible Swarm" (as opposed to the previous, ill-fated Grand Swarm) to protect it from another surprise enemy attack. Nothing could get through the impenetrable cordon of almost four hundred ships.

"He still entertains somewhat grandiose illusions of his own importance," Tsalka declared. "He is impertinent and grasping."

"True," Esshk agreed, "but he is also too often right, concerning the methods of the prey. He was right about the importance they placed on retrieving their castaways from Madura, and I confess I did not see it until too late. An opportunity was lost there, I fear." He hissed a self-deprecating sigh. "He also seems right about sparing some Uul, particularly those with

valuable experience, when a ship—or even an army—is beaten. Not all fall
prey, after all, and it does seem to harden them somehow. Besides, their
valuable experience is not then lost. It is difficult starting over with mindless Uul every time we suffer a reverse."

"A most dangerous precedent, I will say it again," Tsalka objected.
"Our Way has worked well for millennia. It is not for us to make changes
on a whim." He sniffed. "Your 'philosophical hobbies' will place you in
grave danger one day, General; mark my words. You will strain your famil-
ial relations with the Celestial Mother too far, and even she will not indulge you."

"Perhaps," Esshk agreed, "but our Way has struck a snag this time, it
seems. Improvisation is often dangerous, but I do command here, Excellency. I will take Kurokawa's advice, follow his 'tactics,' give him his head, to
a degree. For now. I can always cut it off at my leisure. Consider it an experiment. If I am wrong"—he hissed the equivalent of a shrug—"I will
destroy myself."

"If you are wrong, dear General," Tsalka replied, "I doubt you will be
allowed that honor, and neither will I."

Walker steamed away from the pier shortly before dark to join the frigates
in the Makassar Strait. The next morning, as soon as the sun was up, the
Catalina clattered its way into the sky on what, it was hoped, might be its
final flight. At the old fitting-out pier, two huge barges had been brought
alongside. One was equipped with a respectable pile driver—even by Navy
standards—for driving pier pilings into the bottom of Baalkpan Bay. Both
it and the other barge were crowded with empty casks and great long posts,
like telephone poles. Yard workers and a large force of unskilled laborers
scurried about on each, making final preparations and casting off lines.

Chief Gray and Dennis Silva were on yet a third barge, along with
Dean Laney, Randal Hale, Sandy Newman, Pack Rat, and six other Lemurian helpers. This particular barge was attached in tandem to the others by
a long, thick cable ultimately leading to *Mahan*'s fantail. When the final
lines were taken in, Gray sent a signal to be relayed up the awkward train.
Ever so slowly *Mahan* strained against the weight, and one by one the
barges began to move. The third barge had to wait longer than the others,
since its cable was twice as long. The reason was its cargo. Securely lashed
to the broad, flat deck were all but twenty of *Walker*'s and half of *Mahan*'s
MK-6 depth charges. Both ships had been blessed by a full allotment of the
antisubmarine weapons when they fled Surabaya, and until now, except as
"anti–mountain fish" weapons, no one had thought of a way to use them.

Unlike the MK-6 magnetic torpedo exploder they'd had so much
trouble with, there was nothing at all wrong with the MK-6 depth charges.

They were ridiculously unsophisticated weapons, and had remained virtually unchanged since the Great War. Each consisted of a can roughly the size of a forty-gallon drum, filled with six hundred pounds of TNT. Hydrostatic pressure detonators activated when they reached a preselected depth. Their very simplicity made them remarkably reliable weapons—at least as far as their designed function was concerned. The only problem was, when used against a submarine's tough pressure hull, they had to sink to within twenty yards just to damage the target, ten yards or less to have a serious chance of destroying it. In practice, against a radically maneuvering submarine, they were extremely inefficient. Gray often compared their use to a blindfolded man shooting at bats with a pistol.

Theoretically, the detonation of six hundred pounds of high explosive underneath a *surface* target would have more gratifying results. That was, after all, the desired effect of the MK-6-equipped torpedoes. Therefore, Lieutenant Sandison had been charged with the task of inventing a way to make the depth charges do what the torpedoes wouldn't.

"This'll never work," Silva proclaimed grandly as the line of barges eased into the bay. He was sitting atop one of the sixty cylinders clustered together on the barge. "'Ash cans' are supposed to *blow up* when they go in the water." He arched an eyebrow and looked at those around him. "We're all gonna die."

"Shut up, you maniac," Gray growled. "Besides, what does it matter to you? At least you'll die happy." Silva hadn't returned until morning after he disappeared with Pam and Risa the previous afternoon.

"Yeah," grumped Hale. "The dame famine's bad enough without you making it worse. Two of 'em's already taken. That leaves only two left, well, 'sides the new ones. But they left last night on *Humfra-Dar*."

Silva regarded him with feigned astonishment. "Why, whatever do you mean?"

Laney stepped in front of him, fists at his side. "Silva, if you don't shut the hell up, I'm gonna stuff your hatrack."

"Lighten up, Laney," Silva said. "If you're that hard up, get yourself a 'Cat gal. You'd be surprised how adventurous they are!"

Laney blinked at him. "You just never quit!"

Silva arched his eyebrows again.

"You're one sick bastard, Silva," Randal Hale said, shaking his head, but there was speculation in his voice.

"That's enough!" Gray commanded. "We got enough unnatural things to worry about today—like turnin' depth charges into mines!"

"How are we gonna do that, anyway?" Newman asked.

"See those big posts on the first barge?" They nodded. "We'll drive 'em into the bottom with that pile driver, and tie a depth charge to it a few feet underwater. If any of the post is still sticking up, we'll cut it off. Then, if a ship runs into it, hopefully it'll snap off and the charge'll sink. When it gets to twenty feet, *boom*! Got it?"

Silva cocked his head. "What are we gonna do in the main channel? Too deep to sink poles."

"We'll hang a charge underneath however many of those barrels it takes to keep one up, and anchor the whole thing to the bottom."

"They'll see them, won't they?" questioned Hale.

"Maybe," Gray agreed. "But what are they gonna do about it? We'll rig it so's they can't squeeze between 'em without hitting another. Top it off by putting out way more barrels than we have depth charges too. It'll be just a matter of tying an anchor to 'em and heavin' 'em over the side. That's how we'll leave a clear channel for *Walker* to come back through, without it lookin' like there is one."

Newman looked thoughtful. "Might work," he said. "Now I know why we're on such a long cable, though. I guess we're the ones setting the charges?"

Gray nodded. "With this box of bombs, if one of 'em slips after we set it, the flashies won't even find enough to make it worth their while."

Pete Alden stood on Nakja-Mur's balcony with the High Chief of Baalk-pan, Letts, Shinya, Bradford, and Sandra Tucker. The kid was off with O'Casey. The balcony made an ideal observation post from which they could see the vast panorama of the city's bristling defenses in the late-afternoon sun. The regiments had been moved into their positions, and *Big Sal* was now moored by the shipyard dock. She had a spring in her cable so she could fire her augmented battery into the flank of any force trying to land there, or anywhere along the waterfront. Her sails were stowed, and like all the defenses, she held plenty of water barrels ready to defend against firebombs. Because it was such an obvious place for them to direct the battle, they'd already made plans to abandon the Great Hall if *Amagi* came into the bay. Even with high-rise dwellings all around, the Great Hall and its Sacred Tree stood out quite prominently. It would be a prime target for the battle cruiser's initial salvos. Nakja-Mur was horrified that the Sacred Tree might be damaged, but there was nothing they could do to prevent it. Secondary command posts had been established in strategic locations.

Karen Theimer had worked wonders setting up a central hospital and ambulance corps, and the surgeons and nurses who'd learned their trade with the Allied Expeditionary Force were now fully integrated into the system. Sandra was in overall command of the medical effort, from the central hospital. Karen was her exec, and the other nurses would supervise the two main field hospitals in north and south Baalkpan. Smaller aid stations were established near every defensive position, supervised by talented veterans such as Selass. Sandra hated that she wouldn't be with *Walker* during the coming fight, but there was no question where she'd be most needed. Jamie Miller could care for any casualties the ship might have. Other than her personal feelings, she had no excuse to be aboard.

Without *Mahan*'s generators to run the new transmitter, it had been stowed in a deep, safe bunker. *Walker* would remain in constant contact through light and flag signals, as well as the crystal receivers Riggs had constructed, which required almost no electricity. The experimental batteries they'd built had plenty of juice for them, so Matt could keep overall strategic command even while fighting his ship. Hopefully. Even if everything went exactly according to plan, however, *Walker* would be fighting for her life. Her exposure to the enemy was *the* part of the plan everything else depended on, so that was where he had to be. Sandra still wished she could be with him. The frustration of the evening before had only heightened her longing, as well as her conviction that they *had* been a "couple of dopes" all along. She envied Karen her happiness and her ability to show open, natural affection for the one she loved.

She suddenly realized someone had spoken to her. "What was that?" she asked, shaking her head.

"Do you have any questions or requirements, Lieutenant Tucker?" Letts asked. Gone was the tongue-tied suitor of short months before. Alden would have command of the "land battle" they expected, but Letts was still acting as Captain Reddy's chief of staff.

"Uh, just the disposition of the child, Becky, and Mr. O'Casey."

"I thought you might keep the girl at the central hospital—what's the dope on her, anyway?" Only Bradford and Nakja-Mur knew, and they didn't answer. "Well, if you'll do that, I'll keep O'Casey with me. I'd like to see what he's made of."

Sandra nodded. "Other than that, then, everything's under control," she said.

"Good. Mr. Alden?"

Pete shrugged. "We're about as ready as we can be without reinforcements. *Mahan* signaled a few minutes ago that they're nearly finished laying the mines." He shook his head. "It's a miracle nobody got blown up doing that. Otherwise, the only thing I have to add is that Lieutenant Riggs is finally satisfied with the visibility of the semaphore tower in Fort Atkinson. His guys on the southwest wall couldn't see it through those last few trees and they cut them down. Oh, yeah, I sent Lord Rolak and the First

Aryaal to reinforce the two hundred Sularans, and Mr. Brister's artillery-men in the fort. I also think Shinya should command the independent force we talked about."

Letts nodded agreement. "That's what the captain said too."

Pete looked at Shinya. Ever since he returned, not only from the trip to Manila, but from Aryaal with the AEF, Pete's friend had been very quiet. "I want to deploy the First Marines, the Tenth Baalkpan, and the warriors from *Aracca* to a forward position defending the south and west approaches against any enemy landing." He held up his hand. "You're *not* to pull a Custer's Last Stand, or some Jap equivalent! I don't want you getting tangled up in anything you can't handle. I mainly want you out there to keep some small force from coming ashore and cutting us off from the fort."

"The First Marines are under strength," Shinya said absently. "They had losses at Tarakan and B'mbaado."

"Yeah, well, maybe we can fill 'em out with rifle-trained guys from the Second. Will you do it?"

Very seriously, Shinya nodded, and Pete peered intently at him. "Say, you aren't going to cut your guts out or anything if you have to pull back, are you?"

Tamatsu chuckled. In spite of his mood, he was surprised by the question. "Not unless you tell me to. We don't have the luxury of engaging in such selfish gestures. Besides, that would only increase whatever dishonor I might earn by retreating. It would give aid and comfort to the enemy by contributing to their commissary." Everyone laughed at that, including Shinya. But then a strange expression crossed his face and he grew silent again.

"So that's it, then?" Letts asked skeptically. Alden looked speculative but didn't reply. "Nothing at all?"

"Well, yes, actually," said Courtney Bradford. He motioned to himself and Nakja-Mur. "What about us? What shall we do?"

Letts looked at him, surprised. "I just assumed you'd help in the hospital. The way you're always dissecting stuff—you certainly know how to handle a knife."

Bradford drew himself up. "My dear sir, as I've made no secret, I fancy myself something of a naturalist. It's a hobby. I've a great deal of experience cutting things up, but virtually none putting them back together. Certainly you understand the difference? Of course you do!" He shook his head. "No, just give me a rifle—point me where you need me most, I say. Besides, my recent observations about Grik behavior might prove crucial."

"Trust me, Mr. Bradford, everybody's up on your 'observations,'" Pete interrupted. "But no offense; if things get bad enough we need your one rifle, we'll all be bugging out! I'll give you a Krag—but I'd consider it a personal favor if you'd use it to help guard the hospital. I'm sure Captain Reddy would appreciate it as well. Will you put yourself at Lieutenant Tucker's service?"

Bradford pursed his lips. "Well, if you insist on putting it like that . . ."

"That still leaves me," said Nakja-Mur. "I've grown old and fat, but I was a warrior once. Not much of one, I admit. This is the first time in the memory of the Scrolls that Baalkpan has ever faced war, but I should be defending my people."

"You are," Letts assured him. "You're leading your people, and your courage is an example to them, as well as us. Besides, I need you beside me throughout the battle. I may need your advice or skill at dealing with people. Also, if something happens to me, you're the only one who can see the whole picture. You'll have to step in as Captain Reddy's chief of staff."

"Very well," Nakja-Mur said somberly. "I accept. I will watch you closely to know what to do if that unfortunate event comes to pass. I pray it does not."

"Me too," Alan Letts fervently agreed.

One by one, Sandra, Bradford, and finally Nakja-Mur left the balcony to continue their preparations. Only Shinya and Alden remained. Pete suspected Tamatsu had been waiting to talk to him alone.

"I will be honored to command the independent force," he said at last, "but I wanted you to know I have been engaged in a struggle of . . . honor."

"I know," Alden said simply. "Adar told me."

Shinya looked surprised. "And yet you still trust me to do this thing?"

"Sure. Otherwise I wouldn't have brought it up. Why, don't you trust yourself?"

Tamatsu only shook his head in amazement. "You Americans. You assume a great deal. Even I didn't know, until a few moments ago, which side of the struggle would prevail. And yet you had no doubts?"

"Nope." Alden sighed. "Look, you said whatever was eating you was a matter of honor, right? I know you pretty well by now, I think. The honorable thing to do in this situation is pretty clear—as long as you're not going to commit Harry-Carry."

A ghost of a smile crossed Shinya's face, but he shook his head. "It isn't that simple. I gave Captain Reddy my parole, and I've since engaged in numerous activities for the common good, I think. That wasn't inconsistent with my concept of honor. This . . ." He paused. "This is different. If I continue to help you, even to the extent of aiding you against my own people, I will be committing treason in their eyes—and mine. Whatever the reason, and wherever we are, my people and yours are at war, Sergeant Alden." He took off his hat and scratched his short hair. "However . . ." He stopped again. "Such an interesting word, don't you think? 'However.' I wonder if it was ever intended to be so vague, yet so profound at the same time," he mused darkly. "However, for whatever reason, *Amagi*'s commander supports the side of purest evil in this war. There can be no honorable explanation for that. On its face, that would seem to make my decision simpler, yet it does not. My people do not have the freedom to choose which policies of our government we will support. As far as *Amagi*'s crew are concerned, ordinary seamen and junior officers—men like me—*Amagi*'s commanding officer is the direct representative of the emperor. Whatever has befallen them, they will follow him because of that, whether or not they believe he is right." He searched Alden's face for understanding. "You see it as misplaced obedience to a corrupt commander, and perhaps it is. But to my people, a commander's dishonor does not reflect upon those under his command, as long as they follow his orders. Regardless of the commander's motive, obeying him is the honorable thing for *them* to do. Do you see now why I have had such difficulty with this decision? Through their captain, the crew of *Amagi* have become tools of the Grik. Through their honorable service, they are assisting in the commission of evil. That's the most tragic irony of all.

"So you see, I have not been agonizing over which side is in the right; even from my different perspective, that is obvious. The decision I faced was whether to revert to my status of noncombatant parolee, or openly betray my people, whose honor has already been betrayed by their leader." He took a deep breath. "I have made that decision. Perhaps my long association with Americans has corrupted me, but I begin to see that blind obedience to a dishonorable command can't obviate the final, greatest responsibility of honor: to do the right thing. I grieve for my countrymen who have not realized that yet, but I cannot stand idly by."

"You Japs are so weird," Alden said quietly. "No offense. What made you make up your mind?"

Shinya considered. "First, it was my realization that, if the roles were reversed, and *Walker* had somehow come into association with the Grik, Captain Reddy would never have aided them as *Amagi* has. If he tried, the crew wouldn't have supported him. The way the crew of *Mahan* finally decided they could no longer support Captain Kaufman, regardless of rank, is a good example. Then, when King Alcas ordered the surprise attack on *Walker* that killed Mr. Donaghey, Captain Reddy hanged the saboteurs. I saw no injustice there. They were only following orders, but to do such a thing while negotiations were underway—and after we saved them from the Grik—collective guilt couldn't fail to stain the perpetrators."

Alden nodded. "Now you know why we were so mad about Pearl Harbor."

Shinya grimaced. "Perhaps." He looked out over the wind-ruffled bay.

In the far distance was *Mahan*'s battered outline. The low-lying barges and toiling men and Lemurians were barely visible. Preparing.

"In any event, as I said, I will be honored to command the independent force, if you still desire it. The duty will be heavy, should I face my countrymen. I cannot deny that. But it is also, clearly, my duty." He paused. "As it is my duty to ask for the Second instead of the First Marines. You will need the riflemen as a reserve, whereas if I have to fight, it will be the shield wall and spears."

"All right," Pete agreed, "and you're right. Just remember your promise not to gut yourself if anything goes wrong." They shared another small smile. "You know what you're supposed to do. If things get too hairy, pull back to Fort Atkinson or the Baalkpan wall." He shrugged. "They may not put anyone ashore there at all; flank attacks don't seem their style. We rolled up their flanks time and again on B'mbaado, and it always took them by surprise. That stuff Mallory said about Tjilatjap keeps coming back to me, though, so keep your eyes peeled."

The sun was near the jungle horizon when the last cluster of barrels went into the dappled sea. As powerful as he was, Silva hurt all over from the backbreaking chore of manhandling the heavy depth charges. He tried to use his grimy T-shirt to wipe the burning sweat from his eyes, but the shirt was so soaked it only made it worse. He glanced at the mouth of the bay. He was surprised *Walker* hadn't returned and was struck by the irony of that. On the world they came from, she'd been an insignificant, expendable asset, a relic of an almost ancient war—in terms of technological advancement. She hadn't been in the same league with her smallest modern counterparts in the Japanese Navy. Most of her sisters weren't even frontline warships anymore; they'd been converted to seaplane or submarine tenders, minelayers, transports, even damage-control hulks. . . . Now Dennis was surprised she wasn't already back from facing maybe a hundred enemy ships, with only three sailing frigates to assist her. Nobody else seemed to think it was a big deal either, and he guessed that was really more of a testament to their faith in her captain than the dilapidated ship herself. Still . . .

Several times during the afternoon, they thought they heard the faint booming of *Walker*'s guns, and duller, rippling broadsides of muzzle-loading cannon. Maybe not. The wind was wrong, and the fighting had to be closer than they'd expected if it was so, but regardless, *Walker* and her little fleet were doing their job: buying the time they needed to finish their little surprise.

He looked at the evidence of their hard day's work. Across the lightly choppy water, hundreds of clustered barrels bobbed from the shallows on

one side of the channel to the other. Some supported a deadly cargo. Beyond the barrels, and even mixed with them where they could, they'd set
the posts supporting even more explosives. The minefield looked more
impressive than it was, and the first storm that came along would carry it
away. Eventually the barrels would leak and the depth charges would sink
and detonate without warning. That was one of the main reasons they'd
waited so long to prepare the "surprise"; so it would be fresh and ready
when the enemy came. He noticed there was a kind of vague pattern to the
floating shapes, and it occurred to him the pattern was broken along the
side of the channel they were on. It'd be obvious to anybody—especially
some Jap lookout in *Amagi*'s top—there was a free pass right through the
minefield. The other side looked tight, but that was where they'd deliberately set most of the dummies so *Walker* and the frigates would have a safe
path to return. He looked tiredly around. There were still ten depth charges
left, but all the barrels on the barges were gone.

"Hey, Bosun," he said, getting Gray's attention. "I think we missed a
spot." Before Gray could answer, a growing, clattering drone approached
from the southwest. Looking up, they saw the abbreviated outline of the
PBY. "Coming back," Silva muttered. "I wonder how far behind our ship is?"

Another drone was approaching. He looked toward *Mahan*, loitering a
safe distance from the semicircle the barges had formed, and saw a launch
drawing near. A few minutes later it bumped alongside, and Lieutenant
Sandison hopped onto the barge carrying a large, canvas-wrapped object in
his hands.

"Is this the last of them?" he asked.

"Yes sir," Gray replied.

"All right. I want you to set them all for, oh, say, a hundred and fifty
feet; then we'll tie a cable off to one and put it over the side."

"One fifty?" Gray asked, surprised.

"You heard me."

"But the water here's only about eighty feet deep."

"I know. Trust me; you're going to like it." Securing one end of the
rope to the barge, they dropped the depth charge attached to the other
over the side.

"Now," Sandison instructed, "rig all the rest to slide down the rope so
they'll rest together on the bottom. All except one. Chief? I might need
your help with this. I'm a torpedo guy, after all."

"Well, I ain't no depth-charge man," Gray growled. "We ought to have
Campeti." He paused, pointing, while Sandison unwrapped his object.
"What the hell's that?"

"It *used* to be a MK-6, magnetic torpedo exploder. It's the one we took out of that fish we put in *Amagi*—the one that went off. We worked it over, and now it's been redesignated the Silly Six, Sandison Surprise."

"Silly's right. What the hell's it good for?"

"Well, as you can see, there've been a few modifications." He held it up. "First, the contact-exploder mechanism has been entirely removed—leaving just the magnetic trip mechanism . . ."

"Okay."

". . . which is now just a glorified magnetic switch." There was a loud splash behind them as another depth charge rolled over the side. Half a dozen men and Lemurians held the rope taut as it sank. "I will next put the switch back in this waterproof shell canister, with the battle-lantern battery for company. . . ."

"I'll be damned!" Gray muttered, realization dawning.

"Almost certainly," Sandison agreed. "You'll see there're two long wires trailing out of the canister? I want the canister secured tightly to a rope by its handles, the other end of the rope wrapped around the depth charge. Make the distance about sixty-five feet. When you do that, we'll wrap these two wires around the cable—loosely, with lots of slack—until we get to the charge."

"But how are we going to set it off?" Gray asked. "If we try to run those wires in through the hydrostatic fuse, the damn thing'll leak."

Sheepishly, Bernie fished a hand grenade from his pocket. Two more wires ran out of the top where the fuse had been, and it was carefully sealed around them. "I got this from Reavis. He had the duty."

"Why that little . . . !" Silva began, gasping from exertion.

"Don't be too hard on him, Dennis. Spanky gave me a note."

Gray just shook his head. Another heavy splash. "So," he said, pointing to another object. "What's that? It looks like a big-ass cork."

Sandison nodded. "It's a float for a Lemurian fishing net. Buoyant as hell. I can't remember what they call it; ask one of your guys." He gestured around. "Whatever it is, I think it's 'Cat for 'big-ass cork.' It'll hold our trigger up."

Gray stared, hands on his hips. "You know? If that crazy gizmo works, it'll probably be the first time in the history of the war against the Japs one of those magnetic bastards did anything right."

"Maybe," Sandison agreed; then he pointed to the open lane in the minefield that led to it. "But if it doesn't, we'll have even more reason to curse them—only we probably won't be able to."

Gray nodded as another depth charge splashed over the side. "Yeah. Thank God this ain't the main deal. I'd hate to think everything was riding on it."

Silva stopped heaving on the next depth charge in line and wiped his brow. "What the *hell* do you mean, this ain't the main deal?" he demanded between gasps for air. "We been doin' all this work for a *sideshow*?"

Shortly after 2100 that night, the new construction frigates, USS *Tolson* and USS *Kas-Ra-Ar,* displayed the proper lantern-light recognition signals, and were allowed to pass under the guns of Fort Atkinson. *Mahan* was waiting for them, having returned the barges to the yard. Now she signaled them to heave to and wait for a launch to bring a pilot to take them safely through the minefield. As the ships passed in the night, Jim Ellis saw they'd taken quite a pounding, and though their masts still stood they didn't look new anymore. Of *Walker* and *Donaghey* there was no sign for almost another hour. Finally a flare went up, declaring an emergency, and *Walker* appeared, towing the wallowing, dismasted hulk of Lieutenant Garrett's ship. The launch took Gray across so he could guide the two ships inside the bay. With her searchlights sweeping the surface of the water, the old destroyer picked her way into the clear, where *Tolson* took up the tow so she could move her battered sister to the new fitting-out pier that served the frigates. Reunited with *Mahan*, *Walker* and her own sister steamed back toward the city.

Matt yawned and rubbed his face while Gray sipped the coffee Juan had given him, and finished his report on the mining operation. It sounded like they'd managed a better job than expected. Like Gray, Matt was dubious about the last mine they'd set, but agreed it was worth a try. He thanked the Bosun and leaned back in his chair, stretching his shoulder muscles experimentally. They ached, but not much worse than the rest of him. He thought about how hard it must have been for the detail that set the mines, and imagined they were much sorer than he was. It had been a long day for everyone.

Walker and her little squadron had indeed met the advance enemy force, and Matt now suspected their hundred-ship estimate had been conservative. He also believed they'd engaged the cream of the Grik fleet that day: most of their cannon-armed ships. One had been larger than the others, painted white, just like the curious ship Ben said had grappled with *Revenge*. He wondered what their significance was. He blinked his tired eyes. Not that it mattered as far as this one was concerned: *Walker* had destroyed it, along with as many others as she could, given the restriction Matt had placed on ammunition expenditure. Campeti had tried to destroy mainly gunships, to spare their frigates, but there'd still been plenty to occupy the new ships. *Tolson, Kas-Ra-Ar,* and *Donaghey* fought splendidly, savaging their foes with spectacular results—but there'd just been so many. . . . Lieutenant Garrett, in particular, fought his ship brilliantly—he had the most experience, after all—and maybe a little recklessly too. His ship wound up surrounded, where *Walker* couldn't support her, fighting both sides at point-blank range. It had been a stirring, frustrating scene—the way it must have felt to watch Hawkins hurl himself at the Spanish Armada. In the end, *Donaghey* managed to destroy her tormentors, but Garrett's ship was so badly damaged she might never fight again. Garrett survived—somehow—unscathed, but his sailing master exec, Taak-Fas, was dead, along with almost half his crew. Torpedoman Chapelle, his "master gunner," was lightly wounded.

The battle ended near dark, uncomfortably close to the clustered Balabalangen islands and the bay. The sea was littered with derelict Grik ships, but those that could—about twenty—uncharacteristically fled back the way they'd come, and the destroyer didn't pursue. The enemy retreat was surprising enough, but it was also well coordinated, and that set off warning bells in Captain Reddy's mind. There was no smoke on the horizon that would indicate *Amagi* was near, but he felt the prickly suspicion of a trap nevertheless. It was as if, even as they tried to hold the enemy away, the Grik were attempting to force them back, to shrink their scouting range. Their mission, to prevent the enemy from approaching close enough to discover or interfere with the placement of the minefield, had been accomplished. But the Grik might have accomplished their objective as well, and Matt had to wonder who'd actually won the battle. Mallory flew over several times during the day, but with no radio they had to rely on spotty visual signals. As night fell and his Morse lamp became more visible, Mallory did confirm sighting the main enemy force northeast of Pulau Sebuku, clustered protectively around the battle cruiser. The news wasn't unexpected, although it was dispiriting. Deep down Matt had continued to hope that, given enough time, *Amagi* might still just roll over and sink. For a fleeting instant he had a poignant thought of his father and the scorn he'd have heaped upon such wishful thinking. He sighed.

Wishful thinking wouldn't solve their ammunition problems, either. *Walker* had sortied with another twenty of the "new" shells, reloaded with a solid copper projectile and black powder. As Ellis reported, the projectile worked okay, after a fashion. They went off, and even flew reasonably straight, but with a much lower velocity than the targeting computer was accustomed to, so local control was the only way to go. It also took every one they had to sink six ships. It went without saying that the copper projectiles would be worse than useless against *Amagi*. Sandison hadn't been pleased to learn how the rounds performed when Ellis first told him. He, Garrett, and Campeti had plenty of ideas how to improve them, but they just didn't have the time. They'd have to fight with what they had. He shook his head.

Looking out to starboard, Matt made out *Mahan*'s outline in the dark as the other ship closely paced them. It occurred to him that this was only the second time they'd steamed together since being reunited at Aryaal. That other time was only a brief foray when they'd played tug-of-war for *Mahan*'s propeller. Now, even if they were making only ten knots, Matt felt a sudden exhilaration. The sound of the blowers so close together, and the swish of the sea as they parted it between them, left him with a sense of companionship he'd missed. Jim Ellis was over there, on that other bridge, and Matt wondered what he was thinking. Maybe the same thing. He suddenly wished it were daylight so the people they defended could see the two destroyers steaming side by side in the bay. The sight might bolster their morale—at least until they saw what they were up against.

Without warning, Matt had a chilling premonition that this was the last time *Walker* and *Mahan* would ever be in formation again. As hard as he tried, he couldn't shake the thought. It was as though the swishing sea were a ghostly voice warning the elderly sisters to say their final farewell, because one, at least, was doomed. Which one? he wondered with a heavy heart. Or would both face destruction when *Amagi* steamed into the bay? The moment ended when they neared the dock, and both ships reduced speed. *Mahan* went first to the fueling pier, where her bunkers were quickly filled. Then she moved briefly to the dock, where over half her crew went ashore, leaving fifteen human and twenty Lemurian volunteers aboard— just enough to operate her during the short part she would play. Half her remaining ammunition was off-loaded as well. It had been agreed that *Walker* would need it more than she.

In less than an hour, *Mahan* cast off once more, just as *Walker* was beginning to fuel. As she crept away from the lights on the dock, the jury-rigged Morse lamp on her port bridge wing quickly flashed: "Good hunting. Farewell." Ellis emphasized his message with a long, harsh toot on *Mahan*'s steam whistle.

"Send, 'Good hunting, God bless,'" ordered Matt. While *Walker*'s Morse lamp clacked, he watched *Mahan* fade into darkness, until she was visible no more.

Near the end of the midwatch, Dennis Silva was supervising the transport of vital tools and machinery from the torpedo workshop to their— hopefully—temporary storage, in hardened bunkers ashore. Everything that could be spared—the lathe, mills, cutters and bits, extra torches and acetylene bottles, their meager supply of spare parts—was being off-loaded . . . just in case. Dowden and a small detail had carried all the ship's papers, logs, charts, manuals, and other documents ashore a short time earlier. Even the conduits and bundles of long-bypassed wiring were being stripped from the ship to save the copper wire. Earl Lanier, Ray Mertz, and Pepper gravely removed the restored Coke machine themselves. All told, it was a difficult task, and even though Dennis appreciated the necessity and approved the captain's foresight in ordering it, the implications were ominous and disheartening.

He'd never been so tired. It had been a grueling day, and even his apparently inexhaustible and irrepressible energy had limits, it seemed. Laney would soon replace him with the morning watch, however, and hopefully he'd get a few hours' sleep. The captain had already told them the morning general quarters alarm wouldn't sound. He stopped on the pier, shuffling back from the bunker, and looked at the ship for a moment. She seemed strangely fuzzy in the humid, hazy air, and ephemeral sparks flew like fireflies from last-minute repairs. Her weirdly diffused searchlights beamed eerily downward, illuminating her decks and casting long, twisted shadows. They made her glow like some unearthly, mournful specter, and completing the surrealistic scene, a lively tune squeaked vaguely from Marvaney's phonograph. Silva felt a sudden chill, and sensed he was moving toward his grave. He shuddered.

"She does look rather 'creepy,' as you would say," came a girlish voice from the gloom, and the mighty Dennis Silva nearly pissed himself.

"What're you doin' here, goddamn it?" he demanded more harshly than he meant to.

"I came to see you."

"Me?" He stopped, peering down at Rebecca's tiny form. "What for? Why ain't you with O'Casey or Lieutenant Tucker?"

"I 'gave them the slip,' and each thinks I am with the other. Besides, you are my other protector, and I'm perfectly safe."

"Sure, you're safe as can be around here, even without a watchdog. Least for now. 'Cats are swell folks. But what'd you wanna see me for?"

Rebecca sighed. "Dennis Silva, you are the most vile, crude, wildly depraved creature. . . . I never suspected such as you might even exist. The spectacle you made of yourself when we arrived! I would scold you for your shamelessness if I suspected you understood the concept of shame, but somehow"—she took a breath and shook her head—"I have come to care for you . . . to a small degree. I never had a brother, and have always been thankful for it—properly so, it seems—for I find myself thinking of you more and more in that unsettling role. My sense of propriety demands I despise you—and I do!—yet . . . I also find, like a brother, I suppose, I can't help but love you just a bit as well." She grimaced, as if at the foul taste of the words.

Silva cracked. Perhaps it was exhaustion or indigestion, or perhaps some soot from *Walker*'s stacks got in his eyes, but suddenly his face was wet with tears, and he'd gathered the girl in a tight embrace. "I'm a rowdy old scamp," he agreed huskily into her hair. "Can't help it. But I'd be proud to take you on as my little sister, if you make me. Maybe you can teach me a little about that word, 'shame,' you mentioned. Right now, though, you got to run along. I got to get that old ship ready for a fight, and pretty as she is, she's got a quirk or two ol' Silva's got to straighten out."

"You are unloading things from her in case she sinks!" Rebecca cried, suddenly tearful as well.

"Naw, she can't sink. We're just gettin' a buncha loose junk out of the way. You'd be amazed how cluttered a place can get with nothin' but sloppy guys livin' there."

"You're lying. You need me, you and poor Lawrence as well. I can't help but think something dreadful will happen to you both without me to watch over you—and just think how terrified he will be: his first battle, and no one to comfort him. . . . I don't think anyone really likes him, you know."

"I like him, even if he is a lizard," Dennis assured her. "I already said I was sorry for shootin' him."

"It's not the same. I must spend the battle aboard your ship. . . ." She paused, desperate. "You need me! You will need me before the battle is done; I know it!"

"Now, now, little girls underfoot is the last thing we need in a fight. Lieutenant Tucker's gonna need you, though, and that's a fact." He set her down, wiping his eyes. "An' one thing I need you to do, if it comes to it, is tell my gals I love 'em all. Would you do that? It's Pam and Risa. I know you don't approve, but I do love 'em both." He smiled. "And you too, doll . . . I mean . . . sis."

Rebecca burst into tears again, and clung to him like a rock in a confused, breaking sea.

"Now run on. I got stuff to do, or the Griks won't have to get me; the captain will."

"Very well." She sniffed, releasing him. "Please tell Lawrence—"

"I will. So long now."

She watched him turn and walk tiredly—dejectedly, it seemed—to join a group of Lemurians who'd passed them while they spoke, and together they crossed the gangway onto the ship. Still sniffling, Rebecca stood in the shadows for quite a while, looking back and forth. Eventually, convinced there'd be no more arrivals, she strode purposefully in the direction she knew she was supposed to go.

*L*ieutenant Perry Brister, *Mahan*'s former engineering officer, was standing on the southwest wall of Fort Atkinson before the sun came up. It was dank and humid and totally dark. There was no moon, and the stars were obscured by a heavy, drizzly overcast that had moved in during the night. The fort was entirely exposed to the elements, and there was no higher promontory nearby to protect it from the wind or shade it from the sun. If a Strakka ever directly struck it, the damage would be severe. It did enjoy the highest elevation for miles around, strangely enough, and the best view of the strait. It was strange, because, like other little geographic things now and then, Perry didn't remember the elevation on the point where the fort was constructed being quite this high in "the old world." He wasn't complaining, but it often struck him as odd. Everyone always said the planet was the same, just everything living on it was different. That wasn't always the case, according to Bradford's "ice age" theory, and Perry agreed that whatever was responsible for all the big differences probably had something to do with the little ones too. Whatever the reason, Fort Atkinson was a lot better situated than it would have been built on the same stretch of ground back home.

He fiddled nervously with his binoculars. He wanted to raise them and take a look, but it was too early for that. By doing so, he'd only confirm his unease to the defenders gathered nearby. He cleared his throat and clasped his hands behind his back.

"Good morning, Mr. Bris-terr," greeted Muln-Rolak from the gloom. The elderly Lemurian held two cups of "coffee." His English was still barely understandable, but Brister had become fairly fluent in 'Cat. He replied in that language.

"Morning, Lord Rolak," he said, accepting one of the cups. He looked curiously at the other. "I thought you guys didn't like this stuff. Only use it for medicine?"

Rolak chuffed. "I need medicine today."

Perry nodded. He took a tentative sip and grimaced. "If bad taste is the measure of an effective dose, this stuff ought to cure you."

"I need it to wake me up," Rolak confessed. "I didn't sleep well last night." He scratched at an eye with one of his clawed fingers. "I've been a warrior all my life, and have fought many battles." He blinked. "I've not always won, but I've usually enjoyed myself—and I always survived. Until the Grik came to Aryaal, I never faced the fear that I might not." He uttered a grunting laugh. "Now I face that fear every day." Subconsciously, Perry was fingering the binoculars again. Rolak gestured around them. "These warriors feel it too. All of them. They wouldn't be sane if they didn't." He made a coughing sound that passed for a wistful sigh. "This is not a fun war." He glanced ruefully at Brister and pointed at the binoculars. "So take a look if it makes you feel better. I doubt anyone will notice."

Perry felt himself blushing. "You did," he said.

Rolak blinked with humor. "But that is because I am drinking coffee."

Slowly the sky began to brighten, and nervous, eager eyes stared hard at the strait. The sun would rise behind them—at least that was the same—so there'd be no silhouettes. They'd have to wait until the sun actually illuminated the water below.

"I see them!" came a shout, and Perry did look then. He squinted hard through the binoculars and adjusted them with his thumb.

"Where?!" he shouted in reply.

"Right *there*!"

He quickly looked up and saw a 'Cat pointing down toward the very mouth of the bay, and he jerked the glasses back to his face.

"My God."

The squiggles he'd seen and written off as wave tops suddenly resolved themselves into scores of ships packed impossibly close. He'd been looking mostly at the horizon, beginning to emerge. Looking too far. The thing he'd dreaded to see in the distance was already *here*.

"Load your guns!" he shouted at the top of his voice. "Batteries A, B, and C! Remember your training, and choose your targets!" He snatched a bleary-eyed 'Cat who'd appeared behind him. It was one of his runners. "Quick, to the semaphore tower! Have them fire the flare to signal the city the attack has begun!" He turned back to the front. Beside him was one of the massive thirty-two-pounder guns, resting on a naval carriage like the ones they'd developed for the Homes. The weapon's crew was in the final stage of preparing it to fire. A gunner poured priming powder into and on the vent, and another 'Cat stood ready with a smoldering linstock. Perry looked at Rolak and shook his head with frustration. Then, tilting it back, he opened his mouth.

"*Commence firing!*"

Matt raced to the bridge, still tucking in his shirt. For once he hadn't bothered to shave. In the distance, through the windows, he saw stabbing flashes of fire as the guns of Fort Atkinson hurled their missiles down upon the still-unseen targets below. He felt and heard a deep, shuddering thunder, and the glass panes in the pilothouse rattled with each report.

"Sound general quarters! Tell Mr. McFarlane to light off number two. Where's Gray? Pass the word: single-up all lines, and prepare to get underway!"

Campeti relayed the commands into the talker's headset. Reynolds had gone to the head, and he raced back up the ladder and snatched the set from Campeti's hand.

"Sorry, sir," he mumbled. Matt didn't even notice. He was still issuing orders.

"Signal Mr. Alden—send a runner too—and make sure HQ's aware the attack's underway!"

"Aye, aye, Captain."

Chief Gray was heard on the foredeck, bellowing at the line handlers.

"What's our pressure?"

"Two hundred pounds on three and four, Captain. All night long," Campeti quickly replied. "Just as ordered."

"Very well."

Suddenly there was a bright flash of light in the mouth of the bay, and burning debris soared high.

"Whoo-ee!" shouted Norman Kutas, standing behind the wheel. "Something just blew the hell up!"

"Quiet on the bridge!"

"Captain," came Reynolds's voice, "all stations report manned and ready, except torpedoes! Mr. Sandison has placed his division at the Bosun's disposal—except the smoke generators, and they're manned and ready."

"Very well. Cast off all lines."

Juan Marcos appeared on the bridge, accompanied by a haggard Lieutenant Garrett. Instead of the usual carafe, Juan held a large, wrapped bundle in his hands.

"Mr. Garrett, what are you doing here?" Captain Reddy demanded.

"Sir," Garrett replied formally, "my command is incapacitated, out of the fight. I've moved her to a safe anchorage—I hope—and request permission to resume my previous post here, for the duration of this action."

Matt glanced at Campeti, who shrugged.

"No complaints from me, Skipper. He's a better gunnery officer than I am. 'Sides, we might need more than one before this is over."

"Very well, Mr. Garrett, you have my permission." Matt looked at Juan. "What are you here for?"

"I promised to bring you this, Cap-tan," he replied with quiet dignity. "Lieutenant Tucker sent it out a short while ago. I did not want to wake you."

Matt began to send Juan away, but something in the steward's manner made him reconsider. Instead he took the bulky package and curiously peeked under the folds. He blinked in surprise and glanced back at Juan, a soft look of wonder on his face.

"Lieutenant Tucker commissioned it," Juan explained. "She said you once told her we had seen such a thing, and you admired it greatly. The one who made it would take no payment."

"That was . . . generous," Matt said huskily. Gingerly he handed the package to Garrett. "Have this run up, if you please. On the foremast halyard."

Pete Alden was on the balcony of the Great Hall again, but this time with a far larger group: official gawkers, for the most part, who should have been at their posts. In spite of all their preparations, the attack had come so swiftly and unexpectedly, a measure of confusion was inevitable. Letts was shouting for them to disperse. From Alden's perch, much of the mouth of the bay was obscured by the south headland, and even as the day began to brighten and the overcast burned away, he could see only the mast tops of the enemy ships. It reminded him of a forest of toothpicks. Fort Atkinson was invisible as well behind a shroud of dense white smoke gouting continuously from the active guns and drifting lazily toward the city. It was accompanied by a constant rumbling sound. *It must be hell for the gunners*, he thought: gasping and choking and going deaf in the dense, sulfurous haze. He didn't know how they could even see their targets. Somehow they could, evidently, because even as he watched, another geyser of flames erupted among the clustered masts.

"The fort's really pounding them," Letts observed beside him. Most of the gawkers had finally fled, although Pete saw many Lemurians still crowding the nearby dwellings, trying to catch their first glimpse of the enemy.

"Not hard enough," Pete growled, pointing at the part of the bay they could see. A phalanx of Grik Indiamen had appeared around the headland.

"They'll be in the minefield soon," said Letts. "Too soon. Do you think it'll stop them?"

Pete shrugged. "It might slow them down. Bunch them up. That'll give the fort more time to hammer their flank."

"Look!" cried Nakja-Mur, pointing westward, toward the middle of the bay. Under the brightening sky, *Walker* lanced across the placid water at a flat sprint. Gray smoke streamed aft from three of her rusty funnels, and white water curled from her bow beneath the proud, faded numbers and churned along her side. She was rust blotched and streaked, and all the patches and welds gave her once-sleek hull a leprous look, even at the distance from which they viewed her. But her sad, frail appearance wasn't nearly enough to offset the impression of bold determination she managed to affect. Straight out behind her high foremast, brilliant and new in the first rays of the sun, streamed a huge American flag. Alden raised his glasses and saw words embroidered on the broad stripes: *Makassar Strait, 1*[st] Java Sea, Escape from Surabaya, 2nd Java Sea (Salissa), The Stones, B'mbaado Bay, Aryaal, and simply *Nerracca*. The names of *Walker*'s major actions.

"Now, isn't that just the damnedest thing you ever saw?" Letts managed to say. Pete only nodded. With the size of the lump in his throat, he didn't trust himself to speak.

Another, different rumbling boom came from across the bay. They watched a dirty gray upheaval of water and debris gush skyward from among the leading Grik ships. The red-painted hull directly over the explosion lifted bodily into the air, breaking its back. It sank quickly beneath the settling spray. Several ships nearby looked mortally damaged, and masts plummeted into the sea or fouled other ships as they listed.

"It worked!" Letts shouted, clapping his hands. "My God, what a mess!" Nakja-Mur clasped his paws together in a gesture of thanks.

"Yeah," muttered Alden, "but they're still pushing through. Look at those coming up behind. They're not even stopping for survivors!"

Letts nodded, his joy draining away. "The captain—and everybody with the AEF, for that matter—told me the Grik show no concern at all for losses. I guess I didn't really believe it. Only at the end of the Battle for Aryaal, when all was lost, did they finally break."

"It's like they think they're winning, no matter what, as long as they're on the attack," Pete agreed, remembering Bradford's observations. Another depth-charge mine exploded, causing similar destruction to the first. The Grik sailed inexorably forward. *Walker* was nearer the enemy now, well within range of her guns. She slowed to a near halt short of the minefield and turned to port, presenting a three-gun broadside. Four, if one counted the three-inch gun on the fantail. In this instance, even it would have effect.

"She's at point-blank range!" Letts said excitedly. "She can't possibly miss from there, even with the new shells!" With simultaneous puffs of white smoke, *Walker* opened fire. Copper bolts slashed into the approaching ships near their waterlines. Another mine detonated, and more Grik ships and warriors were swept away. The entire center of the enemy advance had been thrown into disarray by the mines and the lonely four-stacker with the huge, streaming flag. Fort Atkinson continued its uncontested slaughter as well, firing down into the ships that waited to push forward. The semaphore tower was barely visible through the smoke, but a runner arrived with a hasty report. Brister had sent that many of the heavy copper balls were crashing completely through and out the bottoms of their victims, and the closer reaches of the entrance to the bay were clotted with settling hulks. In spite of the initial uncertainty, it looked like the battle was under control.

Another runner appeared, her yellow eyes wide and blinking with excitement and fright. "The Grik are landing on the south coast, east of the fort!" she gasped. "*Amagi* has been sighted to the south, accompanied by another large force!"

"Very well," Pete replied without inflection, but his chest tightened with the news. *Under control, my ass,* he thought. *It hasn't even started yet.* He turned to Letts and Nakja-Mur. "I ought to be down on the south wall, the way things are shaping up."

Letts shook his head. "Not yet, Sergeant. The landing in the south might be a feint." Alden raised a skeptical eyebrow. He didn't believe the Grik were that subtle. "Even if it's not," Letts persisted, "sooner or later they're going to get past *Walker.* She doesn't have the ammunition to hold them forever. When that happens, it might get hairy on the waterfront in a hurry. The only way you can be two places at once is if you're right here, where you can direct all the defenses." He shook his head again, apologetically, looking at the man almost twice his age. "But you're the Marine. I'm just a supply officer."

A rueful grin spread across Alden's face as he looked at the fair-skinned . . . kid, in front of him. "You're right. I *am* a Marine, and this standing around is kind of tough to do. But you're not just a supply officer anymore; you're the goddamn chief of staff!" His eyes twinkled. "So the next time I start to go off half-cocked, just keep yankin' my leash!"

Perry Brister could barely talk. His voice was hoarse, and his throat hurt from all the yelling. Not that it mattered to most of the crews manning the big guns on the south and west sides of the fort; they were probably deaf as posts by now, and no longer needed his direction anyway. Their task was simple, if physically exhausting. As long as there were Grik ships below, they'd keep blasting them apart. They couldn't get them all, of course—there were just too many—but there was no question the Grik knew they were in a fight. As the supply of ready ammunition dwindled, and more had to be brought from the magazines, their rate of fire inevitably fell off, and an ever-increasing number of the enemy slipped through the gauntlet of fire. Also, the guns of the fort simply wouldn't reach clear across the mouth of the bay, and the enemy seemed to have realized that at last. More and more hugged the distant shore. Still, the slaughter Fort Atkinson had worked so far was beyond anything Brister had expected, and the sea frothed with flashies around the burning, sinking ships.

Brister's most pressing concern, however, was what was taking place on the other side of the fort. Scores of small boats plied to and fro between half a hundred Grik ships and the shore. The guns on that side were smaller than those facing the sea—twelve-pounders—and were emplaced to defend against a landward assault. So far they'd been silent. Now those that would bear began firing at the boats full of warriors as they neared the beach. The range was extreme, and they had almost no chance of hitting the anchored ships, but an occasional lucky shot spilled a score or more Grik into the deadly surf. In spite of that, a truly terrifying number of the enemy had begun assembling onshore, their garish banners flapping overhead.

"Look!" cried Lord Rolak, pointing. A peninsula of the thick, impenetrable jungle running east and west between the coast and Baalkpan City had been spared the axes of the defenders, all the way up to the Fort Atkinson road. On the other side of the road, across a wide avenue allowing the movement of troops, as well as visual communications between the city and the fort, an isolated island of vegetation called the Clump had been allowed to remain. Now, as intended, the jungle acted as a formidable obstacle preventing a rapid advance from that direction. The only clear avenue of approach lay through a narrow gap between the jungle and the fort itself. What aroused Rolak's attention was the disciplined column of Lemurian troops marching up the road out of the drifting haze.

Even as Brister raised his glasses, he saw a battery of four field pieces manhandled forward of the column, deploying in the gap. He felt a surge of sympathy for the gunners. The only large domestic animals the local Lemurians used were the pygmy "brontosauruses." They were ideal for leisurely, long-distance transportation of heavy burdens, including artillery, but wholly unsuited to rapid tactical maneuvers. They were surprisingly quick in a sprint, but had no endurance. Besides, they were difficult to control. When frightened or confused, they were at least as dangerous to their owners as to the enemy. Rolak told him Aryaal had maintained a small number of them as warbeasts, and Captain Reddy himself had actually ridden one into battle. Perry was skeptical, and even Rolak admitted they weren't much good for anything beyond mobile observation points. In any event, he wished there were some local equivalent of a horse. By the time the guns were in position, their sizable crews were clearly winded.

"Cease firing on the boats!" Brister croaked. "Target the concentration on the beach!"

"Perhaps we should hold fire until they are closer?" Rolak suggested. "I believe the main assembly area is nearly a thousand tails distant."

"Yeah. But they're so bunched up, all we have to do is shoot in among them. We'll get a few with every shot—even with solid shot. Maybe it'll make 'em think."

"I doubt it," Rolak remarked. "It's gratifying to slay them even at such a great distance, however."

"Sure is. The farther the better."

North of their position, Major Shinya's force began deploying from column into line, a short distance behind the guns. At the sight of them the Grik on the beach uttered a collective ululating shriek and surged toward the gap, even while others continued landing behind them. "Here they come," Brister breathed.

"I agree completely with your previous statement," Lord Rolak remarked. "Farther was better." He stepped back from the wall and drew his long, curved sword. "First Aryaal! Sularan volunteers! Stand to!"

The devastation and slaughter on the bay was beyond incredible. The minefield had worked better than anyone hoped, and flames leaped high and spread from ship to ship. The debris and shattered timbers were so dense in the water, Matt was becoming concerned for *Walker*'s screws as she cruised slowly back and forth, firing into the mass of enemies. *Tolson* and *Kas-Ra-Ar* had finally joined the destroyer and added their guns to the massacre. The entire center of the Grik advance had ground to a halt. Dozens of ships were hopelessly entangled and had created a massive blockage in the channel. Only a few of these carried cannons, and their return fire was wild and desultory. So far, *Walker* and her consorts had suffered only superficial damage. Occasionally enemy firebombs arced out of the wreckage of ships, but the American squadron stayed beyond their range. The effort to use the things was far more dangerous to the Grik themselves. Matt was bitterly convinced that, with enough ammunition, his little squadron could stop this prong of the invasion all by itself.

They didn't have enough, however. All the new copper bolts they'd taken aboard last night had been expended, and they'd dipped dangerously into their reserve of high-explosive shells. They'd discovered their star shells were highly effective against the wooden hulls of the enemy, able to penetrate and then set them afire when they burst. But they had only about ten salvos left, and they might need them for illumination when darkness fell. There were still a fair number of armor-piercing rounds in the magazines, but they'd been even less effective than the copper bolts against wooden-hulled ships. They just punched a four-inch hole in one side and out the other, and almost never exploded. It was better to save them for later. Riflemen and machine gunners fired at the barrels floating among the enemy ships. Many were decoys, of course, and a lot of ammunition was wasted sinking them. Silva tried to remember which ones were which, and concentrated only on those he felt sure supported a depth charge. Occasionally he was rewarded by a resounding blast and another expanding column of debris and spray.

The center, for the moment, was secure. The chaos and frustration there had become so intense, Grik could be seen actually fighting *one another* from ship to ship. It was on the flanks that things were getting out of hand. Ship after ship managed to squirm past the blockage and make its way into the clear. Some fell victim to the shallow water mines, but others got through. On the east side of the bay they came under the guns lining the southern waterfront, and a terrible destruction was heaped upon them. Regardless of losses, the Grik bored in, literally running their ships aground on the open beach between the Clump and the southwest wall of the city. Even as the warriors leaped into the surf and were shredded by the terrible fish, mortar bombs fell on the ships and set them ablaze. And *still* they came. What was more, an increasing number of the enemy were making it ashore. Whether because there were just so many of them or the carnivorous fish were strutted with their flesh was impossible to say. Whatever the reason, the road to Fort Atkinson was in growing danger of being cut.

Matt couldn't do anything about that. If *Walker* moved closer to the waterfront, not only would she interfere with the gunnery from the city wall, but she risked accidental damage herself. Steel or not, the old destroyer's thin skin wouldn't stop a thirty-two-pound ball. She could do something about the Grik squeezing through the open lane in the channel, near the west side of the bay, however. Signaling the two frigates to hold where they were, she altered course and sprinted in that direction. An agonized, droning noise rose over the sound of the blower, and the PBY flashed by overhead, a depth charge slung beneath each wing, set to detonate at its minimum depth. *Just one more flight*, Matt hoped fervently as she passed.

Just one more . . . With luck, Mallory would continue to contribute to the devastation in the center, while *Walker* raced to secure the flank.

With the snarling, hissing sound of a raging sea, the mass of Grik warriors crashed against the shield wall of the Second Marines and the Tenth Baalkpan, deployed across the gap. Still more lapped against the base of Fort Atkinson itself. Sheets of arrows and bounding round shot had torn at them as they charged, and still they came. At three hundred yards, canister and grape from the field battery, as well as the fort, scythed down great gaping swaths of the berserker horde, and still they came. Crossbow bolts and arrows from both sides passed one another in midair, to drive home in shields and flesh. With their smaller, less effective shields, the Grik were savaged by this final fusillade, but even then they didn't falter. The clash of shields, the shrieks and screams, the bellowed curses, and the ring of weapons merged into a single cacophonous thunderclap of sound when the armies came together. The Lemurian line sagged in two places: first in the center, where the heaviest blow fell, where the walls of the Marines and the Guards came together. Second was at the point where the Guard right was anchored to the fort. Shinya bolstered the center by wading into the fight with his own guards and staff. It was, effectively, the only reserve he had. The pressure on the right was relieved when the two hundred Sularans under Lord Rolak's command sortied from the fort behind the line, and drove a wedge into the brief gap the Grik had created.

Shinya's modified cutlass parried and slashed across the top of the shield in front of him. Gaping jaws clamped down and tried to wrench it away, and a spear wielded by one of his staff drove into the top of the creature's head. Tamatsu crouched down and slashed beneath the shield at feet and ankles on the other side as the wall began to stabilize. His wrist jarred painfully when the blade struck bone, and he was rewarded by a muted wail. A foot slammed down on his sword, pinning it to the ground. With all his strength he twisted the blade and wrenched it back, sharp side up. If there was a scream that time, it was drowned by others. His arms were already throbbing with pain. His left was in the shield straps, and the unending blows were starting to be felt. The awkward angle at which he was using his sword sent fire into his right chest and shoulder. The initial defiant yelling of the Lemurians had all but stopped, to be replaced by the panting and grunting of disciplined troops holding the wall, and heaving against the weight of ten times their number. Their only words were cries of instruction or encouragement to those behind, and the spears of the second rank remorselessly thrust and jabbed.

"Major Shinya!" came a cry behind Tamatsu. He spared a glance in that direction and saw an American shoulder his way through the second line. Without another word, the man rested the muzzle of a BAR atop Shinya's shield and held the trigger down for a magazine's burst, sweeping it back and forth. Then he dragged someone forward to take Tamatsu's place. "C'mon, sir! You got more important shit to do!"

Without resisting, and still a little numbed by the fighting and the close report of the automatic rifle, Shinya allowed himself to be dragged out of the wall. Behind the spearmen, he looked at the sailor. He'd seen him before, he supposed, but they'd never met.

He'd called him sir.

"What are you doing here, ah . . ."

"Torpedoman First Russ Chapelle. USS *Mahan*, originally. *Donaghey* now." He had to scream to be heard over the roar of battle. "I said I was bored, and Alden sent me and Flynn and some of his sub pukes up the Fort Road. I'm such a dumb ass. We barely made it! Lizards is landin' hand over fist!"

Flynn joined him, panting. "God, what a snafu! Except there's nothin' 'normal' about *this* situation! Captain Reddy wasn't kiddin' when he said he'd pulled us out of a fryin' pan just to throw us in a fire!"

Shinya whirled and looked at the hell below the fort, but couldn't see beyond the Clump to tell what was happening to the north. "I left Ramic and his warriors from *Aracca* to guard that approach," he insisted.

Russell nodded. "They're moving up here. There's nothing they could do. Goddamn lizards took us by surprise—started runnin' their ships right up on the beach. Ol' Ramic never even had a chance to deploy."

"We're completely cut off?"

"Looks that way. There's no way back to the city with the lizards between us and there. If we hit 'em in the rear we might get through, but the Baalkpan guns would have to quit shooting or risk hitting us." He shrugged and pointed past the shield wall, beyond the fighting and screaming and blood. "Besides, I don't think they're gonna let us disengage."

Shinya agreed. His eyes flitted back and forth, between the fort, his own force, and the road. Ramic's column was approaching at the double-quick. Individually, the warriors from *Aracca* Home couldn't have looked less like soldiers, with their multicolored pelts and bright kilts, but together the *Aracca* regiment moved like the crack veteran infantry they were. "All right then, Torpedoman Chapelle, Chief Flynn," he said with a sharp nod. "This is what we're going to do. . . ."

Some of Shinya's staff managed to extricate themselves from the fighting and gathered around. Several were bleeding. Ramic hurried up, gasping for breath. He seemed oblivious to the swarms of crossbow bolts falling around him until he got behind the protection of the shield wall.

"I'm sorry," he said simply. "I had no choice but to join you here."

Shinya nodded. *Nobody* hated the Grik more than Ramic—not after the loss of *Nerracca* and his son. If there was anything he could have done to prevent the landing, he would have. Tamatsu was just glad Ramic hadn't sacrificed himself and his warriors in a hopeless attempt. "Of course," Shinya said. "Now, as soon as you shake out of column, the *Aracca*s will directly reinforce the shield wall. Relieve as much pressure as you can."

"Yes! We *must* hold here!" Ramic agreed. The others nodded, but Tamatsu sighed.

"Impossible. We have only three regiments. If we had twice that, and the rifle company, we could hold forever, no matter what the Grik send against us—but the troops weary already." He shrugged. "And the rifle company is in reserve in the city. We'll bleed them awhile yet, but then we must fall back on the fort. The left flank will begin to collapse backward, refusing the flank as it does." He looked at them nervously. "I know we've never practiced anything remotely like this, but the Tenth did very much the same against the walls of Aryaal, so I know we can do it. The Grik will try to get around the flank as it moves, and we must not allow that." A crossbow bolt skated off his helmet, and he shook his head irritably. "We'll pull the guns out of the line to cover our flank. Hopefully the pressure will ease when we no longer block the road."

"Yes." Ramic snorted. "We will have opened the gate to their objective!"

Shinya looked at him. "Perhaps. But our new objective must be the preservation of the fort so it can remain a thorn in their side." He gestured at the bay. "Perhaps you've not seen, U-Amaki, Ramic-Sa-Ar! Fort Atkinson has already avenged *Nerracca* manyfold!"

Ramic blinked his rage and suppressed frustration, and replied through clenched teeth, "My revenge won't be complete until the Grik are *extinct*, and the iron ship that aids them lies at the bottom of the sea!"

Nakja-Mur was numbed to silence. So great was his shock over what he beheld, he'd been unable to speak for some time. He still stood beside Letts and Alden, and outwardly he was calm, but his claws dug deep furrows in the balcony rail. The slaughter was incredible—and so utterly alien. As he told his companions earlier, he'd received training as a warrior in his youth, but Baalkpan had forever been at peace. He'd known, theoretically, that he might one day have to fight, but the possibility seemed so remote he'd never truly contemplated what war might be like. The training sessions were viewed as rough, structured play by himself and his young companions, and little more than a way to vent excess energy by his parents. Now he saw war for the very first time, and the scale and scope and violence of it all were appalling.

The nature of the enemy added yet another dimension to the overall horrific effect. They came as inexorably as the tide, entirely oblivious to loss. Baalkpan Bay was a cauldron of destruction and fire, and the air was thick with choking smoke that completely blocked the midday sun. *Kas-Ra-Ar* was burning, and *Tolson* stood by, collecting her crew and spitting hate at the tangled swarm threatening to overwhelm her. *Walker* couldn't be seen, and if not for regular reports from the magical crystal receivers, they'd have no idea if she even yet lived. Beyond the southwest wall, more and more Grik streamed ashore. Propelled by the freshening breeze, they deliberately crashed their ships onto the beach. That was yet another act entirely alien to Nakja-Mur, and one even his American friends hadn't foreseen.

The Grik that made it to the beach were destroyed as effortlessly as insect pests by the cannons, arrows, and mortars of his people. Even from his distant perch, he saw their mangled corpses lying in dark, grotesque heaps. Yet still they came. Driven by some incomprehensible, maniacal madness, the Grik forged through the storm. There were just too many to stop them all. It was like holding back the sea with a fishnet. He caught occasional glimpses of a sizable force through the haze, beginning to assemble in the jungle cut on the Fort Atkinson road. Beyond that, the fort itself was invisible through the smoke.

Nakja-Mur looked at his human companions. He was still unable to judge their emotions by the confusing face moving that they did. A grin was a grin, and a snarl was a snarl, but their eyes—so expressive among his own people—told him nothing. And, of course, they didn't have tails. The tension in their unmoving stance was clear enough, however. Suddenly, even over the tumult, they heard a deeper, prolonged rumble. It was more like an earthquake or distant volcanic blast than anything else he could imagine. They glanced at one another uneasily. A different female runner approached them. "The road is cut!" she cried in near panic.

"Calm, child!" Nakja-Mur soothed, none too calm himself—at least inwardly. "You must not show fear, lest it spread to those around you!"

The young female lowered her eyes and blinked. "Of course. I am shamed."

"Not at all!" Nakja-Mur retorted. "Now, what is your message?"

"Tower one reports a signal from the fort: Major Shinyaa has withdrawn within its walls. His force is mostly intact, and they continue to engage the enemy, but the landing force is free to move on the city. The fort is under heavy attack, but Lew-ten-aant Brister believes they can hold for now."

"Did they estimate the size of the landing force?" Alden demanded.

The runner nodded, eyes wide. "Sixteen to twenty thousands—but the landings continue."

"Very well—thanks." He turned to the others. "As soon as they join the ones in the cut, they'll probably come right at us."

"You don't think they'll wait for further reinforcements?" Letts asked.

Pete shook his head. "Not their style. The first try, anyway. I think now it *is* time for me to go."

Letts nodded. "By all means."

"What of the threat from the bay?" Nakja-Mur asked nervously.

"You two will have to handle it. The defenses are stronger there, and the lizards'll have to land right in their teeth. It'll be very difficult to consolidate their force. They already have in the south. I think that's where the main threat lies."

Alden turned back to the runner. "First Marines, Fifth Baalkpan and Queen Maraan's Six Hundred will prepare to advance to support the south wall."

"Reserves already?" Letts asked.

Pete shook his head. "Do the math. The First Baalkpan and the few Manila volunteers are all we have on the south wall. That's about twelve hundred, counting artillery. There's no way they can stand against twenty or thirty thousand. I wish the rest of the Manila troops had arrived in time! We'll pull the Second Aryaal off the north wall and add them to the central reserve." He cocked his head to one side when the strange thundering sound resumed. Realization struck.

"Son of a bitch! *Amagi* must be in range. She's shelling the fort!"

"Thank you, Lieutenant Brister," said Shinya between deep, ragged breaths. "You timed that perfectly, I believe."

Brister waved his hand and grated, barely above a whisper, "Your withdrawal was what was perfect. I never would have believed it."

Shinya had to strain to hear him. "We lost two of the field pieces," he brooded. "Their crews managed to spike them, but . . ." He shook his head. "It was that double load of canister from each of your guns just as we came over the wall that kept them off us long enough to re-form."

"Later you may admire each other's prowess," Rolak growled tersely. His own part in the successful maneuver had not been inconsiderable. "Right now there is still a great battle underway."

The fighting along the north and west walls of the fort was still fierce, but the pressure was easing. It was as if, sensing greater prey ahead, the majority of the Grik were content to leave the fort isolated and continue their push toward the city. Beyond the fighting on the wall, the seething mass sluiced through the gap and down the road. Midage younglings scurried behind the lines, distributing bundles of arrows. Guns barked, spraying their deadly hail into the flank of the mass, mowing great swaths through the rampaging mob, but for all the attention the bulk of the enemy paid them, they may as well not have bothered. "Cut off and bottled up," Chapelle grimly observed.

Brister's runner returned. "The message got through," he announced with evident relief. "The tower confirmed receipt."

"At least Baalkpan knows what's coming." Brister sighed hoarsely.

A high-pitched, deepening shriek forced its way above the din. It sounded like a dozen locomotives barreling directly toward them with their whistles wide open.

"Holy Christ!" Perry blurted, eyes going wide. "I forgot about the Japs!" He threw himself to the ground. Even as he fell upon it, the earth rushed up to meet him and the overpressure of titanic detonations drove the air from his lungs. Clods of dirt, jagged splinters, and various debris rained down, and a heavy weight fell across his back. For a moment he could only lie there, trying to draw a breath. Finally he succeeded, but the air was filled with chalky dust, despite the damp night before, and he coughed involuntarily. The weight came off and he was dragged to his feet. Chapelle's face appeared before him, looking intently into his eyes. Then it disappeared. Brister shook his head, trying to clear it, and looked around.

A smoking crater was less than forty yards away, and bodies were scattered in all directions. One belonged to the runner who'd just spoken, and most of his head and part of his shoulder had simply disappeared, as if a super lizard had snatched a bite. Another shell had landed on top of the north wall, leaving a big gap surrounded by dazed and broken troops. He wondered why the Grik weren't already pouring through, and lurched toward the wall and climbed to the top. "Form up! Form up!" he rasped over and over to those standing near. He doubted they could hear him. Even to himself he sounded as if he were shouting through a pillow. Rolak joined him, clutching his bloodied left arm to his side, and together they stared beyond the wall.

Ironically, most of the shells had fallen on the Grik. More smoking craters, surrounded by dripping gobbets of steaming flesh and shattered bone, formed a rough semicircle beyond the fort, extending about two hundred yards into the gap. Many of the enemy closest to the impact points were stunned into motionlessness, while others tried to force their way back through the press in panic. Those were mercilessly slaughtered.

"That's something to see," Brister muttered. "Panicked lizards."

"Understandable under the circumstances," Rolak agreed. "But few seem affected."

"Yeah. But remember Bradford's theory, and the way they acted at the

Battle of Aryaal—you were there! When they were suddenly and unexpectedly attacked by overwhelming force, they flipped."

Rolak nodded.

"Interesting. Friendly fire indeed," Brister mused. He looked at Rolak. "Shinya?"

"Alive. He ran toward the west wall to see what damage there was. A Jaap bomb fell there."

More shells began to fall.

"Quick!" Brister grabbed Rolak, and together they tumbled into the crater in the wall. Several defenders fell in on top of them, just as massive explosions pounded the fort again. Only one shell fell among the Grik this time. Brister brushed away debris and peered out of the hole. Most of the enemy were drawing back from the fort. In spite of the terrible damage they'd taken, they knew what *Amagi*'s true target was. Perry was up and running.

"Where are we going?" the old Lemurian asked, struggling to keep up.

"They're trying to silence our guns! I have to make sure they think they have; otherwise they really will!" They came to a stop near the center of the fort to find the signal tower shattered.

"Damn!" Brister swore. He ran toward the west wall again. "Cease firing, cease firing!" he shouted with his damaged voice. He could see one of his guns already destroyed. Another tearing-canvas shriek sent everyone to the dirt this time. The concussion was so great it literally hurled him onto his back. Gasping, he sat up. With everything left to him, he shouted at the top of his lungs, even while debris was still in the air.

"Cease firing!"

With unspeakable gratitude he heard the command repeated, and the surviving crews stepped haltingly, dazedly from their guns. Another was wrecked by the most recent salvo.

"What are you doing?" Shinya demanded harshly, suddenly standing before him. "If you think you can surrender—"

"Surrender, hell!" Brister somehow managed. "*Amagi* doesn't want to waste shells on us! She's only trying to knock out our guns! If she thinks she's succeeded, she'll leave us alone!"

Shinya crossed his arms in front of him, face very stern. "This fort has a mission! You cannot accomplish it by hiding from the enemy! Lieutenant Brister, I had thought much more highly—"

Perry scrambled to his feet. "Now listen to me, you Jap bastard . . . !" he croaked.

Lord Rolak and Russ Chapelle managed to keep them apart.

"What have you in mind?" Rolak asked in a reasonable tone.

"Listen!"

"What?"

"Just listen! What do you hear?" Brister walked to the wall beside one of the guns and peered over it. In the middle distance *Amagi* was clearly visible, surrounded by her grotesque brood.

"What do you hear?" Rolak asked, and Brister sighed.

"Nothing. It worked. They've stopped." For the moment the only sounds were the screams of the wounded, the crackling of fires, and the surflike noise of the Grik flowing past the wall. He pointed at the bay for Shinya's benefit. "Look down there. We've sunk everything in range! Nothing else can even come into this part of the bay without running onto the wreckage of their friends. The battery's done all it can! Despite all our shooting, the enemy's getting past us now by hugging the far shoreline. That's *not* in range, although the guys have been giving it hell. If we keep firing, all it'll accomplish is to get us slaughtered." He paused and looked at their faces. "Together, counting my gunners, we have close to three thousand troops in this fort. We may all die anyway, but I have an idea that might make it more worthwhile than just standing and getting pasted." A shout rose up from the other side of the fort.

"It would seem our friends are preparing to return," Rolak stated dryly.

"Swell. Can the guns on *that* side of the fort keep firing?" Chapelle asked.

"God, I hope so," answered Brister. "Just don't shoot at the bay anymore!"

"I still don't know what you hope to accomplish by this!" Shinya hissed low, as they trotted back across the center of the fort.

"Maybe nothing," Brister replied. "Maybe everything."

Pete Alden's new forward command post occupied a multistory dwelling belonging to one of Baalkpan's more affluent textile merchants. Like many of her class, she hadn't originally been a member of the "run away" party, but she'd joined it quickly enough when *Fristar* abandoned the defenders. Pete didn't care. All that mattered was that the dwelling afforded an excellent view of the entire south wall. The enemy facing it continued to swell far beyond the initial force that landed north of the Clump and occupied the fort road. Ever since the fort was cut off, thousands upon thousands of lizards had poured through the gap, up the road, and out through the cut, where they deployed into a mile-wide front with their backs to the jungle. Round shot bounded through their ranks from across the killing field the People had cut with such effort. Each shot killed some of the enemy, plowing through their densely packed ranks, but the fire had a negligible real effect. Pete thought it was probably good for the gunners' morale, though, faced as they were with what stood before them. If the Baalkpan defenders had a wealth of anything, it was powder and shot for their guns. Let them shoot.

He'd have been happy to let the mortars fire as well, and they might have wreaked some real havoc, but they didn't have as many of the bombs, and the range was a little far—for now. His reserve mortar teams were rushing from the center of the city, and when they arrived he'd have thirty of the heavy bronze tubes at his disposal. He hoped the copper, pineapple grenade–shaped bombs would dilute the force of the Grik assault when it came, preventing it from hitting his defenses as a cohesive mass. Canister ought to blunt the spearhead; hopefully the bombs would shatter the shaft. Now all he could do was wait and listen as the reports flooded in.

Chack and Queen Maraan scaled the ladder behind him from the level below. A signaler escorted them to his side.

"The First Marines have deployed in support of the Manila volunteers," Chack said, saluting. As always, the powerful young 'Cat wore his dented helmet at a jaunty angle, and a Krag was slung over his shoulder.

"The Six Hundred and the Fifth Baalkpan are in place as well," Safir Maraan reported in a husky tone. She was dressed all in black, as usual, and her silver armor was polished to a high sheen.

"Good," Alden murmured. "We're going to need them."

"It's certainly shaping up to be a most memorable battle," the queen observed.

"And how," said Chack, using the term he often heard the destroyermen use. He stood on his toe pads and peered out over the wall. From across the field beyond came the familiar strident, thrumming squawk of hundreds of Grik horns, and the hair-raising, thundering staccato of tens of thousands of Grik swords and spears pounding on shields commenced. "I think they're about to come," he said, turning to Pete. "With your permission?"

"You bet. Give 'em hell."

For just an instant, as he passed her, Chack paused beside Safir. Reaching out, he gently cradled her elbow in his hand. They blinked at each other, and then he was gone. The Orphan Queen's eyes never left him until he disappeared from sight.

"Gen-er-al Aal-den?" she asked.

Pete nodded, still looking at the enemy. "Yes. Go. I think Chack's right." He turned to look at her. "Be careful, Your Highness. I expect I'll be down directly."

"The waterfront's in for it," Dowden observed, peering through his binoculars. The cork in the center of the enemy advance was out of the bottle, and dozens of red-hulled ships were streaming toward the docks. Most of the mines were gone. Clusters of barrels still floated in the bay, giving the impression that mines remained a hazard, but the Grik avoided those that they could. *Kas-Ra-Ar*'s smoldering wreck had finally slipped, hissing steam, beneath the water of the bay, and Matt had ordered *Tolson*, the last shattered, leaking frigate, to disengage. Her captain, Pruit Barry, signaled a protest, but Matt repeated the order and *Tolson* was retiring sluggishly, reluctantly, from the fight. She'd given a good account of herself, surely destroying the last of the gun-armed enemy ships in the center, but she'd paid a terrible price. Her sails were tattered rags, and her foremast was gone. Matt only hoped she'd reach shallow water before she sank. The heavy guns of the waterfront defenses opened up as the enemy approached and tore them apart, but unlike the plunging fire from the fort, fewer of the hits were immediately fatal or disabling. In their same old way, the Grik just kept charging through.

"Can't be helped," Matt ground out. Her ammunition nearly exhausted, *Walker* had only two objectives left. First, she had to prevent any Grik ships from probing the west inlet of the bay. Not many had tried so far. The lure of the city, as expected, kept most of them drawn in its direction. Mainly, though, *Walker* had to remain visible in the bay until *Amagi* arrived. So far the Japanese battle cruiser was taking her own sweet time. That was as they'd hoped, from a naval perspective, thought Matt, glancing at the setting sun. They'd savaged the Grik fleet without *Amagi* to protect it, and *Walker* would be a more difficult target in the dark. But in the meantime people were dying. There'd been no word from Fort Atkinson since it was smothered beneath several ten-inch salvos. Smoke still rose from there, so fighting clearly continued, but the guns overlooking the entrance to the bay were silent.

A continuous, impenetrable pall of smoke obscured the south side of the city as well, and no one on *Walker* could tell what was going on from her station across the bay. Matt now knew he'd been naive to think he could control the battle from his ship. He could transmit, and presumably someone could hear him, but he couldn't see any of his friends' signals at all. It was beyond frustrating, and there was nothing he could do but trust the people on the spot. They were good people, and his presence probably wouldn't make any difference, but it was nerve-racking all the same. Letts had managed to get a single message to him by means of a small, swift felucca. Several major assaults against the south wall had been repulsed so far, but the last attack had been costly, and actually made it past the moat to the very top of the wall. Most of the casualties suffered by the defenders came from blizzards of crossbow bolts, but the enemy was also employing a smaller version of their bomb thrower they hadn't seen before. Several Grik would carry the machine between them, and once it was emplaced they could hurl a small bomb about the size of a coconut almost two hundred yards. The weapon had little explosive force, but like the larger ones it dispersed flaming sap in all directions when it burst. It was a terrible device, and the Grik had an endless supply.

Most of the reserve had already been committed, but more Grik continued pouring through the gap and up the fort road. Letts had been forced to strip defenders from unengaged sections of the wall, even as the invading army lapped around to the northeast to threaten there as well. With this new attack on the waterfront, things would get tight.

"Send a message to HQ. Tell them they're going to have a lot of company along the dock, and there's nothing we can do about it."

"They probably know that already, Skipper."

Matt shrugged. "All the same . . ." The rattling drone of distressed motors distracted him, and he looked again toward the wreck-jumbled harbor mouth. The PBY was returning from somewhere beyond, its latest load of depth charges gone. Gray smoke streamed from the starboard engine, and the plane, less than a hundred feet in the air, clawed for altitude.

"Mallory must've tried to drop on *Amagi*," Larry said. "Crazy bastard. Now the plane's shot to pieces! I thought you told him to stay away from her."

Matt nodded. He had. He also knew Mallory's view of the battle was better than anyone else's. Only Ben Mallory knew exactly how the enemy was deployed, and he must have thought things were desperate indeed to try to tip the balance single-handedly. *Amagi* must be getting close, and Ben must have thought the defenders couldn't take it.

The plane rumbled by, heading for the north inlet, where a backup landing ramp and fueling pier had been established. Up close now, Matt saw it was riddled with holes, and a wisp of smoke trailed the port engine as well. Ben obviously had his hands full just keeping it in the air. The navigation lights flashed Morse.

"*Amagi*," Dowden said.

As they watched, orange flames sprouted around the port engine and leaped along the wing, consuming leaking fuel. Black smoke billowed.

"Oh, no," Matt breathed.

The plane turned into the failing engine, but with an apparently herculean effort, Ben managed to straighten her out with the big rudder and claw for the nearest shore.

"Come *on!*" someone murmured.

Even as the lumbering fireball fought for altitude, however, throttles at the stops, the fight ended with a suddenness as appalling as it was inevitable. The port support struts gave way, and the plane staggered in agony. An instant later the wing around the engine, weakened by fire, simply folded upward. Flaming fuel erupted, spewing from the sky with a heavy, distant *whoosh!* and the brave PBY Catalina and its gallant crew plummeted into the sea.

"Get a squad of Marines into the launch to look for survivors," Matt said huskily. By his tone he didn't expect them to find any. "Then you'd better resume your station, Larry," he added, referring to the auxiliary conn. With only the Grik to fight so far, he'd allowed Dowden to remain on the bridge.

"Aye, aye, Captain," Larry said, still staring at the erratic plume of smoke hovering above the burning, sinking wreckage of the plane. He took a deep breath and looked at Matt. "Good luck, sir."

"You too."

Keje-Fris-Ar paced the battlement spanning the width of his Home, his fond eye tracing details he'd so long taken for granted. Even if all went well, his ship—his Home—would likely be reduced to a smoking, sunken wreck in the shallow water off the fitting-out pier. The distant sound of battle in the south had become a living, gasping, thundering throb, and the guns behind the fishing fleet wharf had begun booming as the Grik drew ever closer to his beloved *Salissa*. They were so densely packed he couldn't even count them. Far to the west, he saw *Walker* beneath her massive flag, racing to intercept a red ship that had strayed too close to the inlet. Tiny waterspouts erupted around the Grik as one of *Walker*'s machine guns came into play. In spite of his dread of what lay in store for his own ship, he felt a surge of guilt, mingled with gratitude for all *Walker* and her people had done for them. What they had yet to do. He sent a prayer to the Heavens for their safety, and added one for *Mahan* as well. The thick smoke had prevented him from seeing the PBY go down.

He knew some still believed the Amer-i-caans had brought this upon them, that the horror they faced was somehow connected to the arrival of the slender iron ships. He also knew that was ridiculous. The Grik had always been there, and today was but a reenactment of that terrible, prehistoric conflict that fragmented and exiled his people. This confrontation had been preordained, inevitable, building to this point over countless generations. The Grik were a scourge, a pestilence, the very embodiment of evil, just as the Scrolls had said. Only distance and the hostile Western Ocean had preserved his people this long. But the Grik managed to cross that distance at last, just as they'd once crossed the water between that distant place the Amer-i-caans called Aa-fri-caa, and the ancestral home of the People.

Keje would never have known that much if *Walker* hadn't come. They'd already done so much for his people, from that first time they helped save his ship until now. If it hadn't been for their timely appearance, the People might already have been scattered again. Keje would certainly be dead. Far from being a party to the evil that descended upon them, Keje believed the Amer-i-caans were a gift: deliverers sent to aid them in this terrible time. That was all very well as far as the People were concerned, but it was terribly unfair to the deliverers. Whatever force for evident good had sent them to this place, its dark counterpart balanced that act by sending *Amagi* to their enemies. Fleetingly, he wished he were facing this battle beside his friend in *Walker's* pilothouse, underneath that great colorful flag. Keje knew he was where he needed to be, however. His duty to his people—his family—dictated that he make this fight here, upon his precious Home.

He felt a presence behind him and turned. There stood his daughter, Selass, holding forth his polished armor. He already wore his finest embroidered jerkin and his old, heavy-bladed scota at his side. Reaching for the armor, he saw that the fur around Selass's eyes was matted with tears, and for the first time in so very long he saw the true face of his daughter once more. Gone was the rebellious arrogance and air of condescension she'd so carefully honed. In its place there remained only a sad, wistful softness. He knew of her friendship with San-draa Tucker, and her dutiful attempts to help the tragic, tormented Saak-Fas come to terms with his ordeal. He also knew of her hopeless love for Chack, the one she'd once spurned. Now she'd lost them both. Saak-Fas had gone to *Mahan*. By all accounts he performed his duty, but Jim Ellis told him that he rarely spoke. Chack had earned distinction and the favor of an exotic foreign queen. The only things Selass had left were her Home and her father, and she stood on the brink of losing them as well. Keje's heart shattered within him, and he took his daughter in his arms.

"Never fear," he told her as softly as his gruff voice allowed. "All will be made right." He squeezed her tight, then gently pushed her away. Behind her stood Adar. "I thought you were ashore," he accused. "Go, take her with you. She belongs at the aid station, not here, and we have 'medics' enough. Besides, this will be a fight for the cannons. Our warriors are behind the fortifications."

"I am going ashore, my lord." Adar gauged the distance to the approaching enemy. More guns along the wall were firing now, and splashes rose among the ships. "We have a moment yet." That said, he spoke no more. He just stared at his lifelong friend.

"You're likely to have a larger 'official' congregation before this fight is done," Keje observed uncomfortably. "I hear Naga has climbed the Sacred Tree."

"To the very top," Adar confirmed. "He prays to the Heavens above the din of battle, so he might be heard."

Keje grunted. "How did he get up there?" He shook his head. "Never mind. He knows the Jaaps may target the tree and the Great Hall?"

"He does. Suddenly he seems aware of quite a lot. He hopes his prayers will protect them."

"Do you think they will?"

"No."

Keje nodded. "Then surely mine won't do much good," he muttered wryly. He looked down. When he spoke again, his voice sounded sad, almost . . . desolate. "Will you pray with me now, Sky Priest?"

Adar blinked rapidly, overcome by emotion. "Of course." Together with Selass and the few others on *Salissa*'s battlement, they faced in the direction the sun had set and spread their arms wide. As one, they intoned the ancient, simple plea:

"Maker of All Things, I beg Your protection, but if it is my time, light my spirit's path to its Home in the Heavens."

The traditional prayer was over, but before they could complete the customary gestures, Adar's voice continued: "I also beseech You to extend Your protection beyond our simple selves to include all here who fight in Your name, even those with a different understanding of Your glory. Ary-aalans, B'mbaadans, Sularans, and the others, all perceive You differently, but they do know and revere You . . . as do our Amer-i-caan friends. Our hateful enemy does not. I know it is . . . selfish of me to ask You to deny so many of Your children their rightful, timely reward in the Heavens, but Maker, we do so desperately need their swords! I beg You not to gather too many in this fight, for even should we be victorious, the struggle must continue, and it will be long, long. Instead, let those You spare be rewarded later, with a brighter glow in the night sky, so all will remember the sacrifice they made!" he lowered his head. "I alone ask this of You. If it is Your will to deny my own ascension in return, so let it be."

The rest of those present stared at him, shocked by the bargain he'd made, and Keje's red-brown eyes were wet with tears. Following Adar's example, together they crossed their arms on their chests and knelt to the deck, ending the prayer at last.

"You take too much on yourself," Keje insisted.

Adar blinked disagreement. "I only wish I had more to offer than my own meager spirit."

"Then you may add mine as well," Keje said, and Adar looked at him in alarm. Once spoken, the bargain could not be taken back. "Idiot. Do you think I would be separated from you in this life or the next, brother?

The boredom would destroy me." He paused. "Two last things; then you must leave. First, if we are victorious but I do not survive, send my soul skyward with wood from *Salissa*." He grinned. "Perhaps the Maker did not hear me. Finally, I will trust you to give Cap-i-taan Reddy my thanks."

Adar embraced him then, wrapping him in the folds of his cloak. "I shall."

"I say," exclaimed Courtney Bradford. "I believe the buggers are hitting the docks!"

The central hospital had been reestablished beneath a long block of elevated dwellings and shops, half a mile southeast of the Great Hall. The sheltered area covered almost six acres, and as the hours passed the space was filling with wounded. Nothing of the battle could be seen from where he stood, gazing westward, but the noise was overwhelming, even over the cries of the wounded.

"I think you're right," Sandra said tersely. "Now put that rifle down this instant and help me with this patient!"

Self-consciously, Bradford leaned the Krag against a massive "bamboo" support and peered at the limp form placed before her. All around them, other nurses and Lemurian surgeons fought their own battles to save the wounded, even while ever more arrived. Many had terrible, purplish red burns, and their fur was scorched and blackened. Others had been slashed by sword or axe, and many were pierced by the wicked crossbow bolts with the cruelly barbed points. There were few minor wounds. Those were tended by medical corpsmen right amid the fighting, or in one of the several field hospitals or aid stations. Those who were able returned to their posts with a bandage and some antiseptic paste on their wound. Only the most severely hurt were brought before Sandra. In spite of the fact that she was, after all, still just a nurse, she'd become the most experienced trauma nurse in the world. An orderly passed by, lighting lamps with a taper.

"I'd love to help you, of course, but I fear there's little point," Bradford said. Sandra spared him a harsh glance, then looked at her patient's face. The jaw was slack and the eyes empty and staring, reflecting the flickering flame. "Dead, you see," Courtney continued bleakly. "Perhaps the orderlies would be good enough to fetch us another?"

Sandra closed her eyes and held the back of her hand to her forehead. It was a classic pose, and for a terrifying instant Bradford feared she would faint, leaving him alone to deal with everything. To his utmost relief, she sighed and wiped sweat from her brow. She strode quickly to a basin and began washing her hands. Surreptitiously Bradford yanked a flask from his pocket and look a long, grateful gulp.

"Yes. I'm sure they will," Sandra said woodenly.

Bradford wiped his mouth and replaced the flask. Then he glanced around. "I haven't seen young Miss 'Becky' since the fighting started. I thought she was in your care."

"So did I," Sandra replied, "but she told me last night that she'd decided to stay with Mr. O'Casey at HQ. Said he's protected her quite sufficiently up till now, and she preferred to stay with him, where she might see more of the 'action.'" Sandra sounded worried, and maybe even a little disappointed. "It's just as well, I suppose. She should be perfectly safe, and"—she gestured at the wounded—"I doubt this is the best environment for a child."

"Perhaps . . ." said Bradford. He lowered his voice. "You do know she represents . . . considerably more than is apparent?"

Sandra nodded. "I suspected as much, but every time Matt seemed about to tell me what it was, there were always other people around. I gather it's a secret?"

"Of sorts," Bradford confirmed, "for now."

Sandra shrugged, gazing at the sea of wounded. "Well, whatever it is, right now I don't much care. I only hope she's safe."

A thundering rumble came from the dock, almost uninterrupted now. They'd grown accustomed to the sound of battle to the south, but this was closer, louder. She looked up worriedly.

"Don't fret, my dear. They'll stop the blighters," Bradford assured her. "It's all part of the plan, you see. Rest assured, I know everything that's going on, and it's all part of the plan." Sandra noticed that Bradford had picked up the rifle again, nervously fiddling with the rear sight.

"I haven't heard *Walker*'s guns for a while," she said, drying her hands and motioning the orderlies to bring another patient.

"Ah, well, of course not! She has limited ammunition, you know. Saving it for the Jappos! Besides, you wouldn't hear her, would you? Not over all that noise!" He waved vaguely westward. "Goodness me!" he said, tilting his head to one side, listening. "They're really going at it!"

On the waterfront, hundreds of firebombs arced through the night sky, leaving thin, wispy trails of smoke. Most fell behind the line, amid shops and storehouses, and erupted with a searing *whoosh!* of roiling flames. One fell directly atop a laboring gun crew, punctuated by a chorus of terrible screams. They were cut mercifully short when the ready ammunition placed nearby exploded. The rest of the guns never even slowed their firing, as the densely packed red-hulled ships drew closer and closer to the dock. Pivoting on her cable, *Big Sal* brought her augmented broadside of twenty heavy guns to bear on the enemy flank, and her well-aimed shots crashed remorselessly through the ships at point-blank range, demolishing those closest to her. But there were so many. With a tremendous shuddering crash, the first Grik ship smashed into the dock, splintering wood, and dropping both its remaining masts upon the anxious horde waiting in the bow. Many were crushed amid piteous shrieks. Regardless, the rest swarmed over the head-rails and onto the dock. Another crash came, and another, as more ships followed the example of the first. The area between the dock and the seawall began to fill with Grik. Some appeared dazed in the face of the onslaught of fire and missiles raining upon them, so close on the heels of their rough landing. Most didn't even pause. They immediately swept into their instinctual, headlong assault. The slaughter was horrific. Mounds of bodies were heaped at the base of the wall as the big guns snapped out, hacking great swaths of carnage into the surging horde. The docks became slippery with blood and gore, but the furious, ululating, hissing shriek continued to grow as more ships grounded, or warriors leaped across to those that had, and found their way into the assault.

As promised, Adar had taken Selass ashore, but he hadn't gone much beyond it himself. Now he paced behind the wall with Chack's sister, Risa, at his side, calling encouragement to *Big Sal*'s warriors, who defended this section. They were heavily engaged. A single Grik warrior either vaulted or was launched entirely over the top of the wall and the warriors behind it. It landed nearby with a crunching thud, and, wild-eyed and slathering, it tried to rise to its feet. At least one of its legs was broken. Risa quickly dispatched it with a meaty *chunk* of her axe, and Adar looked at her appreciatively. "Well-done," he said. "You made that look quite simple."

"It was," she answered disdainfully. "It was crippled."

"Even so. I expect you've had much practice in war of late."

Risa shook her head. "Not much, really, since the fight for *Salissa*. I was on her during the battle before Aryaal. We were late to the fight."

Adar remembered. "Late perhaps, but instrumental. Both you and your brother have much honor due you."

Risa blinked, and with a wry grin she shook her head. "You knew, before this all began, that Chack did not even like to fight? He was afraid of injuring someone."

"I knew," Adar confirmed. "Your mother was perplexed, but proud of his restraint. She was always utterly without fear," he recalled fondly. "Where is she now?"

Risa gestured toward *Big Sal*, invisible through the choking clouds of smoke, except for the stabbing, orange flashes of her broadsides. "Home. She wouldn't leave. She only ever wanted to be a wing runner; now she is a warrior as well."

"We are all of us warriors now, I fear. Even your peaceful brother."

"Even you, Lord Priest?" Risa asked.

"Even I," he confirmed. "Even I have the battle lust upon me, if not the skill or training in war the smallest youngling has received. I yearn to do as you just did—slay the enemy that threatens my people, our way of life, our very existence as a species." He looked at his hands, held out before him. "I do not have the skill for that, and after what I saw . . . once . . . it's frustrating. In a way I envy your brother. The skill I now crave came so easily to him, he never even knew it was there. I understand why the B'mbaadan queen thinks so highly of him. Hers have ever been a warlike people, and must recognize the talent"—he blinked dismay—"the *gift* for war when they see it."

He straightened. "I've learned much, however, about how battles are shaped. Major Shinya and the others have taught me that."

"How is this battle taking shape?" Risa asked, and Adar sighed.

"Very much as planned, I'm afraid."

Risa was confused. "But that is good, surely?"

Adar shook his head. "I believe the single greatest lesson in war we've learned from the Amer-i-caans is to hope for the best, but plan for the worst. Hope is necessary; without it you're defeated before you even begin. But you must plan for the worst, so if it happens you will be prepared." He blinked at her. "I fear this battle is going almost *exactly* as planned."

A roar came from beyond the wall, and a new flurry of bolts rained down beyond them. Warriors tumbled from their posts, and Risa hurried to fill a gap.

"I have no objection," she shouted over her shoulder, "as long as the plan was for victory!"

Perry Brister gulped water from an offered gourd. It soothed the pain in his throat a little, but he doubted it would restore his destroyed voice. Shinya and Rolak also drank as the gourd was passed to them. They gasped their thanks to the youngling who brought it. It had been dark for some hours, but with the fires burning in every direction they could see surprisingly well. Before them now, the coastal plain and the gap were almost deserted. A short while earlier Grik horns had sounded again, from the direction of the city, and as if it had been a dog whistle from hell, the Grik before the fort turned as one and practically fled in the direction of the sound. Across the gap and up through the road cut streamed the Grik as fast as they could, toward Baalkpan. None remained behind to even watch their trapped prey, except the wounded and the dead.

Thousands of Grik bodies lay heaped to the wall, and the three thousand mixed troops occupying the fort had been reduced by nearly a third. Yet they'd held. Now they could begin to prepare for what Brister had been planning ever since he silenced the guns.

"How did you know they would leave?" Shinya finally asked.

"I didn't," Brister rasped. "I thought we'd have to fight through them. Those horn calls must have been a summons for all their reserves. They have to be gearing up for their final push."

They saw nothing of the city besides the flickering light of the fires, and the smoke was so dense they could hardly breathe. Cannon fire still thundered defiantly, however, and bright flashes lit the smoke-foggy sky to the north.

"I suggest we let the troops rest a couple hours, if we can," Brister gasped. "Then we'll form them up."

"I certainly hope you know what you're doing," said Lord Rolak.

Perry shrugged. "Hey, this stunt is mainly based on what you guys told me—and Bradford's cockeyed notions. I have no idea if it'll work. Maybe we'll at least create a diversion."

"It will be better than dying here," Shinya agreed, "trapped and cut off. You were right to silence the guns. There was nothing more they could contribute." He paused. "I apologize."

Brister waved it away. "Nothing to apologize for. I'm sorry I called you a Jap bastard."

Shinya chuckled. "I called you worse. In Japanese."

A runner approached. "Sirs," he said breathlessly, "the iron ship of the enemy is passing into the bay. More Grik ships are leading it in."

They looked to the west. Even in the darkness they saw the black, pagodalike superstructure of *Amagi* silhouetted against the sky. Smoke laced with sparks swirled from her stack, and small shapes moved behind the railings as she steamed relentlessly into the bay. It was a terrifyingly vulnerable moment. The ship was absolutely enormous, and in spite of her litany of imperfectly repaired wounds, she radiated an overwhelming, malevolent power. At this range her main guns were little threat to the fort, but the numerous secondaries and antiaircraft armaments certainly were. In the light of the many fires, the occupants of Fort Atkinson had to be visible. *Surely they see us,* Brister thought.

If they did, they made no sign, and the reason was obvious: the defenders in the fort were helpless. As far as the Japanese knew, the guns were knocked out, and even if they weren't, they'd have no effect against such a leviathan. She'd shelled the fort only to protect her allies, and whoever remained crouching behind its walls was no concern of hers. The Grik would take care of them at their convenience.

In spite of his relief, and his intent that she should, the *fact* that *Amagi* was ignoring them as harmless stoked the rising anger in Perry Brister's soul.

"We're going to make them wish they'd blown us to hell," he croaked.

"Why did we stop firing on the fort?" Kurokawa demanded, entering the bridge behind Sato. So far, the captain had spent the bulk of the "battle" on the flag bridge. Commander Okada spared him a nervous glance. He was shocked to see him wearing a pistol, of all things.

"The enemy there is helpless, sir. We have knocked out their guns."

"Precisely the best time to strike! Wipe them out while they cannot reply."

"Captain," Sato responded stiffly, "they could do little to reply *before* we silenced their guns. Against us, at any rate. Our ammunition is desperately low. I assumed you would wish to save what we have for the American ship. Besides, we don't know what surprises they may have awaiting us."

Kurokawa's face reddened, but he didn't attack as Sato expected. Eventually he even nodded. "Quite right, Commander. We can always pulverize the survivors in the fort at our convenience later. They are clearly cut off."

"Yes, Captain," Sato replied, with a sick feeling in his gut. He'd done everything in his power to avoid this moment, but there'd never been any real chance. He couldn't openly recruit supporters willing to defy the captain, and despite their hideous allies, they would, before this night was done, certainly battle the Americans—their legitimate enemies. To take their side even now would have lost him any support he had. He wondered if his and Kaufman's message got through. Not that it made any difference. His soul seethed with torment, and he knew *Amagi* had become a ship of the damned.

"Any sign of the American destroyer yet?"

"No, sir," he managed. "Signals indicate it has wreaked havoc with our 'allies,' though." Sato couldn't hide the bitter satisfaction in his voice when he made that report. To his surprise, Kurokawa chuckled.

"Excellent! The Americans will have depleted their ammunition as well, and besides, when we destroy them, it will show our barbaric friends who wields the *real* power here. The more Grik the Americans destroy, the more impressive our victory will seem! Let me know as soon as the enemy shows himself!" He paused, then added grimly, "This time, there is no place for him to run."

"The iron ship is entering the bay," General Esshk observed, standing on the quarterdeck of the great white command ship of the Invincible Swarm. So far, as was expected, they'd viewed the battle from a distance. They'd watched the annihilation of the cream of the Swarm as it forced its way past the troublesome fort guarding the mouth of the bay. The Uul that landed on the southern coast seemed to have fared somewhat better.

Tsalka nodded. "At last, perhaps we will gain some advantage for having tolerated those insufferable creatures," he said, meaning the Japanese.

"Kurokawa's plan seems to be working, Lord Regent," Esshk agreed. "His insistence on multiple attacks is contrary to doctrine, and at first glance seems to fly in the face of the very principle of the Swarm—yet never have we been able to utilize so much of our force at once. Many of our Uul have been slain—an unprecedented number, I fear—yet we have certainly 'softened up' the prey in preparation for his mighty ship to enter the bay. He did also put a stop to the slaughter of our ships by the guns in the fort. I am inclined to consider it a brilliant tactic."

"His 'tactics' are indeed effective. Wasteful of Uul, but effective," Tsalka agreed.

"The destruction of the fort of the prey was impressive, and accomplished at such a distance so . . . effortlessly. . . . We would have to watch these new hunters, even if they were not so disagreeable."

"Their power is great"—Esshk nodded—"but so is the power of the prey." He hesitated, then mused aloud, "Worthy prey after all." He glanced at the regent-consort. "Perhaps we should have made the Offer? Never has any Swarm been mauled so. I fear, no matter how this battle turns, even this Invincible Swarm will remain but an empty shell."

"Perhaps," Tsalka agreed, and uttered a long, sad hiss. "But that is the lot of the Uul: to die in the battle of the hunt, doing what they love, what they were bred to do. But there is no way we could have made the Offer. We face the ancient Tree Prey, the ones that escaped! They were not worthy of the Offer before, and long have we hunted them. The prey may have grown since last we met, but it's still the same prey. The Offer cannot be made. Even so, I grieve for the Uul we will lose in this hunt. And I do envy them," he added wistfully.

"Of course. As do I."

Tsalka watched the massive iron ship drive deeper into the bay. "We should advance, I think," he said. "It's not the place of the Hij to gather the joy of the hunt to ourselves, but I would not have it said the New Hunters alone were responsible for success. I fear the Uul look to the iron ship too much as it is."

"I agree," General Esshk replied. "As may we all before this hunt is over."

"Lookout reports Jap battle cruiser, bearing two zero five degrees!" Reynolds shouted. He gulped. "She's coming in."

Walker had been steaming back and forth on the west side of the bay at the mouth of the inlet for over two hours now. To all appearances, she looked as if she were watching the distant battle with impotent frustration, her magazines empty at last. That wasn't far from the truth.

Matt tried to freeze the expression on his face so the searing apprehension he felt wouldn't show. All of *Walker's* actions that day, and now into the night, had been building to this precise moment—when she'd deliberately put herself in *Amagi's* sights. Now that the moment was finally at hand, doubt and fear warred with the certainty of necessity. So far everything had gone as they'd expected. In other words, nothing had broken their way. They'd slaughtered the enemy on a wholesale level beyond comprehension, beyond what any truly sentient species could endure, and reports from the city told of Grik piled as high as the walls. But still they came. It was up to *Walker* and *Mahan* now, just as they'd expected and dreaded. It was up to them to strike a blow that might shatter the enemy's single-minded, maniacal will. To replicate the panic they'd seen in front of Aryaal. Hopefully.

There was no guarantee the enemy would break, even if the plan succeeded. They had only marginal evidence to support Bradford's theory of "Grik Rout." They'd seen it once at Aryaal, and once aboard *Big Sal*. When things had turned suddenly and overwhelmingly against them, and the Grik found themselves on the defense, they'd fled in mindless terror. It was like a dog chasing a bear. The bear was fearless when attacking, but when attacked, its only thought was escape. They were banking everything that the Grik behaved much the same way. There was glaring evidence the reverse was also true, however. When they'd followed the Grik belowdecks on *Revenge*, the creatures had fought like cornered animals. Of course, that was what they'd been, after all. Just as the bear would finally turn on the dog if it were brought to bay, the Grik fought furiously in the hold of the ship. But there'd been no coordination, no discipline, and it had been every Grik for itself. Except the Grik captain. It hadn't fought at all, preferring suicide to capture—very much like what little Matt knew about the Japanese. He still wondered if that was significant.

Gray hadn't seen Grik Rout on Tarakan either. The enemy came ashore and charged and died and killed in the same old way. In the end they'd fought savagely, and the battle raged hand-to-hand—but they'd been cornered too, hadn't they? The sea was at their back, and there was nowhere for them to go. That had to be their weak spot; Lawrence, as safely as possible ensconced in Matt's own quarters, believed it might be so. Now all they could do was pray.

At long last the terrible day had dwindled into twilight, and the twilight into an endless, terrible night. The sky was a muddy pall, shot through with flashes of light. Finally *Amagi* was coming—and *Walker* was the cornered beast.

Matt raised his binoculars. The dim shape of the battle cruiser was edging past Fort Atkinson into the bay. She was screened by at least a dozen Grik ships, probably there to soak up any remaining mines. One of the ships exploded and abruptly sank, even as the thought came to him. *Amagi* adjusted her course, carrying her farther into the cleared lane they'd left for her. Matt tensed. The "special" mine was their last chance to do it the easy way, their last chance to survive, more than likely. The minutes passed, and the dark apparition continued to grow, inexorably. Surely she must have passed over Mr. Sandison's mine by now! He sighed. He'd never really expected it to work. The MK-6 magnetic exploder had let them down so many times, he'd known in his heart it would fail. He was still surprised how let down he felt now that it had once again. That was one break that would have made all the difference.

Matt lowered the glasses and looked at the men around him. He sensed their fear, even in the gloom. They knew their chances were poor, but they also knew they had no choice. Even if they could still flee, they wouldn't choose to, despite the odds. This was the rematch. The game that was called on account of rain almost exactly a year ago would be played out here at last, and the opponent they faced wasn't only the hulking brute they associated with all their trials; it was the Japs. Somehow that seemed profoundly appropriate. The terrible battle raging around them on land and sea would be won or lost. Perhaps what they did here would influence that, but regardless, this was *Walker*'s fight, and *Mahan*'s. Nothing anyone else did could influence *that*. For a moment Matt was silent, remembering the long list of names stricken from the rolls since the last time these three ships met, and he could almost feel the ghosts gathering 'round, expecting him to exact revenge or join them in the attempt. He looked again at the men and 'Cats in the pilothouse, and forced a slight smile.

"Just a few good licks; then we run like hell." He rolled his shoulders and faced the front. Beneath his hand was the back of his chair, bolted to the front of the pilothouse. Part of the ship. Gently, almost lovingly, he patted it. "One more time, old girl," he whispered, then raised his voice. "All ahead full. Make your course zero one zero."

"Ahead full, zero one zero, aye," came the strained reply.

"Mr. Garrett may commence firing as soon as he has a solution. Armor-piercing."

"Aye, aye, Captain," Reynolds said, and repeated the order to the acting gunnery officer. "Sir, Mr. Garrett wants to know if he should withhold a reserve?"

Matt shook his head. "No. Give 'em all he's got."

Even as *Walker* accelerated, her tired sinews bunching for a final sprint, they saw winking flashes and blooms of fire erupt from the Japanese ship.

Kurokawa was just leaving to return to the more spacious flag bridge—a more comfortable vantage from which to view the battle—when he was stopped by the sighting of the American destroyer. He whirled and paced quickly to the windows.

"Where?!"

"Port bow, Captain," Sato said in a quiet, clipped voice. Kurokawa rubbed his hands together with glee.

"Commence firing, Commander Okada! I want that ship erased!"

"Yes, Captain." Sato prepared to relay the order with a heavy heart, but Kurokawa speared him with a cold stare. Sato's tone had finally penetrated the captain's euphoria.

"Commander Okada does not approve the destruction of His Majesty's enemies?" he mocked. Sato turned to him, expression hooded. But before he spoke, something deep inside him snapped and he stiffened to attention.

"On the contrary, Captain. But I remain unconvinced the American destroyer represents His Majesty's chief enemy in this world." He looked pointedly at Kurokawa. "We are about to waste ammunition, lives, and possibly an opportunity as well." Sato knew he'd said too much, and was fully aware of the consequences, but he couldn't stop himself. He no longer would, even if he could. Following his revenge-maddened captain's orders was one thing, but by doing so he was aiding the loathsome Grik. That made him feel loathsome too, and his honor was stained beyond any effort to cleanse it. "Sir, the emperor's greatest enemy in this world can only be the Grik, and you are their tool."

"You are relieved!" screeched Captain Kurokawa. "Place yourself under arrest and await punishment!" Sato only nodded. Suddenly the deck shuddered under his feet and there was a loud explosion from below, in the flag bridge. A sheet of fire enveloped the windows for an instant, and then it was gone.

"Commence firing!" the captain shrieked, then turned back to look at Sato. "Another blow to avenge, and all because of you! Your American friends are not restrained by *your* doubts, I see." Sato did not even challenge the ridiculous statement. He turned to leave the bridge.

"Wait! Fetch your American pet and bring him here! It might amuse him to watch the destruction of the last of his people on this world, and it's only fitting you should see it together—since you will share his fate!"

Kurokawa's sweaty, feverish face was illuminated by the flash from *Amagi's* first salvo in response to the American fire.

"Looks like *Walker's* starting her show," Alden gasped. Then he coughed and hacked for a moment before spitting. Bright flashes of fire and criss-crossing tracers seared the darkness of the bay. Based on positions, and the relative weight of fire, there was no question who was shooting at whom. *Amagi's* forward searchlight winked on and, a mere instant later, died in a spray of sparks and a brief snap of yellow light. Other sharp flashes quickly followed in the same vicinity. *Walker* must be shooting for *Amagi's* bridge, Pete guessed.

"I think the Grik are almost ready too," Chack warned. He pointed across the battlefield to the south. The ground in front of them was covered with dead Grik, and the moat before the wall was so packed with their bodies, the attackers could run straight across without even touching water. The sharpened stakes and other obstacles were so choked with corpses they'd lost most of their effectiveness. Small fires from burning brush and garments cast an eerie red glow upon the scene. A larger fire near the trees, where one of the big Grik bomb throwers was destroyed by a mortar, illuminated the seething mass of enemies beyond. It was impossible to guess how many there were, but it was apparent they'd been heavily reinforced.

"They've called up the last of their reserves," Chack speculated. His usually good English was difficult to understand because his lips were swollen and bloody. His fur was dark with sticky, half-dried blood, and he was limping from a slash on his leg. "After that last attack, they must believe one more heavy thrust must break our line."

"They've pulled out all the stops," Alden agreed. "And it might just work, because we have too. There's nothing left on the north and east walls. Everything's either here or down at the waterfront. The waterfront has bigger guns and more troops, but they're too spread out. It's tough going down there."

"Here as well."

Alden looked at him. "Listen. I don't know what those lizards use for brains, but if it were me, I'd pile as much as I could against a short section of wall, with just enough everywhere else to hold the defenders in place. If they do that, my guess is we'll crack wide-open. I want you to take personal command of the rifle company, and stand ready to hammer them back if they force a breach. Use the B'mbaadans too. Rifles are great for distance work, but up close you're going to need swords to back you up."

"My place is in the line with my Marines," Chack protested.

Alden suppressed a sad smile. "The rifles are your Marines too. I need

someone I trust, who'll wait till they're needed, but won't wait too long."
He paused. "I also need someone who'll keep his head, and knows when it
is too late. If that occurs, pull back immediately. If they knock down the
whole line, save what you can and fall back on the hospital. You'll be in
command of the rear guard, as well as the effort to evacuate into the jungle. Is that understood?"

Chack blinked furiously. "You ask too much! To leave my Homes, my
people . . ."

"I'm not asking shit!" Alden snarled. "I'm *telling* you what you *will* do!
The only thing I'm *asking* is if you understand your duty."

Chack slowly nodded. In the distance the raucous horns began to
blare. The terrible thrumming sound continued to build until it seemed
like thousands of them this time. The thunderous rumble of the shields
rivaled even the nearby guns. Across the field in the flickering light, the
Grik began to move.

Then, from nearby, a low moan was heard that seemed to have nothing to do with the approaching horde. Pete quickly looked in the direction
many heads had turned. On the bay, considerably farther to the north
now, a rising ball of fiery black smoke roiled into the air, briefly illuminating the stricken destroyer beneath it.

"Oh, my God," Alden breathed. "*Walker* . . ."

"Damage report!" Matt bellowed, picking himself up off the deck. He already knew it was bad. He'd felt the heat of the blast, the ship physically
yanked from under his feet. Already her speed was bleeding away. Throughout her sortie against the mammoth battle cruiser, *Walker* had seemed
charmed. Salvo after salvo of her armor-piercing four-inch-fifties slammed
home with telling effect, each shell blessed, kissed, or sent with a hateful
curse. *Amagi's* gunnery went wild, and Matt guessed they must've taken
out her forward fire control. A few shell fragments from near misses, and
some light antiaircraft fire was all the damage the destroyer received in return, in spite of the blizzard of five-and-a-half-inch shells thrashing the
water all around her. Taking advantage of this, *Walker* continued to punish
her adversary for several minutes longer than Matt originally intended; he
just couldn't help himself. Reason finally clawed its way back into his consciousness, however, and finally, reluctantly, he gave the order to turn
away. *Walker* raced up the bay toward the north inlet, making smoke.

By then, hidden in the darkness and her dense curtain of smoke,
Walker had to have been invisible. The wind was still out of the south, and
the man-made cloud spread, wafting around her. She'd ceased firing as
soon as she turned, and all lights were out. Where she headed, there were

no fires or lights to silhouette her, and overhead no moon betrayed her. It must have been just a lucky shot.

"All ahead flank!" Matt shouted as his ship slowed even further. A few shells continued falling, but the fire was desultory now. *They must think they got us*, he realized. Stepping around the chart house and looking aft, he could see why. *Walker* was afire from just behind the bridge to somewhere aft of the amidships deckhouse. The Japanese shell must have penetrated the fuel bunker they'd installed in place of the number one boiler, and blown burning oil all over the ship. Steam gushed from somewhere to rise and mix with the black, greasy smoke. Even as he watched, hoses began to play on the fires.

"Captain!" Reynolds called behind him. "Mr. McFarlane says the number two boiler took a direct hit, and the fuel bunker's been punctured! There's major flooding in the forward fire room—he says it's gone, Skipper— there's nothing he can do. There's also minor flooding in the aft fire room he thinks he can keep under control."

"We're losing steam!"

"Yes, sir. The valve's sprung. He can't cut number two out of the main line from below. He's going to have to do it topside, but the fire . . ."

"Right. Have the hoses concentrate on that area. We've got to have steam!"

Walker slowly drifted to a stop while her crew battled the inferno amidships, and Matt kept expecting another flurry of shells to finish them. For some reason the final salvo never came, even though his ship was an easy target now, burning like a beacon in the night. "Don't want to waste the shells," he mused aloud, watching the Japanese ship once more. "That, or they hope we can keep her afloat and they'll take her later at their leisure."

Chief Gray clambered up the ladder onto the bridge. He was covered with soot, his thinning hair and beard curled by the heat of the fire. "We got problems, Skipper," he said. Matt arched his eyebrows at the ridiculous statement. Gray realized what he'd said, and shrugged. "More problems. The fire main's losing pressure, because we gotta have steam to run the pumps—which Spanky says we ain't gonna get no steam till we can move the fire away from the topside cutoff—"

"Which we can't do without steam for the pumps. I know. Do the best you can. If you can't get to that valve, we can't move."

"Beggin' your pardon, Skipper, but I bet if we even twitch, the Japs'll pound hell out of us."

"That may be, but we can't just sit here like this." He clenched his fists in frustration and paced. "How many did we lose?" he asked at last.

Gray shook his head. "I don't know yet, Skipper. Most of the guys got off the amidships gun platform. That damn Silva deserves a medal. He even saved the machine guns. Got burned some, too. Wasn't for him, a lot more woulda died. Other than that . . . we still have the comm, so we can talk, but the front of the ship's completely cut off from the back as long as that fire's burning. I just don't know."

"Captain . . . Mr. Garrett asks if he should resume firing. There are still a few AP shells left," Reynolds said.

Matt shook his head, looking at the distant enemy ship. "Not just yet." He cleared his throat. "Send a message to HQ. Tell them they'd better already be out of the Great Hall, because it's about to be remodeled."

Amagi had stopped her advance, and now lay reflecting the fires and the glow of battle right in the middle of the bay. Several Grik ships were still nearby. One looked a little larger than the others. Maybe it was one of the white ones like Mallory had seen, Matt thought, as he watched *Amagi's* main gun turrets train out to starboard. They fired.

Amagi's bridge was a shambles. The American gunnery had been remarkably accurate, and several shells impacted uncomfortably close. Two of the bridge officers were dead, and even Kurokawa was lightly wounded when a shell fragment slashed his scalp and severed the brim of his hat. Even so, for the first time since the Strange Storm that brought them here, Captain Kurokawa felt an immense sense of satisfaction course through him. The puny American destroyer responsible for all his aggravation was afire and dead in the water. He'd contemplated finishing her, but she was clearly doomed. He'd let them see the destruction he wrought on the folk they'd tried to protect. That traitor Sato was right about one thing: *Amagi's* ammunition was limited. Better to use it on the city. He was aware the "flagship" had followed them in, and he had an important audience to please.

Without a word, Sato Okada returned to the bridge, escorting the bedraggled, bearded American officer. Kurokawa regarded them both in silent triumph as Kaufman crept unsteadily to the windows and gazed into the darkness at the fiercely burning destroyer. His frail frame convulsed suddenly, as a most unmanly sob escaped him.

"You may use the radio now, Commander Okada," Kurokawa said in English. "Your American friends might appreciate an offer of unconditional surrender. The water will soon be rising, and without any boats . . ." He smiled. "A most unpleasant death, I should think."

"Go to *hell*!" Kaufman snarled.

Kurokawa paused, as if a thought just came to him. "Of course, you deserve my thanks, Captain Kaufman. If not for your capture, and all the important things you've told us, I would never have even known about that destroyer. At least, not before this campaign began. That knowledge was what ultimately made me decide to help the Grik." He looked keenly at the aviator. "Thank you."

Kaufman would have gone for him then. It was as though, for the first time since he'd stepped aboard *Walker* in Surabaya, his wits had finally completely returned. Only a battered, empty shell of the man he'd been remained, but regardless of what the Grik and the Japanese had done to him, he knew Kurokawa was right. They'd broken him, and it hadn't even been that hard. He was already broken when they got him. He *was* responsible. It *was* his fault. For an instant he stared at the Japanese captain, saw the mocking smile.

A hand like iron clasped his withered arm, restraining him before he could strike. It was Sato. Kaufman didn't know what he'd have done: torn out Kurokawa's throat with his teeth, he supposed. It didn't really matter.

"No," came a whispered voice in his ear. It was a voice of resignation, but it came from the only person who'd shown him any compassion at all. He stopped; then, realizing how easily he'd been restrained, he knew it was no use. He lowered his eyes in abject misery, and even above the sound of the crashing guns he heard Kurokawa's thin laugh rise within the confines of the bridge.

Alan Letts heard the incoming rounds. He, O'Casey, and Nakja-Mur, as well as members of the command staff who hadn't yet transferred to the secondary HQ, were preparing to descend the ladder from the lowest level of the Great Hall.

"Down!" Letts screamed, and for the next several moments there was nothing but the overwhelming sound and pressure of titanic detonations. The entire massive structure of the Great Hall sagged beneath them, and there was a terrific crash from above. Oil lamps fell from the walls and rolled away down the sloping floor. One came to rest beside a crumpled tapestry that once adorned the wall of the entrance chamber, and the beautifully woven fabric began to burn. In the eerie silence immediately following the salvo, a deep, rumbling groan could be heard.

Letts scrambled to his feet and looked quickly around. One of the runners had been crushed by a massive limb. It had fallen from the tree far above and crashed down through all three levels of the hall, driving him through the deck on which Alan stood with its jagged stump. The others rose shakily, but Nakja-Mur still lay sprawled. "Quickly!" he shouted at O'Casey. "We've got to get him out now! There may be only seconds before the next salvo!"

Between them and the staff members who'd gathered their wits, they managed to heave the High Chief through the opening and lower him quickly to the ground. By then Nakja-Mur was recovering his senses, and he looked around, blinking surprise. People were running in all directions, and the Great Hall no longer looked quite right. Flames leaped up from nearby structures, and over all there was a wailing, keening sound.

"Take his legs!" Alan yelled. O'Casey could only grab one, but there was plenty of help now. They ran as fast as they could toward the edge of the parade ground, while a sound like a roaring gale and tearing canvas descended upon them.

"Down!"

Even as they dropped, there came again the avalanche of deafening sound and mighty flashes of searing fire as the earth heaved into the sky.

Letts tried to stand, but fell to his knees, stunned by the proximity of the blast. He looked back. Somehow the Great Hall and Sacred Tree still stood, but the building was engulfed in flames. Any shells that actually struck it must have passed right through and detonated on the ground or against the tree itself. Flames licked up and across the huge sloping roof, clawing greedily at the branches above. Smoldering leaves and drifting ash descended all around. Up beyond the light of the fire where the tree disappeared into darkness, they could only just hear Naga's plaintive, wailing chant.

"So now I see war as you are accustomed to it," Nakja-Mur rasped beside him.

Letts glanced down and saw that the High Chief had risen to a sitting position. O'Casey just looked stunned. At least he'd acted, though.

"Nobody ever gets accustomed to it," Alan said, managing to stand. "But yeah, this is the war we left behind when we came here."

"You all tried to tell me, but I never . . ." Nakja-Mur's eyes reflected an expression almost of wonder. He looked back in the direction they'd come. "The Tree . . . !"

Letts motioned the others to grab him. "Never mind the tree! We have to keep moving away from it, in case they aren't satisfied with their handiwork yet."

"The Tree . . ."

The arrival of the wounded at the central hospital had slowed to a trickle. Not that there was any shortage of them, but with the sound of battle coming from everywhere now, Sandra knew more should be arriving, not less. She saw Courtney Bradford talking with one of the young runners, and she quickly finished bandaging an Aryaalan's wounded shoulder and jogged over to where he stood.

"What is it? What's happening?" she demanded. Bradford turned to her, and his face seemed pasty in the torchlight.

"It's . . . it's all going according to plan," he repeated once more.

She glared at him. "It's not!" she snarled. "It can't possibly be! There are no more wounded coming in. Have the field hospitals been overrun?"

"No—no, that's not it at all. Most of the wounded are returning to the fight, and those who cannot must remain where they are for now. The ambulance corps have gone to strengthen the walls."

"But . . . how . . ." She stopped. "We're losing then?"

"Not as you would say *losing*, precisely," Bradford hedged.

"What were you and that messenger just talking about?"

"Um. Well, you see, I've been asked to send whoever can still wield a weapon up to the east wall. It's not engaged—and probably won't be," he quickly added, "but they've taken everyone off it to reinforce those areas that are." He stopped. "We've also been told to prepare to evacuate into the jungle if the word should come. If it does, we must move quickly."

Sandra felt numb. "Is there any word of *Walker*, or . . . or Captain Reddy?" she asked quietly.

Bradford's expression became even more strained, and he placed a hand on her shoulder. "*Walker* is afire, my dear," he said gently, "and dead in the water." He gestured vaguely. "She gave a lovely account of herself but . . ." He shook his head. "The Japs aren't even shooting at her anymore."

Sandra could only stand and stare at him as hot tears came to her eyes. "Mr. Bradford," she said very formally, voice brittle as glass, "would you be so kind as to cover for me here awhile?"

He gawked at her and then looked helplessly around. "Don't be ridiculous! I don't have the faintest idea—"

"Oh, but you do! You've been a tremendous help!" she pleaded.

"I am *not* a doctor!"

Sandra giggled hysterically. "Neither am I!"

Bradford's face became severe. "Listen to me, young lady! You *are* a doctor—the best in the world! There are hundreds of people here who need your help. If you leave now, many may die!" His voice softened slightly. "There's nothing you can do for him, my dear."

Suddenly she was in his arms, sobbing against his chest, and all he could do was stare straight ahead and pat her lightly on the back. A suspicious sensation caused his own eyes to blink.

"There, there. There, there," he said over and over. "All is not lost. I told you there was a plan. That young man of yours may surprise us yet."

A disturbance nearby alerted them to the arrival of several figures, carrying another. A few of the closest wounded recognized the burden, and a cry of alarm rose up.

"What is it?" Sandra demanded, wiping her face on her shirtsleeve. "Let me through!"

"Quick!" said Alan Letts. "It's Nakja-Mur! We got him out of the Great Hall when the Japs started shelling it. He was a little roughed up, but he seemed okay. He even walked a little. Then, all of a sudden, he just collapsed!"

"Get him on the table!" commanded Sandra. Letts, O'Casey, and a couple others set him down, and she shone a light into the High Chief's face. His mouth was slack and his eyes moved lazily from side to side. He seemed unable to focus. She plugged the stethoscope into her ears and listened to his chest. Lemurian hearts sounded different from humans', but she'd learned to recognize those differences. What she heard now wasn't just different; it was wrong. In the midst of all the turmoil and strife, Nakja-Mur's noble heart was fighting a battle of its own.

"Where is Rebecca?" O'Casey suddenly demanded, and Sandra, momentarily distracted, glared at him with wide eyes.

"I thought she was with you!"

Lawrence lay coiled on Captain Reddy's bunk, panting in the heat. He'd heard the sounds of battle and been curious, but then came the tremendous blast, seemingly just aft of where he lay, and he'd grown concerned—mainly that the ship of Rebecca's new friends might have been seriously damaged—and maybe a little that he might have been forgotten. But he wasn't afraid—not in the way Bradford and even, he suspected, the "Grik" might be afraid in a similar situation. He'd endured the Trial, after all. If this was where his existence would end, that was too bad, but so be it. It was getting very hot, though, and he'd have liked to leave the room he was in, but he'd been ordered not to. So there he stayed . . . and panted.

The green curtain parted suddenly, and he blinked in shock when Rebecca's small head poked inside.

"There you are, you silly thing! Come out of there this instant! You will be cooked alive!"

"'Ecky! Here?"

"Of course I'm here," she answered severely. "Where did you expect I'd be? Now come along!"

Without objection, Lawrence obeyed. He'd been given an order, after all. As they passed down the short hallway, they heard the roaring flames and shouted commands nearby. "Do they know you're here?" he asked, already sure of the answer.

"Well, probably not, I suppose. Not everyone, anyway. Mr. Miller and a few of the wounded in the wardroom do—that's where I stowed away! Some of the cabinets are quite spacious. When I popped out and came looking for you, I'm sure he saw me, but he was somewhat busy." Her voice turned grim. "This battle has cost our friends severely, I'm afraid. We must discover some way to be of help."

"How?"

Rebecca chewed her lip. "That's the thing; I haven't the slightest idea. But we'll think of something; we must!"

Jim Ellis watched the battle from *Mahan*'s stark, rebuilt bridge, almost five miles from where *Amagi* loomed, outlined against the burning city beyond. His ship had spent the battle carefully concealed along the shore in the west inlet, covered by foliage and low-hanging branches, in case an inquisitive Grik sneaked past *Walker* for a look, or the enemy spotting plane was a factor after all. Her topsides were blackened with tar and soot mixed with fat, so she'd be virtually invisible in the dark. Now, slowly, she made her way into the bay. The frustrating wait was over at last, and finally it was *Mahan*'s turn.

Amagi's attention had been firmly fixed on *Walker*, just as they'd hoped, but whatever catastrophic injury *Mahan*'s sister had suffered was definitely not part of the plan. The other four-stacker was supposed to be clear, "chased" into the dark, dead-end reaches of the north inlet. Jim watched her burn with a sick, wrenching sense of loss.

The effect was the same, however. With *Walker* afire and apparently no further threat, the last obstacle had been removed, and the Japanese diverted all their attention to reducing Baalkpan to rubble. With any luck, no one would even suspect *Mahan*'s approach. Bernard Sandison stood on the starboard bridge wing, running a final check on the sole surviving torpedo director. Everything had been carefully examined over and over, but it never hurt to check again. They'd have only one chance, and all their hopes were riding on the single MK-10 torpedo in the number one mount. *Almost* all their hopes, Jim amended grimly to himself. If all else failed, he'd added one small addition to the plan.

Mahan had only a skeleton crew aboard, more than half of them Lemurians. All were volunteers. The crew was actually leaner than Jim had led Matt to believe it would be, and damage control might be a problem, but that couldn't be helped. There were full crews for the numbers one and two, four-inch-fifties, as well as the number one torpedo mount. Four people were in the boiler room and two at the throttle station. There was no one at all on the fire-control platform, since the equipment was destroyed. The bridge watch consisted of five, including Jim and Bernie, and all weapons except the torpedo mount were in local control. If all went well, *Mahan* would still have a larger crew than she needed for her task. If things didn't go well . . . *Mahan's* only launch was towing far astern, beyond the worst of her wake. Just in case.

"Ahead two-thirds," Jim almost whispered. He sensed the ship respond with a growing vibration he felt through the soles of his shoes and the increased pitch of the blower. To him the ship was very much alive, with feelings and thoughts of her own. In spite of everything, he'd come to love her in a way he'd never expected when he first set foot on her shattered decks. Even more, he believed she somehow knew how he felt, and what, exactly, was expected of her that night. The two were of one mind, and each had become an extension of the other. *Mahan* was, after all, Jim Ellis's first command.

The closer they got, the larger and more formidable the enemy ship appeared. Blooms of fire erupted from her ten-inch guns as she continued pounding the city. At first *Amagi* had concentrated on the center of Baalkpan, where the Great Hall and Sacred Tree stood. They'd expected as much. It was an obvious target because of the excellent view it afforded of the battlefield. Now the great tree was enveloped in flames, burning with a surprising intensity like some great torch, illuminating everything for miles around. Satisfied with that achievement, the giant guns began hammering the harbor defenses. It was like taking a sledgehammer to an anthill. Doubtless far more Grik were being slaughtered by the dreadful salvos than defenders, but it was also clear they were having the desired effect. Already many guns along critical portions of the harbor wall had fallen silent, and fires raged out of control along the wharf and among the warehouses beyond.

Fires that beautifully backlit *Amagi*. She was a perfect target: stationary, unsuspecting, and highly visible. *Mahan's* approach was from directly abeam of *Amagi's* port side, and at over eight hundred feet in length, it was unthinkable they could miss her. Even so, the tension Jim felt was so intense, he couldn't stand in one place any longer. He began to pace.

"Mr. Sandison?" he asked, clutching nervous hands behind his back.

"Range to target is eleven thousand yards," Bernie replied, his voice strained.

"Very well."

Together they waited in silence with the others as the range wound down. Even as it did, the battle cruiser began raining destruction on *Big Sal*, but not a single shot was fired in *Mahan's* direction.

"Eight thousand yards," Sandison announced.

Jim Ellis stopped his pacing and took a deep breath. "Come left, zero eight zero," he instructed the Lemurian helmsman.

"My course zero eight zero," announced the 'Cat after a few moments' pause.

"God be with us," whispered Jim, and then he spoke aloud: "You may fire your torpedo, Mr. Sandison."

With a shudder they felt through the ship itself, and a muffled *whump-chuff!*, the MK-10 torpedo leaped into the air, surrounded by a shroud of smoke and steam. The fires of the city cast an angry red glare on the burnished metal body, and an instant later the weapon was swallowed by the choppy sea flowing beside the ship. A gush of bubbles rose to the surface, barely visible in the gloom, as the torpedo accelerated toward its target. Just like that, they'd cast the final die. Now all they could do was wait until they rolled to a stop to see what the numbers were.

"Ahead full. Left full rudder! We'll wiggle around a little until we know whether they noticed the impulse charge." As the ship came about, Jim moved to the port wing and raised his glasses. First he looked aft, making sure the sharp turn wasn't too much for the launch to follow; then he looked to *Amagi* as she appeared aft, beyond the funnels.

"Rudder amidships!" he called. *Amagi* was still clearly outlined, still busy with her terrible work. She'd taken no notice of what transpired to port. Jim focused the glasses more carefully, then clenched them in his hands.

"No!" he moaned. A Grik ship was slowly creeping up alongside *Amagi*, the black outline of its masts and sails beginning to obscure the stern of the Japanese ship. "How deep is that fish?" he shouted across the pilothouse. Sandison looked up in alarm and raced to his side.

"Ten feet, more or less."

"*Shit!*" Everyone on the bridge was startled by Ellis's uncharacteristic profanity.

"What?" Bernie asked, then he saw it too. The Grik ship was almost directly abeam of *Amagi* now. "Maybe it'll pass under?" he said anxiously.

"Not a chance! *Revenge* drew thirteen feet, and they're all about the same!" Jim didn't stop to consider that, without her guns, the captured ship had drawn only slightly less than nine feet of water. The ship between *Amagi* and the torpedo was packed with hundreds of warriors, however. In the end, it didn't make any difference. A brightly luminescent column of water snapped the Grik vessel in half, lifting the stern high in the air. The bow section was already half-submerged when the shattered stern crashed down upon it. A loud, muffled *boom* reached them across the distance, almost drowned by *Amagi*'s next salvo. Jim turned to the helmsman and snarled: "Come about!"

Salissa was dying. All her tripod masts were down, and the pagodalike dwellings within them were a shambles. Fires raged unchecked in several portions of the ship, and only a few guns continued to belch defiance at the enemy. She'd been flooded heavily down so she might avoid major damage below the waterline, but she'd sunk much lower than intended now. Occasionally Keje felt her hull grinding against the bottom as the outgoing tide slowly dragged her across it. Before long she would truly rest on the bottom, one way or another, and the way things were going, there'd be no one left to pump her out.

Keje was sitting on his beloved wooden stool, which someone had brought to him when an enormous splinter of wood slashed his leg. He was still on the rampart—what was left of it—and expected that he had only minutes to live. The Grik had made no real attempt to board *Big Sal* as yet; they were too preoccupied trying to break through the wall, and it even looked like they'd succeeded at a couple of points. *Amagi* had made that possible by knocking the wall flat. Somehow the Jaaps must have known they'd been successful and the ensuing salvos were only slaughtering their allies. That was when the mighty guns became devoted to demolishing Keje's Home.

Keje had never seen *Amagi* before this night, and he'd been simply incapable of imagining her power. He knew the Amer-i-caans were afraid of her, and that had given him pause. Because of that he'd known, intellectually, that the Japanese ship was a threat. But deep down, he realized now, he'd really had no idea. They'd been fools to stay and try to resist it! Fools. Cap-i-taan Reddy tried to warn them—to explain what they faced. But he'd been willing to stay and fight, and that had given them heart. Surely it couldn't be that bad? Keje now knew it was. He'd stayed out of pride and disbelieving ignorance. Friendship too, and a sense of duty to his people, but mostly because he hadn't truly known.

Alone, perhaps, among all the People now engaged in this apparently losing fight, Cap-i-taan Reddy and his Amer-i-caans had truly *known* what they faced. But instead of running, they'd elected to stay and defend their ignorant friends. Now, just as *Salissa* Home lay helpless under *Amagi*'s onslaught, *Walker* lay helpless and burning out in the bay. Keje had no idea what had happened to *Mahan*, but he suspected the explosion beyond *Amagi* was probably the result of the weapon she'd been sent to deploy. If that was the case, all was truly lost, and he felt a terrible grief for his friends and his people. Some might get away through the jungle to the east, and perhaps *Mahan* might yet escape. But for *Salissa* and her little sister *Walker,* who'd come to her aid so long ago, Keje was convinced this would be their final fight. Fire blossomed once more from end to end of the massive enemy ship, and he listened to the shells approach. A sudden calm overcame him. At least he'd die with his ship. He hoped the souls of the destroyermen would find their way to wherever it was they belonged, but he also hoped he'd be able to thank them first—and tell them farewell.

"Lookout reports ... some kind of explosion west of *Amagi!*" Reynolds cried. "He said something took out one of the Grik ships on that side. Maybe a loose mine," he speculated hopefully.

Matt closed his eyes and took a deep breath. He knew instinctively that the explosion had been no mine. It was too coincidental and the setup too perfect. He was convinced *Mahan* had made her attack and the Grik ship blundered into the torpedo's path.

"Any reaction from the Japs?"

"No, sir. A searchlight came on for a few seconds and scanned the water close aboard; then it went out. *They* must think it was a mine." Like all of them, Reynolds didn't want to admit their last chance was gone. Then he stiffened, listening to his headset. "We got steam!" he suddenly shouted excitedly. "Spanky—I mean Mr. McFarlane—just reported that they finally managed to make their way to the valve and shut it off! Steam pressure's coming up, and so's the water pressure in the mains!"

"What's the steam pressure?"

"Eighty-five, sir, but coming up fast."

"Very well. What's the status on the amidships guns?"

"Unknown, Skipper. It's still too hot to get up there. None of the ammunition's cooked off, though, so the damage may not be too bad."

"Very well. Ask Spanky to report when he's ready to move."

Thirty minutes later Reynolds announced: "Pressure's up to a hundred and ten. We can move, but just don't goose her ... Lieutenant McFarlane says."

"Right full rudder, starboard engine ahead slow, port, slow astern," Matt commanded by way of response. "If the Japs are still looking at us, let's make 'em think we're just floating in circles," he explained.

Chief Gray reappeared on the bridge, looking even worse than before. This time his hands were bundled in rags, and he raised them up and shrugged when he caught the captain's glance. "Damn valve wheel was hot." *Walker* groaned beneath their feet as she began her turn. "You asked for a casualty report," he said, and Matt nodded. "Four men and nine 'Cats dead. Most of the 'Cats were in the forward fire room. There're also eleven more with major and minor burns. Some real minor, countin' me."

"The men?"

Gray let out a breath. "Mertz, Elden, Hobbs, and Yarbrough. Mertz was tryin' to make sandwiches for us." He snorted. "The galley's wrecked again and the refrigerator too, this time."

"Where was Lanier?"

"In the head. That must be his battle station."

Matt nodded sadly. The list was likely to get longer soon. He watched as the bow slowly came around. He could see *Amagi* now, dark and malignant. The flashes of her guns left bright red blobs across his vision. A new fire burned fiercely near the dock, and he could see the battle cruiser had turned her wrath on *Big Sal*. He felt a white-hot fist clutch his chest. "Left standard rudder. All ahead full! Gunners to the amidships platform, if they're able. Torpedo mount number one, prepare to fire impulse charges! Maybe that'll shake them up!"

Walker heaved against the unaccustomed weight of the flooded fire room, but sluggishly she gathered speed. The heat from aft began to ease, now that they were steering into the wind, and a refreshing breeze circulated inside the pilothouse, scouring away the acrid smoke. Matt looked at Chief Gray, standing beside him. Both knew this was the end, but there was nothing left for them.

Gray grinned. "It's been an honor, Skipper. A *strange* honor, but . . ." He shrugged. "I always knew we'd make an Asiatic Fleet destroyerman out of you, and we damn sure did."

"Thanks, Chief." Matt smiled. Then he raised his voice so the rest could hear. "Thank you all." He turned. "Reynolds, inform Mr. Garrett he may comm . . ." He stopped, looking out across the fo'c'sle. A blizzard of fire and tracers suddenly arced out into the night from *Amagi*'s portside secondary armament. The Japanese must have spotted *Mahan*. Maybe Jim had made the same decision he had. "Commence firing!"

The salvo buzzer rang, but there was only a single report, and a lone tracer arced toward the enemy from the number one gun. They were almost bow-on to *Amagi*, and just like during their first meeting, if *Walker* could get close enough, there was little the Japanese could engage her with from that angle. Some of the heavy antiaircraft emplacements situated high on the superstructure could tear them apart, but so far they were silent. Perhaps they'd been hit during the earlier fight? The ten-inch guns were still trained to starboard, but for the moment they weren't firing. Just about everything on the port side was, however, and there were a series of explosions in the sea much closer to *Amagi* than they'd expected.

"Send a final signal to HQ. Tell them . . ." In his mind Matt saw an image of Sandra Tucker: her sad, pretty face looking up into his as he held her in his arms, tears reflecting the lights of the city that now lay in flaming ruin off the port bow. He shuddered at the thought of all the promise that was lost. He hoped Alan and Karen would survive, and somehow find happiness. "Tell our friends we love them all. God bless."

Walker's deck rumbled as she increased speed, and the buzzer rang again. *Amagi*'s foremost turret had begun to traverse in their direction.

Wham! The number one gun was rewarded with an impact near the enemy's bridge. One of *Amagi*'s port-side searchlights flickered on again, and the beam stabbed down at the water. Matt was amazed to see *Mahan*'s riddled, smoking form illuminated less than four hundred yards from the Japanese ship. Incredibly, a tongue of fire spat from the gun on her exposed foredeck. An almost panicky fusillade churned the sea around the old four-stacker, but few shells were hitting her now. The unsuspected second destroyer had appeared so shockingly close, the gunners were taken completely by surprise. If she could make it just a little farther, she'd be beneath all but *Amagi*'s highest guns. If there was a single blessing in all this, powerful as she was, *Amagi* hadn't been designed for a knife fight.

Mahan was low by the bow, and smoke gushed from a hundred wounds. Her bridge was a gutted wreck, and yet some hand must still be guiding her, because she forged relentlessly ahead, unerringly aimed at *Amagi*'s side. Matt turned his attention back to the battle cruiser. In that instant the sky lit up in front of him, and *Walker* was tossed into the air like a dog would toss a stick. She came back down with a sickening lurch, and a towering column of water cascaded down upon the foredeck. There was another brilliant flash, and the next thing Matt knew he was face-down on the wooden strakes of the pilothouse, covered with broken glass.

His nose felt as if it had been pushed inside his face, and his lips were hot with the taste of blood. He struggled to his feet and shook his head. His hearing was totally gone except for a high-pitched, ringing buzz that sounded just like the salvo alarm. He couldn't focus his vision through the smoke filling the pilothouse and the tears in his eyes. For a moment he thought he was alone, because there was no movement whatsoever around him. Wiping desperately at his face with a suddenly dark and tattered sleeve, he finally saw Norman Kutas trying to rise and resume his post at the wheel. Kutas had blood running from his ears. Matt helped him up, and saw his mouth moving in the flickering light, but couldn't hear what he said. He glanced behind him and saw Reynolds was up, but dazed. Gray was sitting on the deck beside the unmoving form of a 'Cat. Two other men were still down as well. Matt looked through the window.

They were much closer to *Amagi* now. They'd made it under her main battery—which simply couldn't depress enough to fire at *Walker* anymore. They were still racing through a forest of smaller splashes from *Amagi*'s secondaries, however. Matt felt the staccato drumming as tracers probed for *Walker*'s bridge. He wondered why the number one gun was no longer firing and looked down at the fo'c'sle. A long, deep gouge began near the small anchor crane forward, and sprouted into a gaping, jagged hole just in front of the gun. One 'Cat was crawling around on her hands and knees, but the rest of the crew was just . . . gone. Then he saw Dennis Silva's unmistakable form, closely followed by another man and two 'Cats, dash through the sleeting tracers and duck behind the dubious protection of the gun's splinter shield. Each had a pair of shells under their arms.

A 5.5-inch shell exploded against the tall foremast behind and above their heads. With a tortured shriek of tearing steel and the high-pitched wail of the lookout, the whole thing crashed into the sea to starboard. Still secured by a twisted spiderweb of cables and stays, it began pounding against the hull. Two more heavy blows aft pitched Matt forward against his chair. Distractedly, he thought either his hearing was better or the explosions were very loud. Reynolds had recovered himself and was screaming into his microphone in frustration, apparently getting no response. The number one gun fired.

Gray was up now, pointing through the shattered windows. His mouth was moving in a shout, and Matt thought he heard the word *"Mahan."*

"What is it?" Kurokawa demanded, when he heard the excited cries sweeping like a wave across the bridge from port to starboard.

"Enemy destroyer off the port beam, sir! Closing fast!" came the alarmed reply.

"But . . ." Beyond that, he couldn't speak. The American destroyer was in *front* of them! It was still burning—although it did seem to be moving now. . . .

Sato Okada seared him with an expression of utter contempt. "Surface action, *port!*" he shouted. "Commence firing, all guns, *commence firing!*"

Ahead of them, *Walker* had completed her turn. Her bow lit with the flash of her number one gun, and an instant later the forward part of the bridge near the helm exploded in upon them with a terrific blast and a searing ball of flame. From where he lay on the debris-strewn deck, Sato heard Kaufman's gleeful laugh.

Jim Ellis released the wheel and crouched on the splintered strakes just before *Mahan* crashed into *Amagi*'s side at almost fourteen knots. He slammed against the base of the wheel and fell back on the deck. Wincing from the pain of several cracked or broken ribs, he struggled to rise. Impossible. With a gasp, he sprawled backward. Strange, kaleidoscopic lights flashed through the hundreds of holes in the front of the bridge, and cables and shredded conduit dangled from the overhead. *Mahan*'s bridge had drawn a terrifying volume of fire during that final approach. Miraculously, Jim didn't think he'd been badly hit, but he was certain he was the last man alive in the forward part of the ship.

He clenched his teeth against the pain and tried to rise once more. To his surprise, he felt a pair of hands under his arms, helping him to his feet.

"You go!" came an urgent, heavily accented voice. "Go, go! Time . . . small!" Jim shook his head, amazed by how quiet it suddenly seemed. The blower still roared behind him, but the shooting had all but stopped. There was a great rumbling, crunching sound forward, as *Mahan* still drove against the side of the Japanese ship.

"I can't go. I have a job to finish!"

The Lemurian fixed him with intense, desperate eyes, and Jim suddenly realized who it was. "I do!" said Saak-Fas. "I help make ready! I know, I . . . do!" The Lemurian straightened to his full height. "I *need* do!"

Jim looked at him, but it was hard to see through the darkness and the blood running in his eyes. "It's my ship. My responsibility," he gasped. The 'Cat gestured to a form on deck. It moaned.

"'Spons-baal-tee?"

Torn, Jim could only stand rooted to the deck. He felt it beginning to settle. Suddenly the Lemurian blinked and began making his way to the ladder at the back of the pilothouse. "I *do*! No time!" With that, he disappeared down the ladder. Realizing he had no choice, Jim staggered to Bernard Sandison, lying in a pool of blood, and began dragging him toward the ladder.

Saak-Fas stepped lightly down the companionway stairs to the passage leading to the wardroom. The lights were dim and flickering, but that didn't matter; he could see as well in the dark as the Amer-i-caans could in daylight. Down yet another ladderlike stair, he entered the crew's forward berthing space. Water was half a tail deep on deck, and more gushed in through great rents in the side of the ship. Forward he sloshed through the rising water, until he came to the passageway leading to the chain locker. The collision damage was more evident here. The deck was buckled beneath his feet and the water was clammy and slick with oil leaking from ruptured fuel bunkers below.

He'd rarely been *in* the water before, except for baths of course. Other than surf, he'd never stood in seawater up to his waist. That just wasn't done. He felt a chill at the thought that some flasher fish might somehow have wriggled into the ship, but he knew it was unlikely. Most of the holes were probably too small, and besides, it was after dark. He stopped at the entrance to the passageway and looked inside with a sense of growing peace. The ordeal he'd suffered at the hands of the Grik still tortured him. He'd fought to suppress the terror, the agony of that experience, knowing that somehow, if he did, the Heavens would reward him with the opportunity now at hand.

It had been so hard at times, the added misery he heaped upon himself. The rejection of his beloved Selass, his self-imposed isolation from his

people. But everything he did to torment himself further had helped create the buffer that now existed between his mind and the real pain and
lingering terror that threatened to drive him mad. He'd passed the ultimate test, and now the reward was near. He looked fondly at the twelve
half-submerged depth charges jumbled in the passageway by the collision.
He smiled at the feeling of unaccustomed happiness that slowly filled his
being. He'd savor the short additional time he'd give the Amer-i-caan, Ellis, to try to get clear. Then he'd strike a mighty blow against the hated
Grik and finally end his agony in the same, glorious instant.

"Hold them back! *Hold* them!" Pete Alden bellowed. Even as he did, the
volunteers from Manila broke. It was like a heavy cable supporting far too
great a weight. The strands began to separate and fray, snapping and pro-
testing as they did, but inexorably, as the cable began to thin, the strain on
the surviving strands became ever greater. Finally, inevitably, it snapped.
It wasn't really their fault. The small contingent of Maa-ni-lans had received the least amount of training of any of the defenders, and someone on
the other side may have been savvy enough to notice that their short section
of the line was a little softer than the others. They'd been hammered mercilessly ever since the start of the fight as well, and their numbers had dwindled by more than half.

With a wild, triumphant, hissing roar, like the sound of heavy surf
pounding against the rocks, a densely packed mass of Grik sent them reel-
ing back. A wedge was driven between the intermingled First and Fifth
Baalkpan on the left, and Company B, First Marines, and the *Humfra-Dars*
on the right. What ensued was a wild melee like nothing Pete had yet seen
since the long, long battle began.

Bellows of rage and screams of agony intermixed with the harsh
clanging of weapon on weapon and shield on shield. The terrifying jaws
and sickle-shaped Grik swords and claws slashed and tore and hacked
their way through the line, while the defenders did their best to close the
gap. Inexorably, the line peeled away from the break as the defenders
tried, instinctively, to re-fuse their new flanks, and the Grik pressed even
harder. Pete had a sick, sinking feeling in his gut, and he could almost see
the entire line rolling up from within, and marauding, slaughtering Grik
surging unopposed through the city pathways. The end of everything was
as clear before him as if it had already happened.

Suddenly the ripping sound of a light machine gun, one of *Mahan's*
.30's most likely, chattered above the seething, shrieking mass. Then came
the stutter of a Thompson, then two. Soon a steady crackle of rifle fire
joined in. Chack must have committed his rifle company at last. Alden
remembered his last conversation with the remarkable young Lemurian,

and he only hoped he hadn't waited too long after all. For just an instant, the Grik penetration hesitated, confused.

With a wild, high-pitched squall like hundreds of maddened cats, and shouts of "B'mbaado! B'mbaado!" Queen Maraan's personal guard, with their silver sunbursts on jet-black shields, rose from behind the low secondary redoubt and slammed into the teetering Grik with a berserk frenzy. Without hesitation Pete joined the charge, emptying his automatic pistol almost as fast as he could slide magazines into it. His staff joined in, swinging their swords. The counterattacking force was far smaller than the enemy breakthrough, but the effect of the attack was all out of proportion to the numbers involved. The Grik staggered back, away from the devastating blow. Those directly at the point of contact turned to flee in wild-eyed panic. Finding their escape blocked by those behind them, they turned their weapons on their comrades—even as they were cut down from behind.

Pete watched in dumbfounded amazement as the catastrophic breakthrough degenerated into another kind of catastrophe—for the Grik. The battle to escape became a real battle, Grik on Grik, as those caught within the Baalkpan defenses fought against those still trying to get in. Because they were sandwiched between their own kind and the frenzied defenders, the breakthrough was quickly exterminated. And yet . . . something of what happened within the wall seemed to take hold beyond it. A small nucleus of panicked warriors had escaped destruction and continued fighting their way through the press. The entire attack ground to a halt while the situation in front of the breach sorted itself out.

Queen Maraan appeared beside him to his right, looking over the wall. She was panting heavily, bloody sword in hand. "It looked like we would break them for a moment, just as we did at Aryaal," she gasped. "It's like they cannot comprehend defense. If they are not attacking, they are losing." She shrugged. "But they are so many."

Pete stared at her, struck by sudden inspiration. He hadn't been at the Battle of Aryaal, and hadn't seen what she had. In the heat of battle, he'd completely forgotten Bradford's crackpot theory. Then, over her head, and far out in the bay where the flashes of *Amagi*'s guns had become so common, there was another mighty flash, much bigger than the others. A sheet of fire vomited into the sky, and *Amagi*'s stricken silhouette was at the very heart of the massive plume. Many others saw it too, on both sides, and the fighting became almost desultory as thousands of heads turned toward the bay. The noise of the explosion, when it came, was fantastic. Not so much in actual sound, though it was great, but in the sense of size and power it represented over such a great distance.

"My God!" shouted Pete. "It worked! That Goddamn, idiotic, torpedo stunt *worked!*" An enormous, rising, thunderous cheer built throughout the city. *"It worked!"* screamed Pete again as he turned back to look at the stunned sea of Grik. If there was any chance Bradford was right, now was the time to find out. *"Push them!"* he bellowed. "Push them back! Up and at 'em!" He holstered his pistol and unslung his Springfield. "The army will *advance!*"

Walker staggered under the force of the mighty blast, and the rest of the glass in the pilothouse streamed inward like shattered ice. Kutas cried out, reflexively raising his hands to his face. Matt lunged for the wheel. "Chief!" he shouted. "Get this man below!" He spun the wheel hard to port, preventing the completion of *Walker*'s suicidal dash to ram *Amagi* herself. The ship responded sluggishly, and once again it seemed like her speed was dropping off. He was grateful for the reprieve *Mahan* had given them, but horrified by her sacrifice as well. In a hidden corner of his soul, he might have even felt a little cheated. A wave of irrational anger swept over him, and he lashed out at Reynolds.

"I want a report from Spanky *now!*" he shouted.

"I'm *trying*, Skipper!" The young seaman looked close to tears. "I can't get through! I can't get *anything!*"

"I'll find out, Captain!" Gray shouted back, as he helped the blinded, moaning helmsman down the ladder. Matt looked back at *Amagi*. A giant towering mushroom of fire and smoke was still rising and expanding into the dark, hazy sky. At the base of that pyre would be *Mahan*'s shattered remains.

"My God."

He was thankful he couldn't see *Mahan*, as *Walker* ranged down *Amagi*'s opposite side. The battle cruiser was beginning to list heavily to port, and a wide strip of red bottom paint was rising into the light of the burning city. They'd make sure, Matt grimly determined, although he couldn't imagine anyone on *Mahan* having survived. A dreadful, heavy sadness descended upon him when he remembered *Mahan*'s farewell the night before. Jim must have been planning this all along, and never said a word. He continued *Walker*'s slow turn to port, and when Leo Davis appeared and relieved him at the wheel, Matt told him to steer around to the other side of the Japanese ship.

Amagi was engulfed in flames, from just aft of her funnel where *Mahan* struck, all the way to her number four turret. Japanese sailors scurried madly about her decks, dragging hoses and directing streams of water onto the conflagration. Some were removing covers from her lifeboats. Clearly her crew was concerned with more important matters than the battered, smoldering destroyer describing a wide, decrepit turn off her starboard side. It never even occurred to Matt that she wasn't finished yet.

Spanky himself staggered onto the bridge, looking even worse than the chief. Most of his hair was gone, and his skin looked purple and angry. His clothes were a uniform dark gray from the soot and oil that stained them. He wiped his face with his hat.

"I didn't mean to take you from your work, Spanky," Matt told him. "Gray could've brought the word."

"Not this word, Skipper," he said, looking down at the deck. Then he raised his scorched face to Matt's and looked him in the eye. "We're gonna lose the ship." He spoke the words quietly, but they had the effect of a shouted curse. "The forward engine room's flooding, and we can't keep ahead of it in the aft fire room much longer." He sighed. "Hell, there's flooding everywhere. The pumps are overwhelmed. Those last two five-and-a-half's opened us up like a sardine can, aft. You don't even *want* to know what that ten-incher did to us belowdecks."

"How long does she have?" Matt asked him stiffly.

"Couple hours. Maybe three, if nobody shoots any more holes in her. Most of the leaks aren't too bad, but they're *everywhere*." He shook his head. "She's just had enough. We got maybe an hour and a half left for the engines, but after that she's gonna go fast."

Matt slowly nodded, and tried to keep his voice under control. "Thanks, Spanky. Stretch it out as long as you can. I'll try to get some shallow water under her before she goes down." He looked out through the bridge windows. Davis had glanced over his shoulder to listen to the conversation and saw the sudden surprise on the captain's face. He quickly turned back to the front. When they brought the ship about, she should have passed far ahead of the sinking battle cruiser. Now he could see they were headed almost directly at her, and her bow was now reaching for the west. Davis broke the stunned silence himself.

"Holy Toledo! The Japs are underway!" He pounded the wheel under his hands. "They can't *do* that!" As if in answer to his protest, a stream of tracers marched toward the ship. On the fo'c'sle, Silva opened fire without even waiting for orders.

"Grik Rout" was real, and it was happening everywhere. The weary defenders in the south charged up and over their wall with their curious but ferocious high-pitched yell. Alden imagined it was very much like what the old rebel yell of the Confederacy must have sounded like. Demoralized already by the evident destruction of their invincible iron ship, the Grik host recoiled from the onslaught. Once again, they fought viciously among themselves as those in the rear ranks battled to maintain the assault against those who'd already abandoned it. To them, the attack became one against those who would try to prevent their escape. And all the while, the former defenders waded behind them through the carnage, slaughtering them almost without resistance. The panicked Grik in front of them, fighting their own kind, added a substantial force multiplier to the charge.

Across the corpse-choked moat and onto the open plain beyond, the defenders-turned-attackers kept up the unrelenting pressure while somehow, miraculously, maintaining a semblance of shield-wall integrity. The discipline and careful training Alden had insisted on was paying off. Even so, the advance began to slow. The troops were exhausted after the long fight, and the exertion of just climbing over bodies so they could keep slaughtering Grik began to tell. The thousands who fled were being killed by both sides, and the unrouted mass behind them began to move forward bit by bit. The charge finally ground to a halt, and then it was like the field of Aryaal again in yet another way: both battle lines stood in the open without support or protection, and in that situation, the overwhelming numbers of the enemy began to swing the tide back.

Alden slashed with his rifle, butt-stroking and stabbing with the bayonet, as he'd demonstrated so many times on the drill field. His pistol was empty and he had no more ammunition. Before him was a scene from a nightmare hell. Gnashing teeth, slashing weapons, and high-pitched shrieks of pain punctuated the rumbling roar of shields grinding together. The damp earth at his feet had been churned into a bloody, viscous slurry, and the only traction afforded to those holding the shield wall were the mushy mounds of unrecognizable gore half-submerged in the ooze. The frothing, working mass of Grik beyond the shields were illuminated by a red, flickering light from the fires—adding to the unreal, otherworldly aspect of the battle. Chack almost stumbled past him, shouting his name, and Pete grabbed him by the arm. "Where's the rifle company?" he shouted.

"The machine guns are empty, and I ordered the others to stay on the wall. They're of little use in this type of fight. If all had bayonets it might be different. . . ."

"Never mind. You did right. Have them prepare to cover our withdrawal. I'm going to try to pull back to the wall."

"It will be risky. The enemy will sense victory and strike even harder."

"I know, but that's all there is. We can't move forward and we can't stay here. There're just too damn many." Chack blinked reluctant agreement. He turned to run back to the wall and prepare his troops. Then he stopped. Alden looked in the direction he faced and was stunned to see hundreds of Lemurians pouring over the wall and racing over the ground he'd been preparing to yield. More than hundreds, perhaps a few thousand in all, and he had no idea where they'd come from. There simply were no more reserves. Then he saw the proud regimental flags whipping in the breeze as their bearers crossed the wall in the wake of the charge. The Second Aryaal, the Second B'mbaado, and the Third Baalkpan were three he recognized. All were "veteran" units that had been deployed in defense of the shipyard and the north wall.

Screaming their rage, they streamed across the abattoir and surged directly into the faltering line. The weight of their unexpected charge carried the entire shield wall forward into the face of the enemy, and once again there was a distinct change in the Grik. Once again those facing the added spears turned on those behind them, slashing and screaming in panic, and slaying their unprepared comrades before they had a chance to even realize what had happened. The rout began to grow, and the air of terror was even greater this time. As the shield wall churned forward again, it became apparent that many Grik still fighting bore the same wild-eyed expressions as those trying to get away. Something was pushing them from behind, just as the reinforced attack was driving them back. Almost as if it shared a single collective awareness, the entire host suddenly shifted in the one direction it perceived safety might still be found: toward the sea.

What began as a steadily growing tendency to move west quickly built into a panicked rush. Soon the horde of Grik was flowing past the shield wall from left to right with the unstoppable chaotic urgency of a massive, flooding river. Spears continued to slay them as they hurried past, but there was no reaction from those around the victims except, perhaps, to quicken their pace. It was shocking and amazing and dreadful all at once, and a vague cheer began to build as Alden's troops realized that this time there'd be no stopping the rout. Whatever force enabled the Grik to operate with some semblance of cooperation, cunning, and courage had disappeared just as surely as if the strings of a marionette had been cut.

The cheering grew frenzied when the flag of the Second Marines resolved itself in the flickering gloom beyond the raging torrent of Grik.

"It's Shinya! Shinya!" came a gleeful shout at Alden's side. He turned and saw Alan Letts actually jumping up and down and waving his arms in the air. His hat was gone and his red hair was plastered to his scalp with blood and sweat. Mud spattered in all directions as he capered. Pete grinned happily at Letts's enthusiasm, and his unexpected presence. He was obviously right. Somehow the force in Fort Atkinson they'd feared was doomed had managed to break out and attack the enemy in the rear. Not only that, but they'd timed it just about perfectly as well. Now it looked like it would be only a matter of minutes before the forces were reunited, as what once had been the Grik right fled between them.

"Where the hell did you come from?" Alden asked the ecstatic Letts.

"After the Japs pounded the Great Hall, there was something wrong with Nakja-Mur, so we carried him to the hospital." He shook his head. "It looked like everything was falling apart. The lizards broke through on the waterfront, and some are even roaming through the city." He sobered. "*Big Sal* got pasted. I don't know if there's anybody left alive. Anyway, I sent runners to fetch every regiment not actually engaged. Stripped *everything*, and had them converge on the parade ground." He grinned. "Then when *Amagi* blew up, the lizard breakthrough just fell apart. We charged them, and most went scurrying back to their ships!" He laughed gleefully. "The ships're all hard aground, and the surviving gunners on the harbor wall are feedin' the fish with 'em right now! Anyway, we left them with it, and hurried here as fast as we could." He winked. "Good thing too."

"No foolin'!" Pete looked at Chack. "As soon as we link up with the 'lost garrison,' we'll continue to press the enemy! We'll sweep those bastards right into the sea!"

For a moment Chack just stood there, amazed. The Grik that fled before them still outnumbered them by a very large margin. And yet, somehow, they were no longer even warriors. They'd become more like the skuggiks they slightly resembled: dangerous individually, but no more capable of concerted action, and no longer a threat to the city. Many would still die destroying what was left when the army swept forward to finish them, but he agreed completely with Alden's intent to do it now while the panic was fresh. He didn't know if "Grik Rout" would ever fade from such an acute state; they'd never again seen any of the Grik that fled before Aryaal. Nevertheless, they couldn't take any chance it might, and besides, the combined defenders of Baalkpan deserved the slaughter that had been given them.

"It's hard to believe it's almost over," he said at last. Then he ran to detail a runner to make contact with Shinya.

"Almost over," Letts repeated happily; then his smile faded. Out on the water he could see the flames of the battle cruiser, but she wasn't where she'd been before. She was creeping toward the mouth of the bay. Behind her, moving just as slowly, was another, smaller ship, also burning. Tracers arced back and forth between them. Was that *Walker* or *Mahan*? He couldn't tell in the dark. Whichever it was, it wasn't over for her. With a hurried word to Alden, he raced back toward the city.

Amagi was listing hard to port, but somehow she remained afloat. Roaring flames leaped skyward, and black smoke coiled and billowed. Her tall, pagodalike superstructure shimmered in the heat and leaned to the left at a drunken angle. Two of the three aft turrets were still trained to starboard, guns slightly elevated at the angle from which they'd been battering the city and *Big Sal*. They were silent now. Their crews had either been cooked inside them, or abandoned them to the fire spreading swiftly aft. The third turret probably hadn't moved since that day so long ago when the dive-bomber crashed into it. She looked destroyed, yet still she floated. She was underway, and it looked more and more as if she might escape.

Walker had found a seemingly magical place directly astern of *Amagi*, where the battle cruiser could bring nothing heavier than light, fixed, or handheld machine guns to bear on the battered destroyer that dogged her. The problem was, that was all she needed. *Walker*'s bridge and foredeck were a bullet-riddled wreck. Only one of her machine guns still spoke from the fire-control platform, manned by Lieutenant Garrett alone. A steady stream of replacements ran to the number one gun, as those crewing it were killed or wounded. Only Dennis Silva remained of the original four who got it back in action, and he was wounded in a dozen places. Still he stood there, drenched in blood, directing the gun at the retreating ship. An occasional stream of yellow "tobacco" juice arced onto the deck. The shots he fired were few and far between, however. There couldn't be more than half a dozen AP shells left on the entire ship, and those were mainly scattered on the wrecked aft deckhouse, where the number four gun had been knocked out by that last 5.5-inch shell. They had to be found and carried forward the length of the ship.

On the bridge, Leo Davis was dead, hit above the left eye by a rico-chet. The 'Cat who'd replaced him at the helm was also down. Matt now stood there alone, crouched low behind the thin bulwark and the upright compass housing. Communications were cut off throughout most of the ship, and Reynolds was effectively out of it, yet he stayed on the bridge, curled in a fetal position against the chart house bulkhead, still trying to raise the ship's various compartments. They'd heard only by word of mouth that the auxiliary conning station, aft, was destroyed. Its crew—including Larry Dowden—had never known what hit them. Matt mourned Larry, and all the others lost this night. If there was a later, he'd mourn them properly, but without the auxiliary conn, somebody had to steer from the pilothouse. And so it was there, on *Walker*'s bridge, that Matt played tag with the devil.

With the loss of the foremast, the radio was out, and Clancy had been ordered to remove it and place it in the whaleboat—the only boat left. The launch was a shattered wreck, and the other launch never returned from searching for survivors of the PBY. Of course, they'd been steaming at high speed ever since it left. Maybe it was still out there somewhere, vainly trying to catch them.

An intermittent pounding, metallic drumming, came from the front of the pilothouse where bullets struck, but the enemy fire had begun to slacken. Matt saw Spanky crawling across the strakes from the ladders. He was bleeding and seemed disoriented. Matt risked a peek out the window to make sure their position relative to *Amagi* was unchanged. His hat had been snatched off his head during a recent similar check. "Are you all right?" he shouted.

McFarlane shook his head. "I'm shot, Goddamn it. How're you?"

The captain almost laughed. "Nothing, would you believe it?" A throbbing pain resurfaced. "Busted nose, a few scratches," he amended. "How's she holding up?"

"The bow's a sieve, and she's down four feet by the head. I just came from there. A Jap bullet came through the goddamn hull and got me in the goddamn ass! Everybody's out of the aft fire room but the Mice, and they're in water up to their shins. If we don't head for shore right damn now, the fish'll get us all!"

Matt nodded, but at the same time he knew he couldn't give up. *Amagi* might be finished—*Walker* certainly was—but as long as the battle cruiser was afloat, she was a threat. He couldn't break off before the task was done—not as long as they had a single shell for the number one gun. It had to end here, now. If *Amagi* got away and somehow survived, Baalkpan would never survive her eventual return. Worse than that, the sacrifice of all those who'd died and suffered this long day and night would have been for nothing.

"Soon," Matt promised. "We'll break off soon."

"Goddamn it! Why won't that unholy bitch just sink?!" Silva raged into the night. He could barely see through the blood clouding his vision, and he suspected his left eye was ruined. A swarm of paint chips and bullet fragments were the cause. Even so, he could tell *Amagi* was listing twenty-five or thirty degrees—but that was where it stopped. Low in the water and creeping along at barely five knots, the Jap was still underway and entering the center of the channel. He'd thrown shell after shell into her stern, and there'd been no visible effect other than a growing, gaping hole in her fantail. Now, no matter how hard they searched, the runners who'd been bringing him shells couldn't find any more.

Machine-gun bullets still rattled off the splinter shield, but only a few. It was as if the Japanese sailors knew *Walker* had done her worst, and had nothing left to throw at them. They were going to get away.

"Mr. Silva!" came a cry behind him, and he whirled in shock. Through the warped, twisted hatch on the starboard front angle of the superstructure appeared a small girl and a striped lizard.

"What the *hell* are you *doing* here?" he choked. "Goddamn, there's bullets and bombs . . . and we're fixin' to sink! Get your stupid asses under cover, for crissakes!"

Rebecca looked at her companion. "Well, Lawrence, clearly we're not wanted, and apparently they don't need *this* as badly as we thought—with everyone running around looking for them!" It was only then that Silva realized the small girl and large, but still sore lizard were struggling with a heavy, four-inch-fifty shell suspended between them.

Torn, he glanced at the retreating battle cruiser. For the moment the incoming fire had stopped completely. Maybe the enemy gunner was out of ammunition—or he'd simply given up. "Shit!" he groaned disgustedly. "Gimme that; then get the hell outta here!" He sprinted across the blood-slick deck to meet them. "Let me guess: Lieutenant Tucker still thinks you're with O'Casey and vicey-versey?"

"I tried to sto' her," Lawrence announced virtuously, but the girl only grinned.

"My safety is still primarily *your* responsibility, Mr. Silva. I have no control over assumptions others might make," Rebecca stated sternly. "Besides, whether they like it or not, or even know it, my people must be represented in this fight!"

"Skipper's gonna kill me," Silva muttered with absolute certainty, taking the shell in his massive hands. He noticed with a sinking feeling that it was high-explosive. "Here," he said, resignedly, handing it to the loader, "let's make it count!" He glared back at the girl. "I've pulled some stupid stunts, but this . . . at least get behind the splinter shield!"

Rebecca's grin faded. "Your eye!"

"Just a scratch." Silva turned to Pack Rat, the Lemurian pointer. "Well? Quit screwin' around, and let 'em have it!"

"You gonna aim for us?" Pack Rat cried sarcastically. His gunners were all Lemurians, too short to look through the sight and push the trigger pedal too. They could elevate and traverse if he guided them, though. He was positive just a few more rounds would finish *Amagi*, but they just didn't have them. A single HE shell wouldn't make much difference.

"Yeah, if somebody'll load the goddamn thing!" he growled disgustedly. It was then that he saw his trainer was down. "Hey . . . Lawrence! Get your stripey ass on the training wheel!"

Lawrence's jaw went slack. "Trainer? I?"

"Yeah, trainer, you! Step on it!"

The breech slammed shut, and Silva squinted with his good eye through the telescopic sight mounted on the left side of the gun. Only the smallest part of his consciousness even noticed when a tiny hand squirmed its way into his clenched, bloody fist.

"Port a little," he crooned, "port . . . port . . . Good! Up, up . . . Good. Shit! Stop when I say 'good,' damn you! Down . . . Good!" He stepped aside. "Fire!" Pack Rat stomped on the pedal. The gun barked and recoiled backward, but Silva was watching the tracer. It struck right in the middle of the gaping hole aft, and he thought he saw a brief flash deep inside the ship.

"A hit!" Rebecca cried excitedly.

"Woop-te-do. Might as well throw hand grenades at the bastard," Silva explained dejectedly. "Well, that's that," he said, squeezing Rebecca's hand before letting it go. Suddenly he hurt all over, and he was sick inside as well. "Beat feet back to the pilothouse. There's no sense standing around and getting shot if we ain't got no more bullets! I'll tell the captain we're dry." He started to turn.

"Silva, look!" Pack Rat shouted. Dennis did. *Amagi* was suddenly leaning a little farther to port and veering hard right.

"What the hell?" he murmured. "Maybe we hit her steering engine or something?" Whether that was the case, or *Amagi* had simply tired of the dog yapping at her heels and decided to present her remaining broadside of secondary guns and destroy the nuisance that tasked her, Silva had no idea. He knew the latter would be the result, however, and *Walker* heeled as the captain saw it too. Sluggishly, *Walker* turned hard a'port, but her grace and quickness were gone. The short delay was just enough to put her at a disadvantage, and there was nothing she could do. Silva clutched the girl to his side and braced himself for the final fusillade, while *Amagi* continued her sharp turn, out of the main channel, and into the prepared lane they'd left the day before. She was drawing considerably more water this time when she passed directly over the MK-6 magnetic exploder—and the cluster of depth charges it was anchored to.

The sea convulsed around her, just under the number two turret, and her entire bow heaved up upon the gigantic swelling of foam. Then a geyser of spray erupted forth and completely inundated the forward half of the ship. There was very little flash, but the sound of the blast was enormous. *Amagi* collapsed into the hole the charges left in the water, the sea closing over the bow before it shuddered back to the surface like a submarine. Only now, it was . . . crooked . . . somehow. The outline of the ship had visibly changed, and even as they watched, it contorted still more. Water surged near the base of the forward superstructure, but there was red paint visible beneath her pointed bow.

"*Broke her goddamn back!*" Silva bellowed. "I *knew* it would work!"

Pack Rat looked at him incredulously, and Rebecca threw her arms around his waist.

Captain Kurokawa was thrown against the chart table by the force of the blast. His head struck the edge, and he lay stunned for several moments. He comprehended a great roaring, surging sensation, as well as screams and urgent shouts. *Amagi* heaved beneath him, and the deck began to cant. *"Nooooo!"*

He didn't recognize the cry that escaped his lips. It was primordial. Staggering to his feet, he looked about. All the windows were smashed, and sparks fell like fiery rain from shorted conduits on the overhead. The flames that engulfed his ship aft boiled to unprecedented heights—then began to subside. The tilt of the deck was becoming more extreme. "No!" he shrieked again. The bridge seemed deserted of all but bodies. Those who'd left their posts would pay, he grimly swore. Then he saw movement on the blistered bridge wing. Still groggy, Kurokawa recognized the American, Kaufman, by his beard and skinny frame. The man was whooping with savage joy, even as the ship sank beneath him. Fumbling at his side, Kurokawa slipped the Nambu pistol from the leather holster and moved carefully across the sloping deck.

"This is the cost of your madness!" came a feeble shout from beneath the wreckage of the engine room telegraph. Without hesitation, Kurokawa snapped off a shot in the direction of the voice. He was rewarded by a moan of anguish. Looking closer, he peered into the sputtering darkness to see Sato Okada. Just as he thought. He leveled the pistol at the dark form and advanced.

"Your treachery has brought us to this, Commander." His voice was almost calm, but his eyes bulged with maniacal fury. "My strategy to subvert the Grik, and ultimately have them serve us, would have succeeded in the end." He straightened. "It will yet. They will win the battle and the ship will be saved. I will continue to serve the emperor in spite of you, wherever we are!" Carefully, he aimed the Nambu at an eye that seemed to glow in the darkness. "You won't live to see it, however." His finger tightened on the trigger.

More sparks seemed to pour from his eyes, and he crumpled under the force of a blow to the back of his head. He vaguely knew the pistol had fired again as he fell. Rolling over, he looked up in time to see his attacker. Skinny arms raised above his head, clutching a twisted piece of conduit, David Kaufman stood silhouetted against the burning night beyond the windows.

"Wait!" he cried, and to his amazement the man actually did. The final blow didn't fall, and Kaufman stood gasping, waiting expectantly. Kuro-kawa shot him. With a roar of rage, Kaufman raised the pipe to strike, but the Nambu barked again and again, until the conduit clattered feebly against the deck beside Kurokawa's head.

Kaufman was on his knees. "Goddamn sneaky Japs," he murmured, and pitched forward onto his face.

Amagi groaned in agony, and Kurokawa quickly pointed the pistol at Okada, where he still lay trapped. "Where were we?" he asked.

"You were going to shoot me, but you can't anymore. The magazine is empty."

Kurokawa jerked the trigger, but nothing happened. Where did all the bullets go? "No matter!" he barked in frustration. "Your reprieve will be quite short, I assure you! As soon as the battle is over and the damage attended to, I'll have you executed in disgrace!" There was a shuddering rumble deep within the ship, and Sato Okada began to laugh. "Silence, you fool!" Kurokawa raged.

Okada stopped laughing and just looked at him for a moment. "You are the fool, Captain. There will be no repairs!"

Matt and Spanky were both standing now, staring in shock through the empty window frames. Less than four hundred yards away, *Amagi* quickly settled toward the silty bottom of Baalkpan Bay. Her bow broke away and capsized before it went down. The rest of her sank on a relatively even keel. Boats went over the side, and hundreds of white-clad forms scram-bled into them, or as high in the superstructure as they could go. The water wasn't particularly deep, and chances were, much of the ship would remain above the surface. Many would survive. Chief Gray staggered onto the bridge without a word, and even Reynolds stood to see.

Great clouds of steam and smoke gushed skyward aft as the sea closed over the fires. A heavy detonation rumbled across the water, and soot and steam belched from the stack. Finally the savaged fantail disappeared from view with a tremendous, thundering gurgle of escaping air. Only then did a heartfelt cheer erupt from *Walker*'s survivors.

Finally! Matt thought. His entire body felt almost rubbery with relief. *My God . . . Finally!* He closed his eyes briefly in thanks. A few Grik ships frantically tacked past the smoldering wreck, headed for the Makassar Strait. *Walker* had nothing left to shoot at them.

Matt looked at his watch. "Oh two five eight, Mr. Reynolds. Please re-cord it in the log." He looked at Gray. "Now, if only things are going okay ashore," he said grimly, watching the fleeing ships. It was impossible to tell if they were going to reinforce the landing in the south, or just running away. He had no idea if they were winning or losing the battle on land, and all of Baalkpan seemed to burn.

"Survivors?" Gray asked with distaste, gesturing at the boats in the water and the protruding pagoda. Matt shook his head.

"They're fine for now," he said. "If we take time to bring them aboard, they'll just be in the water with us. How fast can we push her without putting too much stress on the forward bulkheads, Spanky?"

McFarlane seemed distracted, concentrating. "Six knots?" he hazarded. "Faster than that and you'll drive her under. Slower and she'll sink before we get there. I expect you'll try to make it to the shipyard?"

Matt nodded sadly. "That's my hope. I'll angle her toward shore, though, just in case she doesn't make it."

He looked back at *Amagi*'s wreck as he spun the wheel for home. "I wish Jim could've seen this," he said.

By some freakish miracle of buoyancy, *Mahan*'s stern still floated. The entire forward part of the ship had been obliterated by the blast, removing the flooded weight that would have quickly pulled the rest of her down. The explosion also heaved the shattered aft section backward against the continued thrust of her single screw. The watertight integrity was completely gone, however, and the stern was filling rapidly. Escaping air shrieked through the many rents, and the deck tilted ever downward.

Jim and two 'Cats had dragged Sandison into the meager protection of the battered aft deckhouse before the huge explosion drove them to the deck. One of the 'Cats was blown over the side, but the other had been there to revive him. Still lying on the deck, Jim watched with stunned bitterness, and a profound sense of betrayal and futility, as *Amagi* began to steam out of the harbor in spite of her massive wound. He'd killed his ship, and who knew how many of her crew, for nothing. Then, to his bleary-eyed astonishment, he saw *Walker* giving chase.

He knew it was a pointless gesture, as futile as his own had been. *Walker* could never finish the monster with only her lonely number one gun, and clearly that was all she had left to fight with. Even so, in spite of his despair, he felt a thrill of pride. In the flickering light he saw that *Walker*'s foremast was down, but someone had removed the big flag and run it up to the top of the shorter mast, aft. It was scorched and torn, but it streamed with a stately, defiant grace. The sight brought tears to his eyes.

He staggered painfully to his feet with the Lemurians' help, and stood unsteadily on the canted deck. The vibration of the engine had subsided at last, and the screw stopped thrashing at the water as it rose into the air. Far across the bay his friend pursued *Amagi*, an occasional flash from the four-inch gun amid the tracers proclaiming that, however hopeless, *Walker* was still in the fight.

The deck lurched beneath his feet. *Mahan* was going fast. He looked down at the unconscious torpedo officer and was grateful that Bernie wouldn't suffer what was to come. He hugged the 'Cat supporting him tightly against his side.

"Cap'n Ellis!" came a cry. Jim whirled and caught a glimpse of a dull white reflection in the water alongside. It was the launch! There was movement aboard, and it was full of men and 'Cats. He'd forgotten all about it—other than a brief suspicion that it had been sunk by the blast.

"Mr. Steele? Is that you?" he cried.

"Aye, sir. Sorry it took so long to come back for you, but with that screw churnin' up the water, we couldn't get close. Better hurry, sir; the old girl's goin'!"

"There's a wounded man up here. Can you give us a hand?"

At that moment his dying ship lurched again, but almost before it registered, he heard a momentous blast. He jerked his head back to the south. *Walker*'s now distant shape was outlined by *Amagi*'s flames, and an enormous cataract of luminous water engulfing the enemy ship.

Wild cheering erupted in the launch, but Frankie Steele's voice remained intent.

"Just slide him down the deck and we'll take him on the boat, Cap'n." He turned to the other occupants of the launch. "Shut up, you guys! I know it's a hell of a thing, but we gotta save the skipper!"

With a final magical image of the sinking battle cruiser etched on his mind, Jim and the Lemurian pushed Sandison down the sloping deck, toward the rising water and waiting hands.

Sandra Tucker and Sean O'Casey sprinted down the pathways of Baalkpan as the all-pervading, haze-gray world began to brighten almost imperceptibly. Fires still burned fiercely in many parts of the city, and soldiers and firefighters with buckets and skin bags of water raced to and fro. Even in the face of the ongoing disaster, however, the mood of those they met was jubilant. They'd won. In spite of everything, they'd won. Bradford ran with them, wheezing from exertion and the weight of the Krag he still carried. He'd come along ostensibly to protect them from marauding Grik— several hundred had broken into the inner city from the waterfront—but Sandra doubted they'd be much of a threat. Most had probably already been killed. She wouldn't have waited regardless. The casualties from the fight for the docks were proportionately greater than anywhere else. The Grik had attempted to land almost a hundred ships there, and *Amagi* had concentrated much of her fire in the area as well. Somewhere behind, the rest of the medical team she'd assembled followed as fast as they could, but she wouldn't wait. Her duty to the wounded would have drawn her anyway, but she'd heard *Walker* was coming in.

Across the cratered parade ground they ran, oblivious to the smoking ashes of the Great Hall and the blackened wreckage of the Sacred Tree, through throngs of celebrating people, and into the desolated trading sector. They finally emerged behind the battered seawall and stared in wonder and horror at the scene before them. It was like the very pit of hell. The colorful, cheerful ambience of the area was entirely gone. In its place was a gray, blood-washed ruin that must have resembled the Great War battlefields of France and Belgium. Bodies were everywhere, friend and foe, but the Grik corpses were beyond number. The earth behind the wall had been churned into a slush of gore, and the stench of death was overpowering. One of the huge cannons still poked through its embrasure, its exhausted crew leaning on it or lying nearby. They were covered in mud and blood, and their pelts were a uniform matted reddish brown. But their white teeth flashed incongruous grins as Sandra approached. They were alive, and they'd won.

She scrambled atop the wall, leaving the one-armed O'Casey struggling clumsily to join her. Beyond, the scene was even worse—if that was possible—except in this case almost all the dead were Grik. Forests of masts protruded from the water, and shattered hulks lay half-submerged against the docks. Fires burned out of control, and she saw some of the enemy still dying even now, writhing in the flames or cringing in parts of the ships not yet burning. Past the dock, and a little to the right, lay the massive sunken carcass of *Big Sal*, her pagodalike habitations blackened by fire, the foremost one still burning. All her masts were gone.

"Wait, my dear!" huffed Bradford behind her. "Please wait just a moment!"

She paid him no heed. Running along the top of the wall, she dashed down past the fitting-out pier and emerged among a large assembly of Lemurians gathered near the shipyard. There'd been no fighting there, almost as if the enemy had deliberately avoided damaging the facility. Probably they had. Because it was mostly clear of Grik, many of the wounded had been carried there, but not everyone present had been injured. Many had come just to see. They were staring seaward, and she looked in that direction.

Two motor launches, the whaleboat, numerous feluccas, and boats of every description strained to nudge or tow *Walker* into the large refit basin. With a rush of terror Sandra saw that the old destroyer had been savaged. Her bridge was riddled with holes, and empty windows gaped. An enormous hole in her foredeck was surrounded by jagged plates peeled back like flower petals. The weather deck was a scorched shambles, and the aft deckhouse had been demolished. The gun once perched atop it had collapsed into the debris and lay on its side, muzzle askew. Most of her length was blackened by fire, and the foremast trailed alongside, tangled in a jumble of cables. Smoke still wafted weakly from her aft funnel—the cantankerous number four boiler—but steam was escaping as well. Less than a foot separated the fo'c'sle from the debris-strewn water, as the bow slowly nudged through the flotsam. Her proud number, 163, was already lost to view. From the aft mast the giant flag still flew, almost shredded now, but stirring fitfully in the light morning breeze. Sandra choked back a sob.

The ship's blood-spattered decks were almost empty, and Sandra assumed most of her survivors had already been removed by the flotilla surrounding her. Several men and 'Cats stood on the fire-control platform, and there was movement on the bridge as well. If Matt still lived, that was where he'd be. She shouldered her way through the throng for a better look, and seeing who she was, most parted and made a lane for her to pass. She didn't notice them, but if she had, she'd have seen the deferential lowered ears and blinks of respect running through the crowd.

Walker edged into the basin and slowed to a stop less than fifty yards from the pier. The overtaxed launches tried to pull her closer, but it was clearly no use. The ship was going fast. As Sandra watched, the aft fire room access trunk opened with a clang, and a mist of steam gushed out. A short female 'Cat crawled onto the deck, then reached back inside the opening. With a mighty heave she pulled first one, then another pale, grimy form into the light. Coughing and leaning on one another, the three quickly shuffled under the amidships deckhouse toward the ladder at the back of the bridge. As if she'd been waiting for that very event, *Walker* finally surrendered herself to the sea. Water crept over the fo'c'sle and coursed into the jagged hole. The rasping blower went silent, but the sound was replaced with a massive, urgent *whoosh* as the bow dipped lower and lower. With a juddering, grinding thump, it struck the silty bottom. There was an almost dying groan as the rest of the ship quickly settled. All that remained above water was the top of the bridge and her four battered funnels resting at a slight angle to port. Most of the flag was still visible too, jostled by the rising, turbulent froth of escaping air.

There was an audible, mournful sigh from the crowd, replaced by a frenzied cheer when a large, bloodied man above the bridge—whom Sandra recognized as Dennis Silva—gave a jaunty wave with one hand, while the other supported a small girl sitting on his shoulders. Tabby and the Mice stiffly ascended the ladder to the crowded platform, and Sandra felt her heart leap into her throat when Matt climbed wearily up from the bridge to join them. She was yelling now too, waving her arms over her head, and tears streamed down her cheeks.

Wherever she came from, there was no doubt: USS *Walker*, DD-163, and her lost and lonely crew had found their way home at last.

EPILOGUE

*D*isaster," Tsalka hissed mournfully. "Utter and complete disaster." The rising sun presided over the beginnings of a bright, brisk morning in the Makassar Strait, and of the almost four hundred ships comprising the Invincible Swarm, less than seventy now accompanied the *Giorsh*, Esshk's flagship, as it sailed back toward Aryaal. To make matters even worse, most of those ships were empty of all but their crews, since they'd been the ones that launched the southern assault. Never in the millennia-long history of the Grik had there been such a catastrophe. Tsalka sighed. "I did not command here, but that will make little difference to the Celestial Mother. I am regent-consort of this territory now, and I am responsible. Would you care to join me, General Esshk, for a final repast? I intend to destroy myself at the midday, with all proper ceremony while it is still due me. You may join me in that as well, if you like."

Esshk leaned on the rail, his claws gouging the white-painted wood as he stared aft at the mighty plume of smoke still hovering over distant Baalkpan. He sighed as well. "I am honored, Lord Regent, but I shall not destroy myself today, nor, I believe, should you. To do so would be selfish, and possibly even a crime against our race."

"But, General," Tsalka hissed in shock, "you know I am no one's prey, and I fear nothing of this world, but surely a quick, clean, honorable death is preferable to what we can expect from the Celestial Mother amid such disgrace?"

"We are disgraced," Esshk agreed, "but not by our actions. We attacked our prey as we have always done, as we have been raised and trained to do: with overwhelming numbers and even more overwhelming arrogance. We are no more disgraced by our actions than the countless Uul we sent to be slaughtered. Our disgrace lies in our arrogance and our stubborn, rote-dominated, unimaginative ignorance! Don't you see? This prey is different from any we have faced before. We thought they were the same as those that escaped us long ago, but we were wrong. Perhaps it was the 'Americans' that changed them, but it really doesn't matter. The point is, they *have* changed, and we have not. You accused me of being a philosopher, and perhaps I am. I hope so, at any rate, because it will take philosophers, not mindless Uul, to defeat this prey in the end—and we must defeat them! Having beaten us, do you think they will be content? Of course not! They will destroy us all if we do not ready ourselves to meet them, and to do that we will have to change." He paused. "And some of those changes must be fundamental."

"But why must we be the ones to attempt this change?" Tsalka almost wailed. "Better to destroy ourselves than face such an impossible challenge!"

"It must be we," Esshk replied, "because we were here. Only we know the truth. Perhaps bearing that truth, knowing the end we face, we will convince the Celestial Mother it *is* truth. That, and something more." He snapped his claws and his personal guards disappeared. They returned escorting a haggard, stained, and bloodied Captain Hisashi Kurokawa, who stood tensely before his "hosts."

"Captain Kurokawa," Esshk greeted him pleasantly, and Kurokawa looked at him in surprise. "You failed to bring the victory we relied on you to achieve, but you are not entirely to blame. I pushed you when you were not ready, I failed to heed what I now believe was your excellent advice, and I forced you to attack in a way not of your choosing. You did not, as you claimed, destroy the flying machine of the prey, but again, that effort was poorly planned and against your more . . . experienced judgment. At any rate, its contribution to their defense was negligible this time, and numerous witnesses attest that it is now, in fact, destroyed. We will speak no more of that. As I said, we relied far too heavily upon your one ship— magnificent as it was—and I have come to accept your radical argument that when the ground from which the hunter strikes disappears from under him, he is not necessarily made prey, or even to blame. I will therefore suffer your continued existence." Kurokawa stifled a gasp, but Esshk continued. "Only one in ten of your Uul shall go to the cook fires for your part in this terrible failure. Far more of our own will feed our remaining host, I assure you, since ours was the greatest failure of all. Choose the food yourself, and choose them wisely, because now we need your knowledge more than ever. We *must have* the wondrous things you promised: the smoking ships, the airplanes, the guns. . . . They are no longer mere trifles to amuse ourselves with; they are essential. You will make them for us."

Kurokawa cared nothing for the additional losses he'd sustain. Barely four hundred of his crew still survived, rescued by *Giorsh* and other ships as they retreated from the bay, but he could spare another forty if he must, if it meant he himself would live. He was just beginning to accept what he'd considered impossible: he would *live*! His fate was now tied inextricably to Esshk's and Tsalka's, and he doubted they were entirely safe themselves, but one thing was certain: he'd just been following orders. On second thought, maybe their fates weren't inextricable. He assumed now they would take him to meet this "Celestial Mother" of theirs, and if she was astute enough to recognize the wonders he could provide, and the threat that made them necessary, perhaps Esshk and Tsalka needed him more than he needed them. He smiled.

Five days after the terrible battle that would be added to the Sacred Scrolls, and ever after remembered as the Battle of Baalkpan, there was a gathering of friends at the shipyard. The air still smelled of smoke, not only from battle, but from the incessant pyres that had burned for the dead. Uncountable Grik bodies had simply been rolled into the sea, and the shoreline seethed with flasher fish as they did their grisly work. Even so, the scent of death lingered, and the mood of those who gathered near the sunken destroyer was already somber.

The great Nakja-Mur, U-Amaki ay Baalkpan, had been carried to the sky along with an unimaginable eleven thousand others. Sandra said his heart failed in the stress and excitement, but most believed it simply broke. Never in the recorded history of the People had there been such traumatic loss of life. The only consolation was that he'd died knowing his people were safe and the victory he'd given everything for was at hand. Along with him, the flames had carried Naga and Ramic-Sa-Ar to the Heavens. Ramic died in the final fighting, knowing at least part of his vengeance was complete. Young Tassana was now High Chief of *Aracca*.

The destroyermen had lost dearly too, and there were graves in Baalkpan now. Thirteen just from *Walker*, including Larry Dowden, Dave Elden, and Leo Davis. They'd been laid beside Tony Scott's empty grave on the parade ground. Several others had gone down with *Mahan*, and their names would be added to a plaque listing all the destroyermen—human and Lemurian—who'd been lost from the start.

Adar wasn't with them. As long as the funeral pyres burned, he'd be very busy. He was High Sky Priest of Baalkpan now, as well as acting High Chief. He'd continue to perform those duties, by acclaim, at least until the rest of the city's people returned. Few doubted his elevation would be permanent. The views of the "runaways" weren't highly regarded, and Adar had made it clear he intended to press the Grik. The vengeance-minded People were more than happy to support that position. At least for now.

Chack and Queen Maraan were expected shortly. It was understood they were betrothed, and they were even more inseparable now than they'd been before the battle. The funeral pyre for *Big Sal*'s dead had already burned but today, B'mbaadan and Aryaalan souls flew together. Chack and Rolak were escorting Safir.

Sandison and Garrett were in the hospital suffering from serious wounds, but both were expected to recover. Others were still there as well: Kutas, Aubrey, Newman, Rodriguez. . . . Silva had lost his eye—and immediately gone AWOL. Only Risa and Pam Cross knew where he was, but no one really worried. It was clear the nurse was taking care of him herself, when she wasn't on duty, and sooner or later he'd turn back up.

Many others were present, however, for what felt like it was shaping into a service for *Walker* and *Mahan* and their many dead. Saan-Kakja, U-Amaki ay Maa-ni-la, was there. She'd come herself, leading her personal Guard of a thousand warriors. It had been her timely arrival off the southern coast that bolstered Brister and Shinya's forces, tipping the balance in their desperate attack on the Grik rear. She'd apologized profusely for arriving so late, but Maa-ni-la was now a firm member of the Alliance, and she pledged that more troops and supplies were on the way.

Keje was using the same crutches Gray once hobbled on, shortened to fit his physique. Somehow he'd survived the almost total destruction of *Big Sal*'s upper levels, and was found by a rescue party the morning after the battle still sitting on his beloved stool. When Adar tried to suggest he should be High Chief of Baalkpan, he'd refused. *Big Sal* was his Home. With the sophisticated Lemurian pumps, coupled with the concept of hoses they'd learned from the Americans, he was sure she'd float again. For now he was content to recuperate, aided by the diligent attention of his daughter.

Shinya, Brister, Flynn, and Alden were there, as were Alan and Karen Letts. Letts's quick thinking in sending out rescue craft had undoubtedly saved most of *Walker*'s crew. Not only had they taken her people off, they'd helped get the ship into shallow water. The happy addition of *Mahan*'s and *Walker*'s launches—once the survivors were transferred—aided in that considerably, and Jim Ellis and Frankie Steele piloted the launch-turned-tugboats throughout.

To everyone's surprise, *Walker*'s launch had actually rescued most of the PBY's crew. Ben Mallory, Jis-Tikkar, and one of the gunners were found clinging precariously on one of the leaking wing floats. Somehow they'd survived the crash and escaped the sinking wreckage. Most of the flashies had been drawn to other parts of the bay. Tikker was in the hospital, but Mallory was, miraculously, uninjured. Sometimes it was like that.

A pilot might break his neck when his parachute opened, or crawl out of a catastrophic crash.

Her Highness Rebecca Anne McDonald, princess of the Empire of the New Britain Isles, still wore battered dungarees, fuming at Silva's behavior and the fact she was now virtually a prisoner of Sandra Tucker and Sean O'Casey. Lawrence and Silva had recounted her exploits during the battle, and if she and her strange Grik-like friend were now heroes of Baalkpan (and represented a possible end to the dame famine to the Americans), they were also never allowed to go anywhere without a particularly attentive escort. Most knew of her status now—such a secret was impossible to keep for long—and it was considered just a matter of time before Jenks and his squadron arrived. Jenks would be disappointed. She intended that her people and her new friends should become allies against the Grik, and though she wanted to go home, she'd already proclaimed that she'd do so only if Captain Reddy took her himself.

Now the gathering stood, silent for the most part, staring at the sad remains of the proud old ship. The flag still flew from the aft mast, and Matt couldn't bear to see it taken down. Not yet. He remembered the first time he'd seen her, riding at anchor in Manila Bay, in another time— another world. He never would have thought back then that he'd mourn her loss like he did. After what they'd been through and all they'd achieved— and lost—it was like a huge piece of his soul had gone to the bottom with her. Sandra stood beside him holding his hand, a concerned expression on her face. All the pretense of professional distance they'd worked so hard to maintain had gone down with the ship. He needed her now, just as badly as one of her patients might who'd lost a leg.

"Do you think they'll come back?" Karen Letts quietly broke the silence.

"Sure," said Gray.

Unconsciously, Karen's hand went protectively to her lower abdomen, and Sandra smiled wistfully. Karen hadn't said anything, but Sandra had suspected. She'd seen the signs.

"We're all on the same footing now, technologically speaking," Gray continued. "All the modern warships are gone, but they know about cannons, and they've still got the Japs to help 'em—if they don't eat 'em."

Before they could go out and claim the Japanese survivors, several Grik ships, including one of the white ones, had taken them off. All they found was a single wounded officer who'd decided to defect to the Americans. He was waiting patiently when they finally arrived, having hidden from the Grik, as well as his own people. For now he was under guard, but he'd told them a great deal—not least of which was how Captain Kaufman met his end. The sad aviator's body had been buried with full honors alongside the others in the little cemetery.

"Not to mention," mentioned Courtney Bradford dryly, "there are still far more of them than there are of us."

"It doesn't matter," Matt said tiredly. "Even if they don't, we have to keep after them. Adar's right; we have to wipe them out." He paused. "They're even worse than we thought, and that's saying a lot. They don't know how to surrender, and they're not going to leave us alone. If we don't chase them now, keep the pressure up, they'll be back eventually, and all this"—he gestured at the destruction all around, but his eyes never left his ship—"will have been for nothing."

"How long do you think we have?" Sandra asked. Matt shrugged and looked at Bradford.

"Difficult to say, of course," the Australian opined. "According to our 'new' Jappo—a Commander Okada, if I'm not mistaken—we did hurt them rather badly. It may take as many as three years to make good their losses in ships and warriors. Five at the absolute most. You do understand I'm only guessing?"

"My God. That fast?" Jim Ellis interjected.

"Most likely." Bradford nodded.

"That means we've only about half that time to strike before they're fully prepared," Keje said thoughtfully.

"How?" whispered Matt. Beyond his earlier statement of fact, he didn't really want to talk long-term strategy just then. His heart wasn't in it. He just wanted to mourn his ship.

"Easy, Skipper." Spanky grinned. "We'll build battlewagons!"

Matt blinked. "What the hell are you talking about?"

"Ever see a walking-beam steam engine? Put one—a *big* one—on something the size of *Big Sal*, stick on some paddle wheels, and pack her full of guns . . .'Cat battlewagons!"

Keje was intrigued. "Steam engines . . . in a *Home*! Remarkable! You must tell me more, Mr. Maac-Faar-Laan." Then he shook his head. "First we must consider, however, that we still need more help." He bowed to Saan-Kakja. "Less now, of course, but Princess Re-beccaa's people will surely appreciate the necessity of our cause. We must send a delegation across the Eastern Ocean. Take her home, Cap-i-taan Reddy; let her speak for us." He glanced at Chief Gray. "In light of our victory, they may be . . . easier to convince than before."

"Not much time for that," Matt murmured dolefully, still looking at *Walker*'s grave. The destroyer's speed would have made communications across such a distance much simpler. He sighed. No point in wishing for the impossible. Unintentionally, Matt was sure, Keje rubbed salt into the wound.

"Why not raise *Waa-kur*?" Keje asked, genuinely curious.

Matt snorted bitter laughter, then blinked apology in the Lemurian way. "I'm sorry. I sure wish we could, but it's impossible."

Keje blinked perplexity. "Why? She is not heavier than *Salissa*, yet I know my Home can be raised."

"Look," said Spanky, "I know you guys have great pumps; I've seen 'em work. But no matter how much air we put in her, it'll just come out faster. We can't dive and weld, so we can't plug the holes. There's no way."

Keje looked at him and blinked surprise. "Have you never wondered how we build something the size of *Salissa* and then float it?"

"Well . . ." Spanky looked flustered. "I just thought you built 'em on land and launched them down a ways, like we did the frigates."

Keje shook his head. "I understand your . . . misunderstanding . . . now. We build smaller ships, like feluccas, like that. But I assure you, we do not build the great Homes on land."

Spanky's eyes widened. "A dry dock?!"

Keje now had everyone's attention. "You have spoken at some length about what you call a 'proper' dry dock," he said with a touch of irritation, "but we make do with a simpler expedient. We build a wall in the sea and pump out the water behind it. That is what we use this very basin for. I thought you knew? Why else put your ship into it? Here it is very simple. We flood down two Homes across the mouth of the basin, and build the walls only between them. It takes many days to pump the water out, but then you may freely work."

"A cofferdam!" Matt shouted triumphantly, and grinned. It was as though the weight of the world had fallen from his shoulders. Dared he hope? "We *didn't* know! By the time we got here, I was just following the boats pulling us in!"

"And I was following the pilot's directions on the felucca!" Jim said. "I bet Frankie was too!"

"At least somebody knew what they were doing!" growled Gray. Everyone laughed.

Rolak, Chack, and Queen Maraan appeared, joining a happier group than they'd expected.

"What have we missed?" Safir asked pleasantly. She was still sad from the funeral, but uplifted as well.

"We're going to raise the ship!" Sandra announced triumphantly, squeezing her captain's hand.

Spanky's brow knitted into a frown. "Still won't work," he said. "I'm sorry. The damage is just too severe. If we had some steel it might be different, but her structural integrity's shot. We can't keep patchin' her with copper plates and rivets."

Faces fell, but Chack only grinned.

"Steel is like iron, is it not? I've heard the term used interchangeably at times."

"Yeah . . . sorta," Spanky replied.

"Then what are you worried about?" He barked a laugh. "Sometimes you Amer-i-caans are so clever I almost think you are gods. But often you miss the painfully obvious." He gestured vaguely over his shoulder toward where *Amagi* lay on the bottom of Baalkpan Bay, broken and gutted by flames, her warped and dreary superstructure still protruding above the water as a constant, grim reminder. "Out there is all the iron in the world!"

What had been a gloomy gathering became almost a celebration of sorts. Voices rose with excited, animated suggestions, punctuated by occasional laughter. Finally, the great victory they'd achieved actually began to *feel* like a victory instead of yet another ordeal they'd somehow managed to survive. Eventually, as the afternoon waned, the friends began to disperse.

Finally alone, as the sun touched the dense jungle horizon, Sandra wrapped her arms around Matt's neck, pulling him down for a joyful, passionate kiss.

"Gotta go," she whispered at last, tears streaking her face. "Work to do."

"I'll be along."

"You'll be all right?"

Matt smiled at her and nodded. "I think I *am*. Right now, finally, I think we all will be." She hugged him tight, and as she disengaged herself, her fingers trailing away from his, her smile turned impish.

"Karen's pregnant," she announced.

Matt was stunned, as all men are by such sudden, momentous statements. "She didn't look any different to me."

Sandra giggled and shook her head. "See you later, sailor," she said, and stepped away into the gathering twilight.

"Huh," Matt said, turning to walk along the dock. Eventually he grinned.

A short distance away he was surprised to encounter the Mice sitting on coiled cables and leaning against a fallen piling. All three had their elbows on their knees and their chins in their hands as they stared glumly at their sunken Home.

"Evening, uh . . . men," he said, inwardly amused by his own confusion regarding how to address them. The trio began to stand and he waved them back. "Why the long faces?" They looked at him as if he were nuts.

Gilbert hopped up anyway, whipping his hat from his head. No matter how crazy he thought he was, there was no way he could answer the skipper sitting down. "Well, sir, beggin' yer pardon, but our ship's, well . . . sunk."

"So? We'll raise her. What's that compared to everything else we've done?" Isak and Tabby both jumped up.

"But . . . beggin' yer pardon too, how we gonna patch her?" Isak demanded.

Tabby suddenly blinked inspiration. "We gonna use iron from that Jap ship, ain't we!" she exclaimed in a passable copy of her companion's lazy drawl.

Isak stiffened. In a voice both excited and scandalized at the same time, he spoke. "Hally-looya, we're gonna get our boilers back . . . but goddamn! Jap iron? It ain't decent!" Catching himself, he yanked his own hat off his head and mumbled, "Sir."

Matt laughed. "Settle down! Steel is steel. Besides, remember all that scrap we sold the Japs before the war? Maybe *Amagi* used to be a Packard!"

He was still laughing when he left them talking excitedly among themselves. Slowly he walked around the basin, inspecting the remains of his ship with a critical eye. Inevitably, looking at her, he became more somber. No question about it: raising and refitting the old destroyer would be a daunting task. But they *had* performed miracles; they could do it again. The mere fact that any of them were still alive was a miracle in itself.

He stopped when he reached the other side of the basin. The ship was farther from him now, and the exposed damage didn't look so bad. An errant ray of the setting sun managed to blink through the jungle on the far side of the bay and cast his long shadow upon the distant pilothouse. That was where he'd been standing when they fought *Amagi* the first time, he reflected, and when they came through the Squall. It was from there that he'd first seen the Lemurians, and directed the first action in their aid. It was probably where he'd first realized he was in love with Sandra Tucker. He'd fought the Battle of Aryaal/B'mbaado Bay and tried to save *Nerracca* from within its confines. And that was where he'd been standing just the other night. . . .

It suddenly occurred to him that *Walker*'s pilothouse, her *bridge*, was where he had become the man he was. More properly, that . . . living . . . ship, and—he couldn't find the words for her crew—had taken the man he'd been and molded, *refined* him into the man he had become. Hot tears stung his cheeks, and, impatiently, he wiped them away. No time for that, and *she* wouldn't want it. As his shadow disappeared and *Walker*'s bridge grew dark, he knew someday, somehow, he'd stand there again. When he did, it would be at the head of a *fleet* that would scour the Grik from existence and secure the safety of his people—regardless of race—and the memory of all those who'd died to make it happen.

DISTANT THUNDERS

FOR: REBECCA—AND MY NIECE, JENNIFER. (I ALWAYS HAVE TO WRITE OR MENTALLY ADD "NIECE" WHEN I THINK OF JENNIFER BECAUSE, IN SO MANY WAYS, SHE WAS ALWAYS THE "DAUGHTER" I NEVER HAD— BEFORE I HAD A DAUGHTER.)

JENNIFER, YOU AND REBECCA COULDN'T BE MORE DIFFERENT, BUT NEVER DOUBT THAT I LOVE YOU BOTH WITH ALL MY HEART

TO: THE MEN AND WOMEN OF THE ARMED FORCES OF THE UNITED STATES—AND THOSE OF ALL NATIONS WHO FIGHT BRAVELY AT THEIR SIDE. PAST, PRESENT, AND FUTURE. GOD BLESS YOU ALL.

ACKNOWLEDGMENTS

As usual, there are some great folks I need to thank: Chief among these are Russell Galen, the best agent in the world, and Ginjer Buchanan, the finest editor anyone could ever hope to have. CPO, (SW-MTS) USN— (Ret.), Bruce Kent ranks near the top as well. He reminded me that I've neglected the EMs and he was right. Granted, there weren't nearly as many things for electrician's mates to *do* on four-stacker destroyers as even I originally thought, but that's because a truly astonishing variety of machinery that would later be electrically powered was either manually or steam operated. That doesn't mean EMs on four-stackers would have been bored. Far from it. They were dealing with the same broken-down, archaic equipment as everyone else; equipment essentially representing the very dawn of the electrical age! Because of that, their contributions would have been particularly difficult and essential. The information Chief Kent kindly supplied, or pointed me toward, was both fun and fascinating. Together we made a number of discoveries that contributed significantly to this story, I believe. If I didn't use the information right, it's my fault, not his.

Dave Leedom, LTC, USAFR, helped, as always, to inspire my aerial high jinks, while keeping my head out of the clouds and my feet on the ground—figuratively speaking. The inimitable (Bad) Dennis Petty continues to provide . . . inspiration . . . and remains a formidable companion during my own unusual adventures. Just so everyone is clear on this, it's *my* turn to shoot *him*—just a little. My parents, Don and Jeanette Anderson, have always inspired me and remain possibly my greatest fans and fiercest critics. My wife, Christine, mostly falls in the general "fierce critic" category, but I guess I'll keep her anyway. James Kirkland and Schuetzen Powder LLC have my deepest appreciation for all their "ballistics testing" support over the years, and all the guys and gals on my gun's crews are still the best in the country. Andy Gillham is the greatest musician alive and I will always fondly—if vaguely—remember the Sasquatch and space alien hunts of our younger years. We never caught any of the boogers, but that never really mattered, did it? Special thanks go to Tom Potter, a fellow historian and "naval thinker" with a brilliant mind. Ha! He'll get it.

Otherwise, the list of usual suspects is long and has been recited before, but I need to add Pete Hodges and Kate Baker to the list. Good friends are hard to find and I treasure all of mine—even Jim. If I forgot to mention anybody or goofed up in any way, it's all Jim's fault. Actually, Jim deserves a lot of credit. He did more in a few brief seconds to disprove the conspiracy theory surrounding the Kennedy assassination than anyone else has done in the last forty-six years. "Magic bullets" do, in fact, exist. We get it, Jim. No need to KEEP proving your point! (Jim is nothing if not thorough, when it comes to science.)

"Weapons more violent, when next we meet."

—*Paradise Lost*

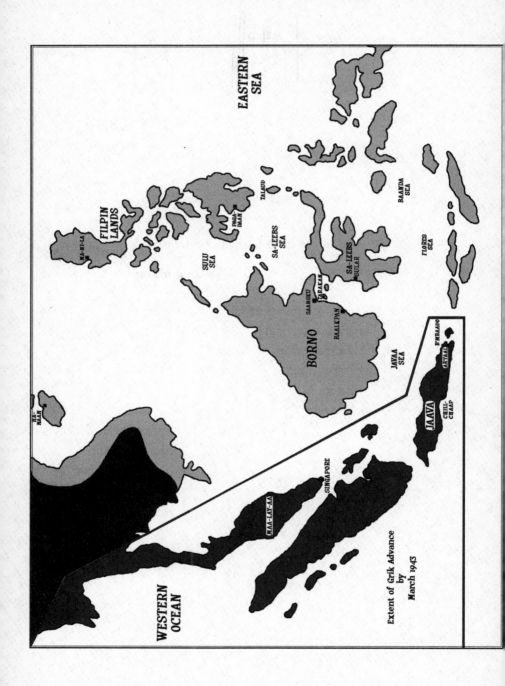

Extent of Grik Advance
by
March 1943

WESTERN OCEAN

EASTERN SEA

FILPIN LANDS

MA-NI-LA

HE-NAAN

SULU SEA

SA-LEERS SEA

TALAUD

PNGA-MAAN

BAANDA SEA

FLORES SEA

SA-LEERS INSULAR

SAANGKU

TARAKAN

BAALKPAN

BORNO

JAVAA SEA

SINGAPORE

MA-LAY-YA

JAAVA

CHIL-CHAAP

TUVU

B'RRADO

U.S.S. WALKER (DD-163)

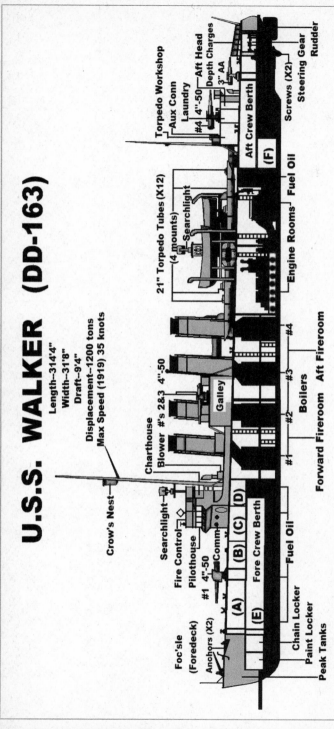

Length–314'4"
Width–31'8"
Draft–9'4"
Displacement–1200 tons
Max Speed (1919) 35 knots

Crow's Nest

Charthouse

Blower #'s 2&3 4"-50

21" Torpedo Tubes (X12)
(4 mounts)

Searchlight

Torpedo Workshop

Aux Conn

Laundry

#4 4"-50 Aft Head

Depth Charges

3" AA

Fire Control
Pilothouse

Searchlight

#1 4"-50

Comm

Galley

Aft Crew Berth

Screws (X2)

Steering Gear

Rudder

Foc'sle
(Foredeck)

Anchors (X2)

(A)

(E)

(B) (C) (D)

Fore Crew Berth

Fuel Oil

Chain Locker

Paint Locker

Peak Tanks

#1   #2   #3   #4

Boilers

Forward Fireroom   Aft Fireroom

Engine Rooms

Fuel Oil

(F)

(A) Cheifs, Warrants, P.O.s Berth
(B) Officer's Quarters
(C) Wardroom
(D) Captain's and Passenger's Staterooms
(E) General Storage & Magazines
(F) General Storage & Magazines

///// *March 1, 1942*

his was NAP 1/c Nataka's last chance. Admiral Nagumo, commanding the First Air Fleet, had ordered Nataka's carrier, *Kaga*, home for repairs. She'd scraped her bottom in the Palau Strait and developed an annoying leak. Now she'd have to leave the war right when things were going so well. Nataka was seriously concerned the war might even be over before she—and, by extension, he—managed to get back in the fight.

He'd already seen a lot of "action" and sometimes felt as if he'd been in the cockpit of his beloved *kanbaku* ever since the beginning of this "new" war against the Americans, British, and Dutch. In all that time however, during all the sorties he'd flown, he hadn't managed to hit *anything* with one of his 250kg bombs! He'd missed the glorious attack on Pearl Harbor; he'd been too sick to hide something that gave him a raging fever and they hadn't let him go. He'd flown many missions since, but now heroes, *immortals*, surrounded him. They'd been his comrades, his peers just a few months before, but they'd accomplished the impossible while he lay sweating in his rack. Somehow, he just hadn't been able to catch up.

Many times now, Nataka had dived with the others in his Navy Type 99 against lonely freighters, destroyers, and even a pair of cruisers. He'd tried to do as he'd been taught, fearlessly braving the black clouds of antiaircraft shells and tracers that rose to meet him. He'd bored in relentlessly at exactly sixty-five degrees and released his bomb at exactly the proper instant—and somehow, he always missed. He'd even missed at Port Darwin! Granted, he hadn't gone after a stationary anchored target; he'd attacked a wildly maneuvering, desperately firing destroyer, but his bomb hadn't even come close! Someone must have finally hit the *norou* old American destroyer; he'd seen it afire and dead in the water when his flight regrouped after the attack, but his dive-bomber must have been the only one to return to *Kaga* that hadn't hit *something*! Even NAP 1/c Honjo, his navigator-gunner, seemed to be losing faith. The two were close—they had to be—but something just wasn't working.

Nataka was a good attack pilot; he *knew* he was. He'd always scored among the very best in practice. Of course, practice targets didn't twist, turn, and lunge ahead at flank speed, churning the sea with their deceptive wakes. They didn't make radical, seemingly impossible turns and belch black smoke at the worst possible moment to spoil his aim. He had to remind himself that there were *men* on his targets now: men who controlled their movements with complete unpredictability. Men who didn't want to die. Now, unless this final "hunting trip" he and Lieutenant Usa had been allowed bore fruit, *Kaga* would steam for Japan before Nataka had a chance to prove himself, before he had a chance to break this terrible curse that seemed to hold him in its grasp!

"There is something building in the east!" Honjo said in his earphones.

Nataka glanced left, beyond the gray-green wing, where a squall line was beginning to form. There were always squalls in these strange seas and sometimes they were intense. They didn't usually form this early in the day, however. "Lieutenant Usa has already seen it," he replied, watching Usa's plane bank left, away from the distant coast they'd been approaching so brazenly. Type 99s were slow and fat; easy prey for any good fighter, even if they were surprisingly agile. Regardless, Nataka wasn't concerned. There were no good enemy fighters in the area. As far as he knew, there were no enemy fighters left at all. Without hesitation, Nataka turned his plane to follow his lieutenant's.

"Maybe a big tanker or some poor, lonely freighter is trying to hide in that squall," Honjo speculated predatorily. Nataka nodded. It was certainly possible. The frequent squalls were the only protection left for those desperate ships fleeing Java. "I just hope, if there is, Lieutenant Usa won't report it," Honjo continued. "Those greedy *bakano* in Second Fleet will want us to lead them to it so they can blast it with their battleships, even if it's a rowboat!"

Nataka nodded again. There'd been a lot of that. Slowly, he eased his plane closer to Usa's and they approached the squall together. Was it just his imagination, or did the rain already seem closer than it should? They were flying three hundred and fifty kilometers per hour, but either the thing was growing much more quickly than any squall he'd seen, or it was moving toward them in an unprecedented fashion. It was also growing darker, and wasn't the usual purple-gray that one usually observed, but rather . . . greenish . . . and livid with dull pulses of lightning. Strange.

"Nataka!" came Usa's clipped, terse voice in his ears. "A ship! Two o'clock, low!"

Nataka suppressed an exasperated sigh. Of course it was low if it was a ship! He strained to see over the black-painted cowling of his engine. *Yes!* All alone on the brilliant purple sea, a lone freighter plodded helplessly along. She looked old, medium-size, with a single stack streaming gray smoke. Perhaps she'd seen them, because she was clearly making for the growing squall.

"We will attack together," Usa said over the radio. "It seems to be the easiest way," he added, almost apologetically, it seemed.

Nataka's face heated, but he made no reply.

"I will approach her port bow," Usa continued. "You will attack from the port quarter. Whichever direction she turns, one of us should have her entire length for his bomb to fall upon!"

"It will be done!" Nataka said, and banked left again, directly toward the squall. "Beloved ancestors!" he muttered, and immediately wondered if anyone heard. If they had, they probably thought he was calling his ancestors to aid him in the attack, but what prompted his words was the squall itself. The thing was monstrous! Not only had it swiftly grown to encompass the visible horizon, but it was practically opaque, not like a squall at all, but like a huge wall of water! He shook himself and glanced at his altimeter. Soon he would begin his dive.

The altimeter had gone insane! The needle spun erratically with wild fluctuations! Not only that, but his compass was distressed as well. As he banked back right, to the north, his compass told him he was flying east! Even as he veered around behind the still tiny ship below, his compass steadfastly insisted that west was north.

"Honjo, I . . ."

"Yes? What is it?"

"Nothing. Usa has circled around while we positioned ourselves. He is beginning his dive!"

"Good luck, Nataka! Let us sink this bastard quickly and get away from that wrongful storm!"

So, Honjo was nervous too. Nataka couldn't count on any of his instruments now. Even his horizon and airspeed indicators were malfunctioning. He pushed the stick forward until the ship's fantail appeared in the telescopic sight in front of his canopy. The target was slow. It couldn't be making more than ten knots at best. He doubted it was capable of any escape sprint, like those so many of his targets had employed. Nevertheless, he engaged the dive brakes to slow his descent. He wanted plenty of time to react if the ship took evasive maneuvers to avoid Usa's attack.

Tracers started rising toward him and a single puff of black smoke erupted in his path. *This sheep has a few little teeth*, he thought, concentrating on his angle of descent. Apparently, the target had managed a feeble burst of speed after all, and he pulled back on the stick just a bit. More tracers came and they seemed brighter than before. Brighter? He risked a quick glance away from the sight. No. The world was darker! The squall was in the west, he *knew* it was in the west, but out-riding clouds above must have blocked the morning sun. *No time.* Usa was nearly upon the target, the gray-green of his plane and the bright red circles on its wings still clearly contrasted against the darker sea. *Excellent!* The ship was turning toward Usa, just as the lieutenant predicted! *Usa might still hit. . . . No!* A massive, dirty plume erupted just off the ship's port bow! Tracers followed Usa's plane as it pulled up, up. . . . But wait! The plane was smoking!

Nataka focused once more on the target. Later there would be time to discover the lieutenant's fate. Hopefully, Usa and his gunner would be all right, but they'd certainly left the ship at Nataka's mercy! Tracers still reached for him and he felt the plane shiver as a few bullets found their mark. He fired his own 7.7-millimeter guns to disperse the defenders. Another black puff materialized to his right and fragments of steel sleeted into his wing. He heard Honjo yell.

Soon, he crooned to himself. His angle was perfect; the target couldn't possibly escape. He had the entire length of the ship from stern to bow for his bomb to strike . . . !

That was the thought NAP 1/c Nataka took to his watery grave. Just as his hand caressed the knobbed lever to release the five-hundred-pound bomb, another pathetic, miraculous black puff appeared less than four feet to his left. Hot steel shredded his canopy and tore away most of his head. More sparkling fragments from the three-inch shell slashed the left wing root and ignited the fuel. The wing fluttered away and the remaining, still dutiful wing sent the flaming wreck into a tight roll that edged it, just slightly, toward the port side of the ship.

With a mighty roar and a blinding flash of flame made even brighter by the dark, eerie squall, the plane and its powerful bomb combined the force of their detonation alongside the old freighter. Technically, Nataka had missed again, but as far as the crew of the SS *Santa Catalina* was concerned, a torpedo couldn't have done much worse.

Santa Catalina's captain quickly assessed the situation. His ship was badly damaged. The near miss forward had opened some seams, but that last stroke left the aft hold quickly flooding. Still, they might just make it. Australia was out of the question, but unlike every other remaining Allied ship in the area, his wasn't bent on escape. The South Java port of Tjilatjap was his destination. Grimly, he ordered as much speed as his old, battered ship could muster; then he stepped out on the bridge wing and stared at the bizarre . . . malignant . . . squall crawling up her wake.

///// *Late March, 1943*

An oppressive smoky haze from the epic battle and resultant, seemingly endless funeral pyres clung to the savaged city and the wide expanse of Baalkpan Bay. Almost three weeks after the Grik invaders churned themselves to offal against Baalkpan's defenses, the smoke and sodden smell of wet, burnt wood still lingered like a sad, ethereal shroud. Captain Matthew Reddy, High Chief of the "Amer-i-caan" Clan, and Supreme Commander of all the combined Allied forces, surveyed the somber scene from *Donaghey*'s hastily repaired quarterdeck as the battered frigate tacked on light, humid, northerly airs toward the mouth of the bay. The water remained choked with the shattered remains of the Grik fleet, causing a real menace to navigation. Occasionally, *Donaghey* thumped and shivered when she struck some piece of floating wreckage and it clunked and shuddered down her side as she passed. It was the first time Matt had returned to the water since that terrible night when the Battle of Baalkpan achieved its cataclysmic peak. Much of the flashing intensity and grief he'd felt had slowly begun to ebb, but the brief interval and the dreary day conspired to reinforce his gloomy mood.

By any objective measure, the battle had resulted in a momentous victory for the Allies, but it came at a terrible cost. The mighty Japanese battle cruiser *Amagi* had accompanied the Grik host, and her shells had shredded the remaining Lemurian ships in the bay and pounded the carefully prepared fortifications to matchsticks and heaps of earth. Lemurian losses had been horrifying, and both precious, aged American destroyers—survivors of the U.S. Asiatic Fleet that had been swept by a mysterious squall from one war (and world) smack into the middle of another—had ultimately been sunk in the battle. *Mahan* (DD-102) was a total loss, having virtually disintegrated herself by ramming the Japanese ship with a load of depth charges set to explode. That blow to *Amagi* had probably been mortal, in retrospect, but she'd still been under way and apparently on the verge of escape. She was finally destroyed by the combination of a lucky, forgotten mine, and the dogged determination of battered *Walker* (DD-163) and her crew, who fought to their final shell despite their own damage and casualties.

USS *Walker* was more fortunate than her sister. She'd managed to crawl back to the shipyard before succumbing to her grievous wounds, and even now, an effort was under way to refloat her. *Amagi* lay on the bottom of Baalkpan Bay, broken and gutted by flames, her warped and dreary superstructure protruding from the water as a constant, grim reminder of that terrible day and night.

Matt himself commanded *Donaghey* for this brief sortie, and it was a slightly awkward situation. He was familiar with *Donaghey*'s historical design, but knew little about actually operating a square-rigged ship. Her assigned captain, Greg Garrett—Matt's former gunnery officer—had become quite a sailor, but he was still recovering from serious wounds. Russ Chapelle, a former *Mahan* torpedoman, had learned quite a bit, however. He'd been the ship's master gunner and was elevated to "salig maa-stir" (sailing master), or executive officer, after *Donaghey*'s own Lemurian exec was killed. Garrett would get his old ship back, or a newer one, when he recovered, but for now, Russ was creditably taking up the slack.

Matt knew Garrett chafed at his inactivity, but his wounds were severe, and Nurse Lieutenant Sandra Tucker insisted he heal completely before exerting himself. All Sandra's patients were important to her, but Greg was human, and humans were an increasingly rare species. The titanic struggle—seemingly destined to encompass the entire locally known world—had already claimed many of the mere handful of humans actively engaged in aiding what was clearly the side of right. No one knew how many Japanese sailors the Grik had saved from *Amagi*, but even if the Grik hadn't eaten them they were, of course, not friends.

According to the charts they'd captured showing the extent of the enemy holdings, the Grik could replace their losses in a shockingly short time. They bred like rabbits and Courtney Bradford theorized that their young reached mature lethality within three to five years. If the remaining Americans and their allies were to have any chance of survival—not to mention victory—they needed all the skills and experience of every last destroyerman. Their window of opportunity would be fleeting and there weren't nearly enough hands and minds for all the work that lay ahead. Matt found it ironic that the ragtag remnants of the Asiatic Fleet who'd wound up here—men once considered the dregs of the Navy by some—were now the indispensable core of innovators: the trainers of the native force they'd need to see them through.

Great work had already been accomplished. They'd begun an industrial revolution of sorts, transforming the nomadic, insular, isolationist Lemurians—people who still reminded many destroyermen of a cross between cats and monkeys—into seasoned professional soldiers and sailors—but those ranks of professionals had been cruelly thinned. Recruitment was constant and Captain Reddy had secured important alliances that would supply the raw material to rebuild their forces, but it would take time to train and equip them, and in spite of their great victory, the war had just begun. The combined human survivors of *Walker, Mahan,* and *S-19* now numbered just over a hundred souls—constituting the known (friendly) human population of this new world—unless somehow, they could befriend the "visitors" who'd appeared that morning beyond the mouth of the bay.

Matt didn't know if their visitors could or would help them, but as much as they needed more friends, they certainly didn't want more enemies. According to Chief Gray, the last meeting between Allied forces and the ships lingering in the strait had been . . . strained. That was one reason Matt wanted *Donaghey* for this meeting. She was the only "home-built" U.S. Navy ship yet made seaworthy again and, scarred as she was, she was the only ship available that should be a match for one of the visitors' powerful steam frigates. Of *Donaghey*'s two sisters, they'd try to salvage *Kas-Ra-Ar*'s guns, but the ship was gone forever. *Tolson* had also very nearly sunk. She'd require much more yard time before she was ready for sea. Several of the massive aircraft carrier–size, seagoing Lemurian Homes had returned after the battle, but impressive as they were, they were too slow to join the delegation. That didn't mean *Donaghey* was approaching the mouth of the bay alone.

Nearly two dozen "prize" ships were taken in serviceable condition after the battle. It would have seemed a great accomplishment, and it was—that they'd been alive to take them. Nevertheless, they'd been the only repairable ships of almost three hundred similar ones—virtual copies of the venerable British East Indiamen their lines were stolen from two centuries before—that had attacked Baalkpan packed with as many as one hundred and fifty thousand Grik warriors. No one would ever know for certain how many there'd actually been. Some of the terrifying, semireptilian Grik had escaped at the end, and many thousands died in the sprawling land battle that had surrounded the city. Far more met their fate in the sea, and the water of the bay had churned for days as the voracious flasher fish fed upon the dead.

Four of those ships now sailed with *Donaghey*, quickly armed with a few cannons each, their once red hulls repainted black with a white stripe between their gunports, according to Matt's new Navy regulations. They'd been cleaned as well as possible and their crews were glad to have them, but they'd never forget who made them. The barbaric nature and practices of their previous owners would taint the ships forever, regardless of how well they were scrubbed.

Matt leaned on the windward taffrail, still gouged and splintered from battle, and focused his intense green eyes on the squadron of strange ships anchored outside the bay—just beyond the reach of the grim-faced gunners serving the heavy cannon of Fort Atkinson. They did look formidable. All were warships, with three masts and sleek-looking hulls. Large half-moon boxes for their paddle wheels and tall, smoke-streaming funnels marred their pleasing lines, but lent a determined, businesslike aspect to their appearance. Matt was impressed by their sophistication. The Empire hadn't quite caught up with the "modern world" the destroyermen had lost, but, in some ways at least, it had advanced to within a generation or two.

The banners streaming above Fort Atkinson caught his attention momentarily: the Stainless Banner of the Trees, Rolak's Aryaalan flag, the gold pennant the Sularans had adopted for their own—and the Stars and Stripes, of course, fluttered from separate poles above the reinforced fortification. The sight of that last flag, and the fact that it still flew after all they'd been through, couldn't help but stir his soul.

Among the sea folk, each of their huge, island-size ships or "Homes" were like nations unto themselves, and their leaders enjoyed co-equal status as "High Chiefs" among their peers. Before the war, those Homes often had clan devices or representative colors, but they hadn't used flags. As "chief" of *Walker*, regardless of her comparative tiny size, Captain Reddy had been afforded the same status as High Chief of the American Clan. With the coming of the war and the Grik Grand Swarm, changes to this age-old system began to evolve. An alliance started to take shape that included not only sea folk, but land folk as well, and a collective, coordinating leadership was required. Nakja-Mur, High Chief of Baalkpan, had been the first leader by default, since his "nation" hosted the other chiefs and, for a time, was the seat of all industry. The city on the southern coast of Borno was also where the first truly decisive engagement had been fought. With Nakja-Mur's death, the leadership of Baalkpan fell to Adar, High Sky Priest of *Salissa*, or *Big Sal*, as the Americans called her. She'd been the first seagoing Home of the Lemurian People to make contact with the Americans.

Amazingly, considering the disparate cultures, a true alliance began to form. Not one merely of expedience, but one designed to unite all willing Lemurians. Keje-Fris-Ar, *Salissa*'s High Chief, had been the first Lemurian to understand the significance and unifying power of flags. He'd directed the creation of the Banner of the Trees, and an infant political union began to take shape.

The stainless Banner of the Trees was composed of a circle of golden tree symbols, one for each Allied Home, surrounding a simple blue star representing the Americans. The star was in the center not to show dominance, but to symbolize that the Americans had been the organizing force, the glue holding everything together during those early, terrible times. Also, unlike the trees surrounding it, the star now represented more than a city-state, personified by a single ship or place. The precedent for that had been set when it became apparent that Captain Reddy was High Chief over both *Walker* and *Mahan*, something difficult for the 'Cats to understand at first, but clearly true. Matt was also acclaimed commander of the first Allied Expeditionary Force and later, all Allied forces. Thus it didn't seem wrong that even though *Mahan* was on the bottom of the sea and *Walker* might never fight again, the single star originally representing two ships, then tiny Tarakan Island, should remain prominent on the flag.

Besides, the United States Navy wasn't dead.

Just as Matt once gave Nakja-Mur a ship he'd captured early in the war so Baalkpan might be represented at sea, so had the bulk of the prizes taken after the Battle of Baalkpan been given, without reservation, to the United States Navy—a navy represented only by Lieutenant Commander Matthew Reddy and his surviving crews. Every Lemurian who joined that crew became a member of the United States Navy and swore to defend a vaguely understood "constitution" against all enemies. Captain Reddy had insisted on that. Therefore, wherever they came from, any Lemurian who swore the oath became a Navy man and a member of the Amer-i-caan Clan for as long as they kept that oath and followed the Americans' strict rules.

Nothing like those rules, or "regulations" as they were called, had ever occurred to any Lemurian, anywhere. The People did as their leaders specifically instructed them, but otherwise, they did as they pleased. No Lemurian leader ever imagined many of their people would willingly submit to the level of discipline demanded by the Americans. The thing was, though the rules were strict, the protections against abuse of power inherent in those rules were equally strict. To their surprise, far more volunteered for the "Amer-i-caan Naa-vee" than for the planned Combined Navy of the Alliance, to be composed of the rest of the prizes and new construction.

Certainly, prestige was a factor, but results were convincing as well. The American Navy had become a tight, close-knit clan of elite professionals who watched out for their own, no matter what they looked like, and it soon became clear the Combined Navy was a nonstarter. For better or worse, the entire Navy—minus the Homes, of course—became Matt's clan, and above every United States ship flew the Stars and Stripes.

That morning, nosing through the last of the debris in the mouth of the bay, everyone crewing *Donaghey* and her prize consorts, human or Lemurian, male or female, was American. Matt was awed by the responsibility, but humbled—and proud—as well.

Raising his binoculars, he focused them on the strange ships they'd sortied to meet. Their guns weren't run out and they were at a distinct disadvantage while anchored, but the men he saw upon their decks appeared tensely vigilant.

"It will be Captain Jenks, I shouldn't wonder," came a small voice. It sounded almost embarrassed.

Captain Reddy glanced at the tiny form beside him. Large jade eyes regarded him with something akin to trepidation, and long, carefully groomed golden locks framed her elflike face. Gone was the tattered waif they'd rescued from Talaud Island, south of Mindanao, with a handful of other civilians and a few S-boat submariners. In her place was this well-dressed, almost regal . . . child . . . possessed of a near adult maturity and resolve. Despite her size and age, her bearing—and presence—made it easy to believe Rebecca Anne McDonald was, well, a princess of sorts. As it turned out, she was the daughter of the governor-emperor of the Empire of the New Britain Isles, and that explained quite a lot that had mystified them before: such as why an entire squadron of warships would search so long and hard for her in a region they hadn't visited in over two hundred years.

"I shouldn't wonder," Matt echoed as amiably as possible, despite his mood and the uncertain situation. The girl had been convinced that Jenks and his squadron would come to their aid. For them to arrive now, so soon after the battle they *had* to have known was brewing, and behave so . . . distantly was irreconcilable with her worldview. Matt motioned to the Bosun, an imposing older man standing nearby with a battered, almost shapeless hat on his head. "Boats is certain of it. He says those are the same ships he . . . met . . . at Tarakan."

"Yep," Chief Bosun's Mate Fitzhugh Gray replied neutrally. "Biggest one's *Achilles*. If Jenks ever named the others, I don't remember. There *were* four of 'em, though."

Gray was a gruff, powerful man, close to sixty, who'd gone a little to seed on the China Station but had since trimmed down and muscled back up considerably. He, at least, had thrived on the activity and adventures they'd experienced since the Squall. He'd also appointed himself Matt's senior armsman and commanded a detail of enlisted humans and Lemurians who'd volunteered for the duty—knowing the man they'd sworn to protect didn't always make it easy. Like Juan Marcos, the little Filipino who'd appointed himself captain's steward, their job had just . . . evolved. Unlike Juan's rank, the Captain's Guard had become an official posting at the urging of Keje and Adar. Keje had even proposed that they make their oath to Adar, who, as chairman or prime minister or whatever he was of the Alliance, was technically the only chief to whom Matt answered. Maybe by his command, they could use the Captain's Guard to keep their Supreme Commander out of harm's way.

Gray refused. He said he'd keep the job he'd already given himself, but he'd sworn an oath when he entered the Navy. That was good enough. Now that his job was official though, he could choose the very best from two battle-hardened and increasingly elite forces: the 1st and 2nd Marines. With the exception of four human destroyermen, the rest of the Captain's Guard were Lemurian Marines.

"What type of signals do your people use?" Matt asked Sean O'Casey who'd joined them by the rail. The powerful, one-armed, dark-skinned man with flowing mustaches had been the girl's companion and protector when the equally lost crew of the U.S. submarine S-19 had taken them from an open boat. The old S-boat had been dragged to this world the same way *Walker* was: through the mysterious Squall. Out of fuel and with nowhere to go, the sub ultimately wound up on a Talaud Island beach. All the sub's passengers were safe—twenty children of diplomats and industrialists, evacuated from Surabaya with four nannies and a nun to care for them— but half its crew had perished in the year before their rescue.

He, and ultimately the girl, had become fonts of information about the Empire, represented by the visiting ships, although both still hedged when asked its exact location. It had been ingrained in them that only secrecy kept their homeland safe, and a lifetime of indoctrination to that effect was hard to overcome. The destroyermen and their allies had learned much about the political situation there, however, and what they knew might prove problematic. O'Casey had actually been evading its authorities because of his participation in a rebellion of sorts, not against the legitimate rulers, but against the Company—the Honorable New Britain Company— that increasingly subverted them.

"Flags, guns, lights, rockets . . . much as ye, it seems, but the meanings are doubtless different."

"What signal for a truce, a parlay?"

"A white flag."

"Some things never change, I suppose. Very well." Matt addressed Chapelle. "Have a white flag run up. The crew will remain at General Quarters."

The ships slowly approached the intruder's squadron until they were close enough to lower one of the surviving motor launches. Matt recognized it as the *Scott*—named for his lost coxswain—as he climbed down into it. Scott had been a true hero, but after the Squall, he'd become terrified of the water—understandable, considering the horrible creatures that dwelt in it here—but he'd been killed on land, by a "super lizard." It had been a terrible, ironic loss.

"Captain Reddy," O'Casey called from the ship. For obvious reasons, he wouldn't be making the crossing. Only later, after the character of their visitors was determined, might he be revealed. "Beware Jenks. As Her Highness has said, he may be a man o' honor, but he has a temper." He grinned beneath his mustaches. "As do ye, I've learned." Matt replied with a curt nod.

Keje-Fris-Ar, High Chief of *Big Sal*, awkwardly found a place beside the captain, favoring his wounded leg. He looked something like a cat-faced bear, and his short, brownish red fur had become increasingly sprinkled with silver. Today it was groomed immaculately. He was dressed in his best embroidered blue smock and highly polished copper scale armor. His battered "scota," or working sword, was at his side—unbound—and on his head was a copper helmet adorned with the tail plumage of a Grik. He grinned, though as usual with his species, the expression didn't touch his red-brown eyes. "That one-armed man has learned you well, my brother. Perhaps it might be best, just this once, to watch that temper of yours. I don't know about you, but I believe we have a sufficient war at present to keep us occupied."

Matt snorted. "I don't know what you're talking about. Sure, I have a temper. So do you. But I don't lose it very often."

"Perhaps," Keje hedged, "but when you do, well . . . you do." He left it at that.

Courtney Bradford descended next, puffing with exertion and trying not to lose the ridiculous, oversize hat that protected his balding pate. Bradford, an Australian, had been a petroleum-engineering consultant for Royal Dutch Shell. He was also a self-proclaimed "naturalist," and despite an absentminded, eccentric personality, he was an extremely valuable man. It was he who showed them where to drill for the oil that had fueled their war effort so far. Of all *Walker*'s company who'd arrived on this "other earth," he'd probably changed the least—personality wise—and still tended to greet each day as a blooming opportunity for discovery and adventure.

"Larry the Lizard," as the men had taken to calling Lawrence, Rebecca's Grik-like pet/companion, scampered down to join them and found a place to perch near the front of the launch. He wasn't as large as their Grik enemies, and his orangeish and brown tiger-striped, feathery fur easily distinguished him from the washed-out dun and brown of the Grik. Otherwise, the physical similarity was striking. He was a kind of "island Grik," a "Tagranesi" he claimed, from somewhere in the Eastern Sea. Apparently a different race from their enemies, he'd become Rebecca's friend and protector. So striking was his similarity to the enemy, Matt had kept him hidden aboard *Walker* until after the great battle out of real concern for his safety. It may have been just as well at the time. Despite their previous, almost pacifistic nature, the Lemurians *hated* the Grik, and he sure looked like one. After the battle however, he'd emerged as something of a hero, and to Matt's honest amazement, the Lemurians had once again displayed their capacity for tolerant adaptability. Somehow, despite his appearance, the 'Cats were able to accept—on Matt's and Adar's word alone—that Larry was on their side. *Walker*'s crew had grown accustomed to him by the time they brought him back to Baalkpan on the eve of battle, but Matt *knew* that under similar circumstances, no equally large group of humans would have embraced Larry as quickly.

The mighty chief gunner's mate Dennis Silva clambered down the rungs last, with Her Highness Rebecca Anne McDonald clinging to his back. Silva winced occasionally, pained by his many wounds, and Matt wished again he'd insisted the big man remain behind. But Silva took his role of protecting the princess seriously and Matt couldn't bring himself to discourage anything the irreverent, depraved pain in the ass actually *wanted* to do—as far as his duty was concerned. Of all of them, Silva might have changed the most—maybe even more than Matt himself. He didn't *seem* much different to the casual observer, despite the patch that covered his ruined left eye. He was still huge, powerful, and still kept his blond hair burred close—even as he let the sun-bleached brownish beard grow longer than everyone knew the captain approved. He remained coarse, profane, and fearlessly reckless, and there was still the more or less unresolved question of what, exactly, constituted the relationship between him, Nurse Pam Cross, and the 'Cat female Risa-Sab-At. Risa's brother, Chack, probably knew, but no one else did . . . for sure. Other than that, however, Silva caused few real problems anymore.

Maybe his wounds slowed him down, but Matt had seen him shoulder more and more responsibility—sometimes of his own accord—even before he was injured. It was as if he'd taken his role as *Walker's* Hercules to heart, and saw it as his personal duty to protect her survivors as best he could—with the possible exception of his primary rival, Chief Machinist's Mate Dean Laney. His protectiveness was particularly focused on the little girl clinging to his back. She had . . . done something . . . to Dennis Silva, and Matt believed the big man would somehow contrive, with his bare hands, to destroy the ship they were about to visit if it threatened the girl in any way.

When all the passengers were aboard, Gunner's Mate Paul Stites advanced the throttle and the launch burbled across the choppy sea to *Achilles'* side. The closer they drew to the "British" ships, the more impressed Matt became. Each Imperial frigate seemed quite well made, and mounted twelve to twenty guns that looked somewhat larger than the American frigates' improved eighteen pounders. Maybe twenty-fours? But the ships simply couldn't be as imaginatively and redundantly reinforced as his own Lemurian-built frigates, and their steam power would be an advantage only until their vulnerable paddle wheels were damaged. Then they'd become a terrible liability. They were more than a match for his "prizes," though, and he had only one frigate to oppose them if it came to that. Of course, there was no way they could enter the bay past the guns of Fort Atkinson and the other big guns they'd quickly emplaced on the southeast entrance. For a melancholy moment, he considered that *Walker* could have taken all of them by herself, but he shook that off. He didn't want to fight them, and despite Gray's assessment, he doubted he'd have to. Most likely, they just wanted to take the girl and go, but it was always wise to consider possibilities—particularly when they weren't necessarily going to get what they wanted.

The barge bumped alongside and Captain Reddy hopped across to an extensive ladder arrangement, complete with manropes that had been rigged while they crossed. Climbing to the top, he saluted the curiously familiar ensign, with the red and white stripes and Union Jack in the field at the ship's stern, then saluted a man he suspected was Captain Jenks, by the description Gray had given him.

"Captain Matthew Reddy, United States Navy. Supreme Commander, by acclamation, of the Combined Allied Forces united under the Banner of the Trees. I request permission to come aboard, sir."

A side party was present, with drums and a pair of trumpets, but they made no sound. The man in the elaborately laced white coat with braided mustaches frowned, then returned the salute with a curious rigidity. "Of course," he said gruffly, apparently somewhat taken aback, "do come aboard." He gestured at the side party. "And please forgive our incivility," he added when he recognized a much cleaned-up Chief Gray reaching the top of the ladder. "We were under the impression your people preferred informal greetings."

"An impression you got when you were rude to us right after a fight," Gray growled over his shoulder. He took the girl from Silva, who'd passed her up from below. Turning, he set her on the deck and glared at Jenks. He pointedly didn't salute the flag or the Imperial officer. Jenks stiffened, but then beamed at the girl before him. At the signal of another officer, the drums rolled loudly and the trumpets blasted a rapid and again tantalizingly familiar fanfare.

"Your Highness!" Jenks exclaimed, going to a knee and sweeping off his hat when the trumpets subsided. Everyone in the vicinity did the same, leaving the Americans standing awkwardly beside the girl.

At that instant, Silva stuck his head over the rail and gawked around, festooned with the evidence of his wounds. His hands were bandaged and blood seeped through the cloth of his white tunic. The garish black patch covering his eye, and the gap-toothed grin that split his bearded face gave him a decidedly piratical air. Faced with an opportunity, he proceeded to prove that nothing could temper his customary irreverent exuberance. "Goddamn," he muttered in the silence, "the skipper just hops aboard and a whole shipload o' limeys surrenders to him!" Jenks's face flushed.

"Silva!" Matt hissed.

"Rise!" Rebecca Anne McDonald said loudly, forcing down a giggle. Behind her, the rest of the occupants of the launch continued to arrive on deck—all of them, even the Lemurians, saluting the flag.

Jenks's face turned even redder, if possible, perhaps with shame over his pettiness. He stood, followed by his officers, and took a step forward. "I'm so glad!" he said to Rebecca, ignoring the other visitors. "Surely it's a miracle. We've found you at last! We'd nearly lost hope, searching much farther and longer than most believed you could possibly survive. Thank God I decided to search among the Ape Folk, thinking they may have taken you in. Only chance brought us to their huge ship, which told us strangers were also searching for others of their kind in waters you may have reached! I believed it possible they may have found you and hurried here, but I honestly cherished little remaining hope!"

"You have found me," the girl agreed, "and I give thanks for your diligence. Sadly, of all those who accompanied me on that ill-fated voyage, only one remained to aid me. Injured though he was, I could not have survived without him. Alas, even he was denied this happy reunion." Rebecca spoke of O'Casey, who'd begged her not to mention him, since he was, after all, a wanted man. But she was determined that he receive his due and, ultimately, a pardon. What she'd said would suffice, however. For now, she'd let him remain anonymous.

"A noble man, surely," Jenks commiserated, "but at least the Empire has you safely back! Their Majesties will be so relieved!"

"How are my parents?" Rebecca asked anxiously.

"Well enough when we left, five months ago, though desolate with worry and grief. Your father blamed himself, you see, for sending you to stay with your uncle, the governor of the Western Isles."

"He sent me to protect me!" the girl insisted.

Jenks glanced at his other visitors again, perhaps wondering how much they'd learned about his nation. "Of course, but . . ."

Matt cleared his throat. "Excuse me, please. This is all very touching and even fascinating, but"—he pointed toward land—"we've recently fought a great battle against a rather large fleet of Grik. I understand you know about them?"

Jenks seemed annoyed by the interruption, but nodded. "From legends, the old logs of the founders." His eyes went wide when Lawrence scrambled aboard. Wide with surprise, but not shock or horror, Matt noticed.

"The young lady . . . Her Highness . . . said you know about his people," Matt said, pointing at the tiger-striped creature gazing about with open curiosity. "I even gather you've been on expeditions to some of their lands. What do you think of them?"

Jenks waved his hand. "Formidable predators, but relatively peaceful. Slow breeders—there aren't many of them on their rocky, jungle isles—mildly intelligent and capable of limited cooperative behavior, but incapable of speech."

Lawrence bowed low and said, "How do you do?"

Jenks's mouth clamped shut and he goggled at the creature before him.

"I must present my particular friend Lawrence," Rebecca added quickly. "He contributed as much to my survival as any other. He speaks very well indeed, as long as he needn't use Ms or Bs or other such words that require . . . lips like ours, I suppose. I haven't learned much of his language, I'm afraid."

"Shows what you know, Jenks," Gray jabbed.

Matt sent him a stern look before turning back to Jenks. "The creatures we fight are a different version of Lawrence: bigger, stronger, just as formidably . . . armed, but who breed like rabbits—you know rabbits?" Jenks nodded. "They breed like rabbits and have mastered ships like the one they stole from your ancient squadron. Now they have cannons, and their only purpose seems to be eradicating all other life they encounter. With me so far?" When Jenks nodded again, Matt continued. "We killed a hundred, maybe a hundred fifty thousand of 'em here a few weeks ago and we lost a lot of people doing it. We have a lot of work to do and not much time to do it. We have to take the fight to them, or someday they'll be back."

"My heartiest congratulations for your victory," Jenks said. "And, of course, you have my country's most profound gratitude for rescuing and protecting Her Highness."

"Thank you, Captain . . ."

"It's 'Commodore,' actually," interrupted one of Jenks's officers. Like the others, he'd remained silent so far, wearing a variety of expressions. There'd been no real introductions on either side and Matt suspected Jenks's officers were as surprised by this breach of protocol as he was. But things were moving fast.

Matt frowned. "Look," he said, "my point is, if they roll us up, they'll keep going. Eventually they'll find you too."

"I'm confident you'll make short work of them, Captain," Jenks said, somewhat condescendingly, "if the carnage I saw on the little island where I met Mr. Gray is any indication."

"That fight was against three ships, Jenks," Gray growled. "*Hundreds* of 'em came here."

"Hundreds of their ships," Matt confirmed, "each filled with hundreds of their warriors. Creatures that look like Lawrence here, but who fight with swords and spears, and now cannons too."

"I'm afraid that can be none of my concern, Captain."

"Maybe not yet, but if we lose, it will be someday. Guaranteed."

"Perhaps. What are you suggesting?" Jenks paused, his mustaches twitching over a smirk. "Surely not an alliance?"

"Essentially, yes."

Jenks shook his head. "I *am* sorry, Captain Reddy, but that's simply impossible. Our duty was to find the princess and we've done so. Her safety is thanks in large part to you, I confess, but our duty now is to return her where she belongs. I'm sensible to the possibility that your arguments may even have . . . merit, but I don't have the authority to get involved. You must understand, my squadron has been engaged in this search for quite some time; time it has been unavailable for . . . other pressing duties. We have even suffered the loss of one of our number, to a leviathan"—he glanced curiously at Gray, as if wondering whether the Bosun had deliberately misled them when they met—"so I seriously don't know what difference my three poor ships might make to your cause." His face betrayed the belief that his "poor" ships would probably make quite a difference indeed. "In any event, even if I had the authority I'd be obliged to refuse. As I've clearly stated, my duty is to return Her Highness to the bosom of her family and no other consideration can prevail."

Rebecca had listened with growing astonishment. Suddenly, she spoke and all eyes fell on her diminutive form. "Then *I* will give you something to consider, *Commodore* Jenks: I refuse to abandon my friends, my *saviors*, while it is in my power to aid them. They are not proposing an alliance only with *you*, you silly man. You already refused Mr. Gray's request for aid when your small squadron might have made a difference. I have proposed they seek an alliance with our country!"

"Ridiculous!" erupted the other officer who'd spoken before, and Matt looked at him again. He wore a mustache much like Jenks's, but so did many others. It seemed to be the style. Unlike the others, he seemed stuffed into his uniform and wore little braid. The braid was unique, though, the gold laced with red. It still struck Matt odd that an apparently comparatively junior member of Jenks's staff would be allowed to speak so freely.

"Perhaps . . ." Rebecca sighed, regarding the man as well. "Perhaps honor *has* become so devalued in my absence. Nevertheless, I will seek an alliance on their behalf and ours. Not only is it the right thing to do after all they've done for me, but it's the sensible course as well. They have dealt the Grik a terrible blow, but the Grik will recover. There will be no better chance to break them forever—before they eventually menace *us*. If we wait and my friends are lost, we will face them all alone and we cannot succeed in that."

"But, Highness!" said Jenks. "Perhaps what you say is true, but I have no choice! I must get you safely home!"

"You do have a choice, Commodore. I have a choice." She glared at the outspoken officer. "The Company may have stripped my family of most of its power, but the governor-emperor is still commander in chief. As the highest-ranking member of his household present, I can order you to help. You might refuse, but I tell you now, if you do, I . . . I will not accompany you home."

"But, Your Highness!" Matt and Jenks both protested at once, but only Matt continued. "We appreciate it, but Jenks is right: we have to keep you safe. Sure, we could use his ships now while we're . . . a little short . . . but his squadron will make little difference, in the end."

Jenks bristled. "I assure you, sir . . ."

"Oh, knock it off! I know exactly what your ships can do, and as I said, we can always use the help. But you really don't know what you're up against." Matt paused, struck by the irony of his argument. A moment ago, he'd been trying to convince Jenks to help. Now he was encouraging him to run away. He sighed. "Look, we want friendship between your people and ours . . . for a lot of reasons, not just this war. And no matter what you think, your three ships can't make much difference in the campaign we're preparing. How likely are we to remain friends with your people if you and the young lady are destroyed defending us?"

"It remains to be seen whether we are indeed destined to be friends," Jenks replied, again glancing at Gray. "That is not my decision to make. For now . . . if—*if*—we join you, it will be solely because it is in the best interests of the Empire."

"Of course we shall be friends!" Rebecca insisted. "We already are. Mr. Flynn and his submersible-boat sailors rescued us from the sea and shared all they had."

Jenks looked at her, even more incredulous. What had she said? Clearly, there was still far more to the princess's story.

Rebecca turned to Matt. "And our ships might make more difference than you think, Captain Reddy," she protested. "There are several hundred armed Marines between them as well."

"Armed with muskets, and with no experience fighting the Grik," Matt mused aloud. He knew the girl had seen their own weapons, but wondered if she truly appreciated the qualitative difference. As an historian, he wasn't sure muskets were much of an advantage over Grik arrows, either. They were probably more lethal and there might be a psychological effect, but arrows reloaded faster.

"Perhaps I might offer a compromise," Courtney Bradford said, speaking for the first time.

"Excuse me," Matt interrupted, risking embarrassing Jenks still further, but it was also possible they needed a brief pause to defuse the mounting tension. "May I present . . . the honorable Courtney Bradford, esquire." Silva barely contained a snort. "He's Minister of Science for the Allied powers. He also has broad diplomatic experience and influence." He shrugged. "And I may as well present the others here. Chief Gray I think you know?" Jenks nodded and worked his jaw. Matt continued. "I understand Mr. Gray's status may have been unclear during your previous meeting. We apparently share some of the same rank designations, and 'chief bosun's mate' doesn't reflect the extent of his responsibilities. He's also my chief, personal armsman, and commands the Captain's Guard. He's not a commissioned officer, but he's the highest-ranking non-commissioned officer in the Alliance. He has commanded detachments including commissioned officers, and in those situations he acts as my direct personal representative."

He waited with some satisfaction while Jenks digested that. "Beside me is Keje-Fris-Ar. *Admiral* Keje-Fris-Ar. In addition to being High Chief of *Salissa* Home and a head of state in his own right, he's assistant chief of naval operations and answers only to me in military matters. His people are not 'Ape Folk.' They call themselves Mi-Anaaka, but our term, 'Lemurians,' doesn't offend them. They were once peaceful, unwarlike people. That's probably how your histories remember them. They've since become some of the best warriors in the world. I wouldn't call them Ape Folk if I were you, because that *does* offend them. I honestly don't know why, since they've never seen an ape, but there it is." Matt suddenly wondered if *Jenks* had ever seen an ape. *Later.* He started to introduce the other members of his party, but they weren't officers. Besides, then he'd have to name Silva, and how would he describe him? The most depraved, dangerous human on the planet? He stifled a chuckle.

Jenks—somewhat reluctantly, it seemed—introduced his officers then. None smiled or offered his hand and most appeared to regard the entire party, the Lemurians in particular, with disdain. Matt dismissed them all as junior copies of Jenks—except the one who'd spoken up. His name was Billingsly, and judging from Rebecca's distasteful glance, he decided to remember him.

"Now, Mr. Bradford, I apologize for the interruption. Please continue."

"My dear," Bradford continued, addressing Rebecca, "you once said when the time came for you to return home, you wanted us, Captain Reddy in particular, to take you. Do you still mean that?"

"Of course."

"Very well. Then I propose that Captain Reddy and other dignitaries escort you home as soon as either *Walker* is . . . repaired . . . or other suitable ships are ready to take you." Bradford realized Jenks knew about *Walker*, their "iron ship," but doubted Captain Reddy was ready to admit that, right now, she was underwater. "That may take some months, but what is that compared to the time you have been gone, after all? The mission will be a diplomatic one with the goal of securing a true alliance. In the meantime, Jenks might dispatch one or two of his ships to bear the happy news of your rescue, but he and *Achilles*, at least, could remain here to augment our fleet until you are ready to leave." He smiled. "That should certainly not interfere with his imperative of protecting you. He should then, of course, accompany you home. Hopefully to return here with reinforcements." He glanced around owlishly. "What do you think?"

"I think this is all a waste of time," Keje growled unexpectedly. He'd learned a lot about the curious face moving of humans and didn't much care for what he saw. He looked at Matt. "They do not want to help us, and now that we have slaughtered the cream of the Grik horde, we have sufficient allies who do. Saan-Kakja has promised many thousands more of her warriors and artisans. Many who fled are now returning, eager to fight. Our fleet is rebuilding and we have more than sufficient iron for our needs, at least for now." He turned back to Jenks. "You have apparently formed the mistaken assumption that we came to you today as suppliants. Not so. Now we have met, it matters little to me if you stay or go, but Adar, High Chief of Baalkpan, chairman and High Sky Priest of the Alliance, would meet with you. He desires friendship, true, but his primary interest in you is . . . historical. He is not naive. We will always welcome friends, but we will not suffer vipers in our midst."

Matt was surprised by Keje's outburst. Who had been warning whom about tempers?

Jenks was also taken aback, as much by Keje's attitude as by his near-perfect command of English. And by what he said, of course. He scrutinized Keje. He'd met other Lemurians on the massive ship coming out from the Philippines. They'd all seemed glad to see him and treated his people with something akin to reverential awe. Just what he would have expected of the simple wogs he thought they were. Wogs extremely talented at building fantastic ships, but wogs. Now he wasn't so sure. He didn't think there was much chance of a real alliance—he glanced at Billingsly—particularly if the Company had anything to say about it. The very word "ally" was too closely associated with "equal partner," and that was out of the question. However, perhaps an arrangement might be made. Besides, speaking of vipers, it might be a very good idea, in the interests of the Empire, for him to learn as much about this Alliance as he could. The Empire had enemies of its own, and though they were preoccupied for now, he suspected these Lemurians and their American friends might someday become formidable enemies indeed, if given reason enough—or allowed.

"Mr. Bradford has made an interesting proposal," he said at last, carefully. "And it might provide the basis for negotiations. I would be . . . honored to meet with your chairman." He glanced at Matt. "I have your word of safe conduct, of course?"

"Of course. We'll escort you under the guns of the fort and provide you with an anchorage. Your people may even have liberty if you give your word they'll behave themselves—and some parts of the city are off-limits. That's not subject to discussion or debate at this point. Perhaps later. In the meantime, any of your people found screwing around in restricted areas will be shot. Understood?"

Jenks bristled again, but calmed himself. "Understood." He turned to Billingsly. "I assume you will want to remain? Very well. Choose someone from your . . . department. He and Ensign Parr will transfer to *Agamemnon* and proceed home with the happy news about the princess. *Ajax* will remain here for now, with *Achilles*. I will draft orders and a brief dispatch." He turned to Matt. "Is that acceptable?"

For some reason, Matt was hesitant. But that had been part of Brad-ford's proposal, after all. "Sure."

"We should have just sent him away with the promise we would bring the girl," growled Keje quietly as the launch burbled back to *Donaghey*. "The girl" was still with them, having refused to part with her friends. She was distressed and confused by Jenks's attitude, not to mention Billingsly's presence. She didn't know Billingsly, but she knew *what* he was. For now, she much preferred to remain among people she trusted unreservedly. That was what she'd whispered to Matt, and he wondered if Keje overheard or just picked up on it too. That might explain his sudden animosity. *Agamemnon* was already piling on sail and beginning to slant eastward. With the freshening breeze, her paddle wheels were free-spinning. "With Jenks hanging around here, he'll see too much," Keje added.

"Possibly." Matt nodded at the Bosun. "Gray's always been a pretty good judge of character and he said Jenks is an asshole." He sighed resign-edly. "Having met him, I'm inclined to agree. But Adar's probably an even better judge. He won't let his fascination with the 'ones who came before' cloud his judgment."

Keje huffed noncommittally. Before ascending to his current lofty title, Adar had been Keje's own High Sky Priest, and the two had been like brothers their entire lives. Keje knew Matt was right, but his own impres-sion of Jenks had been very similar to Gray's. He'd actually been sur-prised by that. According to Matt, his Amer-i-caans and Jenks's people were related in some way. He supposed he'd expected them to behave more alike. Jenks's reaction to Keje's people's situation couldn't have been more different from that of Matt and his destroyermen.

"Besides," said Gray, "he never would've gone for that—just leaving, I mean."

"Right," Matt agreed. "And over time, maybe we can loosen him up. *If* we can make friends with the Brits, and *if* we can trust them, we'll have to bring them up to speed on our programs anyway."

Gray snorted and shook his head. "You know, it sure is weird—not trusting Brits, I mean. Sure, in *our* history we weren't friends all the time, but we were on the same side in the last war, and we were best friends in the war we left behind—both of us fightin' the Japs. Those guys on *Exeter* and *Encounter* and all the others, they were the same as us. They were our guys. We might've gotten in fights in bars, made fun of other, and called other names, but we'd watch out for each other too. This Jenks guy drives it home in no uncertain terms that we ain't on the same side here. Some of the fellas are liable to get . . . confused."

Matt was thoughtful. "Good point, Boats. Make sure everybody knows these aren't the same Brits we knew back home. No fights, no trouble—we *do* want to be their friends—but right now, we're not. We'll have talks, and I'll use the fact that we had a special relationship with the descendants of Jenks's ancestors. Maybe that'll help. But once our visitors know that, we don't want them to take advantage of it either, buddy up to our guys and pump them for information. That sort of thing."

"Aye-aye, Skipper."

A dar, High Chief of Baalkpan, Chairman (by acclamation) and High Sky Priest of the Grand Alliance, paced restlessly in the large conference chamber. He felt uncomfortable in his new role, and truthfully, he would have done almost anything to avoid it. Almost. The problem was, uncomfortable as he felt, there were very few people he personally trusted with the responsibility at this critical and confusing time. Those he did trust already had crucial and possibly even more important roles to play.

Keje could have done it, even though he'd probably never spent six consecutive months on dry land in his life. He was a hero and he'd nearly sacrificed his Home and his life to defend the "land folk" of Baalkpan. Keje had actually been the first acclaimed as High Chief, but he'd flatly refused. He had a Home. Battered and wounded beyond imagination, *Salissa* Home was still his responsibility and he was her High Chief.

Adar understood that. Being Sky Priest of *Salissa* was all he'd ever aspired to himself. Over the last year however, old Naga, High Sky Priest of Baalkpan, had grown increasingly disassociated and Adar had assumed more and more of his duties. Land folk needed a Sky Priest to help chart their course through perilous times, just as sea folk looked to their priests in perilous seas. With Naga's death, and that of the great Nakja-Mur, Adar had been Baalkpan's second choice and he found himself practically drafted to fill the void caused by the loss of both leaders. He really hadn't had a choice. He'd become a prominent, well-known figure to all the diverse elements of the Alliance and he was one of the few people everyone seemed to trust. Ultimately, he'd concluded, the one thing he couldn't do to avoid the job was let someone less committed than him or Keje take it.

He honestly believed Matt could have won the necessary support, even though he wasn't "of the People," but there would have been *some* dissent. They needed unity now above all things, and Matt was far more useful at the point of the spear. They'd never even discussed it, but Adar knew Matt would have agreed. He probably would have been astonished and horrified even to be considered. That left only Adar with the popularity, strength of will, and determination not only to continue the fight, but to carry it to the enemy once more.

He still wore the priestly robes of his former office, but his responsibilities had expanded dramatically. Though all Homes on land or sea were considered equal by tradition, Baalkpan had taken the lead in the war and its leader had gained at least the perception of being a little more equal than other members of the Alliance. Adar agreed with the arrangement in principle; somebody had to be in charge, but he wasn't convinced he was up to the task. Becoming a High Chief was difficult enough, but leading the entire Alliance was something else again. Chairman was the loftiest title he would accept.

He knew he was a better choice than some, since his dedication to "the cause" was unwavering. He spent most of his time convincing less enthusiastic allies that the war wasn't over and all they'd won at Baalkpan was a single battle. Final victory would be achieved only when the Grik were utterly eradicated. That was an argument he could put his heart and soul into, one he'd advocated ever since they'd discovered the true nature of their enemy. He wasn't as confident he was the best choice to *implement* the policy, however. He allowed himself a small grin. Of course, that was what he had Captain Reddy for.

The conference would soon begin and the chamber was filled to overflowing. It wasn't as large as Nakja-Mur's Great Hall had been, but it would be months before that edifice was completely rebuilt. At least the great Galla tree the hall once encompassed had survived the fire. When the first new leaves began to unfold on its charred branches, the People took it as an omen of healing and heavenly favor. It had given them even greater confidence in their choice of Adar to lead them. Adar only wished he were as confident as they. He was beginning to understand the profound difference between strongly advocating a course of action, and ordering that action carried out.

He continued to pace while the expectant chatter grew ever louder. Nakja-Mur would have lounged on a cushion, outwardly calm. Even when inwardly terrified—as Adar had known he often was—he'd always managed an air of confidence, if not always in himself, then in the people he'd chosen to advise him. Adar had many of the same advisors, those who'd survived, and he'd even acquired a curious new one since the return of the evacuated seagoing Homes: a human holy woman, a nun who'd been with the Amer-i-caans Captain Reddy rescued from the amazing diving ship. Matt called its crew "sub-maa-riners," and apparently, their wondrous vessel still lay on the beach of Talaud Island.

The nun, Sister Audry, was an . . . interesting creature. She spoke the Amer-i-caans' tongue with a different sound and Adar had learned she sprang from yet another human clan, the Dutch. He understood she was attractive too, by human standards, yet she had no mate and cited an oath to her God to take none. Adar couldn't imagine why any God—and he was beginning to suspect his Maker of All Things and the human God were one and the same—would require such an oath. Nevertheless, an oath was an oath, whether demanded or freely given. He didn't understand it—yet—but he did respect it. With the scarcity of human females in the vicinity, however, he would have thought she'd face resentment. Not so. All the Amer-i-caans appeared to respect her abstinence as a matter of course, and many sought her out just to talk. Adar did too. On the few occasions they'd had leisure to visit, he'd been charmed by her conviction, personality, and philosophy—even as he'd been troubled by the implications of much of what she'd said.

There was no more devoted servant of the heavens than he, but he was fully aware there were . . . gaps . . . in the dogma of the Sky Priests. He'd once theorized the Amer-i-caans didn't believe that differently than he did. He'd been wrong, but as Matt would say, the devil was in the details. He'd finally concluded that they simply sailed a different path to the same destination. He was learning from Sister Audry that it was a *much* different path . . . and yet . . .

He shook away those thoughts and tried to concentrate on the business at hand. This was a staff meeting, planned days before the strangers from the east arrived. They had much to discuss before Commodore Jenks and his officers entered for their first official audience. Adar had actually already met them. Instead of waiting for the strangers to come to him, as was traditional among the People when visitors called, he'd greeted them on the dock with the full courtesy and fanfare Matt told him they'd expect. Adar was nervous at first in the presence of those he had no doubt were descendants of the "ones who came before," since so much Lemurian liturgy was founded on that ancient visit. But he'd been struck by how different they'd been from what he'd expected. Jenks, in particular, had been formal and polite, but also . . . condescending. Adar quickly shed his initial awe when he realized these representatives of the Empire of the New Britain Isles were mere men, after all: other humans like those he'd come to know. Certainly not holy messengers. They no longer made him nervous, except for whatever . . . worldly significance their presence might imply. That added yet another dimension to his religious ponderings.

Adar was anxious to speak to their leader again, but this meeting was for high-level staff only. Even those residents of Baalkpan who'd begun returning after the battle were not allowed. They'd run before; they might again—this time carrying sensitive information. There *were* foreigners present, but only ones who'd proven themselves steadfast allies.

Saan-Kakja, High Chief of the Fil-pin Lands, was perched rigidly on an ornately embroidered cushion, attended by several of her closest advisors. She and her personal guard had arrived at the height of the land battle for Baalkpan and had helped turn the tide. Since then, more of her troops, artisans, laborers, and beasts of burden—not to mention precious materials—continued to arrive in an uninterrupted stream. Saan-Kakja herself was a spirited, darling creature. She was quite young for her office, but Adar had discovered she had a will of iron. She'd once been led astray by self-serving advisors and seemed determined that it never happen again. She had the most mesmerizing eyes Adar had ever seen: warm and inquisitive like yellow-gold stars, but woe was he they fell upon when they were touched with fire. Adar thanked the Heavens continuously for the alliance Captain Reddy had forged between them.

Safir Maraan, Queen Protector of B'mbaado, was striking as always, her jet-black fur and polished silver breastplate complementing her penetrating eyes. She was older than Saan-Kakja, more experienced, and far more self-assured, but she too was an "orphan queen," and despite the utterly different societies they'd sprung from, she and Saan-Kakja had become fast friends.

Her betrothed, Chack-Sab-At, accompanied Safir. Once a simple, pacifistic wing runner on *Salissa* Home, the amber-eyed, brindled Chack was now a scarred and hardened veteran. Somehow, he'd managed to retain a measure of his irrepressible humor, but it had been tempered by a sharp, worldly wit. He'd seen so much of war already that his innocent youngling's soul was gone forever. He was now a respected warrior, bosun's mate for sunken *Walker*, and a captain of Marines.

General Muln-Rolak, onetime High Protector of Aryaal, also attended Safir. He was old and scarred from many battles—almost to the point of disfigurement. Many of the scars dated from a time when he'd battled Safir's own father. He stood with her now as a trusted friend and colleague. Their lands had once been bitter enemies, but in this war, they fought together as inseparable allies and their relationship had become almost one of father and daughter. Together, at least until Saan-Kakja's regiments were up to strength, they commanded the second-largest army in the Alliance. It was composed of warriors and refugees from both their enemy-occupied homelands on Java.

People of lesser rank stood for the steadfast Sularan regiments who'd remained to fight after the bulk of their own people, across the Makaassar Strait on Sa-leebs, fled in the face of the Grik horde.

Then there were the Amer-i-caans, of course.

Beside Captain Reddy, as always, stood Nurse Lieutenant Sandra Tucker, petite, sandy haired, and much shorter than the towering (by Lemurian standards) man she so clearly loved. Despite her size, she was a dynamo, and through her skill at administration and trauma surgery, a truly astonishing number of People literally owed her their lives. Adar had appointed her Minister of Medicine. With the other surviving nurses who'd come through the Squall—Karen Theimer (Letts), Pam Cross, and Kathy McCoy—she'd created, from scratch, a highly efficient and professional Hospital Corps.

Commander Alan Letts (Karen's new husband) was still chief of staff, and due to his administrative abilities—he'd been *Walker*'s supply officer—Adar had named him Minister of Industry. He'd undergone a transformation from his old Asiatic Fleet days, and Karen was probably responsible for changing the easygoing, arguably lazy, fair-skinned kid from a place called Idaho into one of the most industrious and indispensible logisticians in the Alliance.

Bradford, who emphatically claimed *not* to be an Amer-i-caan, was Minister of Science, and served as plenipotentiary at large.

Commander Perry Brister, *Mahan*'s former engineering officer, was Minister of Defensive and Industrial Works. Lieutenant Commander Bernard Sandison, *Walker*'s torpedo officer, was Minister of Ordnance. The big Marine, Pete Alden, was General of the Army and Marines, and Tamatsu Shinya was his second in command. Lieutenant Steve Riggs was Minister of Communications and Electrical Contrivances, and Brevet Major Ben Mallory was minister for their still nonexistent Air Corps. Ben, like Bernie, was still recovering from serious wounds they'd suffered in the battle.

Adar recognized that he'd bestowed lofty-sounding titles upon them, despite the fact they each had other jobs. It was also clear that, except for "Aahd-mah-raal" Keje-Fris-Ar being Assistant Chief of Naval Operations, and a few other People in charge of agriculture, labor, etc., most of the titles belonged to destroyermen. It didn't matter. After the battle, they were so popular they could all have become kings, but they'd insisted he take the lead. No one would object. Besides, they knew best what they were doing. That being said, everyone except Matt, Sandra, and Pete were new to their "jobs," including Adar, and though he'd never had any difficulty with public speaking before, he decided to let them go first, to set the tone.

He began to call on Matt, but briefly wondered *what* to call him. "Supreme Commander of All Combined Allied Forces" seemed much too stiff and unwieldy for everyday use. Matt had refused the rank of aahd-mah-raal for reasons of his own, but even though there were other aahd-mah-raals now, and many captains, there was no question who was in charge. Adar supposed it didn't matter. There was only one Captain Matthew Reddy. That was how Adar addressed him now, summoning him to speak: "Cap-i-taan Reddy, if you please. Before we begin this discussion in earnest, what was your impression of our visitors?"

Matt appeared thoughtful for a moment. "My initial impression," he began, "was much like Chief Gray's. I thought they were a pack of arrogant jerks. In fact, the more we talked with them—with Jenks, anyway—the stronger that impression became. If I'd had time to think about it, I'm not sure I'd have let them send off a ship."

"What would you have had us do?" Bradford retorted, sensing a reprimand for his compromise. "Hold them hostage? We were not in much of a position to do that. Or were you thinking of holding the girl against her will?"

"Don't be ridiculous, Courtney. Of course not. But the girl doesn't want to go with them; she wants us to take her home. We might have used that as leverage to keep all their ships here. As it stands, they'll know about us, and where we are, long before we're ready to send an expedition to meet them."

"Do you consider them a threat?" Adar asked.

"Sure. Why not?" Matt sighed. "Mr. Chairman, I consider everyone not in this room a threat, because only these people, and those they represent, have *proven* they're not. Do I think these 'new' Brits'll swoop down like the Grik and attack as soon as they know where we are? No. Jenks acted like they had other problems besides us, although neither Rebecca nor O'Casey seems to know what they are. Something that's sprouted up since the two of them have been gone? Maybe." Matt shrugged. "And I don't think they're a threat like the Grik, either. They certainly don't eat people, and I don't think they're much interested in our real estate. They may see us as a rival, though, which we might be soon enough." He looked down at Sandra. "To be honest, based on the technology we've seen, in the months it'll take them to get back to wherever they came from and return here with a sizable force—if that's their intent—we'll have enough of the new weapons we've planned that we'd paste them good. The thing is, they're a threat in the sense that they're a distraction. Just the possibility that they'll send a fleet is enough to pin some of our resources here and in the Philippines when we should be chasing the Grik before they catch their breath."

"No one wants to destroy the Grik more than I, but is haste truly so important?" Adar asked.

"Yes, Mr. Chairman. It's essential."

"But you won't be ready to pursue them for months. These weapons you speak of, this 'technology,' won't be ready for some time."

"True, but we can, *must*, mount *some* operations fairly quickly. And when the new stuff's online, I'd rather use it against the Grik."

Adar nodded. "It seems, then, that we have several imperatives: First, keep the pressure on the Grik; keep them off balance, as you've said. Perhaps we might accelerate the departure of our new Expeditionary Force. Second, we must treat with this Jenks and keep him satisfied that we truly are preparing an expedition to return his lost princess. Try to befriend him and avoid alienating him. Finally, once we do return the girl to her people, we must do everything we can to make friends with them, not only for the benefit of our war effort, but—and I notice you did not mention this—to alleviate the 'dame famine' that afflicts your human destroyermen." The lack of female companionship for Matt's men after an entire year had created what Silva had coined a "dame famine." In the pre-war Asiatic Fleet, it would have been considered extraordinary for the men to "do without" for a couple of weeks.

Matt shifted uncomfortably. "What you say is true, Mr. Chairman. All of it. To accomplish everything you described would be ideal. Lifting the dame famine would sure be a help, too, but I didn't want to mention it, to seem selfish. . . ."

"Nonsense. To . . . abstain as long as most of your people have is unnatural, and cannot be good for them. Rest assured, that imperative is as essential as any other, as far as I am concerned."

"Thank you, Mr. Chairman."

"Now, let us continue with how to accomplish the goals laid before us. Aahd-mah-raal Keje; what of the Navy?"

Keje rose with some difficulty. His leg was stiffening up. He should have been using a cane or something, but he'd refused. "The Navy, Mr. Chairman, doesn't exist, for all practical purposes. *Donaghey* is fit for sea, as are some of the prizes, but it will be weeks before *Tolson* can sail. The shipyards survived major damage in the fighting—I believe the enemy meant to take them intact—so the new construction is proceeding almost uninterrupted. We have abundant hardwood laid up from when we cleared the killing fields around the city. It has remained covered and is drying well. Perhaps we will complete this 'kiln' thing Mr. Brister has begun. The yards are already working around the clock"—he grinned quizzically at

Matt as if wondering if he'd used the phrase appropriately—"and the keels for six more modern warships have already been laid." His grin became eager. "This technique of 'mass production,' where all the parts for each ship are made to a particular plan and any one of them will fit each ship, is truly a wonder. It speeds production amazingly."

Letts nodded. "I'm glad you approve and I'm glad it's working. We'll use the same technique for just about everything, eventually. As soon as we've settled on the various plans"—he winced—"and overcome the . . . reluctance of some of our craftsmen." He looked at Matt and explained. "We've always been amazed by Lemurian ingenuity, and their structural design techniques are beyond anything any wooden human navy ever launched, but they aren't used to blueprints. They just make 'em the way they've always made them. The quality of their craftsmanship is beyond debate, but master shipwrights dominate the shipbuilding industry and they're jealous of their status. They don't much approve of just anybody being able to look at drawings and knock something up."

"Understandable, I suppose," said Matt, "but they're going to have to get used to it." He nodded at Saan-Kakja. "The finalized plans for our first steam frigates have already been sent to Manila, but you'll probably run into some of the same problems."

Saan-Kakja bowed and replied in her almost little-girl voice, "The plans were accompanied by my personal command that they be followed to the letter. I have allowed some innovation within the design parameters, as you suggested, but there will be little variation."

"Fine," said Matt. "Don't want to stifle new ideas, but we need a lot of good ships more than we need a few perfect ones." He turned to Keje and his expression softened. "What about *Big Sal*?"

Keje frowned. "She is refloated," he grumbled. "A simple matter of pumping her out. However, the damage to her upper works was . . . extreme. Your . . . bizarre . . . idea might not only be the best means of returning her to the fight, but the single realistic one as well." He sighed. "I mourn my Home and yearn for her to be as she was, but I might as well yearn for the Grik to leave us alone of their own accord. I fear, with her conversion, our way of life will be altered forever. Will other Homes be changed as well? Will they even *be* Homes anymore, or forever become dedicated weapons of war? What of the wing clans? There is already resistance. How will I sort that out? I also confess that I find it exceedingly strange to rebuild her as a . . . conveyance for weapons that do not yet exist."

"They'll exist," Ben Mallory assured him. "It's going to take time, but there's no question we can do it. Also, knowing the way you 'Cats like gizmos, I bet there'll be less resistance than you expect."

"You've settled on a design, then?" Matt asked.

Adar watched as the conference increasingly shifted from his grasp. He didn't mind. In fact, it was as he'd hoped. Captain Reddy had been somewhat withdrawn since the loss of his ship, but the man was made for command. The situation required that someone step up and take it, and he was the best one for the job. Adar had set the policies, the goals they'd work toward; it was up to his Supreme Commander and the rest of his staff to decide how to implement those policies.

"Sir," Mallory replied, "we've come at this from every angle and run into problems with just about every design." He grinned. "I'd love to have P-40s, but that's just not going to happen. Right now, I'm leaning toward a variation of the old Navy-Curtiss, or NC, flying boats."

"Flying boats?" Matt asked, eyebrows raised. "I thought we'd decided to raze *Big Sal* to a steam-powered flattop. Use her as an aircraft carrier."

"She'll still need to be flat to carry and maybe even launch the planes— like the old *Langley*—but we'll fit her with cranes to lift the planes out of the water. See, the problem is wheels. That, and it would be nice if the aircrews could set the planes down if they're damaged. If they don't float, we're going to lose a lot of guys. Sure not going to fish many out of the drink."

"I see what you mean, but why not floats *and* wheels?"

Mallory scratched a scar under his bearded chin. "Well, believe it or not, Skipper, there's no rubber. I know, it would be all over the place around here back home, but Courtney says even then it wasn't indigenous. Whether anything like it exists somewhere else, who knows." He paused and glanced at the blank faces around him. Of course, Lemurian faces were always blank, but none of them spoke up. "Anyway, there's nothing like it here. Given enough time, we'll probably come up with a synthetic, but our refining capability just isn't that far along yet, and frankly, I don't know how." He looked at Bradford, who shook his head.

"'Fraid not. As Mr. Mallory has suggested, I know there has been some success making a synthetic rubber from petroleum, but I haven't the faintest idea how it's done."

"So in the short term," Mallory continued, "we'd be better off using rigid wheels and some sort of shock-absorbing arrangement. I still think floats are the way to go, though. At least for now." He shook his head. "Believe me, Skipper, I wish that wasn't so. Floatplanes add a lot of problems. They'll likely be bigger, heavier and slower. Payload will be less and they'll have greater power-to-weight requirements. More complicated, too. Basically, like I said, NC flying boats . . . Nancys."

Matt grimaced. "I was proud when I heard we flew those things across the Atlantic—little before my time—and *Walker* was even one of the picket ships before she joined the Asiatic Fleet. But if I recall, only one of 'em made it all the way."

"We'll make 'em better. We have stronger, lighter materials to work with. Hell, most of a British Hurricane is made of wood, and they're pretty good fighters. The toughest thing in the air might be those British medium bombers—what are they . . . or were they? Hell, I can't remember."

"Wellingtons," Bradford supplied, rolling his eyes at the young pilot.

"Right. They may be slow, but they can take punishment. They use the same kind of diagonal bracing the 'Cats use on their big ships. We can do that too. Even the engines shouldn't be too hard. We off-loaded all the machine tools from *Walker* and *Mahan* before the battle and we've been building new machines hand over fist. Maybe we can even get the lathes and stuff off *Amagi*. Then there's the submarine, with all her tools and steel—if we can salvage it. We'll make the engines of iron, but flute the cylinders to save weight. Water cooled, if we can cast the crankcases as well as I think we can . . ."

"Very well," said Matt, almost laughing. "I see you've given this some thought. Have you considered, however, that if the planes have floats and fly off a Navy ship, they can't possibly be part of the Air Corps? All the crews you train to fly them will have to be naval aviators!"

"Hey! Wait a minute!" Mallory shouted good-naturedly, but he was laughed down. They needed the humor but after a moment, Matt sobered.

"Madam Minister of Medicine?" he asked stiffly. Sandra looked up at him with a small smile for the title, but realized Matt had already begun to retreat into his funk.

"Better," she said. "We still have a lot of wounded, but I think the vast majority have turned the corner. A lot have already returned to duty"— she glared at Ben and Bernie—"although some shouldn't have. The Lemurian's polta paste continues to work miracles." She referred to an antiseptic, analgesic, viscous paste made from the still somewhat mysteriously prepared by-products of seep fermentation. Seep was a less refined version of the substance made from polta fruit and was a popular spirit and strong intoxicant. The analgesic properties were fairly straightforward, but Sandra still didn't know why it fought most infections so well. Neither did the Lemurians. They'd had no concept of germ theory when the destroyermen arrived, but they'd had the paste since before recorded history and knew it worked. Before the Squall that transported them here, Sandra had heard of experiments with a type of mold being used to fight infection. She wondered if the same principle was at work here. She didn't know and couldn't even begin to guess without a microscope, but the stuff was a lifesaver that beat sulfonamide all hollow.

"How's Mr. Garrett? And did Silva report to you like I told him?" Matt asked.

"Mr. Garrett's wounds are healing nicely; he just had so many. It's a miracle he survived. Same with Silva, but even though Mr. Garrett's unhappy just sitting around, he does behave. Silva, as you know, is less reasonable. He swooped in for a moment and let Pam Cross patch him up again, but she was going off duty and he took off with her. Frankly, I think she and Risa can make him take it easy better than I ever could." She sniffed, and while others laughed, she noticed a ghost of a smile reappear on Matt's face.

Silva's antics were as legendary as they were infamous. He'd carried on what sometimes appeared a genuine affair with Chack's own sister, Risa-Sab-At. Risa had been captain of *Salissa's* forewing guard, but now they'd amalgamated all the various guards into fewer unified commands. She was now captain of what would become *Salissa's* entire Marine contingent—after they'd undergone the more rigorous training required of Marines. In many ways, Risa was clearly Silva's soul mate, just as reckless and fearless and with the same warped sense of humor. The Lemurians hadn't cared about the rumors surrounding them, rumors Silva and Risa did their best to encourage—only initially—to get Chack's goat. Now, either they seemed determined to get *everyone's* goat—or the rumors weren't really rumors.

The addition of Nurse Pam Cross from Brooklyn to the ménage added a measure of disgust, as well as a grudging respect for the gunner's mate among the human destroyermen. They'd come to accept that Silva might have taken up with a "local gal," whether anything physical was involved or not. They just assumed, naturally (or unnaturally), that there was. For him to then snatch one of the only available dames did breed resentment, but it was more of a wistful "how does he do it" sort. Lurid speculation regarding how the threesome might . . . interact . . . was probably actually good for morale in a roundabout way, and none of them—Silva, Risa, or Pam—would confirm or deny anything.

Three soul mates, Matt chuckled to himself, *two of whom had to come to another world to find each other.* Well, there was nothing he could do about it. He'd once ordered Silva to quit carrying on with Risa, thereby breaking one of his own fundamental rules: Never give an order you *know* won't be obeyed. But in almost every other way, Silva had really straightened up. "Silva's been helping you with ordnance development?" Matt asked Bernard Sandison.

Bernie grimaced. "Yes, sir. When it suits him. He's hurting, I know, so I haven't pushed him yet, but some of his best work has been on 'toys' for himself."

"Do his 'toys' have practical applications?"

"Oh, yeah, but they're not exactly priority items. The man's a diabolical genius when it comes to figuring out new and better ways to kill things, and he does *love* to try them out. It's just . . . his priorities are generally more . . . tactical than strategic."

Matt allowed a genuine laugh then, at Bernie's tact. "You mean he concentrates on 'up close and personal.' Well, we need that too. Give him his head, but try to run him off for a while. He needs to heal up."

"Aye-aye, sir."

"Speaking of that, what have you come up with?"

Sandison shifted on the cushion his wounds made him use. Matt knew the young, dark-haired torpedo officer was highly motivated to please; he still blamed himself for not recognizing the—perfectly good—Mk 10 torpedo among the condemned fish they'd scrounged in Surabaya so long ago. That extra torpedo might have made a lot of difference if they'd known they had it and used it at a different time.

"Right now we're rebuilding to some degree. One of the shops took a hit from *Amagi* and it's a real mess. None of the machinery was badly damaged, thank God, but we're still getting a roof back over it. That said, we've begun to refine some of the projects we were already working on. I think I can give you guncotton, or gun . . . whatever they use for cotton around here, pretty soon. That'll give us a high explosive capability for the four-inch guns. We've already started making exploding shells with a black powder bursting charge, like the ones they used in the last war. Not as good, but . . ." He paused when he saw the captain's grim expression. The only four-inch guns they had were on *Walker*—underwater. They'd salvage the guns, certainly, and maybe the one on the submarine, but they wouldn't know if they could salvage the ship until she was dry. "Anyway," he continued softly, "I wouldn't recommend using it for a propellant charge until we've had a lot more practice with the stuff. Better stick with ordinary gunpowder for now. Same goes for small arms. We just about shot ourselves dry, I'm afraid, and black powder won't work worth a hoot in the automatic weapons. At least not the BARs, thirties and fifties. They gum up too fast.

"That brings up another problem: brass. I've got brass pickers combing everywhere looking for spent shell casings. We're okay on the four-inch guns, and the shells for those are big enough to turn more on a lathe, but we'll have to extrude small-arms brass and . . . I really just don't know how. We can reload what we've got; make it work pretty well, in fact. Before we lost power, we made molds and swages for thirty-, forty-five-, and fifty-cal with grease grooves. We can make bullets out of solid copper, tin, or lead with a gas check of some kind, so they'll work with the fast-twist rifling. Lubed copper bullets work fine in the Springfields and Krags with a slow rate of fire. You can use 'em in the Thompsons and the 1911s too, but they get really filthy. And like I said, when the brass is gone, it's gone—unless we can figure out how to make more."

"I knew about all that stuff," Matt said, "and we'll see what we can do about power. Mr. Riggs, I'll get to you directly. But what about other stuff, Bernie? The 'new' weapons you mentioned?"

"Yes, sir. Personally, I'd love to have torpedoes, but that's going to take a while longer. We've still got the propulsion body of the condemned torp with the crumpled warhead and we're reverse-engineering that, but the precision required . . ." He sighed. "We're just not there yet."

"What can you give me?"

"Exploding four-inch shells and bombs, sir. Lots and lots of bombs. Pretty powerful ones too, eventually—if the guncotton works like I expect." He glanced at Mallory. "I know the bigger ones might not do us a lot of good until we have something to drop them from, but when we do—"

"Don't build them before I find out how much weight the planes'll carry!" interrupted Ben.

"Don't worry." Bernie grinned. "We're working on little ones first, like mortar bombs. In fact, that's what they are." He nodded at Alden. "Pete—the General—and Campeti came up with the idea. Real mortars—the 'drop and pop' kind. Way safer, lighter, deadlier, and with a lot longer range than the ones we've been using. No reason you couldn't drop 'em from an airplane, though."

"Very good," Matt complimented him, "but that still leaves us, in the short term, with a dwindling number of small arms when what I want is more."

"Yes, sir. I'm afraid our best short-term option is still a musket of some kind, like you said. That's one of the things Silva's been fiddling with, although his idea of a musket—"

Matt interrupted. "But I've also said I'm not sure muskets really give us much advantage."

Pete Alden spoke up. "Skipper, I think they will. You're worried about arrows reloading faster and being about as accurate. Normally, that would be true. You're also thinking they're not much advantage over what we've got, but what about the enemy? They don't use longbows. I don't think they can. They're just not built for them, so they're stuck with crossbows, which take about as long to load as a musket and they're not as deadly. Besides, they'll be an improvement in another respect: right now, all our spearmen have to carry a longbow as well. Once they have muskets, with socket bayonets, they can shoot and stick with the same weapon. There might also be a psychological effect on the enemy. Maybe they'll flip and go into one of Bradford's 'Grik rout' fits after a single volley. I'm not counting on it, but they *will* be better than what we've got. As to the accuracy issue, as lame as our industry is right now, that's going to improve. We can already make the barrels much better than they did in the seventeen hundreds, and eventually, smoothbores can be rifled. . . ."

Matt was nodding. "I see what you mean, Mr. Alden. Very well. You're the infantryman and I'll defer to your judgment. I guess we have to be prepared to backtrack a bit before we can leap ahead. At least see what you can do about preparing for simple breechloaders, if you can." He took a breath and looked at Bernie, decision made. "For now, if muskets are what we can do, that's what we'll do." He paused for a moment and glanced uncomfortably around the chamber. "What about . . . that other thing we talked about?"

Sandra gave him a stormy look, but remained silent. She'd clearly already stated her opinion.

Bernie's eyebrows knitted. "You mean . . . the gas?" Matt nodded and Sandison frowned, glancing at Tamatsu Shinya. He sighed. "Making the stuff isn't that big a deal. Mustard or chlorine is dangerous, but not hard. The problem is dispersal—and dispersing it far enough away from *us*, but close enough to the enemy. Wind would always be a factor." He hesitated. "Some may not be all that concerned about ethical issues, as far as the Grik—"

"*I* am concerned about the ethics of such weapons," Shinya interrupted sharply.

Matt looked at him and shook his head. When he spoke, his voice was quiet. "Believe it or not, Colonel Shinya, so am I. So is everyone here. Maybe not for the sake of the Grik, really; I wish God would stomp them all like bugs, but gas is just *wrong*. Using the stuff would take us and our friends to a level almost as bad as the Grik—a level I don't want to be on and I don't want our Lemurian allies to ever see." He took a breath before continuing, now directing his words primarily at Adar, who'd shown an interest in the "wonder weapon." "Gas kills everything. Indiscriminately . . . horribly. It'll kill animals, Grik, 'Cat prisoners—and any of Shinya's people who might be working for the Grik under duress. I *will not* gas 'Cats or men—even Japs who *aren't* working for the enemy against their will."

Matt rubbed his eyebrows. "I know it may be hard for you to understand, Mr. Chairman, but I grew up around guys who somehow survived gas attacks in the Great War and . . . well, 'survived' isn't the best way to put it; 'lingered in misery' is probably better, and they only got a little of the stuff. Honest to God, much as I hate them, it would turn my stomach to gas even the Grik. I'd rather burn them alive. We're going to have to think about this a lot more."

The chamber grew quiet for a moment and Adar was genuinely taken aback by the intensity of Matt's evident revulsion toward what seemed, by description, such an effective and efficient weapon.

"Moral issues aside," Matt continued soberly, "even if we made gas and solved all the problems with delivering it, how do we protect our troops? Unfortunately, we *do* have to think about it and we *do* have to solve that problem, at least. Does anyone honestly think this Kurokawa wouldn't give gas to the Grik if he thought it would benefit him? He's helped them in every other way. Like Ben said, we don't have any rubber, and even if we did, how do you make a gas mask for a Lemurian?" Matt shook his head. "There's no Geneva Convention on this world, governing this war, but we have to decide right now that if we *ever* make gas, it won't be used willy-nilly. Won't be used *at all* unless we're in a jam so tight we don't have any choice." He shrugged and Sandra grasped his hand. He looked at Adar. "That's how I feel, and that's the deal."

Adar said nothing. He had no choice but to agree, but he was perplexed. Clearly, Captain Reddy was extremely sensitive about the subject; all the humans seemed to be. Gas must be a terrible weapon indeed if one was willing to sacrifice the lives of one's own troops to avoid using it.

"We don't even know if Kurokawa and any other Japs are left," said Captain Ellis, speaking for the first time. He'd been Matt's exec on *Walker* before the Squall and had commanded *Mahan* on her suicidal dash. He was currently without a ship, but he was one of Matt's best friends, and Matt was always interested in what he had to say. "We know the Grik 'rescued' a lot of survivors off *Amagi*," he continued, "but they might have eaten them, for all we know."

"Perhaps they did," Shinya grudgingly admitted, saddened by the possibility, but glad they'd changed the subject. "Our prisoner thinks otherwise however." He referred to Commander Sato Okada, the lone survivor the Allies had taken into custody. Matt still hadn't talked to the new Jap directly; he'd been too busy. It was probably time he did, but he honestly wasn't sure how to approach the interview. Shinya had spoken with the prisoner at length and the man was a font of information about Captain Hisashi Kurokawa and the Grik—he hated them passionately and yearned for their destruction—yet unlike Shinya, Okada hadn't put the "old war" behind him. He'd been willing to cooperate with the Americans against the Grik, and if he'd been able to arrange such cooperation before *Amagi* was destroyed, he would have. That didn't mean he was willing to *ally* himself with the enemies of his emperor. Wounded by Kurokawa in the battle, he'd hidden from the Grik "rescuers" and allowed himself to be taken by the Americans and their allies for the sole purpose of supplying information about their common enemies: the Grik—and Kurokawa. Beyond that, as a Japanese officer and a prisoner of war, he had no other reason to live.

Shinya continued. "Okada says this Regent-Consort Tsalka, and their General Esshk are different from other Grik. They may have taken the lesson of their defeat to heart. He believes if they themselves are not killed for their failure, they will try to preserve as many Japanese as they can to help prepare for . . . well, what we are preparing for: our next meeting." He looked at Matt somewhat accusingly. "As Captain Reddy knows, there was a minority faction aboard *Amagi* already . . . frustrated with Kurokawa's command in general, and his association with the Grik in particular."

Matt nodded at Shinya, accepting blame for not telling him he knew some of *Amagi*'s crew were unwilling to aid the Grik. But it hadn't made any difference in the end, as he'd known it wouldn't. With *Amagi* coming for them, they couldn't pick and choose those aboard her they might kill. Shinya knew that, and he also knew that, by not telling him, the captain had been sparing Shinya's own conscience. Nevertheless, his point was sound and heartfelt.

Matt cleared his throat and turned to Riggs. "Now, Mr. Riggs, all these grandiose schemes depend on power. What have you got for us?"

"Simple reciprocating steam engines, Skipper, just like we're planning for the ships, but dedicated to powering generators. Nothing very difficult about building the generators; we still have plenty of copper and there's more coming in. People here already knew how to make wire, even if it wasn't for carrying current. It was mostly for structural reinforcement or ornamentation. We're standardizing most things on one-twenty DC, just like the ship. Nearly everything we have runs off that. We're also going to have to at least wash out *Walker*'s generators when we get them up so we should make new ones as much like hers as we can. We have all the specs, and it's always nice to have spares! The ship's generators are little guys, though, twenty-five kilowatts, about the size of a car engine and transmission. We might need bigger stuff eventually. We'll need some steel, too."

Matt grimaced. "Plenty of steel in the bay," he said, referring to *Amagi*. As soon as *Humfra-Dar* and *Aracca* had returned, they'd moored beside the sunken battle cruiser and begun stripping her exposed upper works. *Amagi* rested in about sixty feet of water, and the eventual plan was to flood down four of the mammoth Homes to build a cofferdam around her. Then they could retrieve the entire ship, piece by piece. Matt didn't even want to contemplate the stresses involved in holding back sixty feet of water, but the Lemurians assured him their ships could take it. Commander Brad "Spanky" McFarlane, *Walker*'s engineering officer, and now chief naval engineer for the Alliance, was convinced they could do it. A lot depended on where *Amagi's* bow had come to rest after breaking away, however. They were fairly certain it was "inside the box," but there was probably other heavy wreckage scattered on the bottom. If one of the Lemurian Homes flooded down on top of any of it, it might cause serious damage.

"Okay," resumed Matt, "but that brings up another issue. Acetylene. We removed all the oxygen and acetylene bottles from *Walker* and *Mahan* before the ... last battle, but with all the repairs we'd made, we're just about dry. We need more, lots more, to break *Amagi*, not to mention repairing *Walker* ... if she can be salvaged."

"Never fear, Captain," proclaimed Bradford cheerfully. "I may know little about synthetic rubber, but acetylene has been around for a hundred years! Quite simple, really."

Matt inwardly groaned. What was "quite simple" to Bradford in theory was rarely as easy in practice as he made it sound. "How do we make it?" he asked guardedly.

"Well, acetylene gas is the natural result of combining water with calcium carbide! It can be safely stored in acetone."

"Okay, where do we get the calcium carbide and acetone?"

"Calcium carbide is made by baking limestone with other easily obtainable ores at extremely high temperatures—I understand an electrical arc furnace is best."

"An electrical arc furnace?" Matt repeated. He looked at Riggs. "*Big* generators."

"Indeed," agreed Bradford. "But the result will be abundant calcium carbide, which we can use for other projects as well—desulfurization of iron, for example, once we get around to making our own. Acetone can be made by distilling wood. We have quite a lot of that, but it is a wasteful process. During the last war, it was made with corn to produce vast quantities. Perhaps we can find some local flora with similar properties. We still need ethyl alcohol anyway, to improve the quality of our gasoline, since tetraethyl lead is certainly out of the question for the foreseeable future!"

"Why do we need 'vast quantities'?" Riggs asked, and Bradford looked at him with astonished eyes.

"Why, if we are ever to make genuine cordite propellants, we must have acetone!"

Matt sighed. "Okay. Letts? Get with Mr. Bradford and Labor and decide what you're going to need." He looked back at Riggs. "That leaves communications, and if we're going to have to cross the whole damn Pacific, or Eastern Sea, to take the young princess home, we'll need sonar, or some other acoustic mountain fish discourager."

They'd found active sonar was the best way to deter the gigantic ship-destroying monsters, or mountain fish, that dwelt exclusively in deep water.

"I don't have anything to tell you on the sonar yet, Skipper, but communications is looking up. We still have all of *Walker*'s radio equipment, and, as you know, I'd already built a decent transmitter here after the Japs bombed our other one. We just didn't have the power to run it. We've begun mass production of even better crystal receivers too. Right now, I'm drawing up plans for a simple, powerful, portable spark-gap transmitter based on a surplus Army Air Corps set I picked up when I was a kid. It was a BC-15A, made in 1918 for airplanes, believe it or not. No tubes or anything really complicated. The only problem with it was that it was pretty . . . broadband . . . as in, all-band. My folks used to get mad as hell when I'd play with it when they were trying to listen to the radio."

Matt laughed. "That's not going to be a problem here. Even if the Japs still have a receiver, we'll be transmitting everything in code. Good work. I guess that still just leaves us with power—power to make the things that make power, I mean."

"Yes, sir. No fast-moving water or anything so, at first, I guess we keep using the method the Mice cooked up. The 'brontosaurus merry-go-round.'"

"Right." Matt glanced at the precious watch on his wrist, then looked at Adar—almost apologetically, it seemed—as if he regretted taking over the meeting. "I guess that's it then. Mr. Chairman, do you have anything to add before our guests are shown in?"

"Nothing for now. I do so enjoy having a plan. Let us speak with these Brits, as you call them, and discover whether anything we learn from them conflicts with our own priorities. I may have something to offer then."

As always, Matt was happy to be back on the water. He sat comfortably in the stern sheets of Scott's launch with Sandra Tucker snuggled tight against him, companionably quiet, ostensibly shielding herself from the occasional packets of spray with his larger form. Her mere proximity seemed sufficient to infuse him with a sense of well-being and optimism that was sometimes so elusive when he was alone with his thoughts. The launch moved through the light chop and the engine burbled contentedly while Matt gazed about the bay, memories of the battle still fresh in his mind. For once, the company and the quality of the day eased the pain those memories brought. His eyes lingered a moment on the two Imperial frigates moored near the fishing wharfs and he felt a twinge.

The Imperial liberty parties had generally behaved themselves, but there had been some incidents. Matt often met with Commodore Jenks, but their discussions were always short and to the point and Jenks invariably asked the same questions: "How much longer must we wait?" and "What progress have you made toward outfitting an expedition to return the princess to her home?" Matt's answers were always the same as well: "Not much longer," and "Quite a bit." The answers were lame and he knew Jenks knew it too. Sometimes Matt got the impression Jenks didn't *expect* a different answer and he asked only so they'd have something to argue about. He was a weird duck and Matt couldn't figure him out. He chased Jenks out of his thoughts and concentrated on enjoying himself.

Sandra was pleased on a variety of levels. She was glad she and Matt no longer had to hide their feelings. She remained convinced it had been the right thing to do, but their ultimately futile attempt to conceal their attraction had added even more stress to their situation. Now, even though their public courtship remained strictly correct, the feel of his large hand unobtrusively enfolding hers seemed comforting and natural. It was amazing how restorative such simple, innocent pleasures could be. The day had a lot to do with her mood as well—their situation always seemed less grim when the sky didn't brood—but she was also pleased with the progress one of her patients was making.

Norman Kutas, quartermaster's mate, was the coxswain today. After the battle, she wouldn't have given odds he'd ever even see again, much less handle a boat. He'd taken a faceful of glass fragments on *Walker*'s bridge, and though she'd worked extra hard to get them all out, the damage had frightened her. But Norm was tough and his eyes were were still intact. Norman would be scarred for life, and those scars were still pink and angry, but he could see. It bothered her that she hadn't been able to save Silva's eye, but in his case there hadn't been anything left to save. At least his empty socket was healing well. Once again she'd been amazed by the healing powers of the Lemurian polta paste.

Courtney Bradford, Jim Ellis, Spanky, and the Bosun were in the boat as well, but they seemed equally charmed by the pleasant day. Either they just weren't inclined to speak, or they were allowing Sandra to treat her most important patient for a while in the best way she could at present. By mutual consent, apparently, all the men knew that a day on the water with his girl was a dose their skipper needed.

Inevitably, however, someone had to break the silence. They were in the boat for another reason too, after all. Just as inevitably, that person was Courtney Bradford.

"I say!" he practically shouted over the noise of the engine, "the military equipment is all well and good, but have they managed to salvage anything *interesting* at all?" he asked. He'd turned to face Matt and had to hold his ridiculous hat on his head with both hands.

Matt shrugged. "Not sure what you mean by 'interesting,' Courtney, but they haven't gotten far into the hull yet. No telling what's in there. We'll see." Bradford turned back to face their destination. Not far away now, the huge pagodalike structures of four Homes protruded from the sea, as if the massive vessels had sunk there in a square. The tripod masts were bare, and massive booms lifted objects seemingly from beneath the sea between them. Matt knew the Homes *were* sunk—in a sense—having flooded themselves down to within thirty or forty feet of their bulwarks. As they drew closer, they saw there was still more freeboard than Matt's old destroyer ever had when fully buoyant. Courtney's question had ruined the moment, but not in an entirely adverse way. They were all anxious to see what had been revealed within the cofferdam formed by the Homes. At last, they'd see what was left of *Amagi*.

Kutas throttled back and the launch gently bumped *Aracca*'s side. Cargo netting of a sort hung down from above and they carefully exited the boat and climbed to the deck. Tassana, High Chief of *Aracca* Home, greeted them with a formal side party and full honors as they'd evolved among the Lemurians that were technically independent of Navy regulations. Her short, silken, gray-black fur glowed with the luster of healthy youth, and around her neck hung the green-tinted copper torque of her office. Her father had been High Chief of *Nerracca*, and when that Home was brutally destroyed by *Amagi*, she became a ward of her grandfather, the High Chief of *Aracca*. She was also his only remaining heir. When he died in the Battle of Baalkpan, she was elevated—at the tender age of twelve—to take his place. Lemurians matured more quickly than humans, but she was still considered a youngling even by her own people. She'd been through an awful lot and was clearly aware she had much to live up to, but Matt suspected she'd do all right. Her father's blood ran in her veins and she had a spine of steel. She also had a lot of help. Keje had practically adopted her, and a better tutor in seamanship and command didn't exist. Already, Keje loved the tragic child as his own, and Tassana adored him as well. In fact, she had quite a serious case of hero worship for just about everyone present, since they'd all been instrumental in avenging the death of her kin.

As always when he stepped aboard one of the enormous seagoing cities of the Lemurians, an awesome sight greeted Matt. The main deck, with the polta fruit gardens lining the bulwark, was normally a hundred feet above the sea, and three huge pagodalike "apartments" towered above it like skyscrapers. The massive tripods that supported the great sails or "wings" soared another two hundred and fifty feet above the deck. Larger than the new *Essex*-class aircraft carriers Matt had glimpsed under construction so long ago, *Aracca* was double-ended, flat-bottomed, and built of diagonally plank-laminated wood that was six feet thick in places. He was always impressed by the incredibly tough, sophisticated design that ensured that she and others like her would last for centuries upon this world's more hostile seas. Looking at *Aracca*, he couldn't imagine any natural force overcoming her. He vividly remembered how vulnerable her daughter Home, *Nerracca*, had been to ten-inch naval rifles, however.

After the ceremonial greeting, the youngling High Chief embraced Matt. He knew she felt great affection for him and he certainly returned it, but hers always made him feel a little awkward. He couldn't convince himself he deserved it. Tassana hugged Sandra next, then Spanky and Courtney. Kutas had stayed with the boat.

"Good morning, my dear!" Courtney said, pecking the High Chief's furry cheek. "We have come to view your progress firsthand! Judging by the increasing quantities of scrap arriving at the shipyard, you must be proceeding beyond our dreams!"

"It goes well," Tassana admitted with a touch of pride. She had the support and assistance of the vastly more experienced High Chiefs of the other Homes, but she was essentially in charge of the project.

"Anybody hurt today?" Sandra asked solicitously.

"A few, not serious. Torch burns, most. The new 'a . . . aa-set-aaleen' does not, ah, reg . . . reg-ulate the same as old, and of course we no have gayges for new torches either."

"It takes a little trial and error, I'm afraid," Courtney commiserated. Raw materials had been their very first priority, so fulfilling their need for more acetylene had dominated all other concerns for a while. The first large steam-powered generator was devoted entirely to the new furnace for cooking limestone, and the stuff was coming in from everywhere. Great, billowing white clouds arose from the crushing grounds near the shipyard, and workers emerged from a day's labor resembling long-tailed spooks. A still for the acetone was much easier to manage, but just as hard to feed. The volatile liquid resulting from the process also tended to evaporate as quickly as it was made, negating tremendous labor, so the quality control required for the combination and compression of the gas was a little haphazard. Courtney had taken personal charge of the project, with Letts's logistical assistance, so he felt a little responsible for each injury sustained.

"The burns not serious," Tassana thoughtfully assured him.

"I'm glad to hear it," Matt said, a little impatient to see the work. "Mind if we take a look?"

"'Course not." Tassana led them up a long stair from the catwalk above the polta garden to the amidships battlement platform above. They strode across it to starboard and peered down over the rail. The view they beheld was amazing and terrible, like something from Dante's *Inferno*. The water level within the cofferdam was considerably lower than that outside, and pumps heaved great geysers into the bay. The main portion of *Amagi* had actually settled atop her own amputated bow, and the scene of tangled, twisted wreckage and destruction was horrifying in a visceral way. The once mighty ship lay exposed down below her main deck and was still quite recognizable, but great arcs of molten steel jetted away from dozens of torches, spewing into the sea and causing a haze of steam to linger in the basin. Heavy booms lifted rusty, unrecognizable chunks, and even small structures. They heaved them across the expansive decks of the Homes and placed them on barges alongside.

"Goddamn," muttered Spanky around his perpetual wad of yellowish Lemurian tobacco leaves. "'Scuse me ladies, but . . . goddamn. Looks like Mare Island down there. Upside down or inside out—whatever—but damned impressive." He looked at Tassana, the usual fond expression he bestowed upon her mingled with respect. "I'm impressed," he repeated. "Keje said you could do it, that I should worry 'bout other stuff, but you know, I admit I was a little skeptical. I had a chief when I was a kid who helped cofferdam the *Maine*, to refloat her, and he told me about it. That was a hell of a job—but this!" He gestured around. "The *Maine* was a rowboat compared to *Amagi*."

"You proud?" Tassana asked eagerly.

"You betcha. You're going to get a lot of leakage, and I'm not sure how you'll manage to get her bottom up, but it looks great so far."

"There already leakage," Tassana admitted, "but pumps stay ahead. Also, when we get to bottom, we sink holes to pump with you hoses. We get bottom."

Spanky shook his head. "I bet you will."

Gray was watching the workers. Now that they weren't on a moving boat, the day had turned hot, and with all the steam . . . "Poor devils down there must be boilin'," he said.

"It . . . uncomfortable," Tassana agreed, "but I go down much . . . The workers . . . cheerful, yes? They cheerful knowing steel they bring up will kill Grik." She grinned. "Some would like to bring up whole ship."

"That might make salvage more convenient," Matt said, "having her closer to the shipyard. But it would take years to fix her. She's torn in half, and that doesn't even count all the damage she took before she got here. And everything on her is just so damn big! We still don't even have cranes remotely big enough to lift her guns."

"Prob'ly have to cut 'em up," Spanky lamented.

Matt shook his head. "I'd rather have her steel now than maybe have *her* a few years from now." He didn't add that they'd need some of that steel to restore his own ship—if it could be done—but Sandra heard it in his voice.

They lapsed into silence for a while, just staring at the monumental undertaking below. There must have been five hundred 'Cat workers on the wreck, cutting, unbolting, swinging heavy sledges, and dragging loose objects to convenient locations for the booms to reach. Their old nemesis resembled nothing as much as a murdered beetle on an ant mound being dismantled, ever so slowly, by the proud but remorseless mandibles of its killers.

Matt shook the thought away. Any sailor hated the breaking yard, but he would *not* attach any sentimentality to that . . . monstrosity that had tormented his dreams and threatened the existence of everything he loved on this world for over a year. He knew *Amagi* herself was not to blame; Captain Kurokawa and the Grik had wielded the weapon she'd been. Still, she'd embodied the threat they posed, and he enjoyed the irony that he and his people would now use her against her former masters. She'd been a scourge, but now she was a precious gift. She wasn't given willingly or received without great cost, but her corpse would provide the bones to which they could attach the sinews of modern war. She'd been the ultimate weapon of the Grik and the Japanese on this world. Now she would help destroy them.

Sandra had noticed the range of expressions that crossed Matt's face. Some she recognized and her heart went out to him. A few confused her. The strange smile that replaced them all left a chill in her bones.

Dean Laney, former chief machinist's mate aboard USS *Walker*, winced and shifted uncomfortably on his stool. Damn, his ass hurt! It had started bugging him a lot lately, and now he had an intermittent case of the screamers, which only aggravated the problem. He sipped his coffee, or "monkey joe," and gazed around. Large, crude machinery hummed, rattled, and roared loudly all around him. The chassis and casings were mostly copper or brass, but some were even made of wood. Only bearings, shafts, chucks, and tool heads were made of real, precious steel, although more and more iron parts and castings were coming from the foundries. Over his head, high in the ceiling beams, leather belts whooped and whirled and spun in all directions around a precarious clockwork of rattling wooden pulleys of various sizes. Having all that motion right over his head sometimes gave him the creeps, but usually he was able to ignore it.

He didn't know what his rank was anymore. Everybody had been getting fancy-sounding promotions, but if he had a new title, word hadn't leaked down to him yet. It didn't really matter, he supposed. It wasn't like he'd get a raise in pay. Besides, his domain had certainly been enlarged. Instead of *Walker's* cramped engineering spaces and modest machine shop, he now oversaw a sprawling, impressive industrial complex. Three long buildings and hundreds of workers were under his direct supervision, and he was responsible for turning out the machines that would make other machines that would ultimately go to the various project directors.

It wasn't as much fun as what Bernie, Ben, and Spanky were doing—making all sorts of swell stuff to use directly against the lizards—but they couldn't do their thing unless he did his. Besides, he never really was a "tight tolerance" guy, he admitted, and the majority of the machines that made machines could be relatively crude.

His wandering eyes fell on a 'Cat machinist almost in front of him. "Hey, you," he grumbled loudly, "watch what the hell you're doing!"

The 'Cat stopped turning the traverse handle, and the coils of brass that had been crawling away from the shaft she was turning abruptly sprang away to join the growing pile around her feet. "What I doing?" she demanded.

Caught off guard, Laney was stumped. Usually, his gruff comments went unanswered. He felt it was his duty to make them periodically to keep the workers on their toes. His face turned red and he stood up—making his ass hurt even more. "You mean you don't *know* what you're doing?" he demanded hotly, questing with his eyes for some fault.

"I know what I doing," came a shockingly abrasive retort. "Do you?"

"Why you . . . ! Just look! Look at all that shit coiled around your feet! It looks like a goddamn tumbleweed! What if that chuck snatches it up? It'll yank you in by the tail and all there'll be is a cloud of fuzz! Who the hell taught you to be a machinist's mate?!"

"Dennis Si-vaa! He teach me good! He make weapons to kill Grik, not stand around all day making big pole less big!"

Laney's eyes bulged. "Silva?! Why, that big malingering ape couldn't machine a proper turd with his ass!" Inwardly, Laney blanched at his own comment. Lately, he literally couldn't do that himself. He forged ahead. "I want you to slip the belt on that machine this goddamn minute, find your chief, and tell him you want to learn how to be a *real* machinist!"

Dean was so intent on his harangue that he didn't hear the sudden *snap-hack!* or the shrill, warning cries of alarm. He *kind* of heard the dull, buzzing *whoosh!* of the broken belt that slapped him on the back of the head.

He was still mad when he woke up in an aid station sometime later, but couldn't remember why. He felt like he'd jumped off a roof headfirst, though.

"Whadami doin' here?" he mumbled. When no answer was immediately forthcoming, he closed his eyes and raised his voice. "Hey, goddamn it! Why am I here?"

"Shut up!" came a harsh, heavenly, female voice. "You want to wake everybody up? Besides, you might burst a vessel!"

Laney opened his eyes and saw Nurse Ensign Kathy McCoy hovering over him.

"It's an angel!" he said wonderingly.

"Nope." Kathy laughed. "Just me."

"You're an angel, all right," muttered Laney, "and there's damn few of you. Scarcer than the kind with wings, I bet. You danced with me a couple o' times at the Busted Screw."

Kathy grimaced. "Yeah. I try to dance with all the fellas. I'd never forget you, though." Laney's eyes went wide and he beamed. "You stomped all over my feet," Kathy explained. "I haven't walked right since."

Destroyed, Laney uttered a groan.

"Head hurt?"

"Yeah. Who hit me? One of those chickenshit monkeys I have to put up with?"

Kathy frowned. "Not who, what. One of those leather belts that runs your machines broke. Conked you pretty good. Didn't break the skin, but you'll have a goose egg the size of a baseball. You guys ought to be wearing helmets in there."

"Mmm. Ought to be doing lots of stuff. We do what we can."

"Yeah. Hey, you hurt anywhere else? You've been squirming around like a worm on a hook, even in your sleep. By the way, now that you're awake, you need to stay that way for a while in case of concussion."

Laney nodded—painfully—but hesitated.

"What? You *are* hurting somewhere else. Where?" Kathy demanded.

"I'd, uh, rather not say. I'm fine."

Kathy nodded. She easily recognized the code words for "I'm not telling a broad about my private agonies." "Okay, without telling me *what* hurts, tell me what it *feels* like."

"Like I'm shitting busted glass!" Laney blurted, then caught himself. "Hey! You tricked me!"

"It's my job," Kathy said. "And it was easy. I won't even ask to do an exam, and I don't really want to. But judging by your physique, your complaint, and your job, I bet you spend a lot of time sitting, right?" Reluctantly, and somewhat indignantly, Laney nodded. "Just as I thought. Hemorrhoids. Piles. You know."

Laney shook his head. "Piles! That can't be it. Sometimes I think I'm gonna die! You can't die from piles . . . can you?"

Kathy almost laughed, but shook her head. "No, and I'll give you something that ought to help, at least a little . . . on one condition."

Laney's eyes narrowed. "Doctors ain't supposed to put conditions on helping folks, are they?"

Kathy shrugged. "Maybe I'm a doctor here, but I'm just a nurse back home. I can do what I want."

"What's the scam?"

"Tell you what. I get a lot of guys—'Cats—in here who work for you. Just like you, they get hurt now and then. Anyway, they're doing important work and they're proud of that. Some would rather be doing something else, and I understand, but your division, or whatever it is, is just as critical as any other—maybe more so—and they know it. They don't mind the work or the hours or even getting hurt, but nearly everyone I see—though anxious to get back to work—is *not* anxious to get back to work for *you*. You're a jerk, Dean. Right now you're a hurt jerk, so I'm trying to be nice. What it boils down to, the 'scam,' I guess, is this: promise to *try* to quit being such a pain in the ass, or I'll let your 'pain in the ass' keep reminding you how you make everybody around you feel. Deal?"

Chief Electrician's Mate "Ronson" Rodriguez heard the exchange between Ensign McCoy and Laney through the thin reed screen that separated them. He'd come in to get his hand fixed after he'd cut it on some of the sharp Lemurian copper wire. Now stitched, disinfected, and bandaged up, he'd been taking his ease for a few moments away from the "powerhouse," the factory he'd been put in charge of where they built, refurbished, and experimented on the various electrical contrivances Riggs was in charge of. The problem was, that stupid ox Laney was always cruising through his shop looking for deserters. Rodriguez knew Laney resented him as a jumped-up electricians' mate third class, and thought he could toss him around with his size and personality. He was wrong.

Ronson might have let him get away with it once, but a lot of things had changed besides relative ratings. Rodriguez had been wounded in action far more often than Laney, and besides Laney's genuinely impressive underwater adventures, Rodriguez had seen a lot bigger "elephants" than the chief machinist's mate. His most recent escapade was the one that finally earned him a nickname. His first name was Rolando, and his shipmates had tried to tag him with "Rolo," "Rodent," and even "Rhonda," but none ever stuck. When *Walker* took that Jap shell in her auxiliary fuel tank in the forward fireroom, somehow Rolando's sweatband and longish hair had caught fire. Silva put him out, but the mental image of him running around on the amidships gun platform like a lit match had left him with "Ronson" Rodriguez, and this time it took.

Since then, he kept his head shaved to his slightly scarred scalp and the only hair he cultivated was a Pancho Villa mustache. The men were allowed trimmed beards and razors were scarce, but the chiefs were allowed a little more leeway by everybody, captain to Lemurian cadet, because in most cases, they'd earned their stripes the hard way. All of *Walker*'s and *Mahan*'s chiefs who hadn't gone to other ships had filled dead men's shoes except Campeti—and the Bosun, of course—but Rodriguez didn't think Laney filled Harvey Donaghey's very well. If Laney felt the same way about him, he could eat turds and chew slow.

The arguments they had over Laney's "defectors" always escalated to bellows of rage and interfered with work in the powerhouse. Laney did know better than to take a swing, and the contention between them always had to be taken to Riggs or Spanky—more lost work in both departments. Riggs and Spanky tried to be fair, but if Laney really needed the deserter in question, the poor bastard got sent back. Rodriguez suspected the two officers were getting as tired of the situation as Rodriguez was, and Laney was probably out on a cracking plank. He wondered whether Kathy McCoy's comments would do any good.

Well, with that bump on his head, Laney would probably leave him alone for the rest of the day, anyway. Time to quit malingering. He stood up from the chair he'd been sitting on, cradling his wounded hand. The throbbing had nearly passed. Neat stuff, that pasty goo, he reflected. Not waiting to be released by the nurse, he ducked out of the aid station and headed back for the powerhouse.

He trudged through the muck of the recent rain and avoided the heavy carts pulled by bawling brontosarries until he saw the smoke rising from "his" boiler. Several 'Cats tended the beast, and it shimmered with heat and suppressed energy. The engine it powered was one of the first they'd built, and it wheezed and blew steam from its eroded and imperfectly packed pistons. He hated the engine and wanted another one, but he had to respect it as well. It had been a prototype, crudely built and not expected to last, but here it was, still chugging away after, well, *thousands* of hours. The generator it turned was also one of their first and he was proud of it. He'd designed it himself, and it was doing fine. Laney's shop had actually made the transmission gears that boosted the RPMs of the slow-turning engine to spin the generator fast enough to provide the calculated voltage, but Laney probably didn't do it himself.

"Silly, useless bastard," he muttered, and opened the fabric flap that covered the entrance to his domain.

"How you hand?" asked one of his new strikers solicitously. Rodriguez didn't remember the 'Cat's name. It was unpronounceable and he hadn't earned a nickname yet, but he'd been one of the deserters he'd succeeded in keeping. The kid was working on one of their simplest products: thermocouples for the vast variety of temperature gauges everybody was screaming for. Essentially all he had to do was join a piece of copper to a piece of iron. When heat was applied to the joint, current was produced. The higher the heat, the more current. The reason he got to keep *this* 'Cat was that when he was trying to explain intangible, invisible free electrons, the little guy actually seemed to understand. He had high hopes for him.

Lemurians in general were almost naturally mechanically inclined and great with practical geometry. They were accomplished jokesters and pranksters and could conceptualize common hypothetical outcomes. They loved gizmos, and if they could *see* something, they could understand it without much trouble. They were very literal-minded, though. When it came to things they couldn't see—like electricity—or even hypothetical outcomes they had no experience with, they had more trouble. He'd been forced to set up a few grade-school demonstrations to let them *see* electricity before he could convince them it was real. He also let them *feel* a little now and then, but had to caution them very carefully about feeling too much of it! He still wasn't sure how much most of his 'Cat electrician's mates and strikers really grasped, but they knew they had to make gizmos to create and harness the semimythical electricity, and they were good about scrupulously following safety regulations. The fact that he'd threatened to give them to Laney if they goofed around with the juice probably helped in that regard.

He waved his bandaged hand at the 'Cat with the unpronounceable name and moved along. He wanted to check on the progress of the portable DC generators they'd been working on when he hurt himself. He was surprised to find Steve Riggs waiting for him at the benches they'd set aside to assemble the things.

"Mr. Riggs! Good to see you, sir."

Steve laughed. "You mean it's good to see me without Laney for a change. Otherwise, you're probably wondering what I'm doing here, getting in the way."

"Well, yes, sir."

"How's the hand?"

Rodriguez raised his hand and flexed the fingers in the bandage. "Fine."

"Good. Look, I really don't mean to pester you, but these transmitters we're putting together are pretty simple affairs. They don't have tubes and their voltage requirements are somewhat critical. I just wanted to see for myself how you're coming along."

"Fair enough." Rodriguez motioned him to a bench where several 'Cats were cleaning up a stack of short, pipe-shaped objects. "Those are the frames. They came out of Laney's shop and they're rough as hell. I have to have the guys file the burrs—with shitty files out of Laney's shop. . . ."

"I get the picture. Laney's a piece of work. Skip it."

"Aye-aye, sir. Anyway, those are the frames. These guys over here are wrapping the field coils." He stopped, self-consciously. "That's how I cut myself. It's great the 'Cats can make wire; I just wish it was a little more, you know, round."

"We'll get to that someday," Riggs said patiently. "For now, just be thankful. We're starting to get a lot of wire out of *Amagi*, but we need it for other stuff."

"Yes, sir. Anyway, there's the pole shoes. We screw 'em to the frame on the inside and it holds the coils in place."

Riggs gestured at a bin with a number of internal assemblies. "Those armatures look like they came out of the Delco factory."

"Thank you, sir. They're a bitch. First we have to turn the shafts on the one little lathe we have. . . ."

"It *is* one of the ship's lathes."

"Yes, sir, thank you, sir. It would be nice if we could get the guys in the ordnance shop to make those, though. Them and the core. We can't make those like they do at Delco. We have to mill the slots on the rotary table. It's still not a huge job, but we're going to need more capacity. We have to make the big generators one at a time, mostly using crap from Laney, and we can't work on those at all while we're doing this."

"The guys at ordnance have their hands full. I'll see if I can get you one of the new, bigger lathes, and maybe a bigger mill. You'll have to make motors for them, though. This isn't a belt-drive shop, and it isn't going to be."

"I understand. Motors we can do."

"So, what are you insulating the coils with?"

"Fiber. Just like the real thing, only we mulch up some of Mr. Letts's gasket material and mix it with some other stuff. Mikey's in charge of that."

"How does it hold up? What about heat?"

"So far, so good. We haven't had the glue-up issues Ben has, for example, and it does insulate well. It's kind of like putty. We cram some in on top of the coils in the core slot too. Anyway, the coils are soldered to the commutator bar."

Riggs inspected one of the brush end frames that a 'Cat was finishing up. "You wave-wound the core, but you're only using two brushes?"

"Yes, sir. We've still got a hell of a spring shortage. We're actually using the same gear springs Ordnance is making for their musket locks! Wave-wound generators will work with two brushes or four. We might want to put four in later."

Riggs pulled the short whiskers on his chin. "Musket springs!" He snorted. "How do the brushes hold up?"

"The springs are fairly stout and they don't have much range of motion. The brushes'll have to be replaced every hundred hours or so, I'm afraid. Since we have to use brass bushings, they'll have to be kept lubed and replaced pretty often too."

Riggs nodded. "Okay, I want a dozen extra brushes, two extra musket springs, and half a dozen bushing sets for each completed generator. What are you doing to regulate the voltage?"

"Well, sir, since you want these things to be wind powered, we've calculated a low cut-in speed and a high charging rate at those lower speeds.

If a serious blow hits, it'll need to be disconnected. If they spin up too fast, centrifugal force will throw the windings out of their slots and thrash the whole thing. To cap the voltage, well, we've got to use a voltage regulator." Rodriguez pointed at yet another group of 'Cats working at a separate bench. "They're making vibrating regulators. I don't think they have a clue what they're doing, but I calculated all the values and gave them the plans. They could all be watchmakers after the war. They won't screw 'em up. Of course, I've got my ammeter to double-check each one. Managed to save *that*."

Riggs smiled. "Very good. Very, very good. If you weren't already in charge, I'd put you there."

"Uh, thanks."

"Now, one more thing; just a little matter, really. How do you plan to refurbish the generators, motors, and other essential equipment on *Walker* after we raise the ship?"

"And this, dear boy, if I'm not much mistaken, is the spleen!" Courtney Bradford leaned back and fanned himself with his sombrerolike hat, as much to clear the vapors of the quickly putrefying creature as to cool himself. It was hot, even in the shade of the trees surrounding the parade ground where the lesson was under way. Abel Cook, his most avid student, leaned forward to view the structure. Abel was thirteen, and he'd long since grown out of the clothes he'd been wearing during his evacuation from Surabaya aboard S-19. Most of the other boys who'd been similarly saved had applied to become midshipmen in the American Navy. Abel had too, but of all of them, he was the only one who'd shown an interest in the natural sciences. Bradford couldn't—and wouldn't—try to prevent the boy from serving, but he saw in the blond-haired, fair-skinned, somewhat gangly teen a much younger version of himself. "We need more of me around here," Courtney had argued with Captain Reddy, and to his surprise, Matt had agreed. Abel was still a midshipman, and naval dungarees had replaced his battered clothes, but Courtney would have him as an apprentice. For a while, at least.

"I believe you're right," the boy replied, his voice cracking slightly. "And that must be the gallbladder," he said, pointing. "It *is* quite large!"

"The better to digest the dreadful things they eat, I shouldn't wonder!" Bradford beamed.

Other students attended the dissection as well, 'Cat corpsmen trainees, and they shuffled forward to look. The cadaver was that of a local variety of skuggik, a much smaller but clearly related species to the Grik. Skuggiks were vicious little scavengers, mostly, and their arms had evolved away, so their external physiology bore marked differences to that of their enemy.

Internally however, they were virtually identical smaller versions. Courtney had attempted to save actual Grik for the demonstrations, but there was no means of cooling them. His modest hoard of postbattle corpses had been revealed by their stench and he'd been forced to surrender them. For now, his little open-air class on comparative biology would have to make do with skuggiks.

"And what is that lobed structure it is attached to?" Bradford asked. "Be silent, Abel," he admonished. "Let someone else answer for a change."

"Lungs!" proclaimed one of the young Lemurians triumphantly. Most of the others snickered.

Bradford sighed. "Would you like another try?"

The 'Cat looked more intently and wrinkled her nose. "You say that other st'ucture is a spleeng? I thought you say spleeng is on lungs?" There was chittering laughter this time.

"Perhaps, my dear, you might consider applying for another posting?"

"It is liver!" burst out another voice. "Big, ugly Grik-like liver!"

"Precisely!" exclaimed Bradford, his gentle chastisement instantly forgotten. His eyes narrowed and he looked at the organ in question. "A rather dry, reeking liver, in fact. Perhaps it's time we called it a day. Our specimen is withering before our very eyes . . . and noses!" He nodded at his assistants. "Please do dispose of this chap with all proper ceremony. We'll continue the lecture tomorrow with a fresh, um, subject. Weather permitting, we may start before the heat of the day!" With that, all but Abel scampered away, glad to escape the stench.

"Well!" said Bradford, still fanning himself and gauging the height of the sun. "Still some hours before dinner, I fear. Most barbarous, this local custom of eating only twice a day! Most barbarous. I'll never grow accustomed to it, and I may not survive." Secretly, he was glad Abel hadn't scurried off with the others. He didn't know why, exactly. He'd always generally loathed children: silly, mindless little creatures. His own son had been different, of course. A rare, exceptional specimen, most likely. He doubted he'd ever see the boy again, or even know if he was alive. He'd gone to fly Hurricanes for the RAF back in '39, and Courtney was slowly growing to accept that pining over his son's fate was pointless. In his heart, the boy would live forever. His ex-wife never entered his thoughts. That left Abel. Maybe that was it? Perhaps the boy was becoming something of a surrogate son? He was clearly unusually bright: unlike the other children who'd been aboard the submarine, he had the sense to seek Courtney's company and he had an insatiable curiosity.

Abel seemed to commiserate with him for a moment about the local customs, but then brightened. "Well, sir, if you're hungry, I'm sure we could find something at the Castaway Cook."

Bradford arched an eyebrow and looked at the boy. The Castaway Cook was a ramshackle, abandoned warehouse a short distance from the shipyard. It had suffered serious damage in the fighting and was really little more than a standing roof when *Walker*'s cook, Earl Lanier, appropriated it as a kind of enlisted men's club. It currently had little value as a warehouse, since there was no pier. In fact, it sported one of the few actual beaches on the Baalkpan waterfront. Earl was a ship's cook, and that was all he was. With his galley underwater, he'd decided he better get back to doing what he knew before somebody made him do something he didn't. Besides, "the fellas is always hungry," he'd explained. He was right. The American destroyermen and submariners he fed were still accustomed to three meals a day, and with all the work there was for everyone, the Lemurian destroyermen and other naval personnel were often hungry too. It was good for morale. The various army regiments were beginning to establish haunts of their own, and with Captain Reddy and Adar's approval had come the stern warning that Marines would also be welcome at Lanier's establishment. Or else.

Earl did a booming business. Besides Pepper, he had five more cooks and half a dozen waitresses. There were also several bartenders and that was what made Bradford's eyebrow rise. The Castaway Cook had another, possibly more common name: the Busted Screw. The entendres of that name were too numerous to count, but the accepted reference was to the party they'd held after replacing *Walker*'s damaged propeller with *Mahan*'s at Aryaal.

Bradford studied the boy's innocent expression. "Well, I suppose," he relented. Together, they dodged the 'Cats and marching troops, stopping now and then to admire various sea creatures on display in the bazaar. Coastal artillery crews drilled on their guns behind reinforced embrasures with augmented overhead protection. Abel watched it all, fascinated, and Courtney felt a growing benevolent affection for the lad.

"Do you ever miss the other children, the ones you were stranded among so long?" Bradford probed.

Abel cocked his head to the side. "I see them now and then," he said thoughtfully, "but we never had much in common, you know. The girls were all—mostly all—ridiculous, squalling crybabies. Miss, uh, Princess Rebecca was the exception, of course."

"Indeed she was. And is. Most extraordinary." Even though Rebecca was also clearly a child, Bradford actually admired her. She had a quick mind and was utterly fearless. With a flash, he suddenly realized that Abel Cook obviously "admired" her as well. "Indeed," he repeated. He motioned toward the martial exercises under way. "Do you wish you had more of that to do? Your, ah, other comrades, the ones old enough, are quite involved in it, you know. Of course you do."

"I do miss it some," Abel confessed. "I'd like to be a soldier or a naval officer." He paused. "I think my father would expect it. Did you know, of all the children aboard S-19, I am the only one whose father was a military man? He was a naval attaché and interpreter for Admiral Palliser." He paused again, and continued more softly. "He was liaison aboard *De-Ruyter* when she went down. I don't . . . I'll never know what happened to him." The boy's lip quivered ever so slightly, but his voice didn't. Bradford knew then that he had far more in common with this lad than he would ever have imagined. "All the other children—the boys, at least—were the sons of important men, but I think Admiral Palliser got me on the submarine himself. Mum was supposed to come, but there wasn't enough room there at the end. Sister Audry offered to leave the boat, but Mum wouldn't have it. The captain, Ensign Laumer, even Mr. Flynn wanted to take her anyway, but that Dutch cow," he said, referring to a somewhat dumpy Dutch nanny in charge of most of the girls, "said it just 'wouldn't do.' Things were 'quite cramped enough as it was.'" Abel's tone turned bitter. "There would have been room for several more people if they'd have just set that one ridiculous woman ashore. I'm sure she weighs as much as a torpedo and occupies three times the space!"

"Now, now," admonished Courtney gently, "I can certainly see your point. But one mustn't be unkind."

Besides Sandra and Karen Theimer Letts, only two other Navy nurses had survived: Pam Cross and Kathy McCoy. Pam was engaged in a torrid part-time affair with Dennis Silva, and for a time that had left only one known, and . . . wholesomely unattached female in the entire world: Kathy McCoy. This intolerable situation had resulted in the increasingly desperate "dame famine." That famine still existed to a degree. The only practical means of truly breaking it seemed to lie in establishing good relations with the Empire, but there were a *few* more women in Baalkpan now. There'd been four nannies, not counting Sister Audry, on S-19 to care for the twenty children of diplomats and industrialists aboard the sub. Two of them, one British and the "ridiculous" Dutchwoman, dropped all pretense of nanny-hood and had taken it upon themselves to "thank" as many of their destroyermen rescuers as they could in the best way they knew how, as soon as they returned to Baalkpan after the battle. Both women were rather plain and had probably landed right in the middle of their version of heaven. Perhaps the dame *famine* was broken, but in spite of terrible losses, the male-to-female ratio was very considerably out of whack. They were only two women, after all, and their energy and gratitude had limits. For now, the dame *drought* still smoldered.

"Besides," Courtney continued, "your mother surely found a far safer transport, in retrospect."

"Possibly," Abel allowed, but his tone sounded unconvinced. For a while, the pair walked in silence.

Beyond the breastworks, they entered what was left of the old warehouse district and followed the strains of music that gradually emerged from the general noise of the nearby industrial productivity. The music came from Marvaney's portable phonograph—a larger, tin resonance chamber had been attached to increase the volume. Bradford didn't recognize the tune, but he rarely recognized any of the music recorded on the depleted, but still large collection of 78s the dead gunner's mate had owned. The surviving records were almost all upbeat American tunes: jazzy, or something the destroyermen called swing. There were a few whimsical Western songs, and some stuff the men called country that sounded more like Celtic chanteys than anything else. Bradford was a classicist, and to his horror he'd learned the late Marvaney had been too, but most of his collection of that sort of music had been used as an object of weight to carry his corpse to the deep. Regardless, all the records were priceless relics now and were carefully maintained. It was rare that two songs were played in a row without a pause to sharpen the needle.

Bradford knew that sometimes, at night, they had live music at the Busted Screw. A small percentage of the Americans had been musicians, of a sort, and like virtually every item nonessential to the two destroyers' final sortie, their instruments had been off-loaded. There were several guitars, a pair of ukuleles, a trombone, and a saxophone from *Walker*. A concertina, a trumpet, and a violin came from *Mahan*. Oddly, a pump organ, of all things, had been aboard S-19. Bradford knew space had been extremely limited on the old submarine and he again wondered vaguely where it had been kept and how they'd managed to get it through a hatch to salvage it. It wasn't much larger than a console Victrola, but still . . . at least there'd been a considerable collection of classical sheet music tucked inside. The original owner was dead, but a lot of the fellows could play a piano. Bradford couldn't, really, but he could read music. He'd attended a concert at the Busted Screw and had to say the sound created by the unlikely orchestra had been . . . unusual. Throw in a variety of Lemurian instruments, and he couldn't quite describe the result. He wasn't without hope that the bizarre ensemble might eventually be arranged into something less cacophonous.

Outside the Screw, on a makeshift hammock slung between two trees on the beach, Earl Lanier lounged in bloated repose. He wore shorts, "go-forwards," and had eyeshades on. There was a large, faded, bluish tattoo of a fouled anchor on his chest, pointing almost directly at a bright pink, puckered scar above his distended belly button. He wore no shirt, and other than a thick mat of dark, curly hair, they were the only things upon his otherwise tanned, ample belly. Beside the hammock stood the battered, precious Coke machine, powered by a doubtlessly clandestine heavy-gauge wire. As Courtney and Abel watched, a black-furred 'Cat with specks of white appeared, complete with a towel over his arm, and took a chilled mug of something from inside the machine and handed it to Lanier. Before Bradford could form an indignant comment, Pepper retrieved another pair of mugs and brought them over.

"One is, ah, you call it beer," he said, knowing Bradford's preference for the exceptional Lemurian brew. He looked at the boy before handing him a mug. "The other is a most benevolent and benign nectar."

"Thank you, dear fellow," Courtney said. "I was just about to ask why you put up with such treatment from that ludicrous creature."

Pepper grinned. "I like cool drinks," he said, and gestured toward the shade of the club, "and so do guys." He shrugged. "No happy Earl, no Coke machine. Also, I like being assistant cook. I like to cook. You wanna eat?"

"Well, now that you mention it . . ." Courtney and Abel followed Pepper under the shade and plopped themselves on bar stools before a planked countertop.

"What'll it be?" Pepper asked as their eyes became accustomed to the shade. "I know you not like fish, but I got fresh pleezy-sore steaks."

"Plesiosaur," Bradford corrected, almost resignedly. "That will be fine. At least they aren't technically fish."

"It is quite good, actually," came a small voice nearby. Bradford squinted and realized that Princess Rebecca sat almost beside him.

"Goodness gracious, my dear!" Courtney exclaimed. "What on earth are *you* doing here?" He glanced quickly around. Abel had suddenly become very still and Bradford suspected, if he could see it, he'd discover a deep blush covering the boy's face. Apparently, sometime during their seclusion on Talaud Island, the young midshipman became smitten with the princess. He wondered if he'd known she'd be here. "And where is that abominable Dennis Silva, your supposed protector?"

Silva popped up from behind the bar like a jack-in-the-box. He teetered slightly. "Right here, Mr. Bradford, and I'm ambulatin' fairly well. Thanks for askin'."

Courtney was taken aback by Silva's sudden, towering presence. He was also just about certain he'd quite understood the word "abominable." Silva had always traded shamelessly in being much more than he appeared to be, and that was doubly true now. Bradford liked the big gunner's mate—chief gunner's mate now—and honestly owed him multiple lives, but if Silva had been frightening before, the eye patch and spray of scars across his bearded face made him positively terrifying. Particularly since Bradford knew Silva's capacity for violence was exponentially greater than his appearance implied as well—and his appearance implied quite a lot. Nevertheless, he stood and faced the apparition with a stern glare.

"Mr. Silva, I find it difficult to believe even you would bring Her Highness to such an iniquitous place. Filthy, sweaty men and Lemurians often gather here and exchange ribald, obscene tales. There is foul speech, and on several occasions one of the Dutch . . . *nannies* . . . we rescued from Talaud has actually performed a striptease! There have been fights, and contrary to regulations, there's often drunkenness. I won't go into your personal life and speculate upon what a poor example you set as a man, but bringing that child with you here is an act of irresponsible depravity!"

Silva leered at him across the counter, and in his best Charles Laughton impression—which wasn't very good—he uttered a single word: "Flatterer!"

Bradford took a breath, preparing to launch another salvo.

"Then what does that say about you, Mr. Bradford, and your bringing Midshipman Cook," Princess Rebecca said, glancing at Abel and offering a small smile. Now that his eyes had adjusted, Bradford clearly saw the blush coloring the boy's face.

"Well," Courtney sputtered defensively, "but that is different, of course! He is young, but he's a warrior and needs male example. Perhaps not as . . . sharply defined an example as Mr. Silva, but . . ."

"Mr. Bradford," Rebecca continued, "I know Mr. Cook and consider him something of a friend." The boy's blush deepened, if that were possible. "You should remember we spent the better part of a year as castaways together. I also know he is barely older than I, and through no fault of his, I expect I have seen considerably more combat. Lawrence and I were aboard *Walker* during the final fight with *Amagi*, if you will recall."

Speechless, Bradford glanced about. Only then did he see Lawrence himself, coiled in the sand like a cat where the sun could still reach him, staring back with what could only have been an amused expression. He was panting lightly, and immediately Bradford's mind shifted gears, wondering why Lawrence would lie in the sun . . . and pant . . . so close to shade. He shook his head.

"Besides," Rebecca said, ending the argument with her tone, "Mr. Silva did not bring me here; I brought him. He is still in some considerable pain from his wounds, you know, and a measured amount of seep helps alleviate that."

"Right," Silva said, resuming his search behind the counter as if he'd lost something. "I'm here for a medical treatment prescribed by medical treaters! I'm on limited, excyooged—excused duty." He vanished again entirely, groping on the floor.

"He's also quite incredibly bored," whispered Rebecca. "Captain Reddy said he must remain here when the expedition to Aryaal departs. He was not pleased. He *understands*, with Mr. O'Casey forced to remain in hiding and Billingsly's spies on the loose, that someone suitably menacing must watch out for me. But . . . he was not pleased."

"Where the devil did it *go*?" came Silva's muted mumble.

"Say, what *is* he looking for down there?" Bradford asked quietly.

Rebecca shrugged sadly. "It could be anything, but usually it's his eye." She shook her head at Bradford's expression. "He has not lost his mind, but he *is* in danger of losing direction." She spoke louder. "And he has clearly had quite enough seep!"

They needed a break from the daily rains, Gilbert Yeager thought. The sun rode overhead, but it wouldn't do much about the humidity. Make it worse, maybe. Didn't matter. The pyres had long since ceased, but black smoke piled into the hazy sky, and the industrial smoke they were making now, combined with the humidity, made every breath an effort. He coughed. Damn, he wished he had a cigarette.

He sighed and took a pouch out of his pocket, stuffing some of the yellow leaves within into his mouth. Chewing vigorously, he tried to get through the waxy, resinlike coating to the genuine tobacco flavor within as quickly as he could. "Gotta be a way to clean this stuff off," he muttered. So far, everything they'd tried to remove the coating so the leaves could be smoked had failed. The native tobacco could be chewed, but it was practically toxic when lit.

The nearest sources of the choking smoke were a pair of crude, but functional locally made boilers. They'd been leveled atop layer upon layer of good firebrick on the once damp shore, but they'd long since cooked all the moisture from the ground around them. They roared and trembled with power in the red light of their own fires that seemed to diffuse upward around them. Dozens of 'Cat tenders tightened or adjusted valves, checked gauges, or scampered off on errands at the monosyllabic commands of another scrawny human, Isak Rueben.

The boilers powered several contraptions—none exactly alike, since each was virtually a handmade prototype—that chuffed along amiably enough, their twin pistons moving methodically up and down. Gouts of steam added even more humidity to the air with every revolution, but at least it was honest steam—not the useless, invisible kind the sun cooked out of the ground. The end use of each machine was a series of shafts, or in one case, a piston-pitman combination. One was a small, prototype ship's engine they were testing for durability. The others spun large generators in crudely cast casings that supplied ship-standard 120 DC electricity to various points.

More engines were under construction that would eventually supply electrical or mechanical power to the pumps that would drain the nearby basin. The mechanical pumps were of a remarkably sophisticated Lemurian design. The electric ones were, like everything else electrical, experimental models Riggs, Letts, Rodriguez, and Brister had conjured up. If Gilbert had any money and if anyone would accept it, he'd lay every dime that the electric pumps would croak the first time they tried them.

Tabby, the gray-furred 'Cat apprentice to the two original Mice, ran lightly up behind him and playfully tagged him on the shoulder, then scampered to where Isak was standing. Hands in his pockets, Gilbert sauntered over to join them. "How they doin'?" he asked, when he was near enough to be heard over the noise.

"Fair," Isak replied skeptically. "Fair to middlin'. They ain't turbines," he accused no one in particular, "but they're engines. Least we got a real job again."

Gilbert nodded. They'd finally trained enough 'Cat roughnecks to take their places in the oilfields, both near Baalkpan and on Tarakan Island. The relief was palpable to them both. They hated the oilfields. Their time in the oilfields back home was what drove them into the Navy in the first place. They'd become firemen, and that was all they really wanted to do. Everyone called them the White Mice, because before the event that brought them here, they never went anywhere but the fireroom and they'd developed an unhealthy pallor as a result. They actually resembled rodents, too, with their narrow faces and thin, questing noses. Nobody ever liked them before, but now everyone treated them like heroes—which they were—Tabby included. First, they'd designed the rig that found oil when the ship was completely out. Then they'd managed to maintain enough steam pressure to get *Walker* to the shipyard after the fight. They were remarkably valuable men, but all their popularity hadn't changed them much. Everyone liked them now, but they still didn't like anybody, it seemed. Except for Tabby.

They'd originally treated the 'Cat like a pet, even though she'd proven herself in the fireroom. She'd even saved both of their lives at the end, by pulling them out of the escape trunk as the ship settled beneath them. Now she was one of them, another Mouse, even if she didn't look anything like one.

"I think they swell," Tabby said, referring to the engines in a passable copy of their lazy drawl.

"Yah, sure . . . for a myoo-zeeum. They're a hunnerd years outta date."

"Buildin' a pair of 'em with three cylinders, triple-expansion jobs—ten times as big—for *Big Sal*, I hear," Isak said.

Tabby's eyes blinked amazement. "Be somethin', to be chief of that."

"You expectin' a promotion?" Gilbert asked accusingly. "Hell, they've made gen'rals an' ad'mrals outta ever'body else, why not you?"

"I never be aahd-mah-raal," she retorted, angry enough to let her language and accent slip. She looked at the engine. "But chief be nice." She turned on Gilbert. "But only if you two be chief-chiefs."

The two men remained apologetically silent for a moment. It was their version of abject contrition. Finally, Isak spoke: "Bosun been to talk to you two?" he asked. Gilbert and Tabby both nodded. "One of us gots to go on the mission they're cookin' up, he says, since they're takin' the first new steam frigates." He pointed at the engine. "They've got one like that, only bigger. That's why we been testin' it to failure." He grunted. "Least this time they're lettin' *us* decide." He looked at Tabby. "An' this time she's in the pool as deep as us. Metallurgy aside, Tabby prob'ly knows these jug jumpers *better* than us. Bosun'd have to find a three-sided coin to make up his mind."

"You just said it," Gilbert accused. "It don't matter what we decide. They'll keep her here just because o' that!"

"Maybe we oughta go ahead an' tell 'em we're sorta related after all," Isak murmured. "Tell 'em we can't bear to be apart." He snickered at his own remark. He and Gilbert had never let on that they were half brothers. There was a certain resemblance often remarked upon, but usually in a mocking fashion. Besides, their last names were different. They'd never told anyone, because not only did they have different fathers, but their mother never married either man. In a sense, they figured that made them each kind of a bastard and a half. Things like that didn't seem to matter as much to them as they once had, but they still saw no need to brand it on their foreheads. "Hell, if it comes to it, I'll go," Isak said. "Kinda got the wanderlust flung on me the last time they busted us up."

"You didn't do any wanderin'," Gilbert accused. "You just stayed on that damn island while me and Tabby went a-wanderin'."

Isak nodded. "Yep. That's what I mean."

"Well," said Gilbert, clearly relieved, "just don't get ate."

With a look around the noisy ordnance shop to make sure no one was paying any particular attention, Dennis Silva clamped the brand-new musket barrel in the mill vise. The barrel was made of relatively mild steel plate, about three-eighths of an inch thick, taken from *Amagi*'s superstructure. Dennis figured they could ultimately salvage enough of the stuff from

Amagi alone to make millions of barrels, if they wanted. The plate had been cut and forged around a mandrel, reamed to its final interior diameter, and turned to its finished contour. Finally, it was threaded and breeched. It was a simple process really, with the equipment they had, but it had just been perfected, and only a few of the barrels were complete. Dennis figured the odds were about even that Bernie would have a spasm when he noticed one missing.

So far, the Captain and "Sonny" Campeti hadn't insisted that Dennis return to his duties full-time—they must have understood he had issues to sort out: some physical, a few domestic. He doubted their forbearance would last much longer. He was malingering, in a sense, and even he was beginning to feel bad about that. There was a lot he could be doing, after all. Should be doing. But he was a blowtorch. He'd go full-blast while there was fuel in the tanks, but when they were empty, they were empty. He'd needed this time to refuel, not only physically, but mentally—to put the "old" Dennis Silva back together. The time was just about right, and if the truth were known, he was actually starting to get a little antsy to return to duty. Besides, he had some ideas.

Carefully focusing his one good eye on the neatly scribed lines he'd drawn on the breech end, he cranked the table up and powered the mill. The cutter spun up and he turned a valve that started misting it with the oily coolant Spanky had devised. Slowly, he turned the crank in front of him. The cutter went through the breech like butter and he turned the other crank on the right side of the table and pulled the cutter back through the breech, widening the gap. Half a dozen more passes gave him the rectangular opening he wanted in the top of the barrel's breech.

"Oops," he mumbled happily, "I guess this barrel's ruined!"

He brushed the chips away and replaced the cutter with another that would leave a rounded, dovetail shape. He measured the depth, traversed the table, and made a single pass at the front of his rectangular cut. Changing the cutter again, to one with a slight taper, he made a final cut at the breech. Looking closely to make sure he'd hit all his lines, he switched off the machine and removed the barrel from the vise.

"God damn you, Silva, what the hell are you up to now?" came an incredulous bellow. A lesser mortal might have at least flinched just a bit despite the almost plaintive note to the shout.

"Goofin' off," Dennis replied mildly. "Cool your breech, Mr. Sandison. Ol' Silva's just keepin' hisself 'occupied,' like you said."

For an instant, Bernie was speechless. "Cool *my* breech? You just hacked a hole in the breech of one of my new musket barrels and you tell me that?" He looked almost wildly around. "Where's Campeti? If you won't listen to me, maybe he can control you! In fact, I want him to *hang* you!"

"Why's ever'body always want to hang me?" Silva asked, as if genuinely curious. "Calm down, Bernie, you'll hurt yourself. You 'cumulated a
extra hole or two in the big fight yourself, if I recall. If you start leakin',
Lieutenant Tucker's gonna get sore, and she'll have the skipper down on
you. He'll make you take a rest, and you'll be countin' waves in the bay at
the Screw while Campeti runs this joint. Besides, just 'cause I'm goofin' off
don't mean I'd dee-stroy a perfectly good musket barrel without a pretty
good reason."

Bernie paused and took a breath. Silva was right. He was a maniac, but
when it came to implements of destruction, if he wasn't actually a genius,
he was at least a prodigy of some monstrous sort. He still had his "personal"
BAR, and was one of the few people allowed to run around with such a prof-
ligate weapon and a full battle pack of precious ammunition. His new favorite weapon however, that he carried just about everywhere he went, was of an
entirely different sort. Bernie glanced at the thing where it leaned near Silva's
workstation with the bag of necessary equipment it required.

It had begun life as an antiaircraft gun aboard shattered *Amagi*, a
Type 96, twenty-five millimeter. The breech had been damaged in the battle
and the flash hider shot away, so Silva "appropriated" it during one of their
early trips to the wreck to salvage anything that remained above water. He
told Sandison what he was doing, and the still painfully wounded (like
nearly everyone) torpedo officer and Minister of Ordnance gave his blessing
to the project. For most of his life, before joining the Navy, Silva had just
been on the loose. For a time however, he'd worked for an old-school gun-
smith near Athens, Tennessee. In that part of the country, even in the mid-
thirties, many guns they worked on were old-fashioned muzzle loaders,
even flintlocks. His time there was probably what made him strike for the
ordnance division in the Navy. In any event, he'd learned a lot about "old-
timey" guns, so Sandison gave him the flintlock from the shortened musket O'Casey had when they rescued him.

Silva turned the Type 96 barrel down as light as he thought was wise
on one of the lathes, breeched it, and fitted it to a crude stock. Then he
made a hollow-base .100-caliber bullet mold like a Civil War Minié ball,
so the bullet would expand and take the gain-twist rifling. He still worked
on it now and then, dolling it up, but what he had was a massive weapon,
weighing almost thirty pounds, with a five-foot barrel. It was amazingly
accurate with its quarter-pound bullet, but the recoil was so horrifyingly
abusive, nobody but Silva had ever even fired it. Probably no human but
Silva *could* fire it more than once without serious injury. He called it his
Super Lizard Gun, and was anxious to test it on one of the allosaurus-like
brutes. He never wanted to go up against one of those incredibly tough
monsters with a .30-06 again.

"So," Bernie said resignedly, "show me why you shouldn't hang. And this had better be something useful!"

"Sure." Silva held up the barrel he'd altered. "Alden wants muskets, and that's fine. That's what we can do right now, so that's how we go. What you're making—*we're* making—is basically an old muzzle-loading Springfield. You settled on cap instead of flint because they're simpler and we can make the caps. Good call. Might want to make a few flintlocks for scouts, explorers, or such in case they wind up out of touch for a while—they can find flint if they run out of caps—but that's beside the point. You're also startin' out with smoothbores because we haven't built a rifling machine yet, and with the way Griks fight, a good dose of buck 'n' ball is just the ticket. Again, fine. The main thing right now is to get guns with bayonets in the hands o' the troops. Eventually, we can take the same guns and rifle 'em, use Minié balls just like ol' Doom Whomper over there. Everything's great, and we move the 'Cats from fightin' like they did in Roman times to the 1860s.

"But the skipper wants breechloaders, and that got me thinking. Everybody seems to figure that means, all of a sudden, we hafta jump from the *old* Springfields to the kind of Springfields we brought with us, our 'oh-threes. That'd be swell, but it's a lot bigger jump than folks would think, and it's bigger than we hafta make."

"It is?"

"Yeah. The Army—our old Army—had the same problem once. After the . . . War Between the States, they had millions of muzzle-loadin' Springfields, see? Thing is, everybody was startin' to go to center-fire breechloaders. Even f . . . likkin' *Spain*. Whaddaya do? This fella named Ersky Allin—er somethin' like that—had sorta the same job as you. Anyway, he figured a way to make center-fire breechloaders outta all them muskets, and it was a cinch!" Silva brandished the barrel again, then fished around on a bench covered with strange-looking objects he'd been working on. He picked something up. "He, this Allin fella, cut the top outta the breech, like I just done, and screwed and soldered this here hinge-lookin' thing to the front of the gap." Silva held the object in place. "The thing on the other side of the hinge is the breechblock—we can cast 'em a lot easier than I milled this one out!—and the firin' pin angles from the rear side to the front center!" He held the pieces together and the breechblock dropped into place with a *clack!*

"I ain't pulled the breech plug out and milled the slot that locks the thing closed, but again, it's a simple alteration. You cut a barrel, put this on, then grind the hammer to where it hits the firin' pin square. All else you gotta add is a easy little extractor!"

Bernie's eyes were huge. "Silva, you *are* a freak-show genius!"

"Nah. Maybe Ersky Allin was, though."

Bernard Sandison looked at Dennis. "How did you do this? I mean, how did you *know* about this?"

Silva shrugged. "I had a couple over the years. First rifles I ever owned. Sometimes huntin' was the only way a fella could stay fed, what with the Depression, and you could buy one surplus at just about any hardware store, or order one from Monkey Wards or Bannerman's for a few bucks."

Bernie shook his head. His childhood and Silva's had been . . . different. "What did they shoot? And how . . . ?"

"That's another neat thing. You're forgin' these barrels on a five-eighths mandrel. Once you ream 'em out smooth, they're about sixty-two-caliber or so. You go ahead and build yer riflin' machine and rifle forty-five- or fifty-caliber *liners* to solder in the old barrels and then chamber 'em! Simple as pie. The first Allin guns they put liners in were fifty-seventy. When they started building rifles like this from the ground up instead of convertin' 'em, they made receivers for 'em an' did 'em in forty-five-seventy. That's a forty-five- or fifty-caliber bullet on seventy grains of powder. Black powder, just like we have now. Both had a pretty high trajectory, but they'd stomp a buffalo to the ground. Probably a lot better for critters around here than a thirty-aught-six. Big and slow gives you big holes and deep penetration. Small and fast gives you small holes, and maybe not so deep penetration. If you're too close, light bullets, even copper jacketed, just blow up on impact and never hit anything vital."

Oddly, Bernie noticed that when Silva was talking ballistics, he didn't sound as much like a hick, but he'd already begun tuning him out. Silva had just solved one of the biggest problems he'd expected to face over the next year or so. It had bothered him for a number of reasons. He'd felt a little like everything they did before they came up with "real" weapons was sort of a wasted effort. Silva's scheme might not give them truly modern weapons, but they were leaps and bounds beyond anything they were likely to face. But what about cartridges?

"These fifty-seventies and forty-five-seventies, what were they shaped like? The shells?"

"Straight, rimmed case," said Silva, grinning. He knew what Bernie was thinking. One of the problems they faced with making new shells for the Springfields and Krags they already had, not to mention the machine guns, was the semi-rimless bottleneck shape. "Even if you haven't solved the problem of drawing cases—which I figure you will—you can turn these shells on a lathe if you have to."

Bernie beamed. "I swear, Silva! Why didn't you just *tell* me you wanted a musket barrel? I'm going to see you get a raise out of this . . . or a promotion, or something! Take the rest of the day off. You're still technically on leave anyway. Go hunting or have a beer! Kill something; you'll feel better!"

"Raise won't do me any good, an' I don't want no promotion. All I answer to is you, Campeti, and the skipper anyway. You can call 'em 'Allin-Silva' conversions, if you want, though."

"You bet! Do whatever you want! I have to talk to the skipper!"

With that, Bernie rushed away with the still-dripping barrel and trapdoor arrangement in his hand. Silva watched him go. "Whatever I want, huh?" Silva said, eyebrow raised.

L ieutenant Tamatsu Shinya, formerly of the Japanese Imperial Navy, and currently brevet colonel and second in command of all Allied infantry forces, unbuckled the belt that held his modified Navy cutlass and pistol. Handing it to the 'Cat Marine sentry at the base of the comfortable dwelling, he climbed the rope ladder to the "ground" floor—roughly twenty feet above his head. It was inconvenient, but virtually all Baalkpan dwellings were built on pilings like this so their inhabitants could sleep secure from possible predators. He reflected that the practice was as much tradition now as anything else, since the city never really slept—even before the war—and over the centuries, dangerous animals had slowly learned to avoid the city carved out of the dense wilderness around it. Now there were fortified berms and breastworks, constant lookouts, and vigilant warriors as well. He wondered as he climbed the ladder if the inconvenient tradition would long survive. At the top, he struck the hatch, or trapdoor, above his head and, raising it, entered.

Once inside, Shinya removed his shoes and stood. A curtain separated the entry chamber from the rest of the dwelling and he passed through it. Finding the occupant seated cross-legged on the floor, facing a small window overlooking the bay, Shinya bowed at the waist.

"Commander Okada," he said in Japanese. "My apologies for disturbing you."

Okada turned then. His uniform had been wrecked and he wore a robe not unlike the ones the Lemurian Sky Priests used. He was older than Tamatsu, but had the same black hair, untinged with gray. He regarded Tamatsu for a moment before dipping his own head in a perfunctory bow.

"At least you still remember how to *behave* somewhat Japanese," Okada observed.

Shinya felt his face heat. He straightened. "And you, sir, it would seem, have learned to behave somewhat like your Captain Kurokawa."

Okada shot to his feet, anger twisting his face. "Still you will compare me to that *kyoujin*?"

"You have called me a traitor on several occasions now. If I am, what are you? I did not surrender when my ship sank; I was captured while unconscious. I had no idea any of my countrymen even existed in this world. I made an honorable accommodation with a former enemy to help confront an evil I am quite certain our emperor would despise. Our primary differences with the Americans are political, and not . . . on anything approaching the levels of our differences with the Grik! You condemn me, yet you supported the actions of a man you know the emperor would have never condoned!" Shinya fumed. He couldn't help it: Okada's attitude infuriated him and he didn't understand it. "Perhaps *General Tojo* would have, but the emperor wouldn't; nor would Admiral Mitsumasa!"

Okada seemed to deflate. "I *tried* to oppose him," he offered quietly. "I helped Kaufman send a warning."

Shinya's voice also lost some of its heat. "Yes, you did. Moreover, you should be proud you did. I too oppose Captain Kurokawa—and the Grik. I do not and will not fight others who do, nor have I done so. I gave Captain Reddy my parole and had no difficulty fighting the Grik. When I learned of your ship, I faced a choice—a choice I was *allowed*, by the way—to abdicate my duty to the troops I command, or risk the possibility I might face you and others like you. I was spared that agony, but I would have done it if forced, because those troops would have been aiding Kurokawa and, by extension, the Grik."

"You make it sound as though I am guilty of aiding that madman simply because I did not rise openly against him sooner! Believe me, I wanted to! But all that would have accomplished is my death before I had any real chance to make a difference." Okada looked down. "In the end, it made no difference anyway."

"It did," Shinya assured him. "You gave us warning. Without that, we would not have been prepared."

"Prepared to kill our countrymen!" Okada almost moaned. "Do you not see? Perhaps you are not a traitor for what you have done, but I can't stop *feeling* like you are, even as I *feel* like one for doing even less. They were *my* men!"

"Yes," Shinya agreed. "But do not think the decision was less difficult for me. Now, to do nothing further, while those same men are in the grasp of such evil, is impossible for me. Don't *you* see?" Shinya waited for a response. When there wasn't one, he sank to the floor across from Okada, who finally joined him there.

"What do you want to do?" Shinya quietly asked.

"I want to go home."

Shinya took a breath. "Unless you have knowledge beyond mine of the mystery that brought us to this world, I fear that is impossible."

Okada looked at Shinya a long moment, weighing the words. Finally, he sighed. "That is not what I meant. Of course I want to go 'home,' but I have no more idea how to do that than you profess to have. No, what I want is to go to that place that *should* be home. The place your allies at least still call Japan."

"Jaapaan," Shinya corrected. "But why? The Lemurians have two land colonies there—a small one on Okinawa and another, larger one on southern Honshu. They have never, by all accounts, encountered any of our people. On this world, Jaapaan is not Japan. Besides, your knowledge of Kurokawa and the Grik is invaluable to those who oppose them."

That was true enough. Thanks to Commander Okada, the humans and Lemurians finally knew more about their enemy now. They still didn't know what drove the Grik to such extremes of barbarity, but they'd learned a little about their social structure. For example, they now knew that the average Grik warrior came from a class referred to as the Uul, which possessed primary characteristics strikingly similar to ants or bees. Some were bigger than others, some more skilled at fighting; some even seemed to have some basic concept of self. All, however, were slavishly devoted to a ruling class called the Hij, who manipulated them and channeled and controlled their instinctual and apparently mindless ferocity. There seemed to be different strata of Hij as well. Some were rulers and officers; others were artisans and bureaucrats. Regardless of their positions, they constituted what was, essentially, an elite aristocracy collectively subject to an obscure godlike emperor figure. Nothing more about their society was known beyond that. The Hij were physically identical to their subjects, but were clearly intelligent and self-aware to a degree frighteningly similar to humans and their allies. They didn't seem terribly imaginative, though, and so far that had proved their greatest weakness.

Shinya persisted. "Don't you want revenge for what Kurokawa has done to the people under his command? *Our* people? Can't you set your hatred of the Americans aside even for that?"

"I do not hate the Americans," Okada stated with heavy irony. "But they are the enemy of our people, our emperor. I cannot set *that* aside. How can you?" Okada shook his head. He didn't really want an answer to his question. "It is true I had hoped, with *Amagi*, to work in concert with the Americans against the Grik, because, like you, I recognize them as evil—perhaps the greatest evil mankind has ever known. I never intended an *alliance* with the Americans, merely a cessation of hostilities. An armistice perhaps. It is not my place to declare peace and friendship with my emperor's enemies"—he glanced with lingering accusation at Shinya— "and no, I would not have broken the armistice. However, with *Amagi*, I could have felt secure that the Americans wouldn't either. In any event, together or independently, we could have carried the fight to the Grik and then inherited this world in the end." He shrugged. "It is a big world. Whether it was big enough for us and the Americans, in the long run, would have been a test for much later—and at least one of us would have survived the Grik." He sighed and looked at Shinya. "An imperfect scheme, perhaps, but a less radical ... departure from my sense of duty than the choice you made."

"An impossible scheme," Shinya stated derisively. "Without the Grik, where would you have been victualed, supplied, repaired? A simple armistice would not have gotten you those things from the Americans and their allies. You would have been at their mercy!"

"No! With *Amagi*, I could have *demanded*! As I am now, a prisoner, I have nothing! Not even honor! I can demand nothing as an equal and I have nothing to even bargain with but what is in my head!"

Shinya stood, talking down to Okada. "No. Impossible," he repeated. "I respect what you did, what you tried to do. You could—*should* be a hero for it instead of a prisoner. But the old world is *gone*! If you had succeeded in the rest of your plan, if you had tried to dictate terms, to conquer support from the Allies, even I would have opposed you."

"Even if it meant killing your own countrymen?"

"Even if it meant killing every man on *Amagi*," Shinya answered quietly. "You say you understand, that you hate the Grik and everything about them. You move your mouth and the right words come out, but you really don't understand, do you? Even now. The Grik are the enemy of everything alive in this world! They ... You haven't ...." He paused, shaking his head. He could see he was wasting his breath. He did respect Okada, but the man was just ... *too* Japanese. He wondered what that said about him?

"I will see what I can do," Shinya said at last. "If you agree to work with the Allies and continue to tell them what you know of Kurokawa and the Grik, I will try to convince them to let you go 'home.' Perhaps there you will find the honor you think you have lost. If so, I hope you can live with it. I doubt it, though. I fear for you, Commander Okada. I fear that someday your misjudgment will fade and the honor I still see in you will rise within your heart and demand a reckoning. Because of the blood we spill on behalf of you and uncountable others, you will die a tortured old man, who missed his opportunity to *be* honorable by mistakenly trying to do the honorable thing."

"What would you have me do?" Matt asked the mustachioed man sitting across the table. The table was split bamboo, with a rough, uneven top, and it served Matt as a desk of sorts in the semi-finished chamber known as the War Room. The chamber was one of many in the "new" Great Hall, still undergoing noisy reconstruction. The irregular surface of the desk didn't really matter much; paperwork was kept to a minimum and consisted of sun-dried skins, like parchment, only not as fine. Usually, the rawhide parchment supported itself well enough to write on.

"What would you have *me* do?" Jenks replied. He was dressed in his best, as always now, for these biweekly meetings. He sat stiffly on a stool in his no longer perfectly white uniform, with its ever so slightly tarnished braid. Under his arm was the black shako with braid that matched his sleeves and collar. It was raining outside and sheets pounded against the hastily covered ceiling and the chamber was humid and damp. Jenks's coat smelled of musty cotton and the half-soaked hat would have added a wet wool and leather odor if the similar wet-'Cat smell hadn't overpowered it. Between them on the desk was a large decanter of purplish amber liquid and two small mugs. Neither mug had been touched.

"I know we haven't often seen eye-to-eye," Jenks understated, "but I do have my duty. I must return the princess to her family—something you promised to help me do—but I don't see any measurable degree of preparation under way to accomplish that task."

Matt cocked an eyebrow at him. "No? We captured two more of your men spying on the shipyard from a boat they'd hired last night. Don't tell me we've caught them all. Surely you have some idea what we've been up to?"

Jenks sat even straighter and his face went hard. "Do you mean to execute those men, like the one you caught a few weeks ago?"

"I *should* hang them," Matt answered darkly. "I told you what the penalty would be if we caught your men snooping around where they don't belong. The entire city has been open to them and they've been treated well, by all accounts. Better than well. Still, you can't resist fooling around where you've got no business."

"If I perceive a threat to the Empire, it is my duty to evaluate it. We have cooperated with every one of your ridiculous requests, languishing here in this place quite long enough for you to prepare an envoy to my people." Jenks's eyes widened slightly in genuine surprise. "Somehow, you have convinced the princess to support you in that. In the meantime, all I get from you are delays, accusations, and, I believe, sir, distortions of truth.

You have done nothing to alleviate my concerns about your Alliance. If anything, those concerns have grown more acute. And my question remains: will you murder these men like you did the last one?"

Matt stood, angry. "We didn't 'murder' anyone! The last man we caught had murdered a sentry to get where he was. He was captured and executed as a murderer and a spy! Would you have done otherwise? Please don't insult my intelligence by telling me you would."

Jenks only sighed.

"Very well," Matt continued, seating himself again. "The men we caught last night did no such thing, and I doubt they saw much either. I'll return them to you, but you'd best restrict them to your ship. If I catch them ashore again, they *will* be hanged!"

Jenks cleared his throat, calming himself. For some time he sat still, staring at Matt as if appraising him anew. "Just so," he said at last, with a hint of resignation. "And you have my appreciation and . . . my apology. You won't see *them* again. I cannot assure you that there will be no more spies, however."

Matt looked closely at the man. He'd spoken the word "spies" with distaste. Did he mean he wouldn't make that assurance, or couldn't? This wasn't the first time Matt got the impression that some things happened on and off Jenks's ship over which he had little, if any, control. He wondered if the vague admission was a crack in Jenks's facade, or if he was merely tiring of the aggrieved role he seemed to think was expected of him. By somebody. Matt merely nodded. He doubted he'd get an admission if he continued to press, and he wanted to use Jenks's comparative openness while he had the chance.

"I do assure you we're doing all we can to prepare the expedition as quickly as possible. As I've said, a reconnaissance of Aryaal is part of that, and a reconnaissance in force is essential—thus the delay. That has to be our first priority. We need to know what's going on there before we dare weaken our defenses here. Our estimates of the Grik may be entirely wrong—they have been before," he added bitterly. "Besides, you've been here only a little more than two months. Bradford said it might take a few. My definition of 'a few' is three or more. Isn't it the same with you?" Matt thought he detected the most subtle of smiles flash across Jenks's face.

"Indeed. But one can always hope for the best, and 'a few' is a somewhat vague expression." Jenks's tone hardened slightly. "Just as your notion of what these Grik are capable of seems vague as well. Come, you defeated them badly when last they came. Surely you cannot be as . . . concerned . . . about them as you claim?"

Matt leaned against the backrest he'd had installed on his stool and regarded Jenks for a moment, rubbing his chin. "Tell you what. I'm about to have an interview with a man who probably knows more about them than anyone alive. Why don't you join us? You may find it . . . enlightening." Matt took Jenks's silence as agreement and rang a little bell. Instantly, the War Room door opened, revealing a small, dark Filipino who eyed Jenks doubtfully. "Juan, please have General Alden and Colonel Shinya escort the prisoner inside."

Juan stood straighter, as if at attention. He'd been *Walker's* officer's steward before the war, and he'd since evolved into Matt's personal steward and secretary. No appointment to that effect had ever been made; Juan just took it upon himself. By sheer force of will, he'd made it stick.

"Of course, Cap-i-tan," he said. "Should I bring coffee?"

Matt hid a grimace at the prospect of Juan's coffee, or at least the stuff that passed for coffee here. Back when he'd had the real stuff to ruin, Juan's coffee had been ghastly. With the ersatz beans he now had, it had improved to the point that it was only vile. Still . . . "No, that's not necessary, but thanks."

With a somber bow, Juan closed the door. A moment later it opened again, revealing three other men whom Juan ushered to seats across the desk. All had recently arrived and were soaked to varying degrees. Once they sat, Juan left the chamber, discreetly closing the door behind him.

"Commodore Jenks, I understand you've met General Alden and Colonel Shinya?" There were nods. "Then may I present Commander Sato Okada, formerly of the Japanese battle cruiser we're stripping in the bay?" Jenks nodded, but Okada continued staring straight ahead.

"Yes, well. I've now spoken with Commander Okada on several occasions and I've discovered he prefers to remain aloof from civilities. You must understand that before we . . . came to this world, his people and ours were at war." Matt's expression darkened. "Quite bitterly at war, as a matter of fact, and that war almost certainly still rages. Since we rescued him from his sunken ship, we've come to an . . . understanding regarding our association. By his choice he remains a prisoner of war. In recognition of the threat posed by the Grik, however, and in exchange for transportation to that region that *would* have been Japan, he's willing to answer any questions about the enemy to the best of his ability. He was *Amagi's* first officer, and as such had frequent direct, personal contact with the Grik. More than anyone else from his ship, in fact, since his former commander, Captain Kurokawa, forced him to perform most of their correspondence. Okada believes this was mainly a form of punishment, since Kurokawa knew how much he loathed their 'allies.' Ask him whatever you want. If you don't believe me about the menace we all face—your precious Empire as well—you must believe him. He's as objective a source as you'll find. You see, he doesn't like us much either."

"Who's to say the information he gives you is genuine, then?" Jenks demanded. "Perhaps he inflates the threat to discourage you from attacking while his own people are still in their hands."

Okada spoke through clenched teeth. His enunciation was careful, if heavily accented. "If this . . . British man doubts my word, I will say nothing to him. I do not even understand why I am here. Surely you have already told him everything I have said. Americans and British are the same. Both are enemies of my emperor. You act in concert and remain as one people, despite your supposed split."

"Hmm," said Matt, "I'm sorry, Commander. Clearly, you *don't* understand. Commodore Jenks is no more British than you are." For an instant, Okada's facade dropped to reveal an expression of confusion while Jenks sputtered. Matt plowed on. "His *ancestors* were British, mostly, from what the princess says, but they came to this world the same way we did before the United States even existed. I've tried to persuade him to accept the historical bond that's existed between our two countries for the last few decades, but he professes not to believe it. If he does, he doesn't care. So don't think of him or his people as enemies of your emperor; they're not. Remember your history. When his people last came through here, Japan was closed to them. They knew it was there, of course, but they knew little of the people who inhabited it. They were too busy in China and India."

"I *am* British, sir. I am a subject of the Empire of the New Britain Isles," Jenks retorted hotly. He glanced at Okada. "But I am no enemy of yours. I apologize for forming my question so tactlessly. Please tell me, in your opinion, how serious is this supposed Grik threat?"

Okada regarded Jenks for a moment, evaluating the sincerity of the question. Finally, he relaxed slightly, and as he spoke, it was clear that evil, shrouded memories marched across his thoughts. "They are a threat beyond imagination. You are familiar with the shape of the world, from your ancient charts?" Jenks nodded. "Besides their recent conquests in Malaysia, they control all of India, the Arab coast, and at least eastern Africa almost to the cape. I believe their imperial capital, where their 'Celestial Mother' resides, is on Madagascar, one of their earlier conquests. They have no sense of honor as even an Englishman might recognize it. Their individual warriors have no sense of honor at all. They are voracious predators who exterminate all in their path, feasting not only on the bodies of their victims, but on their very own dead. They eat their *young*—a practice I have seen with my own eyes—and they have eaten . . . members of my own crew when we failed to conquer Baalkpan on our first attempt. All failure is considered a failure of spirit, and those who fail are considered prey to be devoured. That is why we aided them, why Kurokawa aided them: through fear of being preyed upon if we refused. Kurokawa may have had other reasons of his own, but for the vast majority"—his eyes drooped—"for me, it was fear."

"But what of the battle here?" Jenks demanded. "Surely such a defeat must have hurt them."

Okada looked wistful. "I certainly hope it did. Nevertheless, I have *seen*. I have been to Ceylon, where their teeming hordes are beyond number. I have seen how they so readily replaced the ships and warriors destroyed in their first offensive against Aryaal and this place. A grace period may have been won, but it will be short. They breed rapidly, and if they do *not* eat their young, within five years they may return with three times what they lost—and still maintain control of their frontiers."

"My God," Jenks muttered.

"Nothing we haven't told you before," Alden growled.

"True, perhaps, but . . ."

"Tell you what," Matt said, making a decision he'd been pondering for days. "Now that you have a fresh perspective on why we're in such a hurry and why our expedition to return your princess has received a lesser priority, I'll take you to the shipyard myself. Just you. I don't know what other agenda your spies may have, but I'll let you see what we're working on and let you decide whether we're doing it to fight the Grik, or threaten your Empire. All I ask is that, on your *honor*, you don't divulge what you see, but I'll leave the evaluation up to you."

Jenks seemed flustered at first, but quickly regained his composure. "That is . . . generous of you, Captain Reddy, particularly considering the previous prohibitions. But I cannot possibly swear not to report what I see if, in my estimation, it poses a threat to my Empire."

Matt sighed. "I thought that was understood. Look, I don't really like you very much and I know you don't like me. But I'd have thought, by now, you'd have accepted the fact that we really do want to be friends with your people. If we become friends—real friends—we'll share all the technology we show you. In spite of what you may believe, it's considerable. I wouldn't let you see it at all if I thought you'd still doubt our preparations are devoted to defeating the Grik." He paused, deciding to go for broke. "But face it: we're aware there are . . . elements of your own crew—officers— over whom you seem to have little control. Elements much more interested in their own political agenda than they are the safety of this Alliance, definitely. Maybe even the safety of your own precious Empire—as that safety is envisioned by the princess. I think given the choice, your vision of your Empire more closely reflects hers than you might be at liberty to admit. All I'm asking is, if you don't get the impression that our preparations are geared toward striking your country, don't immediately spill what you see to those other 'elements' I spoke about. Keep an open mind."

Jenks considered. Here was a chance he'd craved—to see what the Americans and their furry allies were up to beyond their guarded barricades. He wouldn't admit it, but he already knew a little. A few spies had gotten through. But he hadn't been told everything they'd discovered either. There was much truth in what Captain Reddy said about those "other elements," just as there was truth in the man's observation that Commodore Jenks was less than pleased about how those elements operated, or about their influence over his government. He would have to step carefully, but he sensed an opportunity.

"Very well," he said, "I can give my word to that." He smiled sardonically, his sun-bleached mustaches quirking upward. "So long as it is not generally known I have done so."

Matt almost mirrored his expression. "Oh, I don't think it'll hurt for folks to know I've given you a tour. No way to hide it anyway, so we might as well give them a show. But we won't tell anyone you promised not to blab if you don't feel like it. All I ask is, once we enter the secure area, give us the benefit of the doubt."

"On that you have my word, Captain Reddy."

Matt nodded and glanced at his watch. "Very well. I have another interview to attend to. If you'll excuse me for an hour, maybe we can put some of your suspicions to rest." Matt's gaze rested on Okada. "Thanks for your cooperation, Commander." He rang the bell again and Juan reappeared.

"Cap-i-tan?"

"Juan, ask the Marine sentries to escort Commander Okada back to his quarters, if you please; then send in Ensign Laumer." He stood and extended his hand to Jenks. For the first time, the Imperial took it without any apparent hesitation. "I don't believe this will take all that long, actually. Juan will see that you're comfortable and provide any refreshments you might ask for."

"Thank you, Captain. I look forward to our outing."

When Juan closed the door behind the three, Matt resumed his seat and took a deep breath.

"You're sure this is a good idea, Skipper?" Alden asked.

"You got me. I don't know what else we can do. We can only stall the man so long—and his beef is valid. We've been playing him for time and he knows it. If we don't show him *why*, the 'incidents' will only increase—understandably—and sooner or later, any chance we might've ever had for an alliance with his Empire will go over the side." Matt shook his head. "No, it's time we put our cards on the table. Besides, Her Highness, Becky"—he grinned—"knows everything we're up to. It's not fair to ask her to continue keeping secrets from her own people."

"Except these political officers, these Company wardens," Shinya reminded him.

"Of course." Rebecca and O'Casey had told them about the Company watchdogs aboard Jenks's ship, and had described their function in a way that brought the Nazi SS or Gestapo to Matt's mind. Or maybe the Soviet naval political officers Shinya referred to was a better analogy. Either way, they were sinister and apparently powerful figures, and, given the opinions of O'Casey and the princess, dangerous and subversive as well. Matt had been waiting for some sign that Jenks didn't necessarily work with them hand in glove before he made his earlier invitation. Rebecca was certain he didn't, and even O'Casey—who had his own reasons to be wary of Jenks—agreed, but Matt had to be sure. After Jenks's veiled admission, he thought he was. Of course, Jenks could have suspected their concerns and put on an act. . . . Matt shook his head. He couldn't believe it. He didn't like Jenks, but he grudgingly respected him. The few times he'd actually spoken to Commander Billingsly, he'd decided there couldn't have been more difference between his and Jenks's *character*, at least.

Jenks might be an asshole, but somehow Matt sensed he was an honorable, even gentlemanly asshole. Billingsly was just an asshole, with no class at all. He remained as arrogant and condescending as Jenks had been when they first met, and his open, blatant, almost hostile bigotry toward the Lemurians was offensive and unsettling. If all the Honorable New Britain Company was like Billingsly, Matt's destroyermen and their allies might have as much to fear from them as they did from the Grik. But Jenks was pure Navy, according to O'Casey, and Matt was very glad that seemed to make a difference. For a number of reasons.

"Yeah," Matt resumed, "we'll have to convince Jenks to keep them in the dark. I think we can, once we show him what we're up to—and then offer to let him see some of the stuff in action! If he accepts, and I bet he will, maybe we'll have some time to work on him." There was a knock at the door.

"Enter."

Juan swept the door open and Ensign Irvin Laumer stepped inside, hat under his arm, and stood at attention. He was towheaded and lanky, but not particularly tall, and he didn't look quite old enough for the uniform he wore. The seriousness of his expression meant he did have some idea why he was there, however, and Matt felt a tug of uncertainty. From what he'd heard of Laumer, he had high hopes for the boy. The kid had good sense, clearly. He'd been the highest-ranking survivor of S-19's complement, but he'd allowed the more experienced chief of the boat take de facto command. The decision must have been a tough one, because Laumer didn't *seem* the type to defer responsibility. Hopefully that meant, like any good officer, he knew when to take responsibility and when to delegate it. Matt's main concern now was that maybe Laumer felt he had something to prove.

Actually, he did, in a way. All of Matt's senior officers, human and Lemurian, were veterans of fierce fighting now. All but Laumer. If the ensign was ever going to be followed where he led, he *did* have to prove himself, Matt reflected. He only wished Laumer's baptism didn't have to be on such a difficult and potentially important mission. He'd love to send Spanky or Brister, or any of half a dozen others, but he couldn't. They were just too necessary where they were. The simple, hard fact of the matter was that Laumer was the only one he could spare with the experience and technical expertise.

"Sir, Ensign Laumer, reporting as ordered!"

"At ease, Ensign," Matt replied mildly, and gestured at the stool Jenks had just vacated across the desk. "Please have a seat." Irvin sat, still rigid, upon the creaky stool. "Coffee?"

"Uh, no, thank you, sir."

Matt waited a moment, staring at the ensign. He decided to get straight to the point. "I want that submarine," he said simply.

Irvin Laumer nodded. He'd obviously expected as much. "I'll get it for you, sir, if it's the last thing I do."

Alden grunted. "Son, that's the point. We want it, sure, but we don't want it to be the last thing you do. You or the people you'll command."

Matt glanced at the Marine and nodded. "Exactly. We've discussed this at some length and decided your mission will have a hierarchy of agendas. First, of course, you must determine whether she can be salvaged at all. She might not even *be* there anymore. Remember too, given the nature of some of the creatures on this world—and under its seas—it's not imperative that we get the submarine back *as* a submarine, if you get my meaning."

Laumer looked troubled, but nodded. "Yes, sir, I think I do."

"You must *know* you do, because that's the deal. If she's still there, it'll be up to you to decide if you can get her off the beach. Don't fool around too long trying if it's not practical. If you can, swell. You'll have fuel, and Spanky, Gilbert, and Flynn all say at least one of her diesels ought to come to life. If you can get her under way, hopefully Saan-Kakja can provide an escort to get you to Manila. After that, bring her here if you can, but that's not essential either. What is essential is the stuff she's made of. Decide quickly if you can get her off, because if you can't, you've got to strip her— and I mean *strip* her! I want her engines, batteries, wiring, screws, gun, bearings, instruments, sonar—hell, I want every *bolt* you can get out of her; is that understood? Even if you get her all the way back here we might strip her anyway, so that's the absolute top priority. Like I said—and I can't stress this enough—we need what she's made of more than we need her. Her whole, intact carcass would be nice—she's got as much steel as *Walker*—but this is strictly a 'bird in the hand' operation. Get what you *know* you can get."

Irvin gulped. "I understand, Captain."

"Very well. Now." Matt leaned back in his chair. "We can't afford to send much with you, but you'll get what we can spare. You can have five of your submariners if you can get them to volunteer. Concentrate on those with critical engineering and operating skills."

"Flynn?" Irvin asked.

Matt shook his head. "No. Two reasons. First, we need him here. Second, and don't take this wrong; he assured me he has the utmost respect for you, but . . . to be honest, he's had enough of subs in these waters." Matt shrugged. "I already asked him, but . . . well, let's just say we've had a little experience with people who've been through too much and pushed too far." Matt was thinking of his old coxswain Tony Scott. "Sometimes they lose focus and make mistakes," he added in a quiet tone. "We'll use Flynn in the shipyard for now, but he's asked for an infantry regiment, if you can believe that." To Matt's surprise, Laumer actually smiled.

"Yes, sir, I can believe it."

Instead of asking the ensign to elaborate, Matt pushed on: "You'll have two of the prize ships to transport equipment and personnel, and bring back what you can salvage. You won't command the ships, obviously, but you'll be in overall command of the expedition."

"Thank you, sir," Laumer said. "Thanks for the opportunity."

Matt grimaced. "There may be plenty of 'opportunity' to get yourself killed, and I'm ordering you to avoid that. Period. Otherwise, besides those previously mentioned, your orders are to depart Baalkpan aboard the prize USS *Simms* in company with another prize sloop. . . ." He shook his head. "We're really going to have to sort that out."

The destroyermen, 'Cat and human, found it difficult and confusing to use the old terms for sailing warships. A small faction insisted "sloops" ought to be destroyers and "frigates" should be cruisers. This caused contention among the frigate sailors, who thought *they* ought to be destroyers and sloops were mere gunboats. God only knew how weird it would get when they had even bigger ships—and seaplane tender/carriers like *Big Sal*. The fact was, no one of either race wanted to give up the title "destroyerman," no matter what they served on.

"Anyway," Matt continued, "you'll escort *Placca-Mar*." He hoped he said it right. His 'Cat was finally improving, as was his pronunciation. "She's the Home Saan-Kakja's returning to the Filpin Lands aboard, along with plans and some of the large machinery we've completed. Colonel Shinya and the prisoner will also be aboard. The colonel will be escorting Commander Okada, but his primary mission is to take charge of training Saan-Kakja's troops in Manila. While you're with *Placca-Mar*, you'll be under Colonel Shinya's direct command, and if you run into any marauding lizards, his orders will supersede any I've given you today. In other words, feel free to disobey the one about avoiding opportunities to get yourself killed, because you *will* defend Saan-Kakja to the last. Understood?"

Irvin gulped, but nodded. "Aye-aye, sir."

"Barring incident, you'll depart company with *Placca-Mar* in the Sibutu Passage, hug the Sulu Archipelago to Mindanao, and proceed to your destination."

"What about mountain fish, if we run across any?" Irvin asked hesitantly, and Matt looked at him, scratching the back of his neck.

"Sparks—I mean Lieutenant Commander Riggs—is working on stuff. So's Ordnance. I also hope to squeeze some advice out of Jenks, if I can. We'll do everything possible to make sure you have solid communications as well, but"—he shrugged—"who knows? You might wind up on your own."

Irvin knew the entire mission was a test of sorts, as much for the captain to evaluate him as for him to evaluate himself. He'd missed all the fighting and really had little reason to expect such an opportunity—and an opportunity was how he viewed it. Somehow he'd prevail. He had to.

"I've been on my own before, Captain," he said at last. "Sort of. Before you took us off Talaud in the first place, we didn't even know what had happened. Even if we lose communications, I'm confident we'll manage."

Matt looked at him for a long moment, then glanced at the others in the chamber. "I sincerely hope so. I implied earlier that you're the only man we can spare for this, but remember, the war's just begun. We can't spare anyone in the long run."

"No, sir."

As was customary by midafternoon, the rain had stopped by the time Captain Reddy, General Alden, and Commodore Jenks gathered at the base of the great, scorched Galla tree. As was also customary, the remainder of the day would be humid and oppressive and the clothes worn by the little group had barely begun to dry before perspiration replaced the moisture. Sandra, Keje, and Alan Letts had joined them. Shinya had departed to prepare the troops for "inspection," and Matt had asked the Bosun not to attend. Chief Gray uncomfortably agreed. His and Jenks's antagonism toward each other was well-known, and Matt wanted the commodore as comfortable about the tour as possible.

A two-wheeled cart appeared out of the bustling activity of the city, the driver reining his animal just short of the overhead that protected them from the incessant dripping. The cart itself looked like an oversize rickshaw, complete with gaudy decorations. The beast pulling it had never been seen in Baalkpan before it and a large herd of its cousins arrived from Manila a few weeks before. It looked a little like one of the stunted bronto-sarries from a distance, although it was smaller and covered with fur. It also had a shorter neck and tail, even if both were proportionately beefier and more muscular. The head was larger too, with short, palmated antlers.

The Fil-pin 'Cats called them paalkas, although Silva's insidious influence had reached Baalkpan before them and here they were almost universally called pack-mooses, even by the local 'Cats. They were herbivorous marsupials, of all things, and Matt was glad to have them. He wondered why no one had ever imported them to Baalkpan before; they were obviously more sensible draft animals than the ubiquitous brontosaurus. They were much more biddable and, from what he'd seen, at least as smart as a horse. They could even be ridden, although no kind of conventional saddle would serve. They were half again as big as a Belgian draft horse, and any rider would have been perpetually doing the splits. Matt primarily wanted them to pull his light artillery pieces and they should be great for that. Shinya and Brister were working on ways the gun's crews could ride them.

Other creatures that *could* be ridden like a horse had arrived from Manila. They were me-naaks, and nobody objected when their name was changed to "meanies." They looked like long-legged crocodiles that ran on all fours, as they should, but their legs were shaped more like a dog's. They ran like dogs too, fast and focused. Their skin was like a rhino-pig's, thick and covered with long, bristly hair, and they had a heavy, plywood-thick case that protected their vitals. Matt was dubious about them, and admitted they were scary. When he'd first seen them in Manila, they'd borne troops in Saan-Kakja's livery, apparently on errands. The crowds gave them a wide berth and Matt had noticed their jaws were always strapped tightly shut. They seemed to obey well enough, and Saan-Kakja had since assured him that they'd make fine cavalry mounts—once he'd explained the concept to her—as long as a rider didn't mind the fact that his mount's fondest wish was to eat him.

Cavalry, and the mobility it provided, was something Matt had been wanting for a long time. It wasn't something 'Cats had given a great deal of thought to, since, as little as most of them ever envisioned fighting, they'd *never* envisioned fighting an open-field battle. The terrain just didn't suit. For the campaign taking shape in Matt's mind however, cavalry of some sort—or at least mounted infantry or dragoons—would come as a nasty surprise for the Grik indeed.

"How . . . interesting," observed Jenks, staring at the conveyance.

Matt shook off his reverie and smiled. "More practical than walking." He gestured around at the aftermath of the squall. "Especially in this muck." Sandra smiled at him and gravitated to his side.

Jenks looked at her briefly, then shook his head. Apparently, what he'd been about to say or ask wasn't something he wanted to discuss just then. He peered into the cart. "Is there space for all of us?" he asked doubtfully.

The paalka dragged the cart through the bustling city. There was so much activity that, except for the remaining damage, it was difficult for Matt to tell a massive battle had raged around and through Baalkpan not so very long before. It was easy to remember they were at war however, since much of the seemingly chaotic commotion was geared toward military preparation. Squads of troops squelched by in cadence, either toward or from the expanded drill field. Quite a few of these wore the distinctive black-and-yellow livery of Saan-Kakja.

Matt, Alden, and Letts returned the salute of a platoon of Marines that marched by on the left, heading for the parade ground. Matt had finally allowed the reconstitution of the Marines as an independent force. They'd be needed as such and the 'Cats' various guard (or, increasingly, army) regiments had sufficient veteran NCOs and officers now to lead them. The Marine uniform was also strikingly regular, now that it had become official. It consisted of a dark blue kilt with red piping along the hem for veterans. NCOs sported red stripes encircling their kilts, from the bottom up, to designate their rank. All wore thick white articulated rhino-pig leather armor over their chests as well. Stamped bronze helmets like those the destroyermen wore (except for the ear holes) completed the basic uniform. Baldrics, straps, belts, and backpacks were all black leather, and had become universal among Allied forces.

The "Army" had begun a similar attempt to provide uniforms for its troops, but the colors varied, since its forces represented different members of the Alliance. In the case of Baalkpan, which fielded numerous regiments, the leather armor was a natural dark brown and the kilts were bright green. This was the color of Nakja-Mur's livery and Adar hadn't changed it. The various regiments had gold numbers embroidered on their kilts.

Matt, and everyone else, had been surprised and gratified to learn that the Aryaalan and B'mbaadan regiments (formerly bitter foes) had been integrated by Lord Rolak and Queen Maraan and had chosen red-and-black kilts, also with regimental numbers, and gray leather breastplates.

As much as Baalkpan's industry had recovered, and even leaped ahead after the battle, none of this would have been possible without Saan-Kakja's support. She'd ordered as much material and supplies, and as many troops and artisans, be brought forward as her nation could realistically afford. Until the frontier could be pushed back, Baalkpan remained the front line of the war, and without her aid, another battle like the last would have finished it. Of course, *Amagi* was no longer a threat, but as things had stood, she wouldn't have been needed.

A lot of Baalkpan's runaway population had returned as well. Perhaps goaded by shame that they'd left in the first place instead of defending their home, they set to work with a will. Matt believed that, with the returns and additions, Baalkpan's population was now greater than it had been when his old, battered destroyer first steamed into the bay.

Smoking pitch assaulted their sinuses as the paalka drew them past the expanded ropewalk, and sparks flew from forges as swordsmiths shaped their blades. Iron had been known to the People, but had been little used except for weapons. Now, an abundance of good steel wreckage was available, as well as a new steady supply of iron ore from the interior, and the Lemurians were drawing out of the Bronze Age at last. Matt watched Sandra's face as the sparks fell and sizzled on the damp ground. He knew what she was thinking. The various Lemurian cultures had been very fine, and with some exceptions, almost idyllic before they came here. Now all was in a state of flux, changing forever to meet the necessities of a nightmarish war. For a bittersweet instant, Matt wondered what changes the war back home would bring to America.

They eased through the congested area surrounding the new sawmill. The big, circular blades sprayed chips and sawdust in great arcs, while brontosarries plodded through a slurry of muck, turning a massive windlass that transferred its rotation through a series of gears that spun the great blades. The quaint display of ingenuity had come from the quirky minds of the Mice. They had certainly risen to the challenge of this new world, Matt thought proudly, as had all his destroyermen.

As they neared the waterfront, the buildings were no longer elevated. Instead, all the shops and warehouses stood right at ground level. A great berm lay beyond them with but a single gated opening, and swarms of workers thronged in and out of the bottleneck. A squad of Marine sentries watched keenly for unknown or suspicious faces. Fortunately, the only faces they had to examine closely were human, and the hundred-odd remaining

Amer-i-caans were well-known to them. When the paalka brought them to the gate, the crowd parted and the sentries waved them through.

If anything, the chaos beyond the gate seemed more apparent than in the heart of the bustling city, but only at a glance. Here, the warehouses, workshops, and open-air industry that sprawled around the basin teemed with what only appeared to be disconnected activity. The racket of tools, shouted commands, and roaring furnaces was overwhelming, and smoke and dank steam hung like fog. In the distance, across the yard, the skeletal frames of numerous ships rose above the activity and haze. Matt and his companions quickly perceived the underlying order—they'd all spent considerable time there, after all—and Matt suspected Jenks saw it as well.

"Here we are, Commodore," Sandra said brightly as Matt helped her down from the rickshaw. Jenks hopped lightly down with the unexpected grace of an athlete and stared around with all the indications of amazement. Alden, Keje, and Letts joined them, and while the others stared about with expressions of proud accomplishment, Keje continued glaring at Jenks. He hadn't been in favor of letting this stranger view their greatest secrets and he still didn't trust the man. His initial dislike had only been intensified by the frequent attempts at espionage, and now they were going to give him a guided tour! He trusted Matt's judgment, and intellectually he knew they had little choice, but he still didn't like it.

"Most impressive, my dear," Jenks replied, somewhat awkwardly. He glanced at his escort. "Gentlemen. Most impressive indeed. You have accomplished all this in the three months since your battle?"

"No, sir," said Letts. "The basics were here when we first arrived. We added a lot while we were preparing for the enemy, and not much was damaged in the fighting. Evidently, they wanted these facilities preserved. Baalkpan would've made them a good base from which to go after our other friends—as well as your people, eventually."

"Indeed," came Jenks's noncommittal reply.

Letts looked at Captain Reddy and saw the nod. This was his show now. "If you would all follow me, I'll point out some of the more interesting things we've been working on."

They trudged past furnace rooms from which an endless relay of naked, panting 'Cats pushed wheelbarrows loaded with copper round shot. These they brought to waiting carts, where others stood with heavy leather gloves to transfer the still-hot spheres. There were hisses of steam and scorched wood when the shot dropped on the cart's wet timbers. Most of the party smiled and returned the waves of the workers. Jenks said nothing, but clearly took note.

Moving along, they reached one of the several foundries that now dotted the basin. Great bronze gun tubes, each with carts of their own, waited in patient rows for their journey to the boring and reaming loft. These new guns had rough, sand-cast bores and would still be smooth-bores after reaming, but even as their interior diameters had increased, the quality and sophistication of their shape had improved and the weight of metal they required was much reduced. Most of the original guns that had defended Baalkpan had already been recast, and generally, they could get five or six guns from four of the earlier, much cruder weapons. The next foundry they passed was pouring molten iron under an open-sided shed and gouts of sparks and fiery meteors arced out and sizzled on a damp beam decking roped off for safety.

Jenks saw all this and was much impressed. Matt and Sandra talked excitedly of what they'd accomplished and Letts seemed almost jubilant. Even Keje had lost some of his earlier overt unfriendliness. As often as he must have seen it now, he still seemed to have an air of wonder. A long, high shed stood nearer the water, covering an assortment of bizarre shapes in various stages of evident completion. Before they headed in that direction, the group was distracted by a series of shouts followed by what sounded like a rough volley of musket fire. The noise quickly settled into a sustained roar.

Brevet Major Benjamin Mallory twisted his arm to stretch the aching muscles. His T-shirt and Lemurian-made dungarees were sweat blotched and stained, and a dark rag dangled and swayed from his belt as he grabbed the wrench and strained against the final bolt.

"There," he said to no one in particular, "my built-in torque wrench says that's about right." He stepped back from the odd-looking machine and dragged the filthy rag across his forehead before he plopped the hat back on his head. It was the only item remaining to him that had once been Army brown. The OD pistol belt and leather holster were his, but they were essentially the same as everyone else's. The machine was an en-gine—he hoped. It was a vague copy of an upright, four-cylinder Wright Gypsy that would serve as a prototype power plant for the airframe de-sign they'd—tentatively—settled on. It was inherently more difficult to balance a four-cylinder engine than one with six cylinders, but they were trying to keep things as simple as possible for now. The cylinders them-selves were air-cooled legacies of the crashed PBY, and they'd dredged up as much of the old plane as they could hook from its scattered resting place on the bottom of Baalkpan Bay. They'd recovered only one of the engines, but fortunately, it wasn't the one they'd already removed a couple of damaged cylinders from. It *had* been damaged beyond repair by a couple of holes through the crankcase and a warped crankshaft sustained when the spinning prop hit the water, but twelve cylinders, fifteen pushrods, eleven piston rods, eighteen valves, and nine pistons were still up to spec. They'd serve his purpose of testing the *rest* of the new engine they'd built from scratch.

Seaman (maybe Ensign now, if his transfer came through) Fred Reynolds stood nearby poring over a black-bound book with red writing on it. It was a copy of Brimm and Boggess's *Aircraft Engine Maintenance* they'd found in the tool kit of the PBY's doubtless long-dead flight mechanic. It was exactly like a similar copy Ben had done his best to memorize in pilot training. He liked to think he *had* memorized enough to build something like the simple engine before him on the stand, but when they inevitably went on to build bigger and better things, the wealth of formulas, diagrams, and general tidbits of information including things as mundane as hand file designs would prove invaluable. Even when one considered the relatively large, eclectic library of *Walker*'s dead surgeon, "Doc" Stevens, and the many technical manuals they'd off-loaded from the two destroyers before their final sortie, it was, in many ways, the single most precious book they possessed. Some of Adar's Sky Priest acolytes had already made a handwritten copy, and others were being copied from it.

The book was already invaluable to poor Reynolds, who stared at the pages like they were written in ancient Greek. Ben stifled a chuckle. Apparently, Reynolds had finally decided what to strike for; he wanted to fly. He'd said he wanted excitement, but he was a little guy, and that would have made Ordnance hell—or so he believed. Ben suspected that in reality, the kid was scared to death of Dennis Silva—completely understandable—and since Silva was the most . . . visible representative of that division and had as yet untested limitations on his authority . . . the fledgling Air Corps, or Naval Air Arm, or whatever it would be called, probably seemed like a comparatively safer billet. Ben chuckled aloud at that, unheard over the machine noises emanating from the rest of the shop.

He glanced at the only other human in sight: Commander Perry Brister. Formerly *Mahan*'s engineering officer and now general engineering minister of the entire Alliance, the dark-haired young man was making a final inspection of the fuel line leading to the simple, crude carburetor. Ben knew Perry had other things to do that day, but he'd always liked fooling with small engines, he'd said, and he wanted to be there when they cranked it up.

"Looks good here," Perry rasped. His once soft voice had never recovered from all the yelling he did during the great battle. Ben looked at the two Lemurians poised near the propeller. One, a sable-furred 'Cat with a polished 7.7-millimeter cartridge case stuck through a hole in his ear, grinned.

"You boys ready?" Ben asked.

"You bet," answered the 'Cat Ben called Tikker. Mallory shook his head and grinned. It was Captain Tikker now. Stepping to a small console, he flipped a switch.

"Contact!" he shouted.

"Contact!" chorused the 'Cats, and, heaving the propeller blade up as high as they could reach, they brought it down with all their might. For a moment, the motor coughed, sputtered, and gasped while the 'Cats jumped back. With a jerk, the wooden propeller came to a stop.

"Switch off!" announced Mallory, and the two 'Cats approached the propeller again. They hadn't thoroughly tested the remote throttle adjustment, and Brister stepped forward and squirted a little fuel in the carburetor. Nodding, he joined Ben.

"Contact!"

This time, the propeller spun with an erratic, explosive, *phut, phut, phut!* sound, backfired, burped, then became a popping, vibrating blur. Brister hurried forward, careful of the spinning blades, and tinkered with the throttle linkage. Slowly, the vibration diminished and the smooth roar overwhelmed their cheers.

"This way!" Letts shouted over the din, and they hurried toward the noise. Another shed, smaller than the first and enclosed on all sides, was nearby. Letts moved a curtain aside and the racket flooded out. In he went, and Jenks was swept along with the rest. Oil lamps dimly lit the interior of the shed, but there were small, brightly glowing objects placed near large, complicated-looking machines. Lemurians and a few men toiled at those machines with singular concentration in spite of the noise emanating from another brightly lit area toward the back of the shed. As he passed them, Jenks saw the machines were turning and spinning, throwing coiled pieces of metal aside. They were also noisy—or would have been—without the cacophonous roar. Most were fairly straightforward. He'd seen their like in Imperial factories: lathes, mills, etc. Great leather belts whirled around pulleys attached to the high ceiling and transferred their rotation to the machines. A very few of the machines had no belts whatsoever, but seemed to run off insulated copper cables terminated at the same source as the brilliant white lights. The mystery fascinated him as much as the roar that grew even louder as they approached.

A haze of smoky fumes was gathering in the light, swirling in a strange, artificial wind. In it stood three men and a couple of Lemurians staring intently at a relatively small machine vibrating on a stand. A big paddle of some kind whirled to a blur at one end of it.

"Mr. Mallory!" Matt shouted at one of the men who stood, hands on hips. He turned.

"Captain Reddy!" There was a huge smile on the man's bearded face. "Good afternoon, sir." He motioned at the machine and eyed a set of gauges on his console. "Temps are a little variable on the cylinders, but that's to be expected with an air-cooled in-line. The production models'll be liquid-cooled and heavier, but the horsepower ought to be similar. The main thing is that it looks like we've solved the crankcase and oil pump issues—at least for straight and level." For the first time Mallory noticed Jenks and his smile faded a little.

"It's okay," Matt shouted. "It's time."

Mallory shrugged as if to say, *You're the skipper*, and motioned to one of the 'Cats stationed near another panel. "Bring her up, Tikker!"

The sable-furred 'Cat with a shiny brass tube in his ear nodded and advanced a small lever. Immediately, the noise increased and the paddle-like object whirred even faster, redoubling the gale of wind and noxious fumes. Jenks began to feel a little ill. Sandra coughed violently and patted Captain Reddy on the arm. Matt looked at her and nodded, noting Jenks's expression as well. He patted Mallory, and when he got his attention, he made a "cut it" gesture.

Tikker noticed and backed the throttle down until the engine finally wheezed and died. The sudden, relative silence was overwhelming.

"Mr. Mallory, you're going to choke all your workers," Matt said with a grin. Ben looked around. If anything but excitement made him feel light-headed, it didn't show.

"Well, yes, sir," he said, beaming, "but it works! The damn thing works! Uh, begging your pardon." He glanced at Jenks and his euphoria slipped a notch. "Yeah, it stinks, I guess, but we've been trying to keep things under wraps."

"I know. That's over now." Matt clapped Ben on his good shoulder and nodded congratulations to the others. "Besides, it looks like we'll be ready for flight testing soon and there's no way to keep *that* a secret. I think it's time Commodore Jenks, at least, sees what we're up to."

Jenks finally surrendered to a coughing fit of his own, but when he composed himself, he pointed at the engine. "What is that thing?" he asked. "Some sort of weapon?"

"Not by itself," hedged one of the other workers who'd joined the group. He was a former *Mahan* machinist's mate named "Miami" Tindal.

Tikker stepped closer. "We put it on a plane, and it'll be a weapon," he said excitedly. A lot of Lemurians acted uncomfortable around the Impe-rials and were hesitant to speak to them. Tikker never seemed uncomfort-able talking to anyone.

"What's a 'plane'?" Jenks asked.

Matt looked at Ben. "If you and . . . Captain Tikker would accompany us?" He paused, his amused, understanding eyes on Perry. "You as well, Commander Brister."

Workers raised awnings to vent the exhaust while together, the growing entourage returned to the larger, open shed. There they showed Jenks an array of ungainly contraptions. Some were mere skeletons, made from laminated bamboo strips, cannibalized even before they were complete. A couple had a kind of taut fabric stretched across their bones to which some kind of sealant or glue had been applied. One, the nearest to the shop, rested on a cart or truck much like the earlier gun tubes. This one not only appeared almost finished, but was painted a medium dark blue. There were darker blue roundels—significant devices of some kind, Jenks was sure—in several places, with large white stars and small red dots painted within them.

"So this is it?" Matt asked appreciatively. It didn't look much like the NC craft he remembered seeing pictures of. If anything, it looked like a miniature PBY. The fuselage/hull form was virtually identical, except there was a single open-air cockpit behind a slip of salvaged Plexiglas where the flight deck would have been. Another open cockpit was positioned halfway to the tail, where the PBY had possessed a pair of observation blisters. The large single wing was supported by an arrangement of struts instead of being attached to the fuselage by a faired compartment. It was easy to see the motor would go in the empty space between the wing and fuselage—with the prop spinning mere feet behind the pilot's head.

"What about wing floats?" Matt asked. By the tone of his voice, he was reviving an old argument.

"They'll be cranked down mechanically by the observer/mechanic in the aft cockpit." Ben looked a little sheepish. "I know you wanted to keep it simple, Skipper, but this is a lot simpler than putting fixed floats on a lower wing. Not to mention we don't have to *make* those lower wings." He gestured at one of the incomplete skeletons. "This way she'll be lighter, faster, more maneuverable, and honestly, we should be able to put her down on rougher seas. With that bottom wing so close to the water, I was really worried about that."

"That's fine, Ben. I told you, when it comes to flying you're the boss, and your arguments do have merit. I just want to make sure the things aren't overly complicated. Like the ships, I want a lot of good ones, not a few of the best."

"I agree, sir. But with this design, I think we get a little of both."

Jenks interrupted. "Flying . . . you mean to say that thing will . . . *fly*?"

"Hopefully." Matt nodded toward a large heap of twisted wreckage piled in the space between the two buildings. It was all that remained of the crashed PBY. "That one did."

"Not very well," Jenks observed skeptically, "if its present condition is any indication. And that one is metal. Why not these new ones?"

"You'd be amazed how well it flew," Matt answered wistfully, "and for how long. But our enemy managed to knock it down. Do you think you could shoot down a flying target?"

Jenks didn't answer.

"Anyway, the metal it was made of is called aluminum. It came from our old world, and I don't know when or if we'll ever be able to make it here. We're having enough trouble with iron. When we get that sorted out, we'll try steel—besides what we're salvaging from the enemy ship. I'm afraid the lizards are probably ahead of us there. . . . Anyway, once we get real steel, and plenty of it, you'll be amazed at what we can do."

Sandra pulled him down to whisper in his ear and Matt's face became grim, but he nodded. He straightened and looked Jenks in the eye.

"Now we're going to show you something else," he said. "So far, you probably haven't seen anything that would assure you we aren't a threat to your empire."

"Quite the contrary, Captain," Jenks answered honestly. "I could even argue that what I have seen here today proves you are a threat that should be quashed before you reach your stride, as it were." There was no hostility in Jenks's tone, only a dispassionate statement of fact.

"Very well. I'll prove it to you. I'll show you something that, up until now, we've been willing to kill your spies, if necessary, to keep them from seeing. I guess you could call it an industrial achievement of sorts"—he waved around—"but not like these others. Mainly, it's an admission of vulnerability, I guess, more than anything." His green eyes turned cold. "Something I damn sure wouldn't show you if I was trying to intimidate you with our power. That alone should convince you we mean you no harm."

"Does this have to do with your mysterious iron-hulled steamer you've been hiding from us since we arrived?" Jenks asked quietly.

"Follow me," was all Matt said.

The group gathered on the dock overlooking the old shipyard basin. Oily brown water coiled with tendrils of iridescent purple and blue lapped gently against the old fitting-out pier. It was quiet where they stood, although considerable activity bustled nearby. Four of the great Homes had been flooded down across the mouth of the inlet in two ranks. Work was under way to seal the gaps between them, fore and aft, so there would ultimately be a pair of continuous walls from land to land.

A single "wall" was the customary dry-dock technique Lemurians had always used to build their great ships in the first place. Inspired by that, and realizing the need for a permanent dry dock, Spanky and Perry had designed one. It was a hard sell at first, since the effort required *Walker* to remain on the bottom even longer. Also, even though he helped design the dry dock, Brister had made a reluctant but strong argument against taking labor and resources away from construction of the new Allied fleet. It was actually easier, he'd reasoned, to build entirely new ships than it would be to fix *Walker*. He'd been in favor of using the Lemurian method to refloat the ship—and then only so they could stabilize her and prevent further deterioration. Perhaps someday they could attempt repairs. In the meantime, they should concentrate all their efforts on the new construction. As for the dry dock, it would certainly be a useful convenience, but one they could postpone.

Spanky argued that a permanent dry dock was essential, not only to refloat *Walker*—and do it right—but because the new construction Brister referred to would be much more prone to require repairs below the waterline than other ships the Lemurians built. He vividly remembered how difficult it had been to remove one of *Mahan*'s propellers and install it on *Walker*. With the ravenous nature of the aquatic life on this different Earth, no underwater work could be performed without elaborate preparation. Besides, once they got her up, Spanky wasn't ready to write *Walker* off. No one had any illusions that repairing the badly mauled destroyer would be an easy task; it might even be impossible. But they had to try. They owed her that much.

As commander of all Allied forces, Captain Reddy had to make the decision, and he'd agonized over it, wondering if he was being entirely objective. He wanted his ship back, and everyone (particularly the Lemurians) wanted him to have her. She'd been instrumental in achieving every success they'd enjoyed, and the dilapidated old four stacker had become a powerful symbol to everyone involved in opposing the scourge of the Grik. The problem was, until they could get at her, there was no way to know if she could even be repaired, and Matt was realistic enough to know Brister was right: they *had* to have those new ships.

Spanky, Jim Ellis, and Sandra had been anxious too, but for a different reason. They knew they couldn't influence his decision, but they also knew how important it was not only to the future of the man who had to make it, but to all of their futures as well. Matthew Reddy had lost . . . a piece of his soul . . . when his ship went down. Only when he knew she was safe and afloat and alive did they think he'd gain it back. And he had to gain it back. Spanky's insistent argument that they needed a real dry dock—one way or the other—was finally sufficient to gain Matt's support.

It was still necessary to flood down the Homes—twice as many as would have been required to simply refloat the ship—since they had to create a dry lane in which to work. It would take longer, but the wait would be worth it. The Lemurian city of Baalkpan would have a real, dedicated, honest-to-goodness dry dock, and the implications of that went far beyond simply pumping out and patching up a single battered, overage destroyer.

What Jenks saw was a lot of heavy, new-looking machinery being erected, and he recognized much of it in principle, as well as the strange variety of crude, open air, steam engines. Tarred canvas hoses were coiled in heaps and a pair of large cranes were under construction. Then his eyes rested on the unfamiliar, scarred, and dreary structures protruding from the water. He gasped.

"It has sunk!" he exclaimed. "Your iron-hulled steamer, your *Walker*, was sunk!"

"She was badly damaged in the battle," Matt confirmed woodenly, "and barely managed to make it here. We'll try to refloat her, but we've got no idea if it's even possible. She might be damaged beyond repair."

Jenks turned a sympathetic glance to Matt. He fully understood the trauma of losing a ship and wondered if that might explain a lot of Captain Reddy's distance. Of course, he chided himself, not having known of the loss, he'd possibly been less than sensitive himself. "I didn't know," he managed. "Nobody knew."

"That was our intention. You keep wondering if we're a threat to you, but how are we to know you're not a threat to us?" Matt shook his head. "I don't think you could *conquer* us. No offense, but based on what we've learned from the princess and . . . Well, we're pretty secure here now. We've stood against a more massive assault than I think you could ever mount. Our concern is, we already *have* an enemy and we have to strike as quickly as we can. As much as we'd like to be friends with your Empire, we can't afford to be distracted right now. We have to go after the Grik with everything we have, and that *would* leave us vulnerable here. We're not really even asking for a true military alliance, much as we'd like one. We just want you to leave us alone!"

"Releasing the princess into our care would go a long way toward assuring that," Jenks said with a trace of sarcasm.

"Possibly, but she doesn't *want* to be released, does she?" Sandra suddenly interjected with a passion that disconcerted Jenks. He'd been surprised she was even present. Different people had different customs, but he'd never met any culture that encouraged women to speak so boldly, or even allowed their presence in situations such as this. The rules were different for nobility of course, but the Americans didn't have a nobility. . . . Did they? Perhaps they'd been influenced by the Lemurians. Lemurian females clearly enjoyed a status here the likes of which he'd never seen. Maybe the scarcity of American women gave them more power? No, he rejected that. He knew Miss Tucker held the rank of lieutenant and was their Minister of Medicine. She clearly had real status and felt no constraints in demonstrating it. Odd.

"I think she has more reason to fear for her safety aboard your ship than she does here," Sandra continued. "You may not have noticed, but she's something of a heroine to the people of this city. If they ever found out something happened to her while she was in your care, there probably *would* be war, and there wouldn't be anything I or Matt or anyone else could do about it—even if we wanted to."

She sighed, and Jenks saw the pain on her face. "None of us wants or needs such a stupid, wasteful war. There would be terrible losses on both sides, and no matter who eventually 'won,' both of us would ultimately lose in the end," she said with certainty. "We don't have *time* to let the Grik catch their breath, and we need every warrior we have to face them— just as I think you need all your troops and ships to avert threats of your own. To *your* east, perhaps?"

Her last punch was a good one, judging by Jenks's expression, even if it was just a guess. Rebecca and O'Casey had described other humans east of the empire who had been a growing threat. They hadn't known of any recent, open confrontations, but they'd been gone a long time and Jenks had certainly been jumpy about something from the start. Their revelations had practically pinpointed the location of the heart of the Empire as well.

"Perhaps you are right," Jenks temporized, still overcoming his surprise. "Perhaps we both have more pressing concerns than fighting one another. But even if you are right about that, surely you can see why I personally chafe at this interminable delay? Honestly, how long must my squadron languish here while it might be needed elsewhere?"

Matt pointed to a small forest of masts clustered beyond the point, where the new fitting-out pier was. These were not just more captured Grik ships under repair. They were new ships, built and fitting out along the same lines as the first human/Lemurian frigates that had performed so well in the previous battles. This construction was different however. Structurally as stout and almost identical to their predecessors, these were steam powered with a central screw propeller. Matt disliked what he considered the Imperial's dangerously exposed paddle wheels, and now that they knew the Grik had cannons, he'd insisted they not take any chances that a single lucky hit might put a ship out of action.

"Over there is one of the main reasons I invited you here today. The *main* reason." He paused. "Why don't you see for yourself?" he asked. "In just a few weeks, we'll mount an expedition to assess the situation in

Aryaal, and possibly a few other places. Come with me. By the time we return, we'll know whether or not we can push the Grik on our own terms, or if we'll have to continue preparations for a more costly campaign. Either way, with that knowledge, I hope to be free to escort Her Highness home."

Commander Walter Billingsly was writing furiously in his journal, quill scritching violently on the coarse paper and spattering little drips and blobs among the words. The writing style was a reflection of his personality: get to the point, regardless of the mess, and do it at a furious pace. Today, he was most furious to learn Commodore Jenks had been given a tour of the "apes" industrial center and he had not been officially informed, nor had he been allowed to send any "escorts" along. Jenks's growing independent-mindedness regarding this entire fiasco was becoming increasingly tiresome. His hand stilled when he heard the sounds of the commodore being piped back aboard. Quickly, he capped the inkwell, wiped his quill on a stained handkerchief, and sanded his most recent passage. Closing the leather-bound book, he stood and straightened his overtight tunic and rounded the desk on his way to the door and the companionway beyond.

On deck, he moved to intercept the commodore as soon as the side party was dismissed.

"What is the meaning of this, Jenks?" he demanded quietly, but with an edge. One must always observe the proprieties of the fiction that the Navy actually controlled its ships.

"The meaning of what, *Commander*?" Jenks replied through clenched teeth. He was clearly angered by Billingsly's tone, but also somewhat . . . distracted.

Billingsly straightened, glancing about. He had a lot of men on this ship, some known, others secret, but the vast majority were loyal Navy men. The charade must be maintained.

"Might I have a word with you, sir? In private?"

Jenks seemed to focus. "I suppose," he muttered resignedly. Raising his voice, he addressed Lieutenant Grimsley. "Lieutenant, there will be an unscheduled boat alongside shortly, I shouldn't wonder. They'll request our coaling and victualing requirements for an extended period. Say, two months. Have a list ready when they arrive, if you please."

"Of course, Commodore," Grimsley replied, eyebrows arched in surprise.

Billingsly was equally surprised, but said nothing as he followed the commodore down the companionway to his quarters. Inside, Jenks tossed his still-damp hat on his desk, undid the top buttons of his tunic, and loosened his cravat. Pouring a single small glass of amber liquid, he relaxed into his chair with a sigh. The stern gallery windows were open for ventilation, but it was still oppressively hot. Without waiting for an invitation, Billingsly took a seat in front of the desk.

"I take it the Americans and their Apes have finally agreed to return the princess to us?" he ventured. "Even so, two months would seem . . . uncharacteristically parsimonious. They have not stinted our supplies before, and such a quantity might not see us home."

"Her Highness still insists on returning home with her 'friends,'" Jenks announced. "I spoke with her myself just prior to returning to the ship. You will be glad to know she is well, happy, and thriving," he added with a barb.

"But . . ."

For once, Jenks saw Billingsly's perpetual scowl dissolve into an expression of complete confusion. He had to stifle a sense of amusement and satisfaction over the bloated bastard's discomfiture. "In slightly under three weeks' time, *Achilles* will accompany an Allied squadron to the place they call Aryaal and perhaps points west and north, in an attempt to discover the current dispositions of these Grik of theirs. Captain Reddy made the offer, and after consulting with the princess, I accepted. I consider it an invaluable opportunity to assess the strategic threat posed by the Grik, as well as our hosts. We will be going as observers only and will not engage in hostilities if any do, in fact, occur. If they do, at the very least I will have the opportunity of seeing the Grik for myself and I'll learn quite a bit about the military capability of this Alliance of theirs as well."

Billingsly's scowl returned and deepened while Jenks spoke. "You should not . . . *must* not make a decision like that without consulting me!" he said menacingly.

"I must and I did make the decision, Commander," Jenks replied. "The offer was phrased in a 'take it or leave it, now or never' fashion," Jenks lied smoothly, "and I saw no choice but to accept."

"Of course you had a choice!" Billingsly countered hotly. "They will never send the princess on this 'expedition' of theirs! With the cream of their naval force otherwise engaged, we could easily take her and be gone!"

"Past those bloody great guns in the fort?" Jenks replied, his own voice rising. "You must be mad."

"Plans could be made. They already have been," he hinted. "With a judicious use of force, a few diversions, and a bit of mischief here and there, we could be gone before they could possibly respond."

Jenks paused, considering his next words carefully. He knew they could condemn him of treason in any Company court. A naval inquiry might see things differently, but who was to say how things now stood after their long absence? He had no choice. "You are forgetting their iron-hulled steamer. I have seen it now, and I tell you it could easily catch us even if we proceeded under full steam for the entire trip—which we certainly cannot do. They intend to leave it here to ensure against any such scheme as you suggest."

Billingsly's expression suddenly became blank, unreadable. He took a breath. "A point," he said. Then an incomprehensible thing occurred; Billingsly smiled. The expression was so foreign to his face that it almost seemed to crack under the strain. "You make a valid point," he continued more earnestly. "And I apologize for my earlier rashness. You have clearly scored a coup! A major intelligence-gathering opportunity! I congratulate you."

Taken aback, Jenks stared at the man. Billingsly's mood had changed so abruptly and uncharacteristically, Jenks couldn't avoid a creeping suspicion. But if Billingsly somehow knew he'd lied about *Walker*'s condition, he would have arrested and usurped him on the spot. Wouldn't he? Moreover, the opportunity was just as significant as Jenks had argued, after all. Perhaps the inscrutable Company man had simply recognized that in an apparent flash of insight, just as it seemed.

"Well, then . . ." Jenks said. "Very well."

"I will, of course, remain here aboard *Ajax* in your absence, to continue to advance our interests and ensure the Apes understand we have not forgotten our princess," Billingsly said.

Jenks was actually relieved. He'd expected Billingsly to demand to come along and he really didn't want him breathing down his neck. Captain Rajendra of *Ajax* was a good officer and would keep him in check. Still a little disconcerted by his good fortune, Jenks spoke a little hesitantly: "Of course. Um, I don't expect you to curtail your . . . surreptitious activities, but please do try harder to avoid being caught. A temporary cessation, at least, might actually be in order. Perhaps they'll drop their guard."

"An excellent suggestion, Commodore. Perhaps they will think, with you and *Achilles* away, they have less reason to fear. I will encourage that perception for a time." Billingsly stood. "Perhaps, at long last, we will see some movement here!" he said cheerfully. "By your leave?"

"Indeed."

Commander Billingsly created what he considered a reassuring smile and left the commodore's quarters. In the passageway beyond, his more comfortable scowl returned. "Damn him!" he muttered to himself, a kaleidoscope of thoughts whirling in his mind. He passed a midshipman—he didn't know his name—in the passageway.

"You there. Boy," he snarled.

The youth forced himself to pause, an expression of controlled terror on his face. Billingsly's proclivities were well-known—as was his power to indefinitely delay a midshipman's appointment to lieutenant. "Sir."

"Run along to Lieutenant Truelove, with my compliments, and ask him to join me in my quarters!"

Visibly relieved, the midshipman raced off.

C aptain Hisashi Kurokawa, formerly of His Imperial Japanese Majesty's Ship *Amagi*, followed obediently behind his "masters" as they were escorted
through the dark, dank, labyrinthine passageways
of what was roughly translated as "the Palace of
Creation," toward the Holy Chamber of the Celestial Mother herself. He remained fully erect as he
strode, carefully groomed and outwardly confident in his meticulously
restored uniform complete with all his medals and many other meaningless, gaudy decorations he'd added for effect. Inwardly, he was terrified,
and he'd learned enough about Grik body language—particularly that of
the Hij—to know his masters weren't quite as collected as they tried to
appear. That Tsalka, General Esshk, and Kurokawa had actually achieved
this audience and not merely been killed out of hand seemed a good sign.
At least the Celestial Mother wanted to hear what they had to say. Chances
were, worst case, they'd be allowed to destroy themselves and not simply be
torn to shreds. Regardless, he knew his masters had some fast—convincing—
talking to do if any of them were to have any hope of survival.

Tsalka, still dressed in the fine robes of his office as Imperial Regent-
Consort of Ceylon and "Sire" of all India, had cautioned Kurokawa to say
nothing unless directly addressed, and for once, for his very life, he'd better prostrate himself before the Celestial Mother. A formal bow simply
wouldn't do. Tsalka seemed the most concerned, and he nervously fiddled
with his robes as they drew closer to the chamber. General Esshk was at
least as outwardly calm as Kurokawa. Resplendent in his crimson cape,
bronze armor, and polished, crested helmet, he still reminded Kurokawa
of a fuzzy, reptilian caricature of a Roman tribune. He alone seemed

oblivious to the heavily armed escort that accompanied them and only the occasional nervous twitch of his stumpy, dark-plumed tail beneath the cape betrayed any concern at all.

Of course, to his credit—Kurokawa supposed—Esshk's concern was more for the survival of his species than for himself. He knew how critical were the observations and ideas the three of them brought to this interview. If the Celestial Mother disregarded their arguments—that to defeat the ancient "Prey That Got Away," all the Grik must make profound, fundamental changes to their precious culture that had thrived in its present form for thousands of years—the ultimate foundation of that culture was doomed. Worse, from Esshk's perspective, failure to adapt could mean the extermination of his very species. Somehow, the Celestial Mother, the keeper and protector of that culture, must be convinced that change was essential—at least temporarily—and he, Tsalka, and the Japanese "hunter" named Kurokawa were indispensible as the only possible agents of that change.

Finally, the Holy Chamber opened before them and Kurokawa got his first glimpse of it, and the Celestial Mother herself. The chamber wasn't much different from Tsalka's he'd seen in Ceylon, except in size. Flowering ivies carpeted the floor and crept up the walls, the farthest of which was lost in the distant gloom. They constituted the only real decoration besides the throne itself, situated in the center of the chamber and bathed in sunlight that entered through an opening high above. A complex system of ingenious mirrors made sure that whatever time of day it was, sunlight always reflected downward upon the intricately carved and gilded throne, bathing it with its warming rays. Absently, Kurokawa wondered where the monster sprawled whenever it rained.

The Celestial Mother was immense. He'd been told roughly what to expect by Esshk, but he was still taken aback. She was at least three times as big as Esshk, who was big for a Grik, and she was incredibly, grossly, shockingly obese to such a remarkable degree as to defy imagination. He was instantly reminded of the mythical, flightless Chinese dragons, except the Celestial Mother had none of their sinewy grace. More like a monstrous grub, he thought. Rolls of fat bulged beneath her skin and drooped from the saddlelike throne like half-empty sacks of grain. Jowls hung just as alarmingly around her polished, bleached-white teeth, and her carefully manicured and painted claws extended, unused, much farther than normal beyond fat, stumpy fingers. Her fur was unlike any Grik's he'd seen before, either. Instead of the rather downy, striated, earth-tone covering he was used to, the Celestial Mother was adorned with actual plumage of a reddish gold hue, almost like new copper. It was beautiful. The contrast between the sparkling glory of her coat and the flabby obscenity it covered was striking. He had to remind himself that this ridiculous, virtually helpless creature before him might well be the most powerful being on this earth.

Together, Tsalka, Esshk, and Kurokawa mounted the first step of the triangular stone dais surrounding the throne and the two Grik instantly prostrated themselves. Kurokawa, with a surge of terror, took the gamble he'd been steeling himself for over the months-long journey to this place, ever since the three of them decided what they must do right after the defeat at Baalkpan: still standing, but making an elaborate flourish with his hands, he bowed very low. Tsalka couldn't see him, but he must have known what he'd done because he emitted a barely audible hiss. The Celestial Mother shifted slightly, causing rolls of gelatinous fat to ripple, and regarded him with her relatively small, bloodred eyes.

"So," she hissed, in a surprisingly high-pitched voice, "in addition to treason, incompetence, and a murderous waste of my precious Uul, I must add criminal impertinence to the charges against you." Tsalka practically moaned. Saying nothing, Kurokawa held his pose. "Well, creature, *formerly* of the "Iron Ship Folk," what have you to say for yourself?" The question was the opening Kurokawa had been hoping for.

"My most abject apologies, Your Majesty," he humbly intoned in English—a language he knew she understood, even if she couldn't speak it. "Among my people, this posture conveys the same meaning as that of Regent-Consort Tsalka and General Esshk. If anything, it signifies even greater respect. True warriors do not crawl on their bellies before any . . . being . . . in victory or defeat, and this posture is reserved only for those we consider worthy of our greatest respect and esteem. Forgive me if I have erred in presenting you with the most sincere honor and unreserved respect I am capable of."

The Celestial Mother leaned back, considering, as surprised by the creature's ability to speak so fluently in the "Scientific Tongue" as she was by his . . . interesting excuse. "Arise, Regent Tsalka, General Esshk," she said, almost as an afterthought. She turned her full attention to the general as he rose and her voice became harder. "The Invincible Swarm is defeated," she stated simply. "As you were once considered the greatest living general of our people, and particularly since you chose not to gently destroy yourself, but to come before me with an explanation—knowing your destruction here will *not* be 'gentle'—I will allow you to speak." She glanced at Tsalka. "You are blameless for the actual defeat. You are no general, after all, but I understand you were deeply involved in the planning that led to this disaster, so either you meddled inexcusably or Esshk displayed even greater incompetence by heeding your untrained counsel. Regardless, you have attached yourself to his failure and will share his fate . . . unless you can convince me, as you claim, that you and Esshk, as well as this unwholesome creature you bring before me, deserve to exist." She paused. "No, in fact you must convince me beyond any doubt that your continued existence is essential not only to our ultimate success, but to our very survival as a species."

She allowed them a moment to contemplate that and, with some effort, contorted herself enough so that she could reach the basket of struggling hatchlings beside her throne. Seizing one, she popped it in her mouth and began to chew. Selected by the Chooser, they were the rejects from her own nest, and her favorite snack.

Tsalka cleared his throat and began to speak. The Celestial Mother had succinctly laid it out, and as tall an order as it was, the opportunity was greater than he'd secretly suspected.

"I thank you, Giver of Life. It is true that General Esshk and I took a great risk by coming before you, but not merely for our meager selves. Against the knowledge we bear, our fates are insignificant. We risk your wrath because we *do* believe the existence of our very race is at stake. We have some few advantages, technological miracles our . . . partner in the Hunt has brought us." He gestured with lingering annoyance at Kurokawa. "Those miracles have already been used to some good effect and we have many more at our disposal, not yet implemented. But truly our only hope for survival, I fear, is that some very fundamental changes be made."

"Such as?" the Celestial Mother demanded, still chewing.

Tsalka paused, measuring his next words very carefully. Finally, almost resignedly, he pointed at the basket beside the throne and, by implication, the morsels within. "Well, for example, we must stop eating those. The Choosers cull them because they are not fiercely aggressive. They defend themselves fanatically against their nest-mates that attack them, but are not attackers themselves. Thus they are not considered fit for the Hunt. Distasteful as the concept might be, General Esshk has convinced me that defense is something we must learn to do."

"Defense!" shrieked the Celestial Mother indignantly. "Defense is for prey! We are the predators all other creatures must defend *against*! It has ever been thus! You would rend thousands of years of culture, tradition, based on a single defeat by an incompetently underestimated opponent? If that is the counsel you bring, prepare yourselves for the Traitor's Death!"

Tsalka prostrated himself again, but to his credit, Esshk remained standing beside Kurokawa. Inwardly, Kurokawa trembled with dread, but he knew that if he showed any doubt or fear now, all was lost.

"Giver of Life," Esshk said quietly, "with respect, and my most fervent worshipfulness, my life is, of course, yours to do with as you please, but I beg you to hear us. The Invincible Swarm was destroyed not only because we underestimated our foe—true enough—but because we were culturally

unable to recognize the fact that the simple Tree Prey we met so long ago
might have progressed into Worthy Prey. They have become other hunters
who, in their fashion, have matched our capacity for the hunt. They had
assistance, others like him"—he gestured at Kurokawa—"who taught
them new miracles of war, but they adapted to those miracles more readily than we and used them more effectively. If we do not adapt as well,
they will sweep us from the world."

"Prey?"

"*Worthy* Prey, Celestial Mother. And like other Worthy Prey, they have
become hunters as well. Given time, they will pursue us."

"Then we must mount another Swarm, greater than the one you wasted,
and destroy them forever! Surely they suffered greatly as well. Now is the
time to exterminate them!"

"I would agree . . . but where will we get the Uul, the warriors, for such
a Swarm? Our frontiers are vast, and are we not now in contact with other
Worthy Prey in the south? And in the west as well? I have heard rumors. . . ."

The Celestial Mother waved a hand. "It is true. We always meet new
prey as we expand, and sometimes the great storms deliver others unto
us . . . like your pet, perhaps? This new "Worthy Prey" in the south and
west is weak in numbers, and infests a small, chill, and undesirable land.
We are in no rush to hunt them, and they are no threat to us. We will manage. We always have."

"I propose that this time, you won't," Kurokawa interjected. He recognized the quaver in his voice and hoped the others didn't. "Not without
us," he added more firmly.

"And what makes you so indispensable?" The Celestial Mother's tone
was suddenly low, threatening.

Kurokawa forged ahead, counting his points on his fingers. "First,
you could probably destroy the Tree Folk—prey—as you said, with one
more major campaign, but the losses would be staggering. Where will you
get the troops . . . the Uul warriors? Second, they know your weakness
now." Even Esshk bristled at "weakness," but Kurokawa continued. "No
doubt they have seen and understand your inability to defend. As soon as
they are able, they will attack. They *must*. Most likely, they will do so before you can adequately reinforce your forward outposts, like Aryaal." He
paused and took a deep, tense breath. "Without proper *defensive* tactics
and preparations, those outposts cannot hold. To avoid even further pointless loss of . . . Uul"—he pronounced it "Ool"—"I most respectfully recommend that you evacuate them. The *strategy* of trading land for time is no
disgrace if part of that strategy is to eventually recover what has been lost.
Third, if we gain that time, we can use it to prepare. While the enemy—

the prey—flounders along impotently behind us, extending their lines of supply while ours contract, we can build the cannon-armed armored ships I have proposed. We can make the flying machines, the artillery, and train your . . . *our* troops, our Uul, in tactics that will succeed." Kurokawa shrugged imperceptibly, going for broke. "And yes, those tactics must be defensive at first." He held up a fourth finger. "Finally, when we have built these weapons, trained . . . our troops, swelled their ranks with an entirely fresh generation that has not known defeat, we wait until the prey is over-extended and has stretched his lines of supply to the breaking point. . . ."

"Then attack?" asked the Celestial Mother, suddenly thoughtful.

"Then attack," confirmed Kurokawa. "The enemy does not breed or reach maturity as quickly as you. Break their Army and Navy and they will have no defense. You can then roll them up with ease and conquer every land from here to the Eastern Sea."

The Celestial Mother scratched her jowls. "Interesting," she hissed thoughtfully.

Esshk was staring at Kurokawa. They'd discussed all this before, but it was supposed to be he who presented their argument to the Giver of Life. "Indeed," he said, equally thoughtful.

Alan Letts stood from his place at the long table in the now almost fully restored Great Hall. The formal reception was intended to commemorate that, as well as the other grand undertakings that would soon commence. In spite of a general mood of joviality and goodwill, there was also a bittersweet understanding that they stood, once again, at a crossroads. The tightly knit members of the Grand Alliance that had hurled back the Grik would scatter again. Some would resume operations against the enemy at long last, while others like Shinya and Saan-Kakja would depart for the Filpin Lands, to oversee the development of an even greater arsenal of freedom than Baalkpan could ever be. Laumer's little squadron would accompany Saan-Kakja on his way to perform the perhaps impossible task Matt had set him. Regardless of their missions, the possibility always existed that they would never all be gathered like this again. They'd lost too many friends in this terrible war to take such things for granted. Letts tapped his mug with a knife to gain everyone's attention, and raised it high.

"Ladies and gentlemen, may I propose a toast?"

Matt smiled as he released Sandra's hand under the table and stood with everyone else. He was proud of Letts. Like all of them, he'd come a long way. He'd earned his post as chief of staff and had developed the confidence that went with it. The main reason for that rose to stand beside him. Nurse Lieutenant Karen Theimer Letts, now Sandra's medical chief of staff, had once been rendered almost catatonic by their situation. Her recovery had inspired Letts to apply himself, and they made a good team. Karen's pregnancy was also beginning to show, and that had gained her an almost reverent consideration by the same rough men who might once have resented the depletion of the "dame" supply in the middle of the famine her marriage to Letts had made even more extreme.

"Ladies and gentlemen," Letts repeated, "I give you Saan-Kakja, U-Amaki ay Maa-ni-la!"

The diminutive High Chief of Manila and patriarch of all the Filpin Lands regarded those at the table and the rest of the assembly in the hall. She was even more striking than usual with her fiery, golden eyes and polished, chased-golden breastplate. Her yellow and black clan colors decorated her cape and kilt, and a short, ornately hilted dirk hung from an elaborate belt in a golden sheath. The martial ensemble clashed with her tiny stature and evident youth.

"They're all so *young*," Sandra whispered in Matt's ear, and he squeezed her hand. It was true. He reflected that the veterans of every war probably thought much the same of all the recruits who joined them in battle— even while they themselves seemed young to the veterans of earlier wars. Rarely were the *leaders* quite so young, however. It suddenly struck him that most of the positions of high authority in the Alliance were held by young, comparatively inexperienced . . . amateurs. Saan-Kakja was by any definition, human or Lemurian, little more than a child. The strikingly competent and just as exotic Safir Maraan wasn't much older. Neither was Chack, who'd probably command a Marine battalion before long. Tassana-Ay-Arracca, whose father had perished with *Nerracca*, had risen to High Chief of *Aracca* Home after her grandfather fell in battle. The commander of the growing Sularan Brigade couldn't be much over twenty. General Muln-Rolak was practically ancient, but he wasn't technically a head of state—although Matt suspected that would change when they retook Aryaal. That meant, as representatives of the Alliance, Keje and Adar were the "geezers," since they were in their early forties.

On the human side, Matt knew how young everyone was. The Bosun was around sixty and was the oldest human in the Alliance, but at the august age of thirty-two, Matt was the oldest officer, just after Spanky. If the newly minted Ensign Reynolds was eighteen yet, he'd eat his hat. Of all the Allied commanders, Matt had the most combat experience by far—all of about fifteen months—and here he was, Supreme Commander of all Allied forces. Again, he wondered what Tommy Hart would have thought of that.

Conventional wisdom would imply they were *all* too young for their jobs. The thought was a little intimidating, but Matt wondered if it was true. The old guys back home, commanding their rectangular dreadnoughts, hadn't been doing so hot. It was their stupidity and shortsightedness, to a large degree, that had made Pearl Harbor such a disaster—and even possible in the first place. Matt didn't want to think about the hoary old men in Congress who'd virtually invited the attack by allowing the Navy to wither to a point that it couldn't credibly enforce their threats and policies. Maybe conventional wisdom wasn't always wisdom at all.

He decided, experience aside, it was probably a blessing they were all so young. Particularly the Lemurians. There'd been numerous times when he'd had trouble dealing with older, more entrenched 'Cats. Saan-Kakja's own sky priest, Meksnaak, was a prime example. Nakja-Mur had been exceptional in many ways, but even he'd been a little difficult until his own Home was at stake. Matt knew it had been difficult for the old 'Cat. It was hard for the young ones, watching their whole world change with the exigencies of war, but they could at least *comprehend* change and feel confident they could absorb it, accommodate it, *use* it. It occurred to him then that if all the Lemurian leaders had been a bunch of stick-in-the-mud, geezer bureaucrats—like those back home—they'd all be dead by now.

"It's a good thing they're so young," he whispered back to Sandra. "I think it's made things a lot easier. And besides, it could be a very long war." He saw her nod, and believed she understood more than he'd said.

"Please do sit," Saan-Kakja said when the cheers and stamping feet subsided. Obediently, the crowd returned to their stools or cushions. The request was more than a courtesy. With everyone standing, no one could see her. "Tomorrow I must leave you," she resumed, "and return to my own land. Colonel Shinya and I must oversee a replication, even an enlargement of what you have accomplished here; this 'in-dus-tree.'" She smiled. "Some may not like it. Maa-ni-la has been a refuge for many of the runaways, as you call them, from various lands, and there will be dissent among those who prefer the old ways." Her eyes flashed and her chin rose slightly. "Their obstructionism will not be tolerated. Fear not."

There was more cheering, and Matt realized he needed to talk to her again about her own security. They'd already learned that even Lemurians were capable of appalling treachery.

"Even when I depart, do not think Maa-ni-la has left you. Half my personal guard will go with me, to become officers and form training cadres in the new, changing ways of war, but many more of my people have arrived here since the Great Battle and I shall leave you over five thousands." She looked directly at Matt. "Lead them as you will. My troops are your troops, and I have no doubt you will cherish them as your own."

Touched, Matt bowed his head, acknowledging the compliment. And the responsibility.

"Soon I will return with even more troops, ships, and many new weapons. I look forward to 'raa-di-o' reports from your upcoming expedition, when we will know the enemy's stance. Regardless, I am confident that if we seize this time that has been granted us by your valor and the Heavens above, when we bring our full, combined might against the scourge, we will stamp it out forever!"

Further cheers filled the hall, and, unnoticed at the far end of the table, Billingsly leaned toward Jenks. It was the first time he'd been ashore for an official function and he'd been haughty and uncommunicative throughout. "And still you do not consider them a threat to the Empire?" he hissed. "The force they are planning will be almost as large, and considerably more advanced than that of the vile Dominion that even now menaces our people back home."

Jenks looked at him and blinked. "Don't be ridiculous, Mr. Billingsly. Of course I consider them a threat, but not at present. Look about you! These . . . creatures"—he'd almost said "people," and what would Billingsly think then?—"are clearly preparing to renew their war with an enemy of potentially greater menace even than the Dominion. These Grik are possibly even more savage, if not as depraved."

"They have a Roman priestess among them," Billingsly reminded him darkly.

Jenks frowned. "I have heard that too, though I haven't seen her. From what I understand, there is a difference. The Roman 'faith' as practiced by the Dominion is an abomination, and as much as our ancestors may have disagreed with the old version, they wrote that it became something entirely different on this world. If she is a priestess of the old version who got displaced here as did the others, her fundamental beliefs are not much different from our own." Jenks smiled. "Besides, I have seen no temples or altars or any of the other trappings of the perverted faith. If she serves the Roman Church, as we know it, she certainly hasn't gained many converts."

"I implore you," Billingsly said, with a hint of what might have been true sincerity, "with the child queen gone, the Americans and the bulk of their Army and Navy away, and much of their new construction incomplete, we would have our absolute best opportunity to rescue the princess and be on our way."

Jenks's expression hardened. "And then we *would* be at war with them, fool! Do you think we could take her without bloodshed? Do you think they would ever trust us then? I have given my *word* to accompany their expedition. I could not change that now, nor would I. You think them a threat? Very well. What better way to gauge that threat than by watching how they fight? I would much rather make those observations while they fight someone else than while trading broadsides with them!"

Billingsly's face hardened as well, and he sat back in his chair. Around them, the festive atmosphere resumed after the speeches were done and the smells of unusual dishes reached them as servers came to the table.

"So be it," he muttered to himself, unheard.

*T*wo weeks after Saan-Kakja and Tamatsu Shinya took their leave of Baalkpan in company with (now Lieutenant) Laumer's small squadron, another, considerably larger force prepared to sail. Saan-Kakja departed amid sincere, exuberant fanfare, but though the turnout of well-wishers was even bigger this time, the mood was more somber. The Second Allied Expeditionary Force was not encumbered by any lumbering Homes—those would come later, when they were fully prepared and sent for—but the fleet was still impressive. *Donaghey* was Matt's flagship, back under the command of a much recovered Commander Garrett. *Tolson's* refit was considered sufficient to allow her participation as well. The first two new steam frigates, with their fewer but more powerful thirty-two-pounder smoothbores, were fresh from the new fitting-out docks. A lot depended on them even though this was essentially their maiden voyage and shakedown cruise combined. Jarrik-Fas commanded USS *Nakja-Mur*, and Captain Jim Ellis commanded USS *Dowden*. Ellis would serve as second in command and commodore of the steam element of the fleet if it was detached for independent operations. Additionally, there were now seven former Grik Indiamen that had been razed and rerigged into single-deck corvettes. Observers found it difficult to believe that the far lighter, sleeker-looking ships, glistening with fresh black and white paint, had been reworked from ships originally belonging to their hated foe. The final consensus concerning designations—regardless how they were rated—was that since none of the ships were big enough to be considered "cruisers," all were still destroyers, in a sense. The only difference it made was to morale.

It was an impressive force, considering all were heavily armed, crowded with Marines, and covered with stacked landing craft. Four relatively unaltered Grik ships (except for color) carried Lord Rolak's 2nd Aryaal, Safir Maraan's "Six Hundred" as well as extra field artillery, draft beasts, and other baggage. Ten large feluccas would serve as the eyes of the fleet and dispatch vessels. *Achilles* was also making final preparations for getting under way, her black coal smoke coiling lazily into the light morning air contrasting with the gray smoke of the Allied steamer's oil-fired boilers. The reason for the more somber mood was that this force, at some point, would certainly make contact with the enemy for the first time since the Battle of Baalkpan. There was a sense of confidence that the fleet could handle itself, but no one knew what they would find. Had the enemy withdrawn, or been reinforced? Had the Grik also made unforeseen improvements? They already had crude cannon when they attacked the city. What other surprises might they have introduced since their last meeting? No one knew, and it was frustrating.

They'd grown accustomed to having reports of enemy dispositions from the flying boat, but they were still a week or more away from discovering whether their "new" aircraft would even fly. They were moving forward with the conviction that it would; many more airframes and engines based on the prototype were already being built, but it would take time before *Big Sal*'s conversion was complete, and they still had to train a lot of pilots. Flight training was already under way, in an ingenious simulator that mimicked flight controls, but it remained firmly on the ground when students climbed aboard. What would happen when/if they actually flew?

In many ways, perhaps the greatest test of the Alliance would be faced in the coming days and weeks, and the thought no one was willing to voice was that, for the first time, Captain Matthew Reddy didn't have *Walker* beneath his feet. He wouldn't even be here when they learned, once and for all, whether he ever would again. That simple fact was the source of tremendous unease. In the past, the mere existence of the old destroyer had been a source of considerable comfort and security. They'd fought without her before, but she'd always *been* there, *somewhere*, somehow always ready to come to their aid just in the nick of time. This was the first time the Alliance had engaged in any major military undertaking without *Walker* to back them up.

Nakja-Mur and *Dowden* were tied to the dock, but *Donaghey* was moored beyond them. Scott's launch was waiting to take Matt over after he said his good-byes. Adar, Keje, Spanky, Sandison, Brister, and Letts were all there, but the only one Matt really had eyes for was Sandra Tucker. She and Princess Rebecca had joined them mere moments before, almost out of breath. Sandra had obviously come straight from the hospital, where she'd been working either quite late or very early. Even after all these months, many of those wounded in the battle to save the city required ongoing operations. Her long, sandy brown hair was swept back in a girlish ponytail that accented her pretty face and slender neck.

Everyone knew Captain Reddy and Sandra Tucker were nuts about each other, even though they'd once tried to hide their feelings out of respect for *Walker*'s crew. Of course, the crew probably knew how they felt before they did, and their poignant sacrifice was the source of much sympathy—and respect. Only after the Battle of Baalkpan, when it was clear that *everyone* knew and further denial was pointless, did Captain Reddy and Lieutenant Tucker show any open affection. Even then, public displays were limited to holding hands, an occasional embrace... and spending as much time together as they possibly could. It was obvious their love continued to grow and each was a reservoir for the other's strength, but still they didn't marry or "shack up," as Silva and Cross had apparently done. They did nothing, in fact, that all the surviving destroyermen from *Walker* and *Mahan* couldn't do. The men rolled their eyes in exasperation, called them dopes... and loved them for it.

Alan Letts liked and admired Sandra, as did everyone, but she always made him feel a little guilty. He loved Karen very much, but they'd convinced the captain to marry them when they'd all fully expected to die. Now things had changed, sort of, but his happiness was undiminished. He was guardedly ecstatic that he'd soon be a father. But his very happiness inspired much of his guilt. He couldn't help thinking it wasn't fair for him to be happy when so many of the men were still miserable. And not all those who were miserable were men.

Alan was amazed by Matt and Sandra's self-sacrificing willpower. Again, he compared their situation to two star-crossed lovers from a John Ford western trapped in a Cecil B. DeMille epic, complete with a cast of thousands, monsters, and freak weather events. He noticed, with a surge of relief—for both of them—that as soon as Sandra arrived, she'd unobtrusively inserted her hand into the captain's, and he'd reached to caress her face.

"Do you guys realize yesterday was the sixteen-month anniversary? A year and a third to the very day since we arrived... wherever we are?" Letts interjected into the awkward silence that ensued.

Matt nodded. "Sixteen months since the Squall. Since we escaped the Japs—and watched them sink *Exeter* and *Electra* and *Pope*... since we nearly got sunk ourselves." He shook his head. "We lost a lot of good destroyermen that day. I didn't forget."

"Well . . . maybe you ought not go just yet. The dry dock's finished and we'll be pulling the plug in a few days. Ben's going to fly. . . ."

"It's time to go," Matt said simply. "You and the fellas can handle all that stuff."

Letts nodded reluctantly.

Princess Rebecca stepped forward. "Mr. O'Casey is safe aboard your ship?"

"Stowed away, and no one the wiser." Matt smiled at her concern for the one-armed man.

"I suppose it is best," she reflected. "With Billingsly here and his spies on the loose, I fear they would have discovered him sooner or later. He grows weary of hiding. I do worry about him, though."

"He'll be fine," Matt assured her. "And he *wanted* to go. Like you said, he's tired of staying out of sight. Aboard ship he can *do* something, and the only time he has to be scarce is if Jenks comes aboard." Matt grinned. "Besides, he has full confidence Silva could protect you from a super lizard with his bare hands." He raised an eyebrow. "Where *is* Silva, by the way?"

"Sulking," Sandra said, wryly. "He wanted to go too. Talk about bored! God knows what mischief he'll cause! Until I let Mr. Sandison have him full-time, he was always either trying out his 'toys,' or down at the Busted . . . I mean, the Castaway Cook." She tousled the princess's hair. "Right now, I have 'the duty.'"

Suddenly, Rebecca lunged forward and embraced the captain. He was so surprised that he stood there a moment, hands away from her. Slowly, he lowered them to encompass her and returned the hug. "Do be careful, Captain Reddy," the girl said blearily. "I know your cause is just and I shall miss you, miss you all, terribly. But you must take care! I cannot help but feel you are protecting my people as well as your own, and somehow, all our fates are tied to you in the end!"

A lump had mysteriously formed in Matt's throat. "I'll take care, Your Highness," he muttered self-consciously, "and I'll watch out for your Mr. O'Casey."

He shook hands with the other men and embraced Keje and Adar. That was their way, like Russians, he supposed, but it was like hugging a . . . well, he didn't know what. "We'll see you soon," he said to Keje. "I'll look forward to seeing the first flattop this world has ever known come steaming over the horizon!" He stepped back, but before he could compose himself, Sandra was in his arms. Wolf whistles and howls of delight came from *Nakja-Mur*, tied nearby.

After a reluctantly chaste kiss, Sandra looked up at him, her eyes swimming. "Do be careful, Captain Reddy," she said, repeating Rebecca's words.

I love you, he mouthed, then turned for the launch.

Walker had always gotten under way with an almost spastic energy, as if straining at her moorings like a dog on a leash. The 2nd AEF proceeded more ponderously. The steamers in particular seemed almost reluctant to get under way. *Donaghey* was much quicker. As soon as her cable was up and down, she snatched her anchor from the bottom and surged ahead with the quickening breeze, flag streaming to leeward. She piled on more sail, and soon she was slanting down toward the mouth of the bay. *Tolson* and the corvettes followed in her wake and it was clear the corvettes would be fast, handy ships. Then came the swift feluccas and slower transports. Finally, the steamers began to move. *Nakja-Mur* and *Dowden* slashed at the water with their single, center-mounted screws and began to gain headway with a lot of activity, shouted commands, and considerable noise from their engines and boilers. Steam jetted. It was clear their crews were learning as they went. *Achilles* gained far more efficiently, with her paddle wheels helping her maneuver, but didn't pick up speed as fast. Soon, the entire fleet was steering for the Makassar Strait—and whatever awaited them beyond.

*T*hey came for him as he stepped away from the morning feeding trough. Somehow, on some level, he'd been expecting it. Feeding sounds continued unabated, punctuated by frequent snarls as Uul contended over a particularly choice boiled, meaty bone. He watched as the four specially armored warriors of the Chooser worked their way in his direction through the hissing horde that jostled to and from the trough, and for the slightest instant, he contemplated resistance.

That alone was enough to stun him into immobility. That, and the fact that he realized—*realized*—his sated torpor would allow the warriors to make short work of him. He was armed with only the weapons the Mother had given him. Alone, they would be no match for the armor. There was no mistake. Harshly, they called his name and their eyes were fixed on his. He was the only Uul within the stone feeding chamber who *had* a name, and, resignedly, he moved to meet them.

It was time. He'd had a good life, but now he was old—he knew it was so—and his joints ached and he'd lost several teeth. He'd been just slightly slower in the arena of late and if he noticed it, certainly the Chooser had. He'd still been victorious, and his surge of exultation had been affirmed by the hissing approbation of the Hij spectators, but he knew each of his victories over the last few cycles had been more difficult than the last. It was time for *his* boiled flesh to fill the feeding trough of the Sport Fighters. At least many were his own get, and the tradition would be unbroken. Better to feed his own here than strangers on some distant battlefield, he decided, in an uncharacteristic burst of insight. Still, it would have been better to die fighting.

He'd been a fighter all his life and he'd tasted the chaos and mad joy of major battles often, usually against his own kind. First, he'd merely been one of ten. Through skill he'd eventually become first of ten, then second of twenty—all Grik could count that high; they had two arms, two legs, and sixteen fingers and toes, after all. Time and many battles passed and he was elevated to first of twenty, first of two twenties, and ultimately first of *five* twenties, as high as any Uul could aspire. That was when he'd been taken to the arena for the pleasure of the Hij and given a *name*. He had little sense of the passage of time or how many victories he'd won. Tens of twenties, certainly. All he knew was that he'd been in the arena a long, long time. He'd enjoyed it. But all good things, like life, must end.

"Greetings, Halik-Uul," spoke one of the armored warriors, less harshly than before.

"In the name of the Mother, I greet you," Halik replied easily. Less certainly, he continued, "The Chooser time, now?"

"Indeed," stated another of the warriors. "Your time has come. Your destiny awaits."

Halik didn't know what a "destiny" was. It was probably elevated speech for "cook pot."

"Come," commanded the one who seemed first of four.

Obediently, Halik followed as the warriors led him through the now quieter, staring horde. They passed through the locked gate to the underground chamber and up into the light. Halik blinked as they strode across the arena he'd fought in so many times. He couldn't help but gaze around. He'd never seen it empty before. They reached another gate, and through it, they ascended a gradually spiraling stair. Halik grew slightly confused. He didn't know where the cook pots were, but the smells never reached them when the wind was from this direction. His heart quickened. Maybe they were taking him to a female! Sometimes warriors who'd shown greater strength and skill were allowed that honor before they faced the butchers. If that were the case, it would make his death slightly less unpleasant, at least.

He'd been paired with a female only twice before, and the result had been dozens of squabbling young he'd never seen, for the most part. Some of the survivors, a fair percentage actually, had eventually appeared in the warrior dens destined for the arena. He'd been ordered to train them himself and he'd complied, though at the time, he'd felt no real connection to them. Two he'd ultimately killed in the arena himself. Recently, however, he'd begun to feel a subtle attachment to those of *his* that remained. Perhaps it was pride of a sort that he'd sired such well-developed and cunning warriors. He didn't think much about it; it was just something he felt.

"This way," ordered the first of four when they reached the top of the stair and a passageway forked away from it. They took the passage to the left. It was dimly lit and there was no sound but the clack of claws and foot-pads on the stones. The passageway continued for a considerable distance and his excitement grew. He could *smell* females! Oddly, he didn't think any were present now, but they had passed there recently. Perhaps one awaited him in a chamber nearby? Suddenly, the guards halted him at a chamber entrance that had strange scents, but not those of females, and he was con-fused, disappointed. Regardless, he entered at their command and stood where they placed him.

His eyes had grown accustomed to the dark passage, and the torches that drew his eyes blinded him to the rest of the chamber. He sensed there were others in the room, and one that smelled . . . wrong. Suddenly, one of the guards grabbed him from behind, holding his arms at his sides. An-other grasped his feet. Without warning, yet another guard draped a cloth over his eyes and quickly wrapped it around them and over his snout, ty-ing his jaws securely shut. An instant later, he was released.

Rising terror threatened to overcome him. He'd never expected it to be like this. That they would destroy him he had no doubt, but he'd never expected them to make sport of him when they did. He could see nothing, but oddly, they'd left his hands and feet unrestrained. He waited, gaining control of his fear.

A terrible blow struck him across the belly. It burned like the strike of a sword or a claw and he expected his insides to fall to the floor. Reflex-ively, he grasped at the terrible wound . . . and felt nothing. Another sharp blow slashed at the back of his leg, and he should have fallen with his leg ropes cut . . . but he didn't. Repeatedly the blows fell upon him, and he stood there and took it despite an almost uncontrollable urge to run, to flee, to try to escape toward where he thought the passageway should be. Reaching up, he tore the blindfold and gag from his face, but now his eyes were even more dazzled by the torches.

"Kill me," he gasped, controlling his voice, "but no play at me as hatch-lings with food pets! I fight for The Mother all my life. I honor Her, submit to Her! Kill me!"

"Sounds almost like *pride*, does it not?" came an urbane, well-spoken voice. Something answered in a tongue Halik had never heard. He felt fear again, but not the visceral, dangerous kind of fear, the kind that would make him prey. This was different. Another blow fell across his back, and finally, a mounting rage drove all fear from him and he lashed back. By some fluke, he managed to grasp the weapon and realized it was a whip. He jerked it toward him and then lashed up against the extended arm of his tormentor with his forearm. The whip was his! He reversed the handle and flailed it about himself with practiced ease, creating a wall of lashing leather while his eyes began to adjust. Another blow fell across his back, and with lightning speed, he spun and directed a reply. The whip cracked against the only target he could see—a pair of glowing eyes. He was rewarded with a shriek, and the glowing orbs were extinguished. Every instinct drove him to fall upon his wounded tormentor, but he forced himself to remain in a protective stance, backing toward the wall. He could see the shape of his attackers now, and saw there were others in the chamber as well. The others were gathered to one side and posed no threat, but the three remaining guards were approaching him, in the classic style, and now they had swords.

"A dilemma, Halik-Uul!" said the urbane voice—so calm! "Whatever will you *do*? You are not in the arena now!"

Halik forced his own passion to subside. The voice seemed . . . familiar . . . and on some level, he somehow knew the words were meant as guidance. What *would* he do? He must think! Suddenly, a wild insight took him. This was not a slaughter, a preparation for the cook pots. It was a test! A test to see if the strange thoughts and awareness he'd experienced of late had some greater meaning. What would he do? In the arena, a match like this would be hopeless. One could use only the weapons one brought to the fight. Sometimes things were deliberately staged that way, to see what would happen, but a single whip against three swords was a losing proposition. But he wasn't in the arena! The voice had said so!

His back was almost to the wall; he could feel it with his tail. A quick glance behind revealed one of the torches—although it wasn't a torch. Not like he'd seen before. An iron bracket supported a small glass globe with a burning wick protruding from a funnel shape on top. He didn't know what the liquid in the globe was, but he knew it would burn. He'd used small bombs in the arena before. Just as the guards rushed him, he snatched the globe from the bracket and hurled it at the one on the far left. It shattered and spread burning fluid across the guard's face and torso. He lunged past the conflagration and leaped upon the blinded, moaning guard. He didn't kill him, but instead, snatched his sword from its hand. Sprinting to the opposite side of the chamber, he took a position with his whip in one hand and the sword in the other. The burning guard had flopped on the floor, flailing and rolling, trying to extinguish the flames. That left two. Confidence soared within him. A moment ago, he'd been doomed. He didn't know exactly what the meaning of all this was, but he did know that with a sword and a whip, he could defeat any two warriors with swords he'd ever faced.

"Enough," came the voice. At a gesture from the darkened figure, the guards obediently slew their wounded comrade and dragged him from the chamber. Halik had no doubt they'd have killed him just as thoughtlessly as they had the others, but now was forgotten.

"In the name of the Celestial Mother," came the voice, as placid as it had been from the start, "you may lay down your weapons and no harm will come to you. I even promise they'll be returned. The sword, in particular, you may wish to keep."

Only then did Halik glance at the weapon. He'd also begun to notice things recently, in ways he never had before. Just as a visit with a female might bring pleasure, he'd discovered other things sometimes did. Success in the arena brought intense pleasure, but suddenly, so did the memory of an unusual sunset he'd once seen. Looking at the sword, he realized that the sight of it gave him pleasure as well! It was the most . . . beautiful thing he'd ever beheld. The blade was a type of layered iron he'd seen carried only by generals, and the hilt was elaborately decorated. Gently, he laid it on the floor.

"Come here."

Obediently, Halik did so. When he drew closer, he could finally discern four robed Hij—and some other creature standing with them. He was still too invigorated to take much notice, and his eyes quickly sought the source of the voice.

One of the Hij drew back his robes and revealed himself as a first general, the highest of the high, and a member of the Celestial Mother's very house. Halik flung himself onto the cold stones of the floor.

"He did well," murmured another voice grudgingly. "The fire was a nice touch, and he is the first to have used it. Clever."

Halik certainly recognized *that* voice. It belonged to the Chooser himself! He'd heard it many times over the years during the Sports.

"Arise, Halik-Uul," came the first voice again. "The Mother's Chooser will take you from this place and his assistants will prepare you for the usual Holy Rites of Elevation. You and I will talk again, and I look forward to conversing with you as one Hij to another."

After Halik was led, dazed, from the chamber, General Esshk looked at Kurokawa. "An interesting recruiting method you have devised. It tests their wits as well as their discipline, ability, and resistance to the Urge. Ultimately, it tests their obedience as well. Most interesting." He glanced at the bloodstains. "Perhaps a trifle wasteful."

"Perhaps," Kurokawa agreed, "but for the war we must prepare for, one Halik is worth a hundred of those others. Maybe a thousand."

Esshk hissed a sigh. "I believe you speak truth, or this activity would not be allowed. There is resistance, however. The Celestial Mother remains unconvinced, but she is willing, at least, to experiment." He glanced in the direction Halik had been taken. "That Uul is not unique, but he is rare and we will need many, many more like him."

"The Chooser opposes us?"

"The Chooser opposes all change. Nevertheless, the hatchling proposal progresses. We will see."

LOGBOOK
OF THE
U.S.S WALKER (DD-163)
DD Rate, COMMANDED BY:
M. P. REDDY, LIEUTENANT COMMANDER, USNR
DESTROYER SQUADRON 29
Attached to: **ABDAFLOAT**

Commencing: 0000, **July 1, 1943,**
at: Baalkpan—formerly Balikpapan
and ending: 1943

LIST OF OFFICERS

Attached to and on board of the USS WALKER (DD-163), commanded by <u>M.P.</u> <u>REDDY, Captain, USNR,</u> during the period covered by this Logbook, with date of reporting for duty, detachment, transfer, or death, from 1 July 1943, to 31 July 1943

NAME	RANK	DATE OF DUTY	DETACHED
M.P. REDDY	Lt. Cmdr/Capt.	5 Sept. 1941	Commanding*
*TDY Commanding 2nd Allied Expeditionary Force.			
J.G. ELLIS	Lt./Capt.	6 Sept. 1941	XO*
*TDY Commanding USS Mahan 1 Mar. 1942. Commanding USS Dowden 23 June 1943			
B. McFARLANE	Lt./Cmdr.	18 Oct. 1938	Engineering*
*TDY Minister of Naval Engineering, Baalkpan. Commanding salvage/refit operation USS Walker.			
B.L. SANDISON	Lt./Cmdr.	1 Nov. 1941	Torpedo*
*TDY Minister of Ordnance, Baalkpan.			
G.C. GARRETT	Lt./Cmdr.	8 Oct. 1941	Gunnery*
*TDY Commanding USS Don aghey.			
S.B. CAMPETI	2CPO/Lt.Cmdr.	9 May 1940	Ordnance*
*TDY B.L. SANDISON			
P.J. BRISTER	Lt./Cmdr.	6 Sept. 1942	Asst. Engineering*
*TDY Minister of Defensive and Industrial Works, Baalkpan.			
S.H. RIGGS	1CPO/Cmdr.	12 Aug. 1940	Comm & Navigation*
*TDY "Minister of Communications and Electrical Contrivances," Baalkpan.			
A.G. LETTS	Lt./Cmdr.	15 May 1941	Commisary & Supply*
*TDY "Minister of Industry and Chief of Staff 'President' of Baalkpan."			
S.M. TUCKER	Lt.	28 Feb. 1942	Medical Officer*
*TDY Minister of Medicine, Baalkpan			
J.R. MILLER	Lt.	22 June 1941	Medical Officer*
*TDY 2nd Allied Expeditionary Force.			

(This page to be sent to Bureau of Navigation monthly with Log sheets)

UNITED STATES SHIP WALKER (DD-163) Tuesday, Sept. 2, 1943
00-04 As before. No problems to report. Woke up pumping detail and inspection party so they could begin final preparations.
Sonny Campeti, Lt. Cmdr. USN

04-08 As before. Pump boilers at full steam pressure despite leaks. Detail reports all in readiness. Inspection party discovered and repaired a faulty joint in the #4 main pipe. Split ends were the cause—like we have seen before. Inspection parties will continue to observe all joints throughout the operation.

Bernard L. Sandison, Lt. Cmdr, USNR

08–12 As before. Weather clear. Water smooth on the bay. Slight easterly wind. Conditions optimum. 0800 mustered all hands and fed them at their stations. No absentees. Final visual inspection of all lines and seals. Heard reports from divisions. Lemurian Homes Humfra-Dar and Woor-Naa standing by to assist with ship-board pumps. Engaged primary pumps 0920. Observed first streams of water being expelled from dry dock basin. Engaged in brief verbal celebration.

Brad McFarlane, Cmdr, USN

12–16 *Not* as before. 1350 observed slight reduction of water level around exposed super-structure of ship. Having difficulty controlling exuberance of all divisions. Self included. Large numbers of civilians have come down to the dock to observe. Detached Marines from other duties to make sure they did not interfere. No question of deliberate interference, just do not want them underfoot and causing distractions. Water flow is difficult to estimate but best guess is 6000 gpm.

Brad McFarlane, Cmdr, USN

16–20 Pumps steaming as before. (Great relief to use that phrase again.) Two minor casualties in the water pipes repaired. Pump engine running well and within Mr. McFarlane's expectations. *Humfra-Dar* has added her pumps to the operation. Water level dropping slowly still, but noticeably. His Excellency, Adar, High Chief of Baalkpan, appeared briefly at the dock to inspect the proceedings. Informed Cmdr. McFarlane that a celebration of thanksgiving and appreciation would commence at 1900. Celebration seems general already at 1700. Chief Laney took a banca boat out to the protruding aft mast of the ship and ran a new ensign up. Tattered remnants of the old ensign (there since the Battle of Baalkpan) were removed and carefully brought ashore. Letts took them in his charge.

PERRY BRISTER, CMDR, USN

20–24 Lights rigged. Water flow uninterrupted. No stoppages. Cmdr. McFarlane has allowed the hands to join the celebration by divisions. Inspection details to remain in place by rotation. A damn good day.

Steven P. Riggs, Cmdr., USN

Approved:

Examined:

Riggs held a lighted Zippo so he could see, and Spanky signed his name by "Approved" at the bottom of the page. Then he handed the log to Letts, who signed beside "Examined." Before he closed the log on the previous day, Letts glanced up at the date and shook his head.

"Five days late for the 'year and a third,' but close enough, I guess."

"That's one of the reasons I pushed so hard to pull the plug yesterday. Give the guys something to celebrate so they wouldn't dwell on what we left behind. What we lost," Spanky replied.

Letts returned the log to Spanky, who handed it to Campeti, who had the watch again. They were all tired, but *nobody* was going to oversee this operation but *Walker*. Sandra Tucker had arrived, looking disheveled, but as anxious as they were for her first glimpse of the ship. Now she stood beside them, peering intently into the predawn gloom of the dry-dock basin at the still only vaguely defined shape.

They stood on what had once been the old fitting-out pier, but was now merely a walkway between massive wooden cranes and equipment sheds. The skeletons of still more new warships rose on the other side of the basin, silhouetted against the new dawn. Until recently, when the dry dock neared completion, the new ships had remained the priority projects. Now, for just a few days, work on them would slow while a large percentage of the laborers concentrated on another task. Steam and smoke jetted from crude, noisy engines while 'Cat "snipes in training" crawled all over them, oiling every conceivable point of friction. Some spun the huge, amazingly efficient Lemurian-designed pumps, and others powered generators that ran electric pumps of human design. The jury was still out on which were better, but Spanky was pretty sure the 'Cat machines would last longer. Hoses pulsed and brown water coursed into the sea beyond the dry-dock wall.

Together, Sandra, Spanky, Alan, Campeti, and Bernie, a growing crowd of human and Lemurian sailors and Marines, sleepy civilian revelers, and finally, to no one's real surprise, Adar himself, watched the dawn gradually reveal what the ravages of seawater and battle had done to USS *Walker*. Throughout the night, while most of her crew and the people of the city celebrated her raising, the water level in the dry dock had steadily dropped. Now she lay, with a slight list to port, where she'd settled after her fight with *Amagi*. Almost half of her upper hull was now exposed and every heart sank as they looked upon her.

A clear demarcation showed how much of the ship had remained above the surface when she sank. It was plain to see, about three-fourths of the way up her four slender funnels and about halfway up her aft mast. The forward mast was gone. Automatic weapons had riddled her bridge, but the line glared dark and glistening below her empty pilothouse windows like an angry, oily slash. Above it, the paint was blackened by fire and dark with rust. Below the line she looked . . . even worse.

An entirely new color had been created. Dark brown mixed with tan, with malignant yellow streaks for contrast. A fair amount of blackened green dangled here and there, where rotting vegetation festooned her. Angry red globs and smears were everywhere and of every different hue, as the rust that caused them dried. Slimy gray-black tar pooled and oozed, and covering all was a translucent rainbow slick of oil that had leaked from her ruptured bunkers. Hatches stood agape, revealing dank interiors. Tangled cables drooped down her side, and brackish water gushed from countless holes as the water level in the basin receded below that still inside the ship. Eel-like chopper fish squirmed like maggots on her deck, their vicious jaws gaping and snapping as their gills labored in the morning air. As primitive as they were, it might take them hours to die.

Walker was a corpse, Sandra thought, and they'd been nothing more than ghoulish grave robbers to expose her to the sun. Hot tears ran down her cheeks. Thank God Matthew wasn't there to see it.

"Lord," Sandison murmured, "what are we going to do?"

Spanky patted his arm and sighed. "We're gonna fix her, Bernie."

The way *Walker* rested looked almost normal by the time the first boats went across: listing slightly and a little low by the stern, but the water wasn't much higher than the greasy black boot topping. She was still full of water, however, and jets of varying intensity coursed from her many wounds. As a result, the volume of water the pumps displaced was reduced as the day wore on. If they emptied the basin more quickly than the ship could drain, they ran the risk of causing even more damage. But her crew was restless to get to work, and by early that afternoon, the first repair parties clamored up her slippery side and stood once more on her leaning deck.

Spanky McFarlane put his hands on his skinny hips and stared hard in all directions, his lips grimly set. A short while before, he'd been Minister of Naval Engineering for an infant nation. Right now, for a time, he was *Walker*'s engineering officer again and nothing else. "All right, ladies," he said at last, as men and Lemurians squelched through the ooze, "we got work to do. Mr. Riggs? Take your party to the bridge. Charts, manuals, anything like that we might've missed before are the first priority. Easy does it. If there's anything left of that stuff, it'll go to pieces if you're not careful." He looked quickly around. "Campeti! Where's Mr. Sandison?"

Campeti gestured over his shoulder. "Went tearing ass up to the bridge. We removed the gun director a long time ago 'cause we could get to the platform, but he wanted to see the torpedo directors. He was like a cat havin' kittens!" Campeti caught himself and looked quickly around. Some of the Lemurians were looking at him strangely. "Uh, no offense. Different kinda cats . . . Little buggers . . ." He held his hands close together, but then his face clouded with embarrassment. "Oh, just get to work, damn it."

Spanky shook his head. "Well, until he gets back, or sends for you to help him, I want you to check the four-inch fifties and see if there's anything left of the machine guns on the amidships deckhouse. When you get through with that, put together a detail to salvage as many fire hoses as you can. We'll start rinsing the old girl off." He couldn't stop a grin. "Just think what the Bosun would say if he saw his decks in such a state."

Campeti almost giggled. In spite of the herculean task ahead of them, the spirits of those who'd come aboard were rising. Finally, after the long months of anticipation and helplessness, of toil and labor on other projects, they could get to work on what mattered most to *them*. It almost seemed as if they could sense something within the ship itself begin to stir as well. A renewed sense of purpose. A new lease on life.

"We wanna go down," grouched a reedy voice behind Spanky, and he turned to look at the pair standing there. It was Gilbert Yeager and the silken, gray-furred 'Cat named Tabby. He had to concentrate for an instant, because without Isak Rueben, the scene just didn't add up. Then he remembered Isak was the one they'd decided would accompany the AEF. Understanding complete, Spanky glared at Tabby when he saw she'd stripped almost completely, in the Lemurian way, to the point that all she wore was what looked like a skimpy little skirt. Despite her fine fur, her breasts appeared very human. It was distracting and annoying and she knew it. Sometimes Spanky harbored a secret, superstitious sense that the presence of women (the nurses' first) aboard his ship was what had caused all their problems to start with. He'd finally allowed Tabby to stay in the firerooms at the captain's orders and because she was a damn fine snipe. He'd broken one of his own cardinal rules, however: if something someone is doing bugs you, either make them stop, or pretend it doesn't bug you. In Tabby's case, he'd failed miserably in both respects. He couldn't—wouldn't now—make her go away, and there was no way he could pretend she didn't bug him.

"You're out of uniform, sailor!" he said harshly, almost plaintively. "Again!"

"Dirty work ahead, Chief," she replied with a creditable drawl. "We ain't got enough new uniforms yet to get 'em all scruffed up."

She even sounds like them now, Spanky thought uncomfortably. She was also the only creature alive that the Mice were actually nice to, in their way. As a result of their association, she'd begun to take on many of their less agreeable attributes. But she *looked* like a pinup in a catsuit.

"I don't give a good goddamn! You *will* put on some clothes or I'll have you on report!" he bellowed. "We'll see if you can remember to . . ." He stopped and watched her slowly unroll a T-shirt she'd been holding behind her back.

"Aye-aye, *Mr. McFaar-lane.* I'll throw somethin' on if it make you happy."

"You . . . !" He stopped. She'd done it to him *again*! He whirled and pointed at the very deck access she'd pulled her companions from months before. "Down there. Let me know if the water's draining out of the aft fireroom! I want you to describe every single piece of equipment as it becomes visible!" He ignored them then, and began delegating other tasks to different details. The Mice shuffled away and ducked down the hatch. Once inside, out of earshot, Gilbert began to chuckle.

"I swear, Tabby, you keep waggin' yer boobs at Spanky like that, one o' these days he's gonna bust a vessel—or grab hold of 'em! You know it drives him nuts. Just havin' wimmin aboard ship is enough to cause him fits— then you keep doin' that!"

"He still needs to laugh," Tabby replied. "I like to make him laugh and he will, later. He always does." Her eyes grew unfocused and she continued softly: "And maybe someday he *will* grab 'em." She looked away, but Gilbert could tell she was blinking embarrassment.

Jeez! Gilbert thought, stunned. *Tabby's sweet on Spanky!* "Yeah, well," he said, his chuckle now gone as he peered into the darkness below. The stench was unbearable and the water was still over the top of his beloved boilers. "Ain't much to laugh about right now. Look at this mess!"

The oily water receded slowly, and purplish brown foam swirled and clung to everything as its support drained away. At some point, one of *Walker's* own hoses snaked down through the trunk with a bellowed, "Slide it in!" and moments later, it began to pulse and throb. The drainage picked up. Another hose, new made, joined the first and was soon jolting and juddering alongside it. Gilbert no longer noticed the smell, and as the water went down, he carefully descended to the upper catwalk, creeping slowly so he wouldn't slip in the oily slurry. His beloved fireroom was a dreary sight in the gloom. He didn't dare make a light.

He suddenly remembered finding a dead, bloated cow out in a pasture when he was a kid. It was one of his ma's, and he'd been curious why it died. While he stood there staring at it, its hind legs started to move. At first, he thought he'd met a ghost cow, because there was no question it was dead. He started to run, but something stopped him. He'd never been scared of a live cow. What could a dead one do to him? With that certain mixture of horror and fascination only kids could conjure, he'd watched a medium-size possum come crawling out of the cow's ass!

He'd pondered that occasionally over the years, that possum squirming around up in there. No matter how hungry he got after that, and there'd been some starving times during the Depression, he'd never eaten possum again. Now, looking at his fireroom, he suddenly imagined he knew what the inside of that old cow had looked like to that possum so long ago.

"Go get another hose, Tabby. A water hose!" he shouted. "Might as well rinse some of this shit down while they're suckin' it out!"

The water came from the basin and wasn't by any means clean, but at least the pressure let him blow the worst of the goo away. Also, it didn't hurt that he'd exposed a little of the lighter paint and it grew brighter in the compartment as the sun hung overhead. Soon, he and Tabby were standing on the slimy deck plates. While he aimed the hose, she held it for him. A couple of times, they raised a plate and stuffed one of the drain hoses in the bilge.

"Gonna need some kind of detergent!" he shouted.

"We use wood ashes, make lye soap?"

"I dunno. Lye does goofy stuff. Not much aluminum down here, but there's zinc in brass and galvanize. Shoot lye on that and we get hydrogen gas! I doubt wood ashes'd be pure enough, but it might corrode the hell out of stuff." Gilbert paused and wiped his face with his shirt. It was stiflingly hot. "I wish somebody'd raise those goddamn vents!" he roared. Almost as if they'd heard him—and maybe someone had—the grungy, nearly opaque skylight vents started going up. Soon, the fireroom was relatively bathed in light and at least a little air was getting in. A few more 'Cats soon came to join them. Gilbert felt mildly guilty. He knew everyone was busy, but hell. He and Tabby turned the hose over to their relief and started to go topside for a much-needed drink. He paused.

"You know," he shouted over the gushing water, "speakin' of corrosion, there ain't much here. Not new, anyway. Maybe all this oily, slimy shit did us a favor." He moved to one of the big Yarrow boilers, kicked the latch, and opened the door. A flood of black water gushed out all over him, knocking him down. Tabby picked him up, and together they peered inside.

"Ook," Gilbert said. He couldn't see much, but the firebricks were gone. Probably disintegrated when the cool water hit them. The lines looked okay, though, and even if a few had popped, he could fix that. New firebrick had been stockpiled long ago during their previous refits. He gently patted the old boiler. "Hey! We can hose her out! No need to get all black and sooty cleanin' her!"

Tabby looked at him. He was covered from head to foot with black, slimy ooze. She laughed aloud. Gilbert grinned too, realizing how ridiculous the statement was under the circumstances.

"Well, we can," he defended. "Mainly, though"—he patted the boiler again—"we can fix this."

It was nearly dusk and it had been a long, eventful, and mostly happy day in spite of their early misgivings. Faces grew somber a few times when the occasional bone was discovered and reverently removed. There weren't many, and those they found were deeply gnawed. There was no way to identify whose they were and it didn't really matter anyway. Courtney Bradford might have told them whether the bones were human or Lemurian, but it ultimately made no difference. Lemurians traditionally preferred to be burned, so their spirits might rise with the smoke and join those in the Heavens who'd gone before, but regardless how distasteful most Lemurians considered the human practice of burying their remains, many Lemurian "destroyermen" had requested burial like—and beside—their shipmates. Their clan.

All the bones were sent to join those of destroyermen already buried in the little cemetery at the Parade Ground in the center of the city, that lay in the returning shade of the Great Tree of Baalkpan. The tree, and the new leaves sprouting from it, was a symbol of hope that all might be made right in the end—not least because of the graves it sheltered with its mighty boughs.

After the grisly chore of removing the dead was complete, spirits rose again. Not because anyone had discovered that the task before them would be easier than they thought; if anything they were beginning to cope with the fact that it would be much harder. Absolutely everything would have to be painstakingly repaired, including all the little things they hadn't even thought of. But now at least the wondering was over. They knew what they had to do. It would be hard, but they could do it. *Walker* would live again.

Alan leaned across a table erected under a colorful awning on the pier. A tired but upbeat Spanky was using a blueprint he'd hand-drawn from memory to describe some of the below-deck damage he'd seen.

"I was really surprised by how little silt there was in the turbines and boilers. The lube oil in the port reduction gear looks like peanut butter, though. Worn-out seals must have leaked." He shrugged. "Everything'll have to be taken apart piece by piece and cleaned, and the seals and gaskets will all have to be replaced—thank God we have plenty of gasket material! You really came through with that weird corklike stuff!"

Alan nodded self-consciously. "Yeah, well, like I said, Bradford discovered it. Some sort of tree in the northwestern marshes—where all those tar pits are. The trees draw the stuff up in their roots and deposit it in the lower outer layers of their trunks. Bradford says it protects them from insects."

"Whatever. It's good stuff. Mallory swears by it. He ran his little air-plane motor for twenty hours straight the other day and never got a leak. He says it's kind of hard to take stuff *apart* after it's been heated up, though. It sort of glues things together. He's calling it the 'Letts Gasket' and says you ought to take out a patent, since you're the one who figured out the application."

"I'll be sure to share my wealth with Courtney."

Adar had joined them, and when the laughter subsided, he addressed Alan. "What is a 'patent'?"

Alan looked at him and his expression turned serious. "Well, it's sort of a reward, I guess. It's a way people are rewarded for coming up with good ideas. Where we come from, laws protect those ideas from being used by other people. For example, if I invented a new gizmo—say the 'Letts gasket'—and got a patent on it, nobody else could swipe my idea and make the same thing without my permission. Usually, people would pay . . . or, ah, trade for permission."

Adar blinked concern. "Among our people there are clans or guilds that possess secret skills only they may pass on. That has caused many of my problems with the shipwrights. Is that much the same? Are you telling me you want permission to use your 'gaas-kets'?"

"No, Adar. It was a joke. 'My' gasket material is at everyone's disposal! I'm afraid we do need to have a long talk about that sort of thing when we get a chance, though."

Alan knew he was going to have to sit down with Adar one of these days and figure out some sort of financial system. Right now, everyone was highly motivated by the war effort and there was little grumbling about long hours, depletion of resources, and a somewhat lopsided distri-bution of labor and wealth. Before the war, Lemurian finance was based on an age-old, carefully refined, and fairly sophisticated barter system. Every-thing was worth exactly so much of something else. Even labor was valued in such a way. Some types of labor were worth more than others, but "wages" were still calculated by time-honored equivalent values. So much time in the shipyard, for example, was worth so many measures of gri-kakka oil, or grain, or seep. One length of fabric was worth so many weights of copper or fish, and so on. Obviously, people didn't carry their "wealth" around with them, or always even have possession of it, but everyone kept careful tabulations of who owed what to whom. To Alan, it was all pro-foundly confusing and inefficient, but he could see how it had worked for so long and, admittedly, well.

The problem was, right now there was an awful lot of activity and production under way and nobody was being "paid" anything. The situation struck a lot of the destroyermen as downright Stalinist, or at least mildly Red. With so much time ashore to think about such things, there'd been increased grumbling over how many barrels of gri-kakka oil a month being in the U.S. Navy was worth. The guys were fed and their booze at the Busted Screw was free, but the time was approaching when they might want to *buy* something. Going back to the old barter system was almost impossible too, since no one had been keeping tabs for a long time now. They'd have to start all over from scratch, and Alan knew from experience how hard it was to clear the books when it came to trades and favors.

He'd been reluctant to approach Adar about the problem because the guy already had so much on his plate. There was the war, of course, and the question of what to do about Jenks. Sister Audry and the presence of the descendants of the "ancient tail-less ones" had him all stirred up about religious matters, and he was walking a tightrope while he tried to figure that out. All were serious matters, but the financial cloud beginning to loom had the potential to eclipse all those other concerns. Somehow, Alan and Adar had to make time for this talk. Soon.

Adar sighed. "Very well. I think I know what you mean and you are right. If we had been keeping track, the people's surplus—guarded by Nakja-Mur and now myself—would have been gone long ago. With everything else . . . I do not look forward to that talk, but I welcome your suggestions." He motioned to the ship in the deepening gloom. "What have you discovered . . . besides bones?" His tone was suddenly urgent. "Can you fix her? You do understand she has become something of a . . . talisman to my People. Younglings carve images—icons of her, almost like Sister Audry's saints. The good sister speaks of your Lux Mundi, ah, Jesu Christo, and I must give that issue much thought." He paused. "Perhaps very much was lost in translation long ago. In any event, right now *Walker* is seen as the savior of my People—the People of Baalkpan and many others. Can you comprehend how important she has become to all of us?"

"Yeah," said Spanky, uncharacteristically quiet. "I wouldn't go runnin' around calling her a 'savior' or anything if I was you"—he glanced at Letts—"but we can damn sure comprehend how important she is. Trust me."

*T*he sky was perfect. There were just enough puffy clouds to provide an occasional respite from the overhead sun, and the blue was so pure and fresh from horizon to horizon that the contrast with the clouds was as sharp as a knife. Matt had spent a great deal of time staring at the sky over the last few days, since he now knew from experience that they were entering the stormy time of year. Currently, the sky meant them no harm and the sea retained that glorious, possibly unique purplish hue he found so difficult to describe. The steady cooling breeze blew up just enough chop to give it character. Gentle whitecaps magically appeared, sparkling under the sun, then vanished like unique little lives. Ahead lay the northeast coast of B'mbaado and the broad bay beyond. B'mbaado was not as thickly forested as Java, but from his perspective now, all Matt could see was a brilliant bluish green, turning golden at the top. If he lived to be a hundred, he'd never be able to reconcile the sheer, exotic, primordial beauty he beheld all around him with the savage lethality that lurked behind the mask.

Donaghey was an absolute joy, and he understood why Garrett loved her so. She and the other "first construction" frigates were built at the same time, but by the old methods. Unlike the new construction, there were subtle differences from one to the next. *Tolson* was a proud, stout ship and had a proud record too, but no matter what her crew did, she just didn't have *Donaghey*'s speed and grace. Her bow was blunter, her beam a bit wider, her shear not as sharp. She was formed a little more like her Grik counterparts. *Donaghey*'s builders had made everything just a bit more extreme. The result was that the flagship of the 2nd Allied Expeditionary

Force was also its fastest element, besides the feluccas, and she could outrun them with the wind abaft the beam.

Tolson cruised not far behind, but the steam frigates were in the distance, laboring to keep up. They were screened by the altered corvettes whose characteristics, as expected, were respectable, and Matt grinned to think how frustrated their skippers must be. The problem wasn't that the steamers were terribly slow; they weren't. They were faster than anything they'd seen of the Grik under any circumstances. They were much faster even than *Donaghey* when the wind was still.

With a good wind, the steamers were faster—and far more economical—under sail, but their paddles and screws caused drag and there was nothing they could do about that. On one of the new ships, *Nakja-Mur*, they'd tried a solution attempted in the previous century. Her screw was designed to be raised and lowered by means of a complex system that had slowed her construction considerably. The scheme worked, after a fashion—and at least it hadn't failed catastrophically—but it didn't really do much for her speed. Even with the screw retracted, there was still the large, blunt sternpost to consider. She did steer better however. Jim Ellis complained that *Dowden*'s steering was "mushy" unless she was under power.

The new engines hadn't really had a test yet. They'd gotten the ships under way and out in the Makassar Strait without anything flying apart, but since the discovery that they only slowed the ships while under sail, they'd been secured. Matt wished he'd been able to test them further while they were close to home, but what if he needed them later and they'd already failed? It was a balancing act of necessities. Eventually he *would* need them. He just wished he knew whether he could count on them.

As usual, Matt and Greg Garrett were standing companionably silent on the quarterdeck. It was a custom they'd observed many times. Sometimes there just didn't need to be words. Matt knew Jim understood it too. The three of them had been through so much together, small talk was often not only superfluous, but distracting Safir Maraan and Lord Rolak ascended to the quarterdeck and caught their eyes. Matt smiled at them and waved them over. The B'mbaadan and Aryaalan troops were mostly on other ships, but Chack was aboard with most of his 2nd Marines. Rolak went where Matt went; he was still insistent on that, but Matt suspected Safir was aboard because of Chack. They weren't "officially" mated yet, but it was just a matter of time. Matt expected a formal announcement and ceremony to cap the liberation of B'mbaado.

"Cap-i-taan," Safir greeted him.

"My lord," said Rolak.

"Queen Protector, Lord Rolak," Matt replied. He looked at Rolak. "Feeling better?" The old warrior grimaced and blinked irritation.

"A glorious day and a beautiful ship!" said Safir. She'd grown almost giddy with excitement the closer they came to her home. With luck, it would be hers again. Hers and her people's.

"Indeed they are," Matt agreed. "And as for the ship, I think I love her!" he admitted.

"You can't have her, Skipper," Garrett said with a grin. "I just got her back!"

Matt chuckled. "Don't worry, Greg. I think peeling her paint with tweezers would be easier than getting you off this ship." He nodded past the masts and taut canvas forward. "There's your coastline, Your Majesty, and not a Grik ship in sight. You'd think they'd at least have a few pickets out, but we haven't seen a thing." He shook his head. "Silly to expect them to think like us, but we *know* they've picked up a *few* ideas."

"It is a sight I have long craved," Safir admitted wistfully. "I am excited, I admit, but some of your uneasiness tugs at me as well."

"Am I uneasy?" Matt asked. "I suppose. I wish we had a little recon . . ." He avoided saying, *I wish we had the PBY,* for the ten thousandth time, but they all knew what he meant. "This steaming—I mean *sailing*—blindly into a situation we know nothing about reminds me too much of old times. I'd almost rather we had to chase down and pound on a few scouts. Besides"—he grinned predatorily—"it would be fun."

"'Fun,' he says." Garrett chuckled. "Remember what happened last time *I* had a little 'fun.'"

"But surely this is different," rumbled Rolak. "Even a large fleet would be no match for us now, and if there are no Grik to sound the alarm, the surprise of our arrival will be all the greater."

"In a perfect world," Matt agreed. He didn't elaborate on how imperfect he considered this world to be. "But they've had as much time to recover as we have. Okada didn't think they could bring anything forward for a while, but with what we know they left in Aryaal when they moved on Baalkpan, they wouldn't need to, to make it a damned bloody fight." He looked at Safir. "I've no doubt we'll win, but I'm always counting the cost. I have to. Besides, we know the Grik can surprise us—they've done it before—and if they didn't eat Kurokawa, he might've helped them arrange something . . . unexpected."

Two Marines tromped up the companionway. One was clearly Chack, still wearing his battered American helmet at a jaunty angle. The other seemed vaguely familiar, but Matt couldn't place him. He was uncomfortably aware that unless he knew them well and their coloration or dress was distinctive, he had a hard time telling one 'Cat from another. The two Marines drew close and saluted.

"Cap-i-taans," Chack said. "Lord Rolak"—he smiled slightly—"Your

Highness. I beg to report the discovery of this . . . creature . . . in my own ranks!"

Rolak peered more closely at the Marine. "By the Sun God's tail! Lord Koratin, you have lost much weight!"

Koratin! Now Matt remembered. He'd been a big wheel in Aryaal and had even been an advisor to its murdering king, Rasik-Alcas! He'd met him briefly when they retook the city right before the evacuation. For some reason, Rolak hadn't hanged him and Matt had forgotten all about him.

"Indeed!" replied Koratin. "I feel like a youngling again! I have always maintained that martial exercises strengthen the mind, body, and character."

"Character!" Rolak huffed. "I have occasionally—and briefly—wondered what happened to you after our last meeting. I assumed you were aboard *Nerracca* when she was lost, since you hadn't been insinuating yourself in the business of the Alliance. Yet here you stand, proving once again your consummate skill for survival!"

"Here I stand, Lord Rolak," Koratin answered, suddenly less ebullient.

Chack cleared his throat. "It seems Koratin enlisted in the First Baalkpan as a private as soon as he arrived in the city. He doubted he would be popular in an Aryaalan regiment. . . . In any event, he distinguished himself in battle and was therefore eligible to apply for Marine training." Chack blinked irony. "He graduated 'boot camp' as a squad leader corporal."

As things now stood in the Lemurian Marine Corps, only combat veterans could be considered for promotion. If there were ever peace, that might change, but for now the system worked well.

Rolak glanced incredulously at the twin red "stripes" on Koratin's kilt. "You *earned* corporal's stripes," he said, astonished. "That is more than you ever did in any previous post."

"True," Koratin agreed, "and I cherish those two stripes more than the finest robe I ever wore." His voice was still soft. "I owed it to my younglings. To all the younglings of our people, Lord Rolak. This, at least, I think you will believe."

Rolak nodded and looked at Matt. "Koratin was never evil. Vain, venal, and grasping, but not evil. I did not hang him because I believed he truly tried to stop Rasik and warn us of his treachery." He grumbled a chuckle. "It did not harm his case that Rasik was trying to kill him when we entered the city."

"You trust him?" Safir asked, surprised.

"I trust his dedication to younglings. That was never in doubt. Even at his worst, he often told noble tales and performed dramas for younglings in open forum. Moral dramas that taught principles he never used to live by."

"I was corrupt," Koratin agreed. "I thought I controlled my destiny. I knew my failings, yet I tried to set an example of integrity beyond myself so the younglings of our city might become better beings than I." He looked at Matt. "I have heard the words of your Sister Audry when she has come among the troops and I know not what power guides all things, whether it is the Sun God, or this other God of yours. Maybe they are the same." He shrugged. "But now I know that no one can hope to control destiny; it has a will of its own, its own plans for all of us. We are but leaves swept into a whirlpool not of our making. We do our best; that is all we can do, but in the end, in this arbitrary new way of war, our fates are in the hands of whichever God truly watches over us. Ultimately, we can only hope He will consider us fit company for the ones He has chosen to reward."

Taken aback, Matt could only stare. He hadn't known Sister Audry's "ministry" had penetrated so deeply. She hadn't built a cathedral next to the Great Hall, so he figured she was keeping things low-key. He knew she'd helped many of his men who felt lost and confused, regardless of denomination, but thought she'd otherwise confined her discussions with Adar. He hoped they didn't return to Baalkpan to find it locked in a holy war. "Jesus," he whispered.

"Carry on, Corporal Koratin," he said at last. "You're dismissed." When salutes were exchanged and Koratin was gone, he looked almost helplessly at Chack and the others. "What were we saying about surprises?"

"Are you sure he can be trusted?" persisted Safir. "Perhaps this is another of his dramas, and he speaks . . . most strangely."

Rolak looked thoughtful. "I don't think he performs; he was never that good. He was always strange, however. Chack?"

Chack blinked and shook his head. "His squad respects him, even the Aryaalans among them. When I said he distinguished himself in battle, it was something of an understatement."

"Let him be," Matt decided. "I guess we'll see. He's right about one thing: none of us knows our destiny." He glanced toward the now barely visible passage between B'mbaado and the distant Sapudis. "Or what we'll find in that bay."

They pushed on through the day and into the night. Matt sent a detail of 'Cats to Jenks's ship to serve as pilots, and keen-eyed Lemurian lookouts spied carefully ahead for shoals or enemy ships. A quarter moon gave more than sufficient light for them to warn of any danger. All night, the tension ratcheted up, and Garrett shortened sail on Matt's orders so the fleet could consolidate. Two hours before dawn, he gave the order for all ships to advance in line abreast and come to general quarters. If they encountered the enemy, they'd execute a turn to port on a signal from the flagship, and form a battle line. *Achilles* would maneuver to keep the battle line between herself and the Grik.

With the sun, they were close enough to see the remains of distant Aryaal through binoculars. Matt raised his precious Bausch & Lombs and adjusted the objective. It was still too far to make out any real details of the city, but except for a few jutting masts here and there that marked the graves of some recent Grik wrecks—possibly survivors of the Battle of Baalkpan that could make it no farther—there were no enemy ships in the bay.

"They're gone," he muttered in wonder.

"Maybe not," Garrett warned. "Maybe their ships are gone, but they might still have an army here, waiting to pounce on us as we disembark."

Matt grunted. He wouldn't put it past them. Still, unless they'd known they were coming—and he couldn't imagine how they would—there would have been *something* here. Supply ships if nothing else.

"May I?" asked Sean O'Casey. The big, one-armed man had joined them by the rail. He'd been bored throughout the voyage and had asked to be used as an engineer on one of the steamers, but Matt wanted him close for his insights regarding Jenks. The Imperial commodore had come aboard to dine a couple of times and Matt always wanted to know what O'Casey had to say about what they discussed. O'Casey remained hidden whenever Jenks was aboard, but his insights regarding Jenks were confusing. He was clearly wary of the man, but there was a subliminal thread of respect intertwined with a deep-seated resentment that remained imperfectly explained. Matt was never sure how much of what O'Casey had to say about Jenks was colored by whatever had apparently passed between the two men. In any event, according to O'Casey, Jenks hadn't avoided any real questions except Matt's occasional attempt to get him to confirm his suspicions regarding the location of the Imperial capital. Even O'Casey still wouldn't divulge that, as a matter of principle, but he knew Matt's guess was essentially correct. Matt didn't ask O'Casey anymore and O'Casey didn't disseminate. It was understood.

Garrett handed O'Casey his binoculars and the big man steadied them against a stay. "Impressive fortifications," he admitted. "'Twould be a costly chore ta storm. There's little ta see beyond the walls, however. Naught but that one fancy structure."

"That was the king's palace," Rolak confirmed. He was old, but his eyes were still far sharper than the average human's. "We burned the rest in the face of the Grik advance," he added sadly. "We left them nothing upon which to sustain themselves." He shook his head and his eyes were moist. "Aryaal was once a mighty, beautiful kingdom."

"It will be again," Matt assured him.

More officers and important passengers began gathering by the rail for their first glimpse of Aryaal or B'mbaado City. Safir's city across the strait had been undamaged by the fighting, but they'd burned it too. Now all they could see were the sad ruins atop the cliff. The fleet continued its advance, the heavily loaded corvettes angling toward the front when Matt ordered the signal aloft. Smoke coiled from the steamer's funnels as their boilers were lit. When they had steam, they'd maneuver inshore with their troops as well.

It was almost surreal. They'd come expecting a savage fight, but as best they could tell, there was nothing to face them. The entire environ seemed too quiet, almost devoid of life. Everything had the look of recent abandonment, and the closer they drew, the more apparent it became. The docks were strewn with debris and every small boat had been dragged ashore and shattered. Nothing at all remained of the dockside shantytown that had once served the cities' modest fisheries. Nothing but bare, scorched ground.

Then they smelled it. It began as a hint, a tantalizing ghost, but as they continued to approach and the wind came more from the shore, they caught the stench of death. Matt had smelled death many times now, in all its ghastly varieties. He'd smelled the decomposing Grik carrion at Baalkpan and on the plain below the very walls he looked upon. He knew what human dead smelled like: burnt, drowned, festering in the sun. This was different. It was something like what he'd smelled in the belly of *Revenge* after they'd taken that ship from the Grik, although there, there'd been a slimy, humid, mildewed edge. Regardless, he now recognized the growing, all-pervading stench of putrefying Lemurians.

"Left them naught ta sustain themselves, ye say?" O'Casey whispered, and tried to hold the glasses still. Matt redirected his binoculars. There'd been a disconnect, he supposed. He'd noticed the thousands of stakes driven in the ground surrounding Aryaal's walls, but must have assumed they'd been some new entanglement or defensive measure constructed by the Grik. Now he saw that atop each stake was a severed Lemurian head. Some were mere skulls by now, and they were still too distant for details, but many hung, slack-jawed, with tissue still attached. Some were quite fresh. Safir Maraan, bold warrior that she was, nearly lost the binoculars she'd borrowed when she lurched to the rail and vomited into the sea. Chack went to her and murmured soft words.

"My God!" exploded Garrett. "We can't have left that many behind! We got them *all*, Captain! Mr. Ellis and I." His tone became pleading. "We took everyone we could—everyone who came to the rendezvous! Maybe some didn't make it, but . . . my God!"

"I'm sure you got all you could, Greg," Matt said, his voice wooden. "But they were here a long time. Long enough to scour Java clean of all the 'prey' we never had a chance to save. The people of Bataava, the other cities . . ."

Rolak jerked his sword free of his belt and desperately cast his eyes about for something to cleave. With a wail of anguish, he finally buried the point in the deck. Even Garrett didn't scold him.

"Do you think they're gone then?" Safir asked, stepping to face him. Her eyes were pools of horror and Chack supported her as though she might faint. Her usually immaculate silver-washed breastplate had been splashed with the contents of her stomach.

"Yeah. I think so." His lips curled in a snarl. "Why else do *that*?"

"What do you mean?" asked Chack. "We know they collect skulls . . . 'trophies' of their prey."

"But they didn't *collect* them!" Matt insisted. "They left them here like that! Maybe not all of them are gone, and keep that in mind when you go ashore, but I bet most are. For some reason, they've abandoned this place and they knew, eventually, we'd return." He gestured at the city and the literally thousands of stakes. "And they wanted to make sure, when we did, we'd see *that*!"

"Skipper," Garrett said quietly, "I think if Mr. Bradford were here, he'd say something profound, about the lizards being more sophisticated than we thought, or something like that. I bet they did this as a warning. To scare us. Make us stay away."

"You're probably right. Maybe they are more sophisticated, or maybe Kurokawa put them up to it. Doesn't matter." He looked at those around him, then forced himself to look at the city again. "I think they'll find it has an opposite effect than they intended. Just like Pearl Harbor." By now, most of the 'Cats knew the significance of that reference. "I want to exterminate them like the vermin they are." He paused, then spoke to Garrett. "Signal the corvettes to disembark their troops as planned. Form a perimeter around the landing area. The steamers will cover the landing with their heavy guns. Once we have a beachhead, we'll put the rest of the troops ashore, again, just like we planned. Whether the landing is contested or not, I want everybody acting like it is. Good practice. Finally, send a signal to *Achilles*, with my compliments, and ask Commodore Jenks if he'd care to accompany me ashore." Matt's face hardened. "I think it's high time our reluctant British friends saw the true face of our enemy."

Captain Reddy met Jenks's boat at the dock. Rolak was with him, along with the old warrior's staff. The only other human was Chief Gray, looming behind his captain with a Thompson submachine gun. The gun had once been Tony Scott's personal weapon and it hadn't saved him in the end—but he hadn't had it with him, had he? Gray was determined that Captain Reddy would always have him *and* the weapon at his back whenever he was at risk. Jenks stepped out of the boat with another white-coated figure. Both held perfumed cloths over their faces. Four of the red-coated, bare-legged Imperial Marines stepped ashore as well, bright muskets on their shoulders.

Jenks was watching the rapid, professional deployment of the Marines the 600, and the slightly less practiced arrival of the Army regiments. Once ashore however, the Army seemed as competent as the others. Matt sensed that Jenks was a little surprised and perhaps slightly daunted by what he saw. The Marines established a perimeter near where the old breastworks once had been, and Safir's 600—who trained with the Marines to the same rigorous standards—deployed across the road leading to the main gate. The Army regiments, in their multicolored leather armor and kilts, took supporting positions as the Marines broadened the beachhead. Four light guns were off-loaded and placed, by sections, in the center and on the right flank. Nothing stirred across the vast plain on the left.

Slowly, the steamers nudged their way closer to the dock. General Alden led the rest of the forces ashore and soon the area within the perimeter teemed with troops. In two hours, they had four thousand battle-tested, well-trained *soldiers* from every Allied power probing slowly forward and automatically preparing defensive positions around the perimeter. The steamers moved away and joined the frigates, where they could defend against any attack from the sea, while covering the ground force with their guns. It struck Matt how differently this landing was going from the first one they'd made on these very shores. Then, it had been dark and chaotic, and the Army was largely untested. It wasn't quite as big either. He was confident that if he'd brought these troops ashore back then, they could easily have defeated the nearly twenty thousand Grik despite Rasic's treachery, without any help from Aryaal at all. The weapons were the same as before, even though there'd been some familiarization training with the new prototypes. Full-scale production was just beginning when they left, and there was no sense "trickling" the new weapons in. The main difference between this Army and the old was, literally, a level of professionalism that came only with experience and confidence.

Alden and Chack approached and saluted. Alden was the overall field commander and the various regimental commanders would have already reported to him. "Skipper," he said, "we've pushed nearly to the gates." He scowled. "Close enough to get a good look at all the heads." He glanced at Jenks appraisingly. "Lord Rolak's supporting the Second Marines and the

Six Hundred with the First and Third Aryaal. He begs the . . . ah . . . privilege of being the first to enter his city."

Matt nodded. "Very well. Chack, you and Queen Maraan let him through, but I want you both to support him closely. No telling what surprises the enemy may have left. Form a perimeter inside the gate, in that open area around the big fountain like we did last time. Use other supporting regiments. After the plaza's secure, proceed to secure the rest of the city. Once we're sure the enemy's gone, we'll form details to take those damn heads down."

"Aye-aye, sir," Alden and Chack chorused, and trotted off. Matt turned to Jenks, who'd remained mostly silent since coming ashore.

"A most impressive display, Captain Reddy," Jenks said. His tone held no irony.

"I guess you could do it better, though," muttered Gray sarcastically. Despite the slightly more cordial relations between Jenks and his captain, the Bosun hadn't thawed.

Jenks rounded on Gray, snatching the kerchief from his face. "It was a genuine compliment, *Mr.* Gray. I do grow weary of your attitude, however. You have harbored a grudge for long months now and perhaps I provoked it. If so, I sincerely apologize in the presence of"—he waved toward the countless pikes—"these tragic dead. That said, and the apology made, I will gladly oblige you if you insist on a confrontation." Jenks took a breath and suddenly gagged violently. "Excuse me," he muttered, and, stepping a short distance away, he retched. His companion, kerchief still in place, joined the commodore while he continued to heave and gasp.

Gray was stunned. "I'll be damned," he managed. "That Bakelite Brit can bend a little after all." He lowered his voice. "Even if it did break him to do it."

"Leave him be, Boats. He's been 'bending' quite a bit lately. More than you know. And seeing that"—he nodded at the city—"could break anybody. We've kind of gotten used to it," he said bitterly, "and it still makes me want to puke."

Jenks finally composed himself and returned to face them. His color was ashen. "My apologies again, gentlemen." His voice was rough.

"No need," said Matt, almost gently.

"I . . . guess I'm sorry too," said Gray. "I didn't mean to make you move your hanky . . . and . . . blow."

It was all Matt could do, even under the circumstances, to keep from cracking up. The Bosun had always had a talent for the backhanded compliment, apology, or . . . anything. Jenks looked at the big man intently for a moment before deciding to accept Gray's . . . statement.

"Actually, as I was saying," continued Jenks, forcing himself to keep the kerchief from his face, "your landing was most impressive. Very businesslike and coordinated. And somewhat ominous to a"—he glanced again at the heads—"a *neutral* observer such as myself."

"Surely you practice such things? Your Marines, for example."

"Certainly, but you have clearly had much more practice, on a considerably larger scale of late. My nation relies as heavily on naval power as does yours. Even more so, I'd wager, but we rarely engage in major land actions. The most recent of those was several years past. As you know, there are just under a hundred Marines aboard my ship, and I'm sure they could have come ashore just as creditably. But even their modern weapons might not have added much punch to your force."

Matt avoided commenting on Jenks's definition of "modern weapons" and the dubious advantage Matt considered muskets to be over the Lemurian's powerful longbows, but he knew his troops had won Jenks's respect. It remained to be seen whether that was a good thing or not.

The wind veered slightly and a gentle, merciful breeze diverted most of the stench northeast, toward B'mbaado. That or their noses were growing desensitized. Flags flapped and popped within the perimeter where the command staff awaited the first reports from the city. They'd heard no shots, but it was possible they might not have. The few rifle-armed scouts might have penetrated far enough by now that the ruins and the breeze could swallow the reports of their Krags. Eventually however, a runner appeared in the gateway and raced down through the ranks until he stood before Matt.

"General Rolak's compliments, Cap-i-taan Reddy," announced the 'Cat with surprisingly little accent. "The city is secure from the north gate, halfway to the south. There is no sign of the enemy other than a few . . . curious corpses. The Royal Palace has also been secured, and General Rolak begs you to come to him."

Matt arched an eyebrow. "Any resistance? Casualties?"

"No casualties, sir . . . but there *is* resistance—of a sort. Nothing to be concerned with," the 'Cat added with a snort, "but something my general prefers you see for yourself."

Matt shrugged and looked at Gray. "Very well. Tell him we'll be along."

Gray hitched his pistol belt and shouted for an orderly to assemble the rest of the Captain's Guard, some of whom were still aboard ship. Matt rolled his eyes, but knew it was pointless to complain. He looked at Jenks.

"Care to join us?"

They entered the city and the entourage was joined by an even larger security force that escorted them to the Royal Palace. Pete Alden met them there, reporting that Rolak and Queen Maraan were inside. Chack was leading his troops on a deeper penetration of the city. As the runner had told them, Alden confirmed that the only signs of the enemy were some "strange" corpses, but cryptically added that they *had* discovered a few Grik. Matt was curious, but knew if there was a threat, they'd have told him. They probably just wanted him to see whatever it was in the same context they'd first viewed it. Sometimes, context was important, and maybe they didn't want to prejudice his perceptions. The palace was filthy and full of reeking droppings. Matt wondered whether the enemy had done that deliberately. Surely even the Grik couldn't live amid such filth? The ships they'd captured hadn't been *clean*, but they hadn't been defiled to this extent.

Alden paused before a macabre scene. A Grik—or was it?—was staked to heavy beams resembling an inverted cross. It flashed through Matt's mind that the thing had been *crucified* right here in the palace! Its tail had been hacked off and was nowhere in sight. All the claws were torn away, leaving mere jagged stumps of fingers and toes. It looked like even some of the creature's teeth had been knocked out. Both eyes were missing from the desiccated corpse but whether they'd been gouged out by scavengers or during the evident "entertainment" was impossible to guess. By the amount of dark, dried blood spattered all around, it had clearly been alive for at least part of the process.

"That's not an ordinary Grik," Gray said.

"Yeah," agreed Matt. "The fur color's wrong. It looks more like one of those aborigine Griks we saw on Bali."

"Wow," muttered Gray. "Bastards must not get along. Wonder why they didn't just eat him?"

"He's not the only one," Alden said. "And there's something else you need to see."

They followed the Marine up a long, winding stair that landed upon another wide chamber, not quite as filthy as the one below. Pete then advanced to a high-arched, guarded doorway. "Open it," he said to one of the guards, and the 'Cat pushed the heavy door inward. Pete glanced back, his face grim, and made a "follow me" motion with his head.

Rasik-Alcas, king of Aryaal, sat upon what had so briefly been his ornate golden throne. The throne had suffered the ravages of the Grik and was now somewhat the worse for wear—but so was Rasik-Alcas. His once elaborate robes were dingy and weather-beaten, faded and stained. His pelt was a loose shroud draped over what had been a powerful frame. His cheeks were hollow and his whiskers were long and shaggy. Within the well-defined skull, however, large eyes still shone bright with hatred and madness. Currently they were locked upon those of Lord Muln-Rolak, standing just a few feet away, his sword point held casually—and unwaveringly—less than an inch from Rasik's nose.

"My lord," Rolak said, addressing Matt, "we were mistaken. Somehow, the beast still lives. Clearly, the punishment we expected for him was far too mild." He grinned horribly. "Or perhaps even the Grik could not stomach the thought of eating him!"

Matt's first reaction was one of rage. He hated Rasik-Alcas more than any living creature—but he hadn't known he was living, had he? The bastard was responsible for the death of Harvey Donaghey, and probably Tom Felts and half a dozen other destroyermen as well. God knew how many Lemurian lives were lost to his treachery. Matt started to order Rolak to hack the miserable murderer down. Then his hand strayed to his Academy sword. He'd do it himself! Pulling the sword free with a snarl, he took a step forward.

"Ah, Skipper?"

"What, Pete?" Matt snapped.

"Well, hold on just a second. Please."

Matt paused, blood thundering in his ears, and looked back at Alden. The chamber was large, but much was in shadow. Large, arched passages that once opened upon a balcony were covered over with planks. The full heat of the day pounded against the wooden barriers, radiating inward. It was hard to see anything, though, except for Rasik and Rolak, who stood in a beam of light that must have been purposely channeled to rest upon the throne.

"We ain't alone in here, Skipper," Pete said.

For the first time, Matt peered hard into the gloom. Evidently, Gray did too, because there came a muttered, "Shit!" and the unmistakable sound of the Thompson's bolt being yanked back.

"My God," Matt said. He could now discern other figures in the chamber that he'd missed in his single-minded concentration on the Aryaalan king. Half a dozen forms stood stationary along the walls, each covered by two or more Marines. At first, he thought he must be imagining things, that the gloom was playing tricks on his vision, but he quickly realized that wasn't the case. They were lizards. Grik. He'd seen quite enough of the monsters to identify them at a glance. These were the real thing, not aboriginals or a different species like Lawrence. These were the exact same creatures they'd come here to fight, but here they stood, almost alone, and their reaction to the situation wasn't right at all.

"What the hell's going on here, Mr. Alden?" Matt demanded, pausing his killing advance on Rasik.

"Damned if I know, Skipper. We came in here and found 'em like this: Rasik on his fancy chair and a bunch of lizards standing around like guards. His guards. Lord Rolak went to kill the bastard and he told the Griks to defend him! It's been like this since: Rolak ready to stick Rasik and the lizards ready to fight. Wouldn't be much of a fight," he added, "but, well, I figured you ought to see it."

"Rolak?"

"The beast says they are his 'children,' his 'pets.' They do seem willing to defend him. Just as odd, he spoke to them in the language of the People, which he must have taught them."

"Ask *them* what this is all about!" Matt ordered.

"I tried. I think they even answered me, but I could not understand. They seemed to understand me, though, and I managed to get them to lower their weapons, at least."

Matt had never personally met the Aryaalan king, but that didn't matter. They knew each other through their deeds. He was glad he'd finally polished his 'Cat enough to vent his rage without an interpreter: "Rasik, you sick bastard! I figured when we left you here, you'd wind up on a stick! I thought that a fitting punishment for what you did. Even then, I never dreamed you'd collaborate with these monsters! They killed your people, your city! Have you seen what they did outside? Have you even *been* outside?"

Rasik turned his gaze upon the captain, the hate and madness still bright. "I did not 'collaborate,' you fool! I fled! I went into the wilderness with my few loyal guards and we evaded the Grik and sometimes killed them. We even fed upon them, on occasion," he added with some satisfaction. "But I *stayed* when all my people left me, left our sacred city to the Grik! *You* are to blame for what has befallen us! You led this evil here! If you had not come, all would be as it has always been. We would have defeated the first, smaller Grik horde and then turned our attention back to B'mbaado! Well, that city is mine now too, as is all of Jaava! None remain to contest me; even the Grik have fled! But I stayed. I *stayed*! All this land is *mine*!"

Rasik's rant was so wildly untrue and preposterous, Matt couldn't even bring himself to respond to it. Instead, he looked at the Grik guards. "Not all the Grik fled, it seems. If you didn't collaborate with them, why do they protect you?"

"A simple thing. They collaborated with *me*. They are not the same as the vermin that infested my city. They are some of those that scattered after the battle I so wisely kept my warriors"—Rasik paused and glared at Rolak—"*most* of my warriors from joining. My companions and I hunted them at first," he admitted, "like any Grik. We did not know the difference. When we discovered they *were* different, we ... allowed them to enlist in our army of liberation! Never have there been such loyal troops! Lift a finger against me and they will strike you down and eat your bones!" Rasik chuckled and it sounded like a wood rasp dragged across a rock.

"We came to hurl the invaders from my city and discovered it all but abandoned! The horde must have learned that I was coming to reap my revenge! All that remained were a few feral Grik, like are known to inhabit the islands nearby. Their masters must have left them here." Rasik flicked his wrist. "We disposed of them."

Matt wondered whether the crucified creature downstairs was one such Rasik had "disposed" of, and if all had been given similar treatment.

"Where are your other 'companions,' *king*?" asked Rolak. The word "king" dripped sarcasm.

"They were like you, *Lord* Rolak," Rasik replied matter-of-factly, with equal sarcasm. "They were disloyal. They disobeyed me *just like you* and I was forced to punish them."

"So," Matt said, taking a few steps closer. "Now you're the uncontested king of all Aryaal, all Java—with nothing but a handful of Grik for subjects!"

"My people will return!" Rasik hissed. "They will return now that I have driven the Grik away!"

"You didn't drive them away," Matt retorted harshly, unable to stomach Rasik's lies any longer. "'Your' people did!" He paused. "*They* did it, Rasik, and they *have* returned! They've come back to scour this city and make it their own again. They left you, sure enough, but they left you here to die."

"You did that!" Rasik screeched.

"Yeah, I did, and I'm sorry. I should have killed you then, like your people said I should!"

"Guards!" shouted Rasik, turning toward "his" Grik.

"Wait!" yelled Matt, in Lemurian. "You say you think they'll understand me?" he quickly asked Rolak.

"Yes, lord . . . if you are careful about your accent!"

Matt ignored the jibe. "You . . . you Grik warriors," he said carefully. "Listen to me. This creature is evil. . . . Do you know what that means?" Rasik prepared a shouted retort, but Rolak waved his sword point to regain his attention. "He has led you down a false path, a dark path . . . a wrong path. He does not want what is best for you, only for himself. He sacrificed his own people to his selfishness and he's ready to do it again. To sacrifice you." Matt rubbed his eyes, hoping he was getting through. "If you try to fight us, you will die. That's the truth. You won't even get any of us." He nodded toward the Marines covering each of the creatures. "If you put your weapons down and come with us, you'll be well treated; I promise! You'll never be 'prey,' and you'll never have to be afraid again. I'm the commander of the forces that defeated you to begin with, the forces that defeated your Invincible Swarm and finally drove your people from this city. I have the power to make this promise, and it *is* a promise! Think of it! Plenty of food, nothing to fear"—he looked at Rasik—"and no more dying at the whim of a wild, unfeeling traitor. A traitor that made prey of his own people and would do the same to you!" There was total silence. "*Think* on it!"

Suddenly, with what almost sounded like a whimper, a sword fell to the floor. Then another. Incredulous, Rasik squirmed on his throne to see, but anything he might have said was silenced when Rolak's blade caressed his neck. The rest of the Grik weapons hit the floor with a cacophonous crash and Matt felt a wild feeling of relief . . . and something else.

"Goddamn," muttered Gray. "Skipper, you just talked to Grik!"

I just talked to Grik! Matt screamed to himself. *What does it mean? What* can *it mean?* Quickly but carefully, since no Grik was ever unarmed, the Marines rounded up the prisoners—*Grik prisoners!*—and led them from the chamber. Matt took a deep breath and looked around. Pete still seemed speechless, as shocked as he was, and Jenks—he'd forgotten Jenks was even there—was looking at him with a very strange expression. He turned back to Rasik.

"Well," he said. "Left to die again. Somehow, you just don't inspire much loyalty, *King* Alcas!"

"Am I to die?" Rasik asked. His madness seemed to have passed with his illusion of power and his eyes had grown wide with fright.

"Just as soon as it can be arranged," Matt promised him.

"I would *so* enjoy killing him, my lord," Rolak crooned.

"Me too, but we need to do it right. For now, we've got a hell of a mess to clean up around here," he said grimly. "Then we've got to decide what to do next. Maybe even learn something from our prisoners." He stopped and shook his head. He needed time to wrap his mind around that. He wished Bradford were here! Or Lawrence. Maybe Rebecca's companion would have some insight. "I want to push on toward Singapore, see what things are like there. Maybe we can take it back too. For some reason, the enemy seems to be abandoning his forward outposts. Anyway, we'll be stuck here for a little while. There'll be plenty of time for a trial for 'His Majesty' and we'll boost morale for his former subjects with a proper, first-class hanging." He glanced at his watch and turned to leave. "Carry on, gentlemen."

"Wait!" cried Rasik. Matt kept walking. "*Wait!*" Rasik screeched with the voice of a terrified youngling. Matt paused in the doorway.

"What?" he snapped. "I've got a lot to do, and as far as I'm concerned, you're to blame for most of it. We might have *saved* some of those people out there on poles if it wasn't for you, damn you! The sooner you're dead, the happier I'll be!"

"After I'm dead," Rasik said, gaining a little control over his voice, "you will never know what I found while I wandered in the wilderness!"

"What you found?"

"Yes. I think you might find it quite interesting . . . possibly even worth my life."

"C ontact!" Ben Mallory shouted, warning Tikker that things were about to happen. Fast. They'd just completed the exhaustive, perhaps even mildly paranoid checklist he'd devised in the naive hope he'd somehow managed to foresee every glitch and imponderable characteristic his "creation" might throw at them. In spite of his excitement, Ben was more than a little nervous. He knew airplanes—particularly the high-performance pursuit planes he'd trained in—but in spite of the workmanlike proficiency he'd gained in the old PBY Catalina, he'd known it had a lot of idiosyncrasies he'd never figured out. Most of them probably had to do with its being a seaplane. His takeoffs and landings had never been all that hot, and that still bothered him. Now he was about to try to fly a seaplane that, essentially, *he'd* designed, without the benefit of any of the cumulative wisdom that had gone into the Catalina. Maybe "nervous" wasn't really the right word.

The water of the bay was a little restless, with a light, uneven chop, but the wind was right and the sky seemed docile enough. The X-PB-1, as he referred to the plane, or "Nancy," as everyone else had taken to calling it, after his first, ill-considered description, floated in the middle of the bay where it had been towed by *Mahan*'s launch, and all the area for a good distance in every direction had been cleared of harbor shipping. Other boats bobbed at regular intervals, ready to race to their aid if something . . . unpleasant happened. Ben hoped it wouldn't. Experiments had shown that if they crashed into the water, even in the bay, they had a life expectancy of between four and six minutes before the "flashies" arrived and tore them to shreds. Of course, they had to survive the crash itself before that little tidbit of information would be relevant.

Ben was unhappy about the seemingly universally accepted moniker. The plane hadn't ultimately wound up looking anything *like* a Nancy—one of the NC, or Navy-Curtiss, flying boats. It still looked more like a miniature PBY to him, although a comparison to a Supermarine Walrus was probably even closer. He was damned if he'd even mention *that*.

"Contact," Tikker confirmed, while Ben stood precariously and turned toward the propeller. He felt as if he were attempting the feat in a canoe. He almost fell when an errant wave bounced the port wing float and slapped the starboard float against the sea.

"Jeez!" he chirped, trying to brace himself. He reached back and grasped one of the blades. At least he felt confident about the propeller. They'd "tracked" it while the engine was on the stand, and run it at different RPMs to check for resonant vibration and balance. The first one flew apart and nearly killed "Mikey" Monk, but they quickly improved the design. Bernie and Campeti finally came up with a scheme for a machine like a Springfield stock carver that they could use to make perfect props every time, as well as musket stocks. He pushed the blade up as high as he could reach, then brought it down with all his might. Much to his gratification, his prototype engine coughed instantly to life, and with a burbling, liquid fart, the propeller blades blurred before him. His back screamed in agony as he pulled something important trying to keep from falling into the prop. *Improvement number one*—he winced—*some kind of rail behind the cockpit for the pilot to hang onto so the engine doesn't eat him!*

Painfully, he turned and tried to get in the seat, but tripped on the stick and sprawled forward, across the windscreen. The stick poked him savagely in the crotch. He had no idea what kind of sound he made over the suddenly coughing engine, but doubted it was very manly. Aft, behind the motor, Tikker sprang up like . . . well, a cat, and hosed fuel at the carburetor with one of *Mahan*'s bug sprayers. The engine farted again, ran up, then started to cough. Somehow, Ben managed to form an objective thought: *Okay. Have to figure out a whole new startup procedure.* He slid down into his wicker seat and for a moment just sat there, gasping sympathetically with the motor while trying to remember where the throttle was through the waves of pain. His vision cleared as the tears evaporated and he pushed the suddenly visible throttle knob forward. Tikker had been keeping the engine alive with the bug sprayer, but now it caught and settled into a healthy-sounding rumble.

Before he could grab it, Ben's six-page checklist flew past his face, into the prop, and showered Tikker with confetti. *Oh, well*, he thought. *Saves me the effort of tearing it up.* He settled in his seat, getting a feel for things, and put the control surfaces through their paces once more. So far, so good. The engine had settled down and sounded swell. He felt the plane begin to accelerate slightly beneath him and glanced up. *That's funny. What's the launch doing there?* The boat was racing straightaway, almost directly in front of him. *Oh. Damn. There's the city, too!* The plane must have bobbed around in a circle while he was concentrating on getting it started and staying alive. He pushed the right rudder pedal to the floorboard, and the plane began turning south again, completing the circle it had begun on its own. *Enough*, he thought. *The vaudeville show's over. Time to get this crate in the air!* He yelled for Tikker to hang on, but doubted the 'Cat heard him. He realized improvement number three was some kind of voice tube so he could communicate with his air crew.

Pointing roughly toward the mouth of the bay, he advanced the throttle. The propeller became invisible and the awkward-looking craft picked up speed. *Okay, fairly responsive. Let's give it some more!* He pushed the throttle to the stop. His creation had no flaps. The PBY hadn't had any and he'd hoped they wouldn't be needed. It was a seaplane, after all, and runway length shouldn't be an issue. He'd hoped. "C'mon," he muttered. The engine roared behind him, a little quieter now, and the prop was spinning—disconcertingly close—as fast as it could. The plane increased speed until it began to skip across the top of the water, but he couldn't seem to get it up. "C'mon!" he yelled, pulling back a little on the stick. The nose came off the water, but he *felt* it catch the wind! "Whoa!" he yelped, pushing back on the stick just a bit. His heart raced and he wondered how close he'd come to flipping the plane on its back. *CG—center of gravity—is too far aft. I was afraid of that*, he thought. *Too much ass in her britches, like a P-39.* He wondered why he'd done that. Was he trying to make a pursuit ship out of a floatplane? Chances were she'd be pretty nimble, but he was growing more concerned about the plane's stability. He concentrated on holding the stick where it was, still building speed. *Might need flaps after all*, he thought.

Suddenly, amazingly, the hull left the water and the contraption was in the air! He risked a glance back at Tikker, but the 'Cat was whirling madly on the crank that retracted the wing floats. He looked to the side. Sure enough, the floats were coming up—slowly. *Damn. Need a little more mechanical advantage there.* The floats had seemed to come up fast enough when they tested them, but that was on dry land, with no drag. *Number five.*

Once the plane was off the water, it practically rocketed into the sky. Again, he wondered if there was some seaplane mystery he was unaware of. He eased back on the stick and knew they had enough thrust at last to keep the nose from trying to flip them. He'd actually foreseen that to a degree, and intended that the high-mounted engine should counteract just such a tendency. He hadn't had any real formula to base his calculations on, but it seemed to be working . . . sort of. That might have been what kept them down so long too, though. *Oh, well, that's what test flights are for!*

He wiped his goggles and realized he was soaked. There'd been enough spray to wet him down pretty good. He'd never gone blind, per se, but a larger windscreen was in order. He'd also have hated to get this wet anywhere but in the tropics. Cold still might be an issue, depending on the ceiling. *Number six.* He started climbing and banking slightly left, intending to ease back toward the city. Slowly, his tension began to ebb. He'd done it! He'd designed and helped build the first airplane ever constructed on this world! A euphoric feeling began to take hold. He'd done it, and he was flying! When the old PBY folded up and fell into the bay during the battle, he'd never dreamed he would survive, much less fly again! He let out a whoop.

He didn't have an altimeter, but thought he was probably about two thousand feet up when he steadied the plane and aimed it at Baalkpan. With any luck, they'd have altimeters soon. There wasn't that much to them, and right then, anything seemed possible. He glanced at his instrument panel. They'd salvaged a few instruments from the Catalina and put them on the prototype whether they had realistic expectations of recreating them or not. They had to know what the plane could do. All the new planes would have a few easy instruments: a compass, an artificial horizon—or clinometer, as the Navy types liked to call it. An airspeed indicator was easy to do. Several temperature gauges would be supplied: one for the crankcase and others for each cylinder head. An oil-pressure gauge had already been successfully tested and was in production. The fuel gauge, at present, was the time-honored floating stick bobbing up and down through a hole in the gas cap. The fuel tank was in the wing above and behind him and he could keep an eye on the "gauge" with a little mirror. They'd need more eventually. They already *had* more than most pilots relied on in the Great War. Ben fiddled with the stick. A little tight, he decided, and he'd like some trim tabs, but overall, the only real problem was a tendency to pitch. *CG, again.* He already hated the propeller so close behind his head. Maybe they needed to turn the engine around. Make it a pusher . . .

He read the gauges instead of just staring proudly at them. Airspeed was better than he'd expected. About ninety. The temps looked good. A little warmer in the rear cylinders, but he'd expected that. Oil pressure was steady, maybe dropping a little, but that was normal as the oil heated up. He looked back at Tikker and caught a huge grin splitting the sable face. A few particles of the checklist still clung in his fur. Ben returned the thumbs-up offered by the only other "experienced" aviator in the Alliance. That thought hit him again. It had been stupid to bring Tikker on this flight. Granted, the 'Cat wasn't *really* experienced, but he had guts and he *had* flown. He'd also done very well in the simulators they'd put together. *Shouldn't have done it*, Ben decided, *but the little guy deserved it.*

Tikker caught his attention again, made a swooping gesture with his hand, and pointed down. Ben saw they were coming up on where *Ajax* was moored. *Oh, no. Why did he have to do that?* Had he *known* Ben's pursuit instincts would kick in, like a dog seeing a rabbit take off? *Can't do it*, Ben decided. *Talk about stupid! No way should I do this! I really probably ought not to. . . .* With a wicked grin, he nodded exaggeratedly.

Pushing the stick forward, he pretended he had a gunsight in front of him and began a shallow dive toward the Imperial frigate. He knew Adar would get hot, and so would the captain when he found out, but what were they going to do? Ground him? The plane started gaining speed. One hundred, a hundred and ten, a hundred and twenty . . . The stick got even tighter, but he waggled his wings just a little and knew he had plenty of control. Closer they sped, and he could see figures running on the deck. He knew just seeing the airplane was probably giving them fits, but there'd been no way to fly it without them knowing, so no one had actually ordered him *not* to buzz the ship. Besides, they still had stuff to test. A hundred and thirty at this dive angle seemed about max, and Ben was really wishing for trim tabs now, but as the mast tops approached, he was pleased to note that when he pulled back on the stick, the strange little plane almost leaped back up into the sky.

Maybe just a little impulsively, he displayed a hopefully universal gesture and yanked the stick to the right, forcing the plane into a slightly tighter climbing barrel roll than he'd perhaps intended.

"Seat belts!" he shouted, as he went inverted. "Number seven!"

There was no danger he and Tikker would fall out—they were sucked *into* their seats—but they were slammed against the left side of their respective cockpits. The tight roll and sharp climb forced Ben's head back—where there was no rest—and he found himself staring right at the blurred propeller just inches away.

"*Shit!*"

Instinctively, Ben pushed the stick forward—maybe a little too much. The aft CG practically pitched the nose out from under them, causing a momentary—but terrifying—negative-G condition. This immediately levitated the fuel in the carburetor and closed the float, starving the engine—not to mention leaving Tikker to clutch the diagonal stringers in the fuselage for dear life. Recognizing that improvement number seven was of *extreme* importance, Ben somehow managed to ease back on the stick, finish the roll, and right the craft before he and Tikker were thrown from the plane.

Airspeed had kept the prop windmilling behind him, and within seconds, as the fuel in the carburetor remembered where to go, the engine coughed and sputtered back to life. Holding the stick in a vise-like grip, Ben looked around. Everything was back to normal and the Nancy seemed to have survived the *stupid, stupid, stupid* gyrations with no apparent damage. He sighed, loosening his grip a little, and took a deep, shaky breath. He almost gagged. *Gas!* There was gas everywhere! He looked at Tikker and saw that the 'Cat was soaked. He was shouting something and pointing up. Ben spun to stare at the little mirror and saw the fuel gauge stick was gone. Worse, so was the gas cap it floated in. *What the hell?!* The pressure of the gas or the air in the tank slapping against it must have blown the cap off, he deduced. Judging by the amount of fuel all over everything, they must have dumped a lot—since most of it wouldn't have landed on them!

He looked down. They were over the city now, and he banked back toward the bay. *I wonder how much fuel we have left?* The engine coughed, gurgled, then roared back to life. *Shit! Not much!*

He turned back to Tikker and made a winding motion over his head. *Get the floats down!* Tikker was already spinning the crank. With a pounding heart, Ben Mallory concluded he was liable to have to attempt yet another stunt he'd absolutely *never* intended for this very first flight: a dead-stick landing on Baalkpan Bay.

Pointing the nose down to build some airspeed, he found he had to keep even more back pressure on the stick to keep the ship level as the engine burped and died completely. The sudden lack of any sound but the wind whooshing through the support struts and control cables was chilling.

"Slow down!" he heard Tikker shriek for the first time.

"Can't!" he shouted back. "Rule number one—when you start training those idiots who volunteered for this—airspeed is life! In our case, we need enough speed to land the damn thing on the water! If we're too slow when we flare out, we'll stall and pancake in. Liable to break something!"

"I thought rule number one was 'no stupid stunts that kill engine!'"

"I . . ." Ben fumed, and concentrated on keeping a steady, gliding descent. Ahead, the bay opened before them again. Damn, they were getting low! 'Cats were scurrying around on the waterfront, dodging this way and that, apparently expecting them to drop right on top of them. He eased back just a bit on the stick—and then held it tight against its tendency to come too far back. *Definitely going to have to change the CG*, he decided. They were over the water now, and he looked for a clear spot to set down.

There wasn't much room. Many of the ships and fishing boats had gathered in this area to stay out of his way.

"A little speed help now?" Tikker demanded.

"Hell, yes. What . . . ?" Tikker hosed the last of the fuel in the bug sprayer at the carburetor. With a "pop!" and an explosive backfire, the engine roared to life and gave him just enough acceleration to level off and make a powered touchdown on the choppy water. He risked a quick glance aft when he heard a shrill cry, and saw Tikker pitch the flaming bug sprayer over the side like an arcing meteor. The backfire must have lit the damn thing!

Whump! The plane practically gouged into the sea, but it had just enough remaining speed and lift to bounce up and skip across a few little waves before settling down for good. The engine gasped, hacked, and the prop spun raggedly to a stop, leaving them bobbing peacefully on the light swells about three hundred yards from shore. Ben finally took a long, deep breath and forcefully released the stick. Tikker said nothing and the two of them merely sat floating on the bay, while the launch approached from seaward.

"Holy shit!" Brister cried when he was close enough to hear. "What the hell were you doing? I thought this was supposed to be a test flight!"

Mikey giggled. "I bet those Brits pissed theirselfs. Way to go, Mr. Mallory."

"It *was* a test flight," Mallory growled. "And it isn't over yet. Tikker, get out and help Mikey with that gas can. I'm taking her up again."

"Are you *nuts*?" demanded Brister, incredulous.

"Maybe, but I've got to figure out a few more things. See if you can find something to plug the fuel tank with. A hunk of that cork stuff you use for bumpers on the boat ought to do." Brister shook his head, but motioned for the man and 'Cat to comply. Shortly, the fuel tank was topped off again and Mikey had whittled a stopper for it. Tikker started to get back in the plane.

"No, you stay here," Ben ordered.

"You kidding?"

"Nope. I want to try her out without your fat ass in her tail. Get some idea how much we need to rebalance things."

"My ass not fat," Tikker replied. "Maybe my head. How you survive without me to save you?"

"See if you can find the bug sprayer. With it empty, maybe it floated." He flipped the switch and started to stand and prop the engine again. "Next one's going to be a pusher," he mumbled, then caught himself. "Hey, give me a piece of that rope while you're at it," he shouted across to the boat. "I need a seat belt!"

Commander Walter Billingsly had been utterly terrified and that just wouldn't do. His one response to fear had always been a killing rage, a need for whomever or whatever caused his fear to suffer the consequences. His terror now past, his rage had lost its heat. It still remained, however, and it would be vented, but it was a cold thing now, an icy ache inside him. By harnessing it and molding it from what it had been into what it was, he had made it a tool, a thing he could use. A thing that would help him when the time came, instead of controlling him.

When the bizarre contraption was towed past *Ajax* and into the open water of the bay, he'd watched with acute interest through his telescope. He'd known about the strange contrivances the Americans and their Ape lackeys were building, but his spies hadn't been quite sure what to make of the things. They reported that they were expected to fly, but neither they nor Billingsly put much credence in that. He'd supposed that was just a fanciful cover story meant as disinformation. Then he *saw* it fly. Amazing! How had these barbarians managed to accomplish something that all the greatest scientists in the Empire had proven was impossible?

He watched while the craft nosed higher and higher into the air and then turned back in his direction. He was excited at first that he'd get a better look at the thing. But then it dove toward him! It grew bigger and bigger in its downward swoop until he was sure it would collide with the ship. In terror, he'd scampered behind one of the great guns for protection, praying for the first time in years. Then, at seemingly the last second, it pulled away with a mighty roar and literally spun on its axis! For a moment during the shocking maneuver, it was silent. In light of what he saw later, he shuddered to think what might happen if such a machine came at them noiselessly in the dark.

He'd watched it zoom over the city, leaning back and forth, then making another silent, simulated attack upon the waterfront! After it was clear, he realized what the true purpose of the machine had to be: a flaming cylinder fell from it and dropped into the water! The machine was a weapon! Of course it was a weapon! It could just as easily have dropped the flaming bomb on *Ajax* as it swooped overhead! The very thought of such an insidious, unsportsmanlike—and utterly effective—device was what truly ignited his terror, beyond the fear he'd felt when he'd thought it was going to ram them. That it could have destroyed them in a single pass and hadn't done so was a clear indication of how the Apes and their Americans considered his presence there. They were not awed by Imperial power as he'd expected them to be. They were contemptuous of it.

They'd clearly intended to frighten him and they had. More significantly, they'd waited until Jenks was a week or more away, which meant they were not trying to frighten *him*. Billingsly's suspicion of Jenks was confirmed. The commodore *had* to have been shown the flying machine during his "tour," and he would have asked about it. Jenks was a fair scientist, to a degree, in his own right. Even if he'd doubted the thing would actually fly, he'd have known that his hosts thought it would. They couldn't have misled him about that. That left only a single possibility: Jenks knew about the flying machine and had said nothing about it.

Billingsly's expression never changed, but inwardly, he roiled. Jenks might command the squadron—such as it remained—and be in charge of all things nautical, and even tactically military. But Billingsly was the supreme representative of the Court of Proprietors, and in matters of intelligence, foreign policy, and even long-term strategy, he was in charge. Jenks had deliberately withheld critical information that profoundly affected all those things. He could claim he hadn't really believed the machine would fly, and it might even be true, but Billingsly didn't believe it. Such a defense might (probably would) get Jenks off at an inquiry since, as a scientist, a respected explorer and naval officer, he couldn't be expected to give credence to claims regarding the feasibility of powered flight.

Walter Billingsly knew better. He believed he understood Jenks more perfectly than perhaps the man knew himself. Jenks would have looked at the contrivance closely. If it was *possible* it might fly—as Walter now knew it irrefutably could—he would have known. And yet he hadn't mentioned it. Did that make him a traitor? Yes.

Billingsly kept many secrets from the commodore, the real nature of *his* "rescue" mission, for one, but Jenks was not supposed to keep any from him. That alone was enough for a charge, if not a conviction. But Walter had been suspicious of many of Jenks's activities of late. This interminable delay, for example, waiting for the Americans to release the girl, was most unseemly. Then, instead of his getting steadily angrier, as Billingsly had, Jenks's attitude toward their "hosts" had appeared to actually thaw somewhat. The most egregious was the tour Jenks had received. The Americans had openly shown Jenks what they'd kept guarded for long months from Billingsly and his spies. Walter suddenly wondered darkly what *other* surprises Jenks might have seen and not told him about!

Now Jenks was gone some hundreds of miles away, an "observer" along to witness a foreign military adventure! Was he an observer? Why did the Americans want him along in the first place? In Billingsly's suspicious mind, no one would show Jenks the things the Americans had without wanting something in return. What did Jenks have? *Achilles*, of course, but the ship and her armaments were not substantially greater than anything the Americans were capable of. What then? Only information. The only thing Jenks had that the Americans could really use was information, and he possessed quite a lot of that.

All around Billingsly, the ship's company grew excited again as the bizarre machine roared by and took to the air once more. None of *them* were terrified, nor had they really been even when the machine came at them. Most shouted and good-naturedly returned the clear gesture the flying man had made. They were excited because a flying machine was a wonder, and they possibly even felt a strange kinship with anyone foolhardy enough to ride one. They were men as used to terrifying adventure as they were to the unending boredom of the last months. But they didn't see things the way he did. They never took the long view of anything. Whatever occurred after their next meal was the distant future. Walter Billingsly knew it was all up to him now, him and the operatives infiltrated into the ship's company. The contingency plan he'd been formulating was coming together nicely, and with some of the recent information he'd obtained, it was looking more practical as well. He needed just a few more pieces of the puzzle to fall into place and he'd be ready to proceed.

He strolled to the rail and watched the flying machine make lazy turns over the bay. His personal mission was more critical now than ever before, but even that had paled somewhat in comparison to the intelligence he'd gathered about these strange folk. He needed to get that intelligence home as soon as he possibly could. Things back there were already in motion and he had no idea how this might influence those long-secret plans. His primary mission was important to their success, but the threat posed by these folk—these other *enemies*—desperately required evaluation by his superiors.

He would no longer worry about Jenks. Surely he was a traitor? Besides, whether he was or wasn't was immaterial in the end. His allegiance was no secret and his presence might have been . . . problematic to the success of Billingsly's primary mission, in any event. Walter had often pondered how best to deal with him when the time came. Aside from the information he might give his American friends, it was probably just as well that he'd gone with them. Realistically, he'd expected a confrontation, a refusal to participate at least. He'd have been astonished if Jenks would have agreed to active cooperation and support. This way, it no longer mattered how Jenks would react. He was certainly in no position to interfere.

nconscious of any irony, newly minted Lieutenant Irvin Laumer stepped forward and extended his hand to Colonel Tamatsu Shinya. Without hesitation, the Japanese former naval officer took it and shook it briskly. The two had become friends, of a sort, during the long voyage, and there had existed a certain bond between them. Both were men driven to succeed and prove themselves, although Irvin didn't know what Shinya needed to prove. He was a loyal officer in Captain Reddy's cadre of companions. (Irvin was well-read and often compared Reddy's relationship with his officers and men to that of Alexander.) He admitted to himself that there might be just a touch of hero worship on his part that made the comparison more apt.

There was no doubt that there were two distinct groups within the Alliance: those who felt comfortable around Captain Reddy and didn't hesitate to express their views to him, and those who were almost afraid to be around the "Great Man." The former category was almost exclusively comprised of those who'd been with him from the start, regardless of race. Irvin still felt like he belonged in the second group. He'd had a tough ordeal—all the S-19s—had, but it wasn't a patch to what Captain Reddy, *Walker*, *Mahan*, and all their crews and allies had been through. Laumer hadn't even been at Baalkpan during the desperate fight. Shinya had. He'd been there from the start like all the others, and he'd certainly earned the companion role, yet he didn't seem to realize it. If he did, he still seemed driven to continue earning it.

Maybe it was because he was a Jap. To this day, not all the Americans truly liked him. They universally respected him, but that wasn't the same.

He'd proven he'd stand even against his own people in this war, if it came down to it, but during one of their talks, he'd admitted to Irvin that it still hurt him, even now. He had no compassion for the Grik, but maybe he needed to keep proving to himself that he actually belonged among his new friends.

"I'll miss you, sir, and our talks," Laumer said.

"As will I," Shinya replied. "I find myself speaking 'Cat so much, it is a pleasure to converse in a . . . human tongue."

Irvin knew what had caused Shinya's hesitation. He probably wished he could talk more with Okada, but he and the other Japanese officer didn't really get along.

"Yes, sir," Irvin answered. "And I really appreciate the 'Cat lessons, too. I'm still not too good at it."

"You will do fine. Besides, most of your command has at least a smattering of English now." Shinya chuckled. "I expect one day the two languages will intermingle!"

"That would sure be weird," Irvin said, imagining the bizarre combination. He took a breath and looked around, nodding farewell to others he recognized. He was awaiting the arrival of Saan-Kakja so he could officially take his leave. As his eyes swept over the massive ship, he was still overcome by the monumental ingenuity that had built her.

The level on which he stood, the battlement, occupied a single deck of the massive central superstructure, and the balcony went all the way around it like a giant wraparound porch. Even as high as he was above the surface of the sea and the ship's center of gravity, any sensation of motion was almost imperceptible. Unfortunately, the mammoth vessel's *forward* motion was almost imperceptible as well, by the standards he was accustomed to. With all her wings set and drawing nicely in the brisk morning breeze, *Placca-Mar*, Saan-Kakja's "Imperial yacht," or whatever it was, was barely making five knots. She was just so damn slow. There was so much to do, and he was anxious to get on with his mission.

Throughout the weeks they'd been at sea since departing Baalkpan, they'd crept northeast through the home waters of the Makassar Strait and entered the Celebes Sea. Their average, excruciatingly slow speed of five to six knots had slowed even further while they picked their way through the tangled, hazardous islands off the northeast coat of Borneo before making their island-hugging journey through the Sulu Archipelago. This tedious, circuitous route allowed them to avoid the abyssal depths of the Celebes and Sulu seas—and the monstrous creatures that dwelt there. Among those they were trying to avoid was one so huge that it actually posed a rare but real threat to ships as large as Lemurian Homes.

Mountain fish they were called by some, or island fish by others.

Whichever it was, it made no difference. The name wasn't idle exaggeration. Irvin had seen one of the things before, when S-19 traversed nearby seas on her way to Cavite—only to discover the Cavite they remembered wasn't there anymore. That was when his now dead skipper decided they needed a place to hole up before their fuel was gone. The resulting odyssey was what had eventually left the sub stranded on Talaud Island.

Finally, after torturous weeks, Meksnaak, Saan-Kakja's Sky Priest, placed them off the western peninsula of Mindanao. Irvin had to take his word. They'd apparently missed the Sibutu Passage in the dark, but finally they'd reached a point where he and his little squadron could part company with the high chief of the Manilos and all the Fil-pin Lands. Despite the frustration goading him to get on with it, he had to admit the ship and the world around it were certainly a beautiful sight. They were on a tack that took them almost directly into the morning sun, and Irvin shielded his eyes against the glare. Lush, unnamed islands speckled the sea directly to starboard, and a larger shore loomed on the horizon. Mindanao, he presumed. Zamboanga. The water was an almost painfully brilliant blue, and was still touched by the golden glory of the new day. It was going to be a hot one, as usual, and eventually the bright, clear sky would give way to rain clouds. Even now, far to the south, a purple squall swept an empty patch of sea.

He hadn't seen the squall that brought the destroyermen and his submariners here. S-19 had been submerged at the time. He had only conflicting descriptions from the destroyermen as to what it looked like. Mostly, they'd said it had been green. He wondered sometimes what he would do if he ever saw one like it. Would he sail into it, hoping it would take him home? Or would he do everything in his power to stay the hell out of its way? He hoped the choice would never come. At least, not until he fulfilled his mission. Somehow, right then, making Captain Reddy proud of him was more important than ever getting home.

He shook his head and looked at his own ship, USS *Simms*. The former Grik Indiaman had been razed like many others and named for Andy Simms, who'd died at the Battle of Aryaal. She was now a United States corvette. She mounted twenty guns and with her once bloodred hull painted black, with a broad white band down her length highlighting the closed, black-painted gunports, she looked nothing at all like her former self. In spite of who originally made her, *Simms* was a heartwarming sight, loping almost playfully along under close-reefed topsails so she wouldn't shoot ahead of her lumbering charge.

She was Irvin's only warship; the other vessel keeping close company had been repainted, rerigged, and repaired, but her lines hadn't been altered. She was a transport, after all. A freighter. It was still a heady sight. He'd gone from an inexperienced kid, glad to have a subordinate take over when things got tough, to a commodore, for all intents and purposes. Deep down, he wasn't sure he was ready. This *should* be Flynn's job, he thought. Flynn was the one who'd brought them through. But Flynn wouldn't—apparently couldn't—do it. That left Irvin, and one way or another he'd accomplish his mission—if it was possible for anyone to—or die trying. He still believed this was a test of sorts and, for an instant, wondered if Captain Reddy understood the depth of Irvin's commitment to prove himself. He doubted it. Irvin didn't fully understand it yet himself. Besides, the captain had literally ordered him to be careful. Irvin appreciated that and he *would* be careful . . . but he *would* succeed, regardless.

"Well, Lieutenant Laumer," Shinya observed, "despite your . . . impatience . . . to leave us, you have one final nicety to perform. Saan-Kakja is here to bid you farewell!"

"Yeah, I'm a little anxious," Laumer admitted. "Is it really that obvious?" Shinya only chuckled.

Saan-Kakja approached, attended by Meksnaak and a trio of other functionaries. As always, Irvin was struck by her presence. She was so small, and much younger even than he was, yet she was beautiful. Not in a "girl" kind of way—at least, not a human girl—but like an exotically colored female tiger would be beautiful. Stunning, magnificent, but also a little "cute," in the fashion one might describe a young, predatory cat. Her eyes were something else too, unlike any he'd seen among all the 'Cats he'd met. Safir Maraan was just as beautiful in her own lethal way, but Saan-Kakja still inspired him with a strange sense of protectiveness as well.

"Lieutenant Laumer," she said, her English much improved, "my priests that chart our path tell me we have reached that point where you will leave us. I shall miss your company when we dine, and I shall miss the company and protection of your noble ships and crews."

Irvin blushed. Saan-Kakja's ship hadn't needed their protection. Hers was probably the most powerful ship left afloat in the world. She'd armed it with cannon before she ever left for Baalkpan, and between the guns Baalkpan lavished on her and the guns constantly arriving from Manila, *Placca-Mar* now mounted sixty of the big thirty-two pounders, and had a couple of the new fifty pounders as well. It would take something like *Amagi* to tangle with her now. "It has, ah, been my honor, Your Excellency. I'll miss you too." He blushed even deeper.

"Mr. Shinya says you will not be entirely on your own," she said with a concerned series of flashing eyelids, "but the transmitter you carry is not as strong . . . as powerful as the one Mr. Riggs has supplied to me. You will be able to receive transmissions, sometimes all the way from Baalkpan, but may not be able to transmit that far yourself. Rest assured, we will hear you and will routinely retransmit any message you send. If mischief of any kind should befall your mission or yourself, do not hesitate to call for help. My brother is High Chief of Paga-Daan, and will receive a communication device similar to yours. He will come to your aid immediately. It will, in fact, be his ships that supply you, if your mission is lengthy."

"Thank you, Your Excellency. On all counts."

Saan-Kakja offered her hand, and for an instant, Irvin didn't know whether to shake it or kiss it. He settled for gently grasping the tiny thing in his own.

"Now, Ir-vin," Saan-Kakja scolded, squeezing firmly with her fingers, "you cannot break me that easily!"

"Of course not, Your . . . my lady."

Saan-Kakja grinned and, with an awkward bow, Irvin stepped away. He shook hands with Shinya again and climbed over the bulwark to descend the rope ladder to the waiting launch below.

"Hell," he muttered to himself, cheeks still hot. "She's not just beautiful; she's downright mesmerizing. Even in kind of a 'girl' way!"

Simms and her consort hauled away to the east, through the Basilan Strait and across the Moro Gulf. Meksnaak had suggested the gulf might be one of their most hazardous passages until they crossed to Talaud, but they met no danger there. A few large gri-kakka surfaced and blew, and some possibly related denizens with short, serpentine necks watched the ships periodically with large, somber eyes, but other than that, all they saw were the myriad seabirds, flying reptiles, and what looked like a cross between the two. Nothing unusual. The birds capered and swooped among the masts, occasionally even snapping at the top men, but the only real harm they caused was the reeking, fishy slurry they dropped and smeared all over the ships. Otherwise, the weather remained fine, the skies no more temperamental than usual, and the sea in no way stirred itself against them.

Irvin wasn't much of a practical sailor yet, and he relied heavily on *Simms*'s actual captain, Lelaa-Tal-Cleraan. She reminded him a lot of Silva's supposed Lemurian sweetheart, Risa-Sab-At, with her brindled fur and quick wit. Unlike Risa, however, Lelaa wasn't a born warrior, and she hadn't even seen action yet. Before getting *Simms*, she'd commanded one of the Navy feluccas. She *was* a born sailor, though, and Irvin was learning a lot from her. She'd translated her skill with the fore-and-aft rigged feluccas to the primarily square rig of *Simms* with astonishing ease. She was a good, patient teacher and well liked by her crew. She lacked any of Saan-Kakja's cuteness factor, but she was young and still handsome in an experienced, practical way. Irvin had every confidence in her, and the two of them had become fast friends.

They tried to keep the Mindanao coast in sight as they worked east-southeast over the next few days. There were islands everywhere, and Lelaa was constantly worried about wind direction, something Irvin, a submariner, had never much considered. Truth be known, he was always more worried about how much water was under the keel and what sort of creatures might be in it. Lelaa was worried too; that was why they hugged the coast—a most unnatural act in a sailing ship. The depths here were unknown, however, and everyone was a little tense as they cruised the edge of the Celebes Sea.

"I like coffee," Lelaa said, staring into her cup with a surprised, wide-eyed blink. She and Irvin were on *Simms*'s quarterdeck enjoying another pleasant morning. "Everyone says it is vile and they don't know how you Amer-i-caans can drink it all the time, but I find it heightens my awareness . . . and I have even come to enjoy the taste. Does that make me strange . . . or even more Amer-i-caan?"

Irvin laughed, then took a small sip from his own scalding cup of "monkey joe." "Well, you've been in the American Navy for some time now, and everybody back home would swear the Navy couldn't function without coffee. I don't think we could've ever won a war without it."

"You have told me of the great battles in your . . . *our* Navy's past. Is that how they won? We drink coffee and our enemies do not?"

Irvin laughed again. "Maybe. If the only difference in a fight is that one side is wide-awake and alert, it might tip the balance. There are other variables, though, that coffee alone can't make up for. Crummy torpedoes, being outnumbered ten to one." His smile faded. "In the war we came from, we drank a lot of coffee, but it wasn't making much difference."

Lelaa took another sip. "I bet it would have, eventually. Maybe in that lost world, it already has."

Irvin grunted.

The alarm bell at the masthead sounded insistently and everyone's gaze turned upward.

"Island fish! Island fish! Three points off starboard bow! Two t'ousand yards! It just came up!"

"Clear for action!" Lelaa shouted, gulping the rest of her coffee and passing the cup to Midshipman Hardee. Hardee had been one of the kids on S-19 and had volunteered to return to her. Now sixteen, he was also the oldest boy who'd been aboard her. "Pass the word for Sparks to wind up his gear!"

"Aye-aye, Captain!" Hardee replied, clutching the cup in both hands. He raced away. "Tex" Sheider, also known as "Sparks," like every communications officer on any Navy ship, scrambled up the companionway from below. He was a small, skinny guy, as many submariners were, and had never seemed to fit his other nickname: Tex. Of course, that didn't matter either. All that mattered was that he was from Texas. There'd once been another Tex on S-19, but he'd suffocated in the battery compartment.

"Captain," Hardee addressed Lelaa. "Sir," he said to Irvin. "I heard the alarm. The guys are winding up the gizmo now." He looked ahead, trying to see the huge fish. A gray-black hump was just visible from deck now. "I sure hope this works," he added nervously.

The Anti–Mountain Fish Destruction Countermeasures, or AMF-DIC, after the British version of sonar—with a couple of extra letters thrown in—were a collection of mostly untried procedures it was hoped would scare the humongous, ship-eating beasts away. All had an acoustic pressure element, which they'd learned through experience might be effective. The first line of defense was literally a giant speaker activated by the ship's communication equipment. A wind-powered generator charged a primitive battery in the "wireless shack" that, when switched through a high-amplitude capacitor, allowed them to boost the output through the simple transmitter Riggs had given them. In this case, instead of routing the jolt of electricity to an antenna, it sent it to a crude speaker mounted firmly to the hull. The result briefly turned the entire ship into a resonance chamber meant to frighten the creatures away.

The second defense, one they knew *could* work when properly applied, was a device most of the destroyermen had been familiar with even though *Walker* and *Mahan* had never been equipped with them. It was a form of "Y" gun that used one of the old muzzle-loading mortars they'd employed in the defense of Baalkpan. A weighted barrel of gunpowder rested upon a rack positioned at the muzzle of the mortar, which allowed them to blast the depth charge into the path of an oncoming mountain fish. They knew the monsters didn't like depth charges at all, and they believed the "Y" gun would work fine—if it didn't blow up the ship.

They had a final defense that Jenks had told them the Imperial Navy used at close quarters: an indiscriminate, simultaneous broadside of every gun on the ship. The resulting concussion seemed to disorient the beasts, and although it made them *very* angry, only rarely did they manage to destroy a ship with their enraged convulsions.

"Stand ready to activate your gizmo, Tex," Irvin instructed. Lelaa nodded. "But wait for the word. I know we want to test it, but if that thing leaves us alone, we'll leave it alone. Right now it's just kind of wallowing there, catching some rays."

"Yeah, but it's right in front of us. What if it won't move? Do we go around it, or blast it?"

Lelaa looked at the sky and the set of the sails. "We blast it," she decided.

"If we go around, we will lose speed, and I want us to be as fast as we can be if we are forced to use the gizmo." She raised her voice. "Signal our consort to lay aft and follow in our wake. Maybe it won't sense us both. No point in making it feel threatened by our numbers."

Irvin glanced at her and she shrugged, her tail swishing uncomfortably. "If there were ten of us, I might try it the other way," she explained, "but with only two, each less than a third its size . . ."

"It moving, Skipper," came the shout from above. "It know we here! It coming this way!"

Lelaa shook her head and looked at Sheider. "Stand by your gizmo, Tex." She gestured at the cluster of copper speaking tubes beside the wheel. "I will give the order."

"Aye-aye, Captain." With a nervous grin at Laumer, he disappeared below.

The giant was not on an attack run but seemed merely interested or curious, so their closing speed was not that great. Unfortunately, a mountain fish's curiosity often included tasting what it was curious about. At six hundred yards, Lelaa strode to the speaking tube and repeated, "Stand by." No one knew what the maximum range of the gizmo might be, but Riggs had figured it would become unpleasant at about five hundred yards. All they would get was one shot every several minutes. In a wind like this, it would take that long for the capacitor to recharge. If Lelaa had any hope of testing the device any closer, she'd have to try it at maximum range first. She started to say, "Fire," but that seemed inappropriate.

"Light it up, Tex."

For an instant, there was nothing. Then, with a jarring suddenness that surprised everyone, the whole skip began to tremble, accompanied by a dull bass rumble beneath their feet. The vibration was so intense, it blurred Irvin's vision. After only a few seconds, the sensation passed.

"What's it doing?" Lelaa shouted above.

"It pissed!" came the shout. "It swim in circle, go ape! Wait! It coming this way, fast! It pissed!"

"Ready the forward "Y" gun!" Lelaa commanded. The gun was already loaded and prepared in all respects, but Shipfitter Danny Porter tracked the oncoming target and shifted the weapon accordingly. The "Y" gun had no sights—it was an area weapon, after all—but Danny had a good eye and was a good judge of distance. He'd been striking for gunner's mate, and his surface action station on the sub had been her four-inch fifty.

"Ready when you are, Skipper," he announced tersely over the voice tube.

"Commence firing when you see fit," Lelaa said. Her voice sounded calm, but tinny. "Try to drop the bomb right on its nose."

For a moment, nothing happened. Danny waited, calculating the ship's slight pitch and the range to the target. He'd been allowed only a couple of tests with the new weapon and was no expert by any means. Suddenly, he stepped back.

"Fire!"

Simms's entire fo'c'sle was shrouded with white smoke and a loud, muffled *whump!* jarred the ship. The barrel-shaped bomb emerged from the smoke and tumbled upward into the sky. For a moment, it seemed to defy gravity as it hung there, wobbling, but growing smaller too. Then it began to fall. Everyone was tense, waiting for the plunge. It looked like Danny had missed, or worse, that the bomb might actually hit the back of the creature. Most supposed that if that happened, it might even die, but it would almost certainly lunge ahead and strike the ship before it did. A large concave splash erupted a hundred feet short of the monster, a little to its left. A pressure cap inside the bomb should detonate at about twenty feet. The sensitive nature of the detonator was always a concern when firing the damn things.

The sea spalled into shattered white marble, and almost immediately, a huge cloud of smoke and spray erupted in the charging fish's path. They saw the beast then, beyond the cloud, practically rear itself out of the water. Another momentous splash followed the first, and they glimpsed massive flukes pounding the sea—away from them!

"It worked!" came Danny's cry, all the way from the fo'c'sle. A huge cheer erupted, echoed by those on their consort astern. They hadn't seen anything, but they must have guessed the second aspect of the AMF-DIC defense had been a success.

"Outstanding!" Irvin said, stepping to join Lelaa near the wheel. Lelaa was smiling toothily. "Please accept my congratulations! We've got to get a message out right away and let everybody know it works!" Irvin's exuberance was tempered a few moments later when Tex appeared on the quarterdeck. His hair was singed and his shirt looked scorched. "What's the matter?" Irvin asked warily, a sick sensation in his gut.

"Transmitter's cooked. Kaput. All that juice was just too much for it. I *told* Clancy we needed a fuse! But nooo!" Tex shook his head disgustedly. "Damn Boston Mick! I'm gonna cool him off—to dirt temperature!—when we get home! One lousy fuse, but he says, 'You know how hard it is to make them?' Not as hard as it is to make a goddamn transmitter!"

"You okay, Tex?"

The smaller, dark-haired man shrugged. "Swell. A little scorched." He looked at his shirt. "I threw the switch, but the transmitter was already on *fire*, so I stifled it with my shirt. Nearly choked myself to death getting it off. Did you know this was the last shirt I had that was made in the U.S. of A.?"

"I'm sorry, Tex. We'll get you another one."

"I want that bastard Clancy's, if he has one left!"

"What about the receiver?" Lelaa inquired. It was a question Irvin should have asked, but Tex was one of his friends. An old shipmate. One of the few left alive.

"I'll get in there as soon as the smoke clears, Skipper. I expect it's fine. It's just a glorified crystal set. Doesn't really even need power. If we didn't short the batteries, we'll still have juice, anyway. If we did short 'em out, once we get to Talaud and set up the steam generator, we'll have more juice than we need. For anything."

"Can you build a new transmitter?" Irvin asked.

"Could be. It ain't hard, and I've got what's left of Riggs's design to work from."

Lelaa looked at Irvin. "I command this ship, but you command the expedition. What are your views? Should we press on, even without two-way communications? This was a hazardous mission to begin with. . . ."

"We press on," Irvin almost interrupted her. "Captain Reddy knows how hazardous it is, and he knew there was a chance we'd find ourselves out of touch. We'll press on," he repeated, "and accomplish our mission. Tex will make a new transmitter. Even if he can't, we have a job to do. A lot of people are counting on us and I won't let them down."

Lelaa smiled. "As I suspected . . . but I had to ask!" She turned to the 'Cat at the helm. "Steady as you go. Our course remains one five zero."

"One fi' zero, ayy!"

W*alker* was about to float again. All
Baalkpan had turned out to watch the
momentous event, it seemed, and no
one really cared anymore if the strangers in the bay knew about it or not. It
was a time of miracles. So incredibly
devastated by the battle that had once
raged here, Baalkpan had become a center of industry, connected with
most of the known world by wireless communication! People had built
aircraft and flown them over this very bay! Aryaal was retaken and Grik
prisoners were on their way here! In the amazing dry dock, weeks of scraping, welding and riveting, heating and rolling Japanese steel into new
plates, and a final, thick coat of red paint had resulted in this collective
achievement. Even if anyone had desired to keep *Walker*'s rebirth a secret,
it wouldn't have been possible. There was no question Imperial spies were
present. In fact, knowing they would be, Letts had counseled Adar to *invite* the Imperial personnel. Their leaders might feel a little foolish learning the ship they'd been so concerned about had been underwater all this
time, but the majority of the Imperial sailors who'd come to watch at least
acted as excited as everyone else.

Water coursed into the dry dock and swirled muddily around the
fresh red paint and wooden braces. Slowly, the polished bronze screws
dipped beneath the torrent and constant shouts of encouragement came
from men and 'Cats on the old destroyer's deck as they relayed reports
from below that all was dry inside. There was a shudder, and the ship
eased ever so slightly from the cradle that had held her upright since the
water was drained from the basin. Cheers reverberated off the many new

buildings when the support beams were heaved from the flood. Line handlers were careful to keep the ship positioned where she was, lest she bump against beams or pilings that were not yet free. Within an hour, all the beams had been withdrawn, and once again *Walker* floated free and easy, supported by her own sleek hull. The pandemonium the sight inspired was difficult to credit, and even more difficult for those who hadn't been there for the battle to understand. Tears erupted from hardened warriors from many clans, and many a Marine was misty-eyed as well.

In some ways, she looked like a different ship. Her guns and torpedo tubes had been removed, as had the big blower, refrigerator, and the tall searchlight tower. A temporary wooden deck was laid over the openings left from the complete removal of her shattered aft deckhouse. The short mainmast aft remained, defiantly flying the Stars and Stripes, but the tall foremast had not yet been reinstalled. The bridge was vacant and the fire-control platform was bare. Everything that could be removed and reconditioned ashore had long since been taken off, and she floated considerably higher in the water than anyone had ever seen her. Still, she floated. All her parts, possessions, and weapons would be returned to her, as would, ultimately, her crew. For now, she floated almost empty of the things that made her what she was; there was no roar of blowers, no machinery noises; she still slumbered, still resting from her grievous wounds, but she was no longer dead. She'd risen from the grave and it was only a matter of time before she'd awake once again.

"Look! Oh, look!" cried Sandra, tears streaking her face.

Beside her, Princess Rebecca hopped up and down, clapping her hands. "Oh, Lady Sandra! Is she not the most beautiful sight?"

Lawrence didn't understand his friend's attachment to the ship. It was but a *thing*. He was thrilled that it would again become the weapon it had once been, and *that* made him happy. He was also glad his friends were happy—for whatever reason. He hopped lightly and clapped too, imitating Rebecca's gestures. Dennis Silva stood beside him, fists clenched at his sides, a sheen over his one good eye. Suddenly, he raised a hand and blew his nose in his fingers. Absently, he started to wipe them on Lawrence's plumage.

"Mr. *Silva*!" Rebecca scolded, suddenly eyeing Dennis.

"A little snot won't hurt him! Runt's gettin' all frizzed out. Prob'ly oughta' comb a little grease in his hair." Under the princess's continued stare, Silva sighed and wiped his fingers on his T-shirt.

Unexpectedly, Lawrence had begun growing a crest on top of his head that Silva compared to a cock roadrunner's. Among the Grik, the only real "crests" of any kind they'd seen had been on dead Hij. Since it was now known the Hij were almost universally older than their Uul warriors, Bradford had ecstatically proclaimed "their boy" must be nearing adulthood, different species or not.

Letts, Adar, and Spanky moved through the throng to join them.

"A hell of a thing," Spanky said, his own eyes a little bright. "I never would've thought it."

"I had no doubts," proclaimed Adar. "Once you were over the shock of losing her and had a plan, I knew, sooner or later, *Walker* would float again. You Amer-i-caans are amazingly ingenious."

"Couldn't have done any of it without *your* equally amazingly ingenious folk," Alan Letts reminded him.

"Where's Karen?" Sandra asked. "She should be here!"

"She's not feeling too well," Alan said, a little self-consciously. "She's no bigger than you, and with her being somewhere around seven months along . . ."

Sandra laughed. "She's big as a house! I know. Don't worry; she's fine. But she is a little big." Her eyes twinkled. "I still say it's twins!"

Alan pretended horror. "Don't say that anymore!"

Over the tumult, they heard a rising drone and looked at the sky. Not to be outdone, the Air Corps was putting in an appearance. Three planes, or ships, as Mallory demanded they be called for some reason, wobbled overhead in a semblance of a formation. He'd finally won approval for his force to be called the Air Corps, even if most of its pilots were naval aviators. His insistence on the seemingly contradictory term confused everyone. Ben would be at the controls of one, Tikker another, and young Reynolds the third. The Air Corps had eight planes now, and with the implementation of Ben's improvements they'd been declared perfected as far as the fundamental design would allow. Within weeks, there'd be two dozen airplanes and they'd face the distinct problem of having more planes than competent pilots.

Sandra hugged herself. It was all finally starting to come together. After all their hard work and sacrifice, she was beginning to feel, well, optimistic. The war had really just started, but with all the new naval construction under way, the professional army they'd begun, the allies they had working along the same lines toward the same goals—they had airplanes, for goodness' sake!—and now with the resurrection of *Walker* . . .

"Mr. Chairman," she addressed Adar, "we must transmit the news to Captain Reddy at once! He'll be so pleased!"

"It has already been done, my dear, with careful observation to details! I expect he is watching the proceedings with us, through the eye of his mind, at this very moment." He grinned and blinked amusement. "I took the liberty of sending your warmest love as well."

Sandra blinked back more tears and hugged the tall Sky Priest.

"Now, ain't that the damnedest thing?" Spanky asked. They all turned to look where he stared. Sister Audry, surrounded by a few dozen 'Cats, was standing near the pier mumbling something none of them could understand. Adar caught a word or two, but over the hubbub, any meaning was lost. The nun finished speaking and brought the fingertips of her right hand to her forehead, down to her stomach, then to her left and right shoulders. The Lemurians with her copied the gesture.

"Say," said Silva, "does this mean our good sister's a 'Catechist?"

"You idiot," Spanky groaned, "you don't even know what that means!"

"Do so!"

"Yeah, he does," Letts confirmed. "And pun aside, he may be right." He looked at Adar. "Mr. Chairman, we've been promising each other a lot of 'talks' lately. Maybe we'd better have one this evening." He glanced around. "Lieutenant Tucker, please join us. Better invite Courtney too, or he'll pout. Spanky, you're Catholic. . . ."

"Sorta."

"I'd like you and Princess Rebecca to attend as well. Princess, you've stated several times that there are others of perhaps . . . similar faith to that of Sister Audry. I think it's time we sort that out, at least. I'll go invite the young nun to our little meeting."

Other eyes watched the proceedings discreetly, through eyelids narrowed with concern.

"I had heard rumors, but I could hardly credit them. Didn't dare to hope," Billingsly muttered to the man beside him. Linus Truelove was Billingsly's most trusted agent and a talented analyst as well. He doubled as *Ajax*'s third lieutenant, hiding his skills beneath a competent but unimaginative, almost oafish facade. His "cover" was easy to maintain. He was a large man, bigger even than the one-eyed protector who often escorted the princess, and even though he pretended drunkenness on occasion, he never drank enough to cloud his quick, devious mind—another advantage he had over the man called Silva, who appeared just as oafish as Truelove pretended to be.

"The enemy grows more capable by the day, and our window of opportunity may close before we are ready."

"We will be ready soon enough," Truelove assured him. "Curtailing our obvious activities has lulled them, I think. Even the guards at their industrial section are not as alert as they were." He grinned wickedly. "I think they are beginning to *trust* us, or at least they no longer have as great a care."

"Possibly. Regardless, when we move it must be as quick and silent as possible. They must not know what has happened for a good many hours and they must not be allowed to interfere once they discover the truth."

"You did not mention 'bloodless' as an imperative. 'Quick and silent' is almost never bloodless," Truelove observed.

"Quick and silent remains the priority."

"Bloodless," repeated Truelove, eyeing Silva. "I doubt that would be possible, regardless. That one, I think, hides behind much the same mask as I. I doubt he will accede 'bloodlessly.' Besides, he is the first I have seen among these barbarians whom I might enjoy testing myself against. He has a reputation."

"Put it out of your mind!" Billingsly snapped. "Perhaps he does, but your 'reputation' must remain secret!"

When the water level inside the basin equalized with the bay, the great gates opened and *Walker* was towed slowly, gently clear of the dry dock. Even as she was tying up to the old fitting-out pier, the dry dock's next inhabitant was being positioned to enter. Keje-Fris-Ar paced nervously back and forth on the strangely abbreviated battlement that remained offset, above the rebuilt deck of his Home.

"This is madness!" he remarked, eyeing the angle of approach. "The dry dock is too small!"

"It is *not* too small, Father," assured Selass, Keje's daughter. She strode each step right beside him and placed her hand comfortingly on his shoulder. "Really, you should not exert yourself so. Your wound . . ."

"My little wound is well healed, thank you," he said gruffly, but then looked fondly at his child. He and Selass had been estranged far too long. First, her choice of a mate had upset him—and then the self-centered fool had the effrontery to die a hero's death! Even before that occurred, she'd developed a hopeless infatuation for Chack-Sab-At, whom she'd first driven away, right into the arms of Safir Maraan! He'd despaired that she might ever become a sensible creature. Perhaps her friendship with Sandra Tucker had helped. She'd even grown civil to Chack's sister, Risa, who commanded *Salissa*'s Marine contingent. Whatever the cause, ever since the Great Battle, she'd been devoted to him and he admitted he was glad their rift had mended.

He stared the length of his ship. His Home was unrecognizable now. Where her great tripods and pagoda apartments once stood, there remained only a huge, flat deck. New quarters were under construction below that deck, but no more would *Big Sal*, as the Amer-i-caans called her, move with the power of the wind and tide that had controlled her every course since her very birth. She was becoming a machine, a ship of war! A thought once so alien to Keje he could never have imagined it. That anyone would build a ship just for war—besides the Grik—seemed unnatural. At least, it had before the Amer-i-caan destroyermen came. But these were unnatural times. *Salissa* had been all but destroyed by the Grik and their Japanese allies, just as *Walker* had. He pondered that a moment.

Was *Walker* not a live thing, even though she was a machine? Captain Reddy and all her people always behaved as if they thought she was. Keje *felt* she was. When they repaired her, would not her soul return to her? It must. Where else would it go? If a body lived, it must have a soul. If *Walker* had indeed been "dead" for a while, perhaps her soul was trapped within her. Or maybe it had rested in the Heavens above, with all the people she'd lost? It was all so confusing! *Salissa* had been nearly as "dead" as *Walker*, but Keje had never felt her soul had left her. That *should* mean her soul would remain with her whether she became a machine or was restored completely to what she was before. His tension ebbed a bit. He'd discussed this with Matt, with Spanky, Adar, and even his daughter. All had different thoughts regarding the soul of a ship, but all completely agreed that, whatever it was, *Big Sal* still had hers. Looking at her now, though, a mere naked hull with a long, flat top, he found it hard to imagine somehow.

"The wings are machines, Father," his daughter reminded him, easily guessing his thoughts. "By our construction and by our design, they harness the wind—a natural element—to our will. We make them, we control them, they move as we direct them. The wings are machines." She nodded toward the gaping hole in the aft center of the broad, flat deck. "The engines, when they are installed, will do the same." She pointed at the shipyard, where the massive contrivances lay covered with sailcloth, awaiting installation. "There they are, Father. They are not wings, but we made them and we shall control them. They will move us as *you* direct them! They will burn gish, yes, and we will no longer be independent of the land folk, but with this terrible war, that time was already past. Those engines will burn gish to make steam—merely heated water and also a natural thing—and that steam will move the engine and turn the propeller that will soon be installed. *Salissa* will move like *Walker*, the very same way!" She paused and chuckled. "Perhaps not as fast . . . but by the same means. If *Walker* has a soul, then surely *Salissa*'s is safe. It might even be proud!"

"Proud?"

"Indeed. Have you not seen the aar-planes? They will be *Salissa*'s! With the guns she still carries and the aar-planes to carry her strength farther than the eye can see, *Salissa* will be the mightiest ship in the world! Mightier even than *Amagi* ever was!"

Keje laughed. "You have been talking to Letts again!" He grew thoughtful. "But Captain Reddy says the same. As much as he loves his ship, he loves aar-planes just as much—and hates not having them!" He sighed, then laughed again. "Did you know I must go to school? I must learn how to handle my own ship all over again! And Mallory says we must form 'operational procedures'!" He shook his head at Selass's concerned blinking. Her tail was rigid with tension. "Fear not! I will be a model pupil! It does amuse me, though."

"What?"

"To 'relearn' how to handle my very own Home, I must practice by controlling their tiny launch!"

They stood together in silence as the great vessel was maneuvered entirely into the basin. Huge bumpers dropped into place and a tally was made of every object that had once supported the destroyer so they'd know nothing protruded from the flat, permanent trestle below. Only then were the pumps engaged.

"How long will it take?" Selass asked.

"A day. Perhaps more. Not as long as it took to empty for *Walker. Salissa* 'displaces' a great deal more water! Is that not a fascinating term? It has no real meaning in situations other than this, because *Salissa* cannot displace enough water to be even noticed in the wide ocean of the world, but here, because of her size, there is far less water in this dry dock, even though the level is the same as before!"

"I have heard the term," Selass admitted, "when the Amer-i-caans discuss the size of the new construction ships. Evidently, they do not weigh the ships themselves, but the water they push aside! How can they do such a thing?"

"Mathematics. They are fiends for it in all things. Everything you see that they have made involves mathematics and the most precise measurements imaginable. It is amazing and stirring, but it makes me somewhat sad as well."

"Why, Father?"

"Well, it is yet another example of how things have changed. Nothing will be built by eye again. Artwork may survive, but the talent, the skills passed down from one maker to the next, will be supplanted by mathematics! The guilds are howling, much like our wing clans did when they learned our Home would lose its wings! I am but an example. I have spent my life learning to move *Salissa* from place to place, and still I do not know everything there is to know about that. Now I must learn to drive a little boat before I will know the *first* thing about moving my Home again."

"You agreed."

"Yes, I did, and it is well. I will move her again, and when I do . . . I am informed"—he grinned—"she will be a weapon the Grik cannot match. I would . . . I *have* sacrificed much for that. So will Geran-Eras when she allows the same alterations to *Humfra-Dar*. But what of the builders, the makers of things? Soon, any leeching pit turner will be able to operate a machine that will quickly make things a shipwright has spent his life learning to build!" He shook his head, part in wonder and part in sadness. "What's more, that pit turner will be able to do it quicker and better and exactly the same every time."

"You sound as if you wish the Amer-i-caans never came."

"No. That is ridiculous. They have saved us. We would be filling Grik bellies if not for them. But in a way, as much as we fought to survive, we, the *People*, also fought for things to remain the same. I know that is what Nakja-Mur fought for, but deep down, even he knew it could never be. I will miss the old ways. It was a good, happy life. If this war ever ends, and it *must* end in victory, I know not what the world will be like. I do know it will be different. Let us just hope it will be different in a good way . . . and that we will live to see it."

"She's up!" Clancy shouted, racing up *Donaghey*'s companionway. Matt and those gathered with him on the quarterdeck turned toward the exuberant outburst. *Donaghey* was moored a short distance from the rebuilding dock and many of the AEF's officers were aboard for a conference of sorts. "She's up and floating and there're no leaks worth a mention! *Walker*'s off the bottom and Lieutenant Tucker sends her love!" There was a resounding cheer and Matt's ears heated just a little.

"Mr. Clancy," he said, unable to summon a frown, "that's wonderful news and I'm glad you shared it with us all, but the last part may have been meant as a private message."

Clancy halted his dash and his face went white. "Uh . . . oh. Ah, sorry, Skipper! I'm so sorry!"

"Oh, shut up," Garrett said, grinning. "That part isn't news!" There was more laughter. "What's the first part say?"

Jim Ellis retrieved the message form and scanned it. He looked at Captain Reddy and Matt nodded. "It's true. *Walker*'s been moved to the fitting-out pier and *Big Sal*'s gone in the tank." He chuckled. "Ben saw fit to celebrate with a flyover. One plane had to land on the bay and be towed in! Let's see. *Tassat* was launched and has been moved to the new fitting-out pier. The new generators are doing swell, but they've had a couple of engine casualties." He looked at Matt. "Hmm. Hope we don't have any out here. Says it wasn't much of a deal, but still." He looked back at the page. "Still no word from Laumer and 'Task Force S-19.' Palmer got that one signal that they were about to try the gizmo, then nothing. He figures it cooked the transmitter." He glanced at Clancy, who'd suddenly stiffened. He and Palmer had argued a lot over the design. "Anyway, they're probably fine. Saan-Kakja arrived safely at her brother's city and they made a successful test transmission of their set—"

"Yes, sir," Clancy interrupted. "I picked it up."

"Wow," said Jim. "Real long-distance comm. Why didn't you tell us?"

"Well, ah . . . you see, they were transmitting the raising of the ship in a kind of blow-by-blow sort of way. . . ."

"Anything else? What about our report of the Grik prisoners?" Matt asked. Jim looked down and chuckled.

"Yeah, it's got a postscript. 'Bradford excited.'"

"Ha!"

"I do wish we could speak to them," Safir mused.

"We can," Alden said. "They just can't talk to us. Maybe when we ship 'em home, Lawrence can talk to 'em."

"I doubt it," said Matt.

"Why not? Most of the 'Cats understand each other okay, except maybe a few of the ones from southern Australia."

"Yeah, but they've been in contact with one another. Look, we now know there's Grik all over the place, or something like Grik. They seem to fill the niche humans did where we came from. There's the Grik we fight, from Africa and Madagascar originally, but there's Grik-like lizards just about everywhere. Lawrence says his people are 'Tagranesi' or something. We've managed to squeeze enough out of Rasik to know the dead aborigines we found here were snatched from Java and the neighboring islands as slave labor and, well, food. I'm sure they don't call themselves Grik."

"I did not even know they were here," Rolak admitted.

"Maybe they haven't been for long, or at least not in any numbers. Our first and only meeting with them on Bali proved to us they were pretty smart. They didn't carry weapons, but then they didn't really need them, did they? They may have been leaking over here from Bali or other islands for a long time and just staying to themselves. As primitive as they were, compared to our enemies, they actually displayed even better tactical sense. Courtney's long believed that Grik behavior has more to do with societal conditioning than anything else."

"That might explain why the prisoners act so different," Ellis speculated. "After we licked them here, they wandered on their own for a while. Maybe they had time to think things over a little."

There was silence for a moment while everyone contemplated the significance of that.

"All the more reason we must not give the enemy more time to think things over," Safir said.

"If I were a member of this Alliance, I would tend to agree with the

Queen Protector," Harvey Jenks said with a touch of irony. It was the first time he'd spoken, beyond civilities, since he'd come aboard. Something had changed in his demeanor ever since he went ashore and saw the aftermath of the Grik occupation for himself. Aryaal and B'mbaado were unusual cities, perhaps unique among Lemurians. Even before the Grik came, they'd been built of stone with stout walls to protect the inhabitants. The devastated architecture was more similar to Imperial construction than any other he'd seen so far, or than he cared to admit. It was as though he'd experienced a premonition of what would happen if the Grik ever threatened his home.

The rabidly gruesome nature of the enemy the Allies faced had been driven in to the hilt as well, and he felt he understood them and their motives much better now. The heads had been taken down and sent to the sky in the fires and much of the debris had been cleared, but the mental image remained. The thaw in his attitude toward the Allies, and Matt in particular, had continued at an accelerated pace. Still, he'd clearly been surprised to be included in this strategy session. He hadn't given any assurances that he was at their disposal or that he'd help them in any way. He *had* begun to consider himself on their side just a little, however.

"Jenks is right," agreed Rolak. "We cannot linger here. Has that vile creature"—he referred to Rasik-Alcas—"spilled any more beans?"

Matt shook his head. "He's told us all he knows about what happened here, and a little more about his activities while in exile, but he knows we've already measured him for a noose. No matter how fair we make it, the outcome of any trial is a foregone conclusion. He's guilty as hell and he knows everybody knows it. When he's not off in the land of Oz, he's sharp enough to be scary. The guy's a real psycho."

"No clues about what he found?" asked Ellis.

Matt shook his head. "The crummy thing is, I think there *is* something. Everything we thought we knew about the Squall that brought us here is changing all the time. First, we thought it was just us and *Mahan*. Then the PBY. Then we learned about *Amagi*. Why wasn't it there when the Squall passed? Okada said they came out of it in the *dark*, probably sometime during the night after we did. Unlike us, they were moving with it, not through it. Is it possible that by staying in it longer, they experienced its effects longer too?" He shook his head. "I doubt even Courtney has an answer for that. Anyway, we now know the sub came through as well. It was pretty far away, judging by the log we brought back, but close enough to hear our fight on the surface. How close was the PBY?" He shrugged. "Up till now, we've assumed we were it, but what if we weren't? That was a big squall and the track it took might have sucked up anything. Why some things and not others? No clue. Maybe the energy or local intensity had something to do with that. Anyway, we need to start thinking about the possibility that other stuff *did* come through, and if it did, we damn sure want to find it before the Japs and Grik do." He snorted. "His Nasty Highness did confirm that they watched a bunch of Japs get off Esshk's ship when it stopped here, roam around unattended, then get back on, so I guess they didn't eat the bastards after all."

"Pity," Ellis said.

"Yeah. The thing is, though, Rasik thinks if he tells us what he found, we'll just kill him anyway. He insists on *showing* us."

"We promised him clemency; what more does he expect?" spat Safir. It was the first time she'd agreed to the "deal" that had been proposed. She hated the very idea of letting Rasik live. Chack, who'd remained uncharacteristically silent, put a hand on her shoulder and stroked it.

"It does not matter," Rolak grumbled. "He still expects to be killed. He views all things in terms of what he would do in our place."

"I'll get it out of him," Alden promised.

Matt laughed. "Pete, I bet you and Boats could get him to confess he painted the moon, but that wouldn't do us much good." He thought for a moment, staring at the bleak shoreline. There was a lot of activity: building a new dock, erecting tents, and preparing materials for structures that would serve as forward supply depots. Few would remain at first, when the Allies moved on. They had more pressing business. Aryaalans and B'mbaadans would return, however, and begin the work of rebuilding.

"Here's the deal," he said at last. "We have to move. The scout we sent to Singapore reports the Grik are pulling out there too. We need to get there before they leave it like this." He gestured shoreward. "We also have to know if Rasik's pulling our chain. He says the things he found are accessible by sea, near Tjilatjap—Chill-chaap." He looked at Jim. "Not *at* Chill-chaap, but near it, so your guys would have missed it when they went ashore there."

Jim winced slightly. They hadn't exactly been *his* guys at that point.

"Here's what we'll do," Matt continued. "You take *Dowden* and a company of Marines and see what Rasik has to show you. If you can do it without puking, try to buddy up to him. He doesn't really know you, after all. Maybe he'll let something slip."

"May I command the Marine company, Captain Reddy?" Chack asked.

Matt hesitated. "I'd rather have you with me, but I guess so. Just don't remind the silly bastard you're the one who trapped him with fire and left him to be eaten by the Grik!"

"He cannot know that," Chack said.

"Right. Say, talk to Koratin. Maybe he can convince him he's on his side. Might get something out of him. Anyway, while you're doing that I'll take the rest of the fleet and all the troops we can transfer out of *Dowden* and head for Singapore. You meet us there if you can. Stay in wireless contact. If something breaks down you can't fix, come back here."

"Aye-aye, Skipper. We'll meet you at Singapore," Jim promised. "If there's a fight, I don't want to miss it."

Chack looked at Safir and caressed her furry cheek. They'd made no announcement at Aryaal after all. They hadn't had the heart. No one felt much like celebrating the reconquest of Aryaal and B'mbaado. "Do not fear, my love. I shall see you at Sing-aapore."

Matt looked at Jenks. "Commodore, if you'd care to dine with me, I'd appreciate it. Juan?" he called, summoning the Filipino who always hovered nearby, "if he has no objection, please escort Commodore Jenks to my quarters. I'll be along directly."

Knowing he was being dismissed, but not resenting it—he *wasn't* a member of the Alliance, after all—Jenks bowed and went with Juan.

Matt turned to Jim. "Take O'Casey with you. I think he's a good guy and he might be a help. Besides, I expect to be spending a lot of time with Commodore Jenks over the next few weeks, and O'Casey needs a break. He can't keep hiding forever."

One of the changes Adar had made during the reconstruction of Nakja-Mur's Great Hall (he still had difficulty considering it *his* Great Hall) was the addition of a number of separate chambers. Some of these were offices, such as the War Room, which was usually occupied by Matt when he was present. Letts had a small office of his own as well. There was also a conference room large enough to accommodate a fair number of attendees while still being relatively cozy. He'd been inspired in this by Keje. In Keje's case, the chamber on *Salissa* wasn't partitioned, but he often had informal, intimate meetings around a simple wooden table supplied with crude stools. In Adar's conference room, the table was bigger of necessity, and there were more stools, but there were also a number of the more traditional cushions for guests to lounge upon. The somewhat uncomfortable stools tended to keep those present awake and relatively alert, but Adar had discovered that often, people he met with needed to contribute only brief reports or accounts. There was no reason for them to suffer while others hashed things out. Many times, for example, he'd watched an exhausted Ben Mallory fall fast asleep on a comfortable cushion while Captain Reddy and the members of his battle line discussed the ramifications of his aerial observations.

Mallory wasn't here for this discussion. Those present were essentially the same ones he and Alan discussed inviting earlier, with the exception of Keje, whom Adar had asked to attend as well. Most of them—Letts, Sister Audry, Rebecca, Sandra, and Keje—joined Adar on stools around the table. Only Spanky and Courtney took advantage of the cushions. Spanky was exhausted after his perpetual "watch-on-watches," and claimed to be only marginally Catholic anyway. Adar got the impression he didn't know why he was there. Courtney was fascinated by the looming discussion, but he always accepted a cushion (and the beer he preferred over seep) when the occasion allowed.

Adar had secretly hoped Alan Letts would start things off, but for once, the light-skinned officer waited for Adar to begin. "Well," he said at last. "I suppose we must hammer things out, as you Amer-i-caans so aptly phrase it. Mr. Letts and I have long planned what he calls an economic discussion, but there appears to be a more pressing matter before us. The economic discussion will . . . *must* happen, I'm sure, but it need not require the presence of some of you. What we must fashion this evening is some sort of accommodation between what appears to be a growing spiritual factionalism." He blinked at Sister Audry.

"I have long enjoyed our brief discussions concerning your faith and how it may have . . . influenced ours historically, but until recently I presumed you understood my fears that openly revealing that faith might contribute to a schism of some kind among our people—right when our growing unity is our greatest advantage. Aryaalans, B'mbaadans, and even Sularans hold substantially different beliefs from most sea folk, and even the People of Baalkpan, yet those differences are primarily matters of interpretation. The fundamental belief system is quite similar. We all revere the Sun and the Heavens, even if we place slightly different emphasis on one or the other, and our understandings of our lives beyond this one are somewhat different as well. Still, the differences are little more profound than the color of our fur. My dear Sister Audry, the differences you preach are far more profound—and potentially more corrosive to the mutual trust and understanding my people have achieved."

"I'm afraid I don't know what you mean," Sister Audry replied in her strangely accented English.

"Of course you do," Adar remonstrated gently. "I consider you a personal friend, and I thought we had an understanding. You assured me you would do nothing to undermine the solidity of the Alliance during this time of trial."

"I have not!" Sister Audry declared. She sighed. "My order is not given to radicalism. It is not even much given to aggressive evangelism. I come from a place that was mostly Mohammadan, after all. Immoderation of speech is not our . . . *my* way, except when it pertains to intellectual works and teaching."

"And yet your 'teachings' have gained a number of converts to your faith," Adar stated as fact. "Ordinarily, I would not concern myself. I cannot dictate faith . . . and I find myself curiously drawn to some of what you say myself. Much requires reconciliation, but it was my understanding that *you* understood our position and would allow me time to consider the merits of our . . . discussions, and decide how best to proceed with that reconciliation. These converts of yours have begun to be noticed, performing unusual rites. Rites that might be misunderstood. That which is strange and poorly understood can bring persecution and factionalism."

"It has not been my intention to abuse your trust, Mr. Chairman. I do what I may for the good of the people and you have my ungrudging obedience. But when people *ask* about the true faith, I must tell them. I cannot *lie*!"

"But there we have our difficulty." Adar drummed his fingers on the wooden tabletop. "Here in Baalkpan we have our own 'true faith.' It may be observed in different ways, but its basic tenets are a source of unity. You preach an entirely different true faith, and that creates doubt and possibly disunity. At this critical time, I fear your revelations."

"What if it's not really a different true faith," Sandra said slowly. "I'm not Catholic. I was raised Presbyterian, but Sister Audry believes much the same as I do. Only the practices are essentially different. Even among your people, there's a single Maker of All Things. I know many of your people believe He is personified by the Sun, and I guess that's understandable. First, there was apparently some misunderstanding passed down from the original tail-less ones, in which your people interpreted the 'Son' to mean the 'Sun.'" Also, even among my people, the sun—as the most impressive object in the heavens and the most obvious life-giving object visible above all things—is often venerated as the embodiment of the Maker. But generally, we believe the Maker, or God, is all-powerful, and as such, He made the sun as well. Why would that concept be so difficult for your people to grasp?"

"Yeah," said Spanky, rousing slightly. "As I said, I'm a little backslid, but I always figured if God *wanted* to be the sun for a while, nobody's going to tell Him He can't. Basically, we're talking a God with even greater powers than some of your folks have ever given him credit for. I like to think, if we can keep Him on our side in this war, the bigger and more powerful He is, the better. Think about it like this: if Sister Audry's right about her interpretation of this probably same Maker of All Things, maybe you shouldn't alienate Him by making her shut her trap. Maybe you should think more, not less, about incorporating her teachings and reconciling things *now* before He throws up his hands and leaves us on our own."

"Cover all our bases, is that what you mean?" demanded Letts.

Spanky shrugged. "Why not? No atheists in trenches—or engine rooms—when somebody's trying to shoot holes in them. What are you all worked up about, anyway?"

"I was always kind of a Mormon," Letts confessed.

"Jeez!"

"See what I mean?"

"What?"

Courtney finished his beer and belched politely. "The problem, Mr. McFarlane, is that there are at least as many different versions of Christianity as there are versions of the various Lemurian faiths. I won't even go into Islam, Hinduism, Buddhism. . . ." He shook his head. "For Catholicism to be the sole representative of human religion on this world might cause some dissent from our very own human ranks!"

Sister Audry glared at Courtney. "I'm sure I don't understand why *you* are even *here*, Mr. Bradford! I gather you are a Darwinist, and little I can imagine could be more corrosive to spiritual unity than the teachings you espouse—that you regularly, openly *engage* in!"

Courtney goggled at the nun. The sudden attack against him came as a complete surprise. He'd expected to have little participation in the discussion—thus the beer—and had accepted the invitation more out of curiosity than any other reason. He had to remind himself that Sister Audry really didn't know him well. "My dear sister," he began, imposing a moderate tone. "I am a Darwinist, as you put it, through evidentiary discovery and understanding, *not* faith. In faith, I do not recognize even you as my superior!" He glanced at Adar and raised a brow. "One of the discoveries, or rather rediscoveries, I've made since coming to your world is that I too am quite the Christian!"

"How utterly preposterous!" scoffed the nun. "How can one possibly be both an evolutionist and a Christian?"

"Quite comfortably and compatibly, I assure you," Courtney said. "In fact, I invariably find the one position complements the other! Even before I came to this fascinating world, I witnessed—*witnessed*, my dear— the endless, unstoppable force of evolution at work on a daily basis. In all of that, I saw the direction of the very hand of God"—he glanced at Adar again—"or the Maker of All Things." He looked back at Sister Audry. "How do *you* define evolution? I define it as physical and behavioral adaptation to any given species' environment or situation. Behavior can adapt quite rapidly. You have adapted somewhat to your circumstances here, have you not? Physical adaptations take more time, and there, I think—if you'll pardon the expression—is the rub between us. Particularly in respect to how those physical adaptations may have been manifested in humanity."

Sister Audry jerked a nod, and Courtney drew himself up on his cushion. "Personally, I do not believe I am evolved from an ape, although I am relatively certain my ex-wife's father was. Such a hairy, bestial, primitive . . . !" He shook his head. "In any event, I don't see that it matters. Why limit God's imagination? I believe He, like any master architect, would perceive the sundry ways in which His various creations might be better formed to suit their conditions. By His hand, those adaptations would begin!"

"Now you sound dangerously like a Freemason! With your notions of an architect!" Sister Audry scowled. The expression looked out of place on her pleasant features.

"In point of fact . . ." Courtney began.

With a look of horror, Sister Audry clutched the silver crucifix between her breasts as if a serpent had been revealed in their midst.

Courtney sighed. "You were undoubtedly taught and sincerely believe that man was made in the image of God. I must pose you some difficult questions: What *is* man? Are we upright apes like my former father-in-law, or are we sentient, spiritual beings capable of comprehending and returning the love of our Maker? What is the image of God? Is it the black one? The red? The brown, yellow . . . or just the white?" He nodded at Adar. "Or might He be covered in fur? You yourself observed no physical disqualification for salvation when you went among the Javanese and Malays to do His work! You continue it here. Does God have a tail? I submit that God is without form—or is of *any* form He chooses! The only 'image' we need concern ourselves with is the spiritual one!"

"But . . . you claim to be a Christian! How can that be? I grant you might be a deist, or some other species of heathen, but how can you claim yourself a Christian?"

"The same way you do, my dear: I have heard and believe the Word. But the Lord Jesus Christ, our *spiritual savior*, appeared only briefly, and his teachings and works were immediately known to but a very few. It was up to others, like yourself ultimately, to spread the knowledge of those works and teachings about. Certainly you don't believe that all those throughout the centuries who lived and died in ignorance of the Word are damned? The loving God I worship would not make beings such as we only to have them suffer such an automatic fate!"

Courtney shrugged, somewhat apologetically. He wasn't much given to proselytizing, or even to sharing his own beliefs so freely. "Perhaps that is your purpose here, my dear," he said more softly. "Your destiny, as it were. But do not reject the possibility that our savior might have come to this place already. If God is capable of creating other worlds such as this, as I certainly *believe* He is, as I believe He is *capable of anything*, perhaps he will send or has already sent his son here as well."

"I don't see the problem," Keje grumbled, surprising everyone. "As I understand it, as Captain Reddy has explained it to me, this Christianity is just another path, another tack sailed to the same destination, to join the Maker of All Things in the Heavens, is it not?" Reluctantly, even Sister

Audry nodded. "Chairman Adar is correct that all those who follow such different paths have put their differences aside, for now, at least, to work for the common good—our very survival. Yet, in his wisdom, he has not prevented the priests of Aryaal or B'mbaado or even Sular from ministering to those souls they tend. Why should Sister Audry be different? Her practices are strange, but to me, so are those of the other priests I mentioned. It seems that a simple statement by Adar that her path is yet another, different one leading to the same place should be sufficient to prevent this persecution he fears. And so what if a few people convert?"

"It is not that simple," Sister Audry protested.

"Let us make it so, at least for now, shall we?" Keje challenged her.

The nun sighed. "Very well. But I will not lie."

"No one is asking that you do," Adar assured her, "but I think my lord Keje has the right of it." He paused, grasping his hands in front of him on the table. He hoped this issue was solved, but he couldn't be sure. Why could nothing be easy? "If no one objects then, I will consider this a closed issue. I will make a formal statement recognizing this Catholic Church and, as has been discussed, proclaim it as yet another path to the Heavens, as far as the Alliance is concerned." Adar blinked imploringly at Sister Audry. "Is that sufficient? For now? Can you at least refrain from antagonizing those who believe differently?"

Sister Audry nodded. "I can. As I have said, I have much practice at that. I will extol the virtues of the Church, *ut in omnibus glorificetur Deus*, but I will say nothing against any other."

"Splendid!" Courtney boomed. "I do so enjoy consensus! Might there be more beer to be had?"

"Sounds okay," Sandra said, "in theory." She looked at Princess Rebecca, who'd said nothing at all during the debate. "What do you think?"

Rebecca looked uncomfortable. "Sounds swell to me," she replied reluctantly. She'd been picking up more and more Americanisms. Courtney sometimes joked that her people might declare war based solely on that. "But the issue may not be closed at all, once we visit my people."

Sandra nodded. She'd gathered enough from Rebecca to understand that the Empire's primary rival was still another human civilization that didn't seem very Catholic at all, despite retaining the name and some of the ceremonies. These others, whom Rebecca referred to only as the Dominion, had inherited many of the cruel and expansive methods and practices of a much earlier Church than was represented by Sister Audry. Apparently, they'd incorporated some radical elements of other "faiths" as well. Rebecca had come to know the nun and she knew a little history, so she understood there were substantial differences between Sister Audry's

Church and what it had become under the Dominion. She wasn't at all sure her people would see any such distinction.

"I guess we'll see," Sandra said.

Marine Corporal Koratin, formerly Lord Koratin, renowned speaker, power broker, and counselor to kings, descended the companionway into the dark, dry hold. Despite his teetering conversion, he automatically thanked the Sun that he wasn't on one of the prize ships. No matter how their new owners tried, they could never quite cleanse the reeking stench of what the Grik had done in them. He'd helped capture a few and the dangling chains, emaciated "survivors," the slippery bones mixed with slimy ballast stones . . . all had been etched on his memory as with acid. In comparison, the hold of USS *Dowden* was a pleasant bower that smelled of fresh, well-seasoned wood, clean ballast, and the honest sweat and musty fur of her hardworking builders. There was only the slightest trace of rancid bilgewater from her new, seeping seams. That was nothing, he thought. *Dowden* was a tight ship, and her seams would only swell tighter.

Dowden's hold wasn't open from stem to stern like Grik ships either. It was highly compartmentalized. He understood the various compartments were even watertight to a degree, making the new steam frigate more difficult for an enemy to sink. He believed it. He was highly impressed with the construction techniques of the sea folk, and with Amer-i-caan designs to draw from, he accepted improvement as a given. He was most impressed by the Amer-i-caans in many ways. That didn't mean he loved them like the sea folk did, or even as the People of Baalkpan and other places had come to. He was genuinely intrigued by the teachings of their Sister Audry, but he didn't care much for their other strange notions of the way things ought to be. He hoped that somehow, the world might one day return to the simpler way it had been before.

The Amer-i-caans struck him as honorable warriors, but mere warriors they'd remained when they could have been kings. True, they'd helped establish a real alliance, the largest ever known, but it was a fragile thing in his cynical view. It would have been better for all if they *had* become kings. An empire was far more stable than any flimsy alliance. But simple warriors they remained—by choice—and all warriors were merely tools. As he had become.

Koratin entered a compartment where no gear was stowed. There was only a short bank of smaller compartments with barred doors across them. The common word was "brig," he believed. He passed the first and nodded genially at the inmate, an Aryaalan Marine like himself, who'd supposedly smuggled a quantity of seep aboard the ship. The prisoner did not react. Koratin came to the next cell and peered inside.

"Lord King," he whispered. "Are you well?"

Rasik-Alcas stirred slightly in the gloom. Confinement was even harder on Lemurians than on humans, but Rasik tried to appear disinterested. Only the slightest twitch of an ear betrayed his stress.

"Come to gloat, Koratin?" he asked at last. "I am king of nothing here, as you well know. This new ship does not yet even have enough vermin for me to rule."

Koratin squatted beyond the bars. "Still, you are a king. By blood. I served your father and I tried to serve you."

"By betraying me?" Rasik flashed, his eyes blinking rage.

"By trying to protect you from your . . . youthful impulses. You *are* young to be king, and when you attempted to destroy the iron ship of the Amer-i-caans, I foresaw the disaster that *did* result."

"You tried to warn them!" Rasik accused.

"I failed. You sent warriors to kill me. They failed. Still there was disaster. You angered the Amer-i-caans and instead of leaving to fight their war elsewhere, they took your city from you." Koratin didn't remind Rasik that they probably would have done it anyway after the Grik advance was discovered. Taking the city was the only way to save the people inside.

"So, you failed to betray me and I failed to kill you. That makes us even?"

"No, Lord King. You might say the one act cancels the other. That leaves us back where we started, if you wish it."

"What?" Rasik laughed. "You would be a king's counselor through iron bars? Why not be king yourself? I understand you have won glory with this ridiculous *Alliance*." He spat the word.

"I could never be king. I am not of the blood. The people would not permit it."

"So you have considered it?"

Koratin shrugged. "I am a political creature, as you know. You will also know I have considered many possibilities." He gestured at himself. "I was a *lord*! I had a great house, many servants, and enough retainers to defeat yours when they came for me! Do you believe I wish to remain a mere warrior? A soldier of lowly rank and status? Do you think me *mad*? I could never be king, but *you* could—and I could have back what I have lost!"

Rasik lowered his head in uncustomary dejection. "I could never be king again. The people hate me. I will be lucky to survive!"

For a moment, Koratin said nothing. He was almost stunned by Rasik's apparent bout of sanity. "Many do hate you," he agreed at last.

"They blame you for the time that was lost in evacuating the city. Some think more might have survived and perhaps even *Nerracca* of the sea folk might not have been destroyed if . . . things had gone differently."

"What do you think, Koratin?"

"I think they may be right. I would have counseled as much, had you allowed me."

Rasik beat his hands against his head. "Easy to say now," he almost moaned.

"But true, Lord King. You know it is."

After several moments, Rasik finally nodded. "It *is* true. You and your love of younglings. I cannot doubt you. You *were* trying to help and I drove you away!"

"Yes, Lord King."

"Well . . . I know you, Koratin! You would not have come to me without a scheme of some sort. What is it? Tell me!"

"There *is* something the Amer-i-caans will want where we go?"

Rasik grew guarded. "Yes."

"Am I correct in assuming you mean to lead them a lengthy, roundabout chase to find it?"

"Why do you ask?" Rasik demanded.

"It is what I would do in your place. You fear they will kill you when they have whatever it is, so you mean to lead them anywhere but where they must go until you have devised another plan."

"What if that were true?"

Koratin sighed. "All the Allied armies have left Aryaal. We sailed for Chill-Chaap this morning. The rest of the fleet moves on the Grik at the land they call Sing-aapore. The people of Aryaal will be returning and they will need a king!"

"But how . . . ?"

"If you have ever trusted me, trust me now," Koratin said. "You must lead the Allies directly to what you found! Give it to them quickly. They will be glad, they might even begin to trust you, and they will *leave*."

"They will kill me!"

"They will not! I have . . . arranged certain things, believe me. Do you think otherwise? That I would not have considered all contingencies? I swear to you, before the Sun in the sky, I will not let the Amer-i-caans harm you! You are my king! I cannot be king! How else will I have what I want?"

"If I do this, if I give them what they want and all goes as you say, how will I then be king again?"

"It is simplicity itself! You *are* king! King Rasik-Alcas! The Allies will leave and you will return overland and simply sit on your throne! I will be there, and you have many more supporters than you know! The first of our people to return to Aryaal will be among the most anxious to see you!"

"I am with you, Lord King!" came a voice from the neighboring cell. "I was in your palace guard! My sword is still yours!"

Koratin looked in the direction of the voice, then stared intently back at Rasik. "You see? When you sit your throne again with your people back in their homes—the homes *you* did not abandon!—who will oppose you then? Who will dare oppose *us*?"

Slowly, Rasik-Alcas grinned. "You always were clever, Koratin. Father said so as well. Too clever for your own good at times, but this time I think you are right. Who indeed will oppose me if I am already on the throne when our people come trickling back? It is not as if they will be great in numbers!"

"True, Lord King," Koratin said grimly. "Very true." He stood. "Is there anything I can bring you?"

"No," Rasik said, bright eyes searching the gloom as if looking for faults in the plan. "None must suspect our scheme. Do any know of our past . . . association?"

"None, Lord King. I am merely a soldier of low rank. No one knows who I really am, or what is in my heart."

"A brilliant subterfuge! Try to discover their plans if you can, but be discreet! Discreet! No one must suspect!"

"Count on it, Lord King."

As Marine Corporal Koratin turned to walk back the way he'd come, he nodded at the other prisoner again. This time, unseen by Rasik, the prisoner nodded back.

*T*alaud Island appeared much as Irvin Laumer remembered it when they'd approached it so long ago in S-19, her diesels gasping on fumes. They hadn't encountered another island fish in the crossing from Mindanao, and Irvin wondered if Silva had actually "sunk" the one that lingered there, as he'd claimed. Surely if he had, another had taken its place? *Walker* had picked one up on sonar, after all. Maybe they had been discouraged. Whatever the reason, he was relieved.

Island fish or no, nothing could protect them and *Simms* from the constant deluge of bird and flying reptile droppings.

"That is the place?" Lelaa asked, approaching him as she wiped at a greenish white smear across her dark fur with a towel. Irvin subdued a chuckle at the captain's expense.

"That's it," he said.

"Where to from here?"

"Around the eastern point. There's a broad lagoon, almost a tiny bay. S-19 was on the beach. There was a little protection but not much. . . . I hope she's still there." He voiced his greatest fear. They knew there'd been storms since they left. A high enough surge could have carried her farther inland, making complete salvage impossible, or it might have even carried her off to sea.

"The mountain on the island smokes," Lelaa observed. "Did it smoke this much when you were here?"

Laumer lifted his binoculars. It was a dreary, hazy, oppressive day. Still, he could see the dull, monochromatic outline of the distant volcano on the island. The smoke was blowing away to the south. "Yeah, maybe.

Sometimes there'd be earthquakes—the ground would move. I don't know. It looks like the thing's a little taller than I remember it."

Midshipman Hardee and Motor Machinist's Mate Sandy Whitcomb were standing with him. Sandy said, "Nah," but Hardee remained silent.

Irvin looked at him. "What do you think?"

"Well, sir, I'm not sure. The top was usually misty when we were here before, and down in the jungle where we spent most of our time, one couldn't see it at all. That being said, I would have to concur with you. It does *seem* taller."

"Hmm. Well, shouldn't make a difference unless it decides to pull a Krakatoa on us." As soon as he said the words, Irvin wished he could take them back. He'd always prided himself on his rationality, but some of the men's superstition had rubbed off on him, he guessed. He noticed the accusing look Whitcomb gave him and smiled uncertainly. "Just kidding, Sandy."

"If it's all the same to 'His Highness,' the new commodore, I wish to hell you wouldn't say shit like that." Sandy gestured vaguely over his shoulder. "Me and the fellas who volunteered to come along did it because it's a job that needs doin' and we like you. We know you've got as much guts as Chief Flynn, but you had the sense to let him take the lead while you learned the ropes. You got more brains than he does, so you're better than him for this caper. As long as you use them brains to accomplish the mission and don't go jinxin' us, we'll get along fine."

Touched and chagrined by the convoluted and somewhat backhanded compliment, Irvin nodded. "Don't worry. Like I said, I was just kidding, but I won't kid about stuff like that anymore. If you want me to throw salt over my shoulder, scratch a backstay, or jump up and down, spitting on myself, I'll do it if it makes you feel better."

Sandy and Hardee laughed. "Nah," said Sandy, "It'ud be funny to see, but none o' that would work anyway."

"What is a Krakatoa?" Lelaa asked.

Sandy rolled his eyes. "A busted toe. A real bad one."

Late that afternoon, they rounded the point. The wind had shifted out of the south and they took in everything but the staysails. The wind cooled them but their progress slowed to a crawl. Irvin wasn't worried. The mouth of the cove he remembered so well was near, and he'd rather creep up on it than tack away and try to find it again from seaward. Better to approach it the same way S-19 had. A call came down from aloft and he knew they'd reached their destination.

"Any suggestions?" Lelaa asked.

"Ah, you'll want to aim for the middle going in. There's just sand, but it shifts around. The lagoon's shaped kind of like a cursive capital E. . . ." He looked at her blank expression and drew one on the bulwark with his finger. "We want the top of the E, the northern end. There's rollers, usually, but it gets calmer when we're in the point's lee. Water there was deeper too."

"Was?"

Irvin shrugged. "Was. Places like this can change every time a storm hits."

"Leadsmen to the bow," Lelaa commanded loudly, then looked back at Irvin. "You were saying?" she asked politely.

Irvin knew she'd just given him another tactful lesson in seamanship. "Ah, that's it. We sail in and anchor as close to shore as the tide will let us. We should see the boat."

Simms crept into the cove, her consort staying well back to avoid any hazards the flagship might encounter. Irvin and all the submariners were on the fo'c'sle staring ahead, passing the binoculars around and listening to the leadsman's shouted depths.

"Goddamn, we should see her by now!" Tex erupted suddenly. He had the glasses.

"Maybe," Whitcomb replied. "The beach they'd left her on was still a mile or so ahead and it was hard to focus the binoculars while the ship passed through the rollers.

Hardee reached for the binoculars. "Here, let me have those a moment, please," he said, somewhat imperiously. Tex handed them over, but then made comic gestures behind the boy's back when he turned. He understood the concept of midshipmen just fine, but he wasn't used to taking orders from sixteen-year-old kids. Hardee put the strap around his neck and quickly scampered up into the foretop—no simple feat with the ship pitching so—and scanned the shoreline from a higher perspective. The Lemurian lookouts probably had better vision than he did, even with binoculars, but none of them had ever seen the submarine before. They didn't really know what to look for.

"There she is!" he suddenly cried down triumphantly.

"Where?" Irvin shouted back.

"About where she was, but . . . all I can really see is the conn tower! It looks like it's leaning toward the sea!"

Irvin looked at the other submariners. When they left, the boat was almost entirely exposed and leaning hard to port—away from the sea.

"Well," he said, "at least she's still here. I guess we'll know the score when we go ashore."

Simms and her consort anchored a quarter mile from the beach, where there'd be plenty of water under their keels even when the tide was out. Irvin was anxious to get a look at the task before them, but decided not to waste a trip ashore just for sightseeing. All the ship's barges went over the side filled with equipment; the disassembled steam engine was their "compact" model, but the parts were still heavy and bulky. The generator was one assembly, and although it wasn't very big, it was heavy. Other tools and equipment went as well, but no camping gear or foodstuffs. They wouldn't have time to establish their outpost that evening, and Irvin wanted to reimpress on everyone the hostile nature of some of the inhabitants of Talaud. Tomorrow they'd build a base camp, assemble the equipment they'd brought, and try to discourage the various predators he felt sure had returned to the area in their absence.

Rowing ashore, Irvin noticed few strikes at the boat. He'd gotten used to the incessant thumping of the flashies in the waters he'd crossed more recently and wondered why there weren't as many here. There were some really big, goofy-looking sharks, he remembered. Maybe that was why. Or maybe it was the deep water all around. He shook his head. Something else for the irrepressible Courtney Bradford to figure out.

His boat nudged ashore and he hopped into the calf-deep water, shoes tied around his neck. Once on the dry sand, he sat down and pulled the battered shoes on his feet. Even while he did so, he looked at the submarine—or what he could see of her. They'd realized, the closer they came to shore, that the boat had been virtually buried in the sand. Not just buried, but sunk in the sand as well. He could easily imagine how it happened. A big storm had lashed the island, maybe even the one that was brewing when they left it. The surge rolled the sub back and forth on the wet, loosening sand, slowly displacing that beneath her, and dragging her down into it. When she was almost level with the beach, the sand collected atop her until all that remained visible was the tower and the four-inch-fifty gun. Irvin stood and approached the boat with the other men.

Lelaa stared at what little was visible in wonder.

"You went under the water in *that*?"

"She's a lot bigger than she looks," Tex said defensively.

"Jeez. She's plumb *buried*!" said Danny Porter. "How the hell are we gonna get her out of *that*!"

Carpenter's Mate Sid Franks laughed. He'd been talking with some of the 'Cats in his division. "Hell, this is the best thing that could have happened!"

"What do you mean?" asked Irvin.

"Well, sir, if she was still high and dry, we'd have had to dig a hole out from under her. No way we could push or pull her in the water. We could have built rollers, I guess, but we would've had to run them out in water deep enough for stuff to eat us. We couldn't have made them stay where we wanted them either. This way, we just dig her out and dredge a channel into the lagoon!"

"Okay, I can see it's easier to dig her out, but how do we dredge your little canal?"

"Easy. Well, not *easy*, but simple, maybe. We securely moor the ships and use their anchors to dredge a trench! Actually, I'm sure one of you geniuses can come up with something better than an anchor—maybe a scoop or something. We scoop the sand, hoist the anchors, or whatever, into the boats, bring it back, and reposition it. Then we do it again."

"We'll have to 'do it again' a lot of times," Danny mused, "but yeah, that'll work better than if we had to relaunch her."

"Everybody hold your horses," Irvin said. The sun had touched the treetops at the jungle's edge. "First, you guys, all but Danny, help get that stuff ashore." He pointed where dozens of 'Cats were carrying crates from the boats to the beach. "Then we get to work tomorrow."

"What are you and Danny going to do?" asked Tex, a little irritated.

"We're going to climb up there"—Irvin motioned with his chin at the conn tower—"and crack the hatch." He took a battle lantern out of the pack he'd been carrying. "You can go on all you want about refloating the old gal, and that's swell, but the first thing I need to do is decide whether there's any point." He sighed. "Hell, fellas, all that banging around might have opened her up like a sardine can. She might be full of water, for all we know."

Suddenly, the ground shivered perceptibly beneath their feet and they heard a dull rumble even above the surf.

"What the hell?"

"Mr. Laumer, look!" Hardee almost shouted. He was pointing southwest, toward the volcano. From where they stood, they couldn't see the mountain itself—the coastal trees were too tall—but they easily saw the gray column of smoke and ash piling into the sky. It seemed to glow just a bit at the bottom, and Irvin wondered if the setting sun was causing it. With the wind now out of the south, they were likely to get some of that ash.

"I sure wish you'd quit doing that," Whitcomb said through clenched teeth. "Think positive, Mr. Laumer. The only thing the matter with her was she was outta fuel. She took a hell of an ash-canning by a Jap tin can. If that didn't open her up, a few little waves ain't goin' to."

Irvin nodded and took his eyes off the tower of smoke. "Okay. I'm sure she's ready for sea," he said, a little sarcastically, "but Danny and I will make that decision and we're going to make it fast. Tomorrow we'll start work on one of two things: refloating S-19 or breaking her up. Captain Reddy himself ordered me—*ordered me*—to make that determination as soon as I laid eyes on her, and that's what I'm going to do. If Danny and I come out of that boat and say we're taking her apart, there won't be any discussions or arguments. Tomorrow we start taking her apart. I know she means a lot to you guys—she means a lot to me too—but Captain Reddy's right. We need what she's made of a lot more than we need *her.* Is that understood?

A little taken aback by Laumer's sudden transformation from an easygoing shipmate to an officer who expected his orders to be obeyed, all the submariners nodded. Lelaa nodded too, in satisfaction.

"That said," Irvin continued, "it's my genuine hope that we can get her out of here in one piece. It would be easier, I think, and then we'd have all of her and not just the stuff we can get at. If we have to break her up, there won't be another trip to bring back more of her. Next time it might all be buried or gone and a lot will go to waste." He shrugged. "And who knows, Captain Reddy might decide we still need a submarine for some reason." He looked at Lelaa, then back at his men. "So now you know how I feel. One way or another, we *will* accomplish our mission and there *won't* be any bitching." He looked at the column of smoke. "And whatever we do, I think we need to do it quick. I have a weird feeling this island isn't too happy to have us back."

That went . . . okay, he thought as he and Danny made their way up the damp dune toward the conning tower. *They're all swell guys, but Captain Reddy's right. Somebody always has to be in charge.* Well, he might not be the best choice, but he was there. Now that the job was at hand and he was off Lelaa's ship, the time had come for him to step up.

There was a space between the four-inch-fifty and the conn tower that was free of sand, for the most part, and he eased onto the rotting strakes. They actually seemed to give a little beneath his weight. Somewhere beneath the sand was the top of the pressure hull but he saw none of it. He hoped it didn't look as bad as what he could see of the conn tower and the exposed areas of the gun. Apparently all the paint had been blasted away and everything was an almost uniform reddish brown. They'd sealed the gun as best they could before they left and he hoped the seal still held. He hoped the submarine's seals still held, for that matter, but his heart began to sink.

"Here," he said, pointing at the gun access hatch on the front of the conn tower, "let's see if we can get in that way."

"Sure," said Danny. The hatch was a new addition, not originally built with the sub, but like many of her sisters, S-19 had been upgraded—a little. Kind of like *Walker* and her Asiatic Fleet sisters, S-19 was literally generations behind the state of the art. They'd had so many accidents with the S-boats, however, many of them fatal, they'd been forced to make a few modifications over the years. The hatch was one. It was intended as a means to pass ammunition to the gun's crew, and as an emergency escape outlet. The ability to escape the dangerous boats had been deemed an important feature. Besides the infamous *Squalus* incident, Irvin remembered hearing about several S-Boat accidents. In one case, the sub sank, leaving nothing but her stern poking out of the open ocean and her surviving crew had to be cut out. Another sinking of a different boat had left the bow exposed, and the crew escaped through a torpedo tube! Regardless how many "escape hatches" the boats now had, far too many of the class had gone down with all hands before the war even started.

"Damn, it's stuck!" Irvin said, trying to undog the hatch. "Give me a hand!"

Danny moved to join him, and together they strained with all their might. No go. "Must've rusted shut," Danny said ominously. Irvin glanced up at a sound and saw Lelaa standing there.

"Let me help." Awkwardly arranged around the small wheel, the three of them gave another tug. To Irvin's consternation and Lelaa's delight, the dog finally spun.

"See? You just needed 'girl help.' I didn't really do anything but touch the handle. You Amer-i-caans say that ships are 'shes' even when you give them 'he' names. Maybe you're right. Girls always listen better to girls."

Danny made a rude noise and spun the wheel to its stop. Looking at Laumer, he raised the hatch.

After the better part of a year exposed to fresh open air, they weren't prepared for the stench that wafted out. It was ungodly, even to Danny. His submariner's brain instantly categorized most of the smells, however, and even as he almost retched and stepped quickly away, his mood brightened a little.

"Aggh! People live in that?" Lelaa gasped.

"No!" Irvin insisted. "At least . . . not this bad. We used to vent her out every day. She spent most of her time on the surface, not all buttoned up. There's months of stink down there that's been baking in the hot sun!"

"A little more than that, Mr. Laumer," Danny said. "There's mold and mildew and other things, but she doesn't smell any gassier than she did when we sealed her up."

Irvin looked thoughtful. Scampering up the rungs to the top of the conn tower, he tried the other hatch, and it spun freely. It had been the one they used most often when they were here before. It clanked open against its stops and he peered into the dark hole. Remembering the battle lantern, he shone it down.

"Doesn't look that bad," he murmured noncommittally. "Smells nasty, but what do you expect? No more gas, so water hasn't gotten to the batteries again."

"Are you going inside?" Lelaa asked. Irvin seemed to consider.

"Well, at first I figured we'd let her air out overnight. Even if it rains, it won't hurt anything, not really. Why?"

"I want to go inside," Lelaa announced. "All I can see is this little thing poking out of the sand. I want to see inside!"

"Okay . . ." Irvin hedged. "It *is* nasty. And it's hot in there too. Maybe not as hot as it used to be when it was in full sunlight . . ."

"Hell, let's go," said Danny. "You told the fellas we'd start to break her or get her out tomorrow, one or the other. They deserve an answer!"

Irvin nodded. "You're right. Let's do it."

One at a time, they descended to the control room below. The smell was ghastly and it felt like breathing a putrid soup, but eventually they grew accustomed to it, even Lelaa. Irvin shone the light around until he settled on the switch he was looking for. It activated the red emergency lighting Spanky had turned on months ago. To Irvin's surprise, the lights still came on, but just barely. There wasn't much juice left at all.

"If we get her dug out, run a cable from the generator, maybe we can charge her up enough to start an engine," Danny said.

"Maybe. Or if the compressed air tanks are still charged, we can turn one over that way. Just give her some fuel, and vroom!" He shook his head. "We're getting ahead of ourselves. Let's see what we've got."

"What are these big poles for, and what are those big, shiny wheels?" Lelaa asked, pointing to port.

"The poles are the periscopes. You know, those two things sticking up on top of the conn tower?"

"One is bent."

"Yeah, it was damaged when the Japs were depth-charging us. Giving us a treatment kind of like what we did to the mountain fish with the "Y" gun. We use them to see above the water when we're under it. Those wheels control the bow and stern planes. They make her go up and down underwater. That, and the amount of water we let in." She looked around.

"Water in here?"

"No. In the ballast tanks. We let water in to go down, and blow it out with compressed air to go back up. That big wheel at the front of the compartment controls the rudder, just like on *Simms*. It makes the boat turn from side to side."

"Sounds simple."

"Believe me, sister. There ain't nothing simple about it!" Danny quipped.

"Hey!" cautioned Irvin. "I don't think 'sister' is an appropriate way to address the captain of a United States ship!"

Danny blinked, then nodded. "Yeah. Sorry. Bein' back here on my old 'sugar boat,' it started to feel like old times."

Lelaa blinked in acceptance. "Then let us be about the business of determining whether we can make it more like old times by getting your 'sugar boat' off this beach!"

They decided to go forward first, since the bow was buried deeper than the stern. The crew compartment looked much like they'd left it: decks clear, racks chained to the bulkhead. They'd removed some of the mattresses for bedding on the island and the others had turned somewhat gray.

"Here's where some of the mildew's from," Danny said. "High humidity got the fart bags!" Irvin pointed the light, nodded, then looked around. It was the most spacious area in the boat and even some of the wooden folding chairs were still secured. A few had come loose, probably when the boat was rolling with the storm. Danny knelt and raised one of the linoleum-covered deck plates and Irvin shone the light.

"Forward battery looks just like we left it." Irvin glanced at Lelaa. "We lost a few batteries in here and had some water coming in. Had to seal off the compartment. Some good fellas died. Gas."

It was a simple statement, but Lelaa could tell the words still hurt. Irvin had already told her the story and explained what happened when seawater and sulfuric acid met. She also knew he'd been a junior officer and the decision wouldn't have been his. She wondered how she would have felt. Probably the same, she concluded. Not guilty, certainly, but pained that she'd survived as a result of such a decision.

"All the passengers were in the torpedo room." Irvin gestured forward. "No torpedoes, so it was the logical place to put them. There's racks in there too."

They moved to the hatch, which had been left standing open. Sure enough, there were quite a few more racks stowed in the compartment. There was also the most confusing conglomeration of pipes, valves, and instruments Lelaa had ever seen. She watched Irvin and Danny inspect a few gauges here and there and make approving or disapproving sounds. They inspected the bilge in the forwardmost area, in front of the fuel tanks.

"Well, she ain't dry," Danny announced, "but she ain't sunk either. Looks about like normal seepage to me."

"So?"

"So we look aft," Danny answered, shrugging.

The aft crew's quarters and officer's country looked much the same. The batteries under the plates looked okay too. There was water in the bilge under the engines, but it hadn't reached the huge machines.

"Those are the engines?" Lelaa asked. She'd seen the steam engines they were building, but the difference in sophistication was stunning.

"Yep," Irvin said. "Two NELSECO diesels. Twelve hundred horsepower combined. They'll move this tub at fifteen knots on the surface, if the sea's calm."

"And they were both running when you ran out of fuel?"

"That's right," said Danny. "They worked the last time we used them." Lelaa looked at him and twitched her tail. She had much to learn about Amer-i-caans, but the statement sounded . . . odd.

"What is in the next compartment?"

"The motor room."

Lelaa *was* confused now. "I have heard you, your people, use the words 'motor' and 'engine' interchangeably," she said. "Why would S-19 need engines *and* a motor?"

Irvin started to laugh, but then realized it was a perfectly good question.

"Motors, actually. Plural. Okay, here's the deal. Unlike the new Fleet Boats, S-19 can run her propeller shafts with a direct drive straight off the diesels. She's actually faster that way. The trouble is, she can only run them one direction—forward. She can't back up or use her screws for maneuvering with the engines. Since she has to use electric motors underwater—they don't burn fuel, make exhaust, or need air; that's how it works—we use the motors for reverse and maneuvering on the surface too. The new system's really better. They don't use the engines for anything but charging the batteries, and the motors do all the work. You've got forward and reverse and all the maneuvering you want all the time." He patted one of the NELSECOs. "But these babies do pretty good."

"I am anxious to see these 'motors,' but you did not answer my question: why is one a 'motor' and the other an 'engine'?"

Irvin and Danny looked at each other.

"Ask Sandy," Irvin said. "He'll know."

Danny nodded agreement, but then turned back to Irvin. "So what's the verdict, Skipper? What do we tell the guys?"

Irvin rubbed his forehead, looked at his two companions, and sighed. "Tomorrow we dig. And I want everybody trying to figure out the best way to dredge a canal this thing'll fit through!"

*U*SS *Dowden*'s anchor splashed into the almost mirror-clear water off the Lemurian city of Chill-chaap. Jim Ellis barely remembered having been there before—he'd had a fever at the time—and it wasn't exactly where its human counterpart, Tjilatjap, had been. The human city was east-southeast of the place the Lemurians had once chosen, and Jim remembered it as it had been in the early, chaotic days of the war they'd left behind. Some ships were still getting in and out when they'd seen the old cruiser *Marblehead* moored there after the pasting she'd taken from Japanese planes. Anyone who saw her was amazed she was still afloat. Her rudder had been jammed hard aport and she was still low by the head. They'd been transferring the wounded ashore, since nobody really expected her to make it out of the area alive. Ellis reflected that he'd never know if she had or not.

Tjilatjap was a dump. The fueling and repair facilities there were inadequate and there were no torpedoes to be had. Worse, from the crew's perspective, there was virtually zero nightlife. Even though it meant steaming back in the teeth of the Japanese storm, he'd actually been glad when they steered for Surabaya once again. He shook his head. That was another time, another world. Where the Tjilatjap he knew should have been, there was absolutely nothing, and never had been. Of the Chill-chaap their Allies had built on the other side of the peninsula, there was nothing left.

Even before the Grik came in force, a raiding party had sacked the city, eaten or taken its inhabitants, and razed much of what remained to the ground. Since then, a year and a half was all it had taken the jungle to reclaim a city almost as old and large as Baalkpan. It was a dreary, creepy sight. Vines and bizarre, spiderweblike foliage covered the ruins, and the old pathways were choked and impassable. From what Ben, Pam, Brister, and Palmer had told him, there were many bones as well. He figured rodents and other things would have eaten the bones by now, but he was glad they wouldn't have to make their way through the once-proud city. According to Rasik, what they sought was a number of miles up the estuary where the river became a swamp.

"Good morning, Cap-i-taan Ellis," came a voice from behind him. He turned and saw Chack standing there, neatly maintained Marine battle dress at odds with the dented American doughboy helmet he wore. He wore a sword suspended from a black leather baldric, and hanging by its sling, muzzle down on his brindle-furred shoulder, was his Krag.

"Morning, Chack. You ready for this?"

"Of course."

Jim nodded. Of course. Chack's steadiness and complete competence were among the constants he'd come to rely on. He still found it hard to believe the young Lemurian had once been a confirmed pacifist.

"Very well. You, me, half a dozen Marines, and Rasik-Alcas. I guess we'll take Isak Rueben in case this 'treasure trove' of Rasik's includes anything he might be needed to evaluate." Jim frowned. Isak had transferred to *Dowden* as chief engineer for the trip, since the ship would be on her own. Isak clearly understood the principles of *Dowden*'s machinery better than anyone else, but he wasn't a very good teacher. Once away from Tabby and Gilbert, he wasn't quite as antisocial as usual, but he didn't delegate worth a damn and tried to do everything himself. He probably needed a break from the engineering spaces as much as the engineering division needed a break from him. "One of the Marines will be Koratin?"

"Yes."

"Do you trust him?"

Chack's tail swished thoughtfully. "In a fight, as a Marine, I trust him. His status as a former Aryaalan noble causes some mild concern. By all accounts, he once lived a life of expediency, taking the tack of best advantage for himself." Chack blinked irony. "That is not necessarily consistent with the accounts of his performance in battle, so perhaps he has indeed changed." Chack shrugged in a well-practiced, very human way. "We will see."

The longboat went over the side and slapped the still water. The Marines escorted Rasik into the boat, followed by Isak, grumbling about the "stupid bulky rifle" he had to carry. Jim knew Isak was proficient with a Krag, but he also knew the wiry little Mouse didn't like wagging one around. The black powder and hard-cast bullet loads they'd made for the weapons had proved fairly effective on animals as big as a midsize rhino-pig, but even the precious few remaining rounds from the Rock Island Arsenal barely got the attention of something the size of a super lizard. No one but Rasik had any idea what sort of monsters they might encounter, and on that subject, at least, he'd remained cryptic.

After a brief word with Muraak-Saanga, his exec and "salig maastir," Jim was last over the side. He alone carried an '03 Springfield with "modern" ammunition and extra stripper clips. He also had his 1917-pattern Navy cutlass and a 1911 Colt. Besides Chack, the Marines he'd handpicked were all armed with their swords and the shorter thrusting spears they preferred. None carried shields. Without the numbers required to form a wall, they'd only get in the way. Two had longbows slung over their shoulders.

Chack barked a command and the oars came out. First and foremost, Chack would always consider himself one of *Walker*'s bosun's mates, and whenever he was in charge of anything on the water, he reverted to that capacity. He moved to the stern and took the tiller himself. Jim settled in for what promised to be a long trip, and with another command from Chack, the oars dipped in unison. "Well, Rasik," Jim said conversationally, "it's your show now." He grinned. "Don't disappoint us."

"You will not be disappointed."

"Swell. I'm glad you want to please. Just to remind you, though, I'll repeat the deal. You show us what you found. If it has any use at all to our war effort, you go free." He gestured to the south. "That's Nusakambangan. It's a pretty big island, and even on my world there was plenty there to survive on." He grinned again. "The Dutch used it as a prison, kinda like an eastern Alcatraz. For some reason, that strikes me as highly appropriate. Anyway, it may not be a palace, but if you managed to scratch out a living in the wild for nearly a year, you should have no trouble there. We'll even leave you weapons."

"I understand. Exile or death."

Jim shook his head. "No. You lead us *straight* to what you found or there won't even be exile, just death. If you try to give us the slip, I'll kill you. If I even start to think you're yanking my chain, I'll hang you in the jungle and leave you for the skuggiks or bugs, whichever get you first. Period. We've come here on your word when my ship's needed elsewhere— when I'd *rather* be elsewhere. If I find out you've been saving your miserable ass just to lead us on a wild-goose chase . . . you'll wish you were in hell for quite a while before you get there."

Methodically, metronomically, almost mechanically, the oars dipped and rose. They were following a major inlet north, and more than once, Jim wished they'd moved the ship farther inland. They didn't have a clue about depths, snags, or sandbars, though, and there was really nothing for it. Eventually the inlet, or river, or whatever it was, began to narrow. So far, they'd seen only the usual wild variety of lizard birds and an occasional crocodile. Once, something large and heavy exploded out of the water near shore and went thrashing into the jungle. No one saw what it looked like. The water eventually grew shallower and opened into a vast swamp filled with fallen trees and stumps. The jungle around it remained dense and apparently impenetrable, and high, misty volcanic peaks were visible in all directions. Jim had no idea if the old Java looked like this around here; he'd never been anywhere but Tjilatjap, but they were always discovering geographic differences here and there. Whatever had changed this world, whether subtle or momentous, was still slowly at work.

A herd or flock—he had no idea what to call it—of strange creatures marched sedately across the swamp some distance away. They looked kind of like giant, fat ducks through his binoculars, but they didn't have wings at all, that he could see, and their very ducklike beaks were proportionately much longer. Their necks were longer too, like a swan's, and their heads bobbed as they moved, swiveling in all directions. Finally, they must have collectively decided the boat was getting too close and they began moving away. Quicker and quicker they moved, with a kind of odd, rolling, waddling motion, and it seemed like the faster they moved, the more panicked they became. One suddenly slammed into an underwater obstruction, a tree or something, and heaved itself up to scamper over it.

"Holy shit, Mr. Ellis!" Isak exclaimed with as much surprise as his voice had ever carried.

The creature's long, gangly, almost delicate-looking legs must have been ten or twelve feet long! Apparently they weren't very strong either, because it was having a hard time clearing the tree. It just kept leaping up, scrabbling pathetically, and falling back to splash in the murky water. What happened next was almost too fast to register in their minds. All they got was an instant-long glimpse of a terrifying jaws clamping tight on the flailing legs and a swirl of some mighty tail. Whatever got the duck thing must have been under the tree, or maybe it came from nearby, drawn by the thrashing sound of distress.

"Holy *shit!*" Isak said again, as the ducklike creature practically capsized, the short, severed stumps of its long legs flailing madly. For an instant, the head popped back out of the water and it *mooed* piteously before the long jaws came again, clamped on the graceful neck, and pulled the head back under.

They kept rowing, a little quicker now, as the capsized corpse continued jerking and heaving as something fed on it from beneath.

"That was . . . a little spooky," Ellis said, controlling his voice. Isak was suddenly peering intently over the side at the dark water, Krag in hand.

Rasik smiled. "A 'spooky' place. You see why I and my followers"—he spit the word—"did not linger here despite our discovery."

"And just where is this 'discovery,' damn you?" Ellis demanded.

"You do not see it?"

"What do you mean? I swear I wasn't fooling! I'll pitch you over the side and let whatever got that big duck have you!"

"A little farther then. Perhaps just a bit to the left. You will see it soon." They did.

"Sweet Olongapo!" Isak exclaimed when Chack suddenly pointed at something nestled against the western shore of the swamp. "It's a god-damn *ship*!"

Closer they rowed until it was clear for all to see. It *was* a ship, heavily corroded, daubed entirely with rust, and almost consumed by the vegetation along the shoreline. If she was one of theirs, she had to have been in pretty sad shape even before being abandoned here for more than a year and a half. She listed toward shore and was clearly a freighter of some kind, with cargo booms, a single funnel, and a straight up-and-down bow.

"Old," said Ellis. "About six, seven thousand tons, by the look of her. How the hell did she get here?"

"Same way we did, I figger," Isak muttered. "Captain, Mr. Bradford, and Spanky was all talkin' about there maybe bein' other stuff scattered around, got sucked here too. The Squall that got us woulda come through here first, maybe not as bad, maybe worse. Somebody said somethin' about local intensity or somethin'." Isak shrugged, but his expression was pensive. "She looks like a dead body that's bobbed up."

They steered closer until they passed under the dangling anchor. The water lapped gently against her rust-streaked side and Jim looked up at the raised-lettered name.

"*Santa Catalina*," he said. "Huh. Never heard of her. Never saw her. She sure wasn't in Tjilatjap when we were."

"She looks sorta like the *Blackhawk*," said Isak in a strange tone, referring to their old Asiatic Fleet destroyer tenderly.

"Yeah. Same as a hundred other ships," Ellis replied. "*Blackhawk* was built as a freighter and bought by the Navy. I bet she's thirty years old, though."

"So," interrupted Rasik. "Are you satisfied now?"

"So far. Don't give me reason to change my mind. Did you go aboard?"

Rasik shook his head and pointed across the swamp to the east-northeast. "We saw it from there. It does not look like anyone is on it, and it would have been a march of many days to reach. The swampland extends far to the north and there are rivers besides."

"So you don't know what she carries? Taking a lot for granted, aren't you?"

"There is much iron. That alone should be worth my life."

Jim grunted. "Where it is, it might as well be on the moon. I can tell she's beached, and probably flooded too."

"Do you want me to kill him, Captain?" Chack asked. "I would enjoy the . . . honor."

Jim shook his head. "No, a deal's a deal. She's worth *something*, even if it's just a boatload of bolts. Let's see if we can squirm through all that growth on her starboard side and try to get aboard."

It took much hacking and chopping, but they finally maneuvered the boat between the ship and shore. She was beached, all right, and that just added to the mystery of her presence here. A number of trees had fallen across her from shore, but there was a stretch of water as well. Also, eerily, rotten cargo nets draped her starboard side, as if the crew had used them to escape.

"Do we trust them?" Jim asked himself aloud, referring to the nets. Without a word, Chack sprang across to the closest one and scampered up. He disappeared over the bulwark. "I guess so," Jim said philosophically.

"You're heavier than Chack," Isak pointed out.

"Yeah, maybe a little. C'mon." He looked at two of the Marines. "You stay here with the boat. Keep your eyes peeled. You others, come aboard—but keep your eyes peeled, too!"

"What about Rasik?" Chack called from above, peering over the side now.

"He comes too. Might as well let him see what bought his life. What's up there?"

"Hard to say. There is much growth and many big boxes. Nobody seems at home. You can tell me what I see when you get here."

The four detailed Marines, including Corporal Koratin, swiftly climbed the nets. Rasik followed with apparent reluctance. Jim went next, followed by a less than enthusiastic Isak Rueben. When he gained the deck, Jim looked around. The ship was an ungodly mess. Vines crawled over everything and debris was strewn about as if large animals had been tearing into things.

"Stay on your toes," Ellis cautioned. "We might run into just about anything." Even as he spoke, his eyes were drawn to a number of large wooden crates still chained to the deck. They were about forty feet long, ten feet high, and maybe six feet wide. The paint had flaked off of most of them, and the wood underneath was black with mold. Other than the weights, around eight thousand pounds apiece, and faded arrows pointing up, the crates were unmarked. "Chack," he said, motioning the 'Cat to take two Marines and begin searching the ship. Isak and one of the Marines paced him as he approached the crates, looking around for something to crack one open.

There was a slight vibration, barely discernible through the leafy carpet and questing roots beneath their feet. Ellis paused, listening, feeling. "Heads up, Chack!" he called as the three Lemurians peered into the darkness beyond an open hatch. "Did you notice something?" Three heads nodded. "Either that was an earthquake or somebody ... some*thing* is running around down below. Try to make torches or something. Don't go where it's dark without a light! Something might get you!"

"Somethin' might get *us*," Isak grumbled. He glanced nervously at the bulwark. "Somethin' that eats giant ducks with ten-foot legs!"

"Shut up. Just look around. Find a fire ax or wrecking bar or something!" Jim ordered.

Chack ran up the mushy ladder to the pilothouse. All the windows were gone and the whole space was badly overgrown. He wrenched open the door to what he assumed was the charthouse or the captain's ready quarters. On *Walker* and *Mahan*, the only two human ships he'd ever been aboard, the two had been one and the same, as well as serving other purposes. The compartment had survived severe invasion, and he snatched up a few rags that had probably been clothes. Shelves held moldy, insect-eaten books. He was beginning to read English a little, but not enough to tell what the books were about. No matter. All books contained precious information and his friends would want them. He kicked over the cot he expected to find and discovered the bottom of the mattress cover was intact. Wrapping up the books and grabbing some other fragments of the mattress cover, he descended back down to his Marines. One was holding a kerosene lantern he'd found by venturing a short distance into the darkness. He shook it with a grin and it made a sloshing sound.

"Kind of beat-up, but almost as good as the ones we make in Baalkpan now, to burn gri-kakka oil. If we use your scraps for torches, we'll be in the dark before we go ten tails—if we don't burn up this dead ship!"

Chack chuckled and, removing his tinderbox from his pack, tossed it to the Marine. "You found it; you light it. Just remember, that's not grikakka oil! If it is like the stuff they use for aar-planes, it might burn *you* up!"

The Marine's grin faded, but soon he had the lantern lit and they entered the darkness beyond the hatch. They moved slowly, two facing forward and one walking backward behind them, all their spears outthrust. Something was in the ship; Chack knew it. It might take forever to search the ship like this, but with its proximity to shore, it was probably unreasonable *not* to expect some kind of threat, whether they'd noticed the vibration or not. They descended a companionway with care and entered a dank passageway. Nothing grew in the darkness, but the deck was mushy and clammy beneath his sandaled feet. It stank and there were occasional large heaps of what might have been excrement.

He stopped and considered. The funnel was aft, so the engineering spaces were as well. Maybe the engine and boilers were salvageable, maybe not. Chances were, the spaces were flooded. He'd spent most of his life aboard massive *Salissa*, and if he'd learned to discern the subtle sensation of buoyancy aboard her, the utter lack of it now convinced him the water level within the ship was probably almost as high as without. That meant they wouldn't be immediately firing up her boilers and steaming out of here. That realization moved her possible cargo to the top of his list of priorities.

"Forward," he said, "to the hold."

He didn't know the layout of the ship, but some things were obvious. The main forward cargo hatch was ahead of them and one deck up. They should find an entrance to the forward hold if they continued down the corridor. There was another heavy vibration, longer this time, and accompanied by a shifting, sliding sound. He glanced at his Marines and saw them exchange nervous blinks in the lantern light. Whatever had infested the ship was big. They couldn't tell where the motion came from because it seemed to resonate through the vessel's very fibers. He handed his short spear to the Marine beside him and unslung the Krag. A hatch gaped before them and they eased slowly toward it. He nodded at the Marine with the lantern, who shone it through the opening. Chack poked his head around the lip and looked inside.

The hold was the largest iron chamber he'd ever seen. Nothing compared to the holds on *Salissa*, which held provisions, barrels of grikakka oil, and other necessities of the Home's long, solitary sojourns, but it was far larger than anything *Walker* could boast. In the meager light of the lantern he couldn't even see how far the space extended, but he imagined one could pile all the cannons yet made by the Alliance in the place. He looked down. There was water, but it didn't look too deep, maybe two tails by the curve of the hull. There were also many more huge boxes, just like the ones they'd seen on deck. He wondered what was in them. Smaller boxes, or crates, were stacked outboard on either side of the larger ones. Some were underwater, others partially so, but most seemed high and dry.

"Should we go down?" asked the Marine he'd handed his spear to. She was a female, young and attractive. Her real name was Blas-Ma-Ar, he suddenly remembered, after spending most of the day trying to recall it.

He could never forget how and when she'd become a Marine, or the ordeal she'd once endured, but the name that always stuck in his mind was the one Chief Gray had given her: Blossom.

"I think not, for now," he answered softly. "Most of what is here looks to be much the same as what is on deck. Let Cap-i-taan Ellis discover what it is. If it is a good thing, we will know we have more of it." He shook his head. "I dislike moving any nearer the dark water below until we know what manner of creature dwells within this . . . human grave of a ship." The others nodded eager agreement and they retraced their steps. A trip through the engineering spaces seemed appropriate now, as they worked their way to the aft hold. In the corridor, they passed staterooms filled with decaying matter. Some doors were shut, and when they forced them open, they were gratified to see far less damage within the compartments. They found a few more books, in much better condition, and one such room even held a modest armory of unfamiliar weapons and rectangular tins of ammunition. These they carried up to the deck in two trips, along with their booty of books, before proceeding aft.

The boiler room was partially flooded, as Chack had suspected, but a meager light filtered through the grungy, vine-choked skylights, making visibility slightly better. They worked their way carefully along the highest catwalk. A sudden flurry of probably nocturnal lizard birds, disturbed by the lantern, frightened them, but Chack quickly recovered. He wanted to see where they went. They swooped around the space shrieking and flapping until they found a large gap between two twisted plates not far above the waterline. Like sand poured from a cup, they burst through into the daylight beyond.

"So she was sunk here," he surmised. "Or damaged elsewhere, and this is where she came to rest. Curious."

Unlike the boiler room, the engine room was relatively dry. There was water, but not much more than might be accounted for by a year and a half of seepage through riveted seams. They wouldn't be steaming her out of here, but the sight of the rusty but intact machinery was encouraging. Finally, they reached the aft hold and here they found their greatest surprise. More crates like those forward, and many smaller crates filled the space. Everything was a jumble, but Chack recognized hundreds of wooden boxes—maybe thousands—spilling rectangular, green metal cans like those that held ammunition for the big Amer-i-caan machine guns. Enough light diffused into the compartment through the murky water to indicate a substantial hole below the waterline.

"Another wound here then," he said. "Probably the fatal one. Still, though tossed about, many of the boxes are dry. Some are right below us," he said, pointing. "It looks like each intact box contains several ammunition cans. Let us claim as many as possible. Proof of the importance of our discovery!" The sight of so much clearly useful ammunition and the better light and visibility subdued his earlier caution. They laid down their burdens and the Marine who'd been holding the lantern descended a ladder to the top of a heap of boxes. Chack was the strongest of the three, so he positioned himself halfway down the ladder, where he might pass the boxes up to Blas-Ma-Ar.

"Here's somethin' might work," Isak said, returning with a small hand maul, a heavy, rusty chisel, and a piece of pipe.

"Sure," Ellis said. "Let's open this one." He'd been trying to choose the worst of the rectangular monstrosities, hoping the mysterious contents were already damaged by the elements and opening it wouldn't make any difference. The crates were unbelievably stout, built to take significant abuse. He hated to crack any of them, fearing he might ultimately only expose the contents to further, more rapid corrosion. But whatever they held, it would be a while before anybody could come retrieve four-ton crates from a swamp! They had to know what was in them.

"Here, give me that," Ellis said. Isak handed over the chisel and Ellis positioned it on a seam. "Now the hammer. If I let you do it, you'll knock my fingers off."

With deft blows, he drove the chisel in, moved it over, and did it again. When he'd loosened an entire seam, he began prying at it with the chisel until they could insert the pipe in the gap. "Give me a hand," he said, and Isak and the Marine leaned on the pipe with him. A tortured *greeech* sound came from the crate. "Again!"

They worked the pipe up and down, much as Jim had done with the chisel, taking occasional anxious looks into the dark interior. "Once more at the top and bottom, and I bet one of us can squeeze in there if we hold it in the middle!" A little more effort and it was done. Jim inserted the pipe in the center of the seam and handed it over. "Pull!" he said. The gap widened and he knocked a few nails over with the hammer. Then he stuck his head inside.

"Great God Almighty!" he said, his voice muffled.

"Well, what the hell is it?" Isak demanded acerbically, losing patience.

For a moment, Jim couldn't speak. Before him, as his eyes adjusted, he saw a bright, greasy metal spindle with only slight surface rust. Beyond was a triangular joint with bolts conveniently screwed into six holes. Still farther in he made out a radiator and the beginnings of a distinctive, Curtiss Green–painted shape that he'd never, *ever* expected to see again. Pulling his head back out, he looked at his companions with wide eyes. "Nail it up tight, fellas," he said. "As tight as you possibly can." He looked around at the other, similar crates and a slow grin spread across his face.

"Well . . . what the goddamn hell *is it*?" Isak demanded.

"Ah, they are pleased. I am so glad!" Rasik said to Koratin. The two had stayed back, near the bulwark, talking.

"So it seems. They also seem to have forgotten all about you."

"How convenient."

"Indeed."

"What is the plan?"

"Simple. Do you see that Marine with the Amer-i-caans? He is one of us. He will continue to distract Cap-i-taan Ellis and the wiry one while we take a boat ride."

"The other Marines?"

"With us."

"How delicious!" Rasik exclaimed. "They meant to maroon me, and I will maroon them! A shame we cannot kill them and take their weapons, but with half our group ordered to remain with the boat . . ."

"Precisely. It might prove dangerous. Now all we need to do is slip back down the net while they exult over their prize! After you, Lord King."

Down in the half-flooded aft hold, they heaved the heavy crates up one after another until Chack's shoulders screamed in agony and the others were panting with exertion. Through their increasingly concentrated toil, none of them noticed when it suddenly grew darker in the chamber for a moment as something moved through the light-giving rent in the ship's side. They felt it, though, another vibration like the others, but clearly *here*.

Chack looked down at the upturned face of his Marine on the diminished stack of crates. "Up!" he shouted. "Out of the hold!" He turned to race up the ladder, to get out of the way. Blas-Ma-Ar heaved frantically against the crates stacked above to make room for him to pass and so neither ever saw what got the other Marine. They heard a heavy splash and felt the entire ship judder slightly. More splashes came when the stack of crates collapsed into the water, but by the time Chack reached the top and spun to offer his hand, the other Marine was gone. There'd been no scream, no shout. Nothing but the splash. Chack snatched his Krag and frantically searched the water. He thought he saw a dark shape near the hole in the ship and fired, but all that apparently accomplished was to create an impenetrable haze of gunsmoke. He roared in frustration and fired again anyway.

"Cap-i-taan! Cap-i-taan!" Blas-Ma-Ar was pulling on his leather armor.

"He is gone!" Chack shook her off and chambered another round. The almost youngling's voice turned hard. "Cap-i-taan Chack-Sab-At, we have lost a Marine. He died bravely doing his duty. How many lives is this ammunition worth? We still have our duty as well!"

Chack took a deep breath. "Very well. You are right, of course. Come, help me with these crates, but stay alert! There may yet be other dangers within this foul place!"

"Was that shots? That was shots!" Jim exclaimed. "Muffled in the ship. Chack!" He looked around. "Hey, where's Koratin and Rasik?"

"They left," the Marine with them said simply.

"*What?* Wait, never mind that now. C'mon!" Jim snatched his Springfield and raced toward the hatch he'd seen Chack and his party enter. "Chack!" he bellowed, and was relieved to hear an answering shout, still muted by decks and passageways. "Where are you? What did you shoot at?"

"We are here," came a closer reply. "We need help with some heavy objects. Most are still stacked in the entrance to the aft hold." Chack finally appeared at the base of the companionway they were looking down. It was dark as pitch.

"Where's your lantern?" Isak asked.

"Follow this corridor behind me, through the engineering spaces. It is not so dark back there. The lantern marks the spot." Chack paused, taking a breath. "Do not enter the aft hold. Something is in there. Something that got one of my Marines. You should be safe enough," he continued brusquely. "I do not think whatever it was can reach as high as the crates we retrieved."

Jim turned to face the Marine who'd stayed with them. "What's this about Rasik? What do you mean, 'they left?'"

Chack had reached the top of the companionway. He was puffing from exertion and repressed emotion, but he interrupted before the Marine could answer. "Cap-i-taan Ellis, we found much ammunition. Good ammunition for the big machine guns. I lost a good Marine to some monster getting it out. Please let us retrieve it while we know the path is clear. I will try to . . . explain the situation with Rasik as I see it when we are done."

Jim started again to demand an immediate explanation, but Chack had already turned to go back for another crate. "Come on," he said to the others.

It still took several trips by all five of them to retrieve the crates and drag them to the bulwark, where the cargo net was. There was indeed much ammunition. For some reason, Jim wasn't surprised to see the boat gone. "All right," he said at last, gasping from his effort, "what gives?"

Chack was breathing hard too, but when he set his last crate down, he turned to Ellis. "I learned a great lesson once, not long ago, from some very wise men." He glanced at Blas-Ma-Ar, puffing up behind them festooned with the odd-looking weapons and the sack full of books. "Sometimes, for their own sake and the sake of the greater good, there are things leaders keep from followers because they do not have 'need to know.' 'Specially if the knowing—and only the knowing—will cause grief or . . . make things harder." Chack's tail flicked dramatically from one side to the other in a gesture that meant much the same thing as "on the other hand."

"There are also some very few rare times when followers decide their leaders don't have 'need to know.' These . . . what-if—hypothetical?—decisions do not come from distrust, animosity, or for any bad reasons at all." His tail flicked again. "It is the esteem they feel for their leaders that makes them happen." He took a final deep breath and continued. "Sometimes, followers see . . . again, hypothetically . . . that a thing must be done. For reasons of honor, integrity, and the greater good of others, there is no choice." He held up a hand. "But, for those same reasons, leaders need not—*must not*—know about the thing that *must be done*."

"That's not good enough, Chack! What the hell's going on? Tell me; that's an order!"

"Very well, but forgive me if my explaining wanders. I've just lost a Marine and I'm maybe 'rattled,' as you say." He sighed. "I'm poorly prepared right now, but may I answer you . . . philosophically?"

"What is this bullshit?" Jim's 'Cat was good, but Chack was speaking English. He must have practiced saying "philosophically" for a while.

"I take that as yes. You of all people know that a leader's honor and authority must be maintained at all costs."

Jim blanched slightly, but he already knew Chack meant no insult.

Chack continued: "He cannot, *must not*, break his word. Not to his crew, or even his prisoners."

Jim's eyes went wide as he finally realized what Chack was saying. "So you're telling me . . ."

Chack shushed him. "A moment. I'm not *telling* you anything. For the sake of our 'philosophical discussion,' say Cap-i-taan Reddy, our supreme commander, was forced to make a decision . . . a terrible accommodation that must torture him . . . even though it was made for the greater good. You, as his friend and follower, are bound to honor that accommodation in his place. You have no choice, no matter how distasteful you find it, even knowing how much it cost Cap-i-taan Reddy to make it in the first place. You would be tempted as his friend to break the accommodation, but that would be against his orders. That would reflect poorly on you and him as well. If, however, unknown to you, a small group of followers—who'd gravely suffered, I add—decided they could not bear this accommodation, and took it on themselves—knowing you would be bound to punish them—to break it without your knowledge . . ."

"They're gonna bump off that Rasik bastard!" Isak said gleefully.

Chack stared hard at the fireman. Under his helmet, his ears were probably slicked back in irritation. "I didn't say that. Nor as I understand it, is that their exact intent."

A short time later, the boat pulled back to the ship with Koratin and the two Marines. Immediately, all those on the ship besides Jim Ellis began passing crates and green metal boxes of ammunition down. Ellis fumed. He was relieved and infuriated at the same time. A plot had been hatched under his very nose—again—and although this time it was apparently done to spare him, he was still angry. Much to Isak's consternation, Jim hadn't revealed what he'd seen in the massive crates. It was just too big and it might be better if it remained a secret. Also, in this case, Isak's opinion wasn't worth much. A short time ago, it wouldn't have occurred to him to keep a secret from Chack, but right now he was mad and a little distrustful. Besides, he realized after he thought about it some more, they were going straight from this place into probable battle. If the Grik captured anyone, God forbid, it was best they have no idea what was in the wrecked ship north of Chillchaap. It wouldn't be difficult for the Grik to launch an expedition to destroy it, because who knew when the Allies would be able to come back themselves? No, this he'd keep to himself for a while until he had a chance to think more about it.

"We've done what we came here to do," he said. "We've found Rasik's 'surprise,' and I know what's in the big crates. This ammo will come in real handy. Hell, it's worth the trip by itself." One of the books Chack had retrieved was the ship's manifest. They'd lugged fifty-five thousand rounds of .50 BMG to the bulwark, and a few thousand rounds of .30-06. According to the pages in the book, there were *two million* more rounds in the ship. Quite understandable when one considered what they were for. A lot would be underwater and some might be ruined, but they'd have the brass and bullets. He tucked the manifest under his arm. He'd look it over some more on the way back to the ship.

He studied Koratin as the Marine corporal worked. It was hard to spot, but there was a little blood on his now slightly grungy white leather armor. "What did you do with Rasik, Koratin? I have to know."

Koratin paused in his labor. "He desired to be set ashore here, instead of on the island," he said simply. "As you Amer-i-caans would say, I owed him one."

Ellis clenched his teeth. "Is he alive?"

"Of course! We left him quite well situated, as a matter of fact." He glanced at the other two Marines. "We left him all our rations and even our spears! He should have no difficulty surviving for a considerable period. I swear to you now, before the Sun sinking yonder, Rasik will never die by our hands!"

Slightly mollified—Aryaalans didn't swear by the Sun lightly—Ellis frowned. "But he might wander back to Aryaal, damn it! That's why I wanted him on the island!"

"It matters little. If he'd wanted across, he could have built a raft. No, I think King Rasik will trouble the Alliance no more. He fully understands he is not wanted!"

"Well . . . you still disobeyed an order! Put yourself and these other Marines on report. I'm tempted to put Chack on report as well, as an accessory of some kind!" Jim looked at Chack. "Philosophical, my ass!"

"He had nothing to do with it!" Koratin objected.

"Maybe not, but he knew."

"He may have *surmised*, Cap-i-taan, but he did not know."

Jim looked at Chack again. Maybe Koratin was right. Clearly, Chack had expected them to kill Rasik. "Very well. For now. Let's hurry up and get the hell out of here. It'll be a long row home, mostly in the dark, and with that giant duck-eating . . . whatever it is, and with what got our Marine, that's kind of a creepy thought!" He shook his head. "What is it with this damn world, where everything wants to eat you?"

"Hey, Cap'n Ellis," Isak said suddenly. Once unaccustomed to making unsolicited comments to officers, the fireman blurted them out all the time now. "It just hit me. The ol' *Blackhawk* used to be *named Santa Catalina* before the Navy bought her! One of her snipes told me once when we was alongside." He shook his head. "Guy was one squirrely bastard. Used to run around ever'where tootin' on a duck call! That's why I remembered it all of a sudden. You know, the duck call . . . ? Well, anyway, it's still kinda weird."

Weird was right, Jim thought. Weird the way Isak's brain worked. A few minutes before, he'd been irate that Jim wouldn't tell him what was in the crates. Then he dredged up something like that.

Rasik-Alcas watched the boat pull away through small gaps in the canopy. They hadn't covered his eyes; they'd only gagged him. Now, through the searing waves of agony, he couldn't even scream. They hadn't taken him far, just a short distance beyond the jungle-choked shore. He'd actually been close enough to hear Koratin reassure Ellis that he wasn't dead! How could any creature lie so amazingly well? Rasik himself hadn't suspected a thing—but of course, he hadn't wanted to. Koratin would have known that! As depraved as Rasik knew himself to be, he'd certainly met his final, evil match—and all because of younglings!

He struggled feebly, but the movement only caused more agony. Koratin and the Marines had pinned his arms to the trunk of a wide subaa tree, right through the twinbones. He couldn't even tear himself free! Not that it would do any good. They'd done the same to the twinbones in his legs and then made a small incision in his belly. Not large enough to bleed him to death, but quite large enough to pull his intestines through. The squirming, tearing sensation had been more than he could bear, and he'd finally passed out. When he awoke, his murderers were gone. Food was scattered on the ground all around him—and his guts had been strung five or six tails away and hung on a limb.

He clenched his eyes shut as biting insects buzzed around his entrails. If only he'd known! How *could* he have known? Not only Koratin's precious, despicable younglings had perished on *Nerracca*—the Home the Japanese destroyed—but so had the younglings or mates of all his conspirators! He *should* have had a way of knowing that. *Would* have, if he'd been thinking clearly! Even so, what did younglings measure against the power Koratin could have had as King Rasik-Alcas's Supreme Minister? Younglings were simple to replace, even a pleasure, but the kind of power Koratin had denied was a priceless, precious thing. It was madness!

Even as Rasik-Alcas considered these imponderables and watched the boat grow small against the setting sun, the tiny, timid night predators began to gather around.

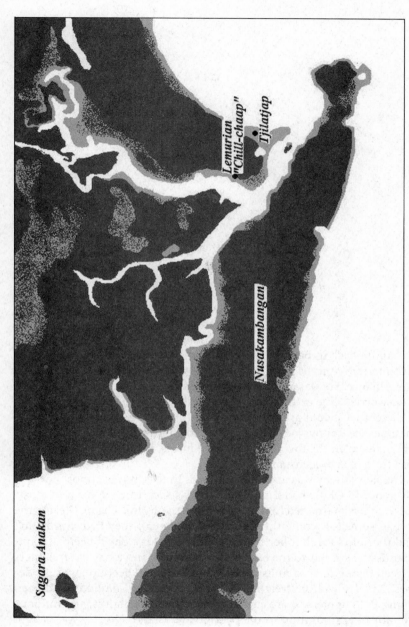

Environs of Tjilatjap

Matt looked at the message form Clancy had handed him. The fact they now had relatively reliable communications was a godsend in many ways. He could keep track of all the various operations under way and he could even exchange semiprivate correspondence with Sandra back in Baalkpan. He got daily updates—when atmospherics didn't interfere—on the progress made on *Walker* and all the other projects of the Alliance. He was a little worried about the silence from Laumer, but not *too* worried. The ex-Grik "tankers" they'd sent with both bunker-grade and diesel fuel should arrive there soon. Still, he'd received so much bad, sometimes calamitous news typed as neatly as their battered typewriters could manage on the dwindling message forms, he always accepted them with a trace of apprehension.

The news today was anything but bad. In fact, it was almost horrifyingly good. Jim Ellis had discovered Rasik's secret in the form of a battered freighter marooned in the swamps north of Chill-chaap. Clearly, the ship had somehow come through the same Squall they had. Jim hadn't found the ship's log, but her manifest told the story. She'd been attempting a mission similar to the one doomed *Langley* and a few old freighters had been trying to accomplish: a last-ditch effort to beef up Java's air defenses. *Langley* and the freighters—including *Santa Catalina*—had been ferrying P-40 fighters, spare engines, tires, parts, fuel tanks, and millions of rounds of ammunition to the beleaguered island. *Langley* was caught short and bombed into a sinking wreck. Matt had heard one of the other freighters made it to Tjilatjap, but since there was no nearby airfield, they'd actually assembled the planes dockside and were attempting to *tow* them overland on refugee-choked roads! He didn't know if they'd ever made it to an airstrip or not. Judging by Jim's report, *Santa Catalina* had been trying to do the same thing.

The only explanation for her condition, position, her very presence in this world, was that she too must have been damaged at sea, passed through the Squall, and arrived at a far different Tjilatjap. The Grik must have already sacked Chill-Chaap and the ship's captain, likely wondering where he was, proceeded as far upriver as he could to preserve his cargo and his ship from the deeper waters. Jim found no trace of the crew or the pilots who would have accompanied the planes. Maybe they were still out there somewhere, but more likely they hadn't survived their contact with this terrible world. Matt shook his head. Much the same would probably have happened to *Walker* and her crew if she hadn't made friends so quickly.

The existence of the ship and her cargo was an incredible stroke of luck, however, maybe even a war winner if they could salvage any of the planes. Jim thought it likely. The manifest totaled twenty-eight aircraft. Curtiss P-40Es! If they saved only half of them, they'd have more than the Philippines had after the first few days of the war. The reason it was horrifying was that Matt wanted those planes *now* and he had no way of getting them. Isak Rueben had said that the ship's engines were probably okay, but the fireroom was a shambles. She was also "kind of sunk," according to the report, so there'd be no salvaging her on a shoestring. An ecstatic Ben Mallory quickly fired back a suggestion from Baalkpan that they immediately launch an expedition to recover the planes. If they could hack an airstrip out of the jungle alongside the ship and somehow power her cargo cranes, they could simply assemble the planes and fly them out.

Matt knew there'd be nothing "simple" about it. The project would require a small army and there'd be no way to keep that secret. They'd also need a higher-grade fuel than the PBY had required and they'd have to cut airstrips everywhere they went to accommodate the planes. He'd been impressed by Jim's initial reaction to remain tight-lipped about the find, but realistically, it probably didn't matter. There was no risk of the Grik or even the Japanese infiltrating their ranks, and if they had spies on the island, they were just as likely to find the ship on their own. If the current Allied offensive was successful, they'd soon have the Grik pushed back almost to Ceylon, making long forays by enemy vessels into the Allied rear even more unlikely. Right now, every ship in Matt's squadron was essential where it was. They'd bottled up the approaches to Singapore and captured or destroyed a few ships—mostly leaving. His assault was essentially awaiting only Ellis and *Dowden*, and the extra weight of metal her broadside might add to the fight. He'd recommend to Adar that they send a small garrison to Tjilatjap and maybe at least begin recovery and stabilization efforts. That made good sense. But right now, his own plate was heaping full.

"A hell of a thing," Garrett commented, reading over his shoulder. "If we'd had those planes in the Philippines, we might still be there."

Matt grunted. "We had a hell of a lot more than that to start with and it didn't matter much. I don't know. MacArthur might have been some kind of Army genius, but he understood even less about his own Air Corps than he did about naval operations." He frowned. "I kind of wish we had him with us now, though. How's Pete's attack plan coming?"

"Pretty good, I think." Garrett looked at Matt. "Pete's done a swell job. I wouldn't be pining for that Army prima donna if I were you."

Matt laughed. "Not 'pining,' but I do wish I had someone else to bounce Pete's plans off of."

"Don't sell yourself short, Skipper. You've done fine onshore." Garrett looked thoughtful. "Besides, you have Rolak and Queen Maraan. Unlike our sea folk friends, they've been fighting on land all their lives. Pete and Safir did a good job chopping up that Grik force on Madura . . . I mean, B'mbaado."

"They sure did," Matt reflected. He took a breath. "Jim should be here in three days. Four at the outside—if the weather holds. Don't forget, this is the stormy time of year!" He chuckled grimly. Protection from the terrible "Strakkas" that struck the region was another reason they needed Singapore in their hands. "We'll pass the word via wireless or couriers for all ships to assemble just west of Bintan Island at that time. We'll have a final conference before we kick off the show."

"You want to invite Jenks?"

Matt nodded. "He's seen *why* we fight now and I think he's more sympathetic than ever before. He'll want to see *how* we fight. I think I'll give him a chance to get in closer this time, if he likes."

Captain Jim Ellis was piped aboard *Donaghey* and received a warm welcome. *Dowden* had made a quick passage, mostly under sail with the stout winds of some distant storm. He was a little surprised to be openly congratulated for his find—he still hadn't told his crew what he'd seen—and only his wireless operator and exec knew what the flurry of transmissions, prodded mostly by Ben Mallory, were about.

"Doesn't matter, Jim," Matt told him. "Adar has already sent a small force to secure the area. He wouldn't let Mallory go; he's still training pilots for the Nancys and he's fit to bust! But if we're successful, he'll have plenty of time to go play with his new toys."

"You're not going to give him a squadron, or wing, or whatever?" Jim asked.

"Hell, no! He's taught some guys and 'Cats to fly, but he's the only man we've got who's ever actually had real pilot training. He majored in aeronautical engineering at West Point, too. Even flew with Colonel Doolittle a few times. How do you think he got the Nancys up so fast?"

"I'll be damned."

"Yeah. He doesn't brag on it. I didn't know it either until he started pitching for the Nancys in the first place. In hindsight, we never should've let him risk his neck so much in that old PBY Catalina."

"But then we'd all be dead."

Matt nodded philosophically. "True. As a matter of fact, if we still had the damn thing, I'd tell him to take it up and scout Singapore for us."

"What do we know?"

"Not much. C'mon, let's adjourn to the wardroom. Juan'll fix you something cool to drink while the rest of the captains and commanders arrive."

Dennis Silva was hunting, as usual, during his free time. Besides being a pleasant diversion for him, it was an increasingly important chore. With so many foreign troops, artisans, and laborers in Baalkpan, the city needed more fresh meat than ever before, and the depleted fishing fleet was stretched to the limit. The ubiquitous polta fruit supplied a wide variety of nutrients the 'Cats, and apparently humans, needed, and other fruits and some vegetables were used as well, but both species needed plenty of animal protein. That left Silva with all the justification he needed to "go a-huntin'" regularly.

He did sometimes find himself craving some of the strangest things, though—stuff he'd always hated. Like beets. The killing grounds around Baalkpan had been planted with many different varieties of tuber and there was a root that tasted a little like beets that he sort of liked. It was odd. He'd always shunned vegetables as superfluous, useless things that took up space on his plate where more meat could have been. Now, some days, he figured he'd kill for a tomato—or a mess of black-eyed peas. Regardless, hunting was necessary. It got him out of the "house," away from the women, and let him kill things on a regular basis.

Pam and Risa were swell, but they had a tendency to coddle him. That could get old, despite the benefits. Technically, he was still sort of convalescing, but he felt as good as he figured he ever would. He was up to full speed working in the factory for Campeti or fooling around with Bernie's projects, but when he had any spare time at all, he headed for the jungle with the Hunter.

The Hunter was a scrawny, almost ancient Lemurian with a silver-streaked pelt and several missing teeth. He was barely taller than Rebecca, but like most 'Cats, he was incredibly strong. His weapon of choice was a massive crossbow that probably weighed as much as he did, and he carried it with a nonchalant ease Silva could only envy. He had guts too. Silva remembered when "Moe" (he called the Hunter Moe, since if the old 'Cat ever had a real name, he didn't remember it) had used *himself* to bait the super lizard that got Tony Scott so Silva could avenge his friend. They'd finally managed to kill the thing, but it was a close call and one of the reasons Dennis had built his massive Super Lizard Gun. So far, he hadn't found any super lizards to test it on. It killed the absolute, literal hell out of the big, dangerous rhino-pigs he and Moe pursued for their succulent meat, but rhino-pigs weren't much of a challenge for the thing. He'd taken to waiting for the creatures to bunch up so he could see how many the gun would kill with a single shot. So far, the record was four.

Enjoyable as any day in the woods was, Dennis and Moe rather doubted they'd get much chance to test the big gun's potential on this trip. In addition to the usual bearers they brought to deal with their kills, Courtney Bradford, Lawrence, and Abel Cook had tagged along. Lawrence's fieldcraft wasn't bad. His species were natural predators, and the little guy had an almost childlike desire to please. He also really liked Silva, even though the big man had shot him once. The fact that his adored Rebecca liked him and considered Silva a demented big brother was probably sufficient explanation. Lawrence wasn't the problem. Courtney Bradford and his young protégé, Abel Cook, still had a lot to learn.

The bearers hung back, letting Dennis and Moe do all the hunting, but Bradford and Cook stayed right up with them. It irked Silva a little, but he figured Abel needed to do more "man stuff" and Bradford was, well, Bradford. He didn't come along often. He was a busy, much-sought-after man. He could be a pain in the ass in the field, making too much noise or chasing after a lizard, but Dennis enjoyed it when he was around. Courtney was a hoot, and too much seriousness was hard on Dennis Silva. He missed the conversation Courtney provided, no matter how bizarre.

"What's that?" Silva whispered as a small, striped reptile that looked like a fat ribbon snake with legs scampered across their path. They were hunting the pipeline cut where they'd killed the super lizard, and the earth was thick and mushy beneath their feet. Moe murmured something unpronounceable and shrugged. Probably not something fit to eat then, Silva decided. Certainly not worth the abuse of a shot. He wondered what Courtney Bradford would have done if he'd seen it. Chase after it on all fours, most likely. At the moment, Courtney was absorbed by retelling the legendary Super Lizard Safari to Abel.

Moe held up a hand and they all froze. He'd sensed something. Motioning them down to the moldy turf, he beckoned them to follow on their bellies. Slowly scooching along almost soundlessly in the damp, rotting material, they moved ahead. Courtney's tale had ceased. Maybe he was starting to get it after all. Moe eased a little farther ahead of them, stopped again, then turned to look back, grinning.

"Rhino-pigs, many," he hissed. "Come up. We have wind so they not smell, but they hear good. Be quiet!"

Even slower, Silva crept forward. Lawrence practically flowed beside him, silent as death. Bradford and Abel brought up the rear. They began to hear the heavy thud of hooves and an incessant, contented grunting. Silva reached Moe's position and peered over a little mound that might once have been a tree.

"Quite a swarm," he acknowledged. "They're just rootin' along. Don't seem too worried. I guess you were right. It takes a while for another super lizard to move in on an old one's territory."

"Too far?" Moe asked.

Dennis calculated the range. It was only about a hundred yards to the pack of animals, but he wanted to get as many as he could with a single shot. That was part of the game as well as his stated "field test" rationale.

"Nah. It oughta do. If anything, we might be too close. Speed don't always mean penetration, an' it ain't like I can reduce my charge." Carefully, he eased the big gun forward.

Rhino-pigs looked much like their cousins back home. Sort of like giant razorbacks with bigger tusks and an odd-looking horn on the top of their heads. At first glance, Dennis hadn't really thought the horn would be good for much, but once he'd seen one take off like a hot torpedo, he'd realized that the forward-hooking horn would be bad news for a taller predator's exposed underbelly. The tusks would slash a man as wickedly as their Alabama brethren. Of course, at six hundred to a thousand pounds, they could just stomp you into paste, too.

"How exciting!" murmured Bradford, joining them at last. "Which one will you take?" Abel said nothing, but he was clearly fascinated.

Dennis eased the gun farther forward until the butt plate rested against his shoulder. He really wasn't looking forward to firing the thing from a prone position. He reached forward and adjusted the rear sight's elevation. As powerful as the weapon was, it had a markedly high trajectory and he'd sighted it in for fifty-yard intervals. When raised, the rear sight stood about four inches high, and the range markers were considerably farther apart the higher they went.

"I'll take 'em as they come," he announced. He was trying a new bullet today. It was essentially the same lead slug he'd used before, but it was capped and cored with a pointed bronze "penetrator." The penetrator made the bullet a little longer, to keep the same weight, and he wasn't entirely sure it would be as stable in flight. He settled in on the stock and peered through the sights. A mighty boar was shoveling great snoutfuls of turf aside as it searched for insects and roots. The clacking, gnashing sounds of tusks were constant.

"You go for big bull . . . boar . . ." Moe said. "I tell when most are best."

"Sure."

"Why not shoot now?" Abel asked. "There are half a dozen behind him."

"Gotta line up their vitals, not just their bodies," Silva answered absently. He checked his priming powder and thumbed the hammer to full cock. Settling back in, he caressed the trigger, waiting for the word.

The wait seemed interminable. A couple of times, Moe tensed, and it seemed like he was about to give the signal, but then he relaxed slightly. Through it all, Silva was as still as stone except for the tiny adjustments he made to his aim, following the vitals of the big boar. Sweat dripped unnoticed down his face and soaked the black patch covering his left eye.

"Now," said Moe, without any warning at all. Almost before the word was fully uttered, Silva squeezed the trigger. The flint leaped forward, scraping a shower of yellow-hot sparks from the frizzen and kicking it open to expose the priming powder. A jet of flame and white smoke erupted in front of Silva's face, and with a horrendous cracking roar, the main charge vomited the quarter pound missile from the barrel—and heaved Silva's shoulder a foot backward. There was a nightmarish shrieking squeal that reverberated in the cut, and through the smoke they saw the big boar perform an almost vertical leaping lunge. He collapsed in the turf, back feet kicking spastically. There was pandemonium among the rest of the herd. Two other dark shapes lay where they'd fallen; another was performing writhing cartwheels. The rest were thundering in all directions like small locomotives gone amok. One large beast came directly at them, and Moe let fly with his massive crossbow, driving a shaft through the charging creature's snout and probably straight into its brain. It collapsed in a heap perhaps a dozen yards short of their position. That fast, all the surviving rhino-pigs were gone, vanishing into the dense growth on either side of the cut.

Silva was standing, already pouring another charge of powder down the massive gun. "Whoo-ee!" he said excitedly. "Good stick, Moe! I figgered I was gonna hafta poke that last one off us with my rifle muzzle!" He shook his head and slapped the holstered 1911 Colt at his side. "Never would've even got my pistol out!"

Lawrence scampered forward with nothing but a short spear. With a peculiar cry, he plunged it into the one still-thrashing pig.

Dennis nodded toward him, smiling. "Junior's growin' up," he said, almost wistfully. "Come on, fellas. Let's see how many we got besides ol' Moe's there!"

Having heard the shot, the bearers were already approaching. They knew whenever Silva fired his big gun, there'd be work to do.

Abel stared at Moe's rhino-pig as they passed it. "Will they clean the beasts here?" he asked.

"Sure. No sense waggin' their guts back. Makes 'em lighter."

"I'd like to watch." He looked at Silva. "Not that I'm finished watching you, sir! You are every bit as fascinating as any entrails, I'm sure!"

Silva blinked. "Yeah, well, thanks." With his rifle fully loaded and at the ready, Silva marched forward to view the carnage he'd created. "Four for sure." He beamed. "Big sumbitches line up, little sumbitches bunch up!" He held out the Doom Whomper. "What a gun!"

"Two 'lood trails!" Lawrence announced. His voice was a little shaky, but he seemed excited. He was spattered with the blood of the pig he'd finished. Dennis sobered.

"Rats. We'll hafta go after 'em, and they're dangerous enough when they ain't hurt and sore at you. Mr. Bradford, why don't you and young Abel here stay and study these boogers while the bearers cut 'em up. Me and Moe"—he glanced at the "lizard"—"and Larry'll track these other ones."

They quickly found the first rhino-pig. It hadn't gone far and had probably bled out within moments of being hit. Silva wasn't sure which one it was in the lineup, but the entry and exit wounds were quite large and about the same size, so he figured it was toward the back. Moe trilled a call to the bearers and, returning to the cut, the three trackers commenced following the final blood trail. This one put them a little on edge, and they'd saved it for last for a reason. Moe said the color of the blood indicated a liver hit. A fatal wound certainly, but not necessarily *immediately* fatal. The more time they gave the beast to die in peace, the less likely it would be to kill one of them when they found it.

They advanced carefully. Rhino-pigs were notorious for playing dead when wounded. Sometimes, their last act was to charge a tracker, taking revenge with its final breath. Moe always said never to approach a "dead" rhino-pig lying on his belly. One that was *really* dead couldn't lie like that; it would always lie on its side. If it was on its belly, it was poised to strike.

They crept along a considerable distance, the blood trail clear and dark, the ground disturbance unmistakable. This was some of the densest jungle Dennis had been in yet. The path they'd once followed while tracking the super lizard was on the east side of the cut and had been fairly easy going, in retrospect. It had been made by an animal dozens of times as big as a rhino-pig. This path wasn't much larger than the animal that left it, and sometimes all of them were forced to their hands and knees. It was like following a shark down a tunnel, Dennis thought uncomfortably. At some point you knew you were bound to run into the bastard, and by then, he was probably turned around and waiting. Raucous cries permeated the jungle and harsh coughs and snorts stopped their progress occasionally. Dennis knew about super lizards and rhino-pigs and many other creatures by now, but only Moe had a real idea what other dangerous predators they were likely to meet. Lawrence proceeded, alert to every movement, his short spear held before him like a sword. *Little lizard's really a pretty good guy to have with you, times like this,* Dennis decided. He knew *he* was in over his depth. He'd never been this far from the cut before.

With considerable relief, they noticed the jungle begin to thin as they approached one of the many clearings probably created by lightning fires. This one was recent, and blackened stumps protruded through the lush, fresh undergrowth. The foliage was really a type of long-leafed grass, Dennis realized, and it was damp and clingy to walk through, even though it was barely calf-high. Lots of herbivores probably frequented places like this, he thought. They heard a squeal. Then another. Lawrence's fur bristled and his eyes became intense as he sniffed the air.

"Just ahead!" Moe told them.

"Not just rhino-'ig," hissed Lawrence with a note of caution.

"What else?" asked Dennis.

"Not sure. Strange, 'ut' a'iliar." He shook his head in frustration. "Like thing I should know."

As quietly as possible, they picked up the pace. There was a little rise, probably formed by burned and rotten deadfall, and they crept up to the peak.

Below them, little more than sixty yards away, three rust-colored Grik, or lizards . . . or something stood around a dead rhino-pig. Their clawed hands held spears that were no more than sharpened sticks, but the points were black with blood. They seemed to be resting from their exertions, or complimenting one another on their prowess, and for the moment, at least, their guard was down.

With a Lemurian curse, Moe brought his crossbow up.

"What the . . . Hey, wait a goddamn minute!" Silva said, pushing the crossbow down. "What the hell? There might be dozens of the bastards!"

"No, just those," Moe said, trying to wrench his weapon free. "They steal our meat! They just big skuggiks!"

"You mean they *live* here?" Silva whispered savagely. "You never said there was jungle Griks on Borno!"

"Like Griks, but not!" Moe insisted. "I tell. Others tell! There not many on Borno, but we kill them when we see them! Let them live on little islands! Not here!"

Suddenly, Silva did remember. He remembered Nakja-Mur mentioning that the Grik on Borneo were primitive and didn't know tools, and they'd been hunted to near extinction. Only on islands like Bali—small or far away—were they left alone. They *had* been told, but he, at least, had forgotten.

"*I* like Grik, 'ut not," Lawrence hissed.

The ground beneath them seemed to shake and the foliage near the trio of lizards exploded into the clearing. Within the confetti of leaves and brush charged a young super lizard! The "Grik," or whatever they were, scattered in three directions. Apparently more interested in live prey than the dead pig, the monster fixed its gaze on one rusty shape and bolted after it with the amazing speed Silva knew the things were capable of.

"Shit!" growled Silva, and rose to a knee. He cocked his big gun and pulled it to his shoulder, raising the stock to his cheek. For an instant, he honestly didn't know what he was doing, but he didn't really need to. Threat assessment had always been one of his strong suits, whether the question was whom to throw the first punch at in a bar, or which target to engage. There *was* that little incident when he'd shot Lawrence, but it was a perfectly understandable mistake and the little guy didn't hold a grudge. . . . His sights found the pocket behind the super lizard's right arm. He eased a little right to lead the target and squeezed the trigger.

The recoil nearly tossed him on his back. It *did* put him on his butt. It was the first time he'd ever fired the Doom Whomper from a kneeling position. Quickly, he reversed the rifle and blew down the barrel, sending a jet of smoke out the vent. Even as he reached for another charge, he was looking to see the results of his shot. At first, there seemed to be no effect. The rusty lizard running for its life dropped to the ground, cowering from the shockingly loud report, most likely. On the other hand, it may have been a final instinctive act of self-preservation. The super lizard was almost upon it. Suddenly, the huge monster just stopped running, as if remembering it had forgotten something in the woods. It swayed a little, caught itself, looked at its prey, and even glared around the clearing. With no further ado, the bulb went out and the beast plummeted to the ground with a rumbling crash.

"Hot damn!" Silva crowed, pouring the charge and seating the bullet atop it. "He may not be a trophy as such critters go, but one shot's one shot!"

"Have care," Moe cautioned. The red-brown lizards were gathering near the one who'd almost bought it, helping it to its feet. Dennis didn't miss the significance of that. All the while, the trio of lizards was staring at them inscrutably. "Those vermin is easy to kill at a . . . far. Up close, they dangerous."

"You leave them lizards be," Silva said.

"Why? We no kill them, them stay here. I told you, them . . . they steal! They dangerous scavengers. Dangerous to hunters. They stay, more come. Be dangerous to city."

"Did ol' Nakja-Mur know you was killin' 'em whenever you saw 'em?" Silva asked.

"Of course. We always kill them when get so close to Baalkpan. Borno is big; them no need be here."

"Does Adar know you're killin' 'em? Does he even know about 'em?" Silva asked. "Bradford woulda had puppies just to gawk at 'em if he'd'a known there was anything so much like Griks right here on Borneo."

Moe didn't answer at first. Even he seemed to realize Dennis was right. "I no see them," he said at last. "I no see 'ungle Griks,' you call them, for five, six seasons. They gone. Good gone, say me." He looked at Lawrence, comprehension dawning. "But they not Griks. Like Griks, but not."

"Larry here looks enough like a Grik that I shot him once," Silva said. "Here you are huntin' with him. Then you rear up and start to kill some lizards that look more like him than they do Griks. I guess I'm sorta confused. Did it ever occur to you to try to *talk* to one of them buggers?" he asked, pointing at the trio still standing, staring back at them. "Did it ever occur to *anybody*? Lord knows I'm not much of a talker myself and I sure ain't one to judge. Killin' a problem's a quicker, more permanent way to solve one than talkin' to it any day, you ask me, but knowin' Larry has made me a little more selective about the lizard problems I kill on sight."

The rusty lizards seemed to decide it was time to go. They gathered their spears but made no move to retrieve the rhino-pig when they went near it. They did look at their multispecies benefactors quite often, however. One of them, maybe the one Silva had saved, pointed at the super lizard with its spear and then pointed it at Silva, adding a resonant cry like a choking goat. Dennis nearly jumped out of his skin when Lawrence replied with something that sounded similar. All three lizards stopped then, looking back, black crests rising on their heads. Another moment passed and then they melted into the trees.

"Goddamn, Larry!" Silva exclaimed. "Don't do that! Most of the time, you talk better than me. That lizard lingo gives me the creeps!"

There was movement in the jungle behind them, but it was only the bearers coming to the sound of Silva's gun. Bradford and Abel were with them. All knew Moe would have finished the rhino-pig with his massive crossbow, so Silva must have found them a more substantial load.

"What did you shoot?" puffed Courtney, leading the others and hastening to join them.

"Teenage super lizard," Silva said offhandedly.

"Splendid, splendid! I do hope you didn't damage the skull this time! I so want an undamaged skull! I wish I'd been here to see it!"

"Honest to God, I wish you'd been here too," Silva said. He went on to describe their encounter.

"Amazing, remarkable!" Courtney looked at Moe. "Does Adar know of these creatures?" he asked, echoing Silva's unanswered question.

"Maybe yes, maybe no," Moe conceded. "Adar is of sea folk. Sea folk know lizards on Bali and other places . . . maybe not here."

"I must speak to him about an expedition to make contact!" Bradford declared.

"That may be a little tough," Silva said. "Ol' Moe here says he and other hunters been killin' 'em on sight for years. Kinda like Injuns." He brightened. "Injun jungle lizards!"

"Oh, dear!" Courtney exclaimed. He turned to Lawrence. "But you spoke to them! What did they say?"

Lawrence flared his new, longer tail plumage and tried to shrug. "I don't know. They could have said, 'Thanks 'or killing the 'ig lizard.'"

"Well . . . what did you say to them?"

"'Good day.'"

"So, what do we know, sir?" asked Chack. He was sitting as close as—probably closer than—was "decent" to Safir Maraan. His reunion with the Orphan Queen had been brief, but almost electric with suppressed passion when Safir arrived on the flagship for the conference.

Matt glanced at Jim and sighed. "Damn little. A week ago, we put a squad of Marines ashore here." He indicated the east-southeast coast of the island on a hand-drawn copy of a Navy chart tacked to the bulkhead. "They've moved to about here." He pointed to the vicinity where the map oddly showed the old British fortress garrison buildings. Whoever had drawn it had made an almost exact copy of *Walker*'s old chart. "Of course, none of this stuff is there." He paused. "In fact, the shoreline's not even exactly the same, and some of these little islands are bigger single islands now. Maybe more proof of Courtney's ice-age theory. Anyway, we'll have to watch the depth going in." He looked around the cramped compartment. "The Marines have set up one of Mr. Riggs's little generators and have been in intermittent contact. Intermittent because they have to move a lot. Evidently, supplies are running pretty low and the Grik are doing a lot of hunting. That doesn't mean they're not expecting us, but it does mean they're spread out a little. Maybe a lot."

"*Are* they expecting us?" Jim asked.

"They have to be expecting *something*. Most of the ships we've captured or destroyed were headed out, probably for Ceylon. Those ships were *packed*, friends. That's why most had to be destroyed. A few supply ships have tried to make it in, but to my knowledge, none has gotten past us. That alone is enough to alarm a savvy Grik Hij that we've cut his sea-lanes. Our spotters say there's a large concentration of enemy troops here." He pointed again at the chart, near where the British repair facilities would have been. "Apparently, it's a burgeoning port facility here as well." He shrugged. "You know, I used to wonder why Lemurians—and this was originally a Lemurian colony of Batavia, I understand—always seemed to pick the same spots for cities that humans did." He scratched his chin. "The old Scrolls might have had something to do with that, but mainly I figure if a place is a good spot for a city or a port, it's a good spot for a city or a port, no matter what species you are!" There were a few chuckles. "Anyway, the spotters also say there are a lot of ships anchored off those facilities, more than they can account for."

"What do you mean?" Jenks asked, speaking for the first time.

"Well, first you have to understand the sheer number of Grik we killed when they came against Baalkpan." He shook his head. "Lots of ships got away, but they were mainly the ones that offloaded their troops on the south coast. I bet they came home nearly empty. They didn't leave them in Aryaal, so they must have brought them here. Second, like I said, the ships we've destroyed were packed, maybe with twice their usual number. That convinces me our scouts have been right all along. They're pulling out of Singapore too."

"Well, that's excellent news, certainly," Jenks proclaimed. "All you need do is wait for them to leave and then take the place over."

"It's not that simple. First, and I really don't expect you to understand this yet, but the Grik don't act that way. They attack. Period. If they're pulling out, somebody up the chain has started thinking *strategically*, and that bugs me. If that's the case, it lends even more importance to our objectives, or eventually, we'll be right back where we started."

"And what are those objectives?"

"Foremost is to kill Grik, of course. The more we kill now, the fewer we'll have to face later. Second, I want as many of those ships as we can get. They may be foul and full of the . . . remains of their sick practices, but they're relatively well made. We need them and I'm afraid they mean to destroy them. Why else send so many troops out on so few ships? Some may have been damaged fighting us, but if they made it here, chances are they're fit for salvage. Third, again according to our spotters, the Grik spent a lot of time and effort on the port facilities. They may not have a dry dock, or otherwise be up to Baalkpan's standards, but they're better than anything in Aryaal. I want those facilities intact." He looked around the compartment, meeting every gaze. "Finally, the spotters have seen a little compound where a few Japs are being held. We have to save them."

There were a few mutters of protest and others looked uncomfortable. A few tails swished indignantly. Matt held up his hands. "I know what you're thinking: what for?" He sighed. "Two reasons, really. No, three. First, chances are, if they were helping the Grik of their own free will they wouldn't be in a compound. Second, we might be able to get some information out of them. They've been to Ceylon and they know what the defenses are like. They've had a far different experience than Commander Okada, and they might even be willing to actively help us. Finally, and most important . . . we just *have* to, is all. If the spotters had seen a compound full of 'Cats, we'd have to save them, wouldn't we?"

"Of course," Safir replied. "But these Jaaps are the enemy too, are they not?"

"Maybe not. Just because some Aryaalans once followed an evil king, are they evil too? Maybe some are, and I'm sure Lord Rolak has his eyes out for any such, but not all. And personally, I'd rather kill each and every one of them with my bare hands than leave them to the fate they might face at the hands of the Grik."

Finally, there were nods in the room, and a few comments of support.

"Very well," Matt continued, "with that, I'll let Generals Alden, Rolak, and Safir Maraan enlighten us with their brilliant plan to accomplish all these objectives." He winced at Pete. "Sorry about the last addition, but I only just heard."

"It's okay, Skipper. I think we can add it in."

"Do you think, General Alden, you might add in some supporting role for *Achilles*?" Jenks asked.

Matt had actually been expecting the offer. He and Jenks might never become friends, but they'd developed considerable mutual respect and even admiration during the commodore's frequent visits aboard *Donaghey*. Matt also knew that the very savagery of their enemy had gnawed at Jenks since he first set foot on the Aryaal dock. He'd slowly come to the same conviction his princess had: sooner or later, the Empire he served most certainly had a stake in this fight.

Pete glanced at Matt and saw him nod. "Why, of course, Commodore. Always happy for another gun platform, especially one as maneuverable as yours."

"My Marines are at your disposal too," Jenks added, "as a reserve if you need it, or possibly as a flanking support of some kind?"

"That's very generous," Alden said, recognizing that the offer was smart as well. Throwing Jenks's untried Marines into a pivotal part of the plan at the last minute might wreck the whole operation, and Pete would never have done it. The Imperial clearly recognized the latter, at least. This way his troops could participate on some level and he avoided the insult of a refusal. Jenks was pretty sharp, Pete decided. "We could use a little more flank security, with all those Grik hunters running around," he said. He advanced to the chart tacked to the bulkhead. "Now, here's the deal. The operation"—he grinned—"is called Singapore Swing. At oh one hundred hours tomorrow morning, the fleet elements will be in position off these beaches, here, here, and here. . . ."

I t was long after dark when Silva's hunting party neared the environs of Baalkpan. The bearers had dragged the masses of meat on travois down to the original riverside fueling pier and transferred it to square, flat barges. From there, they slowly towed the barges to the city behind Scott's launch. As usual, Moe didn't accompany them past the pier, but disappeared into the jungle as soon as the hunt was done. Even Silva didn't know where he lived, and he was probably the closest thing to a friend the old Lemurian had. The sun went down quickly, as was its custom, and for a time the large, voracious insects pestered them as they traversed the estuary. The breeze of the bay protected them a little as they drew nearer the city.

"What the devil?" Silva asked as they caught sight of the old fitting-out pier. The city was lit up like it hadn't been in a long time, and a major party appeared to be under way.

"Most interesting," observed Bradford. "One would like to speculate that they've heard the news of our return after such an auspicious and successful venture as ours today, but I honestly doubt that's the case."

"Nobody invited you to a party neither?" Silva grumped.

"Indeed not. I can't imagine what might have transpired in our absence to cause such revelry. Perhaps the war is over?"

Silva grunted. "We musta missed *something*, but I doubt that's it. Besides, they wouldn't dare win the war without lettin' me in on it. I'm gonna personally poke that Sequestural Lizard Mother through the head with one o' Lanier's U.S.-marked butter knives. I told the skipper so. If she fell off the pot an' broke her neck, I'm gonna be mighty sore."

Abel stirred from where he'd been sleeping curled up next to Lawrence in the stern sheets. "Look!" he said a little blearily. "*Walker* is lit up! Her aft searchlight tower has been reinstalled and they are shining the light about!"

"Ahhh!" roared Silva when the beam rested momentarily on the approaching launch and its train of barges. He shielded his eyes from the painful glare. "Goddamn EMs are horsin' around! They musta managed to twist a couple o' wires together an' thought that was worth a hootenanny!" He chuckled. "Maybe Rodriguez'll point the light at Laney! He can't stand that stupid prick. 'Hey, Ronson, what's that smolderin' pile o' bones?' 'Oh, that's just Laney. Thought I saw a roach on deck!'" Silva laughed.

Abel looked at him in the reflected light—the searchlight beam had passed on—and wondered just how serious the big man was. There were persistent rumors that Silva had actually tried to kill Laney before. Abel usually doubted it. He'd discovered that Silva was particularly skilled at killing things that he *really* wanted dead. But he'd also learned Silva was only slightly more predictable than the weather.

"Hey," Dennis said, addressing the coxswain, "after we drop our load, take us over there, willya?" He was pointing at *Walker*. The coxswain was a Lemurian, one of Keje's officers learning powered-shiphandling skills so he'd at least have some sort of a clue when it came time for *Big Sal* to join the fleet. "Whatever's goin' on, it looks like it has to do with our ship, so I figure anybody that's anybody'll be there. We can report in and find out what's up at the same time."

"You betcha," came the high-pitched response.

The launch's nose bumped against the pier and Silva winced to think what Tony Scott would have said, but he sent Bradford and Abel up the rungs to the dock. Lawrence scampered up without assistance and Silva followed him. There was clearly a party atmosphere, and it seemed as if most of the city had turned out to see the show. It took Dennis only a few minutes to figure out what all the ruckus was about. Through the noise of the revelers, mostly Lemurian but a few human as well, a long-unheard but intimately familiar sound reached his ears. He turned and stared at the ship.

Smoke was rising from the aft funnel, the number four boiler, and the blower behind the still-stripped pilothouse roared with a steady, healthy, reassuring rumble. He'd expected it any day now, just not *today*. He knew the reconstruction of the numbers three and four boilers was almost complete and the starboard engine, that gloriously complicated Parsons turbine, had been carefully overhauled, but the blower motor and both the twenty-five-kilowatt generators had still been in the "powerhouse" when his hunting party set out that morning before dawn. For the longest time, all he could do was stand and stare.

Walker was alive again. She inhaled, exhaled, and her proud heart stirred once more. Her lifeblood flowed to the boiler, where hellish fires flared and water flashed to steam and sang joyously through the pipes to her turbines. At least one refurbished generator fed electricity to her blower and the spotlight. Silva's eye patch felt soggy and his good eye quit working right. Someone was calling his name, but it just didn't register at first. He noticed a slight weight land upon him, pulling his neck forward with small, strong arms. The passionate kiss suddenly inflicted on him finally brought him to his senses and he realized Pam Cross had jumped on him like a kid on a set of monkey bars. The small nurse clung to him and the curves pressed against him brought a smile to his tear-streaked face.

"Why, there you are, my little honeydew!" He still held the massive rifle in his right hand, but his left arm was more than sufficient to support the dark-haired, Brooklyn-born firecracker. "Where's Risa? I kinda missed you gals t'day. Killed me a super lizard! But I wish I'd'a been here, now!"

"Risa's on *Big Sal*, but she'll be heah." Pam giggled. "Probably give you the same kind of welcome . . . except I ain't going to lick you!"

"Always glad to oblige my adorin' ladies!"

Pam hugged him tight. "Gotcha a super lizard with your"—she giggled again—"big gun, huh? That's swell. I'm just glad you're back safe."

Silva pretended innocent confusion. "Say, where'd Bradford run off to? That reminds me. I need to talk to somebody. Mr. Letts or Spanky, I guess. I gotta make a ree-port. We saw somethin' kinda screwy today."

Pam kissed him again and climbed down. "He went over theah, with the kid and the lizard. They're talking to Mr. Letts and Adar already. Hurry back, you big lug."

Silva bowed theatrically. "A hero's toil never ends, m'dear. I'll be back to perform whatever chore you require di-rectly!"

Someone pushed a mug of seep in his hand as he made his way to where Bradford, Letts, Adar, and now Spanky, Sister Audry, and Keje stood. Adar studied him intently.

"Why didn't you kill them?" Adar asked. "Mr. Braad-furd says they looked quite like Grik."

"Yeah, well, they wasn't, was they? Last time I shot somethin' only *looked* like a Grik, he wound up bein' one of my best buddies." Lawrence and Abel had joined them and Silva tousled Lawrence's young crest. The Tagranesi irritably shook his head. "Call me soft if you like, but I've decided shootin' fellas may not always be the best way to say how-dee-do. 'Specially with guns that won't leave much to get acquainted with." He hefted his rifle proudly. "A super lizard with one shot! This thing woulda spattered them little Injun jungle lizards all over the clearin'. Might coulda brung one of 'em back in a snuff can to meetcha."

"Injun lizards?" Spanky demanded.

"I discovered 'em!" Silva said, stubbornly. "I can call 'em what I want." He nodded at Adar. "Question is, what's the dope on 'em? Does his purple presidential holiness think we shoulda killed 'em, captured 'em, or left 'em be?"

Adar was highly accustomed to Silva's irreverent humor by now. He even shared it in good measure. Besides, if anyone had earned the right to make sport of him, or "josh" him a little, as the Amer-i-caans said, Silva certainly had. He wasn't the least offended now.

"Actually, I think you did precisely the right thing. As a Sky Priest of the sea folk who has just lately inherited a land domain, I confess I knew nothing of this species. Nakja-Mur never spoke of them, nor did Naga. I suspect your Moe and other hunters may have been carrying on this war of theirs for generations. Only he and others like him often venture into the wilds around Baalkpan. Nakja-Mur was a thoughtful, wise High Chief and a careful steward. I suspect if he had truly known of your 'Injun lizards,' he would have told us."

"Moe said he did."

"Nakja-Mur never left this city in his life," Adar said. "Naga did, but only by sea. Nakja-Mur also knew of the Grik threat from the west, but didn't truly *believe* it until it was upon him. The same is probably the case with those you saw today. All of us know there are aboriginal tribes of Grik-like creatures. Lawrence is proof of that. But no one ever considered the possibility they might not all *be* Grik in anything other than form. Captain Reddy has sent that they discovered the remains of Grik-like creatures in Aryaal that had apparently been used as slaves or worse. He believes they were like the ones that attacked your shore party when you first came to this world." Adar sighed.

"We have neglected studying these almost mythical creatures long enough—on the islands, and apparently here as well. Perhaps they are yet more enemies, as we have always assumed, but just perhaps"—he glanced at Lawrence and blinked fondness—"they are more like *him* than we could have ever dreamed. We learn more about even the Grik all the time," he added cryptically. He bowed to Courtney Bradford. "You will have your expedition. I want to make contact with these creatures. Perhaps we can even be friends, if they can forgive generations of violence most of us knew nothing about!"

"The only 'expedition' I want is back in the war!" Silva insisted.

"You'll get that," Letts said. "And before much longer." Subtly, during the conversation, Letts and Spanky had turned toward *Walker* so they could stare at the miraculously vibrant . . . living ship. Silva joined them, and eventually, so did all the others. They were here to celebrate her resurrection, after all. Even Sister Audry, who'd done everything she could throughout the day to prevent any spiritual significance from being attached to the event, was moved.

"She still looks a fright, Spanky," Silva said, "but you've done a swell job."

"Everybody has, you moron," Spanky replied gruffly. "Even you."

Silva belched loudly. Seep had that effect on him. So did the local beer, which he'd begun to prefer. Actually, Dennis Silva belched fairly often, regardless. "Try to be nice to a snipe," he grumped, "and what's he do? Slanders and insults." He shook his head. "Where's Loo-tenant Tucker and the munchkin princess? I woulda figured they'd be here for somethin' like this."

Spanky McFarlane looked around. "Well, they *were* here, just a little while ago."

"They went for a cool drink," Adar supplied, "and perhaps they have retired for the night. It is quite late."

"Yeah, well, me and Larry'd better find 'em and report in. I am one of the o-fficial pro-tectors of Her little Highness, after all, and I doubt Larry can stand it much longer without lickin' her er somethin'." Lawrence hissed at Dennis through his fangs, kind of a chuckle for him. "'Sides, Miss Loo-tenant Tucker's prob'ly worn out from dealin' with the little twerp all day!"

The others laughed. Not only did they know Silva was devoted to the girl and considered her anything but a twerp, but they knew Sandra loved the princess like a daughter.

"So long then." Spanky grunted. "And good riddance. Come back and brag when you kill a super lizard with your teeth!"

"That's the very next stunt on my list," Silva called back, heading toward Pam. "And I'll do it too, right after you build a battleship out of a beer can." Reaching the dark-haired nurse, he crushed her in another embrace. "You run along home now. Ol' Silva's kinda tired. Won't be good for more than three or four hours o' labor, I'm afraid. I'll be along directly!"

Pam giggled and moved away through the crowd.

"Mr. Silva?" asked a hesitant voice. It was Abel Cook. "May I accompany you, sir? That is, if you're going to see Lieutenant Tucker and . . . the princess, I would like to join you. To say good evening."

Silva belched at him. "Sure, I guess. What about Mr. Bradford, though? You're kinda his caretaker now, ain't ya? He'll be skunked in half an hour with all the booze down here—Captain Reddy would have a fit! Bradford's liable to puke on Adar or dance nekkid in the searchlight!"

"I'll come right back, I promise!"

"Hmm. You better keep yer grabbers to yourself! I seen how you look at her. You go to gropin' at Her Highness, me and Larry'll eat you!"

"No, sir, Mr. Silva! Never . . . ! I—"

"Oh, come on. If they went for a cold one, maybe they're at the Screw. Neither one's much for booze, but Pepper keeps some juice an' such."

They didn't find them at the Busted Screw; nor were they at the Fem Box, as the female bachelor officers' quarters was called.

"Say," said Dennis, "I wonder where they're at?" He wasn't really worried, but he was growing a little annoyed—and anxious. "Maybe they went to see Sister Audry? She ain't half bad for a gospel shark. Has some brains. Ever'body knows I'm as pious a critter as there is, but if you go jabberin' religion at folks all the time, without a break, pretty soon they'll tune you out—like a worn bearing. That, or they'll get sick o' hearin' it squeal and replace it with a new one."

"What did you say?" asked Lawrence, and Silva laughed.

The party had wound down considerably by the time they realized Sandra and Rebecca weren't at the little hut Sister Audry kept near the fishers' wharf. But Sister Audry wasn't there either. "Now, this is startin' to stink," said Silva. "Only place left they might be is *Big Sal*, in the dry dock, seein' Selass. She and Miss Tucker are pals." He shook his head. "Or maybe they're back where we started, oglin' the ship some more. I doubt it, though. It *is* gettin' late. Way too late for Miss Tucker to be sendin' love letters to the skipper at the wireless shack. *Must* be at *Big Sal!*"

Unconsciously picking up their pace, the man, boy, and Tagranesi headed back toward the shipyard. They met a few revelers on the way, but Baalkpan was a weary city. There were so many wildly different projects under way, employing such a large percentage of the populace, even the all-night bazaar that had once been the center of Baalkpan social life had shrunk to a mere shadow of its former size. Those not actively engaged in the war effort still had to labor: fishing and doing the chores of everyday life for more mouths with fewer hands. Others hunted, as they'd done that day. In any event, what had once been a city that never slept shut down almost entirely after dark these days. Even something as grand as bringing *Walker* back to life couldn't keep most from their bedding too long.

All that remained of the party at the dock were oil lamps and a few sozzled mounds lying on the planks. *Walker*'s blower still rumbled, but there was no light aboard. There was clearly still a lot of electrical work yet to accomplish, and besides the spare bulbs they'd stored ashore before the battle, few of those aboard the ship had survived the fight and subsequent submergence. Still, even darkened, she was alive. Silva noted as they passed her that a wisp of smoke rose from the number four stack and stars shimmered in the heat plume above it. He grinned.

Big Sal wasn't much farther, the once distinctive outline changed forever by the alterations under way. She was still lit and work continued aboard her. Keje was pushing her people relentlessly to finish the job so his Home might have water beneath her again. Silva knew the dry dock gave Keje the willies. *Big Sal* had often been flooded down for a variety of reasons, and she was built in something *like* a dry dock, but she wasn't ever *supposed* to be completely dry again. For her to be totally divorced from her natural element as she now was struck Keje and most of his people as an unnatural thing, worse even than the perverse changes their Home was undergoing.

"Least there'll be somebody there we can ask," Silva muttered. They were crossing the old, smooth ramp once used by the PBY to get her out of the water. There were several other ramps here and there, but this had been the one closest to the shipyard.

Almost across, Lawrence stopped and his head jerked toward the water. "Dennis!" he hissed, using Silva's first name. Usually he tried to say, "Mr. Silva," but it came out mangled. The others noticed the sudden difference and recognized the significance. They stopped.

"What's up, Larry?" Silva asked quietly.

"At the 'ater's edge, there is acti'ity—and the scent o' the ladies!"

Silva's heart pounded in his chest. He'd been using his big gun as a kind of walking stick, and he slowly brought it up, peering hard into the darkness. There was no moon and almost no light, but suddenly he *could* see something outlined against the gentle gray wave tops that lapped at the ramp. "Those Imperial sons o' bitches!" he seethed. "They're *swipin'* the gals!" He looked quickly around. Apparently, they hadn't yet been seen.

"'Kay," he hissed. "Abel, you stay put. If there's a ruckus, run like hell, screamin' your head off!"

"But—"

"Shut up. Larry, see if you can ease down the left side o' the ramp. I'll try to creep up on 'em from this side, close to the edge. We gotta see what's what before we raise the alarm. Don't want anybody panickin'! That said, if either of us sees a chance, we'll kill our way in to the girls. You move, I move, and vicey versey. Got it?"

Lawrence jerked a nod.

Abel was terrified, and a little indignant he'd been left out, but he was also chilled by how quickly and easily the jovial giant and servile, companionable Tagranesi became focused, single-minded killers. He stepped slowly back as the others all but disappeared in the darkness.

Silva began to hear muffled whispers as he drew near. Slowly, eight—no, nine—human shapes resolved themselves, gathered onshore near a longboat. The white paint of the boat had been darkened. Three of the shapes stood a little apart, huddled together, while two others apparently watched over them. *That's gotta be them*, Silva thought. *One's shorter than the others.* He wondered who the third one was. *Must be Sister Audry. She wasn't home neither. Weird.* He paused and took a silent breath. *Them devils are actin' impatient. I wonder what they're waitin' for? They musta had the girls for a while. Why not just scram?*

Being a single-shot muzzle loader, Silva's big gun wouldn't be much use. Now, if the two guards would line up . . . Wait! One was moving away, fumbling with his trousers. With a wicked grin and a slow, fluid motion, Dennis slung the rifle and crept up on the man beginning to relieve himself. Dennis knew the human eye, like any predator's, keyed on motion, but it was always amazing how much movement one could get away with if the motion was slow and smooth.

The pissing man never had a chance.

From behind him, like driving his knuckles into his hand, Silva brought his left palm down on the top left side of the man's head and drove his right fist into the hinge of his jaw. There was a loud crunch, like a slick boot sliding on gravel, when the pointed part of the man's jaw crashed into his brain, but there was no other sound. "Sorry, sir," he hissed aloud, like an underling apologizing for making a noise.

"Silence, fool!" came the hoped-for muffled order.

Dennis eased the dead man to the ground, then slowly pulled his Pattern 1917 cutlass from its sheath. Like his giant rifled musket and his 1911 Colt, he never went anywhere without it. Trying to imitate the pissing man's stride, he moved back toward the prisoners. He had maybe a couple of seconds at best before he was discovered. For one thing, he was much taller than his victim.

A dark form fluttered in the corner of his good eye and he saw Lawrence pounce on the man farthest from him. In the same instant that Lawrence dug his hind claws into the man's chest, clamped his jaws on his throat, and launched himself backward into the darkness, Silva drove the cutlass into the ill-defined torso of the other guard. Both emitted hideous, wrenching screams. He yanked Sandra's gag down under her chin. "Surprise!" he said. "It's me!"

"Our feet first!" Sandra gasped. "It's Billingsly! He's trying to take the princess!"

"I figgered that!" Silva said, hacking at the ropes that bound their feet with just enough slack to walk or stand. A musket fired and a jet of blinding flame flashed from the boat. "Ow!" he said. The ball had grazed his hip. In the darkness, it could just as easily have hit one of the girls.

"Stop them!" someone bellowed. "They mustn't escape!" A pistol flared with a loud *ker-thump!*

"Help! Help!" screamed Abel's voice. "The Imperials are attacking! They are taking the princess! Help!"

Lawrence killed another man and a musket flashed in his direction.

With their feet free, Silva started working on their hands.

"No time!" Sandra shouted. "We're tied together too! We can't run like this!"

"Got to!" Silva replied. "Go!" He unslung his rifle and pointed it at the boat. With a mighty roar that anyone in the city who saw or heard it would recognize, he hoped he'd scuttled Billingsly's escape. Another musket fired from near the top of the ramp. Not the cavalry then, Silva realized. None of the new Springfield muskets had been issued yet. Must be the ones these others were waiting for! He heard Abel scream again, in pain this time. He dropped his rifle and pulled the Colt, flipping the safety with his thumb. "Get down, boy!" he roared, and emptied the magazine in the direction of the shot. "Run!" he shouted at the three ladies. "Run like hell that way!" He spun back toward the boat.

Evidently, he'd miscounted. Other men must have been *in* the boat as well, because there still seemed to be as many enemies as he and Lawrence had started with. He had only the cutlass now. "C'mon, Larry!" he thundered. "Kill 'em all! No pris'ners!"

Gilbert Yeager awoke from a happy, muzzy dream of happy, muzzy steam coursing joyfully through clean, tight pipes and leaping energetically at polished turbine blades. Something was booming somewhere and somebody had definitely stepped on him. Silly, rude bastards! Couldn't they tell he was asleep? Now somebody was shaking him, trying to get him off the miraculously cool pipe where he was listening to the glorious song of steam. "Whatcha fagarattin' ta da boomin' slip!" he demanded indignantly. He sat up, realizing he was still on the warm, damp dock where he'd apparently passed out. He blinked in the darkness. A bright flash not far away lit sparklers in his eyes. "Ahhhg!"

"Somebody's tryin' to swipe the princess!" Tabby said beside him. She was still shaking his head.

"So? Lemme alone!"

"No! We must do something! There is a fight, and Si'vaa and Larry are outnumbered! The princess and Minister Tucker, at least, are in danger!"

Gilbert blinked again. "Well, why the hell didn't you wake me up, goddamn it?" He leaped to his feet with a board in his hand, swayed, then brandished the piece of wood. "Death to whoever the hell it is we're fixin' ta kill!" he screeched. A probably errant pistol ball struck the board and slapped it into his face. He went down as though pole-axed. "I'm *keeled*!" he wailed through busted lips. "I knew it! Just a matter o' time!"

"You ain't killed!" Tabby shouted, trying to drag him to his feet. "But you are drink too much!" She dropped his arm. "Me too," she admitted. Leaving Gilbert where he lay, she ran toward *Walker*, trilling a cry of alarm.

There was much alarm already. Weary as Baalkpan was, most of her sentries were alert. Those who could be. A coast defense gun, situated to protect the shipyard, lit the night with a mighty roar. Another went off and a red alarm rocket screeched into the sky. Bronze pipe-gongs began sounding throughout the city. Spanky McFarlane ran past a still-babbling Gilbert dressed only in his hat and skivvies. There was a .45 in each hand. Mallory and Rodriguez wore only their skivvies, but they both had '03 Springfields. Keje rushed to the scene with half a dozen armed 'Cats. Blindingly, *Walker*'s searchlight flared down on the scene like an angered God. The tableau it revealed was stunning not only in its unexpectedness, but in the magnitude of the implications and the scope of the slaughter.

Commander Billingsly stood behind all three females, who were still tied together, and held a long-barreled pistol pressed painfully under Princess Rebecca's jaw. Another man with blood on his face held a cutlass across the throats of Sandra Tucker and Sister Audry. Five other men still stood, although all seemed wounded to some degree, but there were at least a dozen bodies scattered on the old seaplane ramp. One of them was Dennis Silva.

Silva, at least, didn't seem dead, but he was covered with blood and just sitting on the ground at the women's feet. Lawrence was there too, equally bloody, but apparently uninjured. He was supporting Silva and looking intently at the princess.

"Drop your weapons!" Billingsly demanded.

"Eat shit!" Spanky growled back. "Clearly you don't know who you're monkeyin' around with!"

"I admit to some uncertainty in that regard," Billingsly admitted. "Your man here, the big one, is not dead. I must say both his arrival and his courage came as a significant surprise. It is a shame you force me to kill him." Billingsly nodded at one of his remaining men, who pointed a pistol at Silva's apparently senseless head.

"Ronson, Ben," Spanky said quietly. "You got enough light on your sights?"

"Yeah."

Both Springfields spoke almost as one and the henchman's head geysered up and backward in what appeared an almost neon spray under the harsh light.

Billingsly flinched and drove the pistol more savagely into the princess's neck. "Well," he said, recovering himself. "Touché. A most impressive demonstration of marksmanship! You have saved your man, bravo! It changes nothing, however."

"How's that?" Spanky asked. "At one word from me, these two guys can do the same to you and your pals and this little game'll be over."

"That would be a most unfortunate word for you to give. You see, I have yet another hostage in the boat behind us, a young Mr. Abel Cook, if I don't mistake his name. He is lightly injured, I'm afraid, but he is also in the hands of a most dedicated friend of mine, a Mr. Truelove. He is perfectly prepared to cut that young man's throat, and you can't even see him." Billingsly shrugged. "Mr. Truelove is also performing a number of other tasks, highly specialized for this occasion."

Spanky glanced to his right as a winded Adar and Alan Letts arrived. He knew both would have enough sense to say nothing until they knew more about the situation. "Such as?" Spanky asked.

"Mr. Truelove is holding a hooded lantern over the side of the boat. As long as that colored lantern is visible to my ship, *Ajax*, she will not fire a full broadside of grapeshot into this very gathering. If you carry out your threat I will die, which would certainly disappoint me, but then Mr. Truelove would drop that lantern into the sea and everyone here, including many of you—who I predict are leaders of this ridiculous Alliance—would also die. A most tragic ending to what I had hoped would be a very peaceful little rescue."

"Kidnapping, you mean!" Letts snarled.

Billingsly shrugged again. "Semantics. A great hobby among philosophers, but quite tedious for me, I'm afraid."

"You're bluffing," Spanky declared. "I can still see your ship's lights, riding where they've been for months!"

"A regrettable subterfuge . . . Mr. McFarlane, is it not? A mere anchored raft with lights. I assure you, *Ajax* stands less than two hundred yards offshore this very moment. You could adjust your annoying light to see her if you wish. No? Well then, you should probably take my word."

"You can't possibly expect to get away with this!" Adar remarked forcefully. "We will chase you; we will hunt you! We will never give up! You are committing an act of war against a people who mean you no ill!"

"Oh, I certainly hope so!" Billingsly said. "War with you might suit our plans quite nicely just now! As for pursuit, what will you make it with?" He gestured at *Walker*. "Surely not that. It is not even armed and requires more weeks of repair before undertaking a chase. The bulk of your fleet is elsewhere, and that which is here and nearly ready to sail—your 'new-construction steamers,' you call them—are about to suffer a mischief." He looked about. "Does anyone happen to have the time?"

A red pulse of light engulfed the waterfront and a towering, roiling ball of flame gushed into the heavens. A moment later, there was a second flash, as large as the first, and the thunderous detonations reached them at last.

"My God! The fuel storage tanks!" Letts whispered. "They must have bombed the whole tank battery!" It was true. It also wasn't lost on anyone that the flash had indeed illuminated *Ajax*, just offshore.

"You son of the Devil!" Princess Rebecca finally screamed. "You filthy, vile, reptilian monster! These people needed that fuel to fight the Grik, not *us*, you pathetic fool! You've destroyed us all!"

Sandra, a bloody gag back in her mouth, struggled against the man holding her until he pressed the cutlass tighter, drawing blood. Billingsly silenced the princess with another jab of the pistol.

"There, now!" Billingsly exclaimed cheerfully. "No doubt you will replace the fuel shortly, but I am reliably informed that your new boilers do not thrive on wood or coal." He shook his head. "You may now regard that as an oversight in design, but perhaps not. The oil you use instead seems to have a number of advantages . . . but it *is* frightfully flammable, isn't it? In any event, you have little left with which to chase us! Your better-sailing frigates, gone with the fleet, alas, might have had a chance if the winds favored them, but your steamers will be no faster than we—and helpless if the wind fails! We would have a good start on them regardless. As for your 'prizes,' all the swifter variety of those are either gone as well, or their conversions are not yet complete."

"We will chase you, nevertheless," Adar warned grimly.

"Please do! Be my guest to try, but remember this: for each hostile act on your part, a hostage will fall into the sea with his or her throat cut! The one-eyed giant will die first. He has cost us much and spoiled what would have been a perfect plan. Next, the injured boy. After that, the Roman witch priestess will die, followed by your precious Minister of Medicine, Miss Tucker. I trust things will never proceed that far. If they do and if *Ajax* is ultimately somehow destroyed, the princess will, regrettably, die with the ship. Do as you will. Try what you like." He paused. "Test me," he taunted.

"We will chase you and we will watch you," Adar promised, "and we had better see our people alive when we do!"

"As you will. As I said, you are welcome to try. Beware if I tire of your company, however!"

Billingsly looked about for a moment, apparently pondering, then nodded to himself. Spanky recognized the look of someone who thought he'd covered all his bases. For the life of him, Spanky couldn't figure out what the man might have missed.

"Gather the giant's weapons," he instructed one of his men. He glanced at Spanky and raised his voice. "You will be safe," he assured the reluctant underling. "If they kill you, Truelove will kill the boy. Now hurry; we are leaving this place at last!"

"You'll regret this, Billingsly!" Spanky shouted. He saw Silva move a little and knew at last that the big man still lived. *Oh, Lord,* he thought, but it was something, at least. With a little more certainty, he shouted again, "I *guarantee* you'll regret this!"

"Perhaps," Billingsly replied. "I have few regrets, actually. I'm sure I *would* regret killing these poor souls now in my care. Pray, spare me that."

Somehow, Sandra must have worked her gag loose. Suddenly she shouted out, "Give Captain Reddy my love! Tell him to do whatever he must!" There was a loud slap and a muffled cry. The still-growing mass of warriors, sailors, and townsfolk pushed forward with a growl.

"Now, now!" yelled Billingsly. "That was sensible advice; do what you must! At present, you must let us leave and you must signal your fort to let us pass!"

"We *cannot* just let them leave!" Keje said, moving close to Spanky, Adar, and Letts.

"We have no choice for now," Adar replied heavily. He turned to Letts. "Quickly, have someone pass the word along the waterfront and to Fort Atkinson: do not fire; let them pass! We will save them somehow, but we cannot do it here or now!"

"What about Captain Reddy?" Letts asked. "He's going to flip!"

For a moment, Adar said nothing while he watched the hostages briskly moved into the boat. Someone was bailing water out of it as the oars dipped clumsily and it shoved off, away from the ramp.

"Cap-i-taan Reddy will be mounting his assault on Sing-aapore about now," he said woodenly. "Perhaps it would be best not to tell him just yet. He can do nothing but worry about our situation here, and his attack must proceed. Torn in two directions at once, he might behave rashly."

Keje grunted assent.

"I will never forgive myself for allowing this to happen," Adar continued, "and Cap-i-taan Reddy may not forgive me for keeping it from him, even briefly." He blinked beseechingly at Keje. "But if he is . . . distracted now, and somehow he or our effort suffers for it, our world will not forgive me—for however long it remains."

*A*nd it was such a lovely plan, too," Sean O'Casey said as yet another seething mass of Grik infantry slammed into the shield wall of the 2nd Marines. Chack laughed. The 2nd Marines and 1st Aryaal had met virtually no resistance to their predawn landing in the shipyard district. Even now, in the dawn's dreary, overcast light, cutters and launches were securing the Grik fleet anchored in the harbor. As Captain Reddy had surmised, most of those ships had little more than caretaker crews aboard, and dozens were already making sail to join the Allied support vessels, blue streamers fluttering from their mastheads to identify them as prizes. The Marines and 1st Aryaal actually had plenty of time to deploy to defend the beachhead before the enemy finally "got their shit in the sock," as Alden put it, and gathered a significant force to fall on the defenders.

The Marines in front of Chack and O'Casey heaved back against the onslaught and the cacophony was beyond anything O'Casey had yet experienced. He'd been at Baalkpan and seen the terrible nature of this war firsthand, but never from quite this close. There was a constant, roaring screech of weapons on weapons and shields on shields and Grik cries of agony as weapons pierced or slashed their vitals.

"It is a phalaanx of sorts, or so Cap-i-taan Reddy calls it. He based it on an ancient human formation, but he modified it to better fit our different circumstances!" Chack shouted over the din. "The enemy uses nothing like it. They attack as a mob, without discipline. It seems to be all they know how to do. They *can* bash through by sheer weight of numbers, however."

He nodded toward the left of his line, where it joined with Rolak's. "Can you heft that spear?" he asked.

O'Casey balanced the spear in his right hand, judging the weight. "Well enough," he assured Chack.

"Very well. Stay out of the front rank and beware the crossbow bolts!" With that, Chack called his staff, and together, they waded into the fiercest of the fight. O'Casey had been a soldier once, but he'd never been in a fight like this. The sheer scope was beyond his experience, and the type of fighting quite alien. The biggest battle he'd ever seen before Baalkpan had involved maybe a thousand men on both sides combined. He'd thought it was huge at the time. He'd lost that battle and been branded a traitor. His cause was crushed and he'd barely escaped with his life. Here, Rolak and Chack commanded nearly three thousand, and God alone knew how many Grik they faced. Many thousands more, at least. And yet Chack, whom he'd heard was once a pacifist, seemed unconcerned. He hefted the spear again and plunged ahead with the rest.

Six pounder field guns poked their muzzles through the ranks and spewed deadly, scything hail through the attackers, and two guns preceded Chack's reinforcements into the bulging line. With a pair of thunderclaps and a choking haze of white smoke, the pressure there all but vanished. Still Chack raced into the gap, giving the battered line time to re-form around him. He and his staff bashed with their shields and thrust with their short Marine spears at the regathering swarm. O'Casey found himself right among them, poking inexpertly and a little awkwardly with his own spear. More than once he felt it bite. Even so, he decided he'd probably have to become a pistol man, maybe with a few braces draped around his neck. A swordsman he'd never been. Maybe it was time he learned that art?

"Did you find that exhilarating?" Chack asked, when the last dribble of attackers was repulsed. Chack's white leather armor glistened with bright blood and the incongruous American helmet shone where a sword had skated across it, taking the paint. A slow, rolling, methodical broadside thundered from the frigates on the water. *Donaghey's* eighteen pounders swooshed overhead to impact in the dense but confused enemy rear, while the fewer but heavier twenty-fours of the steamers moaned over the largely Lemurian force, trailing smoke. They detonated over and among the still-gathering Grik and the screams brought a wicked grin to Chack's face. "The new exploding shells, or case shot," he explained. "Wonderfully destructive things, though we don't have many yet. The fuses can be unreliable as well, which adds a . . . delicious uncertainty to their passage overhead!" He watched while another broadside erupted from the covering warships. "Glorious," he breathed happily and turned back to O'Casey.

"It *is* a lovely plan! What did you mean earlier? Do you fear it goes poorly?" Chack asked the one-armed man.

"What do *you* mean? Is this good?" O'Casey gasped.

Chack laughed again. "Everything's swell so far! You do not know *all* the plan, and I do!"

"I thought ours was ta be a blockin' force!" O'Casey seemed exasperated.

"It is! And we block well, don't you think?" He gestured around. "We have already accomplished much of our goal. We are ashore and well placed. We have seized most of the docks and much of the repair yard. We have drawn the enemy's focus and hopefully it will remain fixed upon us for some time to come." He pointed excitedly, watching several squads hurry toward them from the boats. "Ah! The new mortars! Soon we will see something, I think! Soon, but not yet!"

O'Casey had already seen quite a lot. He knew, for example, that he was glad these people were his friends, and he now knew how essential it was that they be friends of the Empire. He keenly suspected that this small force to which he was attached would have made short work of the Imperial Company regiment that had ground his own rebellion to dust. They had no muskets—yet—but they had something far more important: confidence, discipline, and the unwavering certainty that they were *right*.

"Oh, Jenks, ye fool!" he muttered under his breath. "Where'er ye be on this field this day, open yer eyes and do nae aggravate these folk!"

"Now, now, now!" shouted Pete Alden, lowering his binoculars. With the thunder of a hundred drums, the 1st Marines, the 2nd and 4th Aryaal, the 1st Baalkpan, 3rd B'mbaado, and 2nd Sular kicked off their sweeping, or "swinging," advance with around four thousand troops. 'Cats just couldn't do bugles, so they'd settled on drum tattoos and various combinations of short whistle blasts to control large forces on the battlefield. The first few fights had shown the need for something like that, and now they had it. The roar of the drums sent gooseflesh down Matt's arms.

"I agree," Matt said, "it's time." He grinned. "Not that it matters what I think! This is your show, Pete!"

"If it was completely my show, you'd be watching from *Donaghey* right now!" Pete answered harshly. "Promise me you won't wander off? We haven't really been engaged yet, but the pickets I threw out on the flanks report quite a few rambunctious Grik hunting parties, or the like. We expected that and our bowmen and a few of the NCOs with Krags are dealing with them, but I'd sure hate to have to tell Lieutenant Tucker I let you get conked from behind."

Chief Gray pointedly racked the bolt on the Thompson he carried.

Gunner's Mate Paul Stites followed suit with a BAR. "Mind your own chickens," Gray grumbled. Besides Stites, there were four Lemurian Marines in the Captain's Guard detail, and Jenks had a pair of his own polished muskets on their shoulders.

Matt just smiled and shrugged. Harvey Jenks chuckled beside him.

"A magnificent show, Captain Reddy," Jenks said. "I, at least, fully understand your desire to view it firsthand!" He looked at his own distant *Achilles*, whose guns had remained silent thus far. "I almost regret not committing myself entirely to your support—not that it seems you need it!"

"I understand your reasons. It's hard to engage in offensive operations against somebody you're not at war with. I doubt the Grik will notice any distinction, however. Besides, your Marines are on the far left with General Maraan. They're yet another blocking force, but it could be bloody work."

"There, if they must fight, it will be a defensive engagement," Jenks said. "Defending oneself from attack is hardly offensive in nature."

Matt looked at the Imperial. "Again, the Grik will make no distinction. I doubt your own superiors will."

"You wanted us in this war," Jenks said more quietly, seriously. "I've come to believe we belong in it, though God knows we have problems of our own. We may need *your* help someday. How could we possibly ask it of you if we did not make this small gesture?"

Matt grunted. "Your gesture could cost a lot of Imperial lives. Safir says your Marine lieutenant Blair isn't particularly open to her tactical suggestions."

Jenks nodded. "Well, there is little I can do about that. I command my ship and I command the Marines to perform their duties. How they perform those duties is up to Blair, I'm afraid. At best, if the Grik do strike there, our people may learn from one another. At worst . . ." He blinked. "Our people may learn a costly lesson from one another."

Matt shook his head, somewhat surprised Gray had held his tongue. He surveyed the disposition of the troops and all seemed to be shaping up nicely. All but the weather. Ahead, in the west, the general overcast seemed darker as the day progressed. When he spoke, he sounded slightly distracted. He was watching the sky. "I'd hoped your Marines might bolster our lines, like spearmen behind the shields. I'm telling you that a thin pair of ranks, even armed with muskets, *can't* stand against the Grik."

Jenks's smile was brittle. "We'll see." He nodded forward. "Your army will leave us behind while we discuss this, I fear, and General Alden will scold us again."

Chack sensed a change in the Grik host before him. Another attack had been repulsed, but for a long time now, nearly half an hour, there'd been no assault. Leaving O'Casey with his staff, he trotted to where General Rolak directed his end of the line from the roof of a crude warehouse. Scrambling up the ladder, Chack saluted the old Aryaalan warrior.

"Quite a difference between this and our last meeting with these creatures!" Rolak enthused, returning Chack's salute. "Your Marines fight splendidly!"

"As do your troops, Lord. Any sign of Mr. Braad-furd's Grik Rout?" Chack asked.

Rolak frowned and his tail twitched with agitation. "Not yet. They do seem to have their shit in their sock, as General Alden so colorfully put it. This Hij general of theirs expends many lives, but he avoids allowing them to bunch up too deeply. If any panic, the panic spreads less far."

"True," Chack agreed. "But he has sacrificed mass to accomplish this. Twice they might have broken our line if they had supported their assault with greater numbers."

"They are hesitant, I think. Few of these warriors could have been at Baalkpan. All they know is that they lost there, badly. I believe they test new tactics here, within the constraints of their warriors' . . . capabilities."

"Do you really?" Chack asked absently, thinking. "Perhaps. There are no defensive works, other than gun emplacements for their limited artillery. They do not defend as we do, behind breastworks or terrain, or with careful discipline. They defend by attacking." He took a drink from his water bottle. "Do you think that is new? That they make 'spoiling' attacks hoping to slow our advance?"

"How can we truly know what is 'new' to them? Anything they do besides a mass attack is 'new' to us, but it is possible. It may also be that they think they have succeeded. We have achieved our objective, but perhaps they do not know that. Consider: would the Grik do as we have done? Land, attack, secure a defensive perimeter, then stop?" Rolak shook his head. "I doubt they can even comprehend such a strategy."

"You may be right, lord," Chack replied, eyeing the mass of enemies before them. Their numbers continued to swell, but they'd been badly bloodied and corpses were heaped along the length of the perimeter. "We seem to have affixed the enemy's attention entirely upon us. As best we can tell, they have no notion of the main force bearing down upon their left." Chack glanced at one of the Manilo couriers who'd arrived shortly before, mounted on one of the swift "meanies," as Silva called them. The beasts still gave him the "creeps." They looked like larger, more reptilian versions of their enemies, that happened to go about on all fours. The courier had reported only desultory fighting in front of the main force.

Rolak glanced at the darkening sky. "We are liable to have a storm today. A Strakka comes at last, I suspect. It is fortunate that we have secured a safe harbor for our fleet."

Chack had been looking often at the sky himself. "I wish our luck with the weather might have held a few more days. If the gust front hits during the battle, it will confuse things."

"More for them than us, I expect." Rolak grinned. "We have a plan and they do not. At least, what they have of a plan seems to depend upon what we do for a change."

Chack nodded noncommittally. He'd had some experience with plans now, and he knew how fragile they could be. So did Rolak, for that matter. Chack suspected the old warrior of practicing his dry wit upon him. "For myself, I would hope the Strakka holds off a bit longer so our plan might unfold unimpeded," he said.

"You are of the sea folk." Rolak waved his hand. "You would know that better than I." He gestured back to the front. "Perhaps you should return to your Marines. The enemy stirs. Does it appear to you, amidst that mob, that he is shifting his front?" Rolak's teeth appeared in a feral grin. "Perhaps he is preparing to attack in a different direction!"

"Good Lord!" Jenks exclaimed. "Do they always come on like that?"

"Yep," said Gray. The Bosun spat.

"Pretty much every time," Matt confirmed.

The closer Alden's army had approached what they'd identified as the Grik main force, fixed in front of Rolak and Chack, the more crazed attackers had charged headlong against Alden's overwhelming force. At first, they'd come in groups of a dozen or less, shrieking defiantly and waving their weapons. Arrows cut down most of those before they ever came in range of a spear. Then, more Grik charged them from the jungle that bordered the clearing they'd started across. Matt had been secretly amazed they'd made it that far before being noticed, but Manilo couriers or cavalry—or whatever they were—had assured them Chack and Rolak had grabbed plenty of the enemy's attention.

They'd heard the cannonade grow louder as they neared and saw the warships in the bay jockey for more advantageous firing positions. Broadside after broadside sent roiling clouds of billowing smoke across the water. The new mortars were still silent for now, waiting for the Grik to wholly focus on the new threat. Then, shortly before, the dense peninsula of jungle ahead that stood between Alden's and Rolak's converging forces suddenly teemed with thousands of Grik shapes.

"They've finally turned to meet us," Matt had announced aloud, as much for Jenks as Alden. A number of horns blew together, their different tones jumbled and discordant, but they'd seemed a suitable accompaniment to the shrill, growling shrieks of the horde that had erupted from the trees.

Now Jenks could only stare in horror at the elemental force bearing down on them. It was a mob, to be sure, but a huge one, and this first look at a Grik berserker charge was most disconcerting. He wondered how Captain Reddy could just stand there like that, watching them come. Either the man was utterly fearless or his trust in his commanders and troops was truly that profound. Jenks realized that Captain Reddy and his guards had faced this before, but he couldn't imagine anyone ever becoming so inured to it. He stood as well. He was an officer, a gentleman, and possessed a significant measure of personal courage. He admitted to himself that he was terrified, though. Standing in the face of that seething, swarming mass of teeth, claws, swords, and crossbows couldn't possibly be done without some fear. And yet, glancing sidelong at the American officer, this Supreme Commander, he saw no sign of any emotion other than . . . anticipation.

"'Bout . . . now!" Matt said.

As if reading his commander's thoughts, Pete Alden bellowed at the top of his lungs, the order he gave repeated down the ranks and punctuated with whistle blasts.

"Commence firing!"

Twelve pieces of light artillery bucked and spewed dense clouds of smoke and double loads of canister. Arrows whickered into the darkening sky with a terrible, collective "swoosh." Untold hundreds of Grik warriors were swept away with as little apparent effort as the command had taken to give. Others screamed in agony and writhed on the ground, clutching wounds or festooned with arrows.

"Independent, fire at will!" Alden shouted, his voice already a little hoarse after the last command and the choking smoke that followed it.

There were a number of distinct thumping, popping sounds beyond the trees from the direction of the initial landing force. Whistling sounds, dozens, scores, like Jenks had never heard, were punctuated by fearsome but smallish blasts that sent gouts of earth into the sky right among the rear of the enemy host. A few of the "mortar bombs," Reddy had called them, though Jenks had never seen their like, erupted in the trees themselves and sent swarms of splinters into the Grik. The agonized screeching took on a desperate, terrified air.

Then, above it all, there came a roar. It wasn't like the roar of thunder or the marching surf; it was higher pitched, excited, almost gleeful. Despite its tone, it had a profound, unstoppable, elemental urgency that stirred his most primitive thoughts. In contrast to the increasingly agonized and terrified cacophony of the Grik horde, the roar from beyond the trees was confident, eager, remorseless. It was the sound of doom.

"That'll be Rolak and Chack!" Gray boomed happily. "They were the anvil. Probably got mighty sick of it too. Now they're the hammer!"

A large percentage of the Grik, where the mortars still fell, had been transformed from an unstoppable juggernaut into a wild, panicstricken mass. Jenks looked on in amazement while thousands of Grik scrambled in all directions, slaying *one another* with wild abandon. Some ran back the way they'd come, smashing into the howling Lemurian troops and Marines that suddenly erupted from the trees. Others raced north or south, toward the jungle or the sea. Some crashed into the rear of the forward element, still charging the Allied line. Battle erupted there, among the *Grik*, even as the foremost berserkers slammed into the Allied shield wall.

The slaughter was incredible. The mortars stopped falling and the field guns were pulled back to avoid inflicting casualties on the Allied forces now closing on the still-larger Grik army caught between them. The relative sizes of the armies lost all meaning, however, since growing numbers of Grik were now murdering one another. It was insane. The fighting at the shield wall was still wildly intense; the Grik that struck there as a relatively cohesive force still outnumbered Alden's entire command, but that was when the qualitative difference between the combatants was most plainly demonstrated. Nowhere did the shield wall break. It stood like a monolithic cliff in the face of disorganized breakers, and the killing was remarkably one-sided.

Spears thrust and jabbed over, under, and around the front-rank shields, whose bearers pushed with all their might against the battering Grik. Inexorably, General Rolak's force swept through the chaos of the Grik rear, killing any who stood even momentarily. Those who fled from between the closing pincers were mostly ignored, but few seemed to realize this and even fewer had the wherewithal or initiative to take advantage of the fact. Within an hour of the first mortar blasts, the jaws of the pincers clamped shut and all that remained of the battle was a prolonged, remorseless butchery.

Captain Reddy must have noticed Jenks's expression. Perhaps his face was pale?

"Maybe you're wondering why I don't put a stop to it?" Matt's words came in a fierce monotone. "On some level, maybe I still wish I could. But those down there"—he gestured at the dwindling Grik—"won't quit fighting. Hell, half of them are still killing each other!" He shook his head. "I don't know how or why they act the way they do, and frankly, that's not my concern right now. Maybe we'll know someday. Maybe the prisoners we took at Aryaal will help with that. But right now, we'll use this clear weakness of theirs against them as often and mercilessly as we can. There may come a time when they get wise and it won't work anymore." He looked at Jenks again. "Or maybe you're wondering *if* I could stop it?"

Almost without thinking, Jenks jerked a nod.

Matt shrugged. "I don't know that either. You probably can't comprehend what's driven these people, *my* people, down there, to become what they are from what they were. Mostly, they used to be almost instinctively unaggressive. There were exceptions, but all of them have suffered loss like you can't imagine. At least, I don't think you can. Hell, I couldn't have until I came to this world. Maybe the Rape of Nanking comes close . . ." He saw Jenks's uncomprehending blink. "Skip it. Anyway, like you saw at Aryaal, we aren't fighting a civilized enemy, and this isn't anything like a civilized war. The very wickedness of our enemy is what's allowed us to build this army, these *soldiers* I'm so proud of. I don't think anything else would have done it."

Captain Reddy sighed. "*Could* I stop them from hacking the life out of every last Grik down there? Maybe. I tried once, you know, and it didn't work. The Grik give no quarter and *never* ask for it. I don't think they know how. Faced with an enemy like that, what do you think? Even if I could *make* Alden's troops stop killing, the Grik won't. I don't know what made 'tame' Griks out of the ones Rasik had, but it didn't happen in the middle of a fight. Maybe they need time to think things through, and some of the ones who get away will come in later, all peaceable and contrite. For now . . . I have a rule. It used to be 'Never give an order you know won't be obeyed.' 'Know' has become 'believe,' but it still works pretty good. That's my little concession to the gray area of command, and given a choice, I'd much rather err on the side of my people than those monsters down there."

He looked away from Jenks, back at the dwindling fight. There were cheers now. Cheers of survival, pride, and relief. Cheers for Captain Reddy too. "Besides, to answer the last question you never asked: no. Deep down, I don't *want* them to stop. Not after Baalkpan. Not after all *I've* lost."

A meanie galloped up. Well, "galloped" wasn't exactly the right word, but it was blowing hard through flared nostrils and would likely have been panting if its jaws weren't cinched tightly shut. It stared malevolently around. "Cap-i-taan Reddy," cried the Manilo cavalryman from its back. "General Rolak's most fervent compliments and affection! He begs to inform you that when they made their charge, another, smaller Grik force was assembling on his flank. He had no choice but to ignore it when this show kicked off. Since it did not attack his rear as he advanced, he fears it may have wind of the blocking force to the west." The courier motioned toward where the clouds were growing positively malignant. As before, when Matt had seen a growing Strakka, black tendrils had begun to radiate from the dark, brooding core.

Matt looked at Jenks. "After seeing this, are you sure you don't want to urge Mr. Blair to consider General Maraan's suggestions a little more carefully?"

Jenks eyed the semidomesticated beast the rider sat upon. "Is there room up there for me?" he demanded.

"Of course."

Jenks turned to Matt. "Thank you indeed for a most . . . illuminating experience. I believe I would like to . . . strongly counsel Lieutenant Blair to do just that. By your leave, Captain Reddy?"

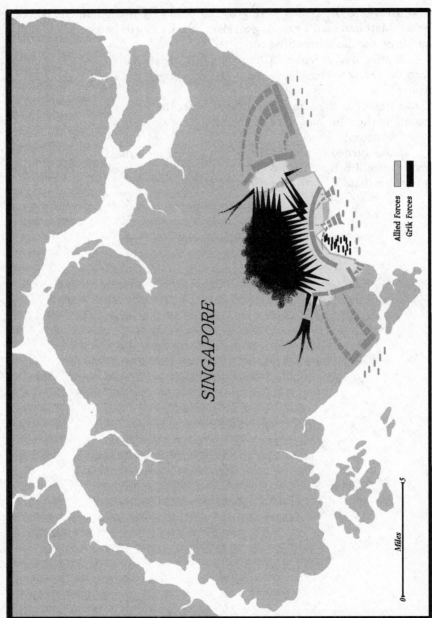

SINGAPORE

Allied Forces
Grik Forces

Miles
0 ⊢———————⊣ 5

Battle for Singapore

*T*he mood in *Donaghey*'s wardroom was mixed that night. The island of Singapore was theirs, essentially, and almost without exception, all the objectives outlined in the plan had been achieved. Casualties were light, considering the relative sizes of the forces involved, and that was reason enough for most of the commanders to feel proud of and comfortable with the victory.

Lieutenant Blair was anything but comfortable. Not only did he suffer from a painful wound across his ribs, but his losses had not been light at all. Jenks and the Manilo courier astride the meanie had arrived at the left-flank blocking force too late to counsel, cajole, or issue orders, and in contrast to the other leaders present, Blair stared at the bulkhead with a stricken, opium-slacked expression.

His Imperial Marines had stood bravely in the face of the Grik tide that swarmed across them. The two aimed volleys of musket fire they'd managed had forced the charging Grik into Safir Maraan's shield wall, but meeting that immovable object, they'd swarmed back around it—and over the left flank "secured" by Blair's Marines. Caught in the process of reloading, and helpless in the face of an enemy the likes of which they'd never faced, the Imperial Marines either broke or were slaughtered where they stood. It was a horrifying thing to see, Safir later confessed to Matt, and she was as furious over the senseless waste of Blair's Marines as she was over the utterly avoidable losses her own flank had suffered before she could pull it back. In her practical, slightly bloodthirsty way, she'd insisted that Blair be hanged.

He wouldn't be, of course. Matt secretly suspected Jenks had far more control over Blair's tactics than he'd confessed, and the Marine Lieutenant had probably just been following orders: orders not to integrate his force with the Lemurians or take *their* orders under any circumstances. Jenks's own horror over the aftermath and his hesitation to censure Blair confirmed as much. If Blair could recover from watching half his men shredded before his eyes, he might be a better officer for it.

Otherwise, all the major port facilities had been secured and the remaining Grik driven into the jungle. Chack's 2nd Marines had joined with Alden's 1st, and together the two regiments stormed the stockade where the Japanese prisoners were held. They were just in time, too. Apparently, some final order had been issued by the now dead (by suicide, as usual) Hij commander that none of the Japanese be taken alive. More than a dozen of the thirty-odd advisor/prisoners had already been killed before the Marines slaughtered their captor/allies. With Matt's permission, the Bosun had accompanied the effort in case his Thompson was needed, and to his reported incredulity, one of the Japanese prisoners actually killed *himself* when he realized that Americans were among their rescuers! The rest of the Japs seemed appropriately grateful for their rescue, after witnessing their comrades die and recognizing their own ultimate fate.

The wardroom heaved and the gimbaled lanterns cast eerie shadows. The leading edge of the Strakka was upon them at last, having waited until the battle was over before descending in all its savage fury. The army still ashore had taken cover as best it could, mostly in the newly constructed Grik warehouses along the dock. Some pickets were still out, and the meanie-mounted Manilos were scouring the jungle for any large Grik concentrations they'd missed. Most reports had any semicohesive groups heading north. No one knew if there was any kind of causeway connecting this Singapore with the Malay Peninsula or not, but one way or another, the overriding imperative of the Grik survivors seemed to be escape. Even the enemy force that broke through on the left was reportedly moving north now, in disarray.

Matt was guardedly optimistic. They'd know more when the storm passed and the weather cleared, but the 2nd Allied Expeditionary Force seemed to have won the first purely offensive battle of the war. They'd engaged in an ambitious multipronged amphibious assault against territory the enemy knew better than they did, and utterly crushed that enemy on his own ground. It was a heady moment and an auspicious beginning to the complex strategic plan he, Adar, Keje, and Alden had initially conceived.

Matt was speaking to Rolak. Unlike Pete, who'd remained ashore, the old warrior wasn't too proud to retreat to the comforts of a warm, dry bed. "Too proud" probably wasn't the best way to put it, Matt decided, seeing the signs of fatigue the day had left on his friend. "Too practical not to," was probably the better choice of words. Chack remained ashore in his stead. The ship tossed on the suddenly malicious sea, jerking up short as her carefully laid anchors kept her in place. The wind screamed through the rigging and was even audible in the wardroom, over the pounding rain that lashed the skylight. It was a *hell* of a storm, Matt thought, but the Allied ships and their rich haul of prizes rode relatively easily in the protected harbor. It was a slow-moving Strakka, and any ship caught on the open ocean would have been in for it. In spades.

"What now?" Jenks asked. He'd come out to *Donaghey* with Matt before the storm struck with all its fury. He was essentially stranded aboard until the sea calmed enough for him to return to *Achilles*.

"Now we wait," Matt replied. "Clancy's been transmitting our action report to Baalkpan, but in this weather, who knows if they'll get anything. He said he's picked up pieces of a reply, but can't make any sense out of it." Matt shrugged. "Not only are we trying to transmit a message through terrible atmospheric conditions, but we can't run the wind generator in weather like this, so he can't even boost the gain on the output. Cheesy, primitive batteries are all we have."

" 'Cheesy' to you, perhaps, but exciting technology to me, I assure you!"

Sean O'Casey suddenly burst into the compartment, waving a wet message form in his hand. His face was hard, enraged, and newly damp dried blood was running down his face like reconstituted tomato soup. Clancy trailed close behind. He looked a little apologetic, but overall his expression was much like O'Casey's.

"Ye must read this, Captain; read it now! Proof at last o' the heinous Empire that creature serves!" He was addressing Matt but his murderous glare was fixed on Jenks.

Matt was momentarily taken aback, but Jenks could only goggle at the one-armed apparition who'd appeared in their midst. Recognition spread across his face and it reddened with discovery and outrage.

"You!" Jenks shouted. "By all that's holy, how . . . ! That you should be *here*!" He turned to Matt. "Captain Reddy, I *demand* an explanation! This man is a wanted criminal—never mind the missing arm; I would recognize him anywhere! He is a traitor, sir, and his appearance here not only confirms it, but for him to appear now, after all these months, is sufficient proof to me that you *knew* he was wanted and yet kept the knowledge of his presence from me!"

"Ye *demand*!" O'Casey almost choked. "Captain Reddy, *I demand* that . . . monster be clapped in irons, his ship seized, an' he be hoisted kickin' to the end of a yard on the first sunny morn' we're granted! Of all the perfidious, lyin', spyin', goats o' the world! I hope ye choke all the day long afore ye gasp yer last!"

"As I said," continued Jenks, his tone ominous, "Mr. Bates is a wanted man. He is a traitor to his emperor and has risen in arms against him and his lawful subjects! I demand that you arrest him at once, or there will be consequences!"

"This is *my* ship," Greg Garrett suddenly exploded, "and *I* demand somebody tell me what the hell's going on here!"

"Yeah," Matt said angrily. "Let's all find out, shall we? What are you even doing here, O'Casey? You were supposed to be on *Dowden*!"

"He was ashore for the fighting today, Captain," Rolak answered. "Chack brought him and said you had told him to 'let O'Casey entertain himself,' or some such. He came aboard here with me."

Matt groaned. "Commodore Jenks," he said, "I was and am aware Mr. O'Casey—or Bates, as you seem to know him—is a fugitive from your government, but he's also the man most responsible for the survival of Princess Rebecca. He lost his arm in the act of saving her, and it was he and some of our submariners who protected and cared for her long before you ever came to call. I'm personally convinced he's not a traitor to your emperor or his household, although other . . . elements within your government might not agree. Ask the princess yourself for her opinion of the man!"

"Aye, that's the problem, Captain Reddy, the blackguard cannae do any such thing!"

"What the hell are you talking about?" Matt demanded. In answer, O'Casey held forth the message form.

"I been trying to clean it up, Skipper," Clancy supplied. "It just didn't make any sense! Finally, O'Casey here comes in the shack wanting to check on things back home. He used to do that now and then when he was here. . . . Anyway, we went over it again and again. There's no mistake!" Clancy glared at Jenks.

Matt took the page after a final glare around the wardroom, and looked at the words.

```
TO ALL MEMBERS OF THE SECOND ALLIED
EXPEDITIONARY FORCE X FROM ADAR COTGA
X GREETINGS AND CONGRATULATIONS ON
YOUR NOBLE VICTORY OVER THE EVIL FOE
X THE GRATITUDE OF YOUR PEOPLE AND
YOUR RACE KNOWS NO BOUNDS X AS
CHAIRMAN OF THE GRAND ALLIANCE
PLEASE ACCEPT MY MOST HUMBLE
APPRECIATION FOR YOUR VALOR AND
SACRIFICE X YOUR SLAIN AND WOUNDED
ARE IN MY PRAYERS X END MESSAGE
```

ADDENDUM:

EYES ONLY M P REDDY CINCAF X
DISTRIBUTE FOLLOWING AS YOU SEE FIT X
AT APPROX 0230 THIS DAY CMDR
BILLINGSLY AND IMPERIAL FRIGATE HIS
COMMAND COMMENCED OFFENSIVE
OPERATIONS AGAINST BAALKPAN-THE
UNITED STATES NAVY-THE GRAND ALLIANCE
X SEVENTEEN ALLIED PERSONNEL KILLED
IN DIRECT ACTION AND BY DELIBERATE
DESTRUCTION OF BAALKPAN HARBOR READY
FUEL RESERVE X APPARENT MOTIVE FOR
ASSAULT IS ABDUCTION OF PRINCESS
REBECCA X REGRET TO INFORM THIS
OBJECTIVE ACHIEVED X ALSO PROFOUNDLY
REGRET TO INFORM THAT OTHER HOSTAGES
TAKEN INCLUDE MINISTER OF MEDICINE
SANDRA TUCKER-SISTER AUDRY-ABEL COOK-
DENNIS SILVA-TAGRANESI LAWRENCE X
SILVA AND COOK BOTH WOUNDED CONDITION
UNKNOWN X UNABLE TO MOUNT IMMEDIATE
EFFECTUAL PURSUIT DUE TO DESTRUCTION
FUEL RESERVE AND THREATS AGAINST
HOSTAGES X COURSE ENEMY SHIP AJAX 050
CONSTANT CONFIRMED BY AIR X REQUEST
DIRECT ORDER BEN MALLORY CEASE
INCREASINGLY EXTENDED OBSERVATION
FLIGHTS X CANNOT EXPRESS DEPTH OF
SHAME X ADAR X END TRANSMISSION

For a long moment, Matt could say nothing. The expression on his face must have told something of the nature of the tale, however, because the shouts and accusations in the wardroom ceased entirely and the only sounds came from the groaning hull, the confused sea, and the moaning storm outside. A rage as pure and hot and black as boiling pitch roiled up inside him as he reread the stilted words. They'd taken Sandra! That was all that registered at first. That maniac Billingsly had taken the one thing he truly cared about on this entire, mixed-up planet! No, that wasn't completely true. He cared about many things; he cared about their friends and the work they'd started here. He cared about the war and defeating the Grik so their friends and works might thrive. He cared about Rebecca,

Sister Audry, Abel, and even Silva ... but almost from the beginning, it had always been Sandra who gave him the strength and will to continue in the face of ... anything. With her love, understanding, and healing way, she'd been the one who brought him back from the brink of despair when he lost his ship. She'd tended his battered, bleeding soul and restored it to something that *could* care again despite the horrors and agonies it had seen and endured. He couldn't lose her! She had become his life! When all was said and done, ultimately, she was *why* he carried on. *As God is my witness*, he swore fervently to himself, *I'll have you back, Sandra! And those who have done this, no matter who they are or where it takes me, are going to* pay!

He flung the sheet at Jenks, who picked it up and started to read. Matt waited a moment longer until he was sure he could control his voice. "Mr. Clancy," he said at last, "write this down." His tone was calm, but iron hard. Clancy fumbled through his notebook until he found a blank page and poised his pencil. "From Matt Reddy, et cetera, to Adar, et cetera. No shame. Even the best hunter can step on a viper." He paused to decide if the analogy was appropriate. Oddly, there were no snakes on Borneo that they knew of. There were deadly poisonous lizards however, and he'd heard them translated and referred to as vipers before—once in reference to Jenks himself, come to think of it. He nodded and continued, thinking hard as he spoke. "I want tankers sent out *today* from the new refinery at Tarakan Island. Use every available ship. We're going to start stockpiling fuel on Mindanao at Saan-Kakja's brother's place. Lots of it. We'll probably leapfrog it east of there as well. Meanwhile, if the Baalkpan tank batteries can't be repaired, we'll start a reserve at the refinery dock up the river, if we have to. I don't care if we have to fill Grik hulks with the stuff. We took enough ships today to make up any supply issues that might arise." He paused and Jenks tried to speak. "Shut up," Matt said, and turned back to Clancy.

"No matter what, we still have to keep the pressure up out here. Baalkpan is to redouble its efforts to get all the steamers, troops, supplies— everything—to Singapore as fast as possible. Keje's got to step on it too. We need *Big Sal* and her planes to scout if nothing else. Finally"—he paused again and took a deep breath—"if Spanky honestly doesn't think *Walker* will be ready to steam ten thousand miles and fight a battle within thirty days, I want all work on her suspended. We don't have the time to waste resources on her."

Everyone in the compartment was flabbergasted. Most still had no idea what had occurred, but if Matt was willing to write *Walker* off, it must have been something ... astonishing. Sensing Captain Reddy's sudden hostility toward the Imperial, Garrett snatched the message form from him.

"General Rolak? I want Chack and a company of the Second Ma-rines," Matt said.

Rolak glanced at the hull and, by implication, the storm outside.

"Now, lord?"

"Right now." He looked at Clancy. "As soon as we're finished here, anyway. Signal 'em to be ready, if you can." Glancing at Garrett, he saw the rage and astonishment begin to spread across his face. "I love the old *Donaghey*, but she's helpless right now," he said, still talking to Clancy. "Signal Mr. Ellis on *Dowden* and have her come alongside as close as he dares. Somebody wake up the Bosun and assemble the Captain's Guard. When *Dowden* arrives, we're going across. We'll try to swoop in close to the dock and pick up Chack's Marines."

"What are we going to *do* about this, Skipper?" Garrett demanded.

Matt's gaze finally fell on Jenks. "First, we're going to take that bastard's ship."

There was an uproar then, with everyone grabbing for the message form and shouting for explanations.

"Enough!" Matt bellowed, and when there was silence, he calmly summed up the situation.

Sensing his position was precarious at best, Jenks cleared his throat. "Captain Reddy, may I speak now?"

"Knock yourself out."

"Captain . . ." Jenks's hand encompassed all present. "Gentlemen, I as-sure you that none of you is more shocked and horrified by this outrage than I. I swear before God that Commander Billingsly has acted not only independently of, but utterly against my direct orders!" He faced Captain Reddy. "Think upon it, sir! We were upon that field together today! Think upon what we discussed! Think of the *blood* that was shed by my country-men! I accept that it may have been shed foolishly, and that is for me to bear, but it is no less precious or sacred for all my pride! Upon *that blood* I swear I am sincere!"

O'Casey balled his single fist and took a step forward. "Sincere, are ye? How sincere were ye when ye crushed me effort tae destroy the likes o' Billingsly long ago?"

"*You took up arms against the throne!*" Jenks shouted. "What was I to *do*? I fancy we were friends once, you and I. The governor-emperor him-self called you friend! He tried—*I* tried to make you see reason, to seek accommodation, but *no*! It has always been all or nothing with you! We could have pushed the Company back, reined it in, but you had to have it *all*; you wanted it *dead*! Instead, by *your* actions, your *rebellion*, you won sympathy for their cause! It was *you* who gave them a majority in both courts and marginalized the governor-emperor to near impotence! It is you, ultimately, who has brought us to *this*!"

O'Casey took another step, but instead of striking Jenks, he suddenly seemed to deflate. It was as if years of self-righteous anger and purpose just drained away and left nothing in its wake. Nothing but a man. He began to sob. "Oh, ye divil, ye prob'ly have the right o' it!" he managed through his tears. "God damn me fer a fool! An' now the very beast I'd hoped ta slay has our sweet princess! God *damn* me!"

Jenks's hand seemed to strain to comfort the big man, but didn't reach quite far enough. "No," he said softly. "God damn *me*. You were right all along, as it turns out. The Company *is* a beast to spawn men like Billingsly. I doubt now that we could have controlled it in the end, regardless. Damn *me* for not joining your cause!"

Stiffly, Jenks faced Captain Reddy. "You have my surrender, sir, and that of my ship." He fumbled at his side for his sword. "I will not fight you. As that note will attest, your people and mine would seem to be at war. *My God*, but this is a stupid, terrible world we live in! In any event, your people are clearly the aggrieved party and I will require none of those under my command to shed their blood in defense of the actions of a lunatic. Or a nation gone mad."

Matt shook his head, as if to clear it. Too much too fast! "Keep your sword, Commodore Jenks," he said at last. "It would seem I'm not at war with *you* after all. But I'm kind of like O'Casey, or Bates, or whoever he is, in one respect: all or nothing. From now on, you're on our side all or nothing, and we're on yours the same way. We're still taking some of the Second Marines aboard *Achilles*, though, you and I. If there's anyone you or anyone you trust even *suspects* of being a Company spy, they'll be sent back here to *Donaghey*'s brig."

Matt looked at Clancy. "Make those signals now, if you please." He turned to Rolak. "Commodore Ellis will assume overall command here until Keje arrives with the rest of the fleet. At that point, Keje will assume strategic command, but you and General Alden will still command the ground troops. Jim will be Keje's exec and chief of staff. Standing orders are and will remain to keep up the pressure on the Grik. Stay focused *here*, on the job that's *here*, and push the bastards any way you can. Follow the plan, but stay flexible; the ability to do that has always been our biggest advantage."

"But . . . of course, lord. But where will you be?"

Matt jerked his chin at Jenks. "I'm going home. With him."

CHAPTER 20

*R*ain battered Adar's Great Hall, where the grim meeting was under way. The air was dank and musty with the smell of wet fur and burning grikakka oil. A broad, hand-drawn map covered a large table in the gloom, and all the major leaders of the Alliance were gathered around it. All who weren't absent or taken from them, at least. Kathy McCoy stood in for Sandra and Karen Theimer Letts. Karen had taken the news of the abductions hard, and with her increasingly difficult pregnancy nearing its peak, Alan had convinced her to let him put her on light duty.

"But surely they're not coming *now*," sputtered Geran-Eras, high chief of *Humfra-Dar* Home. *Humfra-Dar* had been with the Alliance almost from the first, and Geran, the first female High Chief the Americans had known before they met Saan-Kakja, was particularly fond of Matt. Now young Tassana was a High Chief too, and she nodded agreement with Geran's concern.

"It is madness to ride the Strakka!"

Adar nodded miserably. "I fear Captain Reddy has gone quite mad—in that dangerous, special way we have all come to recognize—and it is my fault!"

"Bullshit," Spanky growled. "For the last time, Adar, it ain't your fault! And Captain Reddy hasn't gone mad, he's just mad as hell. I am too—we all are." He paused, watching the nods. "I don't know what kind of seaman Jenks is, but the captain's not going to let him goof around and get them sunk, either. *Achilles* might take a beating, but she's running with the storm. My bet is they just get here faster."

"Your confidence is reassuring," Adar said, "both in Captain Reddy and myself." He sighed. "But what of these other issues? What of *Walker*?"

It was Spanky's turn to sigh. "We'll have her ready," he said simply. "As much as she means to you, she means even more to me. I'm not about to give up on the old girl now. Besides, the skipper's going to need her."

"What remains to be done?" Keje asked.

"About a million things," Spanky admitted, "but we're already working on most of them. If we just quit, the guys working on that stuff will waste a lot of time twiddling their thumbs before they can get up to speed on other projects anyway." He held up his hand, counting off on his fingers. "Just about everything on *Walker* runs on one twenty DC. That's what we've standardized all our industry for. Even if we hadn't rebuilt her little generators, we could probably stick one of our homemade jobs in her. We're still soaking her AC generator, the one she needs for the gyro and a few other things, but we're almost done with it too."

They'd discovered yet *another* use for the ubiquitous polta fruit and the seemingly endless applications to which it lent itself. In this instance, the fermented form of the juice that became the popular intoxicant seep would turn to a variety of vinegar if its ultimate journey toward becoming the curative polta paste was interrupted. They'd made diluted vinegar baths for the generators and other electrical equipment to deoxidize the nonferrous components. The solution was weak enough that it did that nicely without unduly attacking the ferrous parts. This rendered the assemblies clean and corrosion-free for their ultimate disassembly and restoration.

"Thank God at least the gyro itself was dry," Spanky added. He nodded at Rodriguez. "Ronson and his EMs have been running all over the ship, refurbishing distribution panels, breakers, switches, and all that magical electrical shit. Act like a buncha spiders spinnin' wires everywhere instead of webs."

Rodriguez arched his eyebrows, which matched his Pancho Villa mustache quite well. "Come into my parlor," he said, in a passable Bela Lugosi imitation.

Spanky rolled his eyes, but inwardly he was satisfied. Like all of them, Ronson Rodriguez had come a long way. "Hull and structural damage was repaired before we refloated her," he continued. "Her turbines ain't new, or anything like it, but they're in at least as good a shape as they were when she went down. We hadn't been able to do proper maintenance on 'em in forever, so we still had plenty of spare seals and bearings and such. For them, at least. Numbers three and four boilers *are* practically new. Completely rebuilt and clean as a whistle inside and out." He shook his head. "Those Mice . . . Anyway, we're starting on number three. I wanted to put a new boiler where number one used to be, one that *could* burn something besides oil if it had to, but I guess she's still going to need that extra fuel capacity after all. We'll get started on a new, better bunker in there. Thanks to Letts's gaskets, her steam lines are tight as a drum. We're still having trouble with the steering engine, but we'll get it sorted out."

"That is all very well," Keje said. "She can float and she can steam, but what will she fight with, at need?" Spanky looked at Campeti to answer.

"Uh, well, there's good news and bad news. The numbers one, two, and three four-inch fifties are ready to go back aboard. Even made a new, thicker splinter shield for number one outta Jap steel." He looked at Rodriguez. "Your guys'll have to wire 'em in to the gun director, which, thank God, never even got wet." Rodriguez nodded and Campeti went on. "The number four gun and the three incher on the fantail are practically junk. We can save the tubes and breeches, but that's about it. No way can they be ready in thirty days. Same with the torpedo tubes and mounts—not that we have anything to stick in 'em. Three and four were already gone. We can make the number one triple mount work now, if we swipe parts from number two, but without torpedoes, what's the point? I say we leave 'em off for now and fix 'em at our leisure. Who knows? Maybe someday we'll have some torps.

"I do have a little good news. All the old girl's machine guns survived. That gives us two thirties and two fifties to start with. Add the two fifties we fished up from the PBY and all the ammo the skipper's bringing that Ellis found, and we're actually better off there."

"What about putting some of the Jap guns from *Amagi* on her?" Spanky asked.

"Yeah, I was coming to that," Campeti said. "We've got just about all *Amagi*'s secondaries ashore now, and most are in decent shape. There's a fair amount of ammo for 'em, too. Some was wet, but some was in ready lockers above the waterline." He shrugged. "Some cooked off in the fire. Anyway, the only ones I know we could tie into our fire control are the five and a halfs. They have about the same velocity as our own guns, according to what Shinya told Bernie, but they're way too damn heavy to stick on *Walker*. The dual-purpose four-point-sevens are just a little heavier and only a little slower. They might work—at least in local control. They're the best bet, actually. They were mounted higher up and we've already recovered more ammo for them than *Walker* ever carried. If Brister can get the aft deckhouse rebuilt in time, we could mount one of those suckers right where number four used to be."

"You said they're slower, but with us feeding the four-inch fifties black powder, that's not so, is it?" Spanky asked.

"Not right now," Campeti defended, "but we have to standardize on what we have the most of. 'Sides, Mr. McFarlane, hope springs eternal. We still haven't got the new propellants sorted out, but we will someday. Then we can tie 'em all together."

"What about the antiaircraft stuff?"

Campeti looked thoughtful. "We might stick a few of those Jap twenty-five millimeters on the old girl, just for hoots. They're kinda clunky and don't seem good for much. They're not heavy, though, and we've got 'em. Lots of bullets, too."

"Do it," said Letts. "I want the skipper to have as much firepower as we can give him."

Ben Mallory had been murmuring something to Tikker during the exchange. He was utterly exhausted, having flown all day. Captain Reddy never did order him not to fly, but the Strakka had him grounded for now. By the time the storm was past, *Ajax* would surely be out of range. "I got an idea," he said suddenly. All eyes turned to him. "Yeah," he said, thinking fast, "I got a *swell* idea. When you get the ship all put back together, what's going in that empty space where the torpedo tubes used to be? I know the searchlight tower's there, but what else?"

"I don't know," Spanky confessed. "Maybe those popguns Campeti was talking about."

"Why not give her one of the Nancys!" Ben said triumphantly. "Skipper's always going on about recon," he said a little smugly. "Let's give him some!"

Spanky, Letts, Adar, and Keje all looked at one another.

"Would a davit lift one of those cockeyed contraptions of yours?" Letts asked.

"Sure! They don't weigh much. Might have to rig an extension boom. But with all the weight we're saving, even with the Jap stuff you're adding on, there'll be plenty of margin for a plane, fuel, spares and such as well!"

"And I guess you just happen to know somebody who'd volunteer to fly it, too?"

"Well . . . sure." Ben grinned.

Letts looked at Adar, then shook his head. "Great idea, Ben, but not you. We need you to train pilots, not go tear-assing off on your own. Besides, don't forget what Mr. Ellis found. What would we do about that without you?" Ben slumped, but brightened again at the prospect of an expedition to Tjilatjap. Tikker grinned hugely and his tail swished expectantly. "Not you either," said Letts. "As our only other combat-experienced aviator, you'll command *Big Sal*'s air wing, or squadron"—he shook his head—"whatever you're going to call it."

"Then who?" Ben and Tikker demanded simultaneously.

"You said Ensign Reynolds is competent to commence independent operations. We'll ask him if he'd like to volunteer."

"This is all very excellent, but this discussion has strayed somewhat," Adar said. "You have convinced me that *Walker* will be ready. Good. What else must we do? There are other issues at hand."

"Well," said Letts, "*Big Sal* will soon be ready for sea. The new frigates too, as soon as we can fuel 'em. They're finished. We'll put the planes we have on *Big Sal*, and send the fleet off against the Grik. *Humfra-Dar* can then go in the dry dock. We'll send a couple other Homes with the troops we can't put in the frigates. Otherwise, we keep doing what we're doing." He looked around. "Making the tools for them to do the job."

"Indeed," said Adar, "that is as I hoped. We must push the Grik! Whatever support Captain Reddy requires in the east, Saan-Kakja has promised. Already, ships are leaving Manila to intercept and shadow this *Ajax*. We have finally contacted Lieutenant Laumer on Talaud—his transmitter was damaged—and Captain Lelaa's sloop will attempt to intercept *Ajax* as well. We have addressed all we seem capable of, yet *one* serious issue remains."

"Ah!" Courtney Bradford declared, speaking at last. He hadn't had anything to add to the military and logistical discussion, but now his turn had come. "I presume you refer to a certain . . . ticklish physical and somewhat spiritual notion?"

"It is not a *notion*!" Adar insisted. "For such a learned creature, you are so very cavalier with the most fundamental laws of things!"

"Physics," Bradford agreed. "And I assure you Mr. Chairman, I'm not in the least cavalier about that at all! The problem is, as I've so often told you—and not to put too fine a point on it or to intentionally insult you in any way—your understanding of some physical aspects of the world are . . . well . . . wrong." He pointed at the map before them. "According to Captain Reddy's last transmission, Commodore Jenks has at last freely revealed what many of us have long suspected: this Empire of New Britain Isles is centered in a chain we called the Hawaiian Islands! It is quite distant indeed. It is, in fact, according to your, um, *mis*understanding, quite an impossible place for anyone to be, or even exist. You recognize the world is round, like a cannonball, but since gravity pulls *downward*, you believe we here stand either near or upon the very top of the world! I assume this tradition is due to our proximity to the equator and the fact that the midday sun passes almost directly overhead. On its face, that would seem a most sensible and understandable position. I take it, however, from our discussions and a few old sayings I've heard, that you believe anyone who ventures too distant in any direction will plummet into the void of the heavens!"

"That is a simplistic summation, but essentially correct. Of course, one may venture quite far before that occurs. You have shown me maps of where this Mada-gaaskar lies. You insist it is our ancestral home and I doubt it not. The distance and description are consistent with the Scrolls. Clearly one can exist even that far away, since we once did ourselves. The Grik dwell there still, and in places even more distant. But this ... Ha-waa-ee ... It is so far! It is in the Eastern Sea, where monsters even more terrifying than the mountain fish dwell! You cannot lightly ask anyone to venture that far."

"We must, and so will you," Alan Letts said, "because that's where *Ajax* is going."

Bradford pondered a moment. "My dear Adar, I know we have asked much of you and your people in matters of faith. We popped in here and, in some ways, stood many things you've always believed upon their heads. I personally apologize for that. Having one's beliefs constantly under assault is always traumatic, and I *do* respect your beliefs even if they are wrong." He cleared his throat, realizing that didn't come out quite how he'd intended. "I shall ask you a rhetorical question. You are of the sea folk. You have wandered far indeed throughout your life. Perhaps, at times, you have even wandered far enough that you feared you were getting, oh, at least a little close to the dropoff point. True?"

"Perhaps," Adar reluctantly agreed. "Once we voyaged around the bottom of the land you call Aus-traalia. I admit I grew somewhat concerned."

"Tell me, as you drew farther south, did you notice anything extraordinary?"

"It ... was less warm."

"Yes, yes, but what I mean is, did you notice any tendency at all to walk strangely, or lean? Did you feel any sideways pull of gravity at all?" Adar didn't answer, but he seemed frustrated and even a little irritated. "I must point out that we, these other humans and myself, have little better understanding of what gravity *is* than you do. We *have* learned that it works quite well and it is surprisingly consistent wherever one goes, whether here, Australia, or even the other side of the world. No matter where one goes, gravity always pulls downward, toward the center of the world! This, sir, is a fact. When Captain Reddy told you and Keje that he was born and raised on the 'bottom' of the world, he was quite sincere. Most of our American friends are from a land situated on the far side of this globe. I have never been to America, but I can assure you the Americans have, and they did not have to hang upside down, clinging to their land with their fingers!" He looked thoughtful. "Your beliefs are correct in the respect that the sea returns to the sky, but it does not pour off the side of the world to do it; it evaporates and travels upward, much like the smoke of your pyres carries the souls of your dead to the heavens! It is always dreadfully humid here, but surely you've experienced a day or two in your life when the air seemed less thick, less heavy?"

Adar nodded speculatively.

"Then there you have it! That thickness of the air is water being carried into the sky!"

"If this 'gravity' works so well, then why does it not prevent that?" Adar demanded.

Courtney sighed. "It's a long story. I can and certainly will be more than happy to demonstrate the experiments required to prove it to you, but for the moment, I ask only that you trust me—trust us. The ultimate fact remains that, in order to retrieve those who have been taken from us and deal with this . . . situation in the east that threatens to distract us from our bigger business, Captain Reddy will chase them when he arrives. As you have had faith in us before, have faith now; those who go east will *not* fall off the world. They"—he looked defiantly around the chamber—"*we* may well face unknown dangers, but falling into the sky is not one of them!"

Achilles arrived in Baalkpan Bay on the very heels of the Strakka, after what must have been a record passage. She'd sustained some minor damage, but Matt could find no fault with Jenks's seamanship. Stony stares greeted her arrival and the flag she flew as she steamed into the bay and eased up to the dock. Only when Captain Reddy, the Captain's Guard, and Chack's Marines disembarked was there a marked decrease in the hostile tension. Many people still tried to get at the ship and the people aboard, but the company of the 2nd Marines with Chack was more than sufficient to keep the crowd at bay.

Matt strode to meet Adar, Keje, Letts, and Spanky, flanked by Gray, Stites, O'Casey, and the rest of his personal guard. "It's good to see you, Adar," Matt said, receiving the customary embrace. Keje embraced him as well. "I wish it were under better circumstances."

"As do I, my friend. I cannot express—"

"Skip it," Matt interrupted. "It's done. Quit beating yourself up. Now we have to decide what we're going to do about it."

"Yes," Adar agreed. "All has been prepared as you have specified. The wood and charcoal have been brought, as you ordered." Adar pointed at a massive heap. "That is for *Achilles*, I take it?"

"Yeah. Jenks wants to get under way as soon as possible. Can't say I blame him." He looked at Adar, at all the faces present. "And yes, I do trust him. What's weird is, even O'Casey trusts him now. You wouldn't believe the mess they've got at home." He paused. "Or maybe you would. It's sort of like Aryaal and B'mbaado, except it's all mixed-up in one government." He shook his head. "Anyway, that doesn't matter. Jenks might catch them, but I doubt it. He has to try, though, and we might need him." Suddenly, Matt looked at *Walker*, tied securely to the pier. Her upper works had not yet been repainted, except for a few spots where the weather had allowed the painting of some welds and seams. She looked like a patchwork quilt, but she was *whole,* or mostly so. Smoke rose from two stacks and workers shouted and scrambled over her. A strange-looking gun was being lowered onto her rebuilt and slightly reconfigured aft deckhouse. Her force-draft blower gave the distinct impression she was breathing on her own.

"I didn't believe it," he confessed quietly. For a moment, the hard expression he'd worn melted away. "I couldn't let myself." He looked at Spanky. "Mr. McFarlane, my compliments—and my most heartfelt appreciation."

Spanky looked uncomfortable. "Shucks, Skipper, wasn't just me."

"No, but you're the ramrod. Always have been. Looking at you, I doubt you've slept since those bastards took the girls."

Spanky shrugged, glancing down at his stained and filthy self. "Not many have. You're gonna need your ship for this one, Skipper. She's the only thing in the world fast enough to catch them. You've pulled more than one trick out of her hat. I figure she's got plenty more where they came from."

Matt clasped the skinny man's arm. "You bet. How long?"

"Two weeks, Skipper. We'll have her good as new by then. Might be a few quirks—we've basically rebuilt her from the keel up—but that's still a week ahead of schedule."

"I doubt it, if you count the man hours!" Matt chuckled grimly. "Give the guys a little more time off if you can. Don't worry; I'm not going to stop you now!"

Spanky—everyone—grinned relief. They'd been afraid the captain would want to leave immediately. Undoubtedly he did *want* to, but he also knew a fully repaired *Walker* would catch *Ajax* regardless of the head start over the vast distances they were contemplating. One thing bothered Keje, however, and he had to ask.

"What will this Billingsly do with the hostages? He has threatened to kill them if he is harassed. Might he not do that anyway?"

Matt shook his head. "I don't think so, and neither does Jenks. Taking the princess was his objective. According to your accounts of the events, everybody else he took was basically an accident. If he just wanted Rebecca dead, he could have assassinated her many times and just left before anyone got wise." He shook his head. "No, he wants her alive, or this Company he works for does. Probably as a bargaining chip to wring even more power from the governor-emperor. If I know the princess, she's going to be making life miserable for Mr. Billingsly about now. See, not all of *Ajax*'s crew are Company men. Even her captain is a loyalist, according to Jenks. Billingsly wouldn't dare even clap her in irons without risking an open break with what has to be a very divided crew. I bet that will put the princess in a position to demand decent treatment for the hostages."

"I hope you are right," murmured Adar.

"Me too," Matt admitted.

Jenks joined them, saluting. "Please let me express my most abject apologies," he said sincerely. "If I had only known—"

"You stow it too," Matt interrupted. "Everybody's sorry. Okay. We're all on the same side now, so let's get on with it. What do you need?"

"Very well. Some assistance loading the fuel aboard my ship would be appreciated. Our victuals should suffice, but a little more couldn't hurt. Also, after observing the healing effects of your wondrous polta paste, I would beg some of that from you as well."

Adar, still eyeing Jenks suspiciously, motioned to one of his staff standing a discreet distance away. "See to it," he commanded.

"How are we fixed for transmitters and receivers?" Matt asked.

Spanky looked around. "I'll have to ask Riggs. Most have been going in the new ships as soon as they finish 'em."

"See if we can spare a set for Commodore Jenks. I want a couple of spares aboard *Walker* too. I never want to be out of touch again."

"Who'll operate it?" Spanky asked, referring to the one meant for *Achilles*.

"Clancy told me Mr. O'Casey has become fairly proficient. He didn't have much else to do on the voyage out, after all. At least until we transferred him to *Dowden*." Matt looked at Jenks, who was staring at his old nemesis.

"Under the circumstances, I believe that would certainly be acceptable, if Mr. O'Casey—Bates—would be kind enough to agree. In fact, with the discovery that my second officer was one of Billingsly's creatures, I have an opening there as well."

With a strange expression, O'Casey nodded. "Aye, 'twould be . . . interestin' ta sail with ye again, Commodore. On the same side."

Dennis Silva groaned and opened his good eye. He'd actually been awake and alert for some time, but playing possum was a skill he'd learned in China once upon a time, and it had come in handy more than once. When, oh, Chinese gangsters, for example, thought you were down for the count, they were less prepared when you suddenly resurrected yourself and beat them to death with a goofy jade Buddha you didn't know why you had. Life was weird that way, and it always helped to have an edge. He groaned again, making sure the ladies knew he was awake. He hadn't learned much during his possum phase, but he did know everyone was alive, where they were, and that, for the moment, they were alone.

"What hit me?" he grumbled. That was still a mystery. He'd been doing well enough, him and Lawrence, when everything just . . . quit. He knew his head hurt—badly—so something must have conked him. He didn't remember anything else from then, until a short time ago.

"Strange. I would have wagered on 'where am I?' came Sister Audry's voice.

"Wagerin's a sin, Sister," Dennis proclaimed piously. " 'Sides, any fool can tell we're at sea, an' I been in enough brigs to recognize one for what it is, even if I never been in it before."

"The weapon was a bag of musket balls," Princess Rebecca said, moving quickly to sit beside him where he lay on a pair of moldy blankets. "But the man who hit you was a particularly revolting and traitorous coward named Truelove. He seems to be Billingsly's chief minion." She caressed his forehead and then gingerly inspected his wound. "Healing nicely, at last," she pronounced. Silva hadn't yet tried to rise, but he suspected it would be a disorienting procedure.

"Truelove, eh? Big guy? I remember him. Hafta make a point outta returning the favor. I hate leavin' obligations like that undid." He paused, a thoughtful expression on his face. "Knew it had to be a sneak attack. Ol' Abe the newsboy mighta whupped me in a fair fight, but by the time I met him, it wouldn't have been fair. Good fella. Readin' about him's practically what got me in the Navy. Practically."

"You fought splendidly before that coward struck you down!" Rebecca gushed. "Splendidly!"

"Well . . . of course I did! Ol' Larry helped a little, though. Say, how is the little lizardy guy?"

"I okay," came a familiar voice from the gloom.

Sandra Tucker moved into Dennis's field of vision. "Lucky for you, you showed enough sense to keep some polta paste in your shooting bag. Rebecca got it for us. She pretty much has the run of the ship. You probably would have come out of it—you've got a bad concussion, by the way— but we might have lost young Mr. Cook. Before Truelove hit you, he'd evidently fired his last pistol at the boy. The ball took a big hunk out of the top of his shoulder, close to his neck. Not normally a mortal wound, but it became infected quite quickly."

"Well. Yeah, I keep some o' that stuff in there case o' scratches an' such. Be kinda stupid, after all we been through, to die o' some infected scratch. How is the little bugger? Abel, right?"

"I'm here, sir," came a weak voice. "I'm well enough. I did what you said. I yelled and ran for help!"

"And was shot for his efforts too, the brave, silly boy!" Rebecca scolded.

"Oh, well. Ever'body gets shot sooner or later in the Navy. Seems like it, anyway. You done good, boy." Silva finally tried to sit up, but it just wasn't going to happen yet. He growled and lay back down. "So," he said, "what's the scam? Why ain't we been rescued?"

"We're hostages," Sandra said simply. "They've threatened to kill us if our forces molest them. For a couple of days, one of our planes came and buzzed around, but we haven't seen it since the storm."

"A couple o' days! A storm! How long have I been out?"

"Several days. I believe you were in a coma."

"Huh. Damn, no wonder I'm so hungry. Several days on this bucket and we could be anywhere. That's the first thing we gotta figure out: where we are. Then we gotta keep track of our position."

"Why?" Sister Audry asked.

"So we'll know when to get off, of course! If they're keepin' us hostage, our folks won't blow the hell outta this tub! Besides, Dennis Silva ain't *nobody's* hostage!"

"What's your plan?" Rebecca asked eagerly.

"Ain't got one yet. I just woke up, remember? Gimme a minute or two to figure the angles. So, Miss . . . Lieutenant . . . Minister . . ."

Sandra laughed. "Lieutenant will still do."

"Thanks, ma'am. Lieutenant Tucker says you got the run o' the ship?"

"Essentially," Rebecca replied. "That porcine beast must preserve the fiction he has rescued *me* from *you*. No one actually believes it. I spend most of my time down here, after all, but he dares not put me in irons. My behavior is controlled by threats against your well-being."

"You figure there's anybody aboard we can count on?"

"I'm sure of it. There are more Company men aboard *Ajax* than any ship that sailed with the squadron, but not all are traitors. Why, even the captain, Captain Rajendra, is a loyal man! He fairly chafes! He does not know what to do, however. Less than half the crew stands with him."

"The captain himself, eh?" Silva pondered. "Sure you can trust him?"

"Absolutely."

"Then get our position from him. We need maps too. Charts."

"What have you got in mind?" Sandra demanded.

"Well, I'm still conjurin' it up, and me and the boy have a little healin' to do, but it strikes me the last thing we want is to wind up wherever this ship is goin'. Once we're there, there won't be any use for us. There may not be any use for the princess. So somewhere between here and there, we have to switch trains."

Irvin Laumer's eyes jerked open and he leaped to his feet when he heard the scream. Everyone was exhausted and he'd been taking a short siesta in the shade of a leafy lean-to on the beach. Only an idiot would do such a thing under the standing trees on Talaud Island. It took him an instant to realize the scream had come from the workers near the sub. Sprinting through the loose sand, he yanked the .45 from his holster and jacked a round into the chamber.

"What the hell's going on here?" he shouted. The screaming had stopped, but there was still a lot of shouting and confusion around the work site.

"One of the 'Cats was just walking across the gangplank to the boat," Danny Porter said excitedly, "when this jet of water, like a high-pressure hose, knocked him off into the water! As soon as he fell in, something . . . got him!"

Irvin looked at him incredulously, then eased a little closer to the basin they'd begun excavating around S-19. There was a lot of water down there, and nothing they could do about it. Some soaked in through the sand and more came in with the tide when the sea was running high. Sometimes the boat actually floated. "What was it?" Irvin asked.

"How the hell am I supposed to know?" Danny demanded. "There's all kinds of weird, murdering critters running around on this place! It's a miracle we survived here as long as we did before, and we were idiots to come back to it!" Danny brought his voice under control. "And if that ain't enough, we've got *that* thing scaring the water out of everybody!" He pointed at the mist-shrouded volcano in the distance. When they'd been marooned on Talaud Island, the volcano occasionally rumbled and made the ground shake, but for the past few weeks, it had been venting almost constantly. Sometimes it belched heavy clouds of ash that settled on them and got into everything when the wind was right. Sometimes it just made creepy noises. A time or two, they'd had spectacular light shows in the middle of the night. Nobody in their group really knew squat about volcanoes, aside from a few historical accounts, but the overwhelming consensus was that the Talaud volcano was building up to something big.

The problem was, they were stuck there—marooned again, in a sense. *Simms*'s consort had been little more than a freighter, and once she'd off-loaded the equipment, machinery, fuel oil for the steam boiler, and the hopefully required diesel, she'd sailed for Manila for more supplies. *Simms* had remained, lending her crew to the labor and as a safety measure in case, for any reason, they had to abandon the expedition. But even *Simms* and Captain Lelaa were gone now. They'd sailed two days before to rendezvous with a little squadron of feluccas led by Saan-Kakja's brother to intercept and at least pinpoint *Ajax*'s position.

Irvin understood why Lelaa had to go, but it left him and his crew in a pickle. *Simms* had taken the newly repaired transmitter, and the set on the boat was irreparable. Tex was trying to build another set like Riggs's design from the parts at hand, but it was slow going. In the meantime, they were at the mercy of all the terrors *Walker* had once rescued them from—the dangerous predators including the nocturnal tree git-yas, as Flynn had called them, bizarre creatures that looked and acted like a cross between a Grik and a sloth that dropped on unwary prey from above. There were other things, almost ghostly things no one had ever really seen or had a shot at, that could snatch a man and run faster than anything ought to be capable of. Then there was the mountain, of course. Now . . .

"Did anybody get a look at it at all?" Laumer asked of the creature that got the 'Cat.

"Well, it was kind of blotchy," Sid Franks volunteered. As the carpenter, he would now have to repair the damaged gangplank. The jet of water had enough force to blow off the handrail. "It swirled up when it . . ." He stopped, staring at the water.

"So whatever it is, it's still in there?" There were nods and Irvin sighed. "Must be a sea creature. Came out of the water last night when nobody was looking and moved in." He shrugged. "Only one thing for it." He turned to Midshipman Hardee, who, along with a 'Cat who'd been dubbed Spook, had increasingly taken on their ordnance duties. "We have to get rid of this thing before we can get any more work done today. Get some of the grenades and all the small arms. Make sure you issue them to guys who know how to use them."

The armed guards who protected the workers from the denizens of the jungle were summoned, and with the distribution of the four other Krags and the single Thompson (all the small arms had been retrieved from the submarine on *Walker*'s previous visit) a total of eight riflemen, one submachine gunner (Danny), and Irvin Laumer armed with his pistol prepared to face whatever was in the water. Six grenadiers had simple, ingenious devices quite similar to the grenades the Americans were accustomed to. They were virtually identical in form and function, although the fuses weren't as reliable. There could be as many as ten seconds or as few as two before the things went off, so there was never any goofing around after the spoon flew.

Irvin nodded at the first 'Cat grenadier. The idea was to chase the creature aft, toward the screws, where the water was shallower. There they hoped to get some shots at it. The grenades weren't powerful enough to damage the pressure hull of the submarine, but Irvin told them not to throw the things too close to it anyway. With a returning nod, the first 'Cat pulled the pin and dropped his weapon in the water. A few seconds later, a geyser of spume and white smoke erupted into the air with a dull thump, and this was the signal for the next grenade. A high, splashing column of water that dissipated downwind followed another *ker-plunk*. A third grenade went off. Then a fourth. Suddenly, out of the spume of the fifth grenade, something . . . terrifying . . . scrambled up out of the excavation directly at Tex Sheider. At first glance, it looked like a mottled black-and-green spider, but it had a tail sort of like a lobster and long, thin claws to match, making it at least ten feet long. One of the claws clutched the partially shredded body of the 'Cat workman.

"Holy shit!" was all Tex had time to screech before it blew him off his feet with a concentrated burst of seawater. Instantly, the monster lunged at him.

"Well . . . fire, damn it!" Irvin yelled.

Danny opened up with his Thompson, spraying chunks off the beast in all directions. The black powder loads under his bullets created a fog bank of white smoke around him. The thing recoiled from the impacts and writhed in agony. The other riflemen had recovered somewhat from the sudden appearance and attack and were scrambling to shoot without hitting one another. Irvin stepped forward, firing his pistol. He'd never fired any of the new loads before and was surprised not only by the smoke, but by the significantly greater recoil and loud boom that came with every shot instead of the usual sharp bark. The hideous creature turned to face him and he steeled himself for another blast of water. This time, however, there was only a meager, bloody splurt, and as he emptied his magazine, the creature suddenly flopped on its back and began to spasm violently. Irvin ran to Tex and grabbed him by the shirt, dragging him farther from the dying beast. Tex seemed unconscious, and where his shirt had torn, Irvin could see a dark red impact point on his chest.

"Cease firing!" he shouted at the men and 'Cats who were still shooting at the creature. Any twitching movement was sufficient proof to them that more bullets were called for. "Get over here! Help me with this man!"

Irvin was feeling for a pulse when Tex suddenly groaned. "Oh, Jesus, that hurts." He gasped.

"What does?"

"What do you think! It feels like that thing squirted a fourteen-inch shell at me!"

Irvin gently tore the rest of the shirt away. The red mark was already turning black. "Lie still! You may have some broken ribs! No wonder it was able to knock the 'Cat off the gangway! You're lucky it didn't stop your heart."

"I think it did, for a minute."

"Well . . . we don't have a real doctor. Sid knows a thing or two. Should be able to tell if anything's broken. You'll be taking it easy for a while, anyway." He motioned for some 'Cats to move Tex under the lean-to he'd been napping under. "Danny, form a detail to bury our man," he said, referring to the half-eaten 'Cat. "And get that damn nasty thing's corpse out of my sight!"

"Yes, sir," Danny said. Only later did it occur to Irvin that the man had called him "sir." He raised the 1911 Colt and looked at it. Filthy. The new rounds might work okay, but they sure dirtied up a gun. "Mr. Hardee, you and Spook gather up all the weapons that were fired and clean them thoroughly. Step on it, too. No telling when we'll need them again."

Irvin sighed and looked at the submarine while workers either resumed their tasks or performed the duties he'd just ordered. Somehow, he'd managed to last until no one was looking before the shakes overtook him. For a long moment, he just held his trembling hands tight against his sides, waiting for the spell to pass—hoping it was just a spell. He'd been wondering more and more whether he was ready for this. In the past, he'd always had someone to turn to, to turn things *over* to when it started getting rough. Now he was *it*. He had to come to grips with that. Ultimately, that was the real test Captain Reddy had given him, and in an even greater sense it was the test he'd set himself.

So far, in spite of everything, they'd made a lot of progress. S-19 hadn't been badly damaged before it wound up here, just out of fuel. Time and the elements had treated her more harshly than the Japanese did. "Task Force S-19" had done good work and with any luck, they'd get her off eventually. The trouble was, did they have time? Would the island even *let* them go? One thing was almost certain: they'd lose more people before they were done. He hoped it would be worth it, and he hoped he wouldn't lose his mind—or his nerve. He wished Lelaa were here!

Without noticing when it happened, he realized that his hands had stopped shaking. It was just a spell after all, he decided. This time. He looked at the lean-to, where Sid was inspecting Sheider. They were talking in low tones and he even heard a faint laugh. He shook his head and started back toward the sub.

Lelaa was mad as hell. She'd had *Simms* heaved to, just as the commander of the steamer had instructed. Her orders were not to fire on the Imperial ship for any reason, and while she understood the orders, she was still frustrated. Not that it would have done much good. The Imperial frigate was more than a match for her and both sides knew it. Still, this order to heave to only added insult to injury. Two feluccas, the ones she'd been dispatched to meet, had also loosed their sails.

Their mission had been to avoid contact, to observe from a distance and report, but the wind had died away and the steamer came to them. Helpless now, all they could do was what they were told. The enemy (she could think of it as nothing else) steamer closed the distance until she saw a form raise a speaking trumpet.

"I am impressed by your people's persistence," an amplified but distorted voice called, "but this is becoming ridiculous. I can't have you hounding us all the way to our destination! This is the last time I will suffer any interference! The next Allied vessel that crosses my path will be destroyed."

Lelaa quickly motioned for a speaking trumpet as well. Raising it to her lips, she caught herself wishing Irvin were there. She knew her English was better than good, but he'd always just seemed to have a way about him. "Excuse me, please," she called back. "We have neither the desire nor the ability to interfere with your progress. It is you who closed the distance with us. Our mission is merely to ensure that the hostages are safe and well. This is no more than I understand you invited us to do!"

"That is all? You don't mean to menace us with your mighty fleet?" mocked the voice.

Lelaa's tail swished with rage, but she managed a civil reply. "That is all, I assure you."

The man across the water didn't speak for a while, as if he were considering something. Finally he raised the trumpet again. "Since, as I said, this is the last time I will be bothered by you or your Alliance, I will allow you to come across and interview my guests. Come aboard alone. If I see any weapons, you will be fired upon!"

Lelaa lowered her trumpet, stunned. "Hoist out a boat," she said.

Clambering up the side of the Imperial frigate, Lelaa was not met by the sort of side party she'd grown to expect. Instead, a pair of armed men essentially took her into custody and escorted her to a small gathering by the rail. She'd never actually met Princess Rebecca, but she recognized her on sight. She bowed. "Greetings, Your Highness," she said in her most respectful tone. "I trust you and your companions are well?"

"Look. The monkey talks!" muttered a large, dangerous-looking man in the group.

"There, there, Mr. Truelove! Let's attempt to be civil!" admonished another, probably Billingsly, Lelaa decided.

"Well enough," the girl replied. "For now." She seared the one who must be Billingsly with a glare. "But one takes these things day by day."

Lelaa addressed Billingsly. "And what of the other hostages? She says they are well, but where are they? Have you any idea how important they are to us?"

Billingsly smiled. "Honestly, at first I did not. I expected my resolve to be tested and I'd be forced to, um, release a few of them over the side, as it were. Imagine my surprise when that did not occur! We quickly learned the truth of the matter. We knew who the Roman witch was, but good gracious! You *cannot* imagine how amazed we were to discover one of our guests, the noble Minister Sandra Tucker, is practically affianced to your Supreme Commander!" He chuckled. "Honestly, I confess to a professional lapse. I never had any idea, yet the young princess let it slip as if it were common knowledge!"

Rebecca loosed a glare of perfect hatred at Billingsly.

"I'll wager your Captain Reddy was a tad upset? I understand you have some means of rapid communication, so I expect he has been informed."

"He knows," Lelaa admitted, "and I submit that *you* cannot imagine the wrath you have brought down upon yourself!"

"Oh, splendid!"

Lelaa was confused. "In any event, if any of the hostages have been mistreated . . ."

"Not a hair on their heads! They are confined, of course—no end to mischief in a couple of them—but their wounds are healing nicely and they thrive in their accommodations. It *is* a bit cramped, and I'm afraid privacy is at a premium, but no one would say they've been mistreated!" A strange expression crossed Billingsly's face. Unlike most Lemurians Lelaa was good with human face moving, but this was . . . different. "Nor will you be, so long as you behave."

"What . . . what do you mean?"

Truelove laughed and Billingsly's lips quirked into something like a smile. "Why, you will be joining them, of course." He turned to a darker-skinned man with a graying mustache. "Is that ridiculous ship still there? I believe I gave them fair warning that I did not wish to be pestered again! Open fire!"

"What! Wait!" cried Lelaa, struggling against the two guards who'd suddenly seized her arms. "You said 'the next time,' damn you!"

Billingsly turned to her. "When you had the insolence, the gall to raise your speaking trumpet and answer back at me . . . at *me*! You who are not only a lesser species, but a *female*!" Billingsly barked an incredulous laugh. "That *was* the next time. Captain Rajendra, I gave you an order!"

The dark-skinned man replied, clearly forcing his voice to remain calm. "Commander Billingsly, firing on that ship would be an act of willful murder. They are completely unprepared. . . . Their guns are not even run out!"

"Then that should make destroying them all the easier. Destroy one of the other little ships as well; I don't care which, but you may allow one to escape."

"But, Commander!"

Still facing away, Billingsly spoke very clearly. "Destroy those ships, Captain Rajendra, or place yourself under arrest. Which will it be?"

"*Simms!*" Lelaa shrieked at the top of her lungs, hoping someone on the nearby ship might hear. "Hard over! Run!" Truelove backhanded her to the deck.

"Captain Rajendra?" Billingsly prodded.

Rajendra's expression seemed almost desperate as he looked at those around him. This was beyond anything, beyond even the questionable seizure of the princess. This entire episode had been engineered to paint the Navy with the same guilt the Company wore. He could not be part of it! But what of the princess? He feared for her and her friends, and he knew the Company had an unwholesome agenda regarding her. If he was relieved, he would be unable to help her. His eyes sought hers and he saw . . . pleading. She would think him a monster and might not trust him when she absolutely had to. And yet, the ships were doomed. If he refused the order, another would carry it out. Presently, he at least retained command of his ship's movements, if not her actions. He had to preserve that!

"Commence firing," he whispered, barely audible, eyes locked on the princess, pleading for understanding.

"What was that, Captain? I'm a bit hard of hearing today."

"Commence firing, God damn you!" Rajendra bellowed, not caring if Billingsly knew he was shouting at him and not the crew.

Matt stood on *Walker*'s port bridge wing and, for just a while, allowed himself to feel the pure joy of the moment. At long last, his ship was alive again. He felt her sinews coiling for the rush in the vibration of the newly painted rail beneath his hands. Her hasty, impatient breath was in the blower behind the pilothouse. Her muscles were the men and 'Cats who scrambled on the fo'c'sle, a little awkwardly and out of practice perhaps, to single up her lines. Her heart was her own and always had been, but as he stood there, he almost felt her mind merge with his once more, becoming a willing tool for his purpose. Oh, if only Sandra were there, it would be the *perfect* moment. A measure of her old vitality restored, the ship fairly strained against the bonds that clutched her to the land. She was ready for the long voyage ahead, come what may. Together they'd get Sandra back: the old destroyer and her captain.

"Take in the stern lines," Matt commanded, and he waited while the task was performed. "Left full rudder," he called to Kutas, the scarred helmsman. "Port ahead one-third." The dingy water alongside the dock boiled up through the propeller guard and thunderous cheers reverberated from the crowd gathered to see. Matt scanned the crowd for faces as *Walker*'s stern crept away. They were the ones who'd done this, the people of this city he'd grown to love. Partly they'd done it because this ship was their protector, the almost holy talisman that saved them from the Grik. They owed it to her; they needed her still—but the quality of the work they'd done and the inhuman hours that work had required bespoke a labor of love.

Matt nodded his thanks to all of them, not only for what they had done for his ship, but for what he knew they'd done for him.

Some of the faces he saw were less jubilant than others. Adar appeared thoughtful, but he waved encouragingly. Judging by his posture, Keje was downright morose. He'd badly wanted to come, but *Big Sal* would soon join the fleet at Singapore. He couldn't be in two places at once. Besides, his daughter Selass was sailing as *Walker*'s medical officer. They'd become quite close again and he would miss her. Letts looked anxious. He'd complained that he never got to go anywhere, but as Matt had once told him, he'd worked himself out of a job. He had a bigger job now and a very pregnant wife. Riggs looked stoic. Ed Palmer could do his job on the ship, but he couldn't take over ashore. Perry Brister made an obscene gesture at somebody aft and Matt chuckled, spotting Spanky McFarlane waving cheerily from where the number one torpedo mount used to be. Spanky had left Brister in charge of his division in Baalkpan because there was no way *Walker* was steaming off without *him*.

Gazing farther aft, the incongruity of an *airplane* lashed carefully to the deck behind the searchlight tower struck Matt again. Besides never having seen such a thing on a four stacker before, the Nancy just looked so strange and fragile. He knew it would be great having it along—if it didn't fall apart. Mallory had assured him the "ships" were tougher than they looked. Matt hoped the same was true for poor Reynolds. The young aviator seemed somewhat lost and all alone standing near the plane.

"Rudder amidships," Matt called. "Take in the bowline." A few moments later, he added, "All astern, one-third." The old ship groaned a bit as the turbines' gears reversed their thrust, but she did seem . . . tighter than he remembered. As they backed away, the crowd cheered again and Matt kept looking for faces as they grew smaller. Bernie was there, waving happily with the others. He liked his job ashore. Laney was some distance away from him, sitting on a stanchion, probably wondering if he was happy or sad. He caught sight of Pam Cross and Risa standing side by side. Whatever . . . relationship . . . they shared with Silva, they were worried about the big ape, and his heart went out to them. The final face he recognized was that of one of the Mice—Gilbert Yeager—standing all alone with his hands in his pockets. Tabby knew *Walker*'s systems as well as anyone now, and she'd won the toss. Matt was secretly amazed Gilbert hadn't just sneaked aboard anyway. He'd done it before. Still, he was probably the most forlorn figure *Walker* was leaving behind.

"All stop. Right full rudder, all ahead two-thirds!" Matt commanded. The old ship's stern crouched down and water churned. Almost immediately, she began a looping turn to starboard. "Honk the horn, if you please,"

Matt said, and with a shriek of her whistle that drowned any further cheers, *Walker* sprinted for the mouth of the bay.

"Feels good, huh, Skipper," said the Bosun as he and Chack appeared on the bridge. Back aboard his Home, Chack had immediately reverted to his role as bosun's mate. He would have other duties too: his company of Marines would augment the crew, but it also had to drill with the new muskets they'd been issued. Bernie had insisted *Walker* get the first batch.

"Feels good," Matt confirmed. "We'll let things shake down a little; then we'll start running a few drills."

"Gonna be a comedy at first," Gray warned.

"I know. Say, where's Mr. Bradford? I figured he'd be on deck to enjoy the send-off."

"Oh, he's below, still stowing junk he says *you* said he could bring along, for experiments an' such."

Matt laughed. "He hit me with a list and swore he'd stick to it, but I guess I don't really care what he brought as long as it stays out of the way." He shook his head, watching as they left the feluccas and fishing boats in their wake. "God, it feels good to be *moving* again!"

"In case you didn't notice, we were moving along pretty well on *Achilles* in that Strakka!" Chack said dryly.

"Mmm. That was quite the thrill ride, but we were being pushed. It's nice to move that fast on our own!"

They talked amiably until they passed below Fort Atkinson and the report of a gun interrupted their conversation. Then another.

"A salute," Gray said. The guns kept firing. As the number mounted, Matt turned to Gray, who was staring expressionlessly ahead. When they finally stopped at nineteen, Matt's tone was ominous.

"Nineteen guns? *You* told them to do that! Are you out of your mind? That's nuts . . . and think of the wasted powder!"

Gray looked at Matt. "Yeah, Adar asked and I told him. And it ain't nuts! The Secretary of the Navy gets that many, and if you ain't at least that, what are you? You'd better dip the flag or you'll disappoint the boys an' girls in the fort."

Walker turned north-northeast after clearing the point batteries and islands beyond. Sprinting at the glorious speed of twenty-six knots, she reached the refinery island of Tarakan at dawn the next morning. The growth was beginning to reestablish itself after the vicious but comparatively small battle once fought there, and the ensuing great fire that had ravaged the place. To Matt, it still seemed a little odd to see the Stars and Stripes flying over an island where not a single human currently dwelt. All

the workers there were 'Cats—Navy 'Cats, and thus Americans—still. . . .
Walker topped off her bunkers and sped on.

A week before *Walker* sailed, they'd heard the news of *Simms*'s fate,
when a lone felucca returned to Paga-Daan, Saan-Kakja's brother's home.
The transmission had told how *Simms* was approached and destroyed
without warning of any kind. Worse, a felucca under the command of
Saan-Kakja's brother himself was also destroyed. Other than a few of
Simms's crew who'd apparently rowed Captain Lelaa over to *Ajax* to confer
with the hostage takers, there were no other survivors. Saan-Kakja was in
a frenzy, understandably, but she was also ready to declare war on the Empire of the New Britain Isles. Matt had to send his personal assurance that
the Empire itself might not be to blame, and they'd secured a strong alliance with at least one element of the Imperial Navy. He then had to beg
the Paga-Daans to replenish Jenks's ship when it arrived instead of firing on it. Things were spiraling out of control and, for Matt at least, the
all-important war in the west had assumed an almost back-burner status.
Meanwhile, he spent more time trying to smooth things over between his
Allies than he did running his ship—all while pursuing the criminals
who had taken Sandra, the princess, and at least three more of their people.
Those hostages might now include *Simms*'s captain.

Just as they turned west to cut across the Moro Gulf of the Celebes Sea,
they received confirmation that *Achilles* had indeed reached Paga-Daan and
had her fuel replenished. A subsequent transmission from *Achilles*—
O'Casey had apparently finally figured out the device he'd been given—
asked why the Paga-Daans had been so unfriendly. Matt had Palmer send
a message that explained the new situation—and the Paga-Daans immediately replied that they had not been rude to Jenks. Matt finally summoned Bradford and put him in charge of the diplomatic situation and
insisted that it had been his job in the first place.

Walker steamed on, her repaired sonar blasting the depths before her.
The sonar had been a major concern, but all the delicate equipment had
been above water in the charthouse, so it hadn't been as difficult to fix as
originally feared. They'd installed a pair of the "Y" guns—thanks to *Simms*,
they knew those worked—but it was good to be able to cross deep water at
speed. With Bradford finally dealing with diplomacy, Matt was free to drill
his crew and get his ship ready to fight.

"Sound General Quarters," Matt said for the third time that day, and
cringed. Of all the things no one had thought to repair, the general alarm
was becoming the most obvious. Everything else seemed to be working
fine so far, but the alarm, always ill-sounding, now reverberated through
the ship like a goose being choked underwater. Despite the comical sound,
the crews immediately sprang to their stations. The automatic response

had already returned to *Walker*'s veterans, and her new draft was quickly picking up the pace.

Fred Reynolds was the talker (he had to have something to do when he wasn't fussing with the plane) and he began to call out readiness reports from the various stations.

"Engineering reports manned and ready," he said. "Main battery is manned . . . and mostly ready. They're still having a little trouble figuring out who stands where on that Jap gun—I mean, number four." He quickly recited the rest of the litany. Matt noticed that the young ensign visibly paled when he reported for the plane-dump detail. Matt hoped it would never come to that, but if the plane ever caught fire or was otherwise interfering with the performance of the ship or crew in battle, they had to be ready to throw it over the side. He glanced aft and almost barked a laugh. Once again, he saw a pair of 'Cat mess attendants solemnly, carefully, carrying the Coke machine forward to the companionway under Earl Lanier's fierce, watchful supervision. Apparently, Earl was determined that providing for the iconic machine's safety should become as instinctive as any other preparation for battle. It had been severely wounded in action before, and after Earl lovingly and painstakingly restored it to health, he wasn't going to risk it again.

"Lookouts, machine guns, and damage control, all manned and ready. All stations manned and ready, Captain!" Reynolds finally reported.

"Very well," Matt said, controlling his voice and looking at his watch with a dissatisfied frown. The time had actually been pretty good, but he had to maintain appearances. "Secure from General Quarters. Continue steaming as before but maintain condition three. I want a few fingers close to a few triggers. There *are* sea monsters out there, after all."

"Aye-aye, Skipper. Secure from General Quarters and maintain condition three."

In the short bustle that followed, while the crew secured their helmets and other gear, and men and 'Cats slid down the ladder from the fire-control platform above the wheelhouse, Courtney Bradford appeared on the bridge. "How invigorating!" he wheezed after the effort of climbing the steps aft. "The old girl seems as good as new and ready for a scrap! It does my heart a world of good, I must say. It feels almost like old times!"

Matt turned to look at Bradford. "You weren't here for the old times, back before the war. We had some damn good men and we've lost an awful lot of them since, but the few who remain, from *Walker* and *Mahan*, and a few from S-19, have become something a little more than just damn good men. With them, and their Lemurian shipmates, this old can probably has as good a *crew* as any four stacker ever had!"

"Quite," Courtney agreed. "I have always noted how, in the various navies I've grown familiar with, each crew contains all the wildly different varieties of specialized skills to operate and maintain their ship at sea and on far-flung deployments. Oddly, however, I've also seen how the men who possess those skills set themselves apart from one another as distinctly as, well, different races sometimes do. Aboard here, all those different skills have become wonderfully diffused through necessity. Your crew has become much better educated than is the norm, Captain Reddy, and they have accomplished that feat largely on their own."

"You're right, but they've had a lot of help," Matt said. "These 'Cats! They're smart as a whip, but teaching them stuff has helped all the fellas. I've often heard it said that teaching makes a smart man wise. I'm not sure that's true in a classroom, but out here?" He shrugged. "It sure shows you what you *don't* know, and in our situation, you'd better find an answer. Chances are, somebody has one. That's what's caused your diffusion of skills." He waved his hand. "There'll always be rivalries. The 'snipes' and 'apes' wouldn't have it any other way, but that's good for morale. The thing is, after all we've been through and what this crew went through to get this ship back in action, there's probably not a deck ape aboard who couldn't lend a competent hand in the fire-rooms if it came to that. And vice versa. They might gripe, but they could do it and they *would*."

"Speak for yourself, Skipper," said Chief Gray, joining the pair. "Spanky's still mad that I missed most of the slop work. Says I'm *banned* from the engineering spaces! Hell, I wouldn't go down there to piss on him if he caught fire!"

"You see?" Matt said, laughing. "Boats, you're the exception that proves the rule!" He shook his head. "What does that mean, anyway? What a stupid thing to say."

"Indeed," Bradford agreed, lowering his voice. He glanced around as if checking to see who was in earshot. There weren't many secrets aboard *Walker*, not anymore, but Bradford had learned that his theories and observations were sometimes prone to . . . upset sensitive ears. Some of those sensitive ears were already somewhat agitated. Everyone knew *Walker* was steaming inexorably east and there was a very good chance she'd ultimately pass into waters no Lemurian had ever been. The fact that all the humans and a fair number of the Lemurian old hands seemed so unconcerned kept the edge off among the more strictly pious or superstitious. In this case, however, Bradford himself had become suddenly and surprisingly sensitive to the imperative that they minimize stressful contemplations among certain elements of the crew.

Apparently assured there were no panicky types present, he proceeded. "I have in fact been giving that a great deal of thought. As you know, I've been overwhelmed with stimuli, overwhelmed, sir! This world is a cornucopia of delights for a man of my interests. Forgive me if, on occasion, I've been diverted from some fairly obvious conclusions that would've ordinarily struck me with the greatest importance! It's the sheer volume of wonders that's crippled me and I'm but one man. . . ." He paused. "I do hope we may rescue young Mr. Cook. He's been such a great help. . . ."

"Courtney?" Matt prodded.

"Of course. Where was I? Oh, yes. A mere trivial example of my preoccupation is my failure to extrapolate beyond a few observations I made when we first came to this world. Surely you remember when Miss Tucker and I dissected the creature we killed on Bali?"

The day Marvaney died. "Yeah, I remember," Matt said.

"Well, you may recall that Miss Tucker and I disagreed about the physiology of the beast? I said it was more like a bird, with its furry feathers and hollow bones, et cetera, and she said its jaws made it a lizard as far as she was concerned—oh, please don't take this as criticism of the dear woman—but, well, I was right, you see. I admonished her to judge them more by what they *were* like and less by what they *looked* like . . . and I promptly fell into the same trap myself. We bandied the term 'lizard' about for so long, I failed to pursue my original course of study. We *were* a bit busy at the time, as you'll recall.

"In any event, it was the boy Abel who brought it back to my mind; he was quite fascinated with dinosaurs before his unpleasant experiences turned him slightly against them. But the point is we, the scientific community of which I consider myself a part, have always assumed dinosaurs were cold-blooded reptiles! Monstrous beasts, plodding along, lying in the sun like lizards on a rock, but we were wrong! If the fauna of this world is truly descended from the same fauna as our own, there would be a lot of egg on a lot of faces at the Royal Society, if I could ever report!"

"Well . . . that's amazing, Courtney," Matt said dryly, "but what's your point? I'm afraid 'lizards' has pretty much stuck as slang for 'Grik.' I doubt you're going to get folks to start calling 'em 'birds' at this point. Be happy with your win over 'Lemurians.'"

"No! That's not what I'm saying at all!"

"Then for God's sake, for once in your life, say what you mean!" hissed Gray, exasperated. Matt looked at the chief and raised his hand, but couldn't help agreeing with him.

"I'm trying to! Aren't you listening at all?" Bradford asked forcefully, and Gray rolled his eyes. "The thing is, all my various preoccupations pushed some rather more important thoughts from my head. One such was retrieved by your ridiculous comment that the 'exception proves the rule.' I know you don't believe that," he hastened to add, "and neither do I. That brings us to some rather disturbing thoughts I've had regarding our arrival on this world. We already know we must have been given, or been the victims of, some exception to the rules we knew, because, well, here we are."

"Clearly," Matt said.

"We also now know that exception wasn't necessarily an exception at all."

"Shit, Mr. Bradford—'scuse me, Skipper—but just spit it out. I'm getting an 'exceptional' headache trying to figure you out!" Gray whispered, but Matt shushed him. He thought he knew where Bradford was going.

"Very well," Courtney continued, a little stiffly. "Jenks's ancestors came through a . . . phenomenon much like the one we did. They call it the Passage, and it occurred in relatively close geographic proximity to our Squall. We also agree there may have been other similar such episodes over the centuries. Maybe it happens quite often, in fact, but the transportees are otherwise in smaller, more vulnerable ships with smaller crews, who have no means of protecting themselves in this more hostile world. They either don't survive the event, or are lost before locals like the Lemurians discover them and give them aid. The mysterious fate of the crew of the Tjilatjap transport, *Santa Catalina*, and even the original crew of our own lamented PBY would seem to support that theory. As noted, a few men in a fishing boat would have poor prospects of survival.

"We still don't know what all else might have come through our Squall with *us*. Four ships now, counting the transport, plus a submarine and an airplane—that we know of. Now we learn of this Dominion that controls a portion of the Americas. Princess Rebecca is a dear child, but her history is not up to that of Jenks or Mr. O'Casey. They told me that this Dominion was founded by some bizarre combination of survivors from an 'Acapulco' or 'Manila' galleon and remnants of an even older, possibly pre-Columbian American tribe. I won't go into the details of that twisted union at present, but it was the Acapulco galleon that rang the first warning bell."

"What are you talkin' about?" Gray asked. "What's a 'Aca-poolco galleon'?"

"What I'm talking about is that whatever phenomenon transported us to this world may not be nearly as unique as we first believed. Whatever conditions arise to trigger it might—*might*, I say—also ensure that it is a one-way transfer. I don't begin to understand the mechanics of it yet, but that at least seems certain, since we've never encountered any lumbering Lemurian Homes or mountain fish on *our* world." He paused. "Or maybe *that* is the key!"

Captain Reddy and Chief Gray looked at each other. Evidently,

Courtney was on one of his stream-of-consciousness rolls, and they might as well let it run its course.

"What key?" Matt prodded.

"Metal! As far as we know, only recently—relatively speaking—has any quantity of *metal* been abroad on the oceans of this world! Perhaps large quantities of iron contribute some form of electromagnetic aspect to the phenomenon—or the superior conductivity of the bronze guns, copper fittings . . . precious nonferrous metals of our predecessors. . . . Oh, dear me, Captain, an entirely new avenue of contemplation has opened before me!"

"Well, let's finish our little trip down the avenue you were already on, for now," Gray almost pleaded. "What's Aca-poolco got to do with anything?"

"Oh, dear, I do apologize! Let's see, yes. Only that our little Squall was not unique. Probably not even *regionally* unique! There might well be other human civilizations beyond those we know of scattered about this hostile world. Perhaps many more. Now you understand, of course!"

Finally Matt understood. Bradford was right. The question had been sitting there in front of all of them, but they'd just been too busy to notice it and ask. The possible answer chilled him in spite of the warm day. "Aca-pulco galleons were Spanish treasure ships, Boats," he explained. "They sailed once a year or so to Acapulco from the Spanish Philippines loaded with loot. We studied Commodore Anson's circumnavigation at the Academy. He captured one of the things with a fifty-gun ship—*Centurion*, I think it was—and the loot set most of his crew up for life. At least, that's the story."

"So? I mean, it's a neat story and all, but what good is a bunch of Spanish treasure to us?" Gray still didn't get it.

"None," Matt said. "None I can think of now, anyway." He grinned, but then his expression turned serious again. "The problem is, no Aca-pulco galleon would have ever sailed into the Java Sea. If that's indeed what it was, that means whatever happened to us could've happened in other *places* and not just other times, all over the world. Might happen again. To think otherwise would be expecting an exception to these screwy *new* rules."

"Indeed," Bradford said again. "I would think it's inevitable. Something, some force, connects this world with ours. In the past, our world's oceans were vast, mostly empty places, yet there have been many unexplained disappearances there. Perhaps some of those unfortunates wound up here as well. But right now, on our earth, a global war is under way and the seas are packed with many thousands of modern, quite seaworthy vessels. If my theory is correct, I fear it's just a matter of time before we meet another lost traveler like ourselves, and it could happen anytime, anywhere."

For a long moment there was silence on the bridge. Chief Quartermaster's Mate Norman Kutas at the wheel, who'd clearly heard at least the gist of the conversation, finally broke it. "Well, if we do run into somebody else," he said, "I hope to God they're on our side. We got enough folks mad at us as it is."

Glaring at Kutas, Bradford lowered his voice still further. "There is yet another quite bizarre possibility," he said.

"Oh, no," moaned the Bosun.

Bradford ignored him. "Just as we've discovered beyond any serious possible debate that there are *two* earths, as it were, how can we assume there are not many, *many* more?"

Walker put in briefly at Paga-Daan, long enough only for Matt to go ashore and express his sympathies and for his ship to fill her bunkers from one of the tankers moored there. There were two so far and more on the way. Most would probably take their time, creeping along the archipelago and down the Mindanao coast. Matt couldn't blame their captains, but he wanted to make sure the commanders and crews of the ships already there, that had taken the more dangerous route across the Celebes Sea, were recognized. Bunkers full, *Walker* steamed away before sunset, haze blurring the tops of three funnels.

Churning south-southeast, Matt now had a choice to make. He could continue in Jenks's wake until he caught the Imperial within two or three days at most, or he could lose another day and swing south to Talaud. Irvin Laumer and his crew had been out of touch since the loss of *Simms*, and Talaud was a dangerous place. Once he caught up with Jenks he'd be slowed down, regardless, and they had to be closing the gap on Billingsly. *Achilles* was bigger and faster than *Ajax* and she'd been replenished periodically, allowing her to steam ahead in the face of contrary or indifferent winds. But where could *Ajax* refuel? She might have stopped and cut trees for her boiler on any number of islands, but that would have slowed her even more. Matt doubted Billingsly would have done so initially, but chances were the man considered himself safe from pursuit by now. He knew the Alliance had nothing beyond the Philippines, and *Simms* and the feluccas were the last gauntlet he had to pass. He would be in for a surprise.

But what of Laumer? With the full concurrence of his officers, Matt decided he had to check on the young lieutenant's situation and at least leave him a transmitter. They recrossed the Celebes Sea in the dark of night and a severe rain squall, sonar pounding the depths. It was in these very waters, this bottleneck to the vast Pacific—or Eastern Sea—that *Walker* had once encountered *two* mountain fish in close proximity. The sonar had chased one away and they were pretty sure they'd killed the other one, but there was something about the area apparently, maybe the food-bearing currents, that allowed a higher percentage of the monsters to coexist than usual. In any event, in addition to the sonar, they made the crossing with extra lookouts, keen-eyed Lemurians scanning the sea for basking behemoths under the glare of the searchlights. None were seen.

Dawn revealed Talaud's hazy outline under an oppressive gray sky. Campeti was serving as *Walker's* gunnery officer for the voyage and he had the deck. He knocked quietly on the charthouse hatch and opened it a crack. Matt had taken to sleeping on a cot inside, intent even in sleep on the green flashes that lit the quiet sonarman's scope. He liked to be handy if he was needed, but also, even though the new mattresses they'd made for the ship's crew were comfortable, nobody had gotten around to fixing the fan in his stateroom. It got awfully stuffy in there.

"Captain, you awake?" Campeti asked.

"Sure," Matt said, sitting up. He glanced at the sonarman. A 'Cat was usually in the chair, but Fairchild, *Mahan's* chief sonarman or sound man, had taken the watch for this stretch. "Anything?" he asked.

"Nothing, Skipper. We're going too fast to really tell, but since we're trying to scare stuff off instead of hunting, I guess that's a good thing."

Matt grunted. "What's up, Campeti?"

"Talaud's off the starboard bow. It looks . . . kinda queer."

"I'm on my way."

Staas-Fin, one of Ronson's best electrician's mates, stood behind the big brass wheel and Courtney and Spanky were on the bridge when Matt joined them, putting on his hat. He hadn't shaved. Of all the crew, Matt always tried to keep himself clean-shaven, but that was hard to do, sleeping in the charthouse. He needed to see if Staas-Fin, or "Finny," could fix his fan. Otherwise, he might as well give up and grow a beard like the rest of the men. He wasn't ready to let Juan shave him on the bridge in the captain's chair. "What's up?" he repeated.

Spanky pointed at the island. "Well, it looks a little different, for starters," he said.

"Wow," Matt muttered, agreeing. The quiescent volcanic mountain he remembered had grown significantly since he saw it last and the thick haze either came from it, or was the aftermath of some action on its part. The air had an acrid taste. The top of the mountain was lost to view, but there were occasional flashes of light, either from lightning or maybe even lava arcing into the sky.

"Fascinating!" Bradford exclaimed.

"Yeah. I hope our guys are all right," Matt said.

"Hey," said Spanky, "where're all the damn birds?" On their previous visit the ship had been swarmed with lizard birds and even some real birds that pestered them constantly and defecated all over the ship. Nobody replied. They had no answer.

Just before noon, *Walker* rounded the northeast point of the island and entered the wide lagoon where they'd found the submarine. The sky was even blacker, but the air had cleared with a northerly breeze. At least they could breathe. Anchoring in almost the exact spot as before, they swung out the launch and steered for shore. Matt, Spanky, and the Bosun were accompanied by Stites, Chack, and six Marines. The Marines were the ones Chack thought had gained the most proficiency with their muskets.

At first glance, the camp around the submarine looked deserted. A lot of work had clearly been done and the sub itself actually seemed afloat in a basin on the beach. No smoke rose from the generator engine boiler, however, and as they drew near they could see a literal swarm of what looked like bizarre lobster corpses on the beach.

"What the hell?" Gray murmured. The launch's engine seemed to attract someone's attention, because as the bow nudged against the sand, a figure stood up from behind hasty-looking breastworks.

"Captain Reddy, is that you?" came a cry. The men and 'Cats jumped out of the boat and advanced. Other faces, eyes drooping with fatigue, peered over the breastworks as they approached.

"My God, Lieutenant Laumer?" Matt asked incredulously. The scruffy beard and tattered clothes left the man almost unrecognizable.

"Yes, sir, it's me!" Laumer said, grinning. He looked out at the Lagoon. "*Walker*, sir! There she is! Boy, is she a sight for sore eyes! Looks almost new!"

"What happened here, Lieutenant?" Matt asked, glancing at one of the dead creatures. It did look something like a lobster, although it was skinnier, proportionately, and appeared less heavily armored. The head was different and the leg arrangement looked more like a spider's. The pincers were long and tapered like a scorpion's. Most of the corpses looked like they'd been blown open fairly easily with bullets.

"Well, sir, we've been making decent progress on the boat. She should be ready for sea before long. We put diesel in her tanks and have one engine running. The problem is getting her off the beach. We were going to use *Simms* to dredge a channel, kind of kedge it out, but Captain Lelaa hasn't returned from her mission to intercept Billingsly." He looked down. "I was sorry to hear about . . . what happened at Baalkpan."

"Yes, well, chasing him is our business now. I hate to tell you, but Billingsly and *Ajax* destroyed *Simms* and a felucca commanded by the High Chief of Paga-Daan. Captain Lelaa may have been aboard *Ajax* when it happened, but there were few survivors otherwise. I'm sorry," he added when he saw Laumer's stricken expression.

"But . . ." Irvin straightened. "That leaves us in kind of a tight spot," he said.

"I'll say," said Gray. "What the hell happened here?"

Irvin rubbed his nose. "A few weeks ago, one of these things got in our basin. Killed one of our guys. We killed it, but it wasn't easy. Scary as they look, they're not only quick on their feet, but they can squirt a jet of water like a cannon shot!"

"Indeed?" muttered Bradford, stooping to examine the head of one of the things.

"Yeah. Anyway, we didn't see any more for a while, but then, day before yesterday, the mountain let loose, bigger than it has yet. We had critters coming at us out of the woods and we figured we'd better fort up. Next thing we knew, all these spider-lobsters, or whatever they are, started charging up on the beach. It started slow, just a few at a time, but it kept growing, so we threw up another breastwork here until we had a little fort. Dug like maniacs! We finished just in time, because the next thing we knew, there were dozens, hundreds of the things! Just about shot ourselves dry." He shook his head. "The situation looked pretty bleak without more ammo. The new loads work okay, but they sure foul up a gun. The Thompson completely seized up a couple of times and we had to dump it in water."

Matt took a breath and looked longingly at the submarine. "You've done a great job here, Lieutenant, but I think you should prepare to evacuate. We have some ammunition we could leave with you, but not much more than it would take to drive off another assault like this one. Another supply ship is on its way, but it may not arrive in time to kedge out your channel. This mission has already gone above and beyond what I ever expected of you."

Irvin set his jaw. Later, Matt would realize that he probably hadn't chosen those last words very well. "Sir," Laumer said, "with all respect, I think we've earned the right to finish this job." He looked around at the nods of his crew. "We don't know if the spider-lobsters will even come back. It might have been a onetime deal. Lots of weird stuff going on." He gestured at the mountain. "I think it has something to do with that. The thing is, if it blows its top, we'll never get this boat out of here!"

"If it does that, there won't be enough left of any of you to catch in a butterfly net!" Gray said.

Irvin nodded. "Maybe. But damn it, Captain, we're almost done! All we need is a couple of weeks with a ship, an anchor, and a windlass!"

"And no storms to fill everything you've done in with sand!" Gray added.

"That would be nice," Irvin admitted.

Matt rubbed the stubble on his chin. "Like I told you once, we need that boat, but we need you and your people more. Here's the deal. We'll leave you a transmitter and a receiver. If things get hairy, there'll be no goofing around! You call for help, understand? Paga-Daan can have a fe-lucca here to pick your people up in just a few days. Leave all the equipment. The same goes for when the supply ship arrives. Use it however you need to, but if things get bad, get the hell out, understood?"

Irvin sighed with relief. For a moment, he'd seen failure staring him in the face and only Captain Reddy could have pronounced that sentence upon him. No storm or spider-lobsters or even a volcano was going to stop him, but Captain Reddy could have. He saluted. "Thanks, sir. We *will* succeed!"

Matt was moody as *Walker* steamed out of the lagoon and into the open Pacific. He'd begun to realize the effect his words might have had on Laumer, and even though he hadn't meant to, he'd practically challenged the young lieutenant to stay. He felt like a heel. He got up from his chair and stepped to the chart table. Kutas had marked the spot where they should rendezvous with Jenks, according to the latest position fixes O'Casey sent. One more day, maybe two, and they'd slow their sprint and take station with the Imperial frigate, maintaining visual contact, but sweeping east while covering the widest possible area. Apparently, the Empire had a few settlements in the Marshall Islands, but according to Jenks, they were notoriously independent places. Billingsly would find no haven there. He must be making for one of the main islands of the Hawaiian chain, probably New Ireland, as Jenks referred to it. The island was a Company hotbed and the center of its administration. New Scotland— was the primary naval base, and Hawaii itself was New Britain. None of the islands seemed "right" to Matt, when he'd looked at Jenks's charts. Their shapes were distinctly changed from what he remembered. Most geographic differences they'd discovered so far were subtle, but the "Hawaiian" chain was more radically altered. He wondered why that was.

Walker could just barely make it to Hawaii before her bunkers ran dry, but what then? Matt was counting on the tankers following them to the Marshalls—if their crews didn't chicken out or if mountain fish didn't eat them. Regardless, *Walker* would be stuck there until she could refuel. He didn't know what awaited them in New Britain, but he wasn't going to arrive with empty bunkers. All he and Jenks could hope to do was catch Billingsly somewhere in the wide expanses that separated the Carolines.

"We're coming for you, you son of a bitch!" he muttered under his breath.

"Y

ou may tell Captain Rajendra he can ask to speak to the moon if he likes," Princess Rebecca retorted sharply, "and he will be much more likely to get what he wants than by asking to speak to me!"

"But, Your Highness!" the boy in the passageway whispered urgently, "the captain had no choice! If he had refused the order, he would have been placed under arrest! How then could he assist you and your friends?"

"He is a dispassionate murderer," Rebecca proclaimed. "A stain upon the honor of the Navy and the Empire!"

"Now, hold on just a second," Silva whispered in the darkness. It was almost pitch-black in the brig. They were supposed to be asleep, and no lights were allowed at this time of night. "Rajendra wants us to trust him, does he? How does he mean to make us?"

"What do you mean?"

"I mean *why* should we trust him? We need proof. Real proof, not just a extra piece o' cheese."

"Well . . . what do you want?"

"I want my goddamn guns, but I bet they'd be missed. They keepin' 'em in the armory? The magazine?"

"The aft magazine," replied the boy. "It is the most secure place on the ship. The Marines' arms are stored there as well, with ready ammunition. Besides, your largest gun would not fit in a weapons locker."

"Hmm. You're prob'ly right, at that. Tell you what. I want three things. First, I want a key to this here lock."

"But—"

"Lookie here, you want us to trust him or not? It ain't like we're gonna break out an' run loose all over the ship. I just want a key to where I can get us outta here if the time comes. 'Sides, what if the ship gets ate by one o' them big fish? We'd be stuck in here." That thought actually gave Silva the creeps. Earlier that day, the great guns had opened up, firing furiously for some time. Three full broadsides. At first they thought a battle was under way, until they heard the guns had been used to frighten off a mountain fish.

"Very well. I will see what I can do."

"Next thing I want is our position. Our exact position!"

"Why?"

"Never you mind. If we take to trustin' you, we'll tell you why. One other thing. I want a lantern. A little one so we can look at our map in the dark. It's too hard to go over it in the daytime 'cause you never know when somebody's peekin' in the door at us."

"I have a one-sided lantern in my quarters," said the boy. Dennis knew he was a midshipman or something and he actually did trust him, at least. For one thing, the little guy was clearly terrified of Billingsly.

"That sounds fine, just fine. You do that, and maybe I can talk the princess into speakin' a word or two to Rajendra if he happens to mosey by."

"Thank you, sir!"

"You bet. Now run along before you get caught—but before you go, there's one last, final little thing."

"Sir?"

"I want all that stuff tonight, see?"

"I . . . I will do my best," whispered the boy a little shakily. They heard his quiet footsteps retreat.

Silva turned to the others in the brig. He couldn't really see more than dark shapes in the gloom, but he knew where everyone was. "Good work, li'l sister," he said to Rebecca. "He seemed ready to pee himself. I figger somethin's up and Rajendra thinks he'd better do somethin' before it's too late."

"It does seem that way," Sandra said in a worried tone. "Maybe they think they're safe enough from pursuit that they can get rid of the 'extra' hostages."

"I fear that may be the case," Rebecca said. "Billingsly no longer even pretends to care what I do or where I go. Nor does he seem to think it important to maintain the fiction of my status aboard. He may plan to eliminate more than us."

Silva doubted Billingsly was through with Rebecca yet, but she might be right about the rest. "Cap'n Lelaa?" he asked.

"Rajendra is a murderer," she said miserably. She'd been badly traumatized by the destruction of her ship, and for quite a while, all she'd

done was lie curled in a ball in a corner of the cell. Finally, however, she'd
begun to take some interest in their situation. She was a naval officer and
she couldn't indulge in self-pity forever. Silva was glad she was snapping
out of it. When things hit the fan, they were going to have to move fast. He
knew Sandra, Rebecca, and Lawrence had plenty of guts, but though he
didn't dislike her, he considered Sister Audry a deadweight. He didn't
need another one to worry about when the time came.

"Yeah, I guess he's a murderer," Silva said, "but so am I, by most
lights. If the kid's right, he did what he *thought* he had to so's to stay where
he might help Rebecca. I'm not plumb sure that *is* what he had to do, but
I'll give him the doubt for now, 'cause I wadn't there. Somebody else
mighta just blown your ship to hell if he didn't, an' then where'd we be?
He *did* give us a map, even if it's kind of crummy."

They'd spent many days explaining maps to Lawrence, describing them
as pictures of the world from high in the sky, as if drawn by some bird that
could fly higher than the eye could see. It finally began to sink in, and then
they showed him places they'd been: Talaud, the Philippines, even as far
west as Baalkpan, though the map was so out-of-date in that respect as to be
almost useless. Between Lawrence and Rebecca's imperfect memory of how
long and in which directions they'd drifted in her boat with O'Casey, they
pieced together which island or atoll they thought they'd found Lawrence
on in the first place. Finally, from that, Lawrence was able to pinpoint
roughly where he thought his home island was. "There is no land called
Tagran on the chart, though," he'd accused, "and I ne'er saw it fro' the sky. I
think it is this, though," he'd decided, pointing at a rough rendition of what
Silva thought was Yap Island. He'd never been there, but he'd seen plenty of
charts and the screwy name had always stuck with him.

"Okay, I hope you're right," Silva had replied. "So long as they don't
eat us."

Lawrence had glared at him and hissed. "They'll take care o' all o' us.
La'rence 'riends their 'riends! You all heroes, ring La'rence to Tagran Island land," he'd said.

It wasn't much, but it was a chance. An escape attempt to Talaud or
even Mindanao would have been their best bet, but Abel had still been
weak, and tension before and after *Ajax*'s confrontation with Lelaa's ships
had made any attempt then impossible. Now that Billingsly knew there
were no other Allied outposts, security surrounding them had grown lax.
They were down to only two choices: they could stay aboard and risk
whatever fate Billingsly had in store for them, or they could try to get off
the ship and hope Lawrence's Grik-like people would take them in.

For some reason, Silva didn't seem particularly concerned with the
mechanics of escape. He apparently thought Rajendra could be trusted,

for selfish reasons at least, and believed his assistance might be handy, if not necessarily essential. Evidently, he didn't even think he needed the key he'd asked for. He'd probably just thrown in the request as a further test of Rajendra. Ever since he started feeling more like himself, he'd given the impression that escape was just a matter of Sandra deciding when. According to the map, their approximate speed and position, and Lawrence's best estimate regarding which island was his home, "when" would have to be the following night. That was when *Ajax* would pass most closely to the island where he thought his people dwelt.

Their discussion was interrupted by more footsteps in the passageway, followed by a quiet voice at the door. "Your Highness, it is I, Captain Rajendra. Midshipman Brassey is here as well. He says you might speak with me. I tell you it is of the utmost importance that you do. All our lives are at risk."

"What of the lives of Captain Lelaa's crew?" Rebecca hissed.

"I could not stop that!" Rajendra insisted. "I had hoped you would understand!"

So it was as Brassey said and Silva had speculated. There was no doubting the torment and sincerity in Rajendra's tone. Either he was telling the truth or he'd missed his calling as a stage performer. Silva still thought there was one way Rajendra might have prevailed, but there was little point in bringing that up now. "Did you bring the stuff we asked for?" he asked instead.

"Yes. I will open the door and pass them through. . . . Please make no attempt at the moment; I would prefer to help coordinate an escape by being elsewhere when it begins!"

There was a tiny clack as the tumbler in the lock disengaged and the door opened a fraction. A hooded lantern, already lit, preceded a piece of paper with some numbers written on it. Finally, Silva felt the large brass key pressed into his hand.

"Well, you done what we asked," Dennis said, announcing the key transfer. "Whaddaya say, li'l sister?"

"I will trust him," Rebecca replied. "Captain Lelaa?"

"I suppose we have no choice," she said ominously. "For now. But if there is further treachery of any kind—"

"Hush now," said Silva, and his tone hardened. "That goes without even sayin'!" He paused. "Loo-tenant Tucker?"

Sandra cleared her throat. "Tomorrow night, Captain Rajendra, providing the position you gave us corresponds with our calculations, we'll be leaving your ship one way or another. If you can facilitate our escape, it would be appreciated."

"Tomorrow night should work well," Rajendra agreed. "Much later than that might be too late." So. Rebecca was right. "This is what I have done, and can do. You may incorporate as much of it into your plans as you see fit. The carpenter has repaired the launch Mr. Silva shot such a gaping hole through. Tomorrow, I shall have it swung out to tow, to swell the wood. I would prefer the pinnace because it is larger and will carry more, but I have no excuse to put it in the water."

"Sounds fine, but why would we need room for more?" Sandra asked.

"Midshipman Brassey has overheard a certain conversation," Rajendra said stiffly. "Most of you are to be hanged for abducting the princess and holding her against her will. My loyal officers and myself will then be hanged for committing a crime against humanity when we fired on Captain Lelaa's ship without warning." Rajendra's voice was full of irony. "Clearly both are legal fictions concocted by Billingsly to eliminate any story but his own should things at home be different than he suspects, but there it is. Some of us will be coming with you."

"Why not just rise up, take back your ship from these Company bastards?" Sandra asked. "We would help!"

"Impossible. I count perhaps seventy loyalists among my crew, opposed by two hundred. It would be a bloodbath and would ultimately fail."

"There've been longer odds," Silva prodded.

"True, but how could we coordinate any effort? I need be wrong about only one of the seventy and our plans will be undone." He shook his head in the darkness. "I cannot let those who are loyal die to no purpose."

"Okay," Sandra said, "we've got a boat and a few extra passengers. We'll need provisions, a compass, sextant, weapons . . . and a means of getting to the boat in the first place."

"The carpenter is one of us. Provisions and navigational aids have already been stowed in the boat," said Brassey. "If a 'sextant' is like a 'quadrant,' that has been included as well. As soon as night falls, I shall bring sufficient ship's clothing to disguise you all." He cleared his throat. "More care than usual must be taken with Captain Lelaa and, uh, Mr. . . . Lawrence, I presume." Lelaa bristled, but knew it was true. What would they do? Tie her tail around her body?

"Otherwise," Rajendra said, "I will adjust the watch so we will have the greatest number of known loyalists on deck as possible. They will sway out an anchor beneath the bowsprit and allow it to fall back against the hull as though we have struck a leviathan. Action stations will be sounded and we should find our chance in the general confusion."

"Silva?" Sandra asked.

"Not bad," he answered, somewhat distracted. He was mentally adjusting certain elements of his own plan to fit. "Sometimes it's better to do sneaky stuff right out in the open. Slinkin' around in the dark always *looks* sneaky." He spoke in Sister Audry's direction: "Guess you'll have to ditch the nun suit!"

"I will not!"

"Well, you'll have to cover it up somehow, or stash it in something." He turned back toward their visitors. "As for weapons"—he found Brassey's form in the gloom—"I figger the boy an' me an' maybe a few other hands can take care o' that. I want my guns back!"

"Very well," Rajendra said, sounding a little unnerved by something in Silva's tone. "Shall we regard the blow against the bow as our signal to begin, then?"

"I suppose that would be best," Sandra said. "But we must move quickly after that. Where will we gather?"

"On the starboard quarter. The first thing that will happen is that the engine will stop and steam will vent. It will be noisy and add to the confusion. The boat will already have been drawn alongside and each will go over as they arrive. I and some other officers will provide security there by sending anyone whose loyalty is unknown to perform some task or other."

"Sounds swell then," Silva said. "You do your part and we'll do ours. Okay with you, li'l sister?"

"Swell," Rebecca replied.

"Um, there is one other thing," Rajendra said. "Our destination. After we escape, assuming we do, where are we going? Our lives are as much at risk in this venture as yours and it is a terrible sea. You have determined a safe landfall, have you not?"

"Yes," Sandra said, but offered nothing more.

After an expectant but disappointed pause, Rajendra straightened. "Well. Then I suppose we must all trust one another."

"Guess so," Lawrence answered in his distinctive voice.

Late the following night, during first watch, according to Silva, they felt a distinct and surprisingly violent blow strike the ship. Already dressed as Imperial crewmen, with both Lelaa's and Lawrence's tails secured as well as possible (far more difficult in Lawrence's case, and he could hardly walk), they began their escape by evacuating the compartment that had been their prison for weeks. Quickly, they scrambled or shuffled down the corridor, Rebecca and Sister Audry helping Lawrence. Lawrence had a nightcap pulled down over his face, but it was so misshapen the disguise wouldn't stand close scrutiny at all. Lelaa might pass as a ship's boy in the dark, but, of course, neither she nor any other female must speak. Other forms began appearing in the corridor, but Silva burst through them shouting, "Gangway!" in a terrible accent. About then, the alarm bells began to ring, and if anyone noticed the strange, hurrying group in the dark, their attention was quickly diverted.

Up a companionway they lurched, now heading aft across the gun deck as *Ajax*'s crew began assembling at their action stations. Most were confused, barely awake. A few had felt or heard the bump and there was a cacophony of wild, almost panicky speculation. Silva grunted with frustration and suddenly swept poor Lawrence up in his arms. The Tagranesi was slowing them down and Dennis thought he'd draw less attention if he appeared to be injured. There were a few lanterns on the gun deck, but only enough for fighting light—enough that the gun's crews could serve their pieces, but not enough to damage their night vision a great deal, or provide much fuel for a fire. Again, if anyone had begun to grow suspicious of them as they made their way through the building, only slightly controlled chaos, the sudden roar of venting steam distracted them. Reaching the quarterdeck companionway, they ascended and rushed to the starboard rail, where several men were heaving on a line. "Get that boat in, afore somethin' eats it!" one shouted. "I didn' spend two days fixin' it ta pre-vide a toothpick fer one o' them divils!" Clearly the carpenter.

"No, damn your vitals!" Rajendra's voice rose toward another group. "Get you and your party down in the forepeak! Check for sprung timbers! We'll be taking water after a thump like that, I shouldn't wonder!" He raised his speaking trumpet. "Run out the guns! Handsomely now! We must fire before the monster returns!" Another man, burly and dark, approached the captain. "The safety valve has suffered a mischief, I fear," he said in a satisfied tone. "There's no fixin' it either, more's the pity. She'll vent steam till the boiler's cold enough to replace the valve!"

Rajendra glanced about. "Very well. Into the boat with our guests! It will add to the confusion if our engineer cannot be found!"

"Aye, Captain!" The man rushed to the rail. "Over the side with ye, Yer Highness!" he said. "There's a man waitin' below ta catch ye!"

"But what of Lawrence?"

"I can 'anage!" Lawrence said. "As soon as this huge creature puts La'rence down!"

"Dee-lighted, you ungrateful little turd," Dennis said. "Snatch onto that line. You can turn your tail loose in the boat! Maybe you'll be good fer somethin' then." He looked at Rebecca. "After you, li'l sister!"

With only the slightest hesitation, perhaps reliving old memories, the far different person who'd become Princess Rebecca grasped the rope and disappeared into the darkness below. Lawrence went next.

"Now you, Sister Audry!" Dennis ordered, after the engineer disappeared.

"I . . . I'm not sure I can!"

"Sure, you can. It's a cinch. Besides, if you don't go, I'll just drop you over the side and hope you land in the boat."

Audry looked at him, utterly uncertain whether he was serious or not. He'd spoken with the flat firmness of fact. "Very well, *Mr.* Silva," she said sharply.

"Prepare to fire!" Rajendra roared.

"You're next, Loo-tenant Tucker!"

"No. You must get weapons. Where's Midshipman Brassey?"

"Here, ma'am!"

"Good. Lead Mr. Silva to the magazine. Take two of these other men. We need weapons and ammunition! We'll pass well enough up here for now, Mr. Cook and I."

Silva knew she meant to guard against treachery. He wasn't sure how she'd do that, but he also knew it would be pointless and time-consuming to argue with her. "All right, Miss Tucker, we'll be back in a flash!" He turned to Brassey and two of the men who'd been hauling the rope. "C'mon!"

"Fire!" bellowed Rajendra. With a stuttering, rolling, earsplitting bark of thunder, *Ajax* vomited an uneven broadside port and starboard. Silva and his pickup team of commandos vanished in the swirling smoke.

"Follow me," Brassey cried. As he'd explained, *Ajax* had two magazines. The one they sought was aft, beneath the orlop and essentially below the waterline, which afforded it some protection from enemy shot. They met a steady stream of grim-faced, sweaty boys hurrying back to the guns, charges in their pass boxes. Reaching the magazine, they found it virtually deserted, the powder boys having already come and gone. The first compartment had a lantern illuminating racks of muskets. Silva was surprised and joyful to see the Doom Whomper secured at the far end of one rack along with his shooting pouch and belt. From the belt still hung his holster, magazine pouches, cutlass, and '03 bayonet in its scabbard. The bayonet was a respectable "sword" in its own right.

"Hot damn!" he hissed, wrapping the belt around his waist and clipping it in place. He then grabbed his massive rifle. He could see movement in an adjoining compartment through a thick pane of wavy glass. The gunner and his mates, most likely, preparing charge bags.

"Whose side's the gunner on?" Silva asked.

"I don't know," Brassey confessed.

"Okay. You fellas get a double armload o' them muskets and some cartridge boxes. Anything in 'em?"

"There should be a battle load of forty rounds apiece," one of the men supplied. "The door is usually locked and guarded."

"Huh. Well, gather all you can carry and take 'em up." He grinned. "If anybody asks, say it's Billingsly's orders!" While the men did as he said, Silva turned to Brassey. "Loose shot and powder? How 'bout musket flints?"

Brassey pointed. "Those small kegs hold balls and flints, but powder will be in there," he said, referring to the space where the gunner was.

Silva nodded. Taking off the Imperial ordinary seaman's striped shirt, he quickly knotted the sleeves and dropped two thirty-pound kegs of shot and a single keg of flints into it. Tying it all together, he handed it to Brassey, who staggered under the weight. "You handle that?"

"I'll manage," said the youngster.

Seeing the other men festooned with muskets, cartridge boxes, and a few baldrics with cutlasses and bayonets, Silva sent the group on its way. "I'll get powder," he said, shooing them off.

Another shattering broadside shook the ship. Any minute now, the compartment would fill with powder boys again. *Hmm.* Backing out of the magazine, he slipped into a compartment across the passageway, leaving the door open a crack so he could see. He smelled something pungent and glanced behind. "Well, well," he muttered. "Rum, by God!" One of the short, thick black glass bottles must have cracked and soaked the padding around it. There was a sack hanging on a hook and he filled it with the bottles, leaving two aside. Pulling the cork on one, he took a long swig. "Ghaaa!" he hissed appreciatively. Not great, but not bad. He wondered what they used for sugar? Lowering the bottle, he took a length of light line that had probably once bound the padding together and stuck one end into the bottle. Then he wrapped it around the open mouth and tied it. Nothing to do now but wait.

Soon, the boys had all apparently come and gone and he slipped back across the passageway. He held both bottles by their necks between the fingers of his left hand, and drew the cutlass with his right. Anyone who saw the cutlass would know *it* didn't belong. It was longer, straighter—and much better—than anything like it on the ship. He shrugged. Time to do his thing. He'd behaved himself long enough.

"Open up!" Silva growled at the inner door. A short man with spectacles and the almost universal Imperial mustache opened the heavy door and peered out. Silva drove the cutlass into his chest and pushed his way inside. Without a sound, the man slid off the blade and onto the deck when Silva lowered the cutlass and regarded the other man. He was bigger and might require more exercise.

He screamed shrilly.

So much for first impressions, Silva thought, and pinned the man to the bulkhead. The gunner, or mate—whichever he was—screamed even louder.

"Well, shit!" Dennis hissed indignantly, skewering the man again. "I've seen *bunnies* make manlier noises when a dog gets 'em by the ass!" Still sobbing, but mortally wounded, the big man fell to the deck when Silva freed the blade.

Quickly, he laid the cutlass on the gunner's table and hung the rope and rum bottle from a hook on the beam overhead. Snatching up a fifty-pound keg of powder, he hurried to place it in the passageway. He knew he was running out of time. Imperial drill for deterring mountain fish seemed to be three broadsides, and the next would fire any minute. He didn't know what would happen after that. He doubted the powder boys would return the pass boxes to the magazine—there was limited space inside, after all—but *somebody* was liable to come down. He ran back inside, picked up another barrel of powder, and smashed it against the deck.

"I thought I might find you here," came a voice from the armory compartment.

Silva looked up. "Well, how do, Mr. Truelove," he said. "For some reason, I thought you might too." He nodded at the pistol held casually in Truelove's hand. "You gonna shoot that in here?"

Truelove grimaced at the pistol and slid it on his belt, where it hung by a hook. "I don't suppose I really need it. I'm actually quite good with a sword. I've seen you use one, you know, at Baalkpan, before I gave you that little tap on the head. You fight quite . . . dynamically and enthusiastically . . . but your sword work is just that: work. To me, it is play."

"Why'd you conk me then?"

Truelove shrugged. "Unsportsmanlike, I know, but necessary at the time. Perhaps now we might meet each other properly?"

"Sure. Just a couple o' questions first. 'Twixt gentlemen."

Truelove nodded. "Of course. Adversaries should know each other at times like this, and I already know a good deal about you."

"How *did* you know I'd be here?"

"Oh, I don't know. Call it intuition. You *are* a resourceful man. I thought it likely you might take advantage of the situation facing the ship. I don't know what you hope to accomplish, but I've no doubt you have a plan. I almost regret thwarting you. I view you as a fellow professional in a way, and suspect I would have enjoyed seeing your plan unfold."

So, thought Silva, *he's here on a whim. Everything else might still be going swell.* He had no doubt Truelove was better with a sword, since Silva had no proper training at all. A real fight wouldn't do, and besides, it might take too long and draw too much attention. A moment earlier he'd been in a rush. Now he needed to stall. "Why Billingsly?" he asked conversationally. "A fella like you'd go just as far on the right side, I figger."

Truelove laughed. "Well, let us just say that I had gone quite as far as I could in His Majesty's Secret Service, and I like money. Yes, indeed." He nodded at Silva's cutlass and reached for his sword. "Shall we be about it then?"

"Sure, but there's just one thing you may not know about me," Silva said, shaking his head with a conspiratorial grin and a prolonged display of being a man with a great secret.

"Oh?"

The third broadside erupted, jarring the ship and making the lantern in the adjoining compartment jump. Silva launched himself like a torpedo and struck Truelove in the chest with his head before the man could clear his blade. They sprawled together in the armory compartment, and quicker than his opponent could recover, Silva's mighty fists were already slamming into his face like pile drivers. Truelove was still trying to free his sword, but with six inches of the blade free, Dennis paused long enough to grasp the man's hand in his and wrench it to the side, breaking several of Truelove's fingers against the guard and snapping the blade off at the top of the scabbard. He pitched the twisted guard in among the musket stocks. The last thing Truelove might have heard before darkness took him was Silva's final, gasping explanation: "Sometimes I can be a little unsportsmanlike too."

For the moment, Truelove was out. Sore from his leap, Silva struggled to his feet and dragged the heavy, limp form into the magazine. Tearing off a piece of wadding made of something he didn't recognize, he stuffed it into Truelove's mouth and propped him against a heavy upright beam. Finding a spool of slow match, he fiercely tied the man's head to the post, across the gag, then proceeded to secure him quickly and professionally against any attempt to escape. Tearing away a piece of Truelove's shirt, he lit it from the lantern and carefully lit the rum-soaked cord that held the bottle suspended. He had no idea how long the cord would hold, five minutes or half an hour, but he needed to be *gone*.

As he fled the armory, as an afterthought he snatched Truelove's pistol from where it had fallen from his belt, then shut the outer door and locked it with his heavy brass key. He'd taken a chance the same key would work, but he'd expected it would. He knocked the top off the second rum bottle and liberally doused the passageway on both sides of the magazine, taking pains not to spill any right in front of it. Finally, he slung his big rifle and hoisted the keg of powder onto his shoulder. He lit another piece of Truelove's shirt from the lantern in the passageway and pitched it onto the far splash of rum. It lit with surprising fervency. Beyond the sudden flame, he saw a boy's panicked face appear and then quickly vanish, yelling, "Fire!" *Oh, well.* Dropping the lantern on the nearest splash, he hoisted his sack of rum bottles with a clinking sound and dashed up the companionway.

Things on the gun deck had calmed significantly when the leviathan they'd apparently struck failed to reappear. He even caught a snatch of a rumor that the starboard anchor had been discovered hanging in the sea. Maybe it was all just a false alarm. Silva paid no heed. His old maxim of doing sneaky stuff right out in the open seemed to be holding up. If a guy with a strange-looking gun came running by with a keg on one shoulder and a canvas sack on the other . . . he must have a good reason—or whoever had ordered him to did. Cries of "Fire!" began to increase, further distracting the crew. The alarm bell was sounding again when Silva reached the quarterdeck—and saw Billingsly pointing a pistol at Sandra, Rajendra, and Cook.

He was dressed in a probably stylish robe, with clashing colors and frills, and stood in stocking feet. He must have finally emerged from his spacious cabin to investigate all the commotion. Like Truelove, perhaps he suspected something and armed himself. Or maybe he was just paranoid. Regardless, there he stood with his long pistol aimed at Sandra. Again. He was shouting for guards, Marines—anyone—but no one could hear him over the alarm bell, the renewed uproar, and the still-venting steam. He didn't hear Silva either, when the big man stepped up behind him and laid him flat with the sack of rum bottles. To Silva, the wild pistol shot was only slightly more alarming than the mournful crash and tinkle of an unknown number of the little prizes in the sack.

"Silva!" cried Sandra. "Thank God! I don't know whether to yell at you for taking so long, or hug you for showing up when you did!"

He flashed a grin. "A hug'll do, but later! We'd better scram! Over the side with you!" He ran to the rail. "Here, somebody strong'd better catch this!" he said, and tossed the powder barrel at the boat. Next went his sack, and he heard someone cry out when they must have found some broken glass. Sandra and Abel were sliding down the rope.

"You next, Mr. Silva!" Captain Rajendra said. "I must be last to leave my ship!"

"I know that sounds all noble an' shit, but not this time," Silva replied. He nodded at a group of men approaching, cutlasses out. Billingsly was beginning to revive as well. "I can handle 'em a lot quicker than you." Rajendra hesitated; then, with a nod, he left Dennis Silva alone on *Ajax*'s quarterdeck. Almost nonchalantly, Silva popped open the holster flap and drew his beloved 1911 Colt. He'd considered it—and all his weapons—as much a hostage as the rest of them. There was a magazine in the well, but if he remembered, he'd emptied it. Besides, the weight was wrong. Depressing the magazine release with his thumb, the—sure enough—empty magazine clattered on the deck at his feet.

"Stop him, you fools!" Billingsly screamed at the swordsmen. "That is a *repeating* pistol of some sort!" The crewmen hesitated. A few more scampered up the stairs; one was an officer. "Kill that man this instant!" Billingsly shrieked.

Silva fished another magazine out of a pouch on his belt, inserted it, and racked the slide. "Too late," he said, and shot the officer. A large red hole appeared on the white jacket, exactly in the center of his chest, and he toppled backward onto the gun deck. Methodically, he then shot the three closest men and they sprawled on the deck around Billingsly. The other crew, who'd arrived with the officer, fled into the waist. Silva pointed the Colt at the Company warden and grinned hugely, his single eye gleaming. Smoke was beginning to coil up out of the ship and there was a growing panic.

"Well, *Mr.* Billingsly! Just you an' me!" He gestured with the pistol. "'S a wonder you didn't fiddle around with this thing, learn how it works. A fella like you coulda used it—at a time like this!" He laughed.

"Just do it!" Billingsly shouted. "Do you mean to mock me to death? Shoot! I *swear* I will kill you and all your pathetic friends! I'll *hang* that precious princess of yours, damn you!"

Silva's grin vanished and something akin to . . . regret crossed his face. "I already *have* killed you, you stupid, measly son of a goat! And at least you *deserve* killin'. You know, I was kinda groggy at the time, but seems I remember ol' Spanky yellin' somethin' about you not knowin' who you was monkeyin' with." He shrugged. "Now you do."

With that, Silva slid down the rope to the waiting boat below. "Cast off!" he said. "Out oars! Get us the hell outta here!"

"They'll fire on us!" Brassey shouted.

"No, they won't. Row."

Rajendra gave Silva a strange look. "Do as he says. All together!"

"I want this ship turned in pursuit of that boat this instant!" Billingsly shouted.

"There's no steam!" returned *Ajax*'s first lieutenant. "Someone has wrecked the emergency valve! We'll have to let the boiler go completely cold before we can fix it!"

"Then make sail! I want that boat! Where's Truelove? Has anyone seen him?"

"No, sir. We have almost extinguished the fire in the orlop passageway. It is very strange. The fire was deliberately set, but also set in such a way as to make it difficult for us to reach the magazine! With all those flames that close . . . it makes me shudder to think!"

Billingsly's eyes went wide. "Has anyone inspected the magazine yet?"

"No, sir. It is locked, would you believe it? Locked!"

"Quickly! Who has a key?"

The executive officer was taken aback, both by the line of questioning and by Billingsly's intensity. "Why, Captain Rajendra, that traitor, would have one."

"Who else?"

"Only the master gunner."

Billingsly covered his face with his hand. "Get axes! Every man who will fit in that passageway this instant, with axes! You must chop a way into the magazine! There isn't an instant to lose!"

The officer raced off and Billingsly turned to face in the direction the boat had pulled away. It was invisible in the darkness, but he knew they would be watching. Probably that fool Rajendra had no idea, but Silva would be watching . . . and waiting. As he'd said, Billingsly was a man with few regrets, but one nagging little minor regret—letting the hostages live as long as he had—suddenly lunged to the very top of his list.

Truelove managed to open one eye but the other was swollen shut. For several moments he couldn't figure out where he was, why he was there, or why he was so uncomfortable. Slowly it all returned to him. *Unsportsmanlike!* He would have chuckled if he didn't hurt so badly and if something painfully large and well secured wasn't stuffed in his mouth. He'd been in the business long enough to appreciate the work of a professional, even at his own expense. Sometimes, given the nature of that brilliant fool Billingsly and the treacherous cause they served, Truelove couldn't help but appreciate a fellow professional, *especially* when it came at his expense. He'd been at it too long and he'd grown jaded. He *did* like the money, but his heart just wasn't much in it anymore. Another thought would have made him laugh. He'd told his adversary his swordsmanship was work while Truelove's own was play. It suddenly occurred to him that, though that may be true, Silva's . . . "professionalism" was still play, while his own had become work. Such irony.

He could barely move his head, but with his one good eye, he gazed around the compartment. Two dead men. A lot of blood. Wait! He was back in the magazine itself! There were no muskets, just barrels of powder secured all around. *If I'm in the magazine, where is that flickering light coming from?* He looked up, but couldn't quite see. After much wriggling, he managed to force his head back just far enough.

Oh, bravo! he said to himself as the charred rope parted and the burning rum bottle dropped.

The current ran swiftly here and the men and women in the launch had rowed for their lives. All knew *Ajax* might turn at any moment and chase them down, but a couple of those on the boat suspected there might be further reason for gaining distance while they could. *Ajax*'s own momentum and the prevailing wind kept her pointed east, while the current carried the launch and its occupants west-northwest. Therefore, they'd gained almost two miles' distance from the ship when the night suddenly lit with a blinding flash that drew all their stares.

The entire aft half of *Ajax* erupted amid a yellow-red ball of fire, scattering masts, beams, yards, timbers, shards of burning rope and drifting canvas far across the sea. There was little steam left in her boiler, but a great steamy plume shot skyward when seawater touched the hot iron. Another similar blast demolished the forward part of the ship when the other magazine went. The bowsprit was launched entirely out of view like an enormous javelin. *Ajax*'s death took only seconds, but to those in the distant boat, it seemed to last much longer. The rolling, staccato, thunderous punch of the blast finally reached them with a physical jolt, and for what felt like whole minutes, flaming debris, blocks, an entire gun and carriage, bodies—or parts of bodies—rained down to splash amid the already vanishing flames.

"My ship," murmured Rajendra.

"My God, Silva, what have you done?" Sandra whispered.

Dennis stood up in the boat and glared around at the dozen or so survivors. "Why is it ever' time somethin' like this happens, it's 'Lawsy me, what's ol' Silva done now'? I'm sick an' tired of it, hear! Might give a fella the benefit o' the doubt now an' again!"

"Did you . . . do something . . . that might have destroyed that ship?" Rebecca asked quietly.

Dennis looked harshly at her for a moment, then glanced at his feet. "Well . . . what if I did? What were we gonna do? *Row* off from 'em? That wadn't ever gonna work, not after Rajendra and his bunch decided they wanted to come with us! Sneakin' off ourselves was one thing. They wouldn'ta noticed us gone till they came to feed us the next day, and we woulda had a lot of ocean to hide in." He glared at the men from *Ajax* again. "A ship's captain, engineer, carpenter—an' who knows what else—disappear in the middle of a distraction like was necessary to get so many off, somebody's gonna take notice! Somebody *did!*"

Rajendra stood too, slightly jostling the boat. "You . . . murdering filth! You *murder* my ship and all her crew and then have the nerve to say you did it because of *us*? Because we came with you? How would you have escaped without our help—without the help of some of the men you killed this night who had to stay behind?"

"It wasn't *your* ship no more, genius!" Silva bellowed. He was fed up. "You were in the same fix we were. Don't you *dare* stand there an' act all sancti-fidious at *me* when you wouldn't even rear up on your hind legs an' *try* to take your ship back! When *you* blew Cap'n Lelaa's ship outa the water with all *her* people on it! You coulda saved your ship then, if you'd pulled your pistol an' shot Billingsly square betwixt the eyes! That prob'ly woulda been the end of it right there, because whatever else you are, or your crew was, you were the *goddamn captain*! Instead, you said, 'Yes, sir! You're the boss!' an' killed two hundred of *our* folks! Then you slunk around whinin' how it wadn't your fault!"

Silva looked at Sandra, knowing she, at least, would believe his next words. "I had me a little plan to get us off the ship. Mighta worked. We mighta got off without killin' hardly anybody"—he shrugged—"or I mighta still blown up your ship. That was always plan B. When I heard your plan, I figgered it 'ud be easier—an' safer—for *us* an' the *princess*. But only if I dusted off plan B an' made it part o' plan A! Well, the plans worked, yours an' mine, an' here we are. I'm sorry if I killed some good fellas, but I ain't *that* damn sorry." He pointed at the pistol on Rajendra's belt. "You can try to shoot me now, an' maybe that'll prove you ain't as yellow as I think you are, but I'll kill you an' you'll just be dead instead o' helpin' out now, when your princess needs you. Or you can prove you weren't never yellow at all—just confused an' a little scared, in a fix you hadn't come upon before. I've heard that happens to folks. You can prove that by bein' a good captain for what's left of your crew, an' by helpin' Larry an' Captain Lelaa—if she'll have you—navigate our way to the boosum o' Larry's lovin' home."

Slowly, Rajendra sat. Some of what Silva had said must have struck a chord, because he lowered his eyes and then stared at the few distant flickering fires that marked the grave of his ship and crew. His expression was desolate. "Who is to be in charge, then?" he finally asked, controlling his voice.

"Lieutenant—rather, Minister—Tucker," Princess Rebecca said in a tone that brooked no argument. "Now that we're all on the same side, she is the highest-ranking official present, myself excluded. If you prefer, you may consider her as my proxy, but you *will* obey her."

"What about *him*?" asked the engineer, referring to Silva.

"As has been most . . . eloquently . . . presented, if Mr. Silva is to be arrested, I must have Captain Rajendra arrested as well. What purpose would that serve? Mr. Silva will retain his position as my chief armsman and personal protector—provided he at least consults me before destroying any more of His Majesty's property."

Dennis looked at the girl. He'd more than half expected her to despise him for what he'd done, and the relief he felt was indescribable.

"Well," he said, a bit huskily, "I'll sure try."

Sandra took a deep breath. "All right, let's get on with it. Captain Lelaa, you have the helm. Lawrence, assist her with the compass, if you please. Captain Rajendra? I assume this vessel has a sail?"

"Report from the crow's nest, Captain," Reynolds said. "Sail on the horizon, bearing zero one zero."

"Very well. Helm, make your course zero one zero, if you please," Matt ordered. He raised his binoculars.

"Making my course see-ro one see-ro, ay!" replied Staas-Fin at the wheel.

"Uh, Skipper?" Reynolds continued. "Wouldn't this be a good time to put my plane in the water and let me fly over there and have a look?"

Matt restrained the grin that tried to form. Reynolds took his new calling as a naval aviator very seriously, and by all accounts he was a good pilot. He and his small flight and maintenance crew cared for the Nancy meticulously. They'd even worked out a number of the problems associated with stowing, rigging out and recovering the plane, and protecting it from the elements. They still hadn't had a chance to actually fly the thing yet, and partially that was due to the time it required to launch and recover the aircraft. Mostly, Matt admitted to himself, he personally didn't want to risk the valuable, fragile resource the plane represented, or the young, excitable, but steady ensign he'd grown so fond of. So far, in addition to his Special Air Detail duties, Reynolds had been stuck in his old job as bridge talker, for the most part. He was starting to feel a little put-upon and it showed.

"Not just yet, Ensign. The sea's got a little chop to it. Besides, I expect that'll be *Achilles*, based on our position. If we spot anything on the horizon we're slightly less sure of, you can risk your crazy neck in that goofy contraption then."

"Aye-aye, Captain," Fred replied, a little wistfully.

The sail was indeed *Achilles*, and they easily overhauled her at twenty knots by early afternoon. Both ships flew their recognition numbers as they approached, even though each captain would have known the other's ship anywhere. It was a procedure they'd agreed on in advance among themselves—just in case. *Walker* slowed to match *Achilles'* nine knots. It was a respectable pace, considering the wind and the drag of the freewheeling paddles. Jenks was undoubtedly conserving fuel, and running the engine wouldn't have given him a dramatic speed increase in any event. Matt recognized his counterpart standing on the elevated conning platform amidships, between the paddle boxes. Stepping onto the port bridge wing, he raised his speaking trumpet.

"It's good to see you, *Achilles*!" he shouted, his voice crossing the distance between the ships with a tinny aspect.

"You cut a fine figure, Captain Reddy," Jenks replied. "Your beautiful ship is quite the rage aboard here! To have you so effortlessly come streaking alongside within an hour of sighting you has been a marvelous sight to behold, while we here labor along and toil for every knot! I must protest your choice of such a drab color for such an elegant lady, however! Gray, for heaven's sake! And I do fear I perceive a streak or two of rust! Clearly you've had a difficult passage!"

Matt laughed. He couldn't help it. For the first time, perhaps, he caught himself *liking* Jenks.

"Rust, he says!" the Bosun bawled on the fo'c'sle. "Did you hear that, you shif' less pack o' malingerers? If there's a *speck* of rust anywhere on this ship, I want it chipped and painted if you have to hang over the side by your useless *tails!*"

Lord, thought Matt yet again, *in spite of* everything, *some things never change. Thank God*. Of course, in his own way the Bosun was a genius. The man was a hero to the crew—to the entire Alliance—and even "Super Bosun" was an inadequate title. He had the moral authority of a thundering, wrathful God, and his increasing harangues were probably carefully calculated to keep the Lemurian crew from dwelling on the now obvious fact that they'd steamed beyond where any of their kind had ever traveled. Possibly only two things kept the more nervous 'Cats diligently at their duty: the persistent and familiar sense of normal gravity that proved they weren't about to *fall* off the world, and the absolute certainty the Bosun would contrive to *throw* them off if he ever caught them cringing in their racks.

"Maybe we should steam in company for the day and through the night," Matt shouted across. "Then spread out tomorrow. In the meantime, I'd be honored if you and your officers would join us for dinner.

Juan"—he smirked slightly—"and Lanier have been preparing something special in anticipation of your visit."

"Delighted, Captain Reddy. It would be *my* honor."

Dinner was served in the wardroom with as much pomp as Juan could manage. He hovered near the guests with a carafe of monkey joe in one hand, towel draped over his arm. His wardroom breakfasts had become legendary, but he rarely got a chance to entertain. For this dinner, he was at his most formal best, and though mess dress hadn't been exactly prescribed, everyone managed as best they could. Matt's own dress uniform was one of his few prewar outfits Juan had managed to maintain. He'd even sent it ashore with other important items before *Walker*'s last fight.

Earl Lanier entered with as much dignity as possible, carrying a tray of appetizers. He'd somehow stuffed his swollen frame into his own dingy mess dress and wore a long, greasy apron tied around his chest and under his arms that hung nearly to his shins. Laying the tray on the green linoleum table, he removed the lid with a steamy flourish. Nestled neatly around a sauce tureen were dozens of smoky pink cylindrical shapes, decorated with a possibly more edible leafy garnish. Matt's face fell, as did the faces of all the human destroyermen. In his ongoing effort to use the damn things up, Lanier had prepared an appetizer of Vienna sausages, or "scum weenies," as some called them. Juan almost crashed into Lanier, forcing him into the passageway beyond the curtain, where he proceeded to berate him in highly agitated Tagalog.

"Ah, cooks and their sensibilities!" Jenks said, spearing an oozing sausage with a fork. After dipping the object in the sauce, he popped it in his mouth. "Um . . . most interesting," he accomplished at last, forcing himself to swallow.

"Yes, well . . ." was all Matt could manage. The "appetizer" remained little sampled except by Chack and some of the other 'Cats, who actually seemed to like the things. Sooner than expected, Juan returned with the main course: a mountainous, glazed "pleezy-sore" roast. He quickly removed the offending tray. The excellent roast was much more enthusiastically received and consumed with great relish. Juan also brought in some other dishes: steamed vegetables of some sort that tasted a lot like squash, and some very ordinary-looking sautéed mushrooms. There were tankards of fresh polta juice and pitchers of the very last iced tea known to exist on the planet. The ice came from the big refrigerator-freezer on deck behind the blower, and Spanky and Lanier themselves had teamed up to repair it. Ice, and the cold water that came from the little built-in drinking fountain, was always welcome, and of course the truck-size machine allowed them to carry perishables.

The dinner was a huge success, and to Juan's satisfaction, everything was much appreciated and commented on. He might kill Lanier later, but for a time, he was in his favorite element.After the last remove, Jenks spoke up. "A most flavorful dinner." He patted his stomach. "Perhaps too flavorful!" He turned to Juan. "You and Mr. Lanier have my heartiest compliments! Even the iced tea! How refreshing! We usually take tea hot, you know. Even if we had a means of making ice at sea, I don't suppose it has ever occurred to anyone to ice tea before!" He paused, and everyone looked at him with keen interest. Of *course* the Empire would know tea! Planting and growing some of the "founder's" cargo would probably have been one of their first imperatives!

Jenks continued. "I am given to understand that you do not imbibe strong drink aboard your Navy's ships, Captain Reddy. Perhaps that is not a bad policy. In case you might consider an exception, I did bring a very mild, dry port to commemorate our rendezvous. There is just enough for a single short glass for all present, and I intended it as a means for proposing a toast."

Matt nodded. "In that case, Commodore, I'll allow an exception. It's not unheard-of in situations like this when 'foreigners' are aboard. Juan, would you be good enough to fetch glasses?"

A few minutes later, glasses had been positioned and filled by Juan's expert hand. Jenks raised his glass. "It is customary at this time for our most junior officer to offer the first toast to the governor-emperor. I do not expect you to participate, under the circumstances, but I do beg you to give His Majesty the benefit of the doubt in this matter. It is his own daughter who has been taken, after all."

"Very well," Matt agreed. "The benefit of the doubt . . . for now." One of Jenks's midshipmen stood, and all those present, everyone, stood with him.

"Gentlemen," he said, "His Majesty!"

All, including Matt, took a sip. The port was interesting, fruity, Matt decided, and as mild as Jenks had promised. He held out his own glass. "The Grand Alliance, and the United States Navy!" All drank again, but Matt noticed there was the slightest hesitation among a few of the Imperial officers. Inwardly, he sighed.

Jenks held forth his glass. "Hear, hear!" he said forcefully. "And a most formidable Navy it is. We have joined together to embark on a venture essential to both our nations." He paused. "May it ever be thus: that we will forever cooperate as friends, and never meet as enemies!" On that, Jenks emptied his glass, and with no hesitation at all, everyone else in the wardroom followed suit.

"Captain!" Reynolds exclaimed excitedly. "Lookout reports surface contact bearing one two five degrees! It's a sail, Skipper! More than one. He says it looks like three or four!"

"Course?" Matt snapped. *Sails! Here?* Other than Billingsly, who else would be in these waters? According to Jenks, they were still a considerable distance from the closest Imperial outpost. Possibly *four* ships! Could others have *joined* Billingsly?

Reynolds relayed the course request and stood, waiting anxiously for several minutes before the lookout in the crow's nest replied, "Almost reciprocal, Skipper. Lookout estimates contact course is two eight zero! Four ships for sure, sir, under sail!"

"Well," said Courtney Bradford, "of course we all presume those are Imperial ships? If not, personally I'd be willing to lay a wager to it."

"What makes you so sure?" Gray asked. "'Specially after all that stuff you were goin' on about the other day."

Bradford looked oddly at Gray. "Why, I will gladly wager my . . . my *hat* that they are indeed Imperials, coming in response to the ship and message Jenks dispatched when he first arrived in Baalkpan! Considering the time it would have taken that ship to travel to the Imperial homeland, spread the word, outfit another expedition . . . that expedition would be about, well, *here* by now!"

Gray looked at the bizarre sombrerolike hat hanging from Bradford's hand (he wasn't allowed to wear it on the bridge) and shook his head. "I wouldn't want that nasty thing as a gift. 'Sides, when you put it that way, you're probably right."

Matt was already convinced. He'd forgotten all about the ship Jenks was allowed to send away, with news of the princess's survival and rescue. He rubbed his chin, looking at Reynolds. Oh, well, he'd promised. Besides, there were other good reasons. "How do you like the sea, Ensign?" he asked.

Reynolds studied the swells. "Looks fine, Skipper. You'll need to heave to and set us down in the lee. The hard part, actually, will be moving away so we'll have the wind again—without sucking us into the screws."

Matt sighed. Another danger he hadn't really thought of. "Very well. Sound General Quarters and call your division. Have Mr. Palmer signal *Achilles* that we'll reduce speed and await your report."

"Aye-aye, sir!"

After all stations reported manned and ready, Reynolds announced shipwide: "Now hear this, now hear this! The Special Air Detail will assemble and make all preparations for flight operations!" Those members of the Special Air Detail not stationed at the plane as part of the Plane Dump Detail during GQ sprang from their various battle stations and hurried to their new posts. Matt had decided that the ship would always be at general quarters whenever the plane was launched or recovered so everyone would be at their highest state of readiness in the event of an accident. It was then easier to call the larger air detail from their normal battle stations, which, with the exception of the designated observer, were all close by. Observers came from Lieutenant Palmer's comm division.

"Mr. Reynolds, you are relieved," Matt said, gesturing for Carl Bashear to take Fred's headset. Kutas was at the helm, so Fred couldn't hope for better ship handling.

"Aye-aye, sir! Thank you, sir!" Reynolds said, and slid down the stairs behind the pilothouse. Hurrying past the galley under the amidships deckhouse, he heard the diminutive Juan Marcos and the monstrous Earl Lanier still arguing about the night before. He chuckled. He didn't care—he was going to fly! His division, almost entirely 'Cats, had already cleared the tarps from the plane and were arranging the tackle to the aft extended davit when he arrived. This Nancy was his own personal plane, the one in which he'd finished his training. It was one of the new, improved models, infinitely better than Ben's prototype. It looked incredibly frail, but Fred knew appearances were deceiving. He'd botched a landing or two, and it had held together under stresses he'd have thought would tear it apart. He had confidence in the plane and himself. Shoot, he had almost thirty hours in the thing! He climbed up to the cockpit and, as always, looked at the large blue roundel with the big white star and smaller red dot with a mix of pride and a sense of incongruity. The roundel contrasted well with the lighter blue of the wings and fuselage/hull, and all the colors looked right, but the contraption they covered was, while in his eyes a thing of beauty, still strange enough to cause a disconnect between its shape and the familiar colors. He shrugged and climbed in. "Who's my OC?" he shouted, referring to his observer/copilot.

One of Ben's improvements, besides turning the engine around, had been installing auxiliary controls for the observer. It only made sense. Observers didn't have to be pilots—yet—but they had to be familiar with the controls and able to demonstrate at least rudimentary flying skills. Of course, their main job was to observe and transmit those observations via one of the small, portable CW transmitters (originally meant for airplanes) that all the new transmitters in the Alliance were patterned after. There was no battery—Alliance-made batteries were still too heavy—but the "Ronson" wind powered generator and a voltage regulator the size of a shoe box gave them all the juice they needed with little weight. An aerial extended from a faired upright behind the observer's seat to the tail.

Fred looked aft and saw Kari-Faask scrambling into her position. She was a niece of the great B'mbaadan general Haakar-Faask, who'd died so bravely in a holding action against the Grik. Kari wasn't quite as bold and fearless as her uncle, but Fred knew she had plenty of guts. She never made any bones about the fact that she was afraid to fly, for example, but she went up anyway and performed her duties without complaint. Also, despite her still somewhat stilted English, she had a good fist on the transmitter key.

"You okay with this, Kari?" Fred called back to her.

"I good. You be good and no crash us!" she hollered back.

Reynolds could tell *Walker* was heaved to by the sudden wallowing sensation. He quickly checked the function of all the control surfaces and shouted down to the chief of the air detail, "All right, Chief, pick us up and swing us out! Set us down with plenty of slack but don't cut us loose until the engine starts, hear? And keep an eye on those line handlers!"

The Nancy lifted. 'Cats strained at the taglines to keep the plane from swinging with the rolling motion of the ship. Reynolds knew Ben had been hoping to construct some kind of catapult, a sort of abbreviated version of what *Amagi* had had, but there just hadn't been time. Now Reynolds better appreciated Ben's scheme. It wouldn't have made any difference with recovery, but with a catapult, they could have just flown right off the ship. A couple of times, the Nancy swung dangerously close to the davit and Fred clenched his eyes shut, expecting a splintering crash, but somehow, fairly quickly, the plane was over the water and headed down. Now the only immediate concern was giving the plane enough slack that the roll of the ship wouldn't yank her back out of the water and smash her against *Walker*'s side.

Suddenly, Reynolds felt the independent motion caused by water under the plane. There'd been no thump or splash at all. "Switch on!" he yelled, and Kari leaped up to lean against the little railing that kept her body away from the prop. Reaching as high as she could, she grabbed a blade and yanked it down. There was a cough, but nothing else. She repeated the process and was rewarded by a loud, muffled fart and the blades blurred before her. Reynolds advanced the throttle while she fell back into her seat and strapped herself in. This was the signal for the detail on the ship to pull the tagline pins that released all ropes from the plane. Kicking the rudder hard left, Reynolds advanced the throttle still more to gain some distance from the ship.

"All right!" Reynolds shouted, tension ebbing away. "We're on the loose!" Behind them, the ship slowly eased forward, exposing them to the westerly breeze. Turning the Nancy's nose into the wind, Reynolds advanced the throttle to the stop. The new liquid-cooled engine was heavier than Ben's makeshift prototype, but the power-to-weight ratio was actually a little better. It stayed uniformly cooler too, which could be good and bad. They'd need better spring technology before they could do a proper

thermostat. The big, exposed radiator behind the cockpit also negated any
potential speed increase, but having flown a couple of times in the prototype, Fred liked "his" Nancy a lot better. Unlike Ben, Reynolds had also
quickly figured out a major secret to seaplane flying. Maybe it was because
he'd had no preconceptions and just did what came naturally, but he'd
amazed Ben on his third flight by "bouncing" his plane into the air off a
wave top with half the speed and in a third of the distance with which Ben
had ever managed it. Ben had been flabbergasted, amazed, annoyed, and
proud all at once. After he got Fred to first figure out what he'd done,
and second explain—and ultimately show it to everyone else—the practice became SOP.

Fred used the procedure now, and within moments of his applying
full power, the plane was in the air. "Whooee!" he shouted, banking low
over the water. He gradually pulled back on the stick. The Nancy's CG was
still just a little aft, and Ben had constantly pounded it into them not to
fool around with the stick, particularly at low altitude. Slowly, the plane
climbed. In the distance, about ten miles away, he saw *Achilles*. He knew
no one on the Imperial ship had ever seen a man fly, and he was tempted
to cruise over and buzz her. He resisted the impulse, realizing it probably
wasn't appropriate to goof around in the air the first time the skipper let
him fly. He grinned, thinking about what it would be like—Ben had told
him of the chaos he'd caused on *Ajax* that one time. Shaking his head, he
banked a little sharper and flew back toward *Walker*, gently waggling his
wings as he flew over.

In all the wide expanse of the world around them, there was nothing
but sea. He'd never flown over the empty ocean before, at least not beyond
sight of land, and it made him a little queasy. Worse, it was a dull, humid
day and the higher he flew, the more difficult it became to tell where the
sky and the horizon met. He looked at his clinometer and steadied his
wings. As far as he could see, there was no sign of land at all. Just the hazy,
grayish sky and the hazy blue sea below. *Achilles* and *Walker* were there,
of course, and that comforted him, but the only other things in view were
the distant ships the lookout had spotted. It was time to get to work.

"Definitely four ships," he shouted to Kari through the speaking tube,
knowing she would report it, although by now *Walker* and *Achilles* would
probably know that already. There were no ships beyond those, however,
and that would be news. He reported that as well. Closer and closer to the
unknown ships he flew, gaining altitude. Still nothing beyond them but
maybe an atoll or something. He couldn't tell for sure, and it might even
have been a distant squall. But the four ships were clearly alone. "Tell 'em
they're sailing steamers, like *Achilles* . . . and *Ajax*. All have those paddle
box things on their sides. When we get a little closer, I'll take her down a

little and see if we can get a look at their flags. They've *got* flags; I can see that much from here."

A short time later, he was kiting a few thousand feet above the strange ships. He still couldn't see what flag they flew, but they must have noticed him. He couldn't tell if his flying machine had caused any consternation below, but they were taking in sail, and puffs of smoke began streaming from their tall, slender funnels.

"Say, Kari," he shouted, "I don't know what it means, or if they're reacting to us or our ships, but they've lit their boilers. Seems that would mean they want to be able to maneuver. Better send that; then we're going down for a closer look."

"Yes, I send," Kari said. "But stay out of musket shot! If they Jenks people, they muskets are no as good as our new ones, and no *near* as good as you rifles, but they plenty good shoot holes in this 'crate' you get close enough!"

"Don't worry. I plan to stay well clear." He eased the stick forward and began a slow, spiraling descent. "Let's see," he said, mentally kicking himself for forgetting a pair of binoculars. He'd have to remember that in the future. Surely Kari could hold the plane level while he took a look—or he could do the same for her. She was the observer, after all. Maybe with her better eyes . . . "Hey, Kari, if you get a good look at the flag, describe what you see!" he yelled.

Still closer they flew, swooping down to within three hundred feet of the water. The ships looked just like Jenks's, for the most part. One had more gunports, the others fewer, but all followed essentially the same lines and rig. Sooty black plumes rose thick from all four ships now.

"I see flag! Imper'al flag!" Kari confirmed. "Is same as Jenks . . . I think." Something about it, she didn't know what, didn't look exactly right.

A single puff of smoke belched from a gun on the nearest ship.

"They shoot at us!" Kari shouted. "With cannon! We out of range their muskets, but not cannon!"

"Relax," said Reynolds, a little shaky himself, as he banked abruptly away. "We probably just spooked them. That had to be a warning shot telling us to keep our distance. If they were shooting *at* us, I doubt if they'd have used just one. Think about it: they've never seen an airplane before in their lives. They don't know if we're dangerous or not. I can understand them not wanting us too close." He rubbed his windblown face. "From what I could see, they looked like Imperial flags to me too. Send it. Tell Captain Reddy we're coming home and ask him to fly a signal saying what he wants us to do." Fred would be glad when they could make headsets for the observers. His Nancy had one of the simple receivers, and the little speakers Riggs had come up with worked fine, but they couldn't compete with a droning motor. For now, they had to rely on visual instructions from the ship.

"Wilco!" Kari shouted through the speaking tube.

"He says—En-sin Reynolds says—they Imperials, all right. Chase plane off with warning shot," one of Ed Palmer's comm strikers reported. "He ask we hoist signal flags, tell more instructions."

Matt was thoughtful. "A warning shot, huh? Very well." He turned and spoke to the Bosun. "Have him orbit us while we meet the strangers, fuel permitting. He should have plenty and it won't be long. The main reasons I let him fly in the first place were to test his procedures—we had to do that sooner or later—and to get the plane off the ship when we meet these guys . . . just in case."

"Aye-aye, Captain," Gray said, and he strode the short distance to where the signalmen and signal strikers stood, just aft of the charthouse.

"That's most odd," Courtney observed.

"What, the warning shot?" Matt asked.

"Well, that too, but I suspect even our Harvey Jenks would have done that when we first met, had we flown an airplane at him. Imperials do seem to have a rather well-defined societal arrogance. Mr. Jenks has mellowed rather satisfactorily, I think. Actually, though, what suddenly strikes me is that presumably they can see us as well as we can see them by now."

"Sure . . ." Matt glanced at the approaching ships and saw the black smoke above them. They *were* much closer, maybe only six miles away. Under steam and sail, they were probably making ten or twelve knots. *Walker* had slowed to five when the plane took off, but she'd accelerated to fifteen as the Nancy swooped back over the ship, reading the flags they'd hoisted. Matt peered past the port bridge wing and looked north-northwest, where *Achilles* had been keeping pace. He saw that Jenks's ship had closed the distance to about seven miles, and smoke was streaming from her stack now too. "What the hell's going on here? Those ships are clearly heading toward *us*, not Jenks. And why did everybody light their boilers all of a sudden?"

Palmer himself appeared on the bridge. His voice had an edge when he spoke. "Message from *Achilles*, Skipper."

"Okay. What's it say?"

"Commodore Jenks suggests that we not, repeat *not* close with the approaching squadron alone."

"Why not?"

"He doesn't say."

"Well, find out, damn it, because they're sure as hell closing with *us*, and they'll get here before he does!"

"Aye-aye, sir," Palmer said, and left the bridge.

"Slow to one-third," Matt ordered. "Maybe we can reduce our closure rate, at least. I'm not sure showing our heels will make the best impression."

"We ought to go to flank and steam circles around the buggers," Gray muttered to Bradford as he returned.

"While perhaps highly satisfying," Bradford whispered back, arching his eyebrows, "it may also be deemed provocative." He raised his voice. "I think I know why they are concentrating on us, Captain," he proclaimed. "When Jenks dispatched his message, he surely must have reported that Her Highness desired *us* to take her home on *this* ship. No doubt Jenks would have described *Walker* as she had been described to him: a dedicated steamer with an iron hull. No sails. I shouldn't wonder if that's why they are converging on this ship; they believe the princess is aboard!"

"Maybe you're right," Matt replied. "And if it hadn't been for Billingsly's stunt, that would make me feel a lot better. Even so . . . Even if they're all as big a pack of jerks as Billingsly, I can't imagine they'd fire at us and risk hurting the girl. Billingsly took her—and the rest of our people— 'cause he wanted her. He could have just bumped her off at any time."

"Not and lived," Gray growled.

"Good point," Matt agreed. He rubbed his face again. "If they've got twenty four-pounders, like *Achilles*, they can punch holes in us out to what, five hundred yards? Six?"

"I'd think about that, Skipper," Gray agreed. "Probably dent the hell out of us to a thousand. But round shot loses a lot of energy quick. It's buckin' a lot of wind for the weight." He shrugged. "If they've got anything even a little bigger, though, the weight goes up exponentially for just a little more wind resistance. A thirty-two's not buckin' much more wind than an eighteen pounder, like *Donaghey* carries, but it'll punch a hole in us at a thousand!"

Matt made up his mind. "Okay, at two thousand yards, we heave to, broadside. We'll fly a white parley flag, but all batteries will remain loaded, trained, and aimed for surface action starboard. The gun director will concentrate on that big boy that must be their flagship. If they close to fifteen hundred yards, we'll fire a warning shot of our own with the Jap gun aft. Have Chief Gunner's Mate Stites lay it himself, in local control. Tell him to use HE for a really big splash and put it close enough to rain on 'em without hurting anybody, clear?"

Chief Bashear understood that the tactical conversation was over and that orders had been issued. He quickly passed the word. "Skipper?" he asked when he received confirmation. "I oughta be aft." Chief Gray might be the "Super Bosun" of the fleet, but Carl Bashear was *Walker*'s official chief bosun's mate now. Since Gray's self-appointed battle station was the forward part of the ship, near the captain, Bashear's post was aft, near Steele, on the auxiliary conn. Chack was a bosun's mate too, but since he also commanded the Marine contingent, he oversaw things amidships, where he could remain close to his Marines.

"Of course, Boats . . . Bashear," Matt said with only a slight hesitation. Gray would always be "Boats" to him, but "Boats Bashear" had seemed to make Carl happy. "By all means, round up a relief and take your post."

Staas-Fin, or "Finny," quickly arrived to take his place and Carl Bashear was gone. Time passed while all the ships gradually converged. *Achilles* was really cracking on, but even with *Walker*'s speed reduced to slow, Jenks clearly couldn't arrive until shortly after the Imperial squadron reached the two-thousand-yard mark and things began to happen. The squeal of the halyard behind the charthouse announced that the parley flag was on its way up. Reynolds's Nancy flew by ahead, just a few hundred feet off the wave tops. Matt had to admit the thing looked a lot better in the air than it did strapped to his ship.

"I see a white flag going up on the biggest Imperial ship," cried Monk from his lookout post on the starboard bridge wing. About that time, the same report came from the crow's nest.

"Sir," said Palmer, gaining the bridge again, "Jenks says firing the boilers is Imperial SOP when they clear for action! He asks if we are *certain* the ships fly the same flag he does, *exactly* the same? The Imperial Naval jack is basically the same as the national flag—thirteen red and white stripes with red on top and bottom, and the union blue in the field! The Company flag has white on top and bottom with no blue, just a red cross of Saint George! He says the Company revived an older flag to show a distinction!"

"Goddamn, what a crock!" Gray said.

"Not a crock," Matt retorted. "There's definitely historical precedence, and it makes sense. Can anybody tell if there's any blue on those flags? If Jenks thinks it's that important, we'd better find out!"

"Can't tell!" shouted Monk. "All their flags are streaming aft and they're headed right for us! I can see stripes now and then, but that's it!"

"What's on top, red or white?" Matt barked.

"Two thousand yards!" cried Finny.

"Very well, left standard rudder. When we're in position, we'll heave to and maintain position. Flags?" he prompted again.

"I can't *tell* what's on top!" Monk yelled.

"Crow's nest?" Matt demanded.

"White!" said Finny. "No, red! Jeez, Skipper, crow's nest no tell either! Campeti say coming to fifteen hundreds!"

"Gun number four will prepare to commence firing. One shot only," Matt said.

"Fifteen hundreds!" Finny almost squealed.

"Fire number four!"

From aft, they heard the bark of the Japanese 4.7-inch dual-purpose gun. Even over the sound of the blower, the *hssssshk* sound of the projectile in flight was distinctive. A large geyser of spume erupted one hundred yards off the port bow of the largest approaching ship, and spray did indeed collapse upon the fo'c'sle.

"Pass the word to Stites," Matt said. "Well-placed."

For a long moment, there was no response from the ships. Matt was about to order a second shot when Monk reported that the target (odd how it had suddenly become "the target") had begun reefing sails. Still, though, the ships continued toward them.

"I don't like it," Gray said.

"Me either," agreed Matt. "They're reducing sail like they're respecting the warning shot, but they're still steaming right at us. I don't like it at all." He looked to port. "Where's Jenks?"

"Coming up hand over fist, but he's still a couple thousand yards off the port quarter. Sir, he's hoisted a really big flag!" Matt looked. Sure enough, a much larger than usual Imperial national flag had been run up to the peak of *Achilles'* maintop. It was clearly a battle flag, and Matt had seen something similar done a long time ago. *Walker* even had her own battle flag now. Meticulously repaired after the Battle of Baalkpan, and with the name of that battle added to the others embroidered upon it, it lay folded in a place of honor in the center of the signal flag locker.

"Run up our battle flag," Matt said resignedly. "Obviously they understand what it means. That ought to impress them more than another warning shot!"

"Skipper! They're turning!"

Matt looked back to the front. At about eight hundred yards, the four ships executed a very tight turn to port that only paddle wheels would have allowed. They still had the wind, and for a moment, the flags all streamed forward from aft. They were red-and-white flags, without the slightest touch of blue, and just as that realization dawned, the starboard side of all but one of the ships erupted in a solid bank of white smoke.

"All ahead flank!" Matt shouted. "Main battery, commence firing! Somebody yank that white rag down and get our own flag up there!"

Fireman Tab-At, or "Tabby," felt the ship squat down and lurch forward as the throttlemen poured on the steam. She almost fell against the aft bulkhead of the fireroom. Access plates on the deck popped up out of their grooves and slid toward her like big, rectangular blades, and she hopped as they went by to keep from losing her toes. They clanged against the bulkhead behind her. "Feed 'em!" she shouted. "Open 'em up!" They had to increase the flow of air, water, and fuel to keep up with the sudden enormous dump of steam. An instant later, she felt like somebody had put a bucket on her head and started beating it with a stick. As quickly as it began, the heavy drumming ceased, but *Walker* kept picking up speed. The air lock cycled and Spanky emerged from the forward engine room. He was covered with dark fuel oil from head to foot, but his eyes were white as they darted around the compartment.

"Everything okay in here?" he shouted.

"Yeah . . ." Tabby started, then amended, "Yes, sir! A few loose plates. What happened?"

"The bastards fired at us!" Spanky bellowed. "The goddamn sneakin' *bastards!*"

"Who shoot?" Tabby asked, her drawl and English slipping a little.

"Those goddamn Company Brits. Who else?"

"How you get so oily? Engines okay?"

"Yeah. Somethin' punched a hole through one of the saddle bunkers, somethin' *big*. Must be rollin' around in the bilge, 'cause it didn't go out the other side, but it blew oil all over the place. Damage control's on the way. Any of 'em come through here, tell 'em to pump the bilges into one of the two empty bunkers aft. It'll be full of crap, but we can't spare the fuel. Maybe we can separate it out some." He started forward. "Gotta check the forward fireroom!"

"Commander McFaar-lane?" Tabby asked. "Spanky? You okay?"

Spanky stopped and looked back at her. "Swell, kid. Just gotta check on the old rice bowl." He wiped at the oil burning his eyes. "Might be your rice bowl too, now. Chief Aubrey's dead. Whatever came through just kinda smushed his head." He wiped his face again. "Chiefs don't last long down here. Never shoulda picked him. He started out as a torpedoman, for God's sake! Shoulda left him at home!" Spanky sneezed, still wiping his face on his oil-soaked sleeve, and disappeared forward through the swirling, steamy heat of the fireroom.

"Damage report!" Matt bellowed over the rapid salvos of the numbers one, two, and four guns.

"Buncha big dents, three big holes," Finny replied. "One hole through for'ard engine room, make big leak in fuel bunker. One dead, two injured. 'Nother hole through wardroom, spray Selass with few steel pieces, but she okay. Hole through for'ard berthing space not hurt anybody."

"*Damn* them! Their flagship better be a wreck by now!" Matt growled. He raised his binoculars and stared hard at the geysers erupting around the distant ship. Actually, as he thought about it, it would be a miracle if they'd hit anything with their first salvo. They had explosive rounds now, using a black-powder bursting charge just like in the Great War. It was a lot better than the solid copper bolts they'd been forced to use before, and way better than nothing. The problem was, Bernie was still working out some issues with his cordite. They had all the formulas, but the organic material they had to work with was different and produced different properties and burn rates. For now, they were still using black-powder propellant charges, and it took time to work out the differential math on the gun director. Their sudden acceleration to flank hadn't helped. Unconsciously, he opened his mouth, trying to pop his ears. They'd installed one of *Amagi*'s alarm bells to replace the dead salvo buzzer, but Campeti had forgotten to push the button. "Cease firing main battery," he called. "Left full rudder! Come to course one eight five!" He needed to give his fire control crew a break, and the only thing that would allow that was a constant course and speed.

"Left full rudder, aye!" answered Kutas. "Making my course one eight five!" Another enemy broadside churned the sea behind the ship, skating across the wave tops and looking for all the world like a giant shotgun pattern in a duck pond.

"They can't hit a moving target, at least one moving this fast," Matt observed with satisfaction. "Where's Jenks?"

"Starboard quarter. He'll pass astern of us on this course," Gray answered. "He's still headin' right at 'em!"

"Course is one eight five degrees!" Kutas exclaimed.

"Main battery may resume firing as soon as they have a solution," Matt ordered. He'd opened the range and given his gunners a stable platform. *Crack!* Three guns spoke together and smoke gushed aft from number one. *Shssssssssh* . . . Splashes rose.

"Down fifty!" they heard Campeti shout from above. "Match pointers . . . Fire!"

"Good hits, good hits!" cried the lookout in the crow's nest. New splashes erupted around *Walker* and she shuddered from a heavy, booming impact forward.

"Trying to lead us," Matt observed with grudging admiration. That had taken quick thinking and steady nerves. "What's the condition of the first target?"

"She hit pretty bad, it look like. She steam in circle, out of line."

"New target, designate far left steamer," he ordered.

"Campeetee say we can't shoot at her," replied the talker a moment later.

"Why not?" Matt raised his glasses. *Damn, what's Jenks up to? Achilles* was still steaming forward, broad battle flag streaming, and she'd moved almost directly between *Walker* and her target. Splashes began to rise around Jenks's ship.

"Come left to one five zero! Redesignate far *right* enemy ship!" Matt ordered in frustration.

"Making my course one five zero, aye!"

Matt didn't want to close the range and risk any more serious hits, but he *needed* to be closer to support whatever it was Jenks was up to. He studied the enemy battle line through the lingering haze of the day and the gun smoke of battle. What was *left* of the line. The enemy had opened the battle—*started* it, he fumed—in an extremely disciplined fashion, but in the face of *Walker*'s salvos, that discipline had fallen apart. The far left ship he'd meant to engage was rushing headlong for *Achilles*, just as the far right ship had turned toward *Walker*. The largest, presumably most powerful, had made a wide, looping turn to port that now had her steaming away, off the starboard beam of the ship *Walker* was bearing down upon. The only ship that had maintained her position in the original formation seemed to have struck her colors! At that moment, no one was firing at anybody. What a mess.

"Guns one and three will bear on the advancing ship!" shouted the talker.

"Commence firing!" An instant later, the two four-inch fifties boomed.

At a range of only six hundred yards, it was almost like engaging the smaller, slower Grik ships they'd fought; but unlike the Grik, the enemy had at least one heavy gun that would bear forward. Even as *Walker* fired, smoke bloomed on the enemy fo'c'sle. Matt never knew where the round-shot from the big smoothbore went; it didn't hit the ship, but *Walker*'s two exploding rounds found their mark. The first detonated against the fo'c'sle with a thunderclap they eventually heard. Large splinters flew in every direction and the bowsprit dropped into the sea, pulling the foretop down with it. The second shot must have exploded inside the ship, because gouts of smoke gushed from the gunports. Bernie's new shells weren't as devastating as the old high-explosive rounds, Matt decided, but they could still make a mess of a wooden ship. He was about to call, "Cease firing," when the next salvo streaked toward the target. One round struck a paddle box and spewed smoke and debris far across the water. The other went down the throat again, and again there was little apparent effect.

At first.

Suddenly, for an instant, the entire center of the ship seemed to bulge as if her seams were straining against some horrendous inner pressure. In the blink of an eye, the seams burst open like an enormous grenade and the ship blew apart amid an expanding, scalding cloud of sooty steam.

"Cease firing, cease firing!" Matt yelled. "All ahead, flank! Have the boats swung out and rig netting along the sides! Stand by to rescue survivors!"

The Bosun started to dash for the stairs. "Uh, Skipper? Maybe we'd better have some of Chack's Marines handy. If there *are* any survivors, they might try to pull some kind of fanatical Jap-like shit. Remember that one crazy Jap . . ."

"I remember, Boats. By all means, keep a squad of Marines at the ready." He glassed the floating debris that had once been a ship. There *did* appear to be survivors. If so, they didn't have much time to get to them. He looked beyond the wreckage. The bigger ship was still headed away and was piling on sail. With her damaged paddle wheel, she probably hoped to escape with the wind alone. He shook his head. Turning, he saw that the one ship that had apparently "surrendered" was still hove to, and was beginning to drift. Turning still farther, he saw that Jenks and the final enemy combatant would soon pass alongside each other, and they were already going at it hammer and tongs. Gun smoke drifted between them and he could feel the periodic pounding of their guns in his chest. "Signal Ensign Reynolds, if you can get his attention," he said, referring to the pilot still circling the battle overhead. "Tell him to buzz the enemy ship engaging *Achilles*, but stay out of musket shot! Maybe he can distract them or something."

"Holy cow!" Reynolds yelled when the ship about fifteen hundred feet below suddenly just . . . blew up. Kari shrieked when debris peppered the plane and a slender, three-foot splinter lodged in the port wing. "Holy *cow*!" Reynolds shouted again, and then struggled for control when the shock wave hit.

"I got hole between my feet!" Kari cried over the voice tube. "We leak when we land!"

"Yeah," agreed Fred, "I bet that's not the only one either. Who knows what it was. Maybe a nail."

"Big damn nail!"

"Hey, look! *Walker's* coming up fast. Maybe she's going to pick up survivors. She's running up a new signal too. What's it say?"

Kari strained to read the flags as they went up the several halyards on the destroyer's foremast. "Ahh, they spell it. I not so good at spell yet. I know standard message flags good. Not so good with spell flags. They too many!"

Reynolds pushed forward on the stick and banked slightly left. "I'll have a look. Just be sure they know we're full of holes and our gas is half gone. When we set down, they'd better fish us out in a hurry!" He flew closer to the ship, squinting his eyes. "Okay." He paused. "They're not *all* letter flags," he accused.

"What they say?"

"They say, 'Buzz enemy still fighting. Distract from Jenks. Beware mu . . . muskets.' Acknowledge that, will ya?"

"Okay."

Reynolds stood on the rudder and banked right, then began a slow climb. Several minutes later, still gaining altitude, he passed over the ship that wasn't doing anything and continued toward where *Achilles* and her enemy were now locked in a deadly, smoke-belching embrace. "Wouldja look at that!" he exclaimed. The ships had apparently damaged each other's paddle wheels and all they seemed able to do was steam in ever-tightening circles around each other. Both looked shattered, and *Achilles*' foremast was down. The funnel on the enemy ship had been shot away and her deck was choked with smoke.

"Here we go!" Reynolds shouted, and pushed on the stick. The new planes had altimeters, but they weren't very accurate or quick to adjust, so he ignored his now. The airspeed indicator worked just fine and his was starting to crowd the red-painted line. A few hundred feet above the enemy masts, he pulled back on the stick and the Nancy swooped up and away. Something smacked the plane and he heard a low, humming *vooom!* whip past him in the cockpit.

"Captain say you stay *away* from muskets!" Kari shouted.

Fred started to reply that he'd meant to; that he hadn't really realized how low he'd been. Now he was mad. He spiraled upward, gaining altitude for another pass. Pushing the nose over, he lined up on where he thought he'd have a bow-to-stern approach by the time they got there. Fumbling at his holster with his left hand, he pulled out his Colt. "I'll teach you to shoot at *me*, you screwy Brits!" he muttered. He laid the pistol on his lap, then took the stick in his left hand and the pistol in his right. He flipped the safety off.

"We go too low again!" Kari scolded.

Grimly, Fred pointed the pistol over the windscreen, in the general direction of the ship he was diving on. With nothing but ship in front of him, he started yanking the trigger. Drowned by the noise of the engine, all the pistol made was popping sounds, but he suspected the men below might hear it better. The ship was coming up fast and he knew he had to pull out. Easing back on the stick, he heard several more *vooooms!* but nothing hit the plane—until he accidentally shot it in the nose himself as the target disappeared aft.

"Crap!"

He'd shot his own damn airplane! It wasn't much of a hole, really, although he knew there'd be another one below, where the bullet came out. But with the obvious powder burn on the blue paint in front of the windscreen, there'd be no way he could blame the hole on enemy fire. He was lucky he hadn't shot his own foot off!

"Crap, crap, *crap!*"

"What you say?" Kari cried from behind.

"I said 'crap'!"

"Get those men out of the water!" bellowed the Bosun. "I don't care if they *are* sneakin', bushwhackin', traitorous sons o' bitches! The more you let the fish get, the fewer we'll have to *hang!*"

The Bosun's words were meant more for the men they were pulling from the water than the men and 'Cats who were saving them. Oddly, the usual swarm of flasher fish hadn't yet arrived to tear the survivors apart. He couldn't account for that. Maybe the explosion of the ship had driven them away, or maybe there just weren't as many of the damn things in really deep water like this. Regardless, he expected something with an appetite would be along eventually, and judging by the panic with which the Imperial Company survivors were trying to get aboard, they must think so too. They'd made them send the most badly wounded up first and fifteen or twenty horribly burned and scalded men had already been sent to Selass in the wardroom. She'd appeared briefly on deck and seemed fine other than a few glistening spots where she'd applied some polta paste to her "scratches," as she'd called them. Now the less injured were coming aboard and a handful already squatted, hands behind their heads, clustered around the steam capstan. Some simply stared back at the, to them, ridiculously small but unfathomably destructive maw of the number one gun.

"Hurry it up, you pack o' jackals!" the Bosun berated. He pointed at the continuing distant fight between *Achilles* and her foe. "We got friends over there dyin' and more scum like you to kill! You got one minute before I yank these nets and we leave you here!" There were moans and cries from the water, but somehow the men, many still injured, managed to climb or splash along a little faster.

"You are consistent, at least," Chack remarked softly. He'd appeared beside the Bosun still holding his Krag instead of one of the new Springfield muskets. "You are merciless to everyone."

"I ain't merciless," Gray murmured through clenched teeth. "I actually feel sorta sorry for the bastards. I just want 'em scared of us before they come aboard. Make 'em easier for your boys to handle."

For a moment, Chack said nothing, possibly digesting the Bosun's words. "It is . . . strange," he said at last.

"What?"

"All the hu-maans we have ever really known have been our benefactors. They have helped us. It is very . . . disconcerting now to have fought them, and killed . . . so many."

"You helped us kill Japs, and they're sorta human, I guess."

"True, but these"—he gestured at the last of the survivors climbing the cargo netting—"these are more like you. They speak the same language, and more important, to us at least, they are the very descendants of the original tail-less ones, the ones who came before." He paused. "It is . . . hard to know they can be bad, and maybe a little hard to know *you* can kill them without remorse."

"I said I felt sorry for the bastards, didn't I?" Gray demanded quietly. He shrugged. "Hell, I felt a *little* sorry for them Jap destroyermen that got ate—before we met you. But war's war, and it's a damn strange world—whichever the hell world you're from." It was Gray's turn to pause. "Just remember, *they* started this fight here today, and it was friends o' theirs who took Lieutenant Tucker, the princess, your buddy Silva, and all the rest. Friends o' theirs who slaughtered *Simms* and all the 'Cats on board. It's a strange world, sure, but strange as this fight today may seem to you, it's crystal clear to me."

He motioned at the bedraggled survivors, maybe thirty in all, not counting those in the wardroom. "There' a lot more of 'em than I expected, and that's a fact." He turned to Chack. "Take charge of your prisoners, if you please."

C aptain Reddy and Commodore Jenks met that evening aboard HNBC *Ulysses*, the captured enemy flagship. Except for her starboard paddles, she hadn't suffered much. *Achilles* had been badly mauled in her fight with HNBC *Caesar*, and had suffered over seventy killed and wounded. She'd require significant repairs before she could continue on. *Caesar* was in worse shape, and once all her wounded were moved to *Ulysses* and *Icarus*—the ship that surrendered early on—*Caesar* would be allowed to sink.

Jenks's fight was practically over by the time *Walker* steamed to her aid, but the destroyer's appearance had ended any further resistance. Matt then turned his ship in pursuit of *Ulysses*. He'd wondered at the time why she would abandon her consorts so readily, but when she too surrendered as he drew near, and he was forced to endure the sniveling apologies and explanations of the squadron's admiral, he understood. Chack and his Marines remained aboard *Ulysses* while *Walker* towed her back to the other somewhat assembled ships.

Meanwhile, Jenks had gone aboard *Caesar* and *Icarus* and gained a little information. To everyone's complete surprise, the ship *Walker* had destroyed was *Agamemnon* herself, the very same ship that Jenks had dispatched home so long ago. He'd also discovered his own loyal Ensign Parr aboard *Icarus*. *Icarus* had been another Navy ship "pressed" into Company service, and was considered the least reliable in the squadron. It was to her that most of the known Imperial loyalists had been sequestered. The young ensign had recognized *Achilles* and risen up with some trusted men, seized the ship, and promptly surrendered her before she could fire a shot. It was Parr who confirmed the terrible news that only the Company had ever learned the results of Jenks's mission, and more important, that they'd discovered the governor-emperor's daughter alive.

Now Matt and Jenks strode *Ulysses*'s quarterdeck, talking quietly, while both men's guards stood watchfully by. From amidships came the cries of the wounded *Walker* had picked up, as they and the other prisoners were transferred aboard.

"How come you took *Achilles* in like that?" Matt finally asked. "We could have destroyed all four ships from beyond their range."

"That's why I took her in," Jenks replied. "I'm reliably informed that you have a temper, and I feared you would destroy them all once they'd fired at you. Was I wrong?"

Matt shrugged. "I don't think I'd have fired on the ship that surrendered," he said, a little defensively. "I didn't destroy *this* ship."

"Ahh, but by the time you caught her, your passion had faded!"

"Mmm," Matt said noncommittally. He pointed at the wounded and the prisoners coming aboard. "What're we going to do with all of them?"

"I suppose we must convene a court-martial," Jenks replied. "We have many repairs to attend and I understand even your ship was slightly damaged?" Matt nodded, thinking of poor Aubrey. "That should give us sufficient time," Jenks added. "If you've no objection, I think Imperial forms might be most appropriate. Three officers will preside as judges. I would be indebted if you yourself would sit, as well as two other officers of your choosing. I know you're not disinterested, but you have no personal knowledge of any of the defendants. I expect you will also assume not *all* are guilty, as Mr. Parr was not."

"Why don't you do it?" Matt asked. "Even some of your loyalists might object to a foreigner."

"As prosecutor, I cannot preside."

"Oh. Okay then. I'll appoint a couple of others. I don't think taking volunteers would be a good idea just now."

"Perhaps not."

For a while, they just walked together and an awkward silence hung about them.

"How's it feel?" Matt finally asked.

Jenks looked disdainfully at the bloody sling supporting his left arm. "It hurts a bit," he confessed with a grin, "but that wondrous ooze your medical . . . person applied has dulled the edge."

"Good. Shouldn't get infected either. How's O'Casey?"

"Hmm? Oh, Bates. Ha. Utterly insufferable. He wasn't hurt at all, but I confess at times I wished for a ball to take off his head."

"I guess he came up with a number of ways to say, 'I told you so'?"

Jenks looked blank for a moment before realization dawned. "Oh! Oh, yes. An infinite number of ways, and without pause, I might add." Jenks shook his head. "He was right all along. I think I even knew it back then, but the politics of New London are considerably less clear at home than they are out here, at the ends of the earth. I hope someday he will forgive me and we might be friends again." Jenks gestured at his arm. "Now that I know where the *true* infection lies."

"So it would seem," Matt said, and sighed. "And here we are, over a thousand miles from where I ought to be fighting who I ought to be fighting. We still don't know where Billingsly and my people—and your princess—are, but we do know your governor-emperor never knew we even had the girl. This Honorable New Britain Company did, though, and fired on the ship—my ship!—they suspected she was on. The only explanation for that is that now, they want her dead! Apparently, this Company is pulling a major power grab, and everything and everyone both of us cares about might depend, one way or another, on how that turns out. Jeez, if that doesn't put us on the *exact* same side at long last, I don't know what ever would."

"I apologize for all of this," Jenks said quietly. "Everything."

Matt became angry. "Damn it, Jenks, I don't want your apology! Maybe that'll make you feel better for being such a jerk once, but all it does now is cheapen everything we've done—and have to do! I still think we need to be friends, your people and mine, because—as I've been trying to pound into that thick skull of yours—there are bigger threats out there than either one of us can handle on our own. There may be stuff we can't even imagine yet! On top of that, I want my people back, the ones Billingsly took! Maybe you didn't know, but Sandra Tucker, well . . . she's my girl . . . and I want *her* back!"

"I am aware of that," Jenks said softly.

"Yeah? Well, be aware of *this*! That night on *Donaghey* during the Strakka, right after the fight for Singapore when we heard the news, I swore an oath. As God is my witness, whoever took her, whoever's *responsible* for taking her and the others, and for the unprovoked attack on Baalkpan . . ." Matt took a breath and his green eyes were as remorseless as the sea. "You can add *Simms* and my ship here today to the list now, but whoever put all this in motion, *no matter who he is*, is going to *pay!*"

H alik stared greedily at the map laid before him on the table in the brazier-lit chamber. It was a map of all the known world, and the chaotic jumble of mountains and coastlines, rivers and islands fascinated him. He dully remembered, even as a young Uul warrior, occasionally wondering how his Hij commanders could know how the world was shaped and how they knew where to take them to fight. Now he could see, *look down upon*, where he was, and many of the places he'd been before. He'd learned much in the months since his unexpected elevation, but maps and the terrain they depicted still held him almost spellbound. Matching terrain in his memory with what he saw on the maps was like scratching a crude drawing of a beautiful sculpture in the sand, and yet the value was in knowing where that sculpture was. Somehow he could sense that, for his purposes, terrain would become vitally important. It was like the different parts of a shield. Some areas were best for countering the blows of an enemy, while others could be used to great advantage when striking out.

He tore his attention from the map and focused again on Regent Tsalka's words. Words that, in all their infinite variety, he'd learned to understand!

"Singapore will surely fall, if it has not already, and my own province, my very own Ceylon, my beloved India, will be next on the list of the prey!"

"You must stop thinking of them as *prey*, lord. That is essential!" General Esshk scolded—quite harshly, Halik thought. "They are no longer even Worthy Prey, as we began to suspect, but have become hunters themselves, in their own right! Hunters perhaps as cunning as ourselves who fight in a new, unexpected way! Hunters like we have never met or faced before!"

"Yes, yes," Tsalka hissed angrily. "I know your views on this. Perhaps you are even right. But what are we to do? Though we argued for it, it destroys me to concede my very home!"

"We must," said the strange creature Halik knew as General of the Sea Kurokawa. "But we must do it slowly. As slowly as we can possibly manage. We will lose territory, yes, but we have much of that. Time is what we lack. If we can trade land for time, and balance the exchange in our favor, the magical weapons I am preparing will be ready before the enemy—they are *the enemy*, my friends!—before the *enemy* can push beyond the frontier into what you consider your ancient Sacred Land! The invaders will not sully the pure realm of the Celestial Mother herself! If a few regencies or frontier territories must be strategically sacrificed to prevent that, that is what must be done! We *will* reconquer them!"

Halik understood that it revolted Tsalka and Esshk when Kurokawa called them "my friends," but he wasn't sure why. He did know Kurokawa was growing in favor with Her just now. The miraculous weapons he'd begun utterly delighted the Celestial Mother, and she was even beginning to appreciate his strategies. Still, he knew Tsalka in particular thought Kurokawa took too many liberties.

"Enough debate, My Lord Tsalka." Esshk hissed. "She has decided—and in favor of our arguments, for now," he added ironically. "Would you try to change Her mind?" Tsalka said nothing in reply. "Well, then," Esshk growled, "that still leaves us with the issue of *how* we will trade land for time."

Kurokawa's gaze slowly shifted to Halik. "That is a question perhaps best asked of our newest general, is it not? You yourself said he survived the entertainment battles far longer than any before him. He is not old, but he is not young anymore either. He could not have prevailed so long on strength and ferocity alone. My few *Rikusentai*, or naval landing forces, that survived the loss of my ship think he has much promise. Look! Even now he studies us, evaluates us, considers . . . and no doubt forms opinions! I think he is learning that map by heart!" Kurokawa paused, and when he spoke again, he addressed Halik directly.

"Tell us, General, based on the map before you, how would *you* trade land for time? The enemy will come, and for now, we cannot stop him. How would *you* slow him down and bleed him white?"

Even to Rebecca, who had little experience with such things, it hadn't really been much of a storm, but it had been a challenge for an open boat on the wide expanse of the Eastern Sea. After two weeks of diminishing stores, sunburn, and increasingly doubtful navigation, the sudden storm afflicted nearly everyone, particularly the Imperials, with a sense of near hopelessness. Lelaa ignored them as much as possible. She was still confident that if Yap—or Tagran—was where the chart showed it to be, they'd find it.

Whatever she felt inside, Sandra remained a diminutive pillar of strength and steady authority. Her skin was red and peeling and her hair was bleached to a platinum blond, but by force of will alone she managed to maintain discipline and keep Rajendra and his men at work. Sister Audry took solace in her faith and remained stoic, if not cheerful, and set a further example for the men. Dennis Silva, as always, seemed unconcerned about anything. He was the only one among them, with the possible exception of Rajendra, who didn't even seem sunburned. His tanned skin only grew darker and his beard and unusually long hair became almost white.

Rebecca herself maintained an unwavering faith in Sandra Tucker—and Dennis Silva. She did worry about Lawrence and Abel, who, along with the Imperial engineer, suffered cruelly from the heat. Lawrence wasn't accustomed to being in the sun all day without recourse to shade, and Abel was still troubled by his wound.

The Imperials did as Sandra said, but they weren't happy. They feared they were doomed and they hated Dennis. Rebecca watched him become the focus of much of their misery and frustration. He'd destroyed their ship and killed their shipmates, and regardless of their current situation, that was something they all had in common. The reason he'd done it, and even the very reason they'd taken to the boat in the first place, became a blurred and distant memory. Slowly, through the long, miserable days and endless, terrifying nights when strange creatures bumped the boat or distant leviathans blew, it all became Silva's fault.

Outwardly, Silva didn't care. Rebecca considered it possible he even deliberately encouraged their animosity to keep them focused on *anything* but giving up. In reality, she suspected he was more deeply troubled by what he'd done than he'd ever admit. At least, she rather hoped so. Then the storm came.

Proper navigation became impossible, but Lelaa and ultimately Rajendra steered the boat as best they could, following a heading they adjusted constantly based on their calculations of leeway and current. It was an imperfect solution, but by working so closely together they at least temporarily made a sort of peace between them. For four days they fought the storm, reefing the sail to a mere sliver of canvas and shouldering through long, westerly swells. Then the wind shifted out of the south and they scudded along, pitching horribly on the confused, tumultuous sea. It had been Silva, standing in the bow of the boat, inundated by spray, who saw the breakers ahead.

It was probably the swell that saved them. That, and Silva's almost earsplitting bellow of, "Drop the sail *right goddamn now* if you want to live!" Without thought, his order was obeyed, and the boat rode a mountainous wave right over the worst of the shoals. They still struck something, probably coral, that tore a terrible gash in the bottom of the boat. It almost broke the keel, but the boat carried on, quickly filling, until the wave deposited them upon a sandy beach.

Leaping in the surf right along with Silva, Sandra ordered everyone who could move out of the boat. They used each new wave to help them heave their burden farther up the beach. Finally, they could go no farther and they collapsed in the sand. After a while, Sandra roused everyone and had all their stores and weapons taken near the edge of the trees, where the waves shouldn't reach. Then, before she would allow anyone another rest, Sandra ordered that the lightened boat be moved farther from the water as well, and secured to a tree by a stout cable. Only then did everyone collapse again, utterly exhausted, and sleep until the light of day.

Rebecca woke to the sound of surf. Her eyes didn't want to open and seemed glued shut with some sort of crust. She wiped them with her hand and grainy particles fell away. She tried again and this time she could see.

"Mornin', sunshine!" Silva said, and grinned at her. He was sitting cross-legged in the sand with his huge rifle across his lap. On a piece of canvas beside him lay the disassembled parts of his pistol. His cutlass was thrust into the sand nearby.

"Good morning," Rebecca replied. She felt disoriented. She was on dry land at last, but it still seemed to be moving under her. She also wasn't where she remembered being, lying in the sand beside the boat. She was under the shade of a large, strange tree and covered with a scratchy blanket. Beyond the shade, she saw that the storm was entirely over and bright sunshine played upon a much moderated, sparkling sea.

"I hurt everywhere," she complained, sitting up.

"Course you do. You been cooped up in a little room for weeks, then sittin' on yer butt in a boat. Takes a while to get the muscles all loosened up again."

"All is well?"

Silva's grin faded just a bit. "Mostly," he hedged.

"What do you mean?" Rebecca fought down an almost panicked concern. "Is everyone all right? What of . . . What of Lawrence, and Mr. Cook?"

"Oh, ever'body's okay, I guess. Cook's over there, still sleepin'. I figger Larry must've perked right up, 'cause he was already gone, trompin' around, I expect, before I even came around. Most o' them Imperial fellas is still sleepin' too, 'cept Rajendra. Him and Cap'n Lelaa's over there inspectin' the boat." He looked up. "And here comes our overall captain o' everything now."

"At ease," Sandra said sarcastically. "Don't bother to jump up and salute!" She was smiling when she sat in the sand next to Silva. "How do you feel, sweetie?" she asked Rebecca.

"Okay," replied the girl. She glanced warily at the nearby tree. "Are you quite sure there are none of those creatures such as were on Talaud? The ones that climb trees and drop upon prey from above?"

"Ain't seen any," Silva assured her, "and there's no scratch marks like they make." He shrugged. "Who knows, though? Don't worry; I been keepin' my eye out!" He chuckled at his little joke. Suddenly, his face went blank and he stiffened. Seeing his reaction to . . . whatever, the two girls froze as well. Slowly, Silva eased around to look back in the jungle behind him. "Damn you, Larry," he said, "what are you doin' sneakin' around in the bushes? You mighta got shot. Again."

Lawrence practically *slithered* up among them, his eyes darting about. "Quiet!" he insisted. He looked at Rebecca and lowered his head. "I *so* sorry!" he moaned. "I so, *so* sorry!"

"What? What is it, my dear?" Rebecca asked, alarmed.

"I just learn charts and I guess I didn't learn so good, or I did learn good, and still not right!"

"What the hell's that supposed to mean?" Silva hissed.

"I think he means that we are where we set out to go, this Yap Island, but, with Larry not knowing charts or being familiar with all the hundreds of islands around here, Yap isn't the same place as Tagran after all," Rebecca said carefully.

"Yes, yess!"

"How does he know?" Sandra asked.

Lawrence hesitated. "I here . . . again!"

"Before?"

"Yes!"

"You're positive?"

"Yes!"

"Well," said Sandra, relieved, "if he's definitely been here before, he should know where the real Tagran is. Isn't that true, Lawrence?"

Lawrence lowered his head again. "Yes," he hissed.

"Whoa, wait a minute!" said Silva. He fumbled behind him in a pile of things he'd brought from the boat. In a moment, he had the chart in his hand. He pointed at a spot on the map. "This here's Yap, what you thought was Tagran. That's where we are, right?" He pointed southwest. "This here's that scary island you said was the place you went through your trial, where there's all sorts o' boogers you wouldn't ever tell us about." He looked at Lawrence. "There *ain't* nothin' southwest of that but empty ocean, so it *can't* be Tagran."

"No," Lawrence said.

"So if that ain't it and this ain't it, your home must be this spot, northeast of here, right?" Lawrence nodded miserably, and Rebecca and Sandra both looked at Silva questioningly. He exhaled noisily. "What the hell. Whatever doesn't kill you is a hoot, I always say."

"What do you mean?" Sandra asked, but she knew.

"Ladies, Larry here's been beatin' around the bushy fact that we're marooned on Boogerland itself." Silva looked hard at Lawrence. "I ain't scared o' Boogerland. I ain't scared o' much at all anymore. The only thing that *does* scare me is threats to folks I care about. You mighta noticed I tend to react violently to those. Now, I know you ain't supposed to blow about what's runnin' around here, but we're talkin' Princess Rebecca and Miss Tucker now! I don't give a furry shit what you promised or swore to; *I* swear I'll twist your head off your skinny neck if you don't cough up everything you know about this damn place!"

That evening they had a big fire on the beach. In spite of everything, Lawrence had still refused to tell Dennis what he wanted to know, but he had told Sandra and Rebecca. They were females, after all, and no female was ever expected to undergo the trial. Sandra promptly told Silva roughly what they could expect—and it *was* scary. Evidently, they had some time, though. Not much, but apparently, the most dangerous time on the island reached its peak at a certain "season" of the year: the mating season of the semi amphibious "shiksaks" that sometimes even troubled Tagran. It wouldn't be a cakewalk, but maybe, just *maybe* they could be gone by then. In the meantime, they had a lot of work to do, and this first full night on Shikarrak Island, or Boogerland, as Silva continued to call it, would be devoted to a much-needed, watchful rest.

Rebecca was drowsy, but it suddenly dawned on her that she didn't see Silva among the group gathered around the fire. She stood and walked a short distance away, and as her eyes adjusted, she could just make him out, standing short of the surf line.

"Mr. Silva?" she said quietly

"Hmm? Oh."

"You frightened me," she scolded. "I looked about and you were nowhere to be seen!"

"Sorry, li'l sister," he said. "Most o' those fellas over there don't like me much, and I had a little thinkin' to do."

Sandra joined them in the darkness. "What were you thinking about?" She huffed. "Anything besides the obvious?"

Silva actually laughed. "Well, yeah, prob'ly. You know the skipper—Captain Reddy—will be lookin' for us by now."

Sandra sighed sadly. "I know. No matter what else is going on, he'll have dropped everything to come after us."

"After you," Silva stated the fact. "And maybe the munchkin queen here. Don't hurt my feelin's none. I bet he's got *Walker* back by now, and I can almost see her steamin' by out there in the dark, with a fine, big bone in her teeth!" He shook his head. "Thing is, he ain't gonna find us. He's gonna chase Billingsly's dead ass all the way to the New Britain Isles and he ain't gonna find us." He chuckled. "You know what he's gonna think? He's gonna think them Brits are either hidin' you girls . . . or they did somethin' to you."

Sandra and Rebecca were both silent for a moment, suspecting Silva was probably right.

"What do you suppose he'll do?" Rebecca asked at last.

Silva chuckled again. "I don't know, li'l sister, but I guarantee they're gonna hate it."

MEET THE AUTHOR

Photo: © Jim Goodrich

TAYLOR ANDERSON is a gunmaker and forensic ballistic archaeologist who has been a technical and dialogue consultant for movies and documentaries. He is also a member of the National Historical Honor Society and of the United States Field Artillery Association, which awarded him the Honorable Order of St. Barbara. He has a master's degree in history and teaches that subject at Tarleton State University in Stephenville, Texas, when his time allows. He lives in nearby Granbury with his family.